Swords of the North

Robert E. Howard

Introduction by Rusty Burke
Edited by Rob Roehm
and Paul Herman

THE
Robert E. Howard
FOUNDATION PRESS

For Glenn Lord (1931-2011), preserver of Howard's typescripts and manuscripts, god-father of Howard studies, and the greatest fan that ever lived.

Published by The Robert E, Howard Foundation Press by arrangement with Robert E. Howard Properties, Inc.
http://www.rehfoundation.org

Version 2.0

In loving memory of our friend and colleague

Steve Tompkins

(1960-2009)

Acknowledgments

All of the items contained in *Swords of the North* come from Howard's original typescripts, manuscripts, and carbons, with the following exceptions:

"The Cairn on the Headland"—text taken from *Strange Tales*, January 1933; "The Dark Man"—text taken from *Weird Tales*, December 1931; "Feach Air Muir Lionadhi Gealach Buidhe Mar Or"—text taken from *The Junto*, February 1930; "The Frost King's Daughter"—text taken from *The Fantasy Fan*, March 1934, where it appeared as "Gods of the North" (we have restored the title Howard used in his submission letter); "The Gods of Bal-Sagoth"—text taken from *Weird Tales*, October 1931; "The Grey God Passes"—text taken from *Dark Mind, Dark Heart* (Arkham House, 1962); "Kings of the Night"—text taken from *Weird Tales*, November 1930; "The Outgoing of Sigurd the Jerusalem Farer"—text taken from *Verses in Ebony* (Hamilton, 1975); "People of the Dark"—text taken from *Strange Tales*, June 1932; "The Song of the Last Briton"—text from a Glenn Lord transcription; "The Valley of the Worm"—text taken from *Weird Tales*, February 1934; "Viking's Vision"—text from a Glenn Lord transcription.

Note: As it appears here, the text for "Marchers of Valhalla" comes from several incomplete drafts that have been stitched together to make a complete tale. One of the earlier drafts has the following Hyborian reference (compare this to the passage on page 69):

> I am Ishtar, a daughter of a king in dim Lemuria which the sea gulped so long ago. Thoth-amon, the sorcerer of Stygia, hated my father, and to spite him, he put the curse on me of Life ever-lasting! / Oh, man, I have lived for so many, weary, weary ages! I saw Atlantis and Lemuria sink below the waves, and the rise of the Hyborians.

The pages containing the ending of the story have Ishtar using a gem to make Allison remember his past life; the beginning of that draft does not survive, so the same fix used by Glenn Lord in the tale's first publication was employed here: "Seconds only had elapsed since the woman had held the gleaming gem to my gaze" was changed to "Seconds only had elapsed since the woman had gestured before my eyes."

Contents

Appendix 1 - James Allison
Unfinished Tales

Appendix 2 - Cormac Mac Art
Unfinished Tales

Appendix 3 - Turlogh Dubh O'Brien
Unfinished Tales

Miscellanea
Poems and Unfinished Tales

Night Falls on Asgard

By Rusty Burke

I believe that many dreams are the result of ancestral memories, handed down through the ages. I have lived in the Southwest all my life yet most of my dreams are laid in cold, giant lands of icy wastes and gloomy skies, and of wild, wind swept fens and wildernesses over which sweep great sea-winds, and which are inhabited by shock headed savages with light fierce eyes.

—Robert E. Howard to H.P. Lovecraft, ca. January 1931

I was having lunch with the late Steve Tompkins, not only one of the most perceptive of Robert E. Howard critics but also one of the greatest of J.R.R. Tolkien fans, when he surprised me by saying that Howard had created a secondary world as deep and complex as Tolkien's. He wasn't just talking about the essay "The Hyborian Age," written as deep background to the Conan stories. He said that essay, and those stories, were merely part of a larger fabric, an eons-spanning vision of a world across which played vast movements of peoples, and which served as the foundation for virtually the entirety of Howard's corpus. As Steve laid it all out for me that afternoon, it brought many things into focus, and I came to see all of Howard's work, from at least the early story "Men of the Shadows" to the last, unfinished tales (such as "Nekht Semerkeht") as comprising one sweeping epic, much as Tolkien's *Lord of the Rings* is but a part of a larger (secondary-) world history found in *The Silmarillion*, *The Book(s) of Lost Tales*, *The Children of Hurin*, and others. Steve also noted that Howard's secondary world, like Tolkien's, was rooted in "The Northern Thing," W.H. Auden's term for what Steve called "the mythology, many-legended history, and darkness-defying worldview of the ancient Germanic and Norse peoples." That was when Steve proposed to me the contents of the collection you now find in your hands.

Howard's secondary world, of course, is not worked out as systematically as Tolkien's. Howard did not have the luxury of a day job, so he was creating on the fly, as he wrote stories to submit to pulp magazines. But there is a clear self-consistency among all his tales which will readily demonstrate that underlying it all is a coherent vision of a fictional history of the world and mankind, in Tolkien's term a "secondary" world, internally consistent, full of strangeness and wonder, "free from the domination of observed fact," yet quite credible, a world rooted in the familiar if populated with the unfamiliar, a world that combines the ordinary with the extraordinary. Just as Tolkien's "Arda" is our Earth, so too is Howard's world. Tolkien's prologue to LOTR tells us that the hobbits are "relations of ours" who have dwindled in size and numbers since the Third Age of Middle Earth and now hide from us, though they still live in "the North-West of the Old World, east of the sea," i.e., northwestern Europe. In his tales, Howard also makes clear that his stories are set in our world, though in vastly older, mightier ages, and he has a counterpart for the hobbits in his Picts, the most ancient race of humankind, in effect "relations of ours," now diminished in both size and numbers, living largely underground in the remote regions of the British Isles, and avoiding contact with the rest of humanity.

Both Tolkien and Howard make use of what has been called the "Time Abyss," the notion of vast age. For both, the races which inhabit the earth are far more ancient than history can relate, and their tales are set in times which were ancient when the most ancient peoples we can imagine were still young. Though they differ in their details, and in the sources of their inspiration, both authors make use of great cataclysms which alter the face of the lands and seas, and of the movements of entire peoples, *Volkerwanderungen*, across the earth. Both lend an air of verisimilitude to their "histories" of these prehistoric eras through use of ancient texts, Tolkien's *Red Book of Westmarch*, *Lay of the Children of Hurin*, and so on matched against Howard's *Nemedian Chronicles* and "iron-bound books of Skelos." As another means of accessing Deep Time, Tolkien has characters like Gandalf and Galadriel, whose lives and memories are measured in millennia, yet who are young in comparison to Treebeard and Tom Bombadil, whom Gandalf calls the eldest being in the world, and who claims to remember "the first raindrop and the first acorn." Howard makes use of ancients such as Kathulos of Atlantis, of characters who narrate the eons-old history of their race, or, most notably, of characters such as James Allison, a modern-day Texan who remembers his numerous past lives as "a man of that restless race men once called Nordheimr and later Aryans, and today name by many names and designations. Their history is my history, from the first mewling wail of a hairless white ape cub in the wastes of the Arctic, to the death-cry of the last degenerate product of ultimate civilization, in some dim and unguessed future age."

In the work of both authors there is heroism, and romance, and most often their tales end in a victory for the protagonists. Yet in both there is always the sense that the victory, no matter how exhilarating it may seem when won, is but a temporary one, that in the long run there can only be defeat, and loss. Here is "the Northern Thing" that deeply influences both writers. In his seminal essay, "Beowulf: The Monsters and the Critics," Tolkien noted that the "southern gods" (that is, those of the Mediterranean peoples) may have been "more godlike—more lofty, dread, and inscrutable": "They are timeless and do not fear death. Such a mythology may hold the promise of a profounder thought. In any case it was a virtue of the southern mythology that it could not stop where it was. It must go forward to philosophy or relapse into anarchy. For in a sense it had shirked the problem precisely by not having the monsters in the centre—as they are in Beowulf to the astonishment of the critics." The "monsters" he refers to are the Chaos and Unreason which mythological monsters represent, the forces which will overthrow or destroy the cosmos as we know it. "But," Tolkien continues, "such horrors cannot be left permanently unexplained, lurking on the outer edges. . . . It is the strength of the northern mythological imagination that it faced this problem, put the monsters in the centre, gave them victory but no honour, and found a potent but terrible solution in naked will and courage."

"Naked will and courage": no better words could be found to describe what lies at the core of the Howardian hero. Many people familiar with Howard's work only through the movie and comic-book derivatives have criticized him for "glorifying violence." Yet in no Howard story is violence ever glorified. Underlying every victory is the sense that it is just a temporary holding action against the Long Defeat, that nothing has really been won. But even Bran Mak Morn, who perhaps moreso than any other Howard character knows that his efforts are foredoomed to ultimate failure, meets his challenges with "naked will and courage." Howard expressed vividly to H.P. Lovecraft his fascination for such characters: "It is the individual mainly which draws me—the struggling, blundering, passionate insect vainly striving against the river of Life and seeking to divert the channel of events to suit himself—breaking his fangs on the iron collar of Fate and sinking into final defeat with the froth of a curse on his lips."

Years ago, Don Herron asserted, in his essay "The Dark Barbarian," that Howard had "created an intellectual artistic counterpoint" to the "cosmicism" of H.P. Lovecraft and Clark Ashton Smith: "Howard's imaginative sweep is not based in cosmic space, but in humanity itself. In his work one sees a colossal march of the races of man. . . . The rise of the Celtic peoples was a favorite subject. . . ." More recently, Jeffrey Shanks and I have made the case that Howard's act of "subcreation" or "secondary-world-building" is based on history and anthropology, where

Tolkien had based his on languages. Some of the history and a good deal of the anthropology available to Howard has since been discredited, but even if he had some doubts about the "objective truth" of the sources he used for inspiration, he might still have used them. In the letter to *Weird Tales* which launched his correspondence with H.P. Lovecraft, after explaining why he held a different view of the settling of the British Isles than that reflected in Lovecraft's story "The Rats in the Walls," he concluded: "But every man is entitled to his own view and a writer has the right to use any and all theories, no matter how conflicting, in his stories. I may write a story one day upholding a certain theory of science, letters, anthropology or what-not, and the next day, a story upholding a theory directly opposite. A fiction writer, whose job is to amuse and entertain, should give all theories equal scope and justice."

While Howard may have felt free to utilize, for fictional purposes, any theory, it remains that, rather than following the course of so many pulp writers and simply writing individual stories or character series that stand on their own, without any connection with other stories or series, he tied all his tales into one consistent imagined history. I believe that his prefatory statement to "The Hyborian Age" offers an important insight into why he did this: "When I began writing the Conan stories a few years ago, I prepared this 'history' of his age and the peoples of that age, in order to lend him and his sagas a greater aspect of realness. And I found that by adhering to the 'facts' and spirit of that history, in writing the stories, it was easier to visualize (and therefore to present) him as a real flesh-and-blood character rather than a ready-made product." In perhaps the most often-quoted encomium to Howard, H.P. Lovecraft said, "It is hard to describe precisely what made Mr. Howard's stories stand out so sharply; but the real secret is that he himself was in every one of them, whether they were ostensibly commercial or not." Howard created a secondary world, a history of the world through which his characters could play, because it made it easier for him to put himself into the stories. While he could certainly have stuck with actual history, and written well-researched historical tales, this did not appeal to his active imagination. For him, the freedom "from the domination of observed fact" that Tolkien mentioned was of the utmost importance. Hence, the creation of a fictional world. But in order for him to be able to feel that this world was real, and to feel himself a part of it, it had to have a history he could adhere to.

The first real articulation of what I term (honoring Steve Tompkins' love of the German language) Howard's *Weltgesichte*, or World-History, appears in the story "Men of the Shadows," written and submitted to

Weird Tales in early 1926. The story was rejected by editor Farnsworth Wright for the very reasons that it interests us now: "It is too little of a 'story'," he wrote, "despite the vigorous action in the opening pages. It is rather a chronicle of a tribe, a picture of the evolution of a race; and thereby it lacks the suspense and thrill that a story of individual conflict and hopes and fears and drama would have." The story is told from the viewpoint of a Norse mercenary in a Roman legion: they are harried by the Picts until only the Norseman is left alive, and he is captured and brought before the Pictish chief, Bran Mak Morn. When Bran seems inclined to accede to the tender-hearted pleas of his sister and grant the Norseman his freedom, despite the intense animosity between the Picts and Norse, it apparently is the final straw for an ancient wizard. He berates Bran for having "turned from the path" and offending the old gods; Bran insists that he will "lift the Pictish nation out of the darkness of the valley of abysmal savagery." There is a clash of wills between the two, and Bran wins. It is at this point that the old shaman begins his narration of "the tale of the race without name." (An odd designation, since we know they are Picts, and a bit later in the narrative the ancient uses the term.) The story is not included in this volume (it is readily available in collections of Bran Mak Morn tales), so I will describe it briefly in its broad outlines.

Many thousands of years in the past, what we now know as the Rocky Mountains were a chain of islands. To those islands came the Picts, the First Race, who had made the long upward climb "from crawling sea-thing to ape and from ape to ape-man and from ape-man to savage" on "broad and fertile plains" "a thousand miles to the north and west." The Picts settled in the islands and, over the course of millennia, developed into skilled craftsmen, and learned to grow crops: they developed a culture.

To the west of those islands was the continent of Lemuria, where lived the Second Race. In their first encounters with the Picts, when the Lemurians came as raiders, they were "half-human Men of the Sea," "scaly like unto a shark and they could swim for hours under water." Over the centuries, they too slowly made the upward climb.

Then came a mighty cataclysm, and the contours of the world were changed. The sea receded from the Pictish isles, leaving them a range of mountains on what is now the North American continent. Volcanoes raged up and down the coast, driving the Picts to flee eastward, pushing before them the ape-men who inhabited those lands. Lemuria sank, leaving only its highest mountain-tops as islands in the Pacific Ocean.

Then came the great ice fields southward, and the Picts ultimately wandered into South America, "a dank, swampy land, serpent-haunted."

Not liking it there, they made boats and sailed to Atlantis, where lived the Third Race. Howard specifically identifies the Atlanteans as Cro-Magnons. They were no match for the Picts at this time, and were driven into Europe, where they waged war with the beast-men who had earlier fled from the Picts, from South America via a chain of marshy islands into Africa and thence to Europe.

There was a war in Atlantis among the Pictish tribes and the losers fled first to Africa and then settled along the shores of the Mediterranean. Eventually they spread over most of Europe and North Africa, driving the Atlanteans and the "red-haired reindeer men" before them.

Then from the Arctic north came the Celts, the Fourth Race. The Picts had at last met their match, and were forced to flee into the waste places of the world. They fled into Scotland, where they mingled with the red-haired giants, beginning the degeneration of the race. And according to a draft page of the story, "the Nordics followed the Celts."

This is the point that the shaman's narration in "Men of the Shadows" ends, with the eons-spanning history of the Picts being brought up to the time of Bran Mak Morn, perhaps the end of the first century of our era. This ties the whole fictional history firmly into "real" history. It also brings us (at last!) to the subjects of this collection, the Celts and their cousins, the Norse.

* * *

Behind my English name are lines of purely Gaelic Eiarbhins, O'Tyrrells, Colquhouns, MacEnrys, and Norman-Irish Martuins, De Colliers, FitzHenrys. Yet there is a Scandinavian strain at me, for one of the MacEnrys of my line married the daughter of an Irish woman and a red-bearded Dane who first opened his eyes on the cold shores of the Skaggerack.

—Robert E. Howard to H.P. Lovecraft, ca. September 1930

Robert E. Howard fans are generally well aware that he was proud of his Irish heritage. Harold Preece's 1976 essay, "The Last Celt," which lent its title to Glenn Lord's authoritative "bio-bibliography," firmly established the fact, and the more recent publication of his letters, particularly those to Clyde Smith, Preece, and H.P. Lovecraft, left no doubt whatsoever that Robert E. Howard was a proud son of the Gael.

The only problem is, it wasn't entirely true, at least not in the literal sense. Extensive genealogical research, especially the work of Patrice Louinet and Rob Roehm, definitively shows that, despite his efforts to Gaelicize all those surnames, Howard's lineage was primarily English. The Henry line, through his paternal grandmother, does seem to trace back to Ireland (though it was never, so far as we know, FitzHenry, MacEnry,

MacHenry, or McHenry, all spellings given by Howard in various letters), and the Walsers (also through Eliza Henry) were not Scandinavian, but Swiss. Otherwise, the heritage is all English.

Let us, however, set aside the question of why Howard might have invented such an overwhelmingly Irish genealogy, and whether or not he truly believed it. What is important, from a literary point of view, is that it gave him an Irish *persona*. I have described elsewhere the deliberate and methodical process by which Howard developed new *personae* which allowed him to "mentally inhabit" his stories, to essentially *become* a character who might relate such a tale. One of the most important of these was The Celt. Not only did the cultivation of this identity allow him to write the stories found in this volume—the eons-spanning history of the Celtic and Nordic "races"—but it led also to the creation of his Crusader-era heroes (Cormac FitzGeoffrey, Donald MacDeesa, Cahal Ruadh O'Donnell), and to the Cimmerian adventurer for whom he is most widely celebrated. So what is important about Howard's "Irish heritage" is not whether it was historically accurate, but that he accorded it the status of Truth.

Howard's intense interest in matters Irish and Celtic seems to originate sometime near the end of 1928, and to have been encouraged and invigorated by the enthusiasm of his new friend, Harold Preece. According to Preece, it was Howard who initiated it, though: "Bob's interest in Celtica magnified and gave personal meaning to all those derived Scottish, Irish, and Welsh traditions which my family has retained during these aeons in America. But for all my earlier reading in Celtica, he was the teacher and I the almost uncritical pupil." Howard's earliest letters to Preece contain nothing on the topic (though Patrice Louinet notes that in 1928 Howard adopted the Irish "Costigan" cognomen), but beginning in September of 1929 he has clearly taken an avid interest. There was much reading in Irish myth, legend, and history, as well as authors like James Macpherson (of the "Ossian" poems) and Donn Byrne. The lilt of Irish diction began to make itself manifest in Howard's letters, and then in his literary productions. During the earlier development of his "Boxer" *persona*, Howard had transformed himself from a thin, gangly youth to a sturdy and muscular young man through a program of exercise and weight-lifting, then had sparred with friends until he was able to mix it up with any of the gang at the local ice house's informal bouts. In similar fashion he threw himself into the project of making himself an Irishman. Merely reading about it wasn't enough, just as devouring copies of *The Ring* magazine didn't make him a boxer. He had to *be* Irish. And so his Ervin forebears became Eiarbhins, the Tyrrells O'Tyrrells, the Martins and Colliers became "Norman-Irish" Martuins and De Colliers, and so on. He even seems to have made an effort to learn Irish Gaelic, and for some time signed his letters to Tevis Clyde Smith "Fear Dunn" (Gaelic for the "brown man"; Smith was "Fear Finn," the "fair" or "blond man").

The first literary works to emerge from this newly Irish writer were probably "The Ghost in the Doorway" and "Dermod's Bane," both 1929 productions, both fairly traditional ghost stories. But also in 1929 there rolled from Howard's typewriter the epic poem "The Ballad of King Geraint." It is very clearly influenced by and modeled after G.K. Chesterton's lengthy poetical epic, *The Ballad of the White Horse*, of which Howard had become an enthusiastic fan. He had purchased the book on his August 1927 trip to San Antonio with Truett Vinson, the same trip during which he first met Harold Preece. Upon arriving home, he wasted little time in writing to Clyde Smith and quoting extensively from this verse narrative of the Battle of Ethandune (now also known as the Battle of Edington), an encounter in 878 between the West Saxons under Alfred and the Danes and their allies under Guthrum. Because Chesterton wished to portray this as a stand of all the people of Britain against the "heathen" Danes, he gave Alfred as allies Eldred, a Saxon, Mark, a Roman, and Colan, a Gael, to represent the inhabitants of Britain who had "fought for the Christian civilization against the heathen nihilism." He knew that "this work was really done by generation after generation," but, he wrote, "it is the chief value of legend to mix up the centuries while preserving the sentiment; to see all ages in a sort of splendid foreshortening. That is the use of tradition: it telescopes history." I believe this idea was transformational for young Robert E. Howard, and that ultimately it achieves its clearest expression in his creation of The Hyborian Age, but his first use of it is in "The Ballad of King Geraint," in which he seems to be responding to Chesterton by showing that his Anglo-Saxon defenders of England against heathens were themselves at an earlier time the heathens. On both sides Howard assembles a marvelous panoply of legendary and vaguely historical figures, along with some entirely fictional (such as Dulborn the Pict), with tantalizing hints of back-story for many of them. It's a marvelous exercise, and is Howard's first foray into the description of a large-scale battle.

The following two years were the heyday for Howard's writing about the Celts and Norse. Most of the poetry herein was probably composed during this span, as were the stories of his two most notable Irish reavers, Turlogh Dubh O'Brien (first seen in "Geraint") and Cormac Mac Art. The Celtic adventurers Cormac FitzGeoffrey, Donald MacDeesa, and Cahal Ruadh O'Donnel were featured in tales of the Crusades, as were

Normans, an Englishman of Danish heritage, and a mixed crew of "Northmen, Danes, Saxons" who carried Harold, the last Saxon king of England, into an ahistorical exile. The story "Spears of Clontarf," a historical narrative of the pivotal battle in which Brian Boru defeated the Danes in 1014, based largely on the account in P.W. Joyce's *A Short History of Gaelic Ireland*, was submitted to a magazine of historical fiction in June of 1931; when it was rejected by this and other magazines, Howard rewrote it to add a fantastic element in hopes of selling it to *Weird Tales*, but as "The Grey God Passes" it fared no better. Howard finally used some of this material to form the background of "The Cairn on the Headland," which was accepted by *Strange Tales* in January 1932.

In the fall of 1931, Howard sent "The People of the Dark" to *Strange Tales*. In this story we find two harbingers of new directions. The tale is told by a modern-day narrator remembering (after a blow to the head) a past life as "Conan of the Reavers." While this Conan is a Gael of perhaps the 5th century, he is described in familiar terms: "square-cut black mane," "massive naked limbs and powerful torso." Some have argued that this Conan is identical with the Cimmerian; I would not go so far, thinking that he is prototype rather than template, yet given our earlier understanding that all of Howard's tales are a part of a unified history, and given his use of reincarnation and the memory of past lives as a motif, who is to say that, if "Conan of the Reavers" took a blow to the head, he would not remember a past life as a Cimmerian wanderer?

The "remembrance of lives past" theme also leads, in a more direct way, to the James Allison stories, the first of which ("Marchers of Valhalla") was apparently composed about April 1932, during the period in which the first Conan stories were rolling from Howard's typewriter. As noted earlier, in Howard's version of *Weltgesichte*, the Celts are the Fourth Race, coming down from the north to establish their domination over the previous races, and the Nordics, their cousins, follow behind them. The characters Howard created during his "Celtic" phase were primarily Celts, and most particularly Irish Gaels. However, in his Oriental tales we find a number of Norman-Irish, or even straight Norman, characters, as well as a smattering of others (John Norwald, of "Lion of Tiberias," is an Englishman of Danish heritage, for instance). By the time of the James Allison series, Howard seems to have brought together the Celtic and Norse into a single "race," the Nordheimr, or Aryans. (Here he was strongly influenced by his idol Jack London, particularly his novel *The Star-Rover*, "a book that I've read and re-read for years, and that generally goes to my head like wine.") And while the Norse played only a supporting role in the stories of Turlogh and Cormac, in the James

Allison series they finally take center stage, albeit through Allison's earlier incarnations. But look at his names: he is Niord, Hunwulf, Hialmar. He says in "The Valley of the Worm," "My name has been Hialmar, Tyr, Bragi, Bran, Horsa, Eric, and John." Is it possible, I wonder, that Howard has moved on from whatever it was that impelled him to create an Irish ancestry, and to make of himself an Irishman? Is he, in writing about Allison, reconciled to his Englishness?

The Conan series would continue until 1935, though any indebtedness to the "Celtic" persona becomes less and less discernible. Although there were a few later efforts, to my mind the Allison series reaches its triumphant conclusion in "The Valley of the Worm," which Steve Tompkins thought to be perhaps the finest single example of how Howard "wrote himself into...the 'Northern Thing...'" I believe this represents the final effort of "The Last Celt": Howard had moved on, and a new persona, "The Texian," had come to the fore.

A brief note on the arrangement of the stories: Steve suggested arranging the stories based on the History of the Fourth Race, beginning with the Hyborian Age and working toward the modern era. While it does have the odd effect of presenting them in somewhat the reverse of the order in which they were written, given our hopes for the book it seemed to me the best method. Some items, particularly poetry, would be devilishly hard to pin down as to date of composition, anyway. And some, again largely poetry, are difficult to ascribe a historical date: these have been placed in a "Miscellanea" section following those devoted to the unfinished stories of James Allison, Cormac Mac Art, and Turlogh Dubh O'Brien.

Swords of the North

Niflheim

Grim land of death, what monstrous visions lurk
Amid the icy fastness of your hills?
Your crags are hoary and they never melt;
Their blades of ice are deep in Midgard's heart.
They knew uncanny dawns before that time
When in the greyness of a sunless void,
Audhumla burst the sullen frost and saw
The strange-eyed Buri looming into life.
Oh, sombre land, I know what thing ye are!
The seat of Midgard's mysteries are you,
For you are Ymir's cold, inhuman heart
Which feeds all oceans with his sluggish blood.
The sky is rimed with frost—the crusted sun
Rocks down the blue, a shield of frozen flame.
Gigantic shadows rise and loom and live
And burst the links that chain them to the past.
They swirl like grey-limbed giants in the night.
They stalk amid the cold and mocking stars.
Ho! Giant brood of shadows! Find in me
A brother and a master and a slave.
Together we will burst the brains of men
With darksome wisdom from abysmal heights,
With knowledge that the soul cannot withstand.
Aye, I have watched you, reeling o'er the ice,
When mist-grey monsters swirled along the sky
And through my gibbering laughter stabbed the sleet.
Sound out the war-horn's doom for Ragnarok!
Let man's destroyers roar from Jotunnheimr
To rend the world and hurl the oceans down
Till in high Asgard wake the sleeping gods.
Then in the crashing combat of that day,
Let Midgard rise and roar and Ymir wake,
Till bergs of ice roar down to Muspellheim
And all becomes as thou art, Niflheim.

The Frost King's Daughter

The clangor of the swords had died away, the shouting of the slaughter was hushed; silence lay on the red-stained snow. The pale bleak sun that glittered so blindingly from the icefields and the snow-covered plains struck sheens of silver from rent corselet and broken blade, where the dead lay in heaps. The nerveless hand yet gripped the broken hilt; helmeted heads, back-drawn in the death throes, tilted red beards and golden beards grimly upward, as if in last invocation to Ymir the frost-giant.

Across the red drifts and mail-clad forms, two figures approached one another. In that utter desolation only they moved. The frosty sky was over them, the white illimitable plain around them, the dead men at their feet. Slowly through the corpses they came, as ghosts might come to a tryst through the shambles of a world.

Their shields were gone, their corselets dinted. Blood smeared their mail; their swords were red. Their horned helmets showed the marks of fierce strokes.

One spoke, he whose locks and beard were red as the blood on the sunlit snow.

"Man of the raven locks," said he, "tell me your name, so that my brothers in Vanaheim may know who was the last of Wulfhere's band to fall before the sword of Heimdul."

"This is my answer," replied the black-haired warrior: "Not in Vanaheim, but in Valhalla will you tell your brothers the name of Amra of Akbitana."

Heimdul roared and sprang, and his sword swung in a mighty arc. Amra staggered and his vision was filled with red sparks as the blade shivered into bits of blue fire on his helmet. But as he reeled he thrust with all the power of his great shoulders. The sharp point drove through brass scales and bones and heart, and the red-haired warrior died at Amra's feet.

Amra stood swaying, trailing his sword, a sudden sick weariness assailing him. The glare of the sun on the snow cut his eyes like a knife and the sky seemed shrunken and strangely far. He turned away from the trampled expanse where yellow-bearded warriors lay locked with red-haired slayers in the embrace of death. A few steps he took, and the glare of the snowfields was suddenly dimmed. A rushing wave of blindness engulfed him, and he sank down into the snow, supporting himself on one mailed arm, seeking to shake the blindness out of his eyes as a lion might shake his mane.

A silvery laugh cut through his dizziness, and his sight cleared slowly. There was a strangeness about all the landscape that he could not place or define—an unfamiliar tinge to earth and sky. But he did not think long of this. Before him, swaying like a sapling in the wind, stood a woman. Her body was like ivory, and save for a veil of gossamer, she was naked as the day. Her slender bare feet were whiter than the snow they spurned. She laughed, and her laughter was sweeter than the rippling of silvery fountains, and poisonous with cruel mockery.

"Who are you?" demanded the warrior.

"What matter?" Her voice was more musical than a silver-stringed harp, but it was edged with cruelty.

"Call up your men," he growled, grasping his sword. "Though my strength fail me, yet they shall not take me alive. I see that you are of the Vanir."

"Have I said so?"

He looked again at her unruly locks, which he had thought to be red. Now he saw that they were neither red nor yellow, but a glorious compound of both colors. He gazed spellbound. Her hair was like elfin gold, striking which, the sun dazzled him. Her eyes were neither wholly blue nor wholly grey, but of shifting colors and dancing lights and clouds of colors he could not recognize. Her full red lips smiled, and from her slim feet to the blinding crown of her billowy hair, her ivory body was as perfect as the dream of a god. Amra's pulse hammered in his temples.

"I cannot tell," said he, "whether you are of Vanaheim and mine enemy, or of Asgard and my friend. Far have I wandered, from Zingara to the Sea of Vilayet, in Stygia and Kush, and the country of the Hyrkanians; but a woman like you I have never seen. Your locks blind me with their brightness. Not even among the fairest daughters of the Æsir have I seen such hair, by Ymir!"

"Who are you to swear by Ymir?" she mocked. "What know you of the gods of ice and snow, you who have come up from the south to adventure among strangers?"

"By the dark gods of my own race!" he cried in anger. "Have I been backward in the swordplay, stranger or no? This day I have seen four score warriors fall, and I alone survive the field where Wulfhere's reavers met the men of Bragi. Tell me, woman, have you caught the flash of mail across the snow plains, or seen armed men moving upon the ice?"

"I have seen the hoarfrost glittering in the sun," she answered. "I have heard the wind whispering across the everlasting snows."

He shook his head.

"Niord should have come up with us before the battle joined. I fear he and his warriors have been ambushed. Wulfhere lies dead with all his weapon-men.

"I had thought there was no village within many leagues of this spot, for the war carried us far, but you can have come no great distance over these snows, naked as you are. Lead me to your tribe, if you are of Asgard, for I am faint with the weariness of strife."

"My dwelling place is further than you can walk, Amra of Akbitana!" she laughed. Spreading wide her arms she swayed before him, her golden head lolling wantonly, her scintillant eyes shadowed beneath long silken lashes. "Am I not beautiful, man?"

"Like Dawn running naked on the snows," he muttered, his eyes burning like those of a wolf.

"Then why do you not rise and follow me? Who is the strong warrior who falls down before me?" she chanted in maddening mockery. "Lie down and die in the snow with the other fools, Amra of the black hair. You cannot follow where I would lead."

With an oath the man heaved himself upon his feet, his blue eyes blazing, his dark scarred face convulsed. Rage shook his soul, but desire for the taunting figure before him hammered at his temples and drove his wild blood riotously through his veins. Passion fierce as physical agony flooded his whole being so that earth and sky swam red to his dizzy gaze, and weariness and faintness were swept from him in madness.

He spoke no word as he drove at her, fingers hooked like talons. With a shriek of laughter she leaped back and ran, laughing at him over her white shoulder. With a low growl Amra followed. He had forgotten the fight, forgotten the mailed warriors who lay in their blood, forgotten Niord's belated reavers. He had thought only for the slender white shape which seemed to float rather than run before him.

Out across the white blinding plain she led him. The trampled red field fell out of sight behind him, but still Amra kept on with the silent tenacity of his race. His mailed feet broke through the frozen crust; he sank deep in the drifts and forged through them by sheer strength. But the girl danced across the snow as light as a feather floating across a pool; her naked feet scarcely left their imprint on the hoarfrost. In spite of the fire in his veins, the cold bit through the warrior's mail and furs; but the girl in her gossamer veil ran as lightly and as gaily as if she danced through the palms and rose gardens of Poitain.

Black curses drooled through the warrior's parched lips. The great veins swelled and throbbed in his temples, and his teeth gnashed spasmodically.

"You cannot escape me!" he roared. "Lead me into a trap and I'll pile the heads of your kinsmen at your feet. Hide from me and I'll tear apart the mountains to find you! I'll follow you to hell and beyond hell!"

Her maddening laughter floated back to him, and foam flew from the warrior's lips. Further and further into the wastes she led him, till he saw the wide plains give way to low hills, marching upward in broken ranges. Far to the north he caught a glimpse of towering mountains, blue with the distance, or white with the eternal snows. Above these mountains shone the flaring rays of the borealis. They spread fanwise into the sky, frosty blades of cold flaming light, changing in color, growing and brightening.

Above him the skies glowed and crackled with strange lights and gleams. The snow shone weirdly, now frosty blue, now icy crimson, now cold silver. Through a shimmering icy realm of enchantment Amra plunged doggedly onward, in a crystalline maze where the only reality was the white body dancing across the glittering snow beyond his reach—ever beyond his reach.

Yet he did not wonder at the necromantic strangeness of it all, not even when two gigantic figures rose up to bar his way. The scales of their mail were white with hoarfrost; their helmets and their axes were sheathed in ice. Snow sprinkled their locks; in their beards were spikes of icicles; their eyes were cold as the lights that streamed above them.

"Brothers!" cried the girl, dancing between them. "Look who follows! I have brought you a man for the feasting! Take his heart that we may lay it smoking on our father's board!"

The giants answered with roars like the grinding of icebergs on a frozen shore, and heaved up their shining axes as the maddened Akbitanan hurled himself upon them. A frosty blade flashed before his eyes, blinding him with its brightness, and he gave back a terrible stroke that sheared through his foe's thigh. With a groan the victim fell, and at that instant Amra was dashed into the snow, his left shoulder numb from the blow of the survivor, from which the warrior's mail had barely saved his life. Amra saw the remaining giant looming above him like a colossus carved of ice, etched against the glowing sky. The axe fell, to sink through the snow and deep into the frozen earth as Amra hurled himself aside and leaped to his feet. The giant roared and wrenched the axhead free, but even as he did so, Amra's sword sang down. The giant's knees bent and he sank slowly into the snow which turned crimson with the blood that gushed from his half-severed neck.

Amra wheeled, to see the girl standing a short distance away, staring in wide-eyed horror, all mockery gone from her face. He cried out fiercely and the blooddrops flew from his sword as his hand shook in the intensity of his passion.

"Call the rest of your brothers!" he roared. "Call the dogs! I'll give their hearts to the wolves!"

With a cry of fright she turned and fled. She did not laugh now, nor mock him over her shoulder. She ran as for her life, and though he strained every nerve and thew, until his temples were like to burst and the snow swam red to his gaze, she drew away from him, dwindling in the witch fire of the skies, until she was a figure no bigger than a child, then a dancing white flame on the snow, then a dim blur in the distance. But grinding his teeth until the blood started from his gums, he reeled on, and he saw the blur grow to a dancing white flame, and the flame to a figure big as a child; and then she was running less than a hundred paces ahead of him, and slowly the space narrowed, foot by foot.

She was running with effort now, her golden locks blowing free; he heard the quick panting of her breath, and saw a flash of fear in the look she cast over her alabaster shoulder. The grim endurance of the warrior had served him well. The speed ebbed from her flashing white legs; she reeled in her gait. In his untamed soul flamed up the fires of hell she had fanned so well. With an inhuman roar he closed in on her, just as she wheeled with a haunting cry and flung out her arms to fend him off.

His sword fell into the snow as he crushed her to him. Her supple body bent backward as she fought with desperate frenzy in his iron arms. Her golden hair blew about his face, blinding him with its sheen; the feel of her slender figure twisting in his mailed arms drove him to blinder madness. His strong fingers sank deep into her smooth flesh, and that flesh was cold as ice. It was as if he embraced not a woman of human flesh and blood, but a woman of flaming ice. She writhed her golden head aside, striving to avoid the savage kisses that bruised her red lips.

"You are cold as the snows," he mumbled dazedly. "I will warm you with the fire in my own blood—"

With a desperate wrench she twisted from his arms, leaving her single gossamer garment in his grasp. She sprang back and faced him, her golden locks in wild disarray, her white bosom heaving, her beautiful eyes blazing with terror. For an instant he stood frozen, awed by her terrible beauty as she posed naked against the snows.

And in that instant she flung her arms toward the lights that glowed in the skies above her and cried out in a voice that rang in Amra's ears forever after:

Ymir! Oh, my father, save me!"

Amra was leaping forward, arms spread to seize her, when with a crack like the breaking of an ice mountain, the whole skies leaped into icy fire. The girl's ivory body was suddenly enveloped in a cold blue flame so blinding that the warrior threw up his hands to shield his eyes. A fleeting instant, skies and snowy hills were bathed in crackling white flames, blue darts of icy light, and frozen crimson fires. Then Amra staggered and cried out. The girl was gone. The glowing snow lay empty and bare; high above him the witch lights flashed and played in a frosty sky gone mad, and among the distant blue mountains there sounded a rolling thunder as of a gigantic war-chariot rushing behind steeds whose frantic hoofs struck lightning from the snows and echoes from the skies.

Then suddenly the borealis, the snowy hills, and the blazing heavens reeled drunkenly to Amra's sight; thousands of fireballs burst with showers of sparks, and the sky itself became a titanic wheel which rained stars as it spun. Under his feet the snowy hills heaved up like a wave, and the Akbitanan crumpled into the snows to lie motionless.

In a cold dark universe, whose sun was extinguished eons ago, Amra felt the movement of life, alien and unguessed. An earthquake had him in its grip and was shaking him to and fro, at the same time chafing his hands and feet until he yelled in pain and fury and groped for his sword.

"He's coming to, Horsa," grunted a voice. "Haste—we must rub the frost out of his limbs, if he's ever to wield sword again.

"He won't open his left hand," growled another, his voice indicating muscular strain. "He's clutching something—"

Amra opened his eyes and stared into the bearded faces that bent over him. He was surrounded by tall golden-haired warriors in mail and furs.

"Amra! You live!"

"By Crom, Niord," gasped he, "am I alive, or are we all dead and in Valhalla?"

"We live," grunted the Æsir, busy over Amra's half-frozen feet. "We had to fight our way through an ambush, else we had come up with you before the battle was joined. The corpses were scarce cold when we came upon the field. We did not find you among the dead, so we followed your spoor. In Ymir's name, Amra, why did you wander off into the wastes of the north? We have followed your tracks in the snow for hours. Had a blizzard come up and hidden them, we had never found you, by Ymir!"

"Swear not so often by Ymir," muttered a warrior, glancing at the distant mountains. "This is his land and the god bides among yonder mountains, the legends say."

"I followed a woman," Amra answered hazily. "We met Bragi's men in the plains. I know not how long we fought. I alone lived. I was dizzy and faint. The land lay like a dream before me. Only now do all things seem natural and familiar. The woman came and taunted me. She was beautiful as a frozen flame from hell. When I looked at her I was as one mad, and forgot all else in the world. I followed her. Did you not find her tracks? Or the giants in icy mail I slew?"

Niord shook his head.

"We found only your tracks in the snow, Amra."

"Then it may be I was mad," said Amra dazedly. "Yet you yourself are no more real to me than was the golden-haired witch who fled naked across the snows before me. Yet from my very hands she vanished in icy flame."

"He is delirious," whispered a warrior.

"Not so!" cried an older man, whose eyes were wild and weird. "It was Atali, the daughter of Ymir, the frost-giant! To fields of the dead she comes and shows herself to the dying! Myself when a boy I saw her, when I lay half-slain on the bloody field of Wolraven. I saw her walk among the dead in the snows, her naked body gleaming like ivory and her golden hair like a blinding flame in the moonlight. I lay and howled like a dying dog because I could not crawl after her. She lures men from stricken fields into the wastelands to be slain by her brothers, the ice-giants, who lay men's red hearts smoking on Ymir's board. Amra has seen Atali, the frost-giant's daughter!"

"Bah!" grunted Horsa. "Old Gorm's mind was turned in his youth by a sword cut on the head. Amra was delirious with the fury of battle. Look how his helmet is dinted. Any of those blows might have addled his brain. It was an hallucination he followed into the wastes. He is from the south; what does he know of Atali?"

"You speak truth, perhaps," muttered Amra. "It was all strange and weird—by Crom!"

He broke off, glaring at the object that still dangled from his clenched left fist; the others gaped silently at the veil he held up—a wisp of gossamer that was never spun by human distaff.

The Valley of the Worm

I will tell you of Niord and the Worm. You have heard the tale before in many guises wherein the hero was named Tyr, or Perseus, or Siegfried, or Beowulf, or Saint George. But it was Niord who met the loathly demoniac thing that crawled hideously up from hell, and from which meeting sprang the cycle of hero-tales that revolves down the ages until the very substance of the truth is lost and passes into the limbo of all forgotten legends. I know whereof I speak, for I was Niord.

As I lie here awaiting death, which creeps slowly upon me like a blind slug, my dreams are filled with glittering visions and the pageantry of glory. It is not of the drab, disease-racked life of James Allison I dream, but all the gleaming figures of the mighty pageantry that have passed before, and shall come after; for I have faintly glimpsed, not merely the shapes that trail out behind, but shapes that come after, as a man in a long parade glimpses, far ahead, the line of figures that precede him winding over a distant hill, etched shadow-like against the sky. I am one and all the pageantry of shapes and guises and masks which have been, are, and shall be the visible manifestations of that illusive, intangible, but vitally existent spirit now promenading under the brief and temporary name of James Allison.

Each man on earth, each woman, is part and all of a similar caravan of shapes and beings. But they cannot remember—their minds cannot bridge the brief, awful gulfs of blackness which lie between those unstable shapes, and which the spirit, soul or ego, in spanning, shakes off its fleshy masks. I remember. Why I can remember is the strangest tale of all; but as I lie here with death's black wings slowly unfolding over me, all the dim folds of my previous lives are shaken out before my eyes, and I see myself in many forms and guises—braggart, swaggering, fearful, loving, foolish, all that men have been or will be.

I have been Man in many lands and many conditions; yet—and here is another strange thing—my line of reincarnation runs straight down one unerring channel. I have never been any but a man of that restless race men once called Nordheimr and later Aryans, and today name by many names and designations. Their history is my history, from the first mewling wail of a hairless white ape cub in the wastes of the arctic, to the death-cry of the last degenerate product of ultimate civilization, in some dim and unguessed future age.

My name has been Hialmar, Tyr, Bragi, Bran, Horsa, Eric, and John. I strode red-handed through the deserted streets of Rome behind the yellow-maned Brennus; I wandered through the violated plantations with Alaric and his Goths when the flame of burning villas lit the land like day and an empire was gasping its last under our sandalled feet; I waded sword in hand through the foaming surf from Hengist's galley to lay the foundations of England in blood and pillage; when Leif the Lucky sighted the broad white beaches of an unguessed world, I stood beside him in the bows of the dragon-ship, my golden beard blowing in the wind; and when Godfrey of Bouillon led his Crusaders over the walls of Jerusalem, I was among them in steel cap and brigandine.

But it is of none of these things I would speak. I would take you back with me into an age beside which that of Brennus and Rome is as yesterday. I would take you back through, not merely centuries and millenniums, but epochs and dim ages unguessed by the wildest philosopher. Oh far, far and far will you fare into the nighted Past before you win beyond the boundaries of my race, blue eyed, yellow haired, wanderers, slayers, lovers, mighty in rapine and wayfaring.

It is the adventure of Niord Worm's-bane of which I would speak—the root stem of a whole cycle of hero tales which has not yet reached its end, the grisly underlying reality that lurks behind time-distorted myths of dragons, fiends and monsters.

Yet it is not alone with the mouth of Niord that I will speak. I am James Allison no less than I was Niord, and as I unfold the tale, I will interpret some of his thoughts and dreams and deeds from the mouth of the modern I, so that the saga of Niord shall not be a meaningless chaos to you. His blood is your blood, who are sons of Aryan; but wide misty gulfs of eons lie horrifically between, and the deeds and dreams of Niord seem as alien to your deeds and dreams as the primordial and lion-haunted forest seems alien to the white-walled city street.

It was a strange world in which Niord lived and loved and fought, so long ago that even my eon-spanning memory cannot recognize landmarks. Since then the surface of the earth has changed, not once but a score of times; continents have risen and sunk, seas have changed their beds and rivers their courses, glaciers have waxed and waned, and the very stars and constellations have altered and shifted.

It was so long ago that the cradleland of my race was still in Nordheim. But the epic drifts of my people had already begun, and blue-eyed, yellow-maned tribes flowed eastward and southward and westward, on century-long treks that carried them around the world and left their bones and their traces in strange lands and wild waste places. On one of these drifts I grew from infancy to manhood. My knowledge of that northern homeland was dim memories, like half-remembered dreams, of blinding white snow plains and ice fields, of great fires roaring in the circle of hide tents, of yellow manes flying in great winds, and a sun setting in a lurid wallow of crimson clouds, blazing on trampled snow where still dark forms lay in pools that were redder than the sunset.

That last memory stands out clearer than the others. It was the field of Jotunheim, I was told in later years, whereon had just been fought that terrible battle which was the Armageddon of the Æsir-folk, the subject of a cycle of hero songs for long ages, and which still lives today in dim dreams of Ragnarok and Goetterdaemmerung. I looked on that battle as a mewling infant; so I must have lived about—but I will not name the age, for I would be called a madman, and historians and geologists alike would rise to refute me.

But my memories of Nordheim were few and dim, paled by memories of that long, long trek upon which I had spent my life. We had not kept to a straight course, but our trend had been for ever southward. Sometimes we had bided for a while in fertile upland valleys or rich river-traversed plains, but always we took up the trail again, and not always because of drouth or famine. Often we left countries teeming with game and wild grain to push into wastelands. On our trail we moved endlessly, driven only by our restless whim, yet blindly following a cosmic law, the workings of which we never guessed, any more than the wild geese guess in their flights around the world. So at last we came into the Country of the Worm.

I will take up the tale at the time when we came into jungle-clad hills reeking with rot and teeming with spawning life, where the tom-toms of a savage people pulsed incessantly through the hot breathless night. These people came forth to dispute our way—short, strongly built men, black haired, painted, ferocious, but indisputably white men. We knew their breed of old. They were Picts, and of all alien races the fiercest. We had met their kind before in thick forests, and in upland valleys beside mountain lakes. But many moons had passed since those meetings.

I believe this particular tribe represented the easternmost drift of the race. They were the most primitive and ferocious of any I ever met. Already they were exhibiting hints of characteristics I have noted among black savages in jungle countries, though they had dwelt in these environs only a few generations. The abysmal jungle was engulfing them, was obliterating their pristine characteristics and shaping them in its own horrific mold. They were drifting into headhunting, and cannibalism was but a step which I believe they must have taken before they became extinct. These things are natural adjuncts to the jungle; the Picts did not learn them from the black people, for then there were no blacks among those hills. In later years they came up from the south, and the Picts first enslaved and then were absorbed by them. But with that my saga of Niord is not concerned.

We came into that brutish hill country, with its squalling abysms of savagery and black primitiveness. We were a whole tribe marching on foot, old men, wolfish with their long beards and gaunt limbs, giant warriors in their prime, naked children running along the line of march, women with tousled yellow locks carrying babies which never cried—unless it were to scream from pure rage. I do not remember our numbers, except that there were some five hundred fighting-men—and by fighting- men I mean all males, from the child just strong enough to lift a bow, to the oldest of the old men. In that madly ferocious age all were fighters. Our women fought, when brought to bay, like tigresses, and I have seen a babe, not yet old enough to stammer articulate words, twist its head and sink its tiny teeth in the foot that stamped out its life.

Oh, we were fighters! Let me speak of Niord. I am proud of him, the more when I consider the paltry crippled body of James Allison, the unstable mask I now wear. Niord was tall, with great shoulders, lean hips and mighty limbs. His muscles were long and swelling, denoting endurance and speed as well as strength. He could run all day without tiring, and he possessed a co-ordination that made his movements a blur of blinding speed. If I told you his full strength, you would brand me a liar. But there is no man on earth today strong enough to bend the bow Niord handled with ease. The longest arrow flight on record is that of a Turkish archer who sent a shaft 482 yards. There was not a stripling in my tribe who could not have bettered that flight.

As we entered the jungle country we heard the tom-toms booming across the mysterious valleys that slumbered between the brutish hills, and in a broad, open plateau we met our enemies. I do not believe these Picts knew us, even by legends, or they had never rushed so openly to the onset, though they outnumbered us. But there was no attempt at ambush. They swarmed out of the trees, dancing and singing their war songs, yelling their barbarous threats. Our heads should hang in their idol hut and our yellow-haired women should bear their sons. Ho! ho! ho! By Ymir, it was Niord who laughed then, not James Allison. Just so we of the Æsir laughed to hear their threats—deep thunderous laughter from broad and mighty chests. Our trail was laid in blood and embers through many lands. We were the slayers and ravishers, striding sword in hand across the world, and that these folk threatened us woke our rugged humor.

We went to meet them, naked but for our wolf hides, swinging our bronze swords, and our singing was like rolling thunder in the hills. They sent their arrows among us, and we gave back their fire. They could not match us in archery. Our arrows hissed in blinding clouds among them, dropping them like autumn leaves, until they howled and frothed like mad dogs and charged to handgrips. And we, mad with the fighting joy, dropped our bows and ran to meet them, as a lover runs to his love.

By Ymir, it was a battle to madden and make drunken with the slaughter and the fury. The Picts were as ferocious as we, but ours was the superior physique, the keener wit, the more highly developed fighting-brain. We won because we were a superior race, but it was no easy victory. Corpses littered the blood-soaked earth; but at last they broke, and we cut them down as they ran, to the very edge of the trees. I tell of that fight in a few bald words. I cannot paint the madness, the reek of sweat and blood, the panting, muscle-straining effort, the splintering of bones under mighty blows, the rending and hewing of quivering sentient flesh; above all the merciless abysmal savagery of the whole affair, in which there was neither rule nor order, each man fighting as he would or could. If I might do so, you would recoil in horror; even the modern I, cognizant of my close kinship with those times, stand aghast as I review that butchery. Mercy was yet unborn, save as some individual's whim, and rules of warfare were as yet undreamed of. It was an age in which each tribe and each human fought tooth and fang from birth to death, and neither gave nor expected mercy.

So we cut down the fleeing Picts, and our women came out on the field to brain the wounded enemies with stones, or cut their throats with copper knives. We did not torture. We were no more cruel than life demanded. The rule of life was ruthlessness, but there is more wanton cruelty today than ever we dreamed of. It was not wanton bloodthirstiness that made us butcher wounded and captive foes. It was because we knew our chances of survival increased with each enemy slain.

Yet there was occasionally a touch of individual mercy, and so it was in this fight. I had been occupied with a duel with an especially valiant enemy. His tousled thatch of black hair scarcely came above my chin, but he was a solid knot of steel-spring muscles, than which lightning scarcely moved faster. He had an iron sword and a hide-covered buckler. I had a knotty-headed bludgeon. That fight was one that glutted even my battle-lusting soul. I was bleeding from a score of flesh wounds before one of my terrible, lashing strokes smashed his shield like cardboard, and an instant later my bludgeon glanced from his unprotected head. Ymir! Even now I stop to laugh and marvel at the hardness of that Pict's skull. Men of that age were assuredly built on a rugged plan! That blow should have spattered his brains like water. It did lay his scalp open horribly, dashing him senseless to the earth, where I let him lie, supposing him to be dead, as I joined in the slaughter of the fleeing warriors.

When I returned reeking with sweat and blood, my club horridly clotted with blood and brains, I noticed that my antagonist was regaining consciousness, and that a naked tousle-headed girl was preparing to give him the finishing touch with a stone she could scarcely lift. A vagrant whim caused me to check the blow. I had enjoyed the fight, and I admired the adamantine quality of his skull.

We made camp a short distance away, burned our dead on a great pyre, and after looting the corpses of the enemy, we dragged them across the plateau and cast them down in a valley to make a feast for the hyenas, jackals and vultures which were already gathering. We kept close watch that night, but we were not attacked, though far away through the jungle we could make out the red gleam of fires, and could faintly hear, when the wind veered, the throb of tom-toms and demoniac screams and yells—keenings for the slain or mere animal squallings of fury.

Nor did they attack us in the days that followed. We bandaged our captive's wounds and quickly learned his primitive tongue, which, however, was so different from ours that I cannot conceive of the two languages having ever had a common source.

His name was Grom, and he was a great hunter and fighter, he boasted. He talked freely and held no grudge, grinning broadly and showing tusk-like teeth, his beady eyes glittering from under the tangled black mane that fell over his low forehead. His limbs were almost ape-like in their thickness.

He was vastly interested in his captors, though he could never understand why he had been spared; to the end it remained an inexplicable mystery to him. The Picts obeyed the law of survival even more rigidly than did the Æsir. They were the more practical, as shown by their more settled habits. They never roamed as far or as blindly as we. Yet in every line we were the superior race.

Grom, impressed by our intelligence and fighting qualities, volunteered to go into the hills and make peace for us with his people. It was immaterial to us, but we let him go. Slavery had not yet been dreamed of.

So Grom went back to his people, and we forgot about him, except that I went a trifle more cautiously about my hunting, expecting him to be lying in wait to put an arrow through my back. Then one day we heard a rattle of tom-toms, and Grom appeared at the edge of the jungle, his face split in his gorilla-grin, with the painted, skin-clad, feather-bedecked chiefs of the clans. Our ferocity had awed them, and our sparing of Grom further impressed them. They could not understand leniency; evidently we valued them too cheaply to bother about killing one when he was in our power.

So peace was made with much powwow, and sworn to with many strange oaths and rituals—we swore only by Ymir, and an Æsir never broke that vow. But they swore by the elements, by the idol which sat in the fetish-hut where fires burned forever and a withered crone slapped a leather-covered drum all night long, and by another being too terrible to be named.

Then we all sat around the fires and gnawed meat bones and drank a fiery concoction they brewed from wild grain, and the wonder is that the feast did not end in a general massacre; for that liquor had devils in it and made maggots writhe in our brains. But no harm came of our vast drunkenness, and thereafter we dwelt at peace with our barbarous neighbors. They taught us many things and learned many more from us. But they taught us iron-workings, into which they had been forced by the lack of copper in those hills, and we quickly excelled them.

We went freely among their villages—mud-walled clusters of huts in hilltop clearings, overshadowed by giant trees—and we allowed them to come at will among our camps—straggling lines of hide tents on the plateau where the battle had been fought. Our young men cared not for their squat beady-eyed women, and our rangy clean-limbed girls with their tousled yellow heads were not drawn to the hairy-breasted savages. Familiarity over a period of years would have reduced the repulsion on either side, until the two races would have flowed together to form one hybrid people, but long before that time the Æsir rose and departed, vanishing into the mysterious hazes of the haunted south. But before that exodus there came to pass the horror of the Worm.

I hunted with Grom and he led me into brooding, uninhabited valleys and up into silence-haunted hills where no men had set foot before us. But there was one valley, off in the mazes of the southwest, into which he would not go. Stumps of shattered columns, relics of a forgotten civilization, stood among the trees on the valley floor. Grom showed them to me, as we stood on the cliffs that flanked the mysterious vale, but he would not go down into it, and he dissuaded me when I would have gone alone. He would not speak plainly of the danger that lurked there, but it was greater than that of serpent or tiger, or the trumpeting elephants which occasionally wandered up in devastating droves from the south.

Of all beasts, Grom told me in the gutturals of his tongue, the Picts feared only Satha, the great snake, and they shunned the jungle where he lived. But there was another thing they feared, and it was connected in some manner with the Valley of Broken Stones, as the Picts called the crumbling pillars. Long ago, when his ancestors had first come into the country, they had dared that grim vale, and a whole clan of them had perished, suddenly, horribly, and unexplainably. At least Grom did not explain. The horror had come up out of the earth, somehow, and it was not good to talk of it, since it was believed that It might be summoned by speaking of It—whatever It was.

But Grom was ready to hunt with me anywhere else; for he was the greatest hunter among the Picts, and many and fearful were our adventures. Once I killed, with the iron sword I had forged with my own hands, that most terrible of all beasts—old saber-tooth, which men today call a tiger because he was more like a tiger than anything else. In reality he was almost as much like a bear in build, save for his unmistakably feline head. Saber-tooth was massive limbed, with a low-hung, great, heavy body, and he vanished from the earth because he was too terrible a fighter, even for that grim age. As his muscles and ferocity grew, his brain dwindled until at last even the instinct of self-preservation vanished. Nature, who maintains her balance in such things, destroyed him because, had his super-fighting powers been allied with an intelligent brain, he would have destroyed all other forms of life on earth. He was a freak on the road of evolution—organic development gone mad and run to fangs and talons, to slaughter and destruction.

I killed saber-tooth in a battle that would make a saga in itself, and for months afterward I lay semi-delirious with ghastly wounds that made the toughest warriors shake their heads. The Picts said that never before had a man killed a saber-tooth single- handed. Yet I recovered, to the wonder of all.

While I lay at the doors of death there was a secession from the tribe. It was a peaceful secession, such as continually occurred and contributed greatly to the peopling of the world by yellow-haired tribes. Forty-five of the young men took themselves mates simultaneously and wandered off to found a clan of their own. There was no revolt; it was a racial custom which bore fruit in all the later ages, when tribes sprung from the same roots met, after centuries of separation, and cut one another's throats with joyous abandon. The tendency of the Aryan and the pre-Aryan was always toward disunity, clans splitting off the main stem, and scattering.

So these young men, led by one Bragi, my brother-in-arms, took their girls and venturing to the southwest, took up their abode in the Valley of Broken Stones. The Picts expostulated, hinting vaguely of a monstrous doom that haunted the vale, but the Æsir laughed. We had left our own demons and weirds in the icy wastes of the far blue north, and the devils of other races did not much impress us.

When my full strength was returned, and the grisly wounds were only scars, I girt on my weapons and strode over the plateau to visit Bragi's clan. Grom did not accompany me. He had not been in the Æsir camp for several days. But I knew the way. I remembered well the valley, from the cliffs of which I had looked down and seen the lake at the upper end, the trees thickening into forest at the lower extremity. The sides of the valley were high sheer cliffs, and a steep broad ridge at either end cut it off from the surrounding country. It was toward the lower or southwestern end that the valley-floor was dotted thickly with ruined columns, some towering high among the trees, some fallen into heaps of lichen-clad stones. What race reared them none knew. But Grom had hinted fearsomely of a hairy, apish monstrosity dancing loathsomely under the moon to a demoniac piping that induced horror and madness.

I crossed the plateau whereon our camp was pitched, descended the slope, traversed a shallow vegetation-choked valley, climbed another slope, and plunged into the hills. A half-day's leisurely travel brought me to the ridge on the other side of which lay the valley of the pillars. For many miles I had seen no sign of human life. The settlements of the Picts all lay many miles to the east. I topped the ridge and looked down into the dreaming valley with its still blue lake, its brooding cliffs and its broken columns jutting among the trees. I looked for smoke. I saw none, but I saw vultures wheeling in the sky over a cluster of tents on the lake shore.

I came down the ridge warily and approached the silent camp. In it I halted, frozen with horror. I was not easily moved. I had seen death in many forms, and had fled from or taken part in red massacres that spilled blood like water and heaped the earth with corpses. But here I was confronted with an organic devastation that staggered and appalled me. Of Bragi's embryonic clan, not one remained alive, and not one corpse was whole. Some of the hide tents still stood erect. Others were mashed down and flattened out, as if crushed by some monstrous weight, so that at first I wondered if a drove of elephants had stampeded across the camp. But no elephants ever wrought such destruction as I saw strewn on the bloody ground. The camp was a shambles, littered with bits of flesh and fragments of bodies—hands, feet, heads, pieces of human debris. Weapons lay about, some of them stained with a greenish slime like that which spurts from a crushed caterpillar.

No human foe could have committed this ghastly atrocity. I looked at the lake, wondering if nameless amphibian monsters had crawled from the calm waters whose deep blue told of unfathomed depths. Then I saw a print left by the destroyer. It was a track such as a titanic worm might leave, yards broad, winding back down the valley. The grass lay flat where it ran, and bushes and small trees had been crushed down into the earth, all horribly smeared with blood and greenish slime.

With berserk fury in my soul I drew my sword and started to follow it, when a call attracted me. I wheeled, to see a stocky form approaching me from the ridge. It was Grom the Pict, and when I think of the courage it must have taken for him to have overcome all the instincts planted in him by traditional teachings and personal experience, I realize the full depths of his friendship for me.

Squatting on the lakeshore, spear in his hands, his black eyes ever roving fearfully down the brooding tree-waving reaches of the valley, Grom told me of the horror that had come upon Bragi's clan under the moon. But first he told me of it, as his sires had told the tale to him.

Long ago the Picts had drifted down from the northwest on a long, long trek, finally reaching these jungle-covered hills, where, because they were weary, and because the game and fruit were plentiful and there were no hostile tribes, they halted and built their mud-walled villages.

Some of them, a whole clan of that numerous tribe, took up their abode in the Valley of the Broken Stones. They found the columns and a great ruined temple back in the trees, and in that temple there was no shrine or altar, but the mouth of a shaft that vanished deep into the black earth, and in which there were no steps such as a human being would make and use. They built their village in the valley, and in the night, under the moon, horror came upon them and left only broken walls and bits of slime-smeared flesh.

In those days the Picts feared nothing. The warriors of the other clans gathered and sang their war-songs and danced their war-dances and followed a broad track of blood and slime to the shaft-mouth in the temple. They howled defiance and hurled down boulders which were never heard to strike bottom. Then began a thin demoniac piping, and up from the well pranced a hideous anthropomorphic figure dancing to the weird strains of a pipe it held in its monstrous hands. The horror of its aspect froze the fierce Picts with amazement, and close behind it a vast white bulk heaved up from the subterranean darkness. Out of the shaft came a slavering mad nightmare which arrows pierced but could not check, which swords carved but could not slay. It fell slobbering upon the warriors, crushing them to crimson pulp, tearing them to bits as an octopus might tear small fishes, sucking their blood from their mangled limbs and devouring them even as they screamed and struggled. The survivors fled, pursued to the very ridge, up which, apparently, the monster could not propel its quaking mountainous bulk.

After that they did not dare the silent valley. But the dead came to their shamans and old men in dreams and told them strange and terrible secrets. They spoke of an ancient, ancient race of semi-human beings which once inhabited that valley and reared those columns for their own weird inexplicable purposes. The white monster in the pits was their god, summoned up from the nighted abysses of mid-earth uncounted fathoms below the black mold, by sorcery unknown to the sons of men. The hairy anthropomorphic being was its servant, created to serve the god, a formless elemental spirit drawn up from below and cased in flesh, organic but beyond the understanding of humanity. The Old Ones had long vanished into the limbo from whence they crawled in the black dawn of the universe, but their bestial god and his inhuman slave lived on. Yet both were organic after a fashion, and could be wounded, though no human weapon had been found potent enough to slay them.

Bragi and his clan had dwelt for weeks in the valley before the horror struck. Only the night before, Grom, hunting above the cliffs, and by that token daring greatly, had been paralyzed by a high-pitched demon piping, and then by a mad clamor of human screaming. Stretched face down in the dirt, hiding his head in a tangle of grass, he had not dared to move, even when the shrieks died away in the slobbering, repulsive sounds of a hideous feast. When dawn broke he had crept shuddering to the cliffs to look down into the valley, and the sight of the devastation, even when seen from afar, had driven him in yammering flight far into the hills. But it had occurred to him, finally, that he should warn the rest of the tribe, and returning, on his way to the camp on the plateau, he had seen me entering the valley.

So spoke Grom, while I sat and brooded darkly, my chin on my mighty fist. I cannot frame in modern words the clan-feeling that in those days was a living vital part of every man and woman. In a world where talon and fang were lifted on every hand, and the hands of all men raised against an individual, except those of his own clan, tribal instinct was more than the phrase it is today. It was as much a part of a man as was his heart or his right hand. This was necessary, for only thus banded together in unbreakable groups could mankind have survived in the terrible environments of the primitive world. So now the personal grief I felt for Bragi and the clean-limbed young men and laughing white-skinned girls was drowned in a deeper sea of grief and fury that was cosmic in its depth and intensity. I sat grimly, while the Pict squatted anxiously beside me, his gaze roving from me to the menacing deeps of the valley where the accursed columns loomed like broken teeth of cackling hags among the waving leafy reaches.

I, Niord, was not one to use my brain over-much. I lived in a physical world, and there were the old men of the tribe to do my thinking. But I was one of a race destined to become dominant mentally as well as physically, and I was no mere muscular animal. So as I sat there there came dimly and then clearly a thought to me that brought a short fierce laugh from my lips.

Rising, I bade Grom aid me, and we built a pyre on the lake shore of dried wood, the ridgepoles of the tents, and the broken shafts of spears. Then we collected the grisly fragments that had been parts of Bragi's band, and we laid them on the pile, and struck flint and steel to it.

The thick sad smoke crawled serpent-like into the sky, and turning to Grom, I made him guide me to the jungle where lurked that scaly horror, Satha, the great serpent. Grom gaped at me; not the greatest hunters among the Picts sought out the mighty crawling one. But my will was like a wind that swept him along my course, and at last he led the way. We left the valley by the upper end, crossing the ridge, skirting the tall cliffs, and plunged into the fastnesses of the south, which was peopled only by the grim denizens of the jungle. Deep into the jungle we went, until we came to a low-lying expanse, dank and dark beneath the great creeper-festooned trees, where our feet sank deep into the spongy silt, carpeted by rotting vegetation, and slimy moisture oozed up beneath their pressure. This, Grom told me, was the realm haunted by Satha, the great serpent.

Let me speak of Satha. There is nothing like him on earth today, nor has there been for countless ages. Like the meat-eating dinosaur, like old saber-tooth, he was too terrible to exist. Even then he was a survival of a grimmer age when life and its forms were cruder and more hideous. There were not many of his kind then, though they may have existed in great numbers in the reeking ooze of the vast jungle-tangled swamps still farther south. He was larger than any python of modern ages, and his fangs dripped with poison a thousand times more deadly than that of a king cobra.

He was never worshipped by the pure-blood Picts, though the blacks that came later deified him, and that adoration persisted in the hybrid race that sprang from the negroes and their white conquerors. But to other peoples he was the nadir of evil horror, and tales of him became twisted into demonology; so in later ages Satha became the veritable devil of the white races, and the Stygians first worshipped, and then, when they became Egyptians, abhorred him under the name of Set, the Old Serpent, while to the Semites he became Leviathan and Satan. He was terrible enough to be a god, for he was a crawling death. I had seen a bull elephant fall dead in his tracks from Satha's bite. I had seen him, had glimpsed him writhing his horrific way through the dense jungle, had seen him take his prey, but I had never hunted him. He was too grim, even for the slayer of old saber-tooth.

But now I hunted him, plunging farther and farther into the hot, breathless reek of his jungle, even when friendship for me could not drive Grom farther. He urged me to paint my body and sing my death-song before I advanced farther, but I pushed on unheeding.

In a natural runway that wound between the shouldering trees, I set a trap. I found a large tree, soft and spongy of fiber, but thick boled and heavy, and I hacked through its base close to the ground with my great sword, directing its fall so that when it toppled, its top crashed into the branches of a smaller tree, leaving it leaning across the runway, one end resting on the earth, the other caught in the small tree. Then I cut away the branches on the underside, and cutting a slim tough sapling I trimmed it and stuck it upright like a prop-pole under the leaning tree. Then, cutting away the tree which supported it, I left the great trunk poised precariously on the prop-pole, to which I fastened a long vine, as thick as my wrist.

Then I went alone through that primordial twilight jungle until an overpowering fetid odor assailed my nostrils, and from the rank vegetation in front of me, Satha reared up his hideous head, swaying lethally from side to side, while his forked tongue jetted in and out, and his great yellow terrible eyes burned icily on me with all the evil wisdom of the black elder world that was when man was not. I backed away, feeling no fear, only an icy sensation along my spine, and Satha came sinuously after me, his shining eighty-foot barrel rippling over the rotting vegetation in mesmeric silence. His wedge-shaped head was bigger than the head of the hugest stallion, his trunk was thicker than a man's body, and his scales shimmered with a thousand changing scintillations. I was to Satha as a mouse is to a king cobra, but I was fanged as no mouse ever was. Quick as I was, I knew I could not avoid the lightning stroke of that great triangular head; so I dared not let him come too close. Subtly I fled down the runway, and behind me the rush of the great supple body was like the sweep of wind through the grass.

He was not far behind me when I raced beneath the deadfall, and as the great shining length glided under the trap, I gripped the vine with both hands and jerked desperately. With a crash the great trunk fell across Satha's scaly back, some six feet back of his wedge-shaped head.

I had hoped to break his spine but I do not think it did, for the great body coiled and knotted, the mighty tail lashed and thrashed, mowing down the bushes as if with a giant flail. At the instant of the fall, the huge head had whipped about and struck the tree with a terrific impact, the mighty fangs shearing through bark and wood like simitars. Now, as if aware he fought an inanimate foe, Satha turned on me, standing out of his reach. The scaly neck writhed and arched, the mighty jaws gaped, disclosing fangs a foot in length, from which dripped venom that might have burned through solid stone.

I believe, what of his stupendous strength, that Satha would have writhed from under the trunk, but for a broken branch that had been driven deep into his side, holding him like a barb. The sound of his hissing filled the jungle and his eyes glared at me with such concentrated evil that I shook despite myself. Oh, he knew it was I who had trapped him! Now I came as close as I dared, and with a sudden powerful cast of my spear, transfixed his neck just below the gaping jaws, nailing him to the tree trunk. Then I dared greatly, for he was far from dead, and I knew he would in an instant tear the spear from the wood and be free to strike. But in that instant I ran in, and swinging my sword with all my great power, I hewed off his terrible head.

The heavings and contortions of Satha's prisoned form in life were naught to the convulsions of his headless length in death. I retreated, dragging the gigantic head after me with a crooked pole, and at a safe distance from the lashing, flying tail, I set to work. I worked with naked death then, and no man ever toiled more gingerly than did I. For I cut out the poison sacs at the base of the great fangs, and in the terrible venom I soaked the heads of eleven arrows, being careful that only the bronze points were in the liquid, which else had corroded away the wood of the tough shafts. While I was doing this, Grom, driven by comradeship and curiosity, came stealing nervously through the jungle, and his mouth gaped as he looked on the head of Satha.

For hours I steeped the arrowheads in the poison, until they were caked with a horrible green scum, and showed tiny flecks of corrosion where the venom had eaten into the solid bronze. I wrapped them carefully in broad, thick, rubber-like leaves, and then, though night had fallen and the hunting beasts were roaring on every hand, I went back through the jungled hills, Grom with me, until at dawn we came again to the high cliffs that loomed above the Valley of Broken Stones.

At the mouth of the valley I broke my spear, and I took all the unpoisoned shafts from my quiver, and snapped them. I painted my face and limbs as the Æsir painted themselves only when they went forth to certain doom, and I sang my death-song to the sun as it rose over the cliffs, my yellow mane blowing in the morning wind.

Then I went down into the valley, bow in hand.

Grom could not drive himself to follow me. He lay on his belly in the dust and howled like a dying dog.

I passed the lake and the silent camp where the pyre ashes still smoldered, and came under the thickening trees beyond. About me the columns loomed, mere shapeless heaps from the ravages of staggering eons. The trees grew more dense, and under their vast leafy branches the very light was dusky and evil. As in twilight shadow I saw the ruined temple, cyclopean walls staggering up from masses of decaying masonry and fallen blocks of stone. About six hundred yards in front of it a great column reared up in an open glade, eighty or ninety feet in height. It was so worn and pitted by weather and time that any child of my tribe could have climbed it, and I marked it and changed my plan.

I came to the ruins and saw huge crumbling walls upholding a domed roof from which many stones had fallen, so that it seemed like the lichen-grown ribs of some mythical monster's skeleton arching above me. Titanic columns flanked the open doorway through which ten elephants could have stalked abreast. Once there might have been inscriptions and hieroglyphics on the pillars and walls, but they were long worn away. Around the great room, on the inner side, ran columns in better state of preservation. On each of these columns was a flat pedestal, and some dim instinctive memory vaguely resurrected a shadowy scene wherein black drums roared madly, and on these pedestals monstrous beings squatted loathsomely in inexplicable rituals rooted in the black dawn of the universe.

There was no altar—only the mouth of a great well-like shaft in the stone floor, with strange obscene carvings all about the rim. I tore great pieces of stone from the rotting floor and cast them down the shaft which slanted down into utter darkness. I heard them bound along the side, but I did not hear them strike bottom. I cast down stone after stone, each with a searing curse, and at last I heard a sound that was not the dwindling rumble of the falling stones. Up from the well floated a weird demon-piping that was a symphony of madness. Far down in the darkness I glimpsed the faint fearful glimmering of a vast white bulk.

I retreated slowly as the piping grew louder, falling back through the broad doorway. I heard a scratching, scrambling noise, and up from the shaft and out of the doorway between the colossal columns came a prancing incredible figure. It went erect like a man, but it was covered with fur, that was shaggiest where its face should have been. If it had ears, nose and a mouth I did not discover them. Only a pair of staring red eyes leered from the furry mask. Its misshapen hands held a strange set of pipes, on which it blew weirdly as it pranced toward me with many a grotesque caper and leap.

Behind it I heard a repulsive obscene noise as of a quaking unstable mass heaving up out of a well. Then I nocked an arrow, drew the cord and sent the shaft singing through the furry breast of the dancing monstrosity. It went down as though struck by a thunderbolt, but to my horror the piping continued, though the pipes had fallen from the malformed hands. Then I turned and ran fleetly to the column, up which I swarmed before I looked back. When I reached the pinnacle I looked, and because of the shock and surprize of what I saw, I almost fell from my dizzy perch.

Out of the temple the monstrous dweller in the darkness had come, and I, who had expected a horror yet cast in some terrestrial mold, looked on the spawn of nightmare. From what subterranean hell it crawled in the long ago I know not, nor what black age it represented. But it was not a beast, as humanity knows beasts. I call it a worm for lack of a better term. There is no earthly language which has a name for it. I can only say that it looked somewhat more like a worm than it did an octopus, a serpent or a dinosaur.

It was white and pulpy, and drew its quaking bulk along the ground, worm-fashion. But it had wide flat tentacles, and fleshy feelers, and other adjuncts the use of which I am unable to explain. And it had a long proboscis which it curled and uncurled like an elephant's trunk. Its forty eyes, set in a horrific circle, were composed of thousands of facets of as many scintillant colors which changed and altered in never-ending transmutation. But through all interplay of hue and glint, they retained their evil intelligence—intelligence there was behind those flickering facets, not human nor yet bestial, but a night-born demoniac intelligence such as men in dreams vaguely sense throbbing titanically in the black gulfs outside our material universe. In size the monster was mountainous; its bulk would have dwarfed a mastodon.

But even as I shook with the cosmic horror of the thing, I drew a feathered shaft to my ear and arched it singing on its way. Grass and bushes were crushed flat as the monster came toward me like a moving mountain and shaft after shaft I sent with terrific force and deadly precision. I could not miss so huge a target. The arrows sank to the feathers or clear out of sight in the unstable bulk, each bearing enough poison to have stricken dead a bull elephant. Yet on it came, swiftly, appallingly, apparently heedless of both the shafts and the venom in which they were steeped. And all the time the hideous music played a maddening accompaniment, whining thinly from the pipes that lay untouched on the ground.

My confidence faded; even the poison of Satha was futile against this uncanny being. I drove my last shaft almost straight downward into the quaking white mountain, so close was the monster under my perch. Then suddenly its color altered. A wave of ghastly blue surged over it, and the vast bulk heaved in earthquake-like convulsions. With a terrible plunge it struck the lower part of the column, which crashed to falling shards of stone. But even with the impact, I leaped far out and fell through the empty air full upon the monster's back.

The spongy skin yielded and gave beneath my feet, and I drove my sword hilt-deep, dragging it through the pulpy flesh, ripping a horrible yard-long wound, from which oozed a green slime. Then a flip of a cable-like tentacle flicked me from the titan's back and spun me three hundred feet through the air to crash among a cluster of giant trees.

The impact must have splintered half the bones in my frame, for when I sought to grasp my sword again and crawl anew to the combat, I could not move hand or foot, could only writhe helplessly with my broken back. But I could see the monster and I knew that I had won, even in defeat. The mountainous bulk was heaving and billowing, the tentacles were lashing madly, the antennæ writhing and knotting, and the nauseous whiteness had changed to a pale and grisly green. It turned ponderously and lurched back toward the temple, rolling like a crippled ship in a heavy swell. Trees crashed and splintered as it lumbered against them.

I wept with pure fury because I could not catch up my sword and rush in to die glutting my berserk madness in mighty strokes. But the worm-god was death-stricken and needed not my futile sword. The demon pipes on the ground kept up their infernal tune, and it was like the fiend's death dirge. Then as the monster veered and floundered, I saw it catch up the corpse of its hairy slave. For an instant the apish form dangled in midair, gripped round by the trunk-like proboscis, then was dashed against the temple wall with a force that reduced the hairy body to a mere shapeless pulp. At that the pipes screamed out horribly, and fell silent forever.

The titan staggered on the brink of the shaft; then another change came over it—a frightful transfiguration the nature of which I cannot yet describe. Even now when I try to think of it clearly, I am only chaotically conscious of a blasphemous, unnatural transmutation of form and substance, shocking and indescribable. Then the strangely altered bulk tumbled into the shaft to roll down into the ultimate darkness from whence it came, and I knew that it was dead. And as it vanished into the well, with a rending, grinding groan the ruined walls quivered from dome to base. They bent inward and buckled with deafening reverberation, the columns splintered, and with a cataclysmic crash the dome itself came thundering down. For an instant the air seemed veiled with flying debris and stone dust, through which the treetops lashed madly as in a storm or an earthquake convulsion. Then all was clear again and I stared, shaking the blood from my eyes. Where the temple had stood there lay only a colossal pile of shattered masonry and broken stones, and every column in the valley had fallen, to lie in crumbling shards.

In the silence that followed I heard Grom wailing a dirge over me. I bade him lay my sword in my hand, and he did so, and bent close to hear what I had to say, for I was passing swiftly.

"Let my tribe remember," I said, speaking slowly. "Let the tale be told from village to village, from camp to camp, from tribe to tribe, so that men may know that not man nor beast nor devil may prey in safety on the golden-haired people of Asgard. Let them build me a cairn where I lie and lay me therein with my bow and sword at hand, to guard this valley forever; so if the ghost of the god I slew comes up from below, my ghost will ever be ready to give it battle."

And while Grom howled and beat his hairy breast, death came to me in the Valley of the Worm.

The Garden of Fear

Once I was Hunwulf, the Wanderer. I cannot explain my knowledge of this fact by any occult or esoteric means, nor shall I try. A man remembers his past life; I remember my past *lives*. Just as a normal individual recalls the shapes that were him in childhood, boyhood and youth, so I recall the shapes that have been James Allison in forgotten ages. Why this memory is mine I cannot say, any more than I can explain the myriad other phenomena of nature which daily confront me and every other mortal. But as I lie waiting for death to free me from my long disease, I see with a clear, sure sight the grand panorama of lives that trail out behind me. I see the men who have been me, and I see the beasts that have been me.

For my memory does not end at the becoming of Man. How could it, when the Beast so shades into Man that there is no clearly defined line to mark the boundaries of bestiality? At this instant I see a dim twilight vista, among the gigantic trees of a primordial forest that never knew the tread of a leather-shod foot. I see a vast, shaggy, shambling bulk that lumbers clumsily yet swiftly, sometimes upright, sometimes on all fours. He delves under rotten logs for grubs and insects, and his small ears twitch continually. He lifts his head and bares yellow fangs. He is primordial, bestial, anthropoid; yet I recognize his kinship with the entity now called James Allison. Kinship? Say rather oneness. I am he; he is I. My flesh is soft and white and hairless; his is dark and tough and shaggy. Yet we are one, and already in his feeble, shadowed brain are beginning to stir and sting and tingle the man-thoughts and the man-dreams, crude, chaotic, fleeting, yet the basis for all the high and lofty visions that men have dreamed in all the long following ages.

Nor does my knowledge cease there. It goes back, back, down immemorial vistas I dare not follow, to abysses too dark and awful for the human mind to plumb. Yet even there I am aware of my identity, my individuality. I tell you, the individual is never lost, neither in the black pit from which we once crawled, blind, squalling and noisome, nor in that eventual Nirvana in which we shall one day sink—which I have glimpsed afar off, shining as a blue twilight lake among the mountains of the stars.

But enough. I would tell you of Hunwulf. Oh, it was long, long ago! How long ago I dare not say. Why should I seek for paltry human comparisons to describe a realm indescribably, incomprehensibly distant? Since that age the Earth has altered her contours not once but a dozen times, and whole cycles of mankind have completed their destinies.

I was Hunwulf, a son of the golden-haired Æsir, who, from the icy plains of shadowy Asgard, sent blue-eyed tribes around the world in century-long drifts to leave their trails in strange places. On one of those southward drifts I was born, for I never saw the homeland of my people, where the bulk of the Nordheimr still dwelt in their horsehide tents among the snows.

I grew to manhood on that long wandering, to the fierce, sinewy, untamed manhood of the Æsir, who knew no gods but Ymir of the frost-rimed beard, and whose axes are stained with the blood of many nations. My thews were like woven steel cords. My yellow hair fell in a lion-like mane to my mighty shoulders. My loins were girt with leopard skin. With either hand I could wield my heavy flint-headed axe.

Year by year my tribe drifted southward, sometimes swinging in long arcs to east or west, sometimes lingering for months or years in fertile valleys or plains where the grass eaters swarmed, but always forging slowly and inevitably southward. Sometimes our way led through vast and breathless solitudes that had never known a human cry; sometimes strange tribes disputed our course, and our trail passed over the bloodstained ashes of butchered villages. And amidst this wandering, hunting and slaughtering, I came to full manhood and the love of Gudrun.

What shall I say of Gudrun? How describe color to the blind? I can say that her skin was whiter than milk, that her hair was living gold with the flame of the sun caught in it, that the supple beauty of her body would shame the dream that shaped the Grecian goddesses. But I cannot make you realize the fire and wonder that was Gudrun. You have no basis for comparison; you know womanhood only by the women of your epoch, who, beside her, are like candles beside the glow of the full moon. Not for a millennium of millenniums have women like Gudrun walked the earth. Cleopatra, Thais, Helen of Troy, they were but pallid shadows of her beauty, frail mimicries of the blossom that blooms to full glory only in the primordial.

For Gudrun I forsook my tribe and my people, and went into the wilderness an exile and an outcast, with blood on my hands. She was of my race, but not of my tribe: a waif whom we found as a child wandering in a dark forest, lost from some wandering tribe of our blood. She grew up in the tribe, and when she came to the full ripeness of her glorious young womanhood, she was given to Heimdul the Strong, the mightiest hunter of the tribe.

But the dream of Gudrun was a madness in my soul, a flame that burned eternally, and for her I slew Heimdul, crushing his skull with my flint-headed axe ere ever he could bear her to his horsehide tent. And then followed our long flight from the vengeance of the tribe. Willingly she went with me, for she loved me with the love of the Æsir women, which is a devouring flame that destroys weakness. Oh, it was a savage age, when life was grim and bloodstained, and the weak died quickly. There was nothing mild or gentle about us; our passions were those of the tempest, the surge and impact of battle, the challenge of the lion. Our loves were terrible as our hates.

And so I carried Gudrun from the tribe, and the killers were hot on our trail. For a day and a night and a day they pressed us hard, until we swam a rising river, a roaring, foaming torrent that even the men of the Æsir dared not attempt. But in the madness of our love and recklessness we buffeted our way across, beaten and torn by the frenzy of the flood, and reached the further bank alive.

Then for many days we traversed upland forests haunted by tigers and leopards, until we came to a great barrier of mountains, blue ramparts climbing awesomely to the sky, slope piled upon slope.

In those mountains we were assailed by freezing winds and hunger, and by giant condors which swept down upon us with a thunder of gigantic wings. In grim battles in the passes I shot away all my arrows and splintered my flint-headed spear, but at last we crossed the bleak backbone of the range and, descending the southern slopes, came upon a village of mud huts among the cliffs inhabited by a peaceful, brown-skinned people who spoke a strange tongue and had strange customs. But they greeted us with the sign of peace, and brought us into their village, where they set meat and barley bread and fermented milk before us, and squatted in a ring about us while we ate, and a woman slapped softly on a bowl-shaped tom-tom to do us honor.

We had reached their village at dusk, and night fell while we feasted. On all sides rose the cliffs and peaks, shouldering massively against the stars. The little cluster of mud huts and the tiny fires were drowned and lost in the immensity of the night. Gudrun felt the loneliness, the crowding desolation of that darkness, and she pressed close to me, her shoulder against my breast. But my ax was close at my hand, and I had never known the sensation of fear.

The little brown people squatted before us, men and women, and tried to talk to us with motions of their slender hands. Dwelling always in one place, in comparative security, they lacked both the strength and the uncompromising ferocity of the nomadic Æsir. Their hands fluttered with friendly gestures in the firelight.

I made them understand that we had come from the north, had crossed the backbone of the great mountain range, and that on the morrow it was our intention to descend into the green tablelands which we had glimpsed southward of the peaks. When they understood my meaning they set up a great cry, shaking their heads violently, and beating madly on the drum. They were all so eager to impart something to me, and all waving their hands at once, that they bewildered rather than enlightened me. Eventually they did make me understand that they did not wish me to descend the mountains. Some menace lay to the south of the village, but whether of man or beast, I could not learn.

It was while they were all gesticulating and my whole attention was centered on their gestures, that the blow fell. The first intimation was a sudden thunder of wings in my ears; a dark shape rushed out of the night, and a great pinion dealt me a buffet over the head as I turned. I was knocked sprawling, and in that instant I heard Gudrun scream as she was torn from my side. Bounding up, quivering with a furious eagerness to rend and slay, I saw the dark shape vanish again into the darkness, a white, screaming, writhing figure trailing from its talons.

Roaring my grief and fury I caught up my axe and charged into the dark—then halted short, wild, desperate, knowing not which way to turn.

The little brown people had scattered, screaming, knocking sparks from their fires as they rushed over them in their haste to gain their huts, but now they crept out fearfully, whimpering like wounded dogs. They gathered around me and plucked at me with timid hands and chattered in their tongue while I cursed in sick impotency, knowing they wished to tell me something which I could not understand.

At last I suffered them to lead me back to the fire, and there the oldest man of the tribe brought forth a strip of cured hide, a clay pot of pigments, and a stick. On the hide he painted a crude picture of a winged thing carrying a white woman—oh, it was very crude, but I made out his meaning. Then all pointed southward and cried out loudly in their own tongue, and I knew that the menace they had warned me against was the thing that had carried off Gudrun. Until then I supposed that it had been one of the great mountain condors which had carried her away, but the picture the old man drew, in black paint, resembled a winged man more than anything else.

Then, slowly and laboriously, he began to trace something I finally recognized as a map—oh, yes, even in those dim days we had our primitive maps, though no modern man would be able to comprehend them, so utterly different was our symbolism.

It took a long time; it was midnight before the old man had finished and I understood his tracings. But at last the matter was made clear. If I followed the course traced on the map, down the long narrow valley where stood the village, across a plateau, down a series of rugged slopes and along another valley, I would come to the place where lurked the being which had stolen my woman. At that spot the old man drew what looked like a misshapen hut, with many strange markings all about it in red pigments. Pointing to these, and again to me, he shook his head, with those loud shrill cries that seemed to indicate peril among these people.

Then they tried again to persuade me not to go, but afire with eagerness I took the piece of hide and the pouch of food they thrust into my hands (they were indeed a strange people for that age), and grasping my axe, set off in the moonless darkness. But my eyes were keener than a modern man can comprehend, and my sense of direction was as mysterious as a wolf's. Once the map was fixed in my mind, I could have thrown it away and come unerringly to the place I sought; but I folded it and thrust it into my girdle.

I travelled at my best speed through the starlight, taking no heed of any beasts that might be seeking their prey—cave bear or saber-toothed tiger. At times I heard gravel slide under stealthy padded paws, I glimpsed fierce yellow eyes burning in the darkness, and caught sight of shadowy skulking forms. But I plunged on recklessly, in too desperate a mood to give the path to any beast, however fearsome.

I traversed the valley, climbed a ridge and came out on a broad plateau, gashed with ravines and strewn with boulders. I crossed this and in the darkness before dawn commenced my climb down the treacherous slopes. They seemed endless, falling away in a long steep incline until their feet were lost in darkness. But I went down recklessly, not pausing to unsling the rawhide rope I carried slung to my shoulders, trusting to my skill and luck to bring me down without a broken neck.

And just as dawn was touching the peaks with a white glow, I dropped into a broad valley, walled by stupendous cliffs. At that point it was wide, from east to west, but the cliffs converged toward the lower end, giving the valley the appearance of a great fan, narrowing swiftly toward the south.

The floor was level, traversed by a winding stream. Trees grew thinly; there was no underbrush, but a carpet of tall grass, which at that time of the year was somewhat dry. Along the stream where the green lush grew wandered mammoths, hairy mountains of flesh and muscle.

I gave them a wide berth, giants too mighty for me to cope with, confident in their power, and afraid of only one thing on earth. They bent forward their great ears and lifted their trunks menacingly when I approached too near, but they did not attack me. I ran swiftly among the trees and the sun was not yet above the eastern ramparts which its rising edged with golden flame, when I came to the point where the cliffs converged. My nightlong climb had not affected my iron muscles. I felt no weariness; my fury burned unabated. What lay beyond the cliffs I could not know; I ventured no conjecture. I had room in my brain only for red wrath and killing lust.

The cliffs did not form a solid wall. That is, the extremities of the converging palisades did not meet, leaving a notch or gap a few hundred feet wide; the stream flowed through it, and trees grew thickly there. I passed through this notch, which was not much longer than it was wide, and emerged into a second valley, or rather into a continuance of the same valley which broadened out again beyond the pass.

The cliffs slanted away swiftly to east and west, to form giant ramparts that marched clear around the valley in the shape of a vast oval. It formed a blue rim all around the valley without a break except for a glimpse of clear sky that seemed to mark another notch at the southern end. The inner valley was shaped much like a great bottle, with two necks.

The neck by which I had entered was crowded with trees, which grew densely for several hundred yards, when they gave way abruptly to a field of crimson flowers. And a few hundred yards beyond the edge of the trees, I saw a strange structure.

I must speak of what I saw not alone as Hunwulf, but as James Allison as well. For Hunwulf only vaguely comprehended what he saw, and, as Hunwulf, he could not have described it at all. I, Hunwulf, knew nothing of architecture. The only man-built dwellings I had ever seen had been the horsehide tents of my people, and the thatched mud huts of the barley people and other races equally primitive.

So as Hunwulf, I could only say that I looked upon a great hut the construction of which was beyond my comprehension. But I, James Allison, know that it was a tower, some seventy feet in height, of a curious green stone, highly polished, and of a substance that created the illusion of semi-translucency. It was cylindrical, and, as near as I could see, without doors or windows. The main body of the building was perhaps sixty feet in height, and from its center rose a smaller tower that completed its full stature. This tower, being much inferior in girth to the main body of the structure, was thus surrounded by a sort of gallery, with a crenellated parapet, and was furnished with both doors, curiously arched, and windows, thickly barred as I could see, even from where I stood.

That was all. No evidence of human occupancy. No sign of life in all the valley. But it was evident that this castle was what the old man of the mountain village had been trying to draw, and I was certain that in it I would find Gudrun—if she still lived.

Beyond the tower I saw the glimmer of a blue lake into which the stream, following the curve of the western wall, eventually flowed. Lurking amid the trees I glared at the tower and at the flowers which surrounded it on all sides, growing thick along the walls and extending for hundreds of yards in all directions. There were trees at the other end of the valley, near the lake; but no trees grew among the flowers.

They were not like any plants I had ever seen. They grew close together, almost touching each other. They were some four feet in height, with only one blossom on each stalk, a blossom larger than a man's head, with broad, fleshy petals drawn close together. These petals were a livid crimson, the hue of an open wound. The stalks were thick as a man's wrist, colorless, almost transparent. The poisonously green leaves were shaped like spearheads, drooping on long snaky stems. Their whole aspect was repellant, and I wondered what their denseness concealed.

For all my wild-born instincts were roused in me. I felt lurking peril, just as I had often sensed the ambushing lion before my external senses recognized him. I scanned the dense blossoms closely, wondering if some great serpent coiled among them. My nostrils expanded as I quested for scent, but the wind was blowing away from me. But there was something unnatural about that vast garden. Though the north wind swept over it, not a blossom stirred, not a leaf rustled; they hung motionless, sullen, like birds of prey with drooping heads, and I had a strange feeling that they were watching me like living things.

It was like a landscape in a dream: on either hand the blue cliffs lifting against the cloud-flecked sky; in the distance the dreaming lake; and that fantastic green tower rising in the midst of that livid crimson field.

And there was something else: in spite of the wind that was blowing away from me, I caught a scent, a charnel-house reek of death and decay and corruption that rose like an intangible miasma from the fleshy blossoms.

Then suddenly I crouched closer in my covert. There was life and movement on the castle. A figure emerged from the tower, and coming to the parapet, leaned upon it and looked out across the valley. It was a man, but such a man as I had never dreamed of, even in nightmares.

He was tall, powerful, black with the hue of polished ebony; but the feature which made a human nightmare of him was the bat-like wings which folded on his shoulders. I knew they were wings; the fact was obvious and indisputable.

I, James Allison, have pondered much on that phenomenon which I witnessed through the eyes of Hunwulf. Was that winged man merely a freak, an isolated example of distorted nature, dwelling in solitude and immemorial desolation? Or was he a survival of a forgotten race, which had risen, reigned and vanished before the coming of man as we know him? The little brown people of the hills might have told me, but we had no speech in common. Yet I am inclined to the latter theory. Winged men are not uncommon in mythology; they are met with in the folklore of many nations and many races. As far back as man may go in myth, chronicle and legend, he finds tales of harpies and winged gods, angels, and demons. Legends are distorted shadows of pre-existent realities. I believe that once a race of winged black men ruled a pre-Adamite world, and that I, Hunwulf, met the last survivor of that race in the valley of the red blossoms.

These thoughts I think as James Allison, with my modern knowledge which is as imponderable as my modern ignorance.

I, Hunwulf, indulged in no such speculations. Modern skepticism was not a part of my nature, nor did I ever seek to rationalize what seemed not to coincide with a natural universe. I acknowledged no gods but Ymir and his daughters, but I did not doubt the existence—as demons—of other deities, worshipped by other races. Supernatural beings of all sorts fitted into my conception of life and the universe. I no more doubted the existence of dragons, ghosts, fiends and devils than I doubted the existence of lions and buffaloes and elephants. I accepted this freak of nature as a supernatural demon and did not worry my head about its origin or source. Nor was I thrown into a panic of superstitious fear. I was a son of Asgard, who fear neither man nor devil, and I had more faith in the crashing power of my flint axe than in the spells of priests or the incantations of sorcerers.

But I did not immediately rush into the open and charge the tower. The wariness of the wild was mine, and I saw no way to climb the castle. The winged man needed no doors on the side, because he evidently entered at the top, and the slick surface of the walls seemed to defy the most skillful climber. Presently a way of getting upon the tower occurred to me, but I hesitated, waiting to see if any other winged people appeared, though I had an unexplainable feeling that he was the only one of his kind in the valley—possibly in the world.

While I crouched among the trees and watched, I saw him lift his elbows from the parapet and stretch lithely, like a great cat. Then he strode across the circular gallery and entered the tower. A muffled cry rang out on the air which caused me to stiffen, though even so I knew it was not the cry of a woman. Presently the black master of the castle emerged, dragging a smaller figure with him—a figure which writhed and struggled and cried out piteously. I saw that it was a small naked brown man, much like those of the mountain village. Captured, I did not doubt, as Gudrun had been captured.

He was like a child in the hands of his huge foe. The black spread broad wings and rose over the parapet, carrying his captive as a condor might carry a sparrow. He soared out over the field of blossoms, while I crouched closer in my leafy retreat, glaring in amazement.

The winged man, hovering in midair, voiced a strange weird cry; and it was answered in a horrible fashion. A shudder of awful life passed over the crimson field beneath him. The great red blossoms trembled and opened, spreading their fleshy petals like the mouths of serpents. Their stalks seemed to elongate, stretching upward. Their broad leaves lifted and vibrated with a curious lethal whirring, like the singing of a rattlesnake. A faint but flesh-crawling hissing sounded all over the valley. The blossoms gaped, straining upward. And with a fiendish laugh, the winged man dropped his writhing captive.

With the scream of a lost soul the brown man hurtled downward, crashing among the flowers. And with a rustling hiss, they were on him. Their thick flexible stalks arched like the necks of serpents, their petals closed on his flesh. A hundred blossoms clung to him like the tentacles of an octopus, smothering and crushing him down. His shrieks of agony came muffled; he was completely hidden by the hissing, threshing flowers. Those beyond reach swayed and writhed furiously as if seeking to tear up their roots in their eagerness to join their brothers. All over the field the great red blossoms leaned and strained toward the spot where the grisly battle went on. The shrieks sank lower and lower, and ceased. A dread silence reigned in the valley. The black man flapped his way leisurely back to the tower, and vanished within it.

Then presently the blossoms detached themselves one by one from their victim who lay very still and white. Aye, his whiteness was more than that of death; he was like a wax image, a staring effigy from which every drop of blood had been sucked. And a shocking transmutation was evident in the flowers directly about him. Their stalks were no longer colorless; they were swollen and dark red, like transparent bamboos filled to the bursting with fresh blood.

Drawn by an insatiable curiosity, I stole from the trees and glided to the very edge of the red field. The blossoms hissed and bent toward me, spreading their petals like the hood of a roused cobra. Selecting one furtherest from its brothers, I severed the stalk with a stroke of my axe, and the thing tumbled to the ground, writhing like a beheaded serpent. It is a grisly thing to see an inanimate object *die* like an animate being.

When its struggles ceased I bent over it in wonder. The stalk was not hollow as I had supposed, that is, hollow like a dry bamboo. It was traversed with a network of thread-like veins, some empty, and from some of which flowed a colorless sap. The stems which held the leaves to the stalk were remarkably tenacious and pliant, and the leaves themselves were edged with curved spines, like sharp hooks. Once those spines were sunk in the flesh, the victim would be forced to tear up the whole plant by the roots if he escaped.

The petals were each broad as my hand, and thick as a prickly pear, and on the inner side covered with innumerable tiny mouths, not larger than the head of a pin. In the center, where the pistil should be, there was a barbed spike, of a substance like thorn, hard as steel, with a point as sharp as that of a dagger, and narrow channels between the four serrated edges.

From my investigations of this horrible travesty of vegetation, I looked up suddenly, just in time to see the winged man appear again on the parapet. He did not appear to be particularly surprized to see me. He shouted in his unknown tongue and made a mocking gesture, while I stood statue-like, gripping my axe. Presently he turned and entered the tower as he had done before; and as before, he emerged with a captive. My fury and hate were almost submerged by the flood of my joy that Gudrun was alive.

In spite of her supple strength, which was that of a she-panther, the black man handled Gudrun as easily as he had handled the brown man. Lifting her struggling white body high above his head, he displayed her to me and yelled tauntingly. Her golden hair streamed over her white shoulders as she fought vainly, crying to me in the terrible extremity of her fright and horror. Not lightly was a woman of the Æsir reduced to cringing terror. I measured the depths of her captor's diabolism by the frenzy in her shrieks.

But I stood motionless. If it would have saved her, I would have plunged into that crimson morass of hell, to be hooked and pierced and sucked white by those fiendish flowers. But that would help her none. My death would merely leave her without a defender. So I stood silent while she writhed and whimpered, and the black man's laughter sent red waves of madness surging across my brain. Once he made as if to cast her down among the flowers, and my iron control almost snapped and sent me plunging through that red sea of hell. But it was but a gesture. Presently he dragged her back to the tower and tossed her inside. Then he turned back to the parapet, rested his elbows upon it, and fell to watching me. Apparently he was playing with us as a cat plays with a mouse before he destroys it.

But while he watched, I turned my back and strode into the forest. I, Hunwulf, was not a thinker, as modern men understand the term. I lived in an age when emotions were more often translated by the smash of a flint axe than by emanations of the intellect. Yet I was not the senseless animal the black man evidently supposed me to be. I had a human brain, whetted by the eternal struggle for existence and supremacy.

I knew I could not cross that red strip that banded the castle, alive. Before I could take a half dozen steps a score of barbed spikes would be thrust into my flesh, their avid mouths sucking the blood from my veins to feed their demoniac lust. Even my tigerish strength would not avail to hew a path through them.

The winged man did not follow. Looking back, I saw him still lounging in the same position. When I, as James Allison, dream again the dreams of Hunwulf, that image is etched in my mind—that gargoyle figure with elbows propped on the parapet, like a medieval devil brooding over the battlements of hell.

I passed through the strait of the valley and came into the vale beyond where the trees thinned and the mammoths lumbered along the stream. Beyond the herd I stopped and drawing a pair of flints from my pouch, stooped and struck a spark into the dry grass. Running swiftly from chosen place to place, I set a dozen fires, in a great semicircle. The north wind caught them, whipped them into eager life, drove them before it. In a few minutes a rampart of flame was sweeping down the valley.

The mammoths ceased their feeding, lifted their ears and bellowed alarm. In all the world they feared only fire. They began to retreat southward, the cows herding the calves before them, the bulls trumpeting like the blasts of Judgment Day. Roaring like a storm the fire rushed on, and the mammoths broke and stampeded, a crashing hurricane of flesh, a thundering earthquake of hurtling bone and muscle. Trees splintered and went down before them, the ground shook under their headlong tread. Behind them came the racing fire and on the heels of the fire came I, so closely that the smoldering earth burnt the moosehide sandals off my feet.

Through the narrow neck they thundered, levelling the dense thickets like a giant scythe. Trees were torn up by the roots; it was as if a tornado had ripped through the pass.

With a deafening thunder of pounding feet and trumpeting, they stormed across the sea of red blossoms. Those devilish plants might have even pulled down and destroyed a single mammoth; but under the impact of the whole herd, they were no more than common flowers. The maddened titans crashed through and over them, battering them to shreds, tearing, rending, hammering, stamping them into the earth which grew soggy with their juice.

I trembled for an instant, fearing the brutes would not turn aside from the castle, and dubious of even it being able to withstand that battering ram concussion. Evidently the winged man shared my fears, for he shot up from the tower and raced off through the sky toward the lake. But one of the bulls butted head-on into the wall, was shunted off the smooth curving surface, caromed into the one next to him, and the herd split and roared by the tower on either hand, so closely their hairy sides rasped against it. They thundered on through the red field toward the distant lake.

The fire, reaching the edge of the trees, was checked; the smashed, sappy fragments of the red flowers would not burn. Trees, fallen or standing, smoked and burst into flame, and burning branches showered around me as I ran through the trees and out into the gigantic swath the charging herd had cut through the livid field.

As I ran I shouted to Gudrun and she answered me. Her voice was muffled, and accompanied by a hammering on something. The winged man had locked her into the tower.

As I came under the castle wall, treading on remnants of red petals and snaky stalks, I unwound my rawhide rope, swung it, and sent its loop shooting upward to catch on one of the merlons of the crenellated parapet. Then I went up it, hand over hand, gripping the rope between my toes, bruising my knuckles and elbows against the sheer wall as I swung about.

I was within five feet of the parapet when I was galvanized by the beat of wings above my head. The black man shot down out of the air and landed on the gallery. I got a good look at him as he leaned over the parapet. His features were straight and regular; there was no suggestion of the negroid about him. His eyes were slanted slits, his teeth gleamed in a savage grin of hate and triumph. Long, long he had ruled the valley of the red blossoms, levelling tribute of human lives from the miserable tribes of the hills, for writhing victims to feed to the carnivorous, half-bestial flowers which were his subjects and protectors. And now I was in his power, my fierceness and craft gone for naught. A stroke of the crooked dagger in his hand, and I would go hurtling to my death. Somewhere Gudrun, seeing or sensing my peril, was screaming like a wild thing, and then a door crashed with a splintering of wood.

The black man, intent on his gloating, laid the keen edge of his dagger on the rawhide strand—then a strong white arm locked about his neck from behind, and he was jerked violently backward. Over his shoulder I saw the beautiful face of Gudrun, her hair standing on end, her eyes dilated with terror and fury.

With a roar he turned in her grasp, tore loose her clinging arms and hurled her against the tower with such force that she lay half-stunned. Then he turned again to me, but in that instant I had swarmed up and over the parapet, and leaped upon the gallery, unslinging my axe.

For an instant he hesitated, his wings half-lifted, his hand poising his dagger, as if uncertain whether to fight or take to the air. He was a giant in stature, with muscles standing out in corded ridges all over him, but he hesitated, as uncertain as a man when confronted by a wild beast.

I did not hesitate. With a deep-throated roar I sprang, swinging my axe with all my giant strength. With a strangled cry he threw up his arms, but down between them the axehead plunged, and blasted his head to a red ruin.

I wheeled toward Gudrun, and struggling to her knees, she threw her white arms about me in a desperate clasp of love and terror, staring awedly to where lay the winged lord of the valley, the crimson pulp that had been his head drowned in a puddle of blood and brains.

I had often wished that it were possible to draw these various lives of mine together in one body, combining the knowledge of James Allison with the experiences of Hunwulf. Could that be so, Hunwulf would have gone through the ebony door which Gudrun in her desperate strength had shattered, into that weird chamber he glimpsed through the ruined panels, with fantastic furnishings, and shelves heaped with rolls of parchment. He would have unrolled those scrolls and pored over their characters until he deciphered them, and read, perhaps, the chronicles of that weird race whose last survivor he had just slain. Surely the tale was stranger than an opium dream, and marvelous as the story of lost Atlantis.

But Hunwulf had no such curiosity. To him the tower, the ebony furnished chamber and the rolls of parchment were meaningless, inexplicable emanations of sorcery, whose significance lay only in their diabolism. Though the solution of the mystery lay under his fingers, he was as far removed from it as James Allison, millenniums yet unborn.

To me, Hunwulf, the castle was but a monstrous trap, concerning which I had but one emotion, and that a desire to escape from it as quickly as possible.

With Gudrun clinging to me I slid to the ground, then with a dexterous flip I freed my rope and wound it; and after that we went hand in hand along the path made by the mammoths, now vanishing in the distance, toward the blue lake at the southern end of the valley and the notch in the cliffs beyond it.

Marchers of Valhalla

The sky was lurid, gloomy and repellant, of the blue of tarnished steel, streaked with dully crimson banners. Against the muddled red smear lowered the low hills that are the peaks of that barren upland which is a dreary expanse of sand drifts and post-oak thickets, checkered with sterile fields, where tenant farmers toil out their hideously barren lives in fruitless labor and bitter want.

I had limped to a ridge which rose above the others, flanked on either hand by the dry drab post-oak thickets. The terrible dreariness and the grim desolation of the vistas spread before me turned my soul to dust and ashes. I sank down upon a half-rotting log, and the agonizing melancholy of that drab land lay hard upon me. The red sun, half-veiled in blowing dust and filmy lurid cloud, sank low; it hung a hand's breadth above the western rim. But its setting lent no glory to the sand drifts and shinnery. Its somber glow but accentuated the grisly desolation of the land.

Then suddenly I realized that I was not alone. A woman had come from the dense thicket, and stood looking down at me. I gazed at her in silent wonder. Beauty was so rare in my life I was hardly able to recognize it, yet I knew that this woman was unbelievably beautiful. She was neither short nor tall; slender and yet splendidly shaped. I do not remember her dress; I have a vague impression that she was richly but modestly clad. But I remember the strange beauty of her face, framed in the dark rippling glory of her hair. Her eyes held mine like a magnet; I cannot tell you the color of those eyes; they were dark and luminous, lighted as no eyes I ever saw were lighted. She spoke and her voice, strangely accented, was alien to my ears, and golden as distant chimes.

"Why do you fret, Hialmar?"

"You mistake me, Miss," I answered. "My name is James Allison. Were you looking for someone?"

She shook her head slowly.

"I came to look at the land once more. I had not thought to find you here."

"I don't understand you," I said. "I never saw you before. Are you a native of this country? You don't talk like a Texan." She shook her head.

"No. But I knew this land long ago—long, long ago."

"You don't look that old," I said bluntly. "—And you'll pardon me for not getting up. As you see, I have but one leg, and it was such a long walk up here that I'm forced to sit here and rest."

"Life has dealt harshly with you," she said softly. "I had hardly recognized you. Your body is so changed—"

"You must have known me before I lost my leg," I said bitterly. "Although I'll swear I can't remember you. I was only fourteen when a mustang fell on me and crushed my leg so badly it had to be amputated. I wish to God it had been my neck."

Thus cripples speak to utter strangers—not so much a bid for sympathy but the despairing wild cry of a soul tortured beyond endurance.

"Do not fret," she said softly. "Life takes but it also gives—"

"Oh, don't give me a speech about resignation and cheerfulness!" I cried savagely. "If I had the power I'd strangle every damned blatant grinning optimist in the world! What have I to be merry about? What have I to do except sit and wait for the death which is slowly creeping on me by an incurable malady? I have no memories to cheer me—no future to look forward to—except a few more years of pain and woe, and then the blackness of utter oblivion. There has not been even any beauty in my life, lying as it has in this forsaken and desolate wilderness."

The dams of my reticence were broken, and my bitter dreams, long pent up, burst forth; nor did it seem strange that I should pour out my soul to a strange woman I had never seen before.

"The country has memories," she said.

"Yes, but I have not shared in them. I could have loved life and lived deeply as a cowboy, even here, before the squatters turned the country from an open range to a drift of struggling farms. I could have lived deep as a buffalo hunter, an Indian fighter, or an explorer, even here. But I was born out of my time, and even the exploits of this weary age were denied me.

"It's bitter beyond human telling to sit chained and helpless, and feel the hot blood drying in my veins, and the glittering dreams fading in my brain. I come of a restless, roving, fighting race. My great-grandfather died at the Alamo, shoulder to shoulder with David Crockett. My grandfather rode with Jack Hayes and Bigfoot Wallace, and fell with three-quarters of Hood's brigade. My oldest brother fell at Vimy Ridge, fighting with the Canadians, and the other died at the Argonne. My father is a cripple, too; he sits drowsing in his chair all day, but his dreams are full of brave memories, for the bullet that broke his leg struck him as he charged up San Juan Hill.

"But what have I to feel or dream or think?"

"You should remember," she said softly. "Even now dreams should come to you like the echoes of distant lutes. I remember! How I crawled to you on my knees, and you spared me—aye, and the crashing and the thundering as the land gave way—man, do you never dream of drowning?"

I started.

"How could you know that? Time and again I have felt the churning, seething waters rise like a green mountain over me, and have wakened, gasping and strangling—but how could you know?"

"The bodies change; the soul remains slumbering and untouched," she answered cryptically. "Even as the world changes. This is a dreary land, you say, yet its memories are ancient and marvelous beyond the memories of Egypt."

I shook my head in wonder.

"Either you're insane or I am. Texas has glorious memories of war and conquest and drama—but what are her few hundred years of history, compared to the antiquities of Egypt—in ancientness, I mean?"

"What is the peculiarity of the state as a whole?" she asked.

"I don't know exactly what you mean," I answered. "If you mean geologically, the peculiarity that has struck me is the fact that the land is but a succession of broad table-lands, or shelves, sloping upward, from sea-level to over four thousand feet elevation, like the steps of a gigantic stair, with breaks of timbered hills between. The last break is the Caprock, and above that begins the Great Plains."

"Once the Great Plains stretched to the Gulf," she said. "Long, long ago what is now the state of Texas was a vast upland plateau, sloping gently to the coast, but without the breaks and shelvings of today. A mighty cataclysm broke off the land at the Caprock, the ocean roared over it, and the Caprock became the new shoreline. Then, age by age, the waters slowly receded, leaving the steppes as they are today. But in receding they swept into the depths of the Gulf many curious things—man, do you not remember—the vast plains that ran from the sunset to the cliffs above the shining sea? And the great city that loomed above those cliffs?"

I stared at her, bewildered, and suddenly she leaned toward me, and the glory of her alien beauty almost overpowered me. My senses reeled. She threw her hands before my eyes with a strange gesture.

"You *shall* see!" she cried sharply. "You see—what do you see?"

"I see the sand drifts and the shinnery thickets gloomy with sunset," I answered like a man speaking slowly, in a trance. "I see the sun resting on the western horizon."

"You see vast plains stretching to shining cliffs!" she cried. "You see the spires and the golden dome of the city, shimmering in the sunset! You see—"

As if night had shut down suddenly, darkness came upon me, and unreality, in which the only thing that had existence was her voice, urgent, commanding—

There was a sense of fading time and space—a sensation of being whirled over illimitable gulfs, with cosmic winds blowing against me—then I looked upon churning clouds, unreal and luminous, which crystallized into a strange landscape—familiar, and yet fantastically unfamiliar. Vast treeless plains swept away to merge with hazy horizons. In the distance, to the south, a great black cyclopean city reared its spires against the evening sky, and beyond it shone the blue waters of a placid sea. And in the near distance a line of figures moved through the still expanse. They were big men, with yellow hair and cold blue eyes, clad in scale-mail corselets and horned helmets, and they bore shields and swords. One differed from the rest in that he was short, though strongly made, and dark. And the tall yellow-haired warrior who walked beside him—for a fleeting instant there was a distinct sense of duality. I, James Allison of the twentieth century, saw and recognized the man who was I in that dim age and that strange land. This sensation faded almost instantly, and I was Hialmar, a son of the Fair-haired, without cognizance of any other existence, past or future. Yet as I tell the tale of Hialmar, I shall perforce interpret some of what he saw and did and was, not as Hialmar, but as the modern I. These interpretations you will recognize in their place. But remember Hialmar was Hialmar, and not James Allison; that he knew no more and no less than was contained in his own experiences, bounded by the boundaries of his own life. I am James Allison and I was Hialmar, but Hialmar was not James Allison; man may look back for ten thousand years; he cannot look forward, even for an instant.

We were five hundred men and our gaze was fixed on the black towers which reared against the blue of sea and sky. All day we had guided our course by them, since the first red glow of dawn had disclosed them to our wondering eyes. A man could see far across those level, grassy plains; at first sight we had thought that city near, but we had trudged all day, and still we were miles away. Lurking in our minds had been the thought that it was a ghost city—one of the phantoms which had haunted us on our long march across the bitter dusty deserts to the west, where, in the burning skies we had seen mirrored still lakes, bordered by palms, and winding rivers, and spacious cities, all which vanished as we approached. But this was no mirage, born of sun and dust and silence.

Etched in the clear evening sky we saw plainly the giant details of massive turret and grim abutment; of serrated tower and titanic wall.

In what dim age did I, Hialmar, march with my tribesmen across those plains toward a nameless city? I cannot say. It was so long ago that the yellow-haired folk still dwelt in Nordheim, and were called not Aryans, but red-haired Vanir and golden-haired Æsir. It was before the great drifts of my race had peopled the world, yet lesser, nameless drifts, had already begun. We were the travelling of years from our northern homeland. Lands and seas lay between. Oh, that long, long trek! No drift of people, not even of my own people, whose drifts have been epic, has never equalled it. It had led us around the world—down from the snowy north into rolling plains, and mountain valleys tilled by peaceful brown folk—into hot breathless jungles, reeking with rot and teeming with spawning life—through eastern lands flaming with raw primitive colors under the waving palm trees, where ancient races lived in cities of carven stone—up again into the ice and snow and across a frozen arm of the sea—then down through the snow-clad wastes, where squat blubber-eating men fled squalling from our swords; southward and eastward through gigantic mountains and titanic forest, lonely and gigantic and desolate as Eden, after man was cast forth—over searing desert sands and boundless plains, until at last, beyond the silent black city, we saw the sea once more.

Men had grown old on that trek. I, Hialmar, had come to manhood. When I had first set forth on the long trail, I had been a young boy; now I was a young man, a proven warrior, mighty limbed, with great broad shoulders, a corded bull throat, and an iron heart. We were all mighty men—giants beyond the comprehension of moderns. There is not on earth today a man as strong as the weakest of our band, and our mighty thews were tuned to a blinding speed that would make the motions of finely trained modern athletes seem stodgy and clumsy and slow. Our might was more than physical; born of a wolfish race, the years of our wandering and fighting man, and beast and the elements in all forms, had instilled in our souls the very spirit of the wild—the intangible power that quivers in the long howl of the grey wolf, that roars in the north wind, that sleeps in the mighty unrest of turbulent rivers, that sounds in the slashing of icy sleet, the beat of the eagle's wings, and lurks in the brooding silence of the vast places.

I have said it was a strange trek. It was no drift of a whole tribe, men and yellow-haired women and naked children. We were all men, adventurers to whom even the ways of our wandering, warlike folk were too tame. We had taken the trail alone, conquering, exploring and wandering, driven only by our paranoidal drive to see beyond the horizon. There had been more than a thousand at the beginning; now there were five hundred. The bones of the rest bleached along that world-circling trail. Many chiefs had led us and died. Now our chief was old Bragi, grown old on that endless wandering—a gaunt, bitter fighter, one eyed and wolfish, who forever gnawed his greying beard.

We came of many clans, but all of the golden-haired Æsir, except the man who strode beside me. He was Gorm, my blood brother, and a Pict. He had joined us among the jungle-clad hills of a far land that marked the easternmost drift of his race, where the tom-toms of his people pulsed incessantly through the hot star-flecked night. He was short, thick limbed, deadly as a jungle cat. We of the Æsir were barbarians, but Gorm was a savage. Behind him lay the abysmal chaos of the squalling black jungle. The pad of the tiger was in his stealthy tread, the grip of the gorilla in his black-nailed hands; the fire that burns in a leopard's eyes burned in his.

Oh, we were a hard-bitten horde, and our tracks had been laid in blood and smoldering embers in many lands. I dare not repeat what slaughters, rapine and massacres lay behind us, for you would recoil in horror. You are of a softer, milder age, and you cannot understand those savage times when wolf pack tore wolf pack, and the morals and standards of life differed from those of this age as the thoughts of a grey killer wolf differ from those of a fat full-fed lapdog dozing before the hearth.

This long explanation I have given in order that you may understand what sort of men marched across that plain toward that city, and by this understanding interpret what came after. Without this understanding the saga of Hialmar is howling chaos, without rhyme or meaning.

As we looked at the great city we were not awed. We had ravaged red-handed through cities in other lands beyond the seas. Many conflicts had taught us to avoid battle with superior forces when possible, but we had no fear. We were equally ready for war or the feast of friendship, as the people of the city might choose.

They had seen us. We were close enough to make out the lines of orchards, fields and vineyards outside the walls, and the figures of the workers scurrying to the city. We saw the glitter of spears on the battlements, and heard the quick throb of war drums.

"It will be war, brother," said Gorm gutturally, settling his buckler firmly on his left arm. We took up our girdles and gripped our weapons—not of copper and bronze such as our people in far Nordheim still worked in, but of keen steel, fashioned by a conquered, cunning people in the land of palm trees and elephants, whose steel-armed warriors had not been able to withstand us.

We drew up on the plain a moderate distance from the great black walls, which seemed to be built of gigantic blocks of basaltic stone, and Bragi strode from our lines, weaponless, with his hand lifted open, palm outward, as a sign of parley. But an arrow cut into the sod near him, arching from the turrets, and he fell back to our lines.

"War, brother!" hissed Gorm, red fires glimmering in his black eyes. And at that instant the mighty iron gates swung open, and out filed lines of warriors, their war-plumes nodding above them in a glitter of lifted spears, the westering sun striking fire from their burnished copper helmets. They were tall and leanly built, dark of skin, though neither brown nor black, with straight hawk-like features. Their harness was of copper and leather, their bucklers covered with glossy shagreen. Their spears and slender swords and long daggers were of bronze. They advanced in perfect formation, fifteen hundred strong, a surging tide of nodding plumes and gleaming spears. The battlements behind them were lined with watchers.

There was no parley. As they came, old Bragi gave tongue like a hunting wolf and we charged to meet the attack. We had no formation; we ran toward them like wolves, and we saw scorn on their hawk-features as we neared them. They had no bows, and not an arrow was winged from our racing lines, not a spear thrown. We wished only to come to handgrips. When we were within javelin-cast they sent a shower of spears, most of which glanced from our shields and corselets, and then with a deep-throated roar, our charge crashed home.

Who said the ordered discipline of a degenerate civilization can match the sheer ferocity of barbarism? They strove to fight as a unit; we fought as individuals, rushing headlong against their spears, hacking like mad men. Their whole first rank went down beneath our whistling swords, and the ranks behind crushed back and wavered as the warriors felt the brute impact of our incredible strength. If they had held, they might have flanked us, hemmed us in with their superior numbers, and slaughtered us. But they could not stand. In a storm of hammering swords we ploughed through, breaking their lines, treading their dead underfoot as we surged irresistibly onward. Their battle formation melted; they strove against us, man to man, and the battle became a slaughter. For in personal strength and ferocity, they were no match at all for us.

We hewed them down like corn; we reaped them like ripe grain! Oh, when I relive that battle, it seems that James Allison gives place to the mailed and mighty Hialmar, with the war-madness in his brain and the war-chant on his lips! And I am drunken again with the singing of the swords, the spattering of hot blood, and the roar of the slaying.

They broke and fled, casting away their spears, and we were hard at their heels, cutting them down as they ran, to the very gates, through which the foremost streamed and which they slammed in our faces, and in the faces of the wretches who were last in the flight, and who clawed and yammered at the unyielding portals until we hewed them down. Then we, in turn, battered at the gates until a shower of stones and beams cast from above, brained three of our warriors, and we gave back to a safe distance. We heard the women howling in the streets, and the men lined the walls and shot arrows at us, with no great skill.

The bodies of the slain strewed the plain from the spot where the hosts clashed to the threshold of the gates, and where one Æsir had died, half a dozen plumed warriors had fallen.

The sun had set, night was falling. We pitched our rude camp before the gates, and all night we heard wailing and moaning within the walls, where the people howled for those whose still bodies we plundered and cast in a heap some distance away. At dawn we took the corpses of the thirty Æsir who had fallen in the fight, and leaving archers to watch the city, we bore them to the cliffs, which pitched sheer for fifteen hundred feet to the white sandy beach. We found sloping defiles which led down, and made our way to the water's edge with our burdens. There, from fishing boats drawn up on the sands, we fashioned a great raft, and heaped it high with driftwood. On the pile we laid the dead warriors, clad in their mail, with their weapons by their sides, and we cut the throats of the dozen captives we had taken, and stained the weapons and the raft sides with their blood. Then we set the torch to the wood, and shoved the raft off, and it floated far out on the mirrored surface of the blue water, until it was but a red glare, fading into the rising dawn.

Then we went back up the defiles, and ranged ourselves before the city, chanting our war songs. We unslung our bows, and man after man toppled from the turrets, pierced by our long shafts. From trees we found growing in the gardens outside the city, we built scaling ladders, and set them against the walls. We swarmed up them in the teeth of arrow and spear and falling beam, but they poured molten lead down on us, and burnt four warriors like ants in a flame. Then once more we plied our shafts, until no plumed heads showed on the battlements. Under cover of our archers, we again set up the ladders, but as we tensed ourselves for the upward rush that would carry us over the walls, sword in hand, on one of the towers that rose above the gates appeared a figure which halted us in our tracks. It was a woman, such as we had not seen for long years—golden hair blowing free in the wind, milky white skin gleaming in the sunlight. She called to us in our own tongue, stumblingly, as if she had not used the language in many years.

"Wait! My masters have a word for you."

"Masters?" old Bragi spat the word. "Whom does a woman of the Æsir call masters, except the men of her own clan?"

She did not seem to understand, but she answered, "This is the city of Khemu, and the masters of Khemu are lords of this land. They bid me say to you that they cannot stand before you in battle, but they say you shall have small profit if you scale the walls, because they will cut down their women and children with their own hands, and set fire to the palaces, so you will take only a mass of crumbling stones. But if you will spare the city, they will send out to you presents of gold and jewels, rich wines and rare foods, and the fairest girls of the city."

Bragi tugged his beard, loath to forego the sacking and the bloodletting; but the younger men roared: "Spare the city, old grizzly! Otherwise they will kill the women—and we have wandered many a moon where no women came."

"Young fools!" snarled old Bragi. "The kisses and love-cries of women fade and pall, but the sword sings a fresh song with each stroke. Is it the false lure of women, or the bright madness of slaughter?"

"Women!" roared the young warriors, clashing their swords. "Let them send out their girls, and we will spare their cursed city."

Old Bragi turned with a sneer of bitter scorn, and called to the golden-haired girl on the tower.

"I would raze your walls and spires into dust, and drench the dust with the blood of your masters," he said, "but my young men are fools! Send us forth food and women—and send us the sons of the chiefs for hostages."

"It shall be done, my lord," replied the girl, and we cast down the scaling ladders and retired to our camp. Soon then the gates swung open again, and out filed a procession of naked slaves, laden with golden vessels containing foods and wines such as we had not known existed. They were directed by a hawk-faced man in a mantle of bright-hued feathers, bearing an ivory wand in his hand, and wearing on his temples a circlet of copper like a coiling serpent, the head reared up in front. It was evident from his bearing that he was a priest, and he spoke the name, Shakkaru, indicating himself. With him came half a dozen youths, clad in silken breeks, jeweled girdles and gay feathers, and trembling with fear. The yellow-haired girl stood on the tower and called to us that these were the sons of princes, and Bragi made them taste the wine and food before we ate or drank.

For Bragi the slaves brought amber jars filled with gold dust, a cloak of flaming crimson silk, a shagreen belt with a jeweled golden buckle, and a burnished copper headdress adorned with great plumes. He shook his head and muttered, "Gauds and bright trappings are dust of vanity and fade before the march of the years, but the edge of slaughter is not dulled, and the scent of fresh-spilled blood is good to an old man's nostrils." But he donned the gleaming apparels, and when the girls came forth—slender young things, lithe and dark-eyed, scantily clad in shimmering silk—he chose the most beautiful, though morosely, as a man might pluck a bitter fruit.

Many a moon had passed since we had seen women, save the swart, smoke-stained creatures of the blubber-eaters. The warriors seized the terrified girls in fierce hunger—but my soul was dizzy with the sight of the golden-haired girl on the tower, and in my mind there was room for no other thought. Bragi set me to guard the hostages, and to cut them down without mercy if the wine or food proved poisoned, or any woman stabbed a warrior with a hidden dagger, or the men of the city made a sudden sally on us.

But men came forth only to collect the bodies of their dead, which they burned on a lofty promontory overlooking the sea, with many weird rituals.

Then there came out to us another procession, longer and more elaborate than the first. Chiefs of the fighting men walked along unarmed, their harness exchanged for silken tunics and cloaks. Before them came Shakkaru, his ivory wand uplifted, and between the lines young slave youths, clad only in short mantles of parrot feathers, bore a canopied litter of polished mahogany, crusted with jewels, wherein sat a lean man with a curious crown on his high narrow head, and the eyes of a vulture. Beside the litter walked the white-skinned girl who had spoken from the tower. They came before us, and the slaves knelt, still supporting the litter, while the nobles gave back to each side, dropping to their knees. Only Shakkaru and the girl stood upright.

Old Bragi faced them, gaunt, fierce, wary, his deep-lined fierce face shadowed by the black plumes which waved above it. And I thought how much more the natural king he looked, standing on his two feet among his giant fighting men, sword in hand, than the man who lolled supinely in the slave-borne litter.

But my eyes were all for the girl, whom I saw for the first time face to face. She was clad only in a short, sleeveless and low-necked tunic of blue silk, which came a hand's breadth above her knees, and soft green leather sandals were on her feet. Her eyes were wide and clear, her skin whiter than the purest milk, and her hair caught the sun in a sheen of rippling gold. There was a softness about her slender form that I had never seen in any woman of the Æsir. There was a fierce beauty about our flaxen-haired women, but this girl was equally beautiful without that fierceness. She had not grown up in a naked land, as they had, where life was a merciless battle for existence, for man and for woman. But these thoughts I did not pursue to their last analysis; I merely stood, dazzled by the blond radiance of her, as she translated the words of the king, and the deep growled replies of Bragi.

"My lord says to you, 'Lo, I am Akkheba, priest of Ishtar, king of Khemu. Let there be friendship between us. We have need of each other, for ye be men wandering blindly in a naked land, as my sorcery tells me, and the city of Khemu has need of keen swords and mighty arms, for a foe comes up against us out of the sea whom we cannot withstand alone. Abide in this land, and lend your swords to us, and take our gifts for your pleasure and our girls for your wives. Our slaves shall toil for you, and each day you shall sit ye down at boards groaning with meats, fishes, grains, white breads, fruits and wines. Fine raiment shall you wear, and you shall dwell in marble palaces with silken couches and tinkling fountains.'"

Now old Bragi understood this speech, for we had seen the cities of the palm tree lands; but it was at the talk of foes and sword-heaving that his cold blue eyes gleamed.

"We will bide," he answered, and we roared our assent. "We will bide and cut out the hearts of the foes who come against you. But we will camp outside the walls, and the hostages will abide with us, night and day."

"It is well," said Akkheba, with a stately inclination of his narrow head, and the nobles of Khemu knelt before old Bragi and would have kissed his high-strapped sandals, but he swore at them and gave back in wrathful embarrassment, while his warriors roared with rough mirth. Then Akkheba went back in his litter, bobbing on the shoulders of the slaves, and we settled ourselves for a long rest from our wanderings. But my gaze hung on the golden-haired interpreter, until the gates of the city closed behind her.

So we dwelt outside the walls, and day by day the people brought us food and wine, and more girls were sent out to us. The workers came and toiled in the gardens, the fields and the vineyards without fear of us, and the fishing boats went out—narrow crafts with curving bows and striped silken sails. And we accepted the king's invitation at last, and went in a compact body, the hostages in the center, with naked swords near their throats, through the iron-grilled gates and into the city.

By Ymir, Khemu was mightily built! Surely the present masters of the city sprang from the loins of gods, for who else could have reared up those black basaltic walls, eighty feet in height, and forty feet thick at the base? Or erected that great golden dome which rose five hundred feet above the marble-paved streets? As we strode down the broad column-flanked street, and into the broad marketplace, our swords in our fists, doors and windows were crowded by eager faces, fascinated and frightened. The chatter of the market place died suddenly as we swung into it, and the people crowded back from the shops and stalls to give us room. We were wary as tigers, and the slightest mishap would have sufficed to make us explode in a frenzied burst of slaughter. But the people of Khemu were wise, and the provocation did not come. The priests came and bowed before us and led us to the great palace of the king, a colossal pile of black stone and marble. Beside the palace was a broad, open court, paved with marble flags, and from this court marble steps, broad enough for ten men to mount abreast, led up to a dais, where the king stood on occasion to harangue the multitude. One wing of the palace extended behind this court, and against this wing the steps were built. This wing was of older construction than the rest of the palace, and was furnished with a curiously carven slanting roof of stone, steep and high, towering above all other spires in the city except the golden dome. The edge of this carven slope of masonry was but a few feet above the dais, and what was contained in that wing, none of the Æsir ever saw; folk said it was Akkheba's seraglio.

Beyond this open court were the mysterious column-fronted stone houses of the lesser priests, on both sides of a broad, marble-paved street, and beyond them again the lofty golden dome which crowned the great temple of Ishtar. On all sides rose sapphirean spires and gleaming towers, but the dome shone serenely above all, just as the bright glory of Ishtar, Shakkaru told us, shone above the heads of men. I say Shakkaru told us; in the few days they had spent among us, the young princes had learned much of our rugged, simple language, and by their interpretation and by the medium of signs, the priests of Khemu talked with us.

They led us to the lofty portals of the temple, but looking through the lines of tall marble columns, into the mysterious dim gloom of the interior, we balked, fearing a trap, and refused to go in. All the time I was looking eagerly for the golden-haired girl, but she was not in evidence. No longer needed as interpreter, the silence of the mysterious city had engulfed her.

After this first visit, we returned to our camp outside the walls, but we came again, and again, at first in bands, and then, as our suspicions were lulled, in small groups or singly, but we would not sleep within the city, though Akkheba urged us to pitch our tents in the great marketplace, if we disliked the marble palaces he offered us. No man of us had ever lived in a stone house, or within high walls. Our race dwelt in tents of tanned hides, or huts of mud and wattle, and we of the long trek as often as not slept like wolves on the naked earth. But by day we wandered through the city, marveling at the wonders of it, taking what we wished at the stalls, to the despair of the merchants, and entering palaces, warily, but at will, to be entertained by women who feared us, yet seemed to be fascinated by us. The people of Khemu were wondrous apt at learning; they soon spoke our language as well as we, though their speech came hard to our barbaric tongues.

But all this came in time. The day after we first visited the city, a number of us went again, and Shakkaru guided us to the palace of the higher priests which adjoined the temple of Ishtar, and as we entered I saw the golden-haired girl, shining a pudgy copper idol with a handful of silk. Old Bragi laid a heavy hand on the shoulder of one of the young princes.

"Tell the priest that I would have that girl for my own," he growled, but before the priest could reply, red rage rose in my brain and I stepped toward Bragi as a tiger steps toward his rival.

"If any man of us takes that woman it shall be Hialmar," I growled, and old Bragi wheeled catlike at the thick killer's purr in my voice. We faced each other tensely, our hands on our hilts, and Gorm grinned wolfishly and began to edge toward Bragi's back, stealthily drawing his long knife, when Akkheba spoke through the hostage.

"Nay, my lords, Aluna is not for either of you, or for any other man. She is handmaiden to the goddess Ishtar. Ask for any other woman in the city, and she shall be yours, even to the favorite of the king; but this woman is sacred to the goddess."

Old Bragi grunted and did not press the matter. The incense-breathing mystery of the temple had impressed even his fierce soul, and though we of the Æsir had not overmuch regard for other people's gods, yet he had no desire to take a girl who had been in such close communion with deity. But my superstitions were less than my desire for the girl Aluna. I came again and again to the palace of the priests, and though they little liked my coming, they would not, or dared not, say me nay; and with small beginnings, I did my wooing.

What shall I say of my skill at courtship? Another woman I might have dragged to my tent by her long hair, but even without the priestly ban, there was something in my regard for her that tied my hands from violence. I wooed her in the way we of the Æsir wooed our fierce lithe beauties—with boastings of prowess, and tales of slaughter and rapine. And in truth, without exaggeration, my tales of battle and massacre might have drawn to me the most wayward of the fierce beauties of Nordheim. But Aluna was soft and mild, and had grown up in temple and palace, instead of wattle hut and ice field; my ferocious boastings frightened her; she did not understand. And by the strange perversity of nature, it was this very lack of understanding which made her more enthralling to me. Even as the very savagery she feared in me made her look upon me with more interest than she looked on the soft-thewed men of Khemu.

But in my conversations with her, I learned of her coming to Khemu, and her saga was strange as that of Bragi and our band. Where she had dwelt in her childhood she could little say, having no idea of geography, but it had been far away across the sea to the east. She remembered a bleak wave-lashed coast, and straggling huts of wattle and mud, and yellow-haired people like herself. So I believe she came of a branch of the Æsir which marked the westernmost drift of our race up to that time. She was perhaps nine or ten years old when she had been taken in a raid on the village by dark-skinned men in galleys—who they were she did not know, and my knowledge of ancient times does not tell me, for then the Phoenicians had not yet put to sea, nor the Egyptians. I can but guess that they were men of some ancient race, a survival of another age, like the people of Khemu—destroyed and forgotten before the rise of the younger races. But they took her, and a storm drove them westward and southward, for many days, until their galley crashed on the reefs of a strange island where kinky-headed black men swarmed onto the beach and slaughtered the survivors for their cooking pots. The yellow-haired child they spared, for some whim, and placing her in a great canoe, with skulls grinning along the gunwales, they rowed until they sighted the spires of Khemu on the high cliffs.

There they sold her to the priests of Khemu, to be a handmaiden for the goddess Ishtar. I had supposed her position to be holy and revered, but I found that it was otherwise, and the worm of suspicion stirred in my soul against the Khemuri, as I realized, in her words, the cruel and bitter contempt in which they held folk of other, younger races. Her position in the temple was neither honorable nor dignified, and though the servant of the goddess, she was without honor herself, save that no man save the priests were allowed to touch her. She was, in fact, no more than a menial, subject to the cold cruelty of the hawk-like priests. She was not beautiful to them; to them her fair skin and shimmering golden hair were but the marks of an inferior race, comparable to the ebony hide and blubber-lips of a negro. And even to me, who was not prone to tax my brain, came the vague thought that if a blond girl was so contemptible in their eyes, that treachery must lurk behind the honor they gave to men of the same race.

Of Khemu I learned a little from Aluna and more from the priests and the princes. They were very old, as a people. They claimed descent from the half-mythical Lemurians. Once their cities had girdled the gulf upon which Khemu overlooked. But some the sea had gulped down, some had fallen before the black savages of the islands, and some had been destroyed by civil wars, so that now, for near a thousand years, Khemu had reigned alone in solitary majesty. Their only contact had been with the wayward black people of the islands, who, until a year or so before, had come regularly in their long, high-prowed canoes, to trade ambergris, and coconuts, whale's teeth, and coral gotten from among their islands; and mahogany, leopard skins, virgin gold, elephant tusks, and copper ore, procured from some unknown tropical mainland far to the south. The people of Khemu were a waning race; though they still numbered thousands, many of these being slaves, descendants of a thousand generations of slaves, still they were but a shadow of their former greatness. A few more centuries would have seen the last of them, but on the sea to the south, out of sight over the horizon, was brooding a menace that threatened to sweep them all out of existence at one stroke.

The black people had ceased to come in peaceful trade. They had come in war-canoes, with a clashing of spears on hide-covered shields, and a barbaric chant of war. A king had risen among them who had united the warring tribes, and now launched them against Khemu—not their former masters, for the old empire of which Khemu had been a part had crumbled before the drift of the kinky-heads into the isles from that faraway continent which was the cradle of their race. This king was not a black man; he was a white-skinned giant like ourselves, with mad blue eyes and hair crimson as blood. They had seen him, the people of Khemu. By night his war-canoes full of black spearmen had stolen along the coast, and at sunrise the slayers had swept up the defiles of the cliff, slaying the fishermen who then slept in huts along the beach, cutting down the laborers just going to work in the fields, and storming at the gates. The great walls had held, however, and the blacks despaired of the storming and drew off. But the red-haired king had stood up before the gates, dangling the severed head of a woman by its long hair, and shouted his bloody vow to return with a fleet of war-canoes that should blacken the sea, and to raze the towers of Khemu to the red-stained dust. He and his slayers were the foes we had been hired to fight, and we awaited their coming with fierce impatience.

And while we waited we grew more and more used to the ways of civilization, insofar as barbarians can accustom themselves in such a short time. We still camped outside the walls, and kept our swords ready within, but it was more in instinctive caution than fear of treachery—even old Bragi seemed lulled to a sense of security, especially after Gorm, maddened by the wine they gave him, killed three Khemurians in the marketplace, and no blood-vengeance or man-bote for the deed.

We overcame our superstitions and allowed the priests to guide us into the breathless dim cavern of a building that was the temple of Ishtar. We went even into the inner shrine, where sacred fires burned dimly in the scented gloom, and even witnessed the sacrifice of a screaming slave girl on the great black, red-veined altar at the foot of the marble stairs which mounted upward in the darkness until they were lost to view. These stairs led to the abode of Ishtar, we were told, and up them the spirit of the sacrifice mounted to serve the goddess. Which I decided was true, for after the corpse on the altar lay still, and the chants of worship died to a blood-freezing whisper, I heard the sound of weeping far above us, and knew that the naked soul of the victim stood whimpering in terror before her goddess.

I asked Aluna later if she had ever seen the goddess, and she shook with fright, and said only the spirits of the dead looked on Ishtar. She, Aluna, had never set foot on the marble stair that led up to the abode of the goddess. She was called the handmaiden of Ishtar, but her duties were to do the biddings of the hawk-faced priests, and the evil-eyed naked women who served them, and who glided like dusky shadows among the purple gloom among the columns.

But among the warriors grew discontent, and they wearied of ease and luxury, and even of the dark-skinned women, for in the strange soul of the Æsir, only the lust for red battle and far-wandering remains constant. Bragi daily conversed with Shakkaru and Akkheba on ancient times; I was chained by the lure of Aluna; Gorm guzzled each day in the wine shops until he fell senseless in the streets. But the rest clamored against the life we were leading and asked Akkheba what of the foe we were to slay?

"Be patient," said Akkheba. "They will come, and their red-haired king with them."

Dawn rose over the shimmering spires of Khemu. Warriors had begun to spend the nights as well as the days in the city. I had drunken with Gorm the night before and lain with him in the streets until the breeze of morn had blown the fumes of the wine from my brain. Seeking Aluna, I strode down the marble pave and entered the palace of Shakkaru, which adjoined the temple of Ishtar. I passed through the wide outer chambers, where priests and women still lolled in slumber, and heard on a sudden, beyond a closed door, the sound of sharp blows on soft naked flesh, mingled with piteous weeping and sobs for mercy, in a voice I knew. The door was bolted, and it was of silver-braced mahogany, but I burst it inward as if it had been match-wood. Aluna groveled on the floor with her scanty tunic tucked up, before a hatchet-faced priest who with cold venom was scourging her with a cruel, small-thonged whip which left crimson weals on her bare fair flesh. He turned as I entered, and his face went ashy, but before he could move I clenched my fist and gave him a buffet that crushed his skull like an eggshell and broke his neck in the bargain.

The whole palace swam red to my maddened glare. Perhaps it was not so much the pain the priest had inflicted on Aluna—because pain was the most common thing in that old, fierce life—but the proprietorial way in which he inflicted it—the knowledge that the priests had possessed her—all of them, perhaps.

A man is no better and no worse than his feelings regarding the women of his blood, which is the true and only test of racial consciousness. A man will take to himself the stranger woman, and sit down at meat with the stranger man, and feel no twinges of race-consciousness. It is only when he sees the alien man in possession of, or intent upon, a woman of his blood, that he realizes the difference in race and strain. So I, who had held women of many races in my mighty arms, who was blood-brother to a Pictish savage, was shaken by mad fury at the sight of alien men laying hands on a woman of the Æsir.

I believe it was the sight of her, a slave of an alien race, and the slow wrath it produced, which first stirred me toward her. For the roots of love are set in hate and fury. And her unfamiliar softness and gentleness crystallized the first vague sensation.

Now I stood scowling down at her, as she whimpered at my feet. I did not lift her and wipe her tears as a civilized man would have done. Had such a thought occurred to me, I would have rejected it disgustedly as unmanly.

As I stood so, I heard my name shouted suddenly, and Gorm raced into the chamber, yelling: "They come, brother, just as the old one said! The watchers on the cliffs have run to the city, with a tale of the sea black with war-boats!"

With a glance at Aluna, and a dumb incoherence struggling for expression, I turned to go with the Pict, but the girl staggered up and ran towards me, tears streaming down her cheeks, her white arms outstretched pleadingly.

"Hialmar!" she wailed. "Do not leave me! I am afraid! I am afraid!"

"I cannot take you now," I growled. "War and slaughter are forward. But when I return I will take you, and not the priests of all the gods shall stay me!"

I took a quick step toward her, my hands yearning toward her—then smitten with the fear of bruising her delicate flesh, my hands dropped empty to my side. An instant I stood, dumb, torn by fierce yearning, speech and action frozen by the strangeness of the emotion which tore my soul. Then tearing myself away, I followed the impatient Pict into the streets.

The sun was rising as we of the Æsir marched toward the crimson-etched cliffs, followed by the regiments of Khemu. We had thrown aside the gay garments and headpieces we had worn in the city. The rising sun sparkled on our horned helmets, worn hauberks and naked swords. Forgotten the months of idleness and debauchery. Our souls were riot with the wild exultation of coming strife. We went to slaughter as to a feast, and as we strode we clashed sword and shield in rude thundering rhythm, and sang the slaying-song of Niord who ate the red smoking heart of Heimdul. The warriors of Khemu looked at us in amazement, and the people who lined the walls of the city shook their heads in bewilderment, and whispered among themselves.

So we came to the cliffs, and saw, as Gorm had said, the sea black with war-canoes, high prowed, and adorned with grinning skulls. Scores of these boats were already pulled up on the beach, and others were sweeping in on the crests of the waves. The black warriors were dancing and shouting on the sands, and their clamor came up to us. There were many of them—three thousand, at the very least—probably many more. The men of Khemu blenched, but old Bragi laughed as we had not heard him laugh in many a moon, and his age fell from him like a cast-off mantle.

There were half a dozen runways leading down through the cliffs to the beach, and up these the blacks must come, for the precipices on all other sides were unclimbable. We ranged ourselves at the heads of these runways, and the men of Khemu were behind us. Little part they had in that battle, holding themselves in reserve for aid that we did not call for.

Up the passes swarmed the chanting black men, and we saw their king, towering above the huge ebony figures. The morning sun caught his hair in a blaze like crimson fire, and his laughter was like a gust of sea wind. Alone of that horde he wore mail and helmet, and in his hand his great sword shone like a sheen of silver. Aye, he was one of the wandering Vanir, our red-haired kin in Nordheim, and what his long trek, his wanderings, and his wild saga, I know not, but that saga must have been wilder and stranger than that of Aluna's or of ours. By what madness in his soul he came to be king of black cannibals, I cannot even offer a guess. But when he saw what manner of men confronted him, new fury entered his yells, and at his bellow the blacks rolled up the runways like ebony, steel-crested waves.

We bent our bows and our arrows whistled in clouds down the defiles. The front ranks melted away, the hordes reeled backward, then stiffened and came on once more. Charge after charge we broke, and charge after charge hurtled up the passes in blind, wild beast ferocity. The black men wore no armor, and our long shafts tore through hide-covered shields like cloth. They had no skill at archery. When they came near enough they threw their spears in whistling showers, and some of us died. But few of them came within spear-cast and less won through to the heads of the passes. I remember one huge warrior who came crawling up out of the defile like a snake, a crimson slaver drooling from his thick lips, and the feathered ends of arrows standing out from his belly, ribs, neck and limbs. He howled like a mad dog, and his death-bite tore the heel of my sandal as I stamped his head into a red pulp.

Some few did break through the blinding hail and came to handgrips, but there they fared little better. Man to man we of the Æsir were the stronger, and our armor turned their spears, while our swords and axes crashed through their wooden shields like paper. Yet so many there were, but for our advantage in location, all the Æsir had died there on the cliffs, and the setting sun had lighted the smoking ruins of Khemu.

All through that long summer day we held the cliffs, until, when our quivers were empty and our bowstrings frayed through, and the defiles were choked with black bodies, we threw aside our bows, and drawing our swords, went down into the defiles, and met the invaders hand to hand and blade to blade. They had died like flies in the passes, yet there were many of them left, and the fire of their rage burned no less brightly because of the arrow-feathered corpses which lay beneath our feet. They came on and up, roaring like a wave, stabbing with spear and lashing with warclub, and we met them in a whirlwind of steel, cleaving skulls, smashing breasts, hewing limbs from their bodies and heads from their shoulders, till the defiles were shambles where men could scarcely keep their feet on the blood-washed, corpse-littered paths.

The westering sun cast long shadows across the cliff-shaded beaches when I came upon the king of the black men, on a level expanse where the upward trending slope ran level for a short distance before it dipped up again at a steeper slant. Arrows had wounded him, and swords had gashed him, but the mad blaze in his eyes was undimmed, and his thundering voice still urged his gasping, weary, staggering warriors to the onset. Yet now, though the battle raged fiercely in the other defiles, he stood among a host of the dead, and only two huge blacks stood beside him, their spears clotted with blood and brains.

Gorm was at my heels as I rushed at the Vanir. The two blacks leaped to bar my path, but Gorm was upon them. From each side they leaped at him, their spears driving in with a hiss. Yet as a wolf avoids the stroke he writhed between the goring blades, and the three figures caromed together an instant, then one black man fell away, disemboweled, and the other dropped across him, his head half-severed from his body.

As I leaped toward the red-haired king, we struck simultaneously. My sword tore the helmet from his head, and at his terrible stroke, his sword and my shield shattered together. Before I could strike again he dropped the broken hilt and grappled with me as a grizzly grapples. I let go my sword, useless at such close quarters, and close locked, we reeled on the crest of the slope. We were evenly matched in strength, but his might was ebbing from him with the blood of a score of wounds. Straining and gasping with the effort, we swayed, hard braced, and I felt my pulse pound in my temples, saw the great veins swell in his. Then suddenly he gave way, and we pitched headlong, to roll down the slanting defile. In that grim strife neither dared try to draw a dagger. But as we rolled and tore at each other, I felt the iron ebbing from his mighty limbs, and by a volcanic burst of effort, heaved on top, and sunk my iron fingers deep in his corded throat. Sweat and blood misted my vision, my breath came in whistling gasps, but I sank my fingers deeper and deeper, and his tearing hands grew aimless and groping, until with a racking gasp of effort, I tore out my dagger and drove it home again and again, until the giant lay motionless beneath me.

Then as I reeled upright, half-blind and shaking from the desperate strife, Gorm would have hewed off the king's head, but I prevented it. A long wavering cry went up from the blacks and they flinched for the first time. Their king had been the fire which had held them like doom to their fate all day, and now they broke suddenly, and fled down the defiles, and we cut them down as they ran. We followed them down onto the beach, still slaughtering them like cattle, and as they ran to their canoes and pushed off, we waded into the water until it flowed over our shoulders, glutting our mad fury. When the last survivors, rowing madly, had passed to safety, the beach was littered with still forms, and floating black bodies sprawled to the wash of the surf.

Only black bodies lay on the beach and in the shallow water, but in the defiles, where the fighting had been fiercest, seventy of the Æsir lay dead, and of the rest of us, few there were who bore not some mark or wound.

By Ymir, that was a slaying! The sun was dipping toward the horizon when we came back from the cliffs, weary, dusty and bloody, with little breath left for singing, but with our heart glad because of the red deeds we had done. The people of Khemu did the singing for us; they swarmed out of the city in a vast shouting, cheering throng, and they laid carpets of silk, strewn with roses and gold dust, before our feet. We bore with us our wounded on litters. But first we took our dead to the beach, and broke up war-canoes to make a mighty raft, and lade it with the corpses and set it afire. And we took the red-haired king of the black men, and laid him in his great war-canoe, with the corpses of his bravest chiefs about him, to serve him in ghostland, and we gave to him the same honors we gave to our own men.

I looked eagerly for Aluna among the throng, but I did not see her. They had put up tents in the marketplace, and there we placed our wounded, and leeches of the Khemu came among them, and they dressed the wounds of the rest of us. And Akkheba had prepared a mighty victory feast for us in his great hall, and thither we went, dust stained and bloodstained, and even old Bragi grinned like a hungry wolf as he wiped the clotted blood from his knotty hands, and he donned the garb they had given him. But I lingered for a space among the tents where lay those too desperately wounded to walk or even be carried to the feast, hoping that Aluna would come to me. But she did not come, and I went to the great hall of the kingdom, without which the warriors of Khemu stood at attention—three hundred of them, the more to do honor to their allies, Akkheba said.

That hall was three hundred feet in length, and half as many wide. It was floored with polished mahogany, half covered with thick rugs, and leopard skins. The walls were of carven stone, pierced by many arched, mahogany-paneled doors, and towering up to a lofty arching ceiling, and half covered with velvet tapestries. On a throne at the back of the hall, Akkheba sat his throne on a raised dais, looking down at the revelry, and with files of plumed spearmen on either side. At the great board which ran the full length of the hall, the Æsir in their battered, stained, dusty garments and corselets, many with bloody bandages, drank and roared and gorged, served by bowing slaves, both men and women.

Chiefs and nobles and warriors of the city in their burnished harnesses sat among their allies, and for each Æsir it seemed to me there were at least three or four girls, laughing, jesting, submitting to their rude caresses; their laughter rose shrill and strident above the clamor. There was an unreality about the scene to me—a strained levity, a forced gaiety. But I did not see Aluna, so I turned and, passing through one of the mahogany arched doors, crossed a silken-hung chamber, and entered another, dimly lighted, and almost ran into old Shakkaru. He recoiled, and seemed much put out at meeting me, for some reason or another, and I noted that his hand clutched at his robe, which all the priests wore that night, in our honor, Akkheba said.

A thought occurred to me and I voiced it.

"I wish to speak with Aluna," I said. "Where is she?"

"She is at present occupied with her duties and cannot see you," he said. "Come to the temple tomorrow—"

He edged away from me, and in a vague pallor underlying his swarthy complexion, in a tremor behind his voice, I sensed that he was in deadly fear of me, and wished to be rid of me. The suspicions of the barbarian flashed up in me and in an instant I had him by the throat, wrenching from his hand the long wicked blade he drew from beneath his robe.

"Where is she, you jackal?" I snarled. "Tell me—or—"

He was dangling like a puppet in my grasp, his kicking heels clear of the floor, his head bent back almost to the snapping point. With the fear of death in his distended eyes, he jerked his head violently, and I eased my grasp a trifle.

"In the shrine of Ishtar," he gasped. "They sacrifice her to the goddess—spare my life—I will tell you all—the whole secret and plot—"

But I had heard enough. Whirling him on high by girdle and knee, I dashed his brains out against a column, and leaping through an outer door, raced between rows of massive pillars, and gained the street. There was no sound. A breathless silence reigned over all. No throngs were abroad that night, as one would have thought, celebrating the destruction of their enemies. The doors were shut, the windows shuttered. Hardly a light shone, and I did not even see a watchman. It was all strange and unreal; the silent, ghostly city, where the only sound was the strident, unnatural revelry rising from the great feast hall. I could see the glow of torches in the marketplace where our wounded lay.

I had seen old Bragi sitting at the head of the board, with his hands stained with dried blood, and his hacked and dusty mail showing under the flaming silken cloak he wore; his gaunt fierce features shadowed by the great black plumes that waved above him. All up and down the board the girls were embracing and kissing the half-drunken Æsir, lifting off their heavy helmets and easing them of their mail as they grew hot with wine. I saw Gorm near the foot of the board, tearing like a famished wolf at a great beef-bone. Some laughing girls were teasing him, and coaxing him to give them his sword, and suddenly, infuriated by their sport and importunities, he dealt his foremost tormentor such a blow with the bone he was gnawing that she fell, dead or senseless, to the floor. But the high-pitched laughter and wild merriment did not slacken. I likened them suddenly to vampires and skeletons, laughing over a feast of dust and ashes.

I hurried down the silent, hollow-resounding street, crossing the court, and passing the houses of the priests, which seemed deserted except for slaves. Rushing into the lofty pillared portico of the temple—I ran through the deep-lying gloom, groping in the darkness—burst into the vaguely lighted inner shrine—and halted, frozen. Lesser priests and evil-eyed naked women stood about the altar in positions of adoration, chanting the sacrificial song, holding golden goblets to catch the blood that ebbed down the stained grooves in the stone. And on that altar, whimpering softly, as a dying doe might whimper, lay Aluna.

Shadowy was the cloud of incense smoke which gloomed the shrine; crimson as hell's fire the cloud which veiled my sight. With one inhuman yell that rang hideously to the vaulted roof, I rushed, and skulls splintered beneath my madly lashing sword. My memories of that slaughter are frenzied and chaotic. I remember frenzied screams, the whir of steel and the chop and crunch of murderous blows, the snapping of bones, spattering of blood, and the gibbering flight of figures that tore their hair and screeched to their gods as they ran—and I am among them, raging in silent deadliness, like a blood-mad wolf among sheep. Some few escaped.

I remember, clear etched against a murky red background of madness, a lithe naked woman who stood close to the altar, frozen with horror, a goblet at her lips, her eyes flaring—as I caught her up with my left hand and dashed her against the marble steps with a fury that must have splintered every bone in her body. For the rest I do not well remember. There was a brief mad whirling blast of ferocity that littered the shrine with mangled corpses, then I stood alone among the dead, in a shrine that was like a shambles, with streaks and clots and pools of blood, and entrails and human fragments scattered hideously and obscenely about the dark polished floor.

My sword trailed in my suddenly nerveless hand as I approached the altar with dragging steps. Aluna's eyelids fluttered open as I looked down at her, my great hands hanging limply, my whole mighty frame sagging helplessly. She murmured, "Hialmar!" Then her eyelids sank down, the long lashes shadowing the youthful cheek, and with a little sigh, she moved her flaxen head and lay like a child just settling to sleep. All my agonized soul cried out within me, but my lips were mute, with the inarticulateness of the barbarian. But I sank down upon my knees beside the altar, and groping hesitantly about her slender form with my hardened arms, I kissed her dying lips, clumsily, falteringly, as a callow stripling might have done. That one act—that one faltering kiss—was the one touch of tenderness in the whole, hard life of Hialmar of the Æsir.

Slowly I rose, and stood above the dead girl, and as slowly and mechanically I picked up my sword. And at the familiar touch of the hilt, there surged through my brain again the red fury of my race. With a wild terrible cry I sprang to the marble stairs. Ishtar! They had sent her spirit shuddering up to the goddess, and close on the heels of that spirit should come the avenger! No less than the bloody goddess herself should pay for Aluna. Mine was the simple cult of the barbarian. They, the priests, had told me that Ishtar dwelt above and the steps led to her abode. Vaguely I supposed it mounted through misty realms of stars and shadows. But up I went, to a dizzy height, until below me the shrine was but a vague play of dim lights and shadows, and darkness was all around me.

Then I came suddenly, not into a broad starry expanse of the deities, but to a grill of golden bars, and beyond them I heard a woman sobbing. But it was not Aluna's naked soul which wailed before some divine throne, for dead or alive, I knew her cry. In mad fury I gripped the bars and they bent and buckled in my hands. Like straws I tore them aside and leaped through, my killing-yell trembling in my bull throat. In the dim light that came from a torch set high in a niche, I saw that I was in a circular, domed chamber, whose walls and ceiling seemed to be of gold. There were velvet couches there, and silken cushions, and among these lay a naked woman, weeping. I saw the weals of a whip on her white body, and I halted, bewildered. Where was the goddess, Ishtar?

I must have spoken aloud, and in my barbaric Khemuri, for she lifted her head and looked at me with luminous dark eyes, swimming with tears. There was a strange unfamiliar beauty about her, something alien and exotic beyond my reckoning.

"I am Ishtar," she answered me, and her voice was soft as distant golden chimes, though broken now with sobbing.

"You—!" I gasped, "you—Ishtar—the goddess of Khemu?"

"Yes!" she rose to her knees, wringing her white hands. "Oh, man, whoever you are—grant me one touch of mercy, if there be mercy left in the world at all! Cut my head from my body and end this long agony!"

But I drew back and lowered my sword.

"I came to slay a bloody goddess," I growled. "Not to butcher a whimpering slave girl. If you be Ishtar—who—where—in Ymir's name, what madness is this?"

"Listen, and I will tell you!" she cried, hitching herself toward me on her knees, and catching at the skirt of my corselet. "Only listen, and then grant me the little thing I ask—the stroke of your sword!

"I am Ishtar, a daughter of a king in dim Lemuria, which the sea drank so long ago. As a child I was wed to Poseidon, god of the sea, and in the awesome mysterious bridal night, when I lay floating and unharmed on the breast of the ocean, the unseeable god gave to me the gift of Life Everlasting, which has become as a curse in the long centuries of my captivity.

"But I dwelt in purple Lemuria, young and beautiful, while my playmates grew old and grey about me. Then Poseidon wearied of Lemuria and of Atlantis. He rose and shook his foaming mane, and his white steeds raced over the walls and the spires and the crimson towers. But he lifted me gently on his bosom and bore me unharmed to a far land, where for many centuries I dwelt among a strange kindly race.

"Then in an evil day I went upon a galley from distant Khitai, and in a hurricane it sank off this accursed coast. But as before I was borne gently ashore on the waves of my master, Poseidon, and the priests found me upon the beach. The people of Khemu claim descent from Lemuria, but they were a mongrel subject race, speaking a mongrel tongue. When I spoke to them in pure Lemurian they cried out to the people that Poseidon had sent them a goddess and the people fell down and worshipped me. But the priests were devils then as now, necromancers and devil-worshippers, owning no gods save the demons of the Outer Gulfs. They pent me in this golden dome, and by cruelty they wrung my secret from me.

"For more than a thousand years I have been worshipped by the people, who were sometimes given faint glimpses of me, standing on the marble stair, half-hidden in the sacrificial smoke, or were allowed to hear my voice, speaking in a strange tongue as oracle. But the priests—oh, gods of Mu, what I have suffered at their hands! Goddess to the people—slave to the priests!"

"Why do you not destroy them with your sorcery?" I demanded.

"I am no sorceress," she answered, "though you might deem me such, were I to tell you what mysteries the ages have unfolded to me. Yet there is one sorcery I might invoke—one terrible, overwhelming doom—

if I might escape from this prison—if I might stand up naked in the dawn and call upon Poseidon. In the still nights I hear him roaring beyond the cliffs, but he sleeps and heeds not my cries. Yet if I might stand up in his sight and call upon him, he might hear and heed. The priests are crafty—they have shut me from his sight and hearing—for more than a thousand years I have not looked on the great blue monster—"

Suddenly we both started. From the city far below us welled up a strange wild clamor.

"Treachery!" she cried. "They are murdering your people in the streets! You destroyed the enemies they feared—now they turn on you!"

With a curse I raced down the stairs, cast one anguished glance at the still white form on the altar, and ran out of the temple. Down the street, beyond the houses of the priests, rose the clanging of steel, howls of death, yells of fury, and the thunderous war-cries of the Æsir. They were not dying alone. The Khemuri's cries of hate and triumph were mingled with screams of fear and pain. Ahead of me the street seethed with battling humanity, no more silent and deserted. From the doors of shops, hovels and palaces alike swarmed screeching city folk, weapons in hand, to aid their soldiers who were locked in mad battle with the yellow-haired aliens. Flame from a score of fires lighted the frenzied scene like day.

As I neared the court adjoining the king's palace, along streets through which men ran howling, an Æsir warrior staggered towards me, drift of the storm of battle which was raging further down. He was without armor, bent almost double, and though an arrow stood out from his ribs, it was his belly he was gripping with his empty hands.

"The wine was poisoned," he groaned. "We are betrayed and doomed! We drank deep, and in our cups the women coaxed from us our swords and armor—only Bragi and the Pict would not give them up. Then suddenly, the women slipped away, that old vulture of an Akkheba left the feast hall—then the pangs took hold on us! Ah, Ymir, it twists my vitals like a knotted rope! Then the doors swarmed suddenly with archers who drove their arrows upon us—the warriors of Khemu drew their swords and fell upon us—the priests who swarmed the hall tore hidden swords from their robes. Hark to the yelling in the marketplace where they cut the throats of the wounded! Ymir, cold steel a man may laugh at, but this—this—ah, Ymir!"

He sank to the pave, bent like a bended bow, froth drooling from his lips, his limbs jerking in horrible convulsions. I raced into the court. On the further side, and in the street in front of the palace, was a mass of struggling figures, where swarms of dark-skinned men in armor battled with half-naked yellow-haired giants, who smote and rent like wounded lions, though their only weapons were broken benches, arms snatched from dying foes, or their naked hands, and whose lips were flecked with the froth of the agony that knotted their entrails. I swear by Ymir, they did not die alone; mangled corpses were trodden under their feet, and they were like wild beasts whose terrible ferocity is not quenched save with the extinguishing of the last least spark of life.

The great feast hall was burning. In its light I saw, standing on the dais high above the conflict, old Akkheba, shaking and trembling with hideous terror of his own treachery, with two stalwart guards on the steps below him. The fighting scattered out over the court, and I saw Gorm. He was drunk, but his condition did not alter his deadliness. He was the center of a struggling clump of thrusting, hacking figures, and his long knife flashed in the firelight, as it ripped through throats and bellies, spilling blood and entrails on the marble pave.

With a low sullen roar I charged into the thick of them, and in an instant we stood alone in a ring of corpses.

He grinned like a wolf and his teeth champed spasmodically.

"There was the devil in the wine, Hialmar! It claws at my guts like a wildcat—come, let us kill some more of them before we die. Look—the Old One makes his last stand!"

I glanced quickly where, directly in front of the blazing feast hall, old Bragi's gaunt frame loomed among the swarming pack. I saw the flash of his sword and the dropping of men about him that fell like autumn leaves. An instant his black plumes waved over the horde—then they vanished and over the place he had stood rolled the dark wave. The next instant I was leaping toward the marble stairs, with Gorm close at my heels. We smote the line of warriors on the lower steps, and burst through. They surged in behind us to pull us down, but Gorm wheeled and his long blade made deadly play among them, cleaving skulls and slashing bellies. They swarmed in on him from all sides, and there he died as he had lived, slashing and slaying in silent frenzy, neither asking quarter nor giving it.

I leaped up on the steps and old Akkheba, his eyes blazing in terror at the hell his treachery had loosed, and he howled at my coming. My broken sword I had left wedged in a guardsman's breastbone. With my naked hands I charged the two guardsmen at the upper steps. They sprang to meet me, stabbing hard. I caught the driving spear of one and hurled him headlong down the stairs, to dash his brains out at the bottom. The spear of the other tore through my mail and blood gushed over the shaft, but before he could tear it from my flesh for a second thrust, I gripped his throat and tore it out with my naked fingers. Then wrenching forth the spear and casting it aside, I rushed at Akkheba, who screamed and sprang in the air, grasping the scrolled edge of the sloping stone roof behind the dais. Mad terror lent the old one strength and courage. Up the steep slope of the roof he clambered like a monkey, catching at the carved decorations with fingers and toes, and howling all the time like a beaten dog.

And I followed him. My life was ebbing out of the great wound beneath my mail, which was soaked with blood, but my wild-beast vitality was as yet undimmed. Up and up he climbed, shrieking, and higher and higher we rose above the city, until we swayed precariously on the level roof ridge, five hundred feet above the howling streets. And then we were frozen, the hunted and the hunter. A strange, haunting cry rang above the hellish tumult that raged below us, above old Akkheba's frenzied howling. On the great golden dome, high above all other towers and spires, stood a naked figure, hair blown in the dawn wind, etched in the red dawn glow. It was Ishtar, waving her white arms and screaming a frenzied invocation in a strange tongue, which came faintly to us. She had escaped from the golden prison I had burst open—now she stood on the dome, calling upon the god of her fathers, Poseidon!

But I had my own vengeance to consummate. I poised for the leap that would carry us both crashing five hundred feet to death—and under my feet the solid masonry rocked. A new frenzy rang in Akkheba's screams. With a thunderous crash the distant cliffs fell into the sea. There was a long rumbling cataclysmic crash, like the shattering of a world, and to my startled gaze, the whole vast plain waved like a surf, and gave way, and dipped southward. Great chasms gaped in the tilting plain, and suddenly, with an indescribable rumble, a grinding thunder, and a crashing of falling walls and buckling towers, the whole city of Khemu was in motion! Was sliding in a vast chaotic ruin, down to the sea which rose roaring to meet it! In that sliding horror, tower crashed against tower, buckling and toppling, grinding screaming human insects to red dust, crushing them to bits with falling stones. Where I had looked out upon an ordered city, with walls and spires and roofs, all was a mad, buckled, crumpled, splintering chaos of thundering stone, where spires rocked crazily above the ruins, and came thundering down.

Still the dome rode the wrack, and the white glistening figure upon it still screamed and gestured. Then with an awesome roar, the sea stirred and rose, and great tentacles of green foam curled mountain high and roared down over the sliding, rumbling ruins, mounting higher and higher, until the whole southern side of the crushed city was hidden in swirling green waters. But for an instant the ancient roof ridge on which we clung had risen above the ruin, holding its place. And in that instant I leaped and gripped old Akkheba, and his death-shriek yowled in my ear as under my iron fingers I felt his flesh tear like rotten pulp, his thews rip from his bones, and the bones themselves splinter. The thunderings of the breaking world were in my ear, the swirling green waters at my feet, but, as the whole earth seemed to crumble and break, as the masonry dissolved beneath my feet, and the roaring green tides surged over me, drowning me in untold shimmering fathoms, my last fierce thought was that Akkheba had died by my hands, before a wave touched him.

I sprang up with a cry, hands thrown out as if to fend off the swirling waves. I reeled, dizzy with surprize. Khemu and the eld had vanished. I stood on the oak-clad hill, and the sun hung a hand's breadth above the post oak shinnery. Seconds only had elapsed since the woman had gestured before my eyes. Now she stood looking at me with that enigmatic smile that had less of mockery than pity.

"What is this?" I exclaimed, dazedly. "I was Hialmar—I am James Allison—the sea was the Gulf—the Great Plains ran to the shore then, and on the shore stood the accursed city of Khemu. No! I cannot believe you! I cannot believe my own reason. You have hypnotized me—made me dream—"

She shook her head.

"It came to pass, long, long ago, Hialmar."

"Then what of Khemu?" I exclaimed.

"Its broken ruins sleep in the deep blue waters of the Gulf, whither they washed in the long ages that passed after the breaking of the land, before the waters receded and left these long rolling steppes."

"But what of the woman Ishtar, their goddess?"

"Was she not the bride of Poseidon, who heard her cry and destroyed the evil city? On his bosom he bore her unharmed. She was deathless and eternal. She wandered through many lands, and dwelt with many people, but she had learned her lesson, and she who had been a slave of priests, became their ruler. She who had been a goddess in cruel seeming, became a goddess in her right, by virtue of her ancient wisdom.

"She was Ishtar of the Assyrians, and Ashtoreth of the Phoenicians; she was Mylitta and Belit of the Babylonians, Derketo of the Philistines. Aye, and she was Isis of Egypt, and Astarte of Carthage; and she was Freya of the Saxons, and Aphrodite of the Grecians, and Venus of the Romans. The races call her by many names, and worship her in many ways, but she is one and the same, and the fires of her altars are not quenched."

As she spoke she lifted her clear, dark luminous eyes to me; the last lurid sheen of the sunset caught the rippling glory of her hair, dusky as night, framing the strange beauty of her face, alien and exotic beyond my understanding. And a cry broke from my lips.

"*You!* You are Ishtar! Then it is true! And you are deathless—you are the Eternal Woman—the root and the bud of Creation—the symbol of life everlasting! And I—I was Hialmar, and knew pride and battle and far lands, and the bright glory of war—"

"As truly as you shall know them all again, oh weary one," she said softly, "when, in a little while, you shall put off that misshapen mask of broken flesh and don new raiment, bright and gleaming as the armor of Hialmar!"

Then night dipped down, and whither she went I know not, but I sat alone on the thicket-clad hill, and the night wind murmured up from the sand drifts and the shinnery, and whispered among the dreary branches of the post oaks.

"Feach Air Muir Lionadhi Gealach Buidhe Mar Or"

Mananan Mac Lir
The son of the sea
Is sib unto me
At the break of the year.

In the white autumn tides
The ghost drums call
When the midnights fall,
And a ghost ship rides
Where the green waves crawl.

I break the loam
By a Kerry hill—
They beckon me still
Through the purple gloam;
Strange eyes in the foam.

The sea-wind chills
The crumbling stones,
And a ghost harp moans
In the shadowy hills.
But a white sail fills
And a sweep-head drones.

The great white oars
They gleam and bend
And the west wind roars
From the blue world's end;
They call like a friend,
Forgotten shores.

A shadowy white
Mist of starlight
Swirls about me;
I am drawn in the night
To the roads of the sea.

The People of the Dark

I came to Dagon's Cave to kill Richard Brent. I went down the dusky avenues made by the towering trees, and my mood well-matched the primitive grimness of the scene. The approach to Dagon's Cave is always dark, for the mighty branches and thick leaves shut out the sun, and now the somberness of my own soul made the shadows seem more ominous and gloomy than was natural.

Not far away I heard the slow wash of the waves against the tall cliffs, but the sea itself was out of sight, masked by the dense oak forest. The darkness and the stark gloom of my surroundings gripped my shadowed soul as I passed beneath the ancient branches—as I came out into a narrow glade and saw the mouth of the ancient cavern before me. I paused, scanning the cavern's exterior and the dim reaches of the silent oaks.

The man I hated had not come before me! I was in time to carry out my grim intent. For a moment my resolution faltered, then like a wave there surged over me the fragrance of Eleanor Bland, a vision of wavy golden hair and deep-gray eyes, changing and mystic as the sea. I clenched my hands until the knuckles showed white, and instinctively touched the wicked snub-nosed revolver whose weight sagged my coat pocket.

But for Richard Brent, I felt certain I had already won this woman, desire for whom made my waking hours a torment and my sleep a torture. Whom did she love? She would not say; I did not believe she knew. Let one of us go away, I thought, and she would turn to the other. And I was going to simplify matters for her—and for myself. By chance I had overheard my blond English rival remark that he intended coming to lonely Dagon's Cave on an idle exploring outing—alone.

I am not by nature criminal. I was born and raised in a hard country and have lived most of my life on the raw edges of the world, where a man took what he wanted, if he could, and mercy was a virtue little known. But it was a torment that racked me day and night that sent me out to take the life of Richard Brent. I have lived hard, and violently, perhaps. When love overtook me, it also was fierce and violent. Perhaps I was not wholly sane, what with my love for Eleanor Bland and my hatred for Richard Brent. Under any other circumstances, I would have been glad to call him friend—a fine, rangy, upstanding young fellow, clear eyed and strong. But he stood in the way of my desire, and he must die.

I stepped into the dimness of the cavern and halted. I had never before visited Dagon's Cave, yet a vague sense of misplaced familiarity troubled me as I gazed on the high arching roof, the even stone walls and the dusty floor. I shrugged my shoulders, unable to place the elusive feeling; doubtless it was evoked by a similarity to caverns in the mountain country of the American Southwest where I was born and spent my childhood.

And yet I knew that I had never seen a cave like this one, whose regular aspect gave rise to myths that it was not a natural cavern, but had been hewn from the solid rock ages ago by the tiny hands of the mysterious Little People, the prehistoric beings of British legend. The whole countryside thereabouts was a haunt for ancient folklore.

The country folk were predominantly Celtic; here the Saxon invaders had never prevailed, and the legends reached back, in that long-settled countryside, further than anywhere else in England—back beyond the coming of the Saxons, aye, and incredibly beyond that distant age, beyond the coming of the Romans, to those unbelievably ancient days when the native Britons warred with black-haired Irish pirates.

The Little People, of course, had their part in the lore. Legend said that this cavern was one of their last strongholds against the conquering Celts, and hinted at lost tunnels, long fallen in or blocked up, connecting the cave with a network of subterranean corridors which honeycombed the hills. With these chance meditations vying idly in my mind with grimmer speculations, I passed through the outer chamber of the cavern and entered a narrow tunnel, which, I knew by former descriptions, connected with a larger room.

It was dark in the tunnel, but not too dark for me to make out the vague, half-defaced outlines of mysterious etchings on the stone walls. I ventured to switch on my electric torch and examine them more closely. Even in their dimness I was repelled by their abnormal and revolting character. Surely no men cast in human mold as we know it, scratched those grotesque obscenities.

The Little People—I wondered if those anthropologists were correct in their theory of a squat Mongoloid aboriginal race, so low in the scale of evolution as to be scarcely human, yet possessing a distinct, though repulsive, culture of their own. They had vanished before the invading races, theory said, forming the base of all Aryan legends of trolls, elves, dwarfs and witches. Living in caves from the start, these aborigines had retreated farther and farther into the caverns of the hills before the conquerors, vanishing at last entirely, though folklore fancy pictures their descendants still dwelling in the lost chasms far beneath the hills, loathsome survivals of an outworn age.

I snapped off the torch and passed through the tunnel, to come out into a sort of doorway which seemed entirely too symmetrical to have been the work of nature. I was looking into a vast dim cavern, at a somewhat lower level than the outer chamber, and again I shuddered with a strange alien sense of familiarity. A short flight of steps led down from the tunnel to the floor of the cavern—tiny steps, too small for normal human feet, carved into the solid stone. Their edges were greatly worn away, as if by ages of use. I started the descent—my foot slipped suddenly. I instinctively knew what was coming—it was all in part with that strange feeling of familiarity—but I could not catch myself. I fell headlong down the steps and struck the stone floor with a crash that blotted out my senses. . . .

Slowly consciousness returned to me, with a throbbing of my head and a sensation of bewilderment. I lifted a hand to my head and found it caked with blood. I had received a blow, or had taken a fall, but so completely had my wits been knocked out of me that my mind was an absolute blank. Where I was, who I was, I did not know. I looked about, blinking in the dim light, and saw that I was in a wide, dusty cavern. I stood at the foot of a short flight of steps which led upward into some kind of tunnel. I ran my hand dazedly through my square-cut black mane, and my eyes wandered over my massive naked limbs and powerful torso. I was clad, I noticed absently, in a sort of loincloth, from the girdle of which swung an empty scabbard, and leathern sandals were on my feet.

Then I saw an object lying at my feet, and stooped and took it up. It was a heavy iron sword, whose broad blade was darkly stained. My fingers fitted instinctively about its hilt with the familiarity of long usage. Then suddenly I remembered and laughed to think that a fall on his head should render me, Conan of the reavers, so completely daft. Aye, it all came back to me now. It had been a raid on the Britons, on whose coasts we continually swooped with torch and sword, from the island called Eireann. That day we of the black-haired Gael had swept suddenly down on a coastal village in our long, low ships and in the hurricane of battle which followed, the Britons had at last given up the stubborn contest and retreated, warriors, women and bairns, into the deep shadows of the oak forests, whither we seldom dared follow.

But I had followed, for there was a girl of my foes whom I desired with a burning passion; a lithe, slim young creature with wavy golden hair and deep gray eyes, changing and mystic as the sea. Her name was Tamera—well I knew it, for there was trade between the races as well as war, and I had been in the villages of the Britons as a peaceful visitor, in times of rare truce.

I saw her white half-clad body flickering among the trees as she ran with the swiftness of a doe, and I followed, panting with fierce eagerness. Under the dark shadows of the gnarled oaks she fled, with me in close pursuit, while far away behind us died out the shouts of slaughter and the clashing of swords. Then we ran in silence, save for her quick labored panting, and I was so close behind her as we emerged into a narrow glade before a somber-mouthed cavern, that I caught her flying golden tresses with one mighty hand. She sank down with a despairing wail, and even so, a shout echoed her cry and I wheeled quickly to face a rangy young Briton who sprang from among the trees, the light of desperation in his eyes.

"Vertorix!" the girl wailed, her voice breaking in a sob, and fiercer rage welled up in me, for I knew the lad was her lover.

"Run for the forest, Tamera!" he shouted, and leaped at me as a panther leaps, his bronze ax whirling like a flashing wheel about his head. And then sounded the clangor of strife and the hard-drawn panting of combat.

The Briton was as tall as I, but he was lithe where I was massive. The advantage of sheer muscular power was mine, and soon he was on the defensive, striving desperately to parry my heavy strokes with his ax. Hammering on his guard like a smith on an anvil, I pressed him relentlessly, driving him irresistibly before me. His chest heaved, his breath came in labored gasps, his blood dripped from scalp, chest and thigh where my whistling blade had cut the skin, and all but gone home. As I redoubled my strokes and he bent and swayed beneath them like a sapling in a storm, I heard the girl cry: "Vertorix! Vertorix! The cave! Into the cave!"

I saw his face pale with a fear greater than that induced by my hacking sword.

"Not there!" he gasped. "Better a clean death! In Il-marenin's name, girl, run into the forest and save yourself!"

"I will not leave you!" she cried. "The cave! It is our one chance!"

I saw her flash past us like a flying wisp of white and vanish in the cavern, and with a despairing cry, the youth launched a wild desperate stroke that nigh cleft my skull. As I staggered beneath the blow I had barely parried, he sprang away, leaped into the cavern after the girl and vanished in the gloom.

With a maddened yell that invoked all my grim Gaelic gods, I sprang recklessly after them, not reckoning if the Briton lurked beside the entrance to brain me as I rushed in. But a quick glance showed the chamber empty and a wisp of white disappearing through a dark doorway in the back wall.

I raced across the cavern and came to a sudden halt as an ax licked out of the gloom of the entrance and whistled perilously close to my black-maned head. I gave back suddenly. Now the advantage was with Vertorix, who stood in the narrow mouth of the corridor where I could hardly come at him without exposing myself to the devastating stroke of his ax.

I was near frothing with fury and the sight of a slim white form among the deep shadows behind the warrior drove me into a frenzy. I attacked savagely but warily, thrusting venomously at my foe, and drawing back from his strokes. I wished to draw him out into a wide lunge, avoid it and run him through before he could recover his balance. In the open I could have beat him down by sheer power and heavy blows, but here I could only use the point and that at a disadvantage; I always preferred the edge. But I was stubborn; if I could not come at him with a finishing stroke, neither could he or the girl escape me while I kept him hemmed in the tunnel.

It must have been the realization of this fact that prompted the girl's action, for she said something to Vertorix about looking for a way leading out, and though he cried out fiercely forbidding her to venture away into the darkness, she turned and ran swiftly down the tunnel to vanish in the dimness. My wrath rose appallingly and I nearly got my head split in my eagerness to bring down my foe before she found a means for their escape.

Then the cavern echoed with a terrible scream and Vertorix cried out like a man death-stricken, his face ashy in the gloom. He whirled, as if he had forgotten me and my sword, and raced down the tunnel like a madman, shrieking Tamera's name. From far away, as if from the bowels of the earth, I seemed to hear her answering cry, mingled with a strange sibilant clamor that electrified me with nameless but instinctive horror. Then silence fell, broken only by Vertorix's frenzied cries, receding farther and farther into the earth.

Recovering myself, I sprang into the tunnel and raced after the Briton as recklessly as he had run after the girl. And to give me my due, red-handed reaver though I was, cutting down my rival from behind was less in my mind than discovering what dread thing had Tamera in its clutches.

As I ran along I noted absently that the sides of the tunnel were scrawled with monstrous pictures, and realized suddenly and creepily that this must be the dread Cavern of the Children of the Night, tales of which had crossed the narrow sea to resound horrifically in the ears of the Gaels. Terror of me must have ridden Tamera hard to have driven her into the cavern shunned by her people, where, it was said, lurked the survivals of that grisly race which inhabited the land before the coming of the Picts and Britons, and which had fled before them into the unknown caverns of the hills.

Ahead of me the tunnel opened into a wide chamber, and I saw the white form of Vertorix glimmer momentarily in the semidarkness and vanish in what appeared to be the entrance of a corridor opposite the mouth of the tunnel I had just traversed. Instantly there sounded a short, fierce shout and the crash of a hard-driven blow, mixed with the hysterical screams of a girl and a medley of serpent-like hissing that made my hair bristle. And at that instant I shot out of the tunnel, running at full speed, and realized too late the floor of the cavern lay several feet below the level of the tunnel. My flying feet missed the tiny steps and I crashed terrifically on the solid stone floor.

Now as I stood in the semidarkness, rubbing my aching head, all this came back to me, and I stared fearsomely across the vast chamber at that black cryptic corridor into which Tamera and her lover had disappeared, and over which silence lay like a pall. Gripping my sword, I warily crossed the great still cavern and peered into the corridor. Only a denser darkness met my eyes. I entered, striving to pierce the gloom, and as my foot slipped on a wide wet smear on the stone floor, the raw acrid scent of fresh-spilled blood met my nostrils. Someone or something had died there, either the young Briton or his unknown attacker.

I stood there uncertainly, all the supernatural fears that are the heritage of the Gael rising in my primitive soul. I could turn and stride out of these accursed mazes, into the clear sunlight and down to the clean blue sea where my comrades, no doubt, impatiently awaited me after the routing of the Britons. Why should I risk my life among these grisly rat dens? I was eaten with curiosity to know what manner of beings haunted the cavern, and who were called the Children of the Night by the Britons, but in it was my love for the yellow-haired girl which drove me down that dark tunnel—and love her I did, in my way, and would have been kind to her, had I carried her away to my island haunt.

I walked softly along the corridor, blade ready. What sort of creatures the Children of the Night were, I had no idea, but the tales of the Britons had lent them a distinctly inhuman nature.

The darkness closed around me as I advanced, until I was moving in utter blackness. My groping left hand encountered a strangely carven doorway, and at that instant something hissed like a viper beside me and slashed fiercely at my thigh. I struck back savagely and felt my blind stroke crunch home, and something fell at my feet and died. What thing I had slain in the dark I could not know, but it must have been at least partly human because the shallow gash in my thigh had been made with a blade of some sort, and not by fangs or talons. And I sweated with horror, for the gods know, the hissing voice of the Thing had resembled no human tongue I had ever heard.

And now in the darkness ahead of me I heard the sound repeated, mingled with horrible slitherings, as if numbers of reptilian creatures were approaching. I stepped quickly into the entrance my groping hand had discovered and came near repeating my headlong fall, for instead of letting into another level corridor, the entrance gave onto a flight of dwarfish steps on which I floundered wildly.

Recovering my balance I went on cautiously, groping along the sides of the shaft for support. I seemed to be descending into the very bowels of the earth, but I dared not turn back. Suddenly, far below me, I glimpsed a faint eerie light. I went on, perforce, and came to a spot where the shaft opened into another great vaulted chamber; and I shrank back, aghast.

In the center of the chamber stood a grim, black altar; it had been rubbed all over with a sort of phosphorous, so that it glowed dully, lending a semi-illumination to the shadowy cavern. Towering behind it, on a pedestal of human skulls, lay a cryptic black object, carven with mysterious hieroglyphics. The Black Stone! The ancient, ancient Stone before which, the Britons said, the Children of the Night bowed in gruesome worship, and whose origin was lost in the black mists of a hideously distant past. Once, legend said, it had stood in that grim circle of monoliths called Stonehenge, before its votaries had been driven like chaff before the bows of the Picts.

But I gave it but a passing, shuddering glance. Two figures lay, bound with rawhide thongs, on the glowing black altar. One was Tamera; the other was Vertorix, bloodstained and disheveled. His bronze ax, crusted with clotted blood, lay near the altar. And before the glowing stone squatted Horror.

Though I had never seen one of those ghoulish aborigines, I knew this thing for what it was, and shuddered. It was a man of a sort, but so low in the stage of life that its distorted humanness was more horrible than its bestiality.

Erect, it could not have been five feet in height. Its body was scrawny and deformed, its head disproportionately large. Lank snaky hair fell over a square inhuman face with flabby writhing lips that bared yellow fangs, flat spreading nostrils and great yellow slant eyes. I knew the creature must be able to see in the dark as well as a cat. Centuries of skulking in dim caverns had lent the race terrible and inhuman attributes. But the most repellent feature was its skin: scaly, yellow and mottled, like the hide of a serpent. A loincloth made of a real snake's skin girt its lean loins, and its taloned hands gripped a short stone-tipped spear and a sinister-looking mallet of polished flint.

So intently was it gloating over its captives, it evidently had not heard my stealthy descent. As I hesitated in the shadows of the shaft, far above me I heard a soft sinister rustling that chilled the blood in my veins. The Children were creeping down the shaft behind me, and I was trapped. I saw other entrances opening on the chamber, and I acted, realizing that an alliance with Vertorix was our only hope. Enemies though we were, we were men, cast in the same mold, trapped in the lair of these indescribable monstrosities.

As I stepped from the shaft, the horror beside the altar jerked up his head and glared full at me. And as he sprang up, I leaped and he crumpled, blood spurting, as my heavy sword split his reptilian heart. But even as he died, he gave tongue in an abhorrent shriek which was echoed far up the shaft. In desperate haste I cut Vertorix's bonds and dragged him to his feet. And I turned to Tamera, who in that dire extremity did not shrink from me, but looked up at me with pleading, terror-dilated eyes. Vertorix wasted no time in words, realizing chance had made allies of us. He snatched up his ax as I freed the girl.

"We can't go up the shaft," he explained swiftly; "we'll have the whole pack upon us quickly. They caught Tamera as she sought for an exit, and overpowered me by sheer numbers when I followed. They dragged us hither and all but that carrion scattered—bearing word of the sacrifice through all their burrows, I doubt not. Il-marenin alone knows how many of my people, stolen in the night, have died on that altar. We must take our chance in one of these tunnels—all lead to Hell! Follow me!"

Seizing Tamera's hand he ran fleetly into the nearest tunnel and I followed. A glance back into the chamber before a turn in the corridor blotted it from view showed a revolting horde streaming out of the shaft. The tunnel slanted steeply upward, and suddenly ahead of us we saw a bar of gray light. But the next instant our cries of hope changed to curses of bitter disappointment. There was daylight, aye, drifting in through a cleft in the vaulted roof, but far, far above our reach. Behind us the pack gave tongue exultingly. And I halted.

"Save yourselves if you can," I growled. "Here I make my stand. They can see in the dark and I cannot. Here at least I can see them. Go!"

But Vertorix halted also. "Little use to be hunted like rats to our doom. There is no escape. Let us meet our fate like men."

Tamera cried out, wringing her hands, but she clung to her lover.

"Stand behind me with the girl," I grunted. "When I fall, dash out her brains with your ax lest they take her alive again. Then sell your own life as high as you may, for there is none to avenge us."

His keen eyes met mine squarely.

"We worship different gods, reaver," he said, "but all gods love brave men. Mayhap we shall meet again, beyond the Dark."

"Hail and farewell, Briton!" I growled, and our right hands gripped like steel.

"Hail and farewell, Gael!"

And I wheeled as a hideous horde swept up the tunnel and burst into the dim light, a flying nightmare of streaming snaky hair, foam-flecked lips and glaring eyes. Thundering my war-cry I sprang to meet them and my heavy sword sang and a head spun grinning from its shoulder on an arching fountain of blood. They came upon me like a wave and the fighting madness of my race was upon me. I fought as a maddened beast fights and at every stroke I clove through flesh and bone, and blood spattered in a crimson rain.

Then as they surged in and I went down beneath the sheer weight of their numbers, a fierce yell cut the din and Vertorix's ax sang above me, splattering blood and brains like water. The press slackened and I staggered up, trampling the writhing bodies beneath my feet.

"A stair behind us!" the Briton was screaming. "Half-hidden in an angle of the wall! It must lead to daylight! Up it, in the name of Il-marenin!"

So we fell back, fighting our way inch by inch. The vermin fought like blood-hungry devils, clambering over the bodies of the slain to screech and hack. Both of us were streaming blood at every step when we reached the mouth of the shaft, into which Tamera had preceded us.

Screaming like very fiends the Children surged in to drag us down. The shaft was not as light as had been the corridor, and it grew darker as we climbed, but our foes could only come at us from in front. By the gods, we slaughtered them till the stair was littered with mangled corpses and the Children frothed like mad wolves! Then suddenly they abandoned the fray and raced back down the steps.

"What portends this?" gasped Vertorix, shaking the bloody sweat from his eyes.

"Up the shaft, quick!" I panted. "They mean to mount some other stair and come at us from above!"

So we raced up those accursed steps, slipping and stumbling, and as we fled past a black tunnel that opened into the shaft, far down it we heard a frightful howling. An instant later we emerged from the shaft into a winding corridor, dimly illumined by a vague gray light filtering in from above, and somewhere in the bowels of the earth I seemed to hear the thunder of rushing water. We started down the corridor and, as we did so, a heavy weight smashed on my shoulders, knocking me headlong, and a mallet crashed again and again on my head, sending dull red flashes of agony across my brain. With a volcanic wrench I dragged my attacker off and under me, and tore out his throat with my naked fingers. And his fangs met in my arm in his death-bite.

Reeling up, I saw that Tamera and Vertorix had passed out of sight. I had been somewhat behind them, and they had run on, knowing nothing of the fiend which had leaped on my shoulders. Doubtless they thought I was still close on their heels. A dozen steps I took, then halted. The corridor branched and I knew not which way my companions had taken. At blind venture I turned into the left-hand branch and staggered on in the semidarkness. I was weak from fatigue and loss of blood, dizzy and sick from the blows I had received. Only the thought of Tamera kept me doggedly on my feet. Now distinctly I heard the sound of an unseen torrent.

That I was not far underground was evident by the dim light which filtered in from somewhere above, and I momentarily expected to come upon another stair. But when I did, I halted in black despair; instead of up, it led down. Somewhere far behind me I heard faintly the howls of the pack, and I went down, plunging into utter darkness. At last I struck a level and went along blindly. I had given up all hope of escape, and only hoped to find Tamera—if she and her lover had not found a way of escape—and die with her. The thunder of rushing water was above my head now, and the tunnel was slimy and dank. Drops of moisture fell on my head and I knew I was passing under the river.

Then I blundered again upon steps cut in the stone, and these led upward. I scrambled up as fast as my stiffening wounds would allow—and I had taken punishment enough to have killed an ordinary man. Up I went and up, and suddenly daylight burst on me through a cleft in the solid rock. I stepped into the blaze of the sun. I was standing on a ledge high above the rushing waters of a river which raced at awesome speed between towering cliffs. The ledge on which I stood was close to the top of the cliff; safety was within arm's length. But I hesitated, and such was my love for the golden-haired girl that I was ready to retrace my steps through those black tunnels on the mad hope of finding her. Then I started.

Across the river I saw another cleft in the cliff wall which fronted me, with a ledge similar to that on which I stood, but longer. In olden times, I doubt not, some sort of primitive bridge connected the two ledges—possibly before the tunnel was dug beneath the riverbed. Now, as I watched, two figures emerged upon that other ledge—one gashed, dust stained, limping, gripping a bloodstained ax; the other slim, white and girlish.

Vertorix and Tamera! They had taken the other branch of the corridor at the fork and had evidently followed the windows of the tunnel to emerge as I had done, except that I had taken the left turn and passed clear under the river. And now I saw that they were in a trap. On that side the cliffs rose half a hundred feet higher than on my side of the river, and so sheer a spider could scarce have scaled them. There were only two ways of escape from the ledge: back through the fiend-haunted tunnels, or straight down to the river which raved far beneath.

I saw Vertorix look up the sheer cliffs and then down, and shake his head in despair. Tamera put her arms about his neck, and though I could not hear their voices for the rush of the river, I saw them smile, and then they went together to the edge of the ledge. And out of the cleft swarmed a loathsome mob, as foul reptiles writhe up out of the darkness, and they stood blinking in the sunlight like the night-things they were. I gripped my sword hilt in the agony of my helplessness until the blood trickled from under my fingernails. Why had not the pack followed me instead of my companions?

The Children hesitated an instant as the two Britons faced them, then with a laugh Vertorix hurled his ax far out into the rushing river, and turning, caught Tamera in a last embrace. Together they sprang far out, and still locked in each other's arms, hurtled downward, struck the madly foaming water that seemed to leap up to meet them, and vanished. And the wild river swept on like a blind, insensate monster, thundering along the echoing cliffs.

A moment I stood frozen, then like a man in a dream I turned, caught the edge of the cliff above me and wearily drew myself up and over, and stood on my feet above the cliffs, hearing like a dim dream the roar of the river far beneath.

* * * * *

I reeled up, dazedly clutching my throbbing head, on which dried blood was clotted. I glared wildly about me. I had clambered the cliffs—no, by the thunder of Crom, I was still in the cavern! I reached for my sword—

The mists faded and I stared about dizzily, orienting myself with space and time. I stood at the foot of the steps down which I had fallen. I who had been Conan the reaver, was John O'Brien. Was all that grotesque interlude a dream? Could a mere dream appear so vivid? Even in dreams, we often know we are dreaming, but Conan the reaver had no cognizance of any other existence. More, he remembered his own past life as a living man remembers, though in the waking mind of John O'Brien, that memory faded into dust and mist. But the adventures of Conan in the Cavern of the Children stood clear-etched in the mind of John O'Brien.

I glanced across the dim chamber toward the entrance of the tunnel into which Vertorix had followed the girl. But I looked in vain, seeing only the bare blank wall of the cavern. I crossed the chamber, switched on my electric torch—miraculously unbroken in my fall—and felt along the wall.

Ha! I started, as from an electric shock! Exactly where the entrance should have been, my fingers detected a difference in material, a section which was rougher than the rest of the wall. I was convinced that it was of comparatively modern workmanship; the tunnel had been walled up.

I thrust against it, exerting all my strength, and it seemed to me that the section was about to give. I drew back, and taking a deep breath, launched my full weight against it, backed by all the power of my giant muscles. The brittle, decaying wall gave way with a shattering crash and I catapulted through in a shower of stones and falling masonry.

I scrambled up, a sharp cry escaping me. I stood in a tunnel, and I could not mistake the feeling of similarity this time. Here Vertorix had first fallen foul of the Children, as they dragged Tamera away, and here where I now stood the floor had been awash with blood.

I walked down the corridor like a man in a trance. Soon I should come to the doorway on the left—aye, there it was, the strangely carven portal, at the mouth of which I had slain the unseen being which reared up in the dark beside me. I shivered momentarily. Could it be possible that remnants of that foul race still lurked hideously in these remote caverns?

I turned into the doorway and my light shone down a long, slanting shaft, with tiny steps cut into the solid stone. Down these had Conan the reaver gone groping and down them went I, John O'Brien, with memories of that other life filling my brain with vague phantasms. No light glimmered ahead of me but I came into the great dim chamber I had known of yore, and I shuddered as I saw the grim black altar etched in the gleam of my torch. Now no bound figures writhed there, no crouching horror gloated before it. Nor did the pyramid of skulls support the Black Stone before which unknown races had bowed before Egypt was born out of time's dawn. Only a littered heap of dust lay strewn where the skulls had upheld the hellish thing. No, that had been no dream: I was John O'Brien, but I had been Conan of the reavers in that other life, and that grim interlude a brief episode of reality which I had relived.

I entered the tunnel down which we had fled, shining a beam of light ahead, and saw the bar of gray light drifting down from above—just as in that other, lost age. Here the Briton and I, Conan, had turned at bay. I turned my eyes from the ancient cleft high up in the vaulted roof and looked for the stair. There it was, half-concealed by an angle in the wall.

I mounted, remembering how hardly Vertorix and I had gone up so many ages before, with the horde hissing and frothing at our heels. I found myself tense with dread as I approached the dark, gaping entrance through which the pack had sought to cut us off. I had snapped off the light when I came into the dim-lit corridor below, and now I glanced into the well of blackness which opened on the stair. And with a cry I started back, nearly losing my footing on the worn steps. Sweating in the semidarkness I switched on the light and directed its beam into the cryptic opening, revolver in hand.

I saw only the bare rounded sides of a small shaft-like tunnel and I laughed nervously. My imagination was running riot; I could have sworn that hideous yellow eyes glared terribly at me from the darkness, and that a crawling something had scuttered away down the tunnel. I was foolish to let these imaginings upset me. The Children had long vanished from these caverns; a nameless and abhorrent race closer to the serpent than the man, they had centuries ago faded back into the oblivion from which they had crawled in the black dawn ages of the Earth.

I came out of the shaft into the winding corridor, which, as I remembered of old, was lighter. Here from the shadows a lurking thing had leaped on my back while my companions ran on, unknowing. What a brute of a man Conan had been, to keep going after receiving such savage wounds! Aye, in that age all men were iron.

I came to the place where the tunnel forked and as before I took the left-hand branch and came to the shaft that led down. Down this I went, listening for the roar of the river, but not hearing it. Again the darkness shut in about the shaft, so I was forced to have recourse to my electric torch again, lest I lose my footing and plunge to my death. Oh, I, John O'Brien, am not nearly so sure-footed as was I, Conan the reaver; no, nor as tigerishly powerful and quick, either.

I soon struck the dank lower level and felt again the dampness that denoted my position under the riverbed, but still I could not hear the rush of the water. And indeed I knew that whatever mighty river had rushed roaring to the sea in those ancient times, there was no such body of water among the hills today. I halted, flashing my light about. I was in a vast tunnel, not very high of roof, but broad. Other smaller tunnels branched off from it and I wondered at the network which apparently honeycombed the hills.

I cannot describe the grim, gloomy effect of those dark, low-roofed corridors far below the earth. Over all hung an overpowering sense of unspeakable antiquity. Why had the little people carved out these mysterious crypts, and in which black age? Were these caverns their last refuge from the onrushing tides of humanity, or their castles since time immemorial? I shook my head in bewilderment; the bestiality of the Children I had seen, yet somehow they had been able to carve these tunnels and chambers that might balk modern engineers. Even supposing they had but completed a task begun by nature, still it was a stupendous work for a race of dwarfish aborigines.

Then I realized with a start that I was spending more time in these gloomy tunnels than I cared for, and began to hunt for the steps by which Conan had ascended. I found them and, following them up, breathed again deeply in relief as the sudden glow of daylight filled the shaft. I came out upon the ledge, now worn away until it was little more than a bump on the face of the cliff. And I saw the great river, which had roared like a prisoned monster between the sheer walls of its narrow canyon, had dwindled away with the passing eons until it was no more than a tiny stream, far beneath me, trickling soundlessly among the stones on its way to the sea.

Aye, the surface of the earth changes; the rivers swell or shrink, the mountains heave and topple, the lakes dry up, the continents alter; but under the earth the work of lost, mysterious hands slumbers untouched by the sweep of Time. Their work, aye, but what of the hands that reared that work? Did they, too, lurk beneath the bosoms of the hills?

How long I stood there, lost in dim speculations, I do not know, but suddenly, glancing across at the other ledge, crumbling and weathered, I shrank back into the entrance behind me. Two figures came out upon the ledge and I gasped to see that they were Richard Brent and Eleanor Bland. Now I remembered why I had come to the cavern and my hand instinctively sought the revolver in my pocket. They did not see me. But I could see them, and hear them plainly, too, since no roaring river now thundered between the ledges.

"By gad, Eleanor," Brent was saying, "I'm glad you decided to come with me. Who would have guessed there was anything to those old tales about hidden tunnels leading from the cavern? I wonder how that section of wall came to collapse? I thought I heard a crash just as we entered the outer cave. Do you suppose some beggar was in the cavern ahead of us, and broke it in?"

"I don't know," she answered. "I remember—oh, I don't know. It almost seems as if I'd been here before, or dreamed I had. I seem to faintly remember, like a far-off nightmare, running, running, running endlessly through these dark corridors with hideous creatures on my heels. . . ."

"Was I there?" jokingly asked Brent.

"Yes, and John, too," she answered. "But you were not Richard Brent, and John was not John O'Brien. No, and I was not Eleanor Bland, either. Oh, it's so dim and far-off I can't describe it at all. It's hazy and misty and terrible."

"I understand, a little," he said unexpectedly. "Ever since we came to the place where the wall had fallen and revealed the old tunnel, I've had a sense of familiarity with the place. There was horror and danger and battle—and love, too."

He stepped nearer the edge to look down in the gorge, and Eleanor cried out sharply and suddenly, seizing him in a convulsive grasp.

"Don't, Richard, don't! Hold me, oh, hold me tight!"

He caught her in his arms. "Why, Eleanor, dear, what's the matter?"

"Nothing," she faltered, but she clung closer to him and I saw she was trembling. "Just a strange feeling—rushing dizziness and fright, just as if I were falling from a great height. Don't go near the edge, Dick; it scares me."

"I won't, dear," he answered, drawing her closer to him, and continuing hesitantly: "Eleanor, there's something I've wanted to ask you for a long time—well, I haven't the knack of putting things in an elegant way. I love you, Eleanor; always have. You know that. But if you don't love me, I'll take myself off and won't annoy you anymore. Only please tell me one way or another, for I can't stand it any longer. Is it I or the American?"

"You, Dick," she answered, hiding her face on his shoulder. "It's always been you, though I didn't know it. I think a great deal of John O'Brien. I didn't know which of you I really loved. But today, as we came through those terrible tunnels and climbed those fearful stairs, and just now, when I thought for some strange reason we were falling from the ledge, I realized it was you I loved—that I always loved you, through more lives than this one. Always!"

Their lips met and I saw her golden head cradled on his shoulder. My lips were dry, my heart cold, yet my soul was at peace. They belonged to each other. Eons ago they lived and loved, and because of that love they suffered and died. And I, Conan, had driven them to that doom.

I saw them turn toward the cleft, their arms about each other, then I heard Tamera—I mean Eleanor—shriek. I saw them both recoil. And out of the cleft a horror came writhing, a loathsome, brain-shattering thing that blinked in the clean sunlight. Aye, I knew it of old—vestige of a forgotten age, it came writhing its horrid shape up out of the darkness of the Earth and the lost past to claim its own.

What three thousand years of retrogression can do to a race hideous in the beginning, I saw, and shuddered. And instinctively I knew that in all the world it was the only one of its kind, a monster that had lived on. God alone knows how many centuries, wallowing in the slime of its dank subterranean lairs. Before the Children had vanished, the race must have lost all human semblance, living as they did, the life of the reptile. This thing was more like a giant serpent than anything else, but it had aborted legs and snaky arms with hooked talons. It crawled on its belly, writhing back mottled lips to bare needlelike fangs, which I felt must drip with venom. It hissed as it reared up its ghastly head on a horribly long neck, while its yellow slanted eyes glittered with all the horror that is spawned in the black lairs under the earth.

I knew those eyes had blazed at me from the dark tunnel opening on the stair. For some reason the creature had fled from me, possibly because it feared my light, and it stood to reason that it was the only one remaining in the caverns, else I had been set upon in the darkness. But for it, the tunnels could be traversed in safety.

Now the reptilian thing writhed toward the humans trapped on the ledge. Brent had thrust Eleanor behind him and stood, face ashy, to guard her as best he could. And I gave thanks silently that I, John O'Brien, could pay the debt I, Conan the reaver, owed these lovers since long ago.

The monster reared up and Brent, with cold courage, sprang to meet it with his naked hands. Taking quick aim, I fired once. The shot echoed like the crack of doom between the towering cliffs, and the Horror, with a hideously human scream, staggered wildly, swayed and pitched headlong, knotting and writhing like a wounded python, to tumble from the sloping ledge and fall plummet-like to the rocks far below.

An Echo from the Iron Harp

Shadows and echoes haunt my dreams
    with dim and subtle pain,
With the faded fire of a lost desire,
    like a ghost on a moonlit plain.
In the pallid mist of death-like sleep
    she comes again to me:
I see the gleam of her golden hair
    and her eyes like the deep grey sea.

* * * * * *

We came from the North as the spume is blown
    when the blue tide billows down;
The kings of the South were overthrown
    in ruin of camp and town.
Shrine and temple we dashed to dust,
    and roared in the dead gods' ears;
We saw the fall of the kings of Gaul,
    and shattered the Belgae spears.

And South we rolled like a drifting cloud,
    like a wind that bends the grass,
But we smote in vain on the gates of Spain
    for our own kin held the Pass.
Then again we turned where the watch-fires burned
    to mark the lines of Rome,
And fire and tower and standard sank
    as ships that die in foam.

The legions came, hard hawk-eyed men,
    war-wise in march and fray,
But we rushed like a whirlwind on their lines
    and swept their ranks away.
Army and consul we overthrew,
    staining the trampled loam;

Horror and fear like a lifted spear
    lay hard on the walls of Rome.

Our mad desire was a flying fire
    that should burn the Appian Gate—
But the day of our doom lay hard on us,
    at a toss of the dice of Fate.
There rose a man in the ranks of Rome—
    ill fall the cursed day!—
Our German allies bit the dust
    and we turned hard at bay.
And the raven came and the lean grey wolf,
    to follow the sword's red play.

Over the land like a ghostly hand
    the mists of morning lay,
We smote their horsemen in the fog
    and hacked a bloody way.
We smote their horsemen in the cloud
    and as the mists were cleared
Right through the legion massed behind
    our headlong squadron sheared.

Saddle to saddle we chained our ranks
    for naught of war we knew
But to charge in the wild old Celtic way—
    and die or slash straight through.
We left red ruin in our wake,
    dead men in ghastly ranks—
When fresh unwearied Roman arms
    smote hard upon our flanks.

Baffled and weary, red with wounds,
    leaguered on every side,
Chained to our doom we smote in vain,
    slaughtered and sank and died.
Writhing among the horses' hoofs,
    torn and slashed and gored,
Gripping still with a bloody hand,
    a notched and broken sword,

I heard the war-cry growing faint,
drowned by the trumpet's call,
And the roar of "Marius! Marius!"
triumphant over all.

Through the bloody dust and the swirling fog
as I strove in vain to rise
I saw the last of the warriors fall,
and swift as a falcon flies
The Romans rush to the barricades
where the women watched the fight—
I heard the screams and I saw steel flash
and naked arms toss white.

The ravisher died as he gripped his prey,
by the dagger fiercely driven—
By the next stroke with her own hand
the heart of the girl was riven.
Brown fingers grasped white wrists in vain—
blood flecked the gasping loam—
The Cimbri yield no virgin-slaves
to glut the gods of Rome!

And I saw as I crawled like a crippled snake
to slay before I died,
Unruly golden hair that tossed
in wild and untamed pride.
Her slim foot pressed a dead man's breast,
her proud head back was thrown,
Matching the steel she held on high,
her eyes in glory shone.

I saw the gleam of her golden hair
and her eyes like the deep grey sea—
And the love in the gaze that sought me out,
barbaric, fierce and free—
Then the dagger fell and the skies fell
and the mists closed over me.

* * * * * *

Like phantoms into the ages lost
    has the Cimbrian nation passed;
Destiny shifts like summer clouds
    on Grecian hill-tops massed.
Untold centuries glide away,
    Marius long is dust;
Even eternal Rome has passed
    in days of decay and rust.
But memories live in the ghosts of dreams,
    and dreams still come to me,
And I see the gleam of her golden hair
    and her eyes like the deep grey sea.

Kings of the Night

> The Caesar lolled on his ivory throne—
> His iron legions came
> To break a king in a land unknown,
> And a race without a name.
>
> —*The Song of Bran*

The dagger flashed downward. A sharp cry broke in a gasp. The form on the rough altar twitched convulsively and lay still. The jagged flint edge sawed at the crimsoned breast, and thin bony fingers, ghastly dyed, tore out the still twitching heart. Under matted white brows, sharp eyes gleamed with a ferocious intensity.

Besides the slayer, four men stood about the crude pile of stones that formed the altar of the God of Shadows. One was of medium height, lithely built, scantily clad, whose black hair was confined by a narrow iron band in the center of which gleamed a single red jewel. Of the others, two were dark like the first. But where he was lithe, they were stocky and misshapen, with knotted limbs, and tangled hair falling over sloping brows. His face denoted intelligence and implacable will; theirs merely a beastlike ferocity. The fourth man had little in common with the rest. Nearly a head taller, though his hair was black as theirs, his skin was comparatively light and he was gray eyed. He eyed the proceedings with little favor.

And, in truth, Cormac of Connacht was little at ease. The Druids of his own isle of Erin had strange dark rites of worship, but nothing like this. Dark trees shut in this grim scene, lit by a single torch. Through the branches moaned an eery night wind. Cormac was alone among men of a strange race and he had just seen the heart of a man ripped from his still pulsing body. Now the ancient priest, who looked scarcely human, was glaring at the throbbing thing. Cormac shuddered, glancing at him who wore the jewel. Did Bran Mak Morn, king of the Picts, believe that this white-bearded old butcher could foretell events by scanning a bleeding human heart? The dark eyes of the king were inscrutable. There were strange depths to the man that Cormac could not fathom, nor any other man.

"The portents are good!" exclaimed the priest wildly, speaking more to the two chieftains than to Bran. "Here from the pulsing heart of a captive Roman I read—defeat for the arms of Rome! Triumph for the sons of the heather!"

The two savages murmured beneath their breath, their fierce eyes smoldering.

"Go and prepare your clans for battle," said the king, and they lumbered away with the apelike gait assumed by such stunted giants. Paying no more heed to the priest who was examining the ghastly ruin on the altar, Bran beckoned to Cormac. The Gael followed him with alacrity. Once out of that grim grove, under the starlight, he breathed more freely. They stood on an eminence, looking out over long swelling undulations of gently waving heather. Near at hand a few fires twinkled, their fewness giving scant evidence of the hordes of tribesmen who lay close by. Beyond these were more fires and beyond these still more, which last marked the camp of Cormac's own men, hard-riding, hard-fighting Gaels, who were of that band which was just beginning to get a foothold on the western coast of Caledonia—the nucleus of what was later to become the kingdom of Dalriadia. To the left of these, other fires gleamed.

And far away to the south were more fires—mere pinpoints of light. But even at that distance the Pictish king and his Celtic ally could see that these fires were laid out in regular order.

"The fires of the legions," muttered Bran. "The fires that have lit a path around the world. The men who light those fires have trampled the races under their iron heels. And now—we of the heather have our backs at the wall. What will fall on the morrow?"

"Victory for us, says the priest," answered Cormac.

Bran made an impatient gesture. "Moonlight on the ocean. Wind in the fir tops. Do you think that I put faith in such mummery? Or that I enjoyed the butchery of a captive legionary? I must hearten my people; it was for Gron and Bocah that I let old Gonar read the portents. The warriors will fight better."

"And Gonar?"

Bran laughed. "Gonar is too old to believe—anything. He was high priest of the Shadows a score of years before I was born. He claims direct descent from that Gonar who was a wizard in the days of Brule, the Spear-slayer who was the first of my line. No man knows how old he is—sometimes I think he is the original Gonar himself!"

"At least," said a mocking voice, and Cormac started as a dim shape appeared at his side, "at least I have learned that in order to keep the faith and trust of the people, a wise man must appear to be a fool. I know secrets that would blast even your brain, Bran, should I speak them. But in order that the people may believe in me, I must descend to such things as they think proper magic—and prance and yell and rattle snakeskins, and dabble about in human blood and chicken livers."

Cormac looked at the ancient with new interest. The semi-madness of his appearance had vanished. He was no longer the charlatan, the spell-mumbling shaman. The starlight lent him a dignity which seemed to increase his very height, so that he stood like a white-bearded patriarch.

"Bran, your doubt lies there." The lean arm pointed to the fourth ring of fires.

"Aye," the king nodded gloomily. "Cormac—you know as well as I. Tomorrow's battle hinges upon that circle of fires. With the chariots of the Britons and your own Western horsemen, our success would be certain, but—surely the devil himself is in the heart of every Northman! You know how I trapped that band—how they swore to fight for me against Rome! And now that their chief, Rognar, is dead, they swear that they will be led only by a king of their own race! Else they will break their vow and go over to the Romans. Without them we are doomed, for we cannot change our former plan."

"Take heart, Bran," said Gonar. "Touch the jewel in your iron crown. Mayhap it will bring you aid."

Bran laughed bitterly. "Now you talk as the people think. I am no fool to twist with empty words. What of the gem? It is a strange one, truth, and has brought me luck ere now. But I need now, no jewels, but the allegiance of three hundred fickle Northmen who are the only warriors among us who may stand the charge of the legions on foot."

"But the jewel, Bran, the jewel!" persisted Gonar.

"Well, the jewel!" cried Bran impatiently. "It is older than this world. It was old when Atlantis and Lemuria sank into the sea. It was given to Brule, the Spear-slayer, first of my line, by the Atlantean Kull, king of Valusia, in the days when the world was young. But shall that profit us now?"

"Who knows?" asked the wizard obliquely. "Time and space exist not. There was no past, and there shall be no future. NOW is all. All things that ever were, are, or ever will be, transpire *now*. Man is forever at the center of what we call time and space. I have gone into yesterday and tomorrow and both were as real as today—which is like the dreams of ghosts! But let me sleep and talk with Gonar. Mayhap he shall aid us."

"What means he?" asked Cormac, with a slight twitching of his shoulders, as the priest strode away in the shadows.

"He has ever said that the first Gonar comes to him in his dreams and talks with him," answered Bran. "I have seen him perform deeds that seemed beyond human ken. I know not. I am but an unknown king with an iron crown, trying to lift a race of savages out of the slime into which they have sunk. Let us look to the camps."

As they walked Cormac wondered. By what strange freak of fate had such a man risen among this race of savages, survivors of a darker, grimmer age? Surely he was an atavism, an original type of the days when the Picts ruled all Europe, before their primitive empire fell before the bronze swords of the Gauls. Cormac knew how Bran, rising by his own efforts from the negligent position of the son of a Wolf clan chief, had to an extent united the tribes of the heather and now claimed kingship over all Caledon. But his rule was loose and much remained before the Pictish clans would forget their feuds and present a solid front to foreign foes. On the battle of the morrow, the first pitched battle between the Picts under their king and the Romans, hinged the future of the rising Pictish kingdom.

Bran and his ally walked through the Pictish camp where the swart warriors lay sprawled about their small fires, sleeping or gnawing half-cooked food. Cormac was impressed by their silence. A thousand men camped here, yet the only sounds were occasional low guttural intonations. The silence of the Stone Age rested in the souls of these men.

They were all short—most of them crooked of limb. Giant dwarfs; Bran Mak Morn was a tall man among them. Only the older men were bearded and they scantily, but their black hair fell about their eyes so that they peered fiercely from under the tangle. They were barefoot and clad scantily in wolfskins. Their arms consisted of short barbed swords of iron, heavy black bows, arrows tipped with flint, iron and copper, and stone-headed mallets. Defensive armor they had none, save for a crude shield of hide-covered wood; many had worked bits of metal into their tangled manes as a slight protection against sword-cuts. Some few, sons of long lines of chiefs, were smooth-limbed and lithe like Bran, but in the eyes of all gleamed the unquenchable savagery of the primeval.

These men are fully savages, thought Cormac, worse than the Gauls, Britons and Germans. Can the old legends be true—that they reigned in a day when strange cities rose where now the sea rolls? And that they survived the flood that washed those gleaming empires under, sinking again into that savagery from which they once had risen?

Close to the encampment of the tribesmen were the fires of a group of Britons—members of fierce tribes who lived south of the Roman Wall but who dwelt in the hills and forests to the west and defied the power of

Rome. Powerfully built men they were, with blazing blue eyes and shocks of tousled yellow hair, such men as had thronged the Ceanntish beaches when Caesar brought the Eagles into the Isles. These men, like the Picts, wore no armor, and were clad scantily in coarse-worked cloth and deerskin sandals. They bore small round bucklers of hard wood, braced with bronze, to be worn on the left arm, and long heavy bronze swords with blunt points. Some had bows, though the Britons were indifferent archers. Their bows were shorter than the Picts' and effective only at close range. But ranged close by their fires were the weapons that had made the name Briton a word of terror to Pict, Roman and Norse raider alike. Within the circle of firelight stood fifty bronze chariots with long cruel blades curving out from the sides. One of these blades could dismember half a dozen men at once. Tethered close by under the vigilant eyes of their guards grazed the chariot horses—big, rangy steeds, swift and powerful.

"Would that we had more of them!" mused Bran. "With a thousand chariots and my bowmen I could drive the legions into the sea."

"The free British tribes must eventually fall before Rome," said Cormac. "It would seem they would rush to join you in your war."

Bran made a helpless gesture. "The fickleness of the Celt. They cannot forget old feuds. Our ancient men have told us how they would not even unite against Caesar when the Romans first came. They will not make head against a common foe together. These men came to me because of some dispute with their chief, but I cannot depend on them when they are not actually fighting."

Cormac nodded. "I know; Caesar conquered Gaul by playing one tribe against another. My own people shift and change with the waxing and waning of the tides. But of all Celts, the Cymry are the most changeable, the least stable. Not many centuries ago my own Gaelic ancestors wrested Erin from the Cymric Danaans, because though they outnumbered us, they opposed us as separate tribes, rather than as a nation."

"And so these Cymric Britons face Rome," said Bran. "These will aid us on the morrow. Further I cannot say. But how shall I expect loyalty from alien tribes, who am not sure of my own people? Thousands lurk in the hills, holding aloof. I am king in name only. Let me win tomorrow and they will flock to my standard; if I lose, they will scatter like birds before a cold wind."

A chorus of rough welcome greeted the two leaders as they entered the camp of Cormac's Gaels. Five hundred in number they were, tall rangy men, black-haired and gray-eyed mainly, with the bearing of men who lived by war alone. While there was nothing like close discipline among them, there was an air of more system and practical order than existed in the lines of the Picts and Britons. These men were of the last Celtic race to invade the Isles and their barbaric civilization was of much higher order than that of their Cymric kin. The ancestors of the Gaels had learned the arts of war on the vast plains of Scythia and at the courts of the Pharaohs where they had fought as mercenaries of Egypt, and much of what they learned they brought into Ireland with them. Excelling in metal work, they were armed, not with clumsy bronze swords, but with high-grade weapons of iron.

They were clad in well-woven kilts and leathern sandals. Each wore a light shirt of chain mail and a vizorless helmet, but this was all of their defensive armor. Celts, Gaelic or Brythonic, were prone to judge a man's valor by the amount of armor he wore. The Britons who faced Caesar deemed the Romans cowards because they cased themselves in metal, and many centuries later the Irish clans thought the same of the mail-clad Norman knights of Strongbow.

Cormac's warriors were horsemen. They neither knew nor esteemed the use of the bow. They bore the inevitable round, metal-braced buckler, dirks, long straight swords and light singlehanded axes. Their tethered horses grazed not far away—big-boned animals, not so ponderous as those raised by the Britons, but swifter.

Bran's eyes lighted as the two strode through the camp. "These men are keen-beaked birds of war! See how they whet their axes and jest of the morrow! Would that the raiders in yon camp were as staunch as your men, Cormac! Then would I greet the legions with a laugh when they come up from the south tomorrow."

They were entering the circle of the Northmen fires. Three hundred men sat about gambling, whetting their weapons and drinking deep of the heather ale furnished them by their Pictish allies. These gazed upon Bran and Cormac with no great friendliness. It was striking to note the difference between them and the Picts and Celts—the difference in their cold eyes, their strong moody faces, their very bearing. Here was ferocity, and savagery, but not of the wild, upbursting fury of the Celt. Here was fierceness backed by grim determination and stolid stubbornness. The charge of the British clans was terrible, overwhelming. But they had no patience; let them be balked of immediate victory and they were likely to lose heart and scatter or fall to bickering among themselves. There was the patience of the cold blue North in these seafarers—a lasting determination that would keep them steadfast to the bitter end, once their face was set toward a definite goal.

As to personal stature, they were giants; massive yet rangy. That they did not share the ideas of the Celts regarding armor was shown by the fact that they were clad in heavy scale-mail shirts that reached below midthigh, heavy horned helmets and hardened hide leggings, reinforced, as were their shoes, with plates of iron. Their shields were huge oval affairs of hard wood, hide and brass. As to weapons, they had long iron-headed spears, heavy iron axes, and daggers. Some had long wide-bladed swords.

Cormac scarcely felt at ease with the cold magnetic eyes of these flaxen-haired men fixed upon him. He and they were hereditary foes, even though they did chance to be fighting on the same side at present—but were they?

A man came forward, a tall gaunt warrior on whose scarred, wolfish face the flickering firelight reflected deep shadows. With his wolfskin mantle flung carelessly about his wide shoulders, and the great horns on his helmet adding to his height, he stood there in the swaying shadows, like some half-human thing, a brooding shape of the dark barbarism that was soon to engulf the world.

"Well, Wulfhere," said the Pictish king, "you have drunk the mead of council and have spoken about the fires—what is your decision?"

The Northman's eyes flashed in the gloom. "Give us a king of our own race to follow if you wish us to fight for you."

Bran flung out his hands. "Ask me to drag down the stars to gem your helmets! Will not your comrades follow you?"

"Not against the legions," answered Wulfhere sullenly. "A king led us on the Viking path—a king must lead us against the Romans. And Rognar is dead."

"I am a king," said Bran. "Will you fight for me if I stand at the tip of your fight wedge?"

"A king of our own race," said Wulfhere doggedly. "We are all picked men of the North. We fight for none but a king, and a king must lead us—against the legions."

Cormac sensed a subtle threat in this repeated phrase.

"Here is a prince of Erin," said Bran. "Will you fight for the Westerner?"

"We fight under no Celt, West or East," growled the Viking, and a low rumble of approval rose from the onlookers. "It is enough to fight by their side."

The hot Gaelic blood rose in Cormac's brain and he pushed past Bran, his hand on his sword. "How mean you that, pirate?"

Before Wulfhere could reply Bran interposed: "Have done! Will you fools throw away the battle before it is fought, by your madness? What of your oath, Wulfhere?"

"We swore it under Rognar; when he died from a Roman arrow

we were absolved of it. We will follow only a king—against the legions."

"But your comrades will follow you—against the heather people!" snapped Bran.

"Aye," the Northman's eyes met his brazenly. "Send us a king or we join the Romans tomorrow."

Bran snarled. In his rage he dominated the scene, dwarfing the huge men who towered over him.

"Traitors! Liars! I hold your lives in my hand! Aye, draw your swords if you will—Cormac, keep your blade in its sheath. These wolves will not bite a king! Wulfhere—I spared your lives when I could have taken them.

"You came to raid the countries of the South, sweeping down from the northern sea in your galleys. You ravaged the coasts and the smoke of burning villages hung like a cloud over the shores of Caledon. I trapped you all when you were pillaging and burning—with the blood of my people on your hands. I burned your longships and ambushed you when you followed. With thrice your number of bowmen who burned for your lives hidden in the heathered hills about you, I spared you when we could have shot you down like trapped wolves. Because I spared you, you swore to come and fight for me."

"And shall we die because the Picts fight Rome?" rumbled a bearded raider.

"Your lives are forfeit to me; you came to ravage the South. I did not promise to send you all back to your homes in the North unharmed and loaded with loot. Your vow was to fight one battle against Rome under my standard. Then I will aid your survivors to build ships and you may go where you will, with a goodly share of the plunder we take from the legions. Rognar had kept his oath. But Rognar died in a skirmish with Roman scouts and now you, Wulfhere the Dissension-breeder, you stir up your comrades to dishonor themselves by that which a Northman hates—the breaking of the sworn word."

"We break no oath," snarled the Viking, and the king sensed the basic Germanic stubbornness, far harder to combat than the fickleness of the fiery Celts. "Give us a king, neither Pict, Gael nor Briton, and we will die for you. If not—then we will fight tomorrow for the greatest of all kings—the emperor of Rome!"

For a moment Cormac thought that the Pictish king, in his black rage, would draw and strike the Northman dead. The concentrated fury that blazed in Bran's dark eyes caused Wulfhere to recoil and drop a hand to his belt.

"Fool!" said Mak Morn in a low voice that vibrated with passion. "I could sweep you from the earth before the Romans are near enough to hear your death howls. Choose—fight for me on the morrow—or die tonight under a black cloud of arrows, a red storm of swords, a dark wave of chariots!"

At the mention of the chariots, the only arm of war that had ever broken the Norse shield-wall, Wulfhere changed expression, but he held his ground.

"War be it," he said doggedly. "Or a king to lead us!"

The Northmen responded with a short deep roar and a clash of swords on shields. Bran, eyes blazing, was about to speak again when a white shape glided silently into the ring of firelight.

"Soft words, soft words," said old Gonar tranquilly. "King, say no more. Wulfhere, you and your fellows will fight for us if you have a king to lead you?"

"We have sworn."

"Then be at ease," quoth the wizard; "for ere battle joins on the morrow I will send you such a king as no man on earth has followed for a hundred thousand years! A king neither Pict, Gael nor Briton, but one to whom the emperor of Rome is as but a village headman!"

While they stood undecided, Gonar took the arms of Cormac and Bran. "Come. And you, Northmen, remember your vow, and my promise which I have never broken. Sleep now, nor think to steal away in the darkness to the Roman camp, for if you escaped our shafts you would not escape either my curse or the suspicions of the legionaries."

So the three walked away and Cormac, looking back, saw Wulfhere standing by the fire, fingering his golden beard, with a look of puzzled anger on his lean evil face.

The three walked silently through the waving heather under the faraway stars while the weird night wind whispered ghostly secrets about them.

"Ages ago," said the wizard suddenly, "in the days when the world was young, great lands rose where now the ocean roars. On these lands thronged mighty nations and kingdoms. Greatest of all these was Valusia—Land of Enchantment. Rome is as a village compared to the splendor of the cities of Valusia. And the greatest king was Kull, who came from the land of Atlantis to wrest the crown of Valusia from a degenerate dynasty. The Picts who dwelt in the isles which now form the mountain peaks of a strange land upon the Western Ocean, were allies of Valusia, and the greatest of all the Pictish war-chiefs was Brule the Spear-slayer, first of the line men call Mak Morn.

"Kull gave to Brule the jewel which you now wear in your iron crown, oh king, after a strange battle in a dim land, and down the long ages it has come to us, ever a sign of the Mak Morn, a symbol of former greatness. When at last the sea rose and swallowed Valusia, Atlantis and Lemuria, only the Picts survived and they were scattered and few. Yet they began again the slow climb upward, and though many of the arts of civilization were lost in the great flood, yet they progressed. The art of metalworking was lost, so they excelled in the working of flint. And they ruled all the new lands flung up by the sea and now called Europe, until down from the north came younger tribes who had scarce risen from the ape when Valusia reigned in her glory, and who, dwelling in the icy lands about the Pole, knew naught of the lost splendor of the Seven Empires and little of the flood that had swept away half a world.

"And still they have come—Aryans, Celts, Germans, swarming down from the great cradle of their race which lies near the Pole. So again was the growth of the Pictish nation checked and the race hurled into savagery. Erased from the earth, on the fringe of the world with our backs to the wall we fight. Here in Caledon is the last stand of a once mighty race. And we change. Our people have mixed with the savages of an elder age which we drove into the North when we came into the Isles, and now, save for their chieftains, such as thou, Bran, a Pict is strange and abhorrent to look upon."

"True, true," said the king impatiently, "but what has that to do—"

"Kull, king of Valusia," said the wizard imperturbably, "was a barbarian in his age as thou art in thine, though he ruled a mighty empire by the weight of his sword. Gonar, friend of Brule, your first ancestor, has been dead a hundred thousand years as we reckon time. Yet I talked with him a scant hour agone."

"You talked with his ghost—"

"Or he with mine? Did I go back a hundred thousand years, or did he come forward? If he came to me out of the past, it is not I who talked with a dead man, but he who talked with a man unborn. Past, present and future are one to a wise man. I talked to Gonar while he was alive; likewise was I alive. In a timeless, spaceless land we met and he told me many things."

The land was growing light with the birth of dawn. The heather waved and bent in long rows before the dawn wind, as bowing in worship of the rising sun.

"The jewel in your crown is a magnet that draws down the eons," said Gonar. "The sun is rising—and who comes out of the sunrise?"

Cormac and the king started. The sun was just lifting a red orb above the eastern hills. And full in the glow, etched boldly against the golden rim, a man suddenly appeared. They had not seen him come.

Against the golden birth of day he loomed colossal; a gigantic god from the dawn of creation. Now as he strode toward them the waking hosts saw him and sent up a sudden shout of wonder.

"Who—or what is it?" exclaimed Bran.

"Let us go to meet him, Bran," answered the wizard. "He is the king Gonar has sent to save the people of Brule."

2

I have reached these lands but newly
From an ultimate dim Thule;
From a wild weird clime that lieth sublime
Out of Space—out of Time.

—Poe

The army fell silent as Bran, Cormac and Gonar went toward the stranger who approached in long swinging strides. As they neared him the illusion of monstrous size vanished, but they saw he was a man of great stature. At first Cormac thought him to be a Northman but a second glance told him that nowhere before had he seen such a man. He was built much like the Vikings, at once massive and lithe—tigerish. But his features were not as theirs, and his square-cut, lion-like mane of hair was as black as Bran's own. Under heavy brows glittered eyes gray as steel and cold as ice. His bronzed face, strong and inscrutable, was cleanshaven, and the broad forehead betokened a high intelligence, just as the firm jaw and thin lips showed willpower and courage. But more than all, the bearing of him, the unconscious lion-like stateliness, marked him as a natural king, a ruler of men.

Sandals of curious make were on his feet and he wore a pliant coat of strangely meshed mail which came almost to his knees. A broad belt with a great golden buckle encircled his waist, supporting a long straight sword in a heavy leather scabbard. His hair was confined by a wide, heavy golden band about his head.

Such was the man who paused before the silent group. He seemed slightly puzzled, slightly amused. Recognition flickered in his eyes. He spoke in a strange archaic Pictish which Cormac scarcely understood. His voice was deep and resonant.

"Ha, Brule, Gonar did not tell me I would dream of you!"

For the first time in his life Cormac saw the Pictish king completely thrown off his balance. He gaped, speechless. The stranger continued:

"And wearing the gem I gave you, in a circlet on your head! Last night you wore it in a ring on your finger."

"Last night?" gasped Bran.

"Last night or a hundred thousand years ago—all one!" murmured Gonar in evident enjoyment of the situation.

"I am not Brule," said Bran. "Are you mad to thus speak of a man dead a hundred thousand years? He was first of my line."

The stranger laughed unexpectedly. "Well, now I know I am dreaming! This will be a tale to tell Brule when I waken on the morrow! That I went into the future and saw men claiming descent from the Spear-slayer who is, as yet, not even married. No, you are not Brule, I see now, though you have his eyes and his bearing. But he is taller and broader in the shoulders. Yet you have his jewel—oh, well—anything can happen in a dream, so I will not quarrel with you. For a time I thought I had been transported to some other land in my sleep, and was in reality awake in a strange country, for this is the clearest dream I ever dreamed. Who are you?"

"I am Bran Mak Morn, king of the Caledonian Picts. And this ancient is Gonar, a wizard, of the line of Gonar. And this warrior is Cormac na Connacht, a prince of the isle of Erin."

The stranger slowly shook his lion-like head. "These words sound strangely to me, save Gonar—and that one is not Gonar, though he too is old. What land is this?"

"Caledon, or Alba, as the Gaels call it."

"And who are those squat ape-like warriors who watch us yonder, all agape?"

"They are the Picts who own my rule."

"How strangely distorted folk are in dreams!" muttered the stranger. "And who are those shock-headed men about the chariots?"

"They are Britons—Cymry from south of the Wall."

"What Wall?"

"The Wall built by Rome to keep the people of the heather out of Britain."

"Britain?" The tone was curious. "I never heard of that land—and what is Rome?"

"What!" cried Bran. "You never heard of Rome, the empire that rules the world?"

"No empire rules the world," answered the other haughtily. "The mightiest kingdom on earth is that wherein I reign."

"And who are you?"

"Kull of Atlantis, king of Valusia!"

Cormac felt a coldness trickle down his spine. The cold gray eyes were unswerving—but this was incredible—monstrous—unnatural.

"Valusia!" cried Bran. "Why, man, the sea waves have rolled above the spires of Valusia for untold centuries!"

Kull laughed outright. "What a mad nightmare this is! When Gonar put on me the spell of deep sleep last night—or this night!—in the secret room of the inner palace, he told me I would dream strange things, but this is more fantastic than I reckoned. And the strangest thing is, I know I am dreaming!"

Gonar interposed as Bran would have spoken. "Question not the acts of the gods," muttered the wizard. "You are king because in the past you have seen and seized opportunities. The gods or the first Gonar have sent you this man. Let me deal with him."

Bran nodded, and while the silent army gaped in speechless wonder, just within earshot, Gonar spoke: "Oh great king, you dream, but is not all life a dream? How reckon you but that your former life is but a dream from which you have just awakened? Now we dream-folk have our wars and our peace, and just now a great host comes up from the south to destroy the people of Brule. Will you aid us?"

Kull grinned with pure zest. "Aye! I have fought battles in dreams ere now, have slain and been slain and was amazed when I woke from my visions. And at times, as now, dreaming I have known I dreamed. See, I pinch myself and feel it, but I know I dream for I have felt the pain of fierce wounds, in dreams. Yes, people of my dream, I will fight for you against the other dream-folk. Where are they?"

"And that you enjoy the dream more," said the wizard subtly, "forget that it is a dream and pretend that by the magic of the first Gonar, and the quality of the jewel you gave Brule, that now gleams on the crown of the Morni, you have in truth been transported forward into another, wilder age where the people of Brule fight for their life against a stronger foe."

For a moment the man who called himself king of Valusia seemed startled; a strange look of doubt, almost of fear, clouded his eyes. Then he laughed.

"Good! Lead on, wizard."

But now Bran took charge. He had recovered himself and was at ease. Whether he thought, like Cormac, that this was all a gigantic hoax arranged by Gonar, he showed no sign.

"King Kull, see you those men yonder who lean on their long-shafted axes as they gaze upon you?"

"The tall men with the golden hair and beards?"

"Aye—our success in the coming battle hinges on them. They swear to go over to the enemy if we give them not a king to lead them—their own having been slain. Will you lead them to battle?"

Kull's eyes glowed with appreciation. "They are men such as my own Red Slayers, my picked regiment. I will lead them."

"Come then."

The small group made their way down the slope, through throngs of warriors who pushed forward eagerly to get a better view of the stranger, then pressed back as he approached. An undercurrent of tense whispering ran through the horde.

The Northmen stood apart in a compact group. Their cold eyes took in Kull and he gave back their stares, taking in every detail of their appearance.

"Wulfhere," said Bran, "we have brought you a king. I hold you to your oath."

"Let him speak to us," said the Viking harshly.

"He cannot speak your tongue," answered Bran, knowing that the Northmen knew nothing of the legends of his race. "He is a great king of the South—"

"He comes out of the past," broke in the wizard calmly. "He was the greatest of all kings, long ago."

"A dead man!" The Vikings moved uneasily and the rest of the horde pressed forward, drinking in every word. But Wulfhere scowled: "Shall a ghost lead living men? You bring us a man you say is dead. We will not follow a corpse."

"Wulfhere," said Bran in still passion, "you are a liar and a traitor. You set us this task, thinking it impossible. You yearn to fight under the Eagles of Rome. We have brought you a king neither Pict, Gael nor Briton and you deny your vow!"

"Let him fight me, then!" howled Wulfhere in uncontrollable wrath, swinging his ax about his head in a glittering arc. "If your dead man overcomes me—then my people will follow you. If I overcome him, you shall let us depart in peace to the camp of the legions!"

"Good!" said the wizard. "Do you agree, wolves of the North?"

A fierce yell and a brandishing of swords was the answer. Bran turned to Kull, who had stood silent, understanding nothing of what was said. But the Atlantean's eyes gleamed. Cormac felt that those cold eyes had looked on too many such scenes not to understand something of what had passed.

"This warrior says you must fight him for the leadership," said Bran, and Kull, eyes glittering with growing battle-joy, nodded: "I guessed as much. Give us space."

"A shield and a helmet!" shouted Bran, but Kull shook his head.

"I need none," he growled. "Back and give us room to swing our steel!"

Men pressed back on each side, forming a solid ring about the two men, who now approached each other warily. Kull had drawn his sword and the great blade shimmered like a live thing in his hand. Wulfhere, scarred by a hundred savage fights, flung aside his wolfskin mantle and came in cautiously, fierce eyes peering over the top of his outthrust shield, ax half-lifted in his right hand.

Suddenly when the warriors were still many feet apart Kull sprang. His attack brought a gasp from men used to deeds of prowess; for like a leaping tiger he shot through the air and his sword crashed on the quickly lifted shield. Sparks flew and Wulfhere's ax hacked in, but Kull was under its sweep and as it swished viciously above his head he thrust upward and sprang out again, cat-like. His motions had been too quick for the eye to follow. The upper edge of Wulfhere's shield showed a deep cut, and there was a long rent in his mail shirt where Kull's sword had barely missed the flesh beneath.

Cormac, trembling with the terrible thrill of the fight, wondered at this sword that could thus slice through scale mail. And the blow that gashed the shield should have shattered the blade. Yet not a notch showed in the Valusian steel! Surely this blade was forged by another people in another age!

Now the two giants leaped again to the attack and like double strokes of lightning their weapons crashed. Wulfhere's shield fell from his arm in two pieces as the Atlantean's sword sheared clear through it, and Kull staggered as the Northman's ax, driven with all the force of his great body, descended on the golden circlet about his head. That blow should have sheared through the gold like butter to split the skull beneath, but the ax rebounded, showing a great notch in the edge. The next instant the Northman was overwhelmed by a whirlwind of steel—a storm of strokes delivered with such swiftness and power that he was borne back as on the crest of a wave, unable to launch an attack of his own. With all his tried skill he sought to parry the singing steel with his ax. But he could only avert his doom for a few seconds; could only for an instant turn the whistling blade that hewed off bits of his mail, so close fell the blows. One of the horns flew from his helmet; then the axhead itself fell away, and the same blow that severed the handle, bit through the Viking's helmet into the scalp beneath. Wulfhere was dashed to his knees, a trickle of blood starting down his face.

Kull checked his second stroke, and tossing his sword to Cormac, faced the dazed Northman weaponless. The Atlantean's eyes were blazing with ferocious joy and he roared something in a strange tongue. Wulfhere gathered his legs under him and bounded up, snarling like a wolf, a dagger flashing into his hand. The watching horde gave tongue in a yell that ripped the skies as the two bodies clashed. Kull's clutching hand missed the Northman's wrist but the desperately lunging dagger snapped on the Atlantean's mail, and dropping the useless hilt, Wulfhere locked his arms about his foe in a bear-like grip that would have crushed the ribs of a lesser man. Kull grinned tigerishly and returned the grapple, and for a moment the two swayed on their feet. Slowly the black-haired warrior bent his foe backward until it seemed his spine would snap. With a howl that had nothing of the human in it, Wulfhere clawed frantically at Kull's face, trying to tear out his eyes, then turned his head and snapped his fang-like teeth into the Atlantean's arm. A yell went up as a trickle of blood started: "He bleeds! He bleeds! He is no ghost, after all, but a mortal man!"

Angered, Kull shifted his grip, shoving the frothing Wulfhere away from him, and smote him terrifically under the ear with his right hand. The Viking landed on his back a dozen feet away. Then, howling like a wild man, he leaped up with a stone in his hand and flung it. Only Kull's incredible quickness saved his face; as it was, the rough edge of the missile tore his cheek and inflamed him to madness. With a lion-like roar he bounded upon his foe, enveloped him in an irresistible blast of sheer fury, whirled him high above his head as if he were a child and cast him a dozen feet away. Wulfhere pitched on his head and lay still—broken and dead.

Dazed silence reigned for an instant; then from the Gaels went up a thundering roar, and the Britons and Picts took it up, howling like wolves, until the echoes of the shouts and the clangor of sword on shield reached the ears of the marching legionaries, miles to the south.

"Men of the gray North," shouted Bran, "will you hold by your oath *now?*"

The fierce souls of the Northmen were in their eyes as their spokesman answered. Primitive, superstitious, steeped in tribal lore of fighting gods and mythical heroes, they did not doubt that the black-haired fighting man was some supernatural being sent by the fierce gods of battle.

"Aye! Such a man as this we have never seen! Dead man, ghost or devil, we will follow him, whether the trail lead to Rome or Valhalla!"

Kull understood the meaning, if not the words. Taking his sword from Cormac with a word of thanks, he turned to the waiting Northmen and silently held the blade toward them high above his head, in both hands, before he returned it to its scabbard. Without understanding, they appreciated the action. Bloodstained and disheveled, he was an impressive picture of stately, magnificent barbarism.

"Come," said Bran, touching the Atlantean's arm; "a host is marching on us and we have much to do. There is scant time to arrange our forces before they will be upon us. Come to the top of yonder slope."

There the Pict pointed. They were looking down into a valley which ran north and south, widening from a narrow gorge in the north until it debouched upon a plain to the south. The whole valley was less than a mile in length.

"Up this valley will our foes come," said the Pict, "because they have wagons loaded with supplies and on all sides of this vale the ground is too rough for such travel. Here we plan an ambush."

"I would have thought you would have had your men lying in wait long before now," said Kull. "What of the scouts the enemy is sure to send out?"

"The savages I lead would never have waited in ambush so long," said Bran with a touch of bitterness. "I could not post them until I was sure of the Northmen. Even so I had not dared to post them ere now—even yet they may take panic from the drifting of a cloud or the blowing of a leaf, and scatter like birds before a cold wind. King Kull—the fate of the Pictish nation is at stake. I am called king of the Picts, but my rule as yet is but a hollow mockery. The hills are full of wild clans who refuse to fight for me. Of the thousand bowmen now at my command, more than half are of my own clan.

"Some eighteen hundred Romans are marching against us. It is not a real invasion, but much hinges upon it. It is the beginning of an attempt to extend their boundaries. They plan to build a fortress a day's march to the north of this valley. If they do, they will build other forts, drawing bands of steel about the heart of the free people. If I win this battle and wipe out this army, I will win a double victory. Then the tribes will flock to me and the next invasion will meet a solid wall of resistance. If I lose, the clans will scatter, fleeing into the north until they can no longer flee, fighting as separate clans rather than as one strong nation.

"I have a thousand archers, five hundred horsemen, fifty chariots with their drivers and swordsmen—one hundred fifty men in all—and, thanks to you, three hundred heavily armed Northern pirates. How would you arrange your battle lines?"

"Well," said Kull, "I would have barricaded the north end of the valley—no! That would suggest a trap. But I would block it with a band of desperate men, like those you have given me to lead. Three hundred could hold the gorge for a time against any number. Then, when the enemy was engaged with these men to the narrow part of the valley, I would have my archers shoot down into them until their ranks are broken, from both sides of the vale. Then, having my horsemen concealed behind one ridge and my chariots behind the other, I would charge with both simultaneously and sweep the foe into a red ruin."

Bran's eyes glowed. "Exactly, king of Valusia. Such was my exact plan—"

"But what of the scouts?"

"My warriors are like panthers; they hide under the noses of the Romans. Those who ride into the valley will see only what we wish them to see. Those who ride over the ridge will not come back to report. An arrow is swift and silent.

"You see that the pivot of the whole thing depends on the men that hold the gorge. They must be men who can fight on foot and resist the charges of the heavy legionaries long enough for the trap to close. Outside these Northmen I had no such force of men. My naked warriors with their short swords could never stand such a charge for an instant. Nor is the armor of the Celts made for such work; moreover, they are not foot-fighters, and I need them elsewhere.

"So you see why I had such desperate need of the Northmen. Now will you stand in the gorge with them and hold back the Romans until I can spring the trap? Remember, most of you will die."

Kull smiled. "I have taken chances all my life, though Tu, chief councilor, would say my life belongs to Valusia and I have no right to so risk it—" His voice trailed off and a strange look flitted across his face. "By Valka," said he, laughing uncertainly, "sometimes I forget this is a dream! All seems so real. But it is—of course it is! Well, then, if I die I will but awaken as I have done in times past. Lead on, king of Caledon!"

Cormac, going to his warriors, wondered. Surely it was all a hoax; yet—he heard the arguments of the warriors all about him as they armed themselves and prepared to take their posts. The black-haired king was Neid himself, the Celtic war-god; he was an antediluvian king brought out of the past by Gonar; he was a mythical fighting man out of Valhalla. He was no man at all but a ghost! No, he was mortal, for he had bled. But the gods themselves bled, though they did not die. So the controversies raged. At least, thought Cormac, if it was all a hoax to inspire the warriors with the feeling of supernatural aid, it had succeeded. The belief that Kull was more than a mortal man had fired Celt, Pict and Viking alike into a sort of inspired madness. And Cormac asked himself—what did he himself believe? This man was surely one from some far land—yet in his every look and action there was a vague hint of a greater difference than mere distance of space—a hint of alien Time, of misty abysses and gigantic gulfs of eons lying between the black-haired stranger and the men with whom he walked and talked. Clouds of bewilderment mazed Cormac's brain and he laughed in whimsical self-mockery.

3

And the two wild peoples of the north
Stood fronting in the gloam,
And heard and knew each in his mind
A third great sound upon the wind,
The living walls that hedge mankind,
The walking walls of Rome.
—Chesterton

The sun slanted westward. Silence lay like an invisible mist over the valley. Cormac gathered the reins in his hand and glanced up at the ridges on both sides. The waving heather which grew rank on those steep slopes gave no evidence of the hundreds of savage warriors who lurked there. Here in the narrow gorge which widened gradually southward was the only sign of life. Between the steep walls three hundred Northmen were massed solidly in their wedge-shaped shield-wall, blocking the pass. At the tip, like the point of a spear, stood the man who called himself Kull, king of Valusia. He wore no helmet, only the great, strangely worked headband of hard gold, but he bore on his left arm the great shield borne by the dead Rognar; and in his right hand he held the heavy iron mace wielded by the sea king. The Vikings eyed him in wonder and savage admiration. They could not understand his language, or he theirs. But no further orders were necessary. At Bran's directions they had bunched themselves in the gorge, and their only order was—hold the pass!

Bran Mak Morn stood just in front of Kull. So they faced each other, he whose kingdom was yet unborn, and he whose kingdom had been lost in the mists of Time for unguessed ages. Kings of darkness, thought Cormac, nameless kings of the night, whose realms are gulfs and shadows.

The hand of the Pictish king went out. "King Kull, you are more than king—you are a man. Both of us may fall within the next hour—but if we both live, ask what you will of me."

Kull smiled, returning the firm grip. "You too are a man after my own heart, king of the shadows. Surely you are more than a figment of my sleeping imagination. Mayhap we will meet in waking life someday."

Bran shook his head in puzzlement, swung into the saddle and rode away, climbing the eastern slope and vanishing over the ridge. Cormac hesitated: "Strange man, are you in truth of flesh and blood, or are you a ghost?"

"When we dream, we are all flesh and blood—so long as we are dreaming," Kull answered. "This is the strangest nightmare I have ever known—but you, who will soon fade into sheer nothingness as I awaken, seem as real to me *now*, as Brule, or Kananu, or Tu, or Kelkor."

Cormac shook his head as Bran had done, and with a last salute, which Kull returned with barbaric stateliness, he turned and trotted away. At the top of the western ridge he paused. Away to the south a light cloud of dust rose and the head of the marching column was in sight. Already he believed he could feel the earth vibrate slightly to the measured tread of a thousand mailed feet beating in perfect unison. He dismounted, and one of his chieftains, Domnail, took his steed and led it down the slope away from the valley, where trees grew thickly. Only an occasional vague movement among them gave evidence of the five hundred men who stood there, each at his horse's head with a ready hand to check a chance nicker.

Oh, thought Cormac, the gods themselves made this valley for Bran's ambush! The floor of the valley was treeless and the inner slopes were bare save for the waist-high heather. But at the foot of each ridge on the side facing away from the vale, where the soil long washed from the rocky slopes had accumulated, there grew enough trees to hide five hundred horsemen or fifty chariots.

At the northern end of the valley stood Kull and his three hundred Vikings, in open view, flanked on each side by fifty Pictish bowmen. Hidden on the western side of the western ridge were the Gaels. Along the top of the slopes, concealed in the tall heather, lay a hundred Picts with their shafts on string. The rest of the Picts were hidden on the eastern slopes beyond which lay the Britons with their chariots in full readiness. Neither they nor the Gaels to the west could see what went on in the vale, but signals had been arranged.

Now the long column was entering the wide mouth of the valley and their scouts, light-armed men on swift horses, were spreading out between the slopes. They galloped almost within bowshot of the silent host that blocked the pass, then halted.

Some whirled and raced back to the main force, while the others deployed and cantered up the slopes, seeking to see what lay beyond. This was the crucial moment. If they got any hint of the ambush, all was lost. Cormac, shrinking down into the heather, marveled at the ability of the Picts to efface themselves from view so completely. He saw a horseman pass within three feet of where he knew a bowman lay, yet the Roman saw nothing.

The scouts topped the ridges, gazed about; then most of them turned and trotted back down the slopes. Cormac wondered at their desultory manner of scouting. He had never fought Romans before, knew nothing of their arrogant self-confidence, of their incredible shrewdness in some ways, their incredible stupidity in others. These men were overconfident; a feeling radiating from their officers. It had been years since a force of Caledonians had stood before the legions. And most of these men were but newly come to Britain; part of a legion which had been quartered in Egypt. They despised their foes and suspected nothing.

But stay—three riders on the opposite ridge had turned and vanished on the other side. And now one, sitting his steed at the crest of the western ridge, not a hundred yards from where Cormac lay, looked long and narrowly down into the mass of trees at the foot of the slope. Cormac saw suspicion grow on his brown, hawk-like face. He half turned as though to call to his comrades, then instead reined his steed down the slope, leaning forward in his saddle. Cormac's heart pounded. Each moment he expected to see the man wheel and gallop back to raise the alarm. He resisted a mad impulse to leap up and charge the Roman on foot. Surely the man could feel the tenseness in the air—the hundreds of fierce eyes upon him. Now he was halfway down the slope, out of sight of the men in the valley. And now the twang of an unseen bow broke the painful stillness. With a strangled gasp the Roman flung his hands high, and as the steed reared, he pitched headlong, transfixed by a long black arrow that had flashed from the heather. A stocky dwarf sprang out of nowhere, seemingly, and seized the bridle, quieting the snorting horse, and leading it down the slope. At the fall of the Roman, short, crooked men rose like a sudden flight of birds from the grass and Cormac saw the flash of a knife. Then with unreal suddenness all had subsided. Slayers and slain were unseen and only the still waving heather marked the grim deed.

The Gael looked back into the valley. The three who had ridden over the eastern ridge had not come back and Cormac knew they never would. Evidently the other scouts had borne word that only a small band of warriors was ready to dispute the passage of the legionaries. Now the head of the column was almost below him and he thrilled at the sight of these men who were doomed, swinging along with their superb arrogance.

And the sight of their splendid armor, their hawk-like faces and perfect discipline awed him as much as it is possible for a Gael to be awed.

Twelve hundred men in heavy armor who marched as one so that the ground shook to their tread! Most of them were of middle height, with powerful chests and shoulders and bronzed faces—hard-bitten veterans of a hundred campaigns. Cormac noted their javelins, short keen swords and heavy shields; their gleaming armor and crested helmets, the eagles on the standards. These were the men beneath whose tread the world had shaken and empires crumbled! Not all were Latins; there were Romanized Britons among them and one century or hundred was composed of huge yellow-haired men—Gauls and Germans, who fought for Rome as fiercely as did the native-born, and hated their wilder kinsmen more savagely.

On each side was a swarm of cavalry, outriders, and the column was flanked by archers and slingers. A number of lumbering wagons carried the supplies of the army. Cormac saw the commander riding in his place—a tall man with a lean, imperious face, evident even at that distance. Marcus Sulius—the Gael knew him by repute.

A deep-throated roar rose from the legionaries as they approached their foes. Evidently they intended to slice their way through and continue without a pause, for the column moved implacably on. Whom the gods destroy they first make mad—Cormac had never heard the phrase but it came to him that the great Sulius was a fool. Roman arrogance! Marcus was used to lashing the cringing peoples of a decadent East; little he guessed of the iron in these western races.

A group of cavalry detached itself and raced into the mouth of the gorge, but it was only a gesture. With loud jeering shouts they wheeled three spears' length away and cast their javelins, which rattled harmlessly on the overlapping shields of the silent Northmen. But their leader dared too much; swinging in, he leaned from his saddle and thrust at Kull's face. The great shield turned the lance and Kull struck back as a snake strikes; the ponderous mace crushed helmet and head like an eggshell, and the very steed went to its knees from the shock of that terrible blow. From the Northmen went up a short fierce roar, and the Picts beside them howled exultantly and loosed their arrows among the retreating horsemen. First blood for the people of the heather! The oncoming Romans shouted vengefully and quickened their pace as the frightened horse raced by, a ghastly travesty of a man, foot caught in the stirrup, trailing beneath the pounding hoofs.

Now the first line of the legionaries, compressed because of the narrowness of the gorge, crashed against the solid wall of shields—

crashed and recoiled upon itself. The shield-wall had not shaken an inch. This was the first time the Roman legions had met with that unbreakable formation—that oldest of all Aryan battle-lines—the ancestor of the Spartan regiment—the Theban phalanx—the Macedonian formation—the English square.

Shield crashed on shield and the short Roman sword sought for an opening in that iron wall. Viking spears bristling in solid ranks above, thrust and reddened; heavy axes chopped down, shearing through iron, flesh and bone. Cormac saw Kull, looming above the stocky Romans in the forefront of the fray, dealing blows like thunderbolts. A burly centurion rushed in, shield held high, stabbing upward. The iron mace crashed terribly, shivering the sword, rending the shield apart, shattering the helmet, crushing the skull down between the shoulders—in a single blow.

The front line of the Romans bent like a steel bar about the wedge, as the legionaries sought to struggle through the gorge on each side and surround their opposers. But the pass was too narrow; crouching close against the steep walls the Picts drove their black arrows in a hail of death. At this range the heavy shafts tore through shield and corselet, transfixing the armored men. The front line of battle rolled back, red and broken, and the Northmen trod their few dead under foot to close the gaps their fall had made. Stretched the full width of their front lay a thin line of shattered forms—the red spray of the tide which had broken upon them in vain.

Cormac had leaped to his feet, waving his arms. Domnail and his men broke cover at the signal and came galloping up the slope, lining the ridge. Cormac mounted the horse brought him and glanced impatiently across the narrow vale. No sign of life appeared on the eastern ridge. Where was Bran—and the Britons?

Down in the valley, the legions, angered at the unexpected opposition of the paltry force in front of them, but not suspicious, were forming in more compact body. The wagons which had halted were lumbering on again and the whole column was once more in motion as if it intended to crash through by sheer weight. With the Gaulish century in the forefront, the legionaries were advancing again in the attack. This time, with the full force of twelve hundred men behind, the charge would batter down the resistance of Kull's warriors like a heavy ram; would stamp them down, sweep over their red ruins. Cormac's men trembled in impatience. Suddenly Marcus Sulius turned and gazed westward, where the line of horsemen was etched against the sky. Even at that distance Cormac saw his face pale. The Roman at last realized the metal of the men he faced, and that he had walked into a trap. Surely in that moment there flashed a chaotic picture through his brain—defeat—disgrace—red ruin!

It was too late to retreat—too late to form into a defensive square with the wagons for barricade. There was but one possible way out, and Marcus, crafty general in spite of his recent blunder, took it. Cormac heard his voice cut like a clarion through the din, and though he did not understand the words, he knew that the Roman was shouting for his men to smite that knot of Northmen like a blast—to hack their way through and out of the trap before it could close!

Now the legionaries, aware of their desperate plight, flung themselves headlong and terribly on their foes. The shield-wall rocked, but it gave not an inch. The wild faces of the Gauls and the hard brown Italian faces glared over locked shields into the blazing eyes of the North. Shields touching, they smote and slew and died in a red storm of slaughter, where crimsoned axes rose and fell and dripping spears broke on notched swords.

Where in God's name was Bran with his chariots? A few minutes more would spell the doom of every man who held that pass. Already they were falling fast, though they locked their ranks closer and held like iron. Those wild men of the North were dying in their tracks; and looming among their golden heads the black lion-mane of Kull shone like a symbol of slaughter, and his reddened mace showered a ghastly rain as it splashed brains and blood like water.

Something snapped in Cormac's brain.

"These men will die while we wait for Bran's signal!" he shouted. "On! Follow me into Hell, sons of Gael!"

A wild roar answered him, and loosing rein he shot down the slope with five hundred yelling riders plunging headlong after him. And even at that moment a storm of arrows swept the valley from either side like a dark cloud and the terrible clamor of the Picts split the skies. And over the eastern ridge, like a sudden burst of rolling thunder on Judgment Day, rushed the war chariots. Headlong down the slope they roared, foam flying from the horses' distended nostrils, frantic feet scarcely seeming to touch the ground, making naught of the tall heather. In the foremost chariot, with his dark eyes blazing, crouched Bran Mak Morn, and in all of them the naked Britons were screaming and lashing as if possessed by demons. Behind the flying chariots came the Picts, howling like wolves and loosing their arrows as they ran. The heather belched them forth from all sides in a dark wave.

So much Cormac saw in chaotic glimpses during that wild ride down the slopes. A wave of cavalry swept between him and the main line of the column. Three long leaps ahead of his men, the Gaelic prince met the spears of the Roman riders. The first lance turned on his buckler, and rising in his stirrups he smote downward, cleaving his man from shoulder to breastbone. The next Roman flung a javelin that killed Domnail, but at that instant Cormac's steed crashed into his, breast to breast, and the lighter horse rolled headlong under the shock, flinging his rider beneath the pounding hoofs.

Then the whole blast of the Gaelic charge smote the Roman cavalry, shattering it, crashing and rolling it down and under. Over its red ruins Cormac's yelling demons struck the heavy Roman infantry, and the whole line reeled at the shock. Swords and axes flashed up and down and the force of their rush carried them deep into the massed ranks. Here, checked, they swayed and strove. Javelins thrust, swords flashed upward, bringing down horse and rider, and greatly outnumbered, leaguered on every side, the Gaels had perished among their foes, but at that instant, from the other side the crashing chariots smote the Roman ranks. In one long line they struck almost simultaneously, and at the moment of impact the charioteers wheeled their horses sidelong and raced parallel down the ranks, shearing men down like the mowing of wheat. Hundreds died on those curving blades in that moment, and leaping from the chariots, screaming like blood-mad wildcats, the British swordsmen flung themselves upon the spears of the legionaries, hacking madly with their two-handed swords. Crouching, the Picts drove their arrows pointblank and then sprang in to slash and thrust. Maddened with the sight of victory, these wild peoples were like wounded tigers, feeling no wounds, and dying on their feet with their last gasp a snarl of fury.

But the battle was not over yet. Dazed, shattered, their formation broken and nearly half their number down already, the Romans fought back with desperate fury. Hemmed in on all sides they slashed and smote singly, or in small clumps, fought back-to-back, archers, slingers, horsemen and heavy legionaries mingled into a chaotic mass. The confusion was complete, but not the victory. Those bottled in the gorge still hurled themselves upon the red axes that barred their way, while the massed and serried battle thundered behind them. From one side Cormac's Gaels raged and slashed; from the other chariots swept back and forth, retiring and returning like iron whirlwinds. There was no retreat, for the Picts had flung a cordon across the way they had come, and having cut the throats of the camp followers and possessed themselves of the wagons, they sent their shafts in a storm of death into the rear of the shattered column. Those long black arrows pierced armor and bone, nailing men together. Yet the slaughter was not all on one side. Picts died beneath the lightning thrust of javelin and short sword, Gaels pinned beneath their falling horses were hewed to pieces, and chariots, cut loose from their horses, were deluged with the blood of the charioteers.

And at the narrow head of the valley still the battle surged and eddied. Great gods—thought Cormac, glancing between lightning-like blows—do these men still hold the gorge? Aye! They held it! A tenth of their original number, dying on their feet, they still held back the frantic charges of the dwindling legionaries.

Over all the field went up the roar and the clash of arms, and birds of prey, swift-flying out of the sunset, circled above. Cormac, striving to reach Marcus Sulius through the press, saw the Roman's horse sink under him, and the rider rise alone in a waste of foes. He saw the Roman sword flash thrice, dealing a death at each blow; then from the thickest of the fray bounded a terrible figure. It was Bran Mak Morn, stained from head to foot. He cast away his broken sword as he ran, drawing a dirk. The Roman struck, but the Pictish king was under the thrust, and gripping the sword-wrist, he drove the dirk again and again through the gleaming armor.

A mighty roar went up as Marcus died, and Cormac, with a shout, rallied the remnants of his force about him and, striking in the spurs, burst through the shattered lines and rode full speed for the other end of the valley.

But as he approached he saw that he was too late. As they had lived, so had they died, those fierce sea-wolves, with their faces to the foe and their broken weapons red in their hands. In a grim and silent band they lay, even in death preserving some of the shield-wall formation. Among them, in front of them and all about them lay high-heaped the bodies of those who had sought to break them, in vain. *They had not given back a foot!* To the last man, they had died in their tracks. Nor were there any left to stride over their torn shapes; those Romans who had escaped the Viking axes had been struck down by the shafts of the Picts and swords of the Gaels from behind.

Yet this part of the battle was not over. High up on the steep western slope Cormac saw the ending of that drama. A group of Gauls in the armor of Rome pressed upon a single man—a black-haired giant on whose head gleamed a golden crown. There was iron in these men, as well as in the man who had held them to their fate. They were doomed—their comrades were being slaughtered behind them—but before their turn came they would at least have the life of the black-haired chief who had led the golden-haired men of the North.

Pressing upon him from three sides they had forced him slowly back up the steep gorge wall, and the crumpled bodies that stretched along his retreat showed how fiercely every foot of the way had been contested. Here on this steep it was task enough to keep one's footing alone; yet these men at once climbed and fought. Kull's shield and the huge mace were gone, and the great sword in his right hand was dyed crimson. His mail, wrought with a forgotten art, now hung in shreds, and blood streamed from a hundred wounds on limbs, head and body. But his eyes still blazed with the battle-joy and his wearied arm still drove the mighty blade in strokes of death.

But Cormac saw that the end would come before they could reach him. Now at the very crest of the steep, a hedge of points menaced the strange king's life, and even his iron strength was ebbing. Now he split the skull of a huge warrior and the backstroke shore through the neck-cords of another; reeling under a very rain of swords he struck again and his victim dropped at his feet, cleft to the breastbone. Then, even as a dozen swords rose above the staggering Atlantean for the death stroke, a strange thing happened. The sun was sinking into the western sea; all the heather swam red like an ocean of blood. Etched in the dying sun, as he had first appeared, Kull stood, and then, like a mist lifting, a mighty vista opened behind the reeling king. Cormac's astounded eyes caught a fleeting gigantic glimpse of other climes and spheres—as if mirrored in summer clouds he saw, instead of the heather hills stretching away to the sea, a dim and mighty land of blue mountains and gleaming quiet lakes—the golden, purple and sapphirean spires and towering walls of a mighty city such as the earth has not known for many a drifting age.

Then like the fading of a mirage it was gone, but the Gauls on the high slope had dropped their weapons and stared like men dazed—*For the man called Kull had vanished and there was no trace of his going!*

As in a daze Cormac turned his steed and rode back across the trampled field. His horse's hoofs splashed in lakes of blood and clanged against the helmets of dead men. Across the valley the shout of victory was thundering. Yet all seemed shadowy and strange. A shape was striding across the torn corpses and Cormac was dully aware that it was Bran. The Gael swung from his horse and fronted the king. Bran was weaponless and gory; blood trickled from gashes on brow, breast and limb; what armor he had worn was clean hacked away and a cut had shorn halfway through his iron crown. But the red jewel still gleamed unblemished like a star of slaughter.

"It is in my mind to slay you," said the Gael heavily and like a man speaking in a daze, "for the blood of brave men is on your head. Had you given the signal to charge sooner, some would have lived."

Bran folded his arms; his eyes were haunted. "Strike if you will; I am sick of slaughter. It is a cold mead, this kinging it. A king must gamble with men's lives and naked swords. The lives of all my people were at stake; I sacrificed the Northmen—yes; and my heart is sore within me, for they were men! But had I given the order when you would have desired, all might have gone awry. The Romans were not yet massed in the narrow mouth of the gorge, and might have had time and space to form their ranks again and beat us off. I waited until the last moment—and the rovers died. A king belongs to his people and cannot let either his own feelings or the lives of men influence him. Now my people are saved; but my heart is cold in my breast."

Cormac wearily dropped his sword-point to the ground.

"You are a born king of men, Bran," said the Gaelic prince.

Bran's eyes roved the field. A mist of blood hovered over all, where the victorious barbarians were looting the dead, while those Romans who had escaped slaughter by throwing down their swords and now stood under guard, looked on with hot smoldering eyes.

"My kingdom—my people—are saved," said Bran wearily. "They will come from the heather by the thousands and when Rome moves against us again, she will meet a solid nation. But I am weary. What of Kull?"

"My eyes and brain were mazed with battle," answered Cormac. "I thought to see him vanish like a ghost into the sunset. I will seek his body."

"Seek not for him," said Bran. "Out of the sunrise he came—into the sunset he has gone. Out of the mists of the ages he came to us, and back into the mists of the eons has he returned—to his own kingdom."

Cormac turned away; night was gathering. Gonar stood like a white specter before him.

"To his own kingdom," echoed the wizard. "Time and Space are naught. Kull has returned to his own kingdom—his own crown—his own age."

"Then he was a ghost?"

"Did you not feel the grip of his solid hand? Did you not hear his voice—see him eat and drink, laugh and slay and bleed?"

Still Cormac stood like one in a trance.

"Then if it be possible for a man to pass from one age into one yet unborn, or come forth from a century dead and forgotten, whichever you will, with his flesh-and-blood body and his arms—then he is as mortal as he was in his own day. Is Kull dead, then?"

"He died a hundred thousand years ago, as men reckon time," answered the wizard, "but in his own age. He died not from the swords of the Gauls of this age. Have we not heard in legends how the king of Valusia traveled into a strange, timeless land of the misty future ages, and there fought in a great battle? Why, so he did! A hundred thousand years ago, or today!

"And a hundred thousand years ago—or a moment agone!—Kull, king of Valusia, roused himself on the silken couch in his secret chamber and laughing, spoke to the first Gonar, saying: 'Ha, wizard, I have in truth dreamed strangely, for I went into a far clime and a far time in my visions, and fought for the king of a strange shadow-people!' And the great sorcerer smiled and pointed silently at the red, notched sword, and the torn mail and the many wounds that the king carried. And Kull, fully woken from his 'vision' and feeling the sting and the weakness of these yet bleeding wounds, fell silent and mazed, and all life and time and space seemed like a dream of ghosts to him, and he wondered thereat all the rest of his life. For the wisdom of the Eternities is denied even unto princes and Kull could no more understand what Gonar told him than you can understand my words."

"And then Kull lived despite his many wounds," said Cormac, "and has returned to the mists of silence and the centuries. Well—he thought us a dream; we thought him a ghost. And sure, life is but a web spun of ghosts and dreams and illusion, and it is in my mind that the kingdom which has this day been born of swords and slaughter in this howling valley is a thing no more solid than the foam of the bright sea."

Swords of the Northern Sea

"Skoal!" The smoke-stained rafters shook as the deep-throated roar went up. Drinking horns clashed and sword hilts beat upon the oaken board. Dirks hacked at the great joints of meat, and under the feet of the revelers gaunt, shaggy wolf-hounds fought over the remnants.

At the head of the board sat Rognor the Red, scourge of the Narrow Seas. The huge Viking meditatively stroked his crimson beard, while his great, arrogant eyes roved about the hall, taking in the familiar scene. A hundred warriors feasted here, waited on by bold-eyed, yellow-haired women and by trembling slaves. Spoils of the Southland were flung about in careless profusion. Rare tapestries and brocades, bales of silk and spice, tables and benches of fine mahogany, curiously chased weapons and delicate masterpieces of art vied with the spoils of the hunt—horns and heads of forest beasts—thus the Viking proclaimed his mastery over man and beast.

The Northern nations were drunken with victory and conquest. Rome had fallen; Frank, Goth, Vandal and Saxon had looted the fairest possessions of the world. And now these races found themselves hard put to hold their prizes from the wilder, fiercer peoples who swept down on them from the blue mists of the North. The Franks, already settled in Gaul and beginning to show signs of Latinization, found the long lean galleys of the Norsemen bringing the sword up their rivers; the Goth further south felt the weight of their kinsmen's fury and the Saxons, forcing the Britons westward, found themselves assailed by a more furious foe from the rear. East, west and south to the ends of the world ranged the dragon-beaked long-ships of the Vikings.

The Norse had already begun to settle in the Hebrides and the Orkneys, though as yet it was more a rendezvous of pirates than the later colonization. And the lair of Rognor the Red was this isle, called by the Scots Ladhbhan, the Picts Golmara, and the Norse Valgaard. His word was law, the only law this wild horde recognized; his hand was heavy, his soul ruthless, his range the open world.

The sea-king's eyes ranged about the board, while he nodded slightly in satisfaction. No pirate that sailed the seas could boast a fiercer assortment of fighting men than he; a mixed horde they were, Norsemen and Jutes—big, yellow-bearded men with wild, light eyes. Even now as they feasted they were fully armed and girt in mail, though they had laid aside their horned helmets. A ferocious, wayward race they were, with a latent madness burning in their brains, ready to leap into terrible flame at an instant.

Rognor's gaze turned from them, with their great bare arms heavy with golden armlets, to rest on one who seemed strangely different from the rest. This was a tall, rangily built man, deep-chested and strong, whose square-cut black hair and dark, smooth face contrasted with the yellow manes and beards about him. This man's eyes were narrow slits and of a cold steel grey, and they, with a number of scars that marred his face, lent him a peculiarly sinister aspect. He wore no gold ornaments of any kind and his mail was of chain mesh instead of the scale type worn by the men about him.

Rognor frowned abstractedly as he eyed this man, but just as he was about to speak, another man entered the huge hall and approached the head of the board. This newcomer was a tall, splendidly made young Viking, beardless but wearing a yellow mustache. Rognor greeted him.

"Hail, Hakon! I have not seen you since yesterday."

"I was hunting wolves in the hills," answered the young Viking, glancing curiously at the dark stranger. Rognor followed his gaze.

"That one is Cormac Mac Art, chief of a band of reavers. His galley was wrecked in the gale last night and he alone won through the breakers to shore. He came to the skalli doors early in the dawn, dripping wet, and argued the carles into bringing him in to me, instead of slaying him as they had intended. He offered to prove his right to follow me on the Viking path, and fought my three best swordsmen, one after the other, weary as he was. Rane, Tostig, and Halfgar he played with as if they were children and disarmed each of them without scathing him or taking a wound himself."

Hakon spoke a courtly greeting and the Gael answered in kind, with a stately inclination of his head.

"You speak our language well," ventured the young Viking.

"I have many friends among your people," answered Cormac. Hakon's eyes rested on him strangely for a moment, but the inscrutable eyes of the Gael gave back the gaze, with no hint of what was going on in his mind. Hakon turned back to the sea-king. Irish pirates were common enough in the Narrow Seas, and their forays carried them sometimes as far as Spain and Egypt, though their ships were far less seaworthy than the long-ships of the Vikings. But there was little friendship between the races. When a reaver met a Viking, generally a ferocious battle ensued.

They were rivals of the Western seas.

"You have come at a good time, Cormac," Rognor was rumbling. "You will see me take a wife tomorrow. By the hammer of Thor! I have taken many women in my time—from the people of Rome and Spain and Egypt, from the Franks, from the Saxons, and from the Danes, the curse of Loki on them! But never have I married one before. Always I tired of them and gave them to my men for sport. But it is time I thought of sons and so I have found a woman, worthy even of the favors of Rognor the Red. Ho, Osric, Eadwig! Bring in the British wench—you shall judge for yourself, Cormac."

Cormac's eyes roved to where Hakon sat. To the casual watcher the young Viking seemed disinterested, almost bored. But the Gael's stare centered on the angle of his firm jaw and noted the slight ripple of muscle that betrays the controlled tenseness. The Gael's cold eyes flickered momentarily.

Three women entered the feasting hall, closely followed by the two carles Rognor had sent for them. Two of the women led the third before Rognor and fell back, leaving her facing him alone.

"See, Cormac," rumbled the Viking, "is she not fit to bear the sons of a king?"

Cormac's eyes traveled impersonally up and down the girl who stood panting with anger before him. A fine, robust figure of young womanhood she was, quite evidently not yet twenty years old. Her beautiful bosom heaved with angry defiance, and her bearing was that of a young queen rather than a captive. She was clad in the rather scanty finery of a Norse woman, but she was quite apparently not of their race. With her blond hair and blazing blue eyes, coupled with her snowy skin, she was evidently a Celt, but Cormac knew that she was not one of the softened and Latinized people of southern Britain. Her carriage and manner were as free and barbaric as that of her captors.

"She is the daughter of a chief of the western Britons," said Rognor; "one of a tribe that never bowed the neck to Rome, and now hemmed between the Saxons on one side and the Picts on the other, holds both at bay. A fighting race! I took her from a Saxon galley, whose chief had in turn taken her captive during an inland raid. The moment I laid eyes on her, I knew that she was the girl who should bear my sons. I have held her now for some months, having her taught our ways and language. She was a wildcat when we first caught her! I gave her in charge of old Eadna, a very she-bear of a woman, and by the hammer of Thor, the old valkyrie nearly met her match! It took a dozen birchings across old Eadna's knee to tame the spit-fire—"

"Are you done with me, pirate?" flamed the girl suddenly. "If so, let me go back to my chamber, for the hag-face of Eadna, ugly as it is, is more pleasant to my sight than your red beard, swine-face!"

A roar of mirth went up and Cormac grinned thinly.

"It seems that her spirit is not utterly broken," he commented dryly.

"I would not count her worth a broken twig if it were," answered the sea-king, unabashed. "A woman without mettle is like a scabbard without a sword. You may return to your chamber, my pretty one, and prepare for your nuptials on the morrow. Mayhap you will look on me with more favor after you have borne me three or four stout sons."

The girl's eyes snapped blue fire, but without a word she turned her back squarely on her master and prepared to leave the hall, when a voice suddenly cut through the din: "Hold!"

Cormac's eyes narrowed as a grotesque and abhorrent figure came shambling and lurching across the hall. It was a creature with the face of a mature man, but it was no taller than a young boy, and its body was strangely deformed with twisted legs, huge malformed feet and one shoulder much higher than the other. Yet the fellow's breadth and girth were surprizing; a stunted, malformed giant he seemed. From a dark, evil face gleamed two great, yellow eyes.

"What is this?" asked the Gael. "I knew you Vikings sailed far, but I never heard that you sailed to the gates of Hell. Yet surely this thing had its birth nowhere else."

Rognor grinned. "Aye, in Hell I caught him, for in many ways Byzantium is Hell, where the Greeks break and twist the bodies of babes that they may grow into such blasphemies as he, to furnish sport for the emperor and his nobles. What now, Anzace?"

"Great lord," whined the creature in a shrill, loathly voice, "tomorrow you take this girl, Tarala, to wife, is it not? Aye—oh, aye. But mighty lord, what if she loves another?"

Tarala had turned back and now bent on the dwarf a wide-eyed stare in which aversion and anger vied with fear.

"Love another?" Rognor drank deep and wiped his beard. "What of it? Few girls love the men they have to marry. What care I for her love?"

"Ah," simpered the dwarf, "but would you care if I told you that one of your own men talked to her last night—aye, and for many nights before that—through the bars of her window?"

Down crashed the drinking-jack. Silence fell over the hall and all eyes turned toward the group at the head of the table. Hakon rose, flushing angrily.

"Rognor, if you will allow this vile creature to insult your wife-to-be, I at least—" his hand trembled on his sword.

"He lies!" cried the girl, reddening with shame and rage. "I—"

"Be silent!" roared Rognor. "You, too, Hakon. As for you—" his huge hand shot out and closed like a vise on the front of Anzace's tunic—"speak, and speak quickly! If you lie—you die!"

The dwarf 's dusky hue paled to a sickly yellow, but he shot a spiteful glance of reptilian malice toward Hakon. "My lord," said he, "I have watched for many a night since I first saw the glances this girl exchanged with he who has betrayed you. Last night, lying close among the trees without her window, I heard them plan to flee tonight. You are to be robbed of your fine bride, master."

Rognor shook the Greek as a mastiff shakes a rat. "Dog!" he roared. "Prove this or howl under the blood-eagle!"

"I can prove it," purred the dwarf. "Last night I had another with me—one whom you know is a speaker of the truth. Tostig!"

A tall, evil-visaged warrior came forward, his manner a mixture of apprehension and sullen defiance. He was one of those on whom Cormac had proved his swordsmanship.

"Tostig," purred the dwarf, "tell our master whether I speak truth—tell him if you lay in the bushes with me last night and heard his most trusted man—who was supposed to be up in the hills hunting—plot with this yellow-haired wench to betray their master and flee tonight."

"He speaks truth," said the Norseman sullenly.

"Odin, Thor and Loki!" snarled Rognor, flinging the dwarf from him and smashing his fist down on the board crashingly. "And who was the traitor?—tell me, that I may break his vile neck with my two hands!"

"Hakon!" screamed the dwarf, a quivering finger stabbing at the young Viking, while his face writhed in a horrid contortion of venomous triumph. "Hakon, your right hand man!"

"Aye, Hakon it was," growled Tostig.

Rognor's jaw dropped, and for an instant a tense silence gripped the hall. Then Hakon's sword was out like a flash of summer lightning and he sprang like a wounded panther at his betrayers. Anzace screeched and turned to run, and Tostig drew and parried Hakon's whistling stroke. But the fury of that headlong attack was not to be denied. Hakon's single terrific blow shivered Tostig's sword and flung the warrior at Rognor's feet, brains oozing from his cleft skull. At the same time Tarala, with the fury of a tigress, snatched up a bench and dealt Anzace such a blow as to stretch him stunned and bleeding on the floor.

The whole hall was in an uproar. Warriors roared their bewilderment and indecision, as they shouldered each other, and snarled out of the corners of their mouths, gripping their weapons and quivering with eagerness for action, but undecided which course to follow. Their two leaders were at variance, and their loyalty wavered. But close about Rognor were a group of hardened veterans who were assailed by no doubts. Their duty was to protect their chief at all times and this they now did, moving in a solid hedge against the enraged Hakon who was making a most sincere effort to detach the head of his former friend from its shoulders. Left alone, the matter might have been in doubt, but Rognor's vassals had no intention of leaving their chief to fight his own battles. They closed in on Hakon, beat down his guard by the very weight of their numbers and stretched him on the floor, bleeding from a dozen minor cuts, where he was soon bound hand and foot. All up and down the hall the rest of the horde was pressing forward, exclaiming and swearing at each other, and there was some muttering and some black glances cast at Rognor, but the sea-king, sheathing the great sword with which he had been parrying Hakon's vicious cuts, pounded on the board and shouted ferociously. The insurgents sank back, muttering, quelled by the blast of his terrific personality.

Anzace rose, glassy-eyed and holding his head. A great, bleak woman had taken the bench away from Tarala, and now held the blond girl tucked under her arm like an infant, while Tarala kicked and cursed like a trooper. In the whole hall there was but one person who seemed not to share the general frenzy—the Gaelic pirate, who had not risen from his seat where he sipped his ale with a cynical smile.

"You would betray me, eh?" bellowed Rognor, kicking his former lieutenant viciously. "You whom I trusted, whom I raised to high honor—" Words failed the outraged sea-king and he brought his feet into play again, while Tarala shrieked wrathful protests.

"Beast! Thief! Coward! If he were free you would not dare!"

"Be silent!" roared Rognor.

"I will not be silent!" she raged, kicking vainly in the old woman's grasp. "I love him! Why should I not love him in preference to you? Where you were harsh and cruel, he is kind. He is brave and handsome and the only man among you that has treated me with consideration in my captivity. I will marry him or no other—"

With a roar Rognor drew back his iron fist, but before he could crash it into that defiant, beautiful face, Cormac rose and caught his wrist. Rognor grunted involuntarily; the Gael's fingers were like steel. For a moment the Norseman's flaming eyes glared into the cold eyes of Cormac and neither wavered.

"You cannot marry a dead woman, Rognor," said Cormac coolly.

He released the other's wrist and resumed his seat. The sea-king growled something in his beard and shouted to his grim vassals: "Take this young dog and chain him in the cell; tomorrow he shall watch me marry the wench, and then *she* shall watch while with my own hands I cut the blood-eagle in his back."

Two huge carles stolidly lifted the bound and raging Hakon, and as they started to bear him from the hall, he fell silent suddenly and his gaze rested full on the sardonic face of Cormac Mac Art. The Gael returned the glance and suddenly Hakon spat a single word: "Wolf!"

Cormac did not start; not by the flicker of an eyelash did he betray any surprize. His inscrutable gaze did not alter as Hakon was borne from the hall.

"What of the wench, master?" asked the woman who held Tarala captive. "Shall I not strip her and birch her?"

"Prepare her for her marrying," growled Rognor with an impatient gesture. "Take her out of my sight before I lose my temper and break her white neck."

Chapter 2

A torch in a niche of the wall flickered, casting an indistinct light about the small cell, whose floor was of dirt and whose walls and roof were of square-cut logs. Hakon the Viking, chained in the corner furthest from the door, just beneath the small, heavilybarred window, shifted his position and cursed fervently. It was neither his chains nor his wounds which caused his discomfiture. The wounds were slight and had already begun to heal—and, besides, the Norsemen were inured to unbelievable physical discomforts. Nor was it the thought of death that made him writhe and curse. It was the reflection that Rognor was going to take Tarala for his unwilling bride and that he, Hakon, was unable to prevent it. He froze as a light, wary step sounded outside. He heard a voice, with an alien accent: "Rognor desires me to talk with the prisoner."

"How do I know you speak truth?" grumbled the guard.

"Go and ask Rognor; I will stand guard while you go. If he flays your back for disturbing him, don't blame me."

"Go in, in the name of the devil," snarled the guard, "but do not tarry too long."

There was a fumbling of bolts and bars, and the door swung open, framing a tall, lithe form, then it closed again. Cormac Mac Art looked down at the prostrate Hakon. Cormac was fully armed, and on his head he wore a helmet with a crest ornamented with flowing horse hair. This seemed to make him inhumanly tall and, in the flickering, illusive light which heightened the darkness and sinisterness of his appearance, the Gaelic pirate seemed not unlike some sombre demon come to taunt a captive in a shadowy corner of Hell.

"I thought you would come," said Hakon, rising to a sitting position. "Speak softly, however, lest the guard outside hear us."

"I came because I wished to know where you learned my language," said the Gael.

"You lie," replied Hakon cheerfully. "You came lest I betray you to Rognor. When I spoke the name men have given you, in your own tongue, you knew that I knew who you really were. For that name means Wolf in your language, and you are not only Cormac Mac Art of Erin, but you are Cormac the Wolf, a reaver and a killer, and the right-hand man of Wulfhere the Dane, Rognor's greatest enemy. What you are doing here, I know not, but I do know that the presence of Wulfhere's closest comrade means no good for Rognor. I have but to say a word to the guard and your fate is as certain as mine."

Cormac looked down at the youth and was silent for a moment.

"I might cut your throat before you could speak," he suggested.

"You might," agreed Hakon, "but you won't. It is not in you to slay a defenseless man thus."

Cormac grinned bleakly. "True. What would you have of me?"

"My life for yours. Get me free and I keep your secret till Ragnarok."

Cormac seated himself on a small stool and meditated.

"What are your plans?"

"Free me—and let me get my hands on a sword. I'll steal Tarala and we will seek to gain the hills. If not, I'll take Rognor with me to Valhalla."

"And if you gain the hills?"

"I have men waiting there—fifteen of my closest friends, Jutes, mainly, who have no love for Rognor. On the other side of the island we have hidden a long-boat. In it we can make it to another island where we can hide from Rognor until we have a band of our own. Masterless men and runaway carles will come to us and it may not be long until I can burn Rognor's skalli over his head and pay him back for his kicks."

Cormac nodded. In that day of pirates and raiders, outlaws and reavers, such a thing as Hakon suggested was common enough.

"But first you must escape from this cell."

"That is your part," rejoined the youth.

"Wait," said the Gael. "You say you have fifteen friends in the forest—"

"Aye—on pretext of a wolf hunt we went up into the hills yesterday and I left them at a certain spot, while I slipped back and made the rest of my plans with Tarala. I was to spend the day at the skalli, and then, pretending to go for my friends tonight, I was to ride forth, returning stealthily and stealing Tarala. But I reckoned not on Anzace, that Byzantium he-witch, whose foul heart, I swear, I will give to the kites—"

"Enough," snapped Cormac impatiently. "Have you any friends among the carles now in the steading? Methought I noted some displeasure among them at your rough handling."

"I have a number of friends and half-friends," answered Hakon, "but they waver—a carle is a stupid animal and apt to follow whoever seems strongest. Let Rognor fall, with his band of chosen henchmen, and the rest would likely as not join my forces."

"Good enough." Cormac's eyes glittered as his keen brain began racing with an idea. "Now listen—I told Rognor truth when I said my galley was dashed on the rocks last night—but I lied when I said only I escaped. Well hidden beyond the southern point of this island, where the sand spits run out into the surf, is Wulfhere with fifty-odd swordsmen. When we fought through the madness of the breakers last night, and found ourselves ashore with no ship and only a part of our band left alive—and on Rognor's island—we took council and decided that I, whom Rognor was less likely to know, should go boldly up to his skalli and, getting into his favor, look for a chance to outwit him and seize one of his galleys. For it is a ship we want. Now I will bargain with you. If I help you to escape, will you join your forces with mine and Wulfhere's, and aid us to overthrow Rognor? And having overthrown him, will you give us one of his long-ships? That is all we ask. The loot of the skalli and all Rognor's carles and the rest of his ships shall be all yours. With a good long-ship under our feet, Wulfhere and I will soon gain plunder enough—aye, and Vikings for a full crew."

"It is a bargain," promised the youth. "Aid me and I aid you; make me lord of this island with your help and you shall have the pick of the long-ships."

"Good enough; now attend me. Is your guard likely to be changed tonight?"

"Scarcely, I think."

"Think you he could be bribed, Hakon?"

"Not he. He is one of Rognor's picked band."

"Well, then we must try some other way. If we can dispose of him, your escape will hardly be discovered before morning. Wait!"

The Gael stepped to the door of the cell and spoke to the guard.

"What sort of a watchman are you, to leave a way of escape for your prisoner?"

"What mean you?" the Viking's beard bristled.

"Why, all the bars have been torn from the window."

"You are mad!" growled the warrior, entering the cell. He raised his head to stare at the window, and even as his chin rose at an angle following his eyes, Cormac's iron fist, backed by every ounce of his mighty body, crashed against the Viking's jaw. The fellow dropped like a slaughtered ox, senseless.

The keys to Hakon's chains were at the guard's girdle. In an instant the young Viking rose, free of his bonds, and Cormac, having gagged the unconscious warrior and chained him in turn, handed his sword to Hakon who grasped it eagerly. No word was said as the two stole from the cell and into the shadows of the surrounding trees. There Cormac halted. He eyed the steading keenly. There was no moon but the starlight was sufficient for the Gael's purposes.

The skalli, a long rambling structure of logs, faced the bay where Rognor's galleys rode at anchor. Grouped about the main building in a rough half-circle were the storehouses, the huts of the carles and the stables. A hundred or so yards separated the nearest of these from the skalli, and the hut wherein Hakon had been pent was the furthest away from the hall. The forest pressed closely on three sides, the tall trees overshadowing many of the storehouses. There was no wall or moat about Rognor's steading. He was sole lord of the island and expected no raid from the land side. At any rate, his steading was not intended as a fortress but as a sort of camp from which he swooped down on his victims.

While Cormac was taking in all salient points, his quick ears caught a stealthy footstep. Straining his eyes, he glimpsed the hint of a movement under the thick trees. Beckoning Hakon, he crept silently forward, dirk in hand. The brooding shadows masked all, but Cormac's wild beast instinct, that comes to men who live by their wits, told him that someone or something was gliding through the darkness close at hand. A twig snapped faintly some little distance away, and then, a moment later, he saw a vague shape detach itself from the blackness of the trees and drift swiftly toward the skalli. Even in the dimness of the starlight, the creature seemed abnormal and uncanny.

"Anzace!" hissed Hakon, electrified. "He was hiding in the trees, watching the cell! Stop him, quickly!"

Cormac's grip on his arm stayed him from springing out recklessly in pursuit.

"Silence!" hissed the Gael. "He knows you are free, but he may not know we know it. We have yet time before he reaches Rognor."

"But Tarala!" exclaimed Hakon, fiercely. "I'll not leave her alone here now—go if you will—I'll steal her away now, or die here!"

Cormac glanced quickly toward the skalli. Anzace had vanished around the corner. Apparently he was making for the front entrance.

"Lead to the girl's chamber," growled Cormac. "It's a desperate chance—but Rognor might cut her throat when he learns we've fled, before we could return and rescue her."

Hakon and his companion, emerging boldly from the shadows, ran swiftly and silently across the open starlit space which parted the forest from the skalli. The young Norseman led the way to a heavily barred window near the rear end of the long, rambling hall. Crouching there in the shadows of the building, he rapped cautiously on the bars, three times. Almost instantly Tarala's white face was framed dimly in the aperture.

"Hakon!" came the passionate whisper. "Oh, be careful! Old Eadna is in the room with me. She is asleep, but—"

"Stand back," whispered Hakon, raising his sword. "I'm going to hew these bars apart—"

"The clash of metal will wake every carle on the island," grunted Cormac. "We have a few minutes leeway while Anzace is telling his tale to Rognor. Let you not throw it away."

"But how else—?"

"Stand away," growled the Gael, gripping a bar in each hand and bracing his feet and knees against the wall. Hakon's eyes widened as he saw Cormac arch his back and throw every ounce of his incredible frame into the effort. The young Viking saw the great muscles writhe and ripple along the Gael's arms, shoulders and legs; the veins stood out on Cormac's temples, and then before the astounded eyes of the watchers, the bars bent and gave way, literally torn from their sockets. A dull rending crash resulted, and in the room someone stirred with a startled exclamation.

"Quick, through the window!" snapped Cormac fiercely, galvanized into dynamic action.

Tarala flung one limb over the shattered sill—then there sounded a low, fierce exclamation behind her and a quick rush. A pair of clutching hands closed on the girl's shoulders, and then twisting about, Tarala struck a heavy blow. The hands went limp and there was the sound of a falling body. In another instant the British girl was out of the window and in the arms of her lover.

"There!" she gasped breathlessly, throwing aside the heavy wine goblet with which she had knocked her guard senseless. "That pays old Eadna back for some of the spankings she gave me."

"Haste!" rapped Cormac, urging the pair toward the forest. "The whole steading will be roused in a moment—"

Already lights were flaring and Rognor's bull voice was heard bellowing. In the shadows of the trees Cormac halted an instant.

"How long will it take you to reach your men in the hills and return here?"

"Return here?"

"Yes."

"Why—an hour and a half at the utmost."

"Good!" snapped the Gael. "Conceal your men on yonder side of the clearing and wait until you hear this signal—" And he cautiously made the sound of a night bird thrice repeated.

"Come to me—alone—when you hear that sound. And take care to avoid Rognor and his men as you come—"

"Why—he'll most certainly wait until morning before he begins searching the island—"

Cormac laughed shortly. "Not if I know him. He'll be out with all his men combing the woods tonight. But we've wasted too much time—see, the steading is aswarm with armed warriors. Get your Jutes back here as soon as you may. I'm for Wulfhere."

Cormac waited until the girl and her lover had vanished in the shadows, then he turned and ran fleetly and silently as the beast for which he was named. Where the average man would have floundered and blundered through the shadows, caroming into trees and tripping over bushes, Cormac sped lightly and easily, guided partly by his cat-like eyes, mainly by his unerring instinct. A lifetime in the forests and on the seas of the wild northern and western countries had given him the thews, wits and endurance of the fierce beasts that roamed there.

Behind him he heard shouts, clashing of arms and a bloodthirsty voice roaring threats and blasphemies. Evidently Rognor had discovered that both his birds had flown. These sounds grew fainter as he rapidly increased the distance between, and presently the Gael heard the low lapping of waves against the sand bars. As he approached the hiding-place of his allies, he slackened his pace and went more cautiously. His Danish friends lacked somewhat of his ability to see in the dark, and the Gael had no wish to stop an arrow intended for an enemy.

He halted and sounded the low pitched call of the wolf. Almost instantly came an answer, and he went forward with more assurance. Soon a vague huge figure rose in the shadows in front of him and a rough voice accosted him.

"Cormac—by Thor, we had about decided you failed to trick them—"

"They are slow-witted fools," answered the Gael. "But I know not if my plan shall succeed. We are only some seventy to over three hundred."

"Seventy—why—?"

"We have some allies now—you know Hakon, Rognor's mate?"

"Aye."

"He has turned against his chief and now moves against him with fifteen Jutes—or will shortly. Come, Wulfhere, order out the warriors. We go to throw the dice of chance again. If we lose, we gain an honorable death—if we win, we gain a goodly long-ship, and you—vengeance!"

"Vengeance!" murmured Wulfhere softly. His fierce eyes gleamed in the starlight and his huge hand locked like iron about the handle of his battle-axe. A red-bearded giant was the Dane, as tall as Cormac, and more heavily built. He lacked something of the Gael's tigerish litheness but he made up for that in oak-and-iron massiveness. His horned helmet increased the barbaric wildness of his appearance.

"Out of your dens, wolves!" he called into the darkness behind him. "Out! No more skulking for Wulfhere's killers—we go to feed the ravens. Osric—Halfgar—Edric—Athelgard—Aslaf—out, wolves, the feast is ready!"

As if born from the night and the shadows of the brooding trees, the warriors silently took shape. There were few words spoken and the only sounds were the occasional rattle of a belt-chain, or the rasp of a swinging scabbard. Single file they trailed out behind their leaders, and Cormac, glancing back, saw only a sinuous line of great, vague forms, darker shadows amid the shadows, with a swaying of horns above. To his imaginative Celtic mind it seemed that he led a band of horned demons through the midnight forest.

Chapter 3

At the crest of a small rise, Cormac halted so suddenly that Wulfhere, close behind, bumped into him. The Gael's steel fingers closed on the Viking's arm, halting his grumbled question. Ahead of them came a sudden murmur and a rattle of weapons, and now lights shone through the trees.

"Lie down!" hissed Cormac, and Wulfhere obeyed, growling the order back to the men behind. As one man, they prostrated themselves and lay silently. The noise grew louder swiftly, the tramp of many men.

Presently into view came a motley horde of men, waving torches as they scanned all sides of the sullen forest, whose menacing darkness the torches but accentuated. They were following a dim trail which cut across Cormac's line of march. In front of them strode Rognor, his face black with passion, his eyes terrible. He gnawed his beard as he strode, and his great sword trembled in his hand. Close behind him came his picked swordsmen in a compact, immobile-faced clump, and behind them the rest of the carles strung out in a straggling horde.

At the sight of his enemy Wulfhere shivered as with a chill. Under Cormac's restraining hand the great thews of his arm swelled and knotted into ridges of iron.

"A flight of arrows, Cormac," he urged in a passionate whisper, his voice heavy with hate. "Let's loose a rain of shafts into them and then lash in with the blades—"

"No, not now!" hissed the Gael. "There are nearly three hundred men with Rognor. He is playing into our hands and we must not lose the chance the gods have given us! Lie still and let them pass!"

Not a sound betrayed the presence of the fifty-odd Danes as they lay like the shadow of Doom above the slope. The Norsemen passed at right angles and vanished in the forest beyond without having seen or heard anything of the men whose fierce eyes watched them. Cormac nodded grimly. He had been right when he assumed that Rognor would not wait for the dawn before combing the island for his captive and her abductor. Here in this forest, where fifty-odd men could escape the eyes of the searchers, Rognor could scarcely have hoped to find the fugitives. But the fury that burned in the Norseman's brain would not allow him to keep still while those who had defied him were still at liberty. It was not in a Viking to sit still when fired with rage, even though action were useless. Cormac knew these strange, fierce people better than they knew themselves.

Not until the clash of steel had died out in the forest beyond, and the torchlights had become mere fireflies glimpsed occasionally through the trees, did Cormac give the order to advance. Then at double quick time they hastened on, until they saw more lights ahead of them, and presently, crouching beneath the tall trees at the edge of the clearing, looked out on the steading of Rognor the Red. The main skalli and many of the smaller buildings were alight but only a few warriors were seen. Evidently Rognor had taken most of his carles with him on his useless chase.

"What now, Cormac?" questioned Wulfhere.

"Hakon should be here," answered Cormac. Even as he opened his mouth to give the signal agreed upon, a carle rounded the corner of a stable close by, carrying a torch. The watchers saw him alter his leisurely pace suddenly and glance fixedly in their direction. Some motion in the deep shadows had attracted his attention.

"What cursed luck!" hissed Wulfhere. "He's coming straight for us. Edric—loose me an arrow—"

"No," muttered Cormac. "Never kill, Wulfhere, save when it is necessary. Wait!"

The Gael faded back into the darkness like a phantom. The carle came straight for the forest edge, waving his torch slightly, curious, but evidently not suspicious. Now he was under the trees and his outthrust fagot shone full on Wulfhere, where the huge Dane stood in grim silence, motionless as a statue.

"Rognor!" The flickering light was illusive; the carle saw only a red-bearded giant. "Back so soon? Have you caught—"

The sentence broke off abruptly as he saw the red beards and fierce unfamiliar faces of the silent men ranged behind Wulfhere; his gaze switched back to the chief and his eyes flared with sudden horror. His lips parted, but at that instant an iron arm hooked about his throat, strangling the threatened yell. Wulfhere knocked the torch from his hand and stamped it out, and in the darkness the carle was disarmed and bound securely with his own harness.

"Speak low and answer my questions," sounded a sinister whisper at his ear. "How many weapon-men are there left at the steading?"

The carle was brave enough in open battle, but the suddenness of the surprize had unnerved him, and here in the darkness, surrounded by his ruthless hereditary foes, with the demonic Gael muttering at his shoulder, the Norseman's blood turned to ice.

"Thirty men remain," he answered.

"Where are they?"

"Half of them are in the skalli. The rest are in the huts."

"Good enough," grunted the Gael. "Gag him and bring him along with us. Now wait here until I find Hakon."

He gave the cry of a sleepy bird, thrice repeated, and waited a moment. The answer came drifting back from the woods on the other side of the clearing.

"Stay here," ordered the Gael, and melted from the sight of Wulfhere and his Danes like a shadow.

Cautiously he made his way around the fringe of the forest, keeping well hidden in the trees, and presently a slight rustling noise ahead of him made him aware that a body of men lurked before him. He sounded the signal again, and presently heard Hakon whisper a sibilant warning. Behind the young Viking the Gael made out the vague form of his warriors.

"By the gods," muttered Cormac impatiently, "you make enough noise to wake Caesar. Surely the carles had investigated but that they thought you a herd of buffalo—who is this?"

By Hakon's side was a slim figure, clad in mail and armed with a sword, but strangely out of place among the giant warriors.

"Tarala," answered Hakon. "She would not stay hidden in the hills—so I found a corselet that she could wear and—"

Cormac cursed fervently. "Well—well. Now attend me closely. See you yon hut—the one wherein you were confined? Well, we are going to set fire to it—"

"But, man," exclaimed Hakon, "the flame will bring Rognor on the run!"

"Exactly; that is what I wish. Now when the fire brings the carles running, you and your Jutes sally from the forest and fall upon them. Cut down as many as you can, but the moment they rally and make head against you, fall back into the stables, which you can easily do. If you work it right, you should do this without losing a man. Then, once inside the stable, bar and bolt the doors and hold it against them. They will not set fire to it, because many fine horses are there, and you with your men can hold it easily against thirty."

"But what of you and your Danes?" protested Hakon. "Are we to bear all the brunt and danger, while—"

Cormac's hand shot out and his steely fingers sank fiercely in Hakon's shoulder.

"Do you trust me or do you not?" he snarled. "By the blood of the gods, are we to waste the night in argument? Do you not see that so long as Rognor's men think they have only you to deal with, the surprize will be triply effective when Wulfhere strikes? Worry not—when the time comes my Danes will drink blood aplenty."

"Well enough," agreed Hakon, convinced by the dynamic impact of the Gael's will, "but you must have Tarala with you, out of harm's way for the time—"

"Never!" cried the girl, stamping her small foot. "I shall be at your side, Hakon, as long as we both live. I am the daughter of a British prince and I can wield a sword as well as any of your men!"

"Well," Cormac grinned thinly, "easy to see who'll be the real ruler in your family—but come, we have no time to waste. But leave her here with your men for now."

As they glided through the shadows, Cormac repeated his plans in a low voice, and soon they stood at the point where the forest most nearly approached the hut that served as Rognor's prison. Warily they stole from the trees and swiftly ran to the hut. A large tree stood just without the door and as they passed under it, something struck Cormac a heavy blow in the face. His quick hand grasped a human foot and, looking up in surprize, he made out a vague figure swaying limply to and fro above him.

"Your jailor!" he grunted. "That was ever Rognor's way, Hakon—when in anger, hang the first man handy. A poor custom—never kill except when necessary."

The logs of the hut were dry, with much bark still on them. A few seconds work with flint and steel and a thin wisp of flame caught the shredded fibre and curled up the wall.

"Back to your men, now," muttered Cormac, "and wait until the carles are swarming about the hut. Then hack straight through them and gain the stables."

Hakon nodded and darted away. A few minutes more found Cormac back with his own men, who were muttering restlessly as they watched the flames eat their way up the wall of the hut. Suddenly a shout sounded from the skalli. Men came pouring out of the main hall and the huts, some full armed and wide awake, some gaping and half-clad, as though just awakened from a sound sleep. Behind them peered the women and slaves. The men snatched buckets of water and ran for the hut and in a moment the scene was one of the usual confusion attendant to a fire. The carles jostled each other, shouted useless advice and made a vain attempt to stem the flame which now leaped roaring up through the roof and curled high in a blaze that was sure to be seen by Rognor wherever he was.

And in the midst of the turmoil there sounded a fierce medley of yells and a small, compact body of men crashed from the forest and smote the astonished carles like a thunderbolt. Hacking and hewing right and left, Hakon and his Jutes cleft their way through the bewildered Norsemen, leaving a wake or dead and dying behind them.

Wulfhere trembled with eagerness and behind him his Danes snarled and tensed like hunting dogs straining at the leash.

"How now, Cormac," cried the Viking chief, "shall we not strike a blow? My axe is hungry!"

"Be patient, old sea-wolf," grinned Cormac savagely. "Your axe shall drink deep; see, Hakon and his Jutes have gained the stable and shut the doors."

It was true. The Norsemen had recovered from their surprize and prepared to turn on their attackers with all the fury that characterized their race, but before they could make any headway, Hakon and his men had disappeared inside the stable whence came the neighing and stamping of frightened horses.

This stable, built to withstand the inroads of hunger-maddened wolves and the ravages of a Baltic winter, was a natural fortress, and against its heavy panels the axes of the carles thundered in vain. The only way into the building was through the windows. The heavy wooden bars that guarded these were soon hacked away, but climbing through them in the teeth of the defenders' swords was another matter. After a few disastrous attempts, the survivors drew off and consulted with each other. As Cormac had reasoned, burning the stable was out of the question because of the blooded horses within. Nor was a flight of arrows through the windows logical. All was dark inside the stable and a chance flown shaft was more likely to hit a horse than a man. Outside, however, the whole steading was lit like day by the burning hut; the Jutes were not famed as archers, but there were a few bows among Hakon's men and these did good execution among the men outside.

At last a carle shouted: "Rognor will have seen the fire and be returning—Olaf, run you and meet him, and tell him Hakon and his Jutes are pent in the stable. We will surround the place and keep them there until Rognor gets here! Then we shall see!"

A carle set off at full speed and Cormac laughed softly to himself.

"Just what I was hoping for! The gods have been good to us this night, Wulfhere! But back—further into the shadows, lest the flames discover us."

Then followed a tense time of waiting for all concerned—for the Jutes imprisoned in the stable, for the Norsemen lying about it, and for the unseen Danes lurking just within the forest edge. The fire burnt itself out and the flames died in smoking embers. Away in the east shone the first touch of dawn. A wind blew up from the sea and stirred the forest leaves. And through the woods echoed the tramp of many men, the clash of steel and deep angry shouts. Cormac's nerves hummed like taut lute strings. Now was the crucial moment. If Rognor's men passed from the forest into the clearing without seeing their hidden foes, all was well. Cormac made the Danes lie prone, and with heart in his mouth, waited.

Again came the glimmer of torches through the trees, and with a sigh of relief Cormac saw that Rognor was approaching the steading from another direction than that he had taken in leaving it. The motley horde broke cover almost opposite the point where Cormac and his men lay.

Rognor was roaring like a wild bull and swinging his two-handed sword in great arcs.

"Break down the doors!" he shouted. "Follow me, shatter the walls!"

The whole horde streamed out across the clearing, Rognor and his veterans in the lead.

Wulfhere had leaped to his feet and his Danes rose as a man behind him. The chief 's fierce eyes were blazing with battle-lust.

"Wait!" Cormac thrust him back. "Wait until they are pounding at the doors!"

Rognor's Vikings crashed headlong against the stable. They bunched at the windows, stabbing and hacking at the blades that thrust from within. The clash of steel rose deafeningly, frightened horses screamed and kicked thunderously at their stalls, while the heavy doors shook to the impact of a hundred axes.

"Now!" Cormac leaped to his feet and across the clearing swept a sudden storm of arrows. Men went down in windrows and the rest turned bewilderedly to face this sudden and unguessed foe. The Danes were bowmen as well as swordsmen; they excelled all other nations of the North in this art. Now as they leaped from their hiding place, they loosed their shafts as they ran with unerring aim. But the Norsemen were not ready to break yet. Seeing their red-maned foes charging them, they supposed, dazedly, that a great host was upon them, but with the reckless valor of their breed they leaped to meet them.

Driving their last flight of shafts pointblank, the Danes dropped their bows and leaped into close quarters, yelling like fiends, to slash and hack with swords and axes.

They were far outnumbered, but the surprize tolled heavily and the unexpected arrows had taken terrific toll. Still Cormac, slashing and thrusting with reddened sword, knew that their only chance lay in a quick victory. Let the battle be drawn out and the superior numbers of the Norse must win. Hakon and his Jutes had sallied from the stable and were assailing their former mates from that side. There in the first white light of dawn was enacted a scene of fury.

Rognor, thought Cormac, as he mechanically stooped below the sweep of an axe and ran the wielder through, must die quickly, if the coup he wished for was to be brought about.

And now he saw Rognor and Wulfhere surging toward each other through the waves of battle. A Dane, thrusting savagely at the Norseman, went down with a shattered skull, and then with a thunderous yell of fury, the two red-bearded giants crashed together. All the pent up ferocity of years of hatred burst into flame and the opposing hordes halted their own fight mutually to watch their chieftains battle.

There was little to choose between them in size and strength. Rognor was armed with a great sword that he swung in both hands, while Wulmere bore a long-shafted axe and a heavy shield. That shield was rent in twain beneath Rognor's first incredible stroke, and tossing the fragments away, Wulfhere struck back and hewed one of the horns from the Norseman's helmet. Rognor roared and cut terrifically at Wulfhere's legs, but the huge Dane, with a quickness astounding in a man of his bulk, bounded high in the air, cleared the whistling blade and in mid-air chopped down at Rognor's head. The heavy axe struck glancingly on the iron helmet, but even so, Rognor went to his knees with a grunt. Then, even as the Dane heaved up his axe for another stroke, Rognor was up and his mighty arms brought down his great sword in an arc that crashed full on Wulfhere's helmet. The huge blade shivered with a tremendous crash and Wulfhere staggered, his eyes filling with blood. Like a wounded tiger he struck back with all the might of his gigantic frame, and his blind, terrible stroke cleft Rognor's helmet and shattered the skull beneath. Both hosts cried out at the marvel of that blow, as Rognor's corpse tumbled at Wulfhere's feet—and the next instant the blinded giant went down before a perfect storm of swords as Rognor's picked swordsmen rushed to avenge their chief.

With a yell Cormac bounded into the press and his sword wove a web of death above the chief who, having grappled with some of his attackers, now kicked and wrestled with them on the bloody earth. The Danes surged in to aid their leaders, and about the fallen chieftains eddied a whirlpool of steel. Cormac found himself opposed to Rane, one of Rognor's prize swordsmen, while Hakon battled with his mate, Halfgar. Cormac laughed; he had crossed swords with Rane, a lean shaggy wolf of a man, that morning and he knew all he wished to know about him. A quick parry of an overhand stroke, a dazzling feint to draw a wide lunge, and the Gael's sword was through the Viking's heart.

Then he turned to Hakon. The young Viking was hard pressed; Halfgar, a giant, taller than Wulfhere, towered over him, raining terrific blows upon his shield so swiftly Hakon could make no attempt to launch an offensive of his own. An unusually vicious stroke beat his helmet down over his eyes and for an instant he lost touch of his opponent's blade. In that instant he would have died, but a slim, girlish figure leaped in front of him and took the blow on her own blade, the force of it dashing her to her knees. Up went the giant's sword again—but at that second Cormac's point pierced his bull throat just above the mail.

Then the Gael wheeled back, just as a powerful carle raised an axe high above the still prostrate Wulfhere. The point was Cormac's favorite, but that he could use the edge as well, he proved by splitting the carle's skull to the chin. Then, grabbing Wulfhere's shoulders, he hauled him off the men he was seeking to throttle and dragged him, cursing and bellowing like a bull, out of the press.

A quick glance showed him that Rognor's veterans had fallen before the axes of the Danes, and that the rest of the Norsemen, seeing their chief fall, had renewed the fight only halfheartedly. Then what he had hoped for occurred. One of the Norsemen shouted: "The woods are full of Danes!" And the strange, inexplicable panic that seizes men sometimes gripped the carles. Shouting, they gave back and fled for the skalli in a straggling body. Wulfhere, shaking the blood out of his eyes and bellowing for his axe, would have hurled his men after them, but Cormac stopped him. His shouted commands kept the Danes from following the fugitives, who were fortified in the skalli and ready to sell their lives as dearly as only cornered men can.

Hakon, prompted by Cormac, shouted to them: "Ho, warriors, will ye listen to me?"

"We listen, Hakon," came back a shout from the barred windows, "but keep back; mayhap we be doomed men, but many shall die with us if you seek to take the skalli."

"I have no quarrel with you," he answered. "I look upon you as friends, though you allowed Rognor to bind and imprison me. But that is past; let it be forgotten. Rognor is dead; his picked veterans are dead and ye have no leader. The forest about the steading swarms with Danes who but await my signal. But that signal I am loath to give. They will burn the skalli and cut the throats of every man, woman and child among you. Now attend me—if you will accept me as your chieftain, and swear fealty to me, no harm will come to you."

"What of the Danes?" the question was shouted. "Who are they that we should trust them?"

"You trust me, do you not? Have I ever broken my word?"

"No," they admitted, "you have always kept faith."

"Good enough. I swear to you that the Danes will not harm you. I have promised them a ship; that promise I must keep if they are to go in peace. But if you follow me on the Viking path, we can soon get another ship or build one. And one thing more—here stands beside me the girl who is to be my wife—the daughter of a British prince. She has promised me the aid of her people in all our endeavors. With friends on the British mainland we can have a source of supplies from whence we can raid the Angles and Saxons to our hearts' content—with the aid of Tarala's Britons we may carve us out a kingdom in Britain as Cerdic, Hengist and Horsa did. Now, speak, will you take me as your chief?"

A short silence followed in which the Vikings were evidently holding council with each other; then presently their spokesman shouted: "We agree to your wishes, Hakon!"

Hakon laid down his notched and bloody sword and approached the skalli door empty-handed. "And will you swear fealty to me, on the bull, the fire and the sword?"

The great portals swung open, framing fierce bearded faces. "We will swear, Hakon; your wish is our command."

"And when they've found we've tricked them, they'll turn and cut his throat and ours, too," grunted Wulfhere, mopping the blood from his face.

Cormac smiled and shook his head. "They've sworn; they will keep faith. Are you badly wounded?"

"A trifle," growled the giant. "A gash in the thigh and a few more on the arms and shoulders. It was the cursed blood that got in my eyes when Rognor's sword bit through my helmet and into my scalp, as it broke."

"Your head's harder than your helmet, Wulfhere," laughed Cormac. "But here, we must be attending to our wounded. Some ten of our men are dead and nearly all of them slashed more or less. Also, some of the Jutes are down. But, by the gods, what a killing *we* have made this night!"

He indicated the stark and silent rows of arrow-feathered or sword-gashed Norsemen.

Chapter 4

The sun, not yet in the zenith of the clear blue sky, glimmered on the white sails of a long-ship as they spread and swelled to catch the wind. On the deck stood a small group of figures.

Cormac extended his hand to Hakon. "We have hunted together well this night, young sir. A few hours since you were a captive doomed to die and Wulfhere and I were hunted outlaws. Now you are lord of Ladbhan and a band of hardy Vikings, and Wulfhere and I have a staunch ship under our feet—though forsooth, the crew is rather scant—still, that can be overcome as soon as the Danes hear that Wulfhere and Cormac Mac Art need men.

"And you—" he turned to the girl who stood beside Hakon, still clad in the mail that hung loosely on her lithe form. "You are in truth a valkyrie—a shield woman. Your sons will be kings."

"Aye, that they will," rumbled Wulfhere, enveloping Tarala's slim hand with his own huge paw. "If I was a marrying man, I might cut Hakon's throat and carry you off for myself. But now the wind is rising and my very heart quivers to feel the deck rocking under my feet again. Good fortune attend you all."

Hakon, his bride and the Norsemen attending them swung down into the boat that waited to carry them ashore. At Wulfhere's shout, his Danes cast off; the oars began to ply and the sails filled. The watchers in the boat and on shore saw the long-ship stand off.

"What now, old wolf?" roared Wulfhere, dealing Cormac a buffet between the shoulders that would have felled a horse. "Where away?—it is for you to say."

"To the Isle of Swords, first, for a full crew," the Gael answered, his eyes alight. "Then—" he drank in deep the crisp strong tang of the sea-wind, "then, skoal for the Viking path again and the ends of the world!"

The Night of the Wolf

Thorwald Shield-hewer's gaze wandered from the glittering menace in the hard eyes of the man who fronted him, and strayed down the length of his great skalli. He marked the long lines of mailed, horn-helmed carles, the hawk-faced chiefs who had ceased feasting to listen. And Thorwald Shield-hewer laughed.

True, the man who had just flung his defiance into the Viking's teeth did not look particularly impressive beside the armored giants who thronged the hall. He was a short, heavily muscled man, smooth faced and very dark. His only garments or ornaments were rude sandals on his feet, a deerskin loincloth, and a broad leather girdle from which swung a short curiously barbed sword. He wore no armor and his square-cut black mane was confined only by a thin silver band about his temples. His cold black eyes glittered with concentrated fury and his inner passions stirred the expressions of his usually immobile face.

"A year ago," said he, in barbarous Norse, "you came to Golara, desiring only peace with my people. You would be our friend and protect us from the raids of others of your accursed race. We were fools; we dreamed there was faith in a sea-thief. We listened. We brought you game and fish and cut timbers when you built your steading, and shielded you from others of our people who were wiser than we. Then you were a handful with one longship. But as soon as your stockade was built, more of you came. Now your warriors number four hundred, and six dragon-ships are drawn up on the beach.

"Soon you became arrogant and overbearing. You insulted our chiefs, beat our young men—of late your devils have been carrying off our women and murdering our children and our warriors."

"And what would you have me do?" cynically asked Thorwald. "I have offered to pay your chief man-bote for each warrior slain causelessly by my carles. And as for your wenches and brats—a warrior should not trouble himself about such trifles."

"Man-bote!" the dark chief 's eyes flashed in fierce anger. "Will silver wash out spilt blood? What is silver to we of the isles? Aye—the women of other races are trifles to you Vikings, I know. But you may find that dealing thus with the girls of the forest people is far from a trifle!"

"Well," broke in Thorwald sharply, "speak your mind and get hence. Your betters have more important affairs than listening to your clamor."

Though the other's eyes burned wolfishly, he made no reply to the insult.

"Go!" he answered, pointing seaward. "Back to Norge or Hell or wherever you came from. If you will take your accursed presence hence, you may go in peace. I, Brulla, a chief of Hjaltland , have spoken."

Thorwald leaned back and laughed deeply; his comrades echoed his laughter and the smoky rafters shook with roars of jeering mirth.

"Why, you fool," sneered the Norseman, "do you think that Vikings ever let go of what they have taken hold? You Picts were fools enough to let us in—now we are the stronger. We of the North rule! Down on your knees, fool, and thank the fates that we allow you to live and serve us, rather than wiping out your verminous tribe altogether! But henceforth ye shall no longer be known as the Free People of Golara—nay, ye shall wear the silver collar of thralldom and men shall know ye as Thorwald's serfs!"

The Pict's face went livid and his self-control vanished.

"Fool!" he snarled in a voice that rang through the great hall like the grating of swords in battle. "You have sealed your doom! You Norse rule all nations, eh? Well, there be some who die, mayhap, but never serve alien masters! Remember this, you blond swine, when the forest comes to life about your walls and you see your skalli crumble in flames and rivers of blood! We of Golara were kings of the world in the long ago when your ancestors ran with wolves in the Arctic forests, and we do not bow the neck to such as you! The hounds of Doom whine at your gates and you shall die, Thorwald Shield-hewer, and you, Aslaf Jarl's-bane, and you, Grimm Snorri's son, and you, Osric, and you, Hakon Skel, and—" The Pict's finger, stabbing at each of the flaxen-haired chiefs in turn, wavered; the man who sat next to Hakon Skel differed strangely from the others. Not that he was a whit less wild and ferocious in his appearance. Indeed, with his dark, scarred features and narrow, cold grey eyes, he appeared more sinister than any of the rest. But he was black haired and clean shaven, and his mail was of the chainmesh type forged by Irish armor-makers instead of the scale mail of the Norse. His helmet, crested with flowing horsehair, lay on the bench beside him.

The Pict passed over him and ended with the pronunciation of doom on the man beyond him—"And you, Hordi Raven."

Aslaf Jarl's-bane, a tall, evil-visaged chief, leaped to his feet: "Thor's blood, Thorwald, are we to listen to the insolence of this jackal? I, who have been the death of a jarl in my day—"

Thorwald silenced him with a gesture. The sea king was a yellow-bearded giant, whose eyes were those of a man used to rule. His every motion and intonation proclaimed the driving power, the ruthless strength of the man.

"You have talked much and loudly, Brulla," he said mildly. "Mayhap you are thirsty."

He extended a brimming drinking horn, and the Pict, thrown off guard by surprize, reached a mechanical hand for it, moving as if against his will. Then with a quick turn of his wrist, Thorwald dashed the contents full in his face. Brulla staggered with a catlike scream of hellish fury, then his sword was out like a flash of summer lightning, and he bounded at his baiter. But his eyes were blinded by the stinging ale and Thorwald's quick-drawn sword parried his blind slashes while the Viking laughed mockingly. Then Aslaf caught up a bench and struck the Pict a terrible blow that stretched him stunned and bleeding at Thorwald's feet. Hakon Skel drew his dagger, but Thorwald halted him.

"I'll have no vermin's blood polluting my skalli floor. Ho, carles, drag this carrion forth."

The men-at-arms sprang forward with brutal eagerness. Brulla, half-senseless and bleeding, was struggling uncertainly to his knees, guided only by the wild beast fighting instinct of his race and his Age. They beat him down with shields, javelin shafts and the flat of axes, showering cruel blows on his defenseless body until he lay still. Then, jeering and jesting, they dragged him through the hall by the heels, arms trailing, and flung him contemptuously from the doorway with a kick and a curse. The Pictish chief lay face down and limply in the reddened dust, blood oozing from his pulped mouth—a symbol of the Viking's ruthless power.

Back at the feasting board, Thorwald drained a jack of foaming ale and laughed.

"I see that we must have a Pict-harrying," quoth he. "We must hunt these vermin out of the wood or they'll be stealing up in the night and loosing their shafts over the stockade."

"It will be a rare hunting!" cried Aslaf with an oath. "We cannot with honor fight such reptiles, but we can hunt them as we hunt wolves—"

"You and your vaporings of honor," sourly growled Grimm Snorri's son. Grimm was old, lean and cautious.

"You speak of honor and vermin," he sneered, "but the stroke of a maddened adder can slay a king. I tell you, Thorwald, you should have used more caution in dealing with these people. They outnumber us ten to one—"

"Naked and cowardly," replied Thorwald carelessly. "One Norseman is worth fifty such. And as for dealing with them, who is it that has been having his carles steal Pictish girls for him? Enough of your maunderings, Grimm. We have other matters to speak of."

Old Grimm muttered in his beard and Thorwald turned to the tall, powerfully made stranger whose dark, inscrutable face had not altered during all the recent events. Thorwald's eyes narrowed slightly and a gleam came into them such as is seen in the eyes of a cat who plays with a mouse before devouring it.

"Partha Mac Othna," said he, playing with the name, "it is strange that so noted a reaver as you must be—though sooth to say, I never heard of your name before—comes to a strange steading in a small boat, alone."

"Not so strange as it would have been had I come with a boatload of my bloodletters," answered the Gael. "Each of them has a half dozen blood feuds with the Norse. Had I brought them ashore, they and your carles would have been at each other's throats spite all you and I could do. But we, though we fight against each other at times, need not be such fools as to forego mutual advantage because of old rivalry."

"True, the Viking folk and the reavers of Ireland are not friends."

"And so, when my galley passed the lower tip of the island," continued the Gael, "I put out in the small boat, alone, with a flag of peace, and arrived here at sundown as you know. My galley continued to Makki Head, and will pick me up at the same point I left it, at dawn."

"So ho," mused Thorwald, chin on fist, "and that matter of my prisoner—speak more fully, Partha Mac Othna."

It seemed to the Gael that the Viking put undue accent on the name, but he answered: "Easy to say. My cousin Nial is captive among the Danes. My clan cannot pay the ransom they ask. It is no question of niggardliness—we have not the price they ask. But word came to us that in a sea fight with the Danes off Helgoland you took a chief prisoner. I wish to buy him from you; we can use his captivity to force an exchange of prisoners with his tribe, perhaps."

"The Danes are ever at war with each other, Loki's curse on them. How know you but that my Dane is an enemy to they who hold your cousin?"

"So much the better," grinned the Gael. "A man will pay more to get a foe in his power than he will pay for the safety of a friend."

Thorwald toyed with his drinking horn. "True enough; you Gaels are crafty. What will you pay for this Dane—Hrut, he calls himself."

"Five hundred pieces of silver."

"His people would pay more."

"Possibly. Or perhaps not a piece of copper. It is a chance we are willing to take. Besides, it will mean a long sea voyage and risks taken to communicate with them. You may have the price I offer at dawn—coin you never made more easily. My clan is not rich. The sea kings of the North and the strong reavers of Erin have harried we lesser wolves to the edge of the seas. But a Dane we must have, and if you are too exorbitant, why we must sail eastward and take one by force of arms."

"That might be easy," mused Thorwald, "Dane-mark is torn by civil wars. Two kings contend against each other—or did, for I hear that Eric had the best of it, and Thorfinn fled the land."

"Aye—so the sea-wanderers say. Thorfinn was the better man, and beloved by the people, but Eric had the support of Jarl Anlaf, the most powerful man among the Danes, not even excepting the kings themselves."

"I heard that Thorfinn fled to the Jutes in a single ship, with a few followers," said Thorwald. "Would that I might have met that ship on the high seas! But this Hrut will serve. I would glut my hate for the Danes on a king, but I am content with the next noblest. And noble this man is, though he wears no title. I thought him a jarl at least, in the sea fight, when my carles lay about him in a heap waist high. Thor's blood, but he had a hungry sword! I made my wolves take him alive—but not for ransom. I might have wrung a greater price from his people than you offer, but more pleasant to me than the chink of gold are the death groans of a Dane."

"I have told you," the Gael spread his hands helplessly, "five hundred pieces of silver, thirty golden torcs, ten Damascus swords we wrested from the brown men of Serkland , and a suit of chain-mail armor I took from the body of a Frankish prince. More I cannot offer."

"Yet I can scarce forego the pleasure of carving the blood-eagle in the back of this Dane," murmured Thorwald, stroking his long, fair beard. "How will you pay this ransom—have you the silver and the rest in your garments?"

The Gael sensed the sneer in the tone but paid no heed.

"Tomorrow at dawn you and I and the Dane will go to the lower point of the island. You may take ten men with you. While you remain on shore with the Dane, I will row out to my ship and bring back the silver and the rest, with ten of my own men. On the beach we will make the exchange. My men will remain in the boats and not even put foot ashore if you deal fairly with me."

"Well said," nodded Thorwald, as if pleased, yet the wolfish instinct of the Gael warned him that events were brewing. There was a gathering tension in the air. From the tail of his eye he saw the chiefs casually crowding nearer him. Grimm Snorri's son's lined, lean face was overcast and his hands twitched nervously. But no change in the Gael's manner showed that he sensed anything out of the ordinary.

"Yet it is but a poor price to pay for a man who will be the means of restoring a great Irish prince to his clan," Thorwald's tone had changed; he was openly baiting the other now. "Besides, I think I had rather carve the blood-eagle on his back after all—and on yours as well—*Cormac Mac Art!*"

He spat the last words as he straightened, and his chiefs surged about him. They were not an instant too soon. They knew by reputation the lightning-like coordination of the famous Irish pirate which made his keen brain realize and his steel thews act while an ordinary man would still be gaping. Before the words were fully out of Thorwald's mouth, Cormac was on him with a volcanic burst of motion that would have shamed a starving wolf. Only one thing saved the Shield-hewer's life; almost as quick as Cormac, he flung himself backward off the feasting bench and the Gael's flying sword killed a carle who stood behind it.

In an instant the flickering of swords made lightning in the smoky vastness of the skalli. It had been Cormac's intention to hack a swift way to the door and freedom, but he was hemmed too closely by bloodlusting warriors.

Scarcely had Thorwald crashed cursing to the floor than Cormac wheeled back to parry the sword of Aslaf Jarl's-bane, who loomed over him like the shadow of Doom. The Gael's reddened blade turned Aslaf 's stroke and, before the Jarl slayer could regain his balance, death flooded his throat beneath Cormac's slicing point.

A backhand stroke shore through the neck cords of a carle who was heaving up a great axe, and at the same instant Hordi Raven struck a blow that was intended to sever Cormac's shoulder bone. But the chain mail turned the Raven's sword edge, and almost simultaneously Hordi was impaled on that glimmering point that seemed everywhere at once, weaving a web of death about the tall Gael. Hakon Skel, hacking at Cormac's unhelmed head, missed by a foot and received a slash across his face, but at that instant the Gael's feet became entangled with the corpses that littered the floor with shields and broken benches.

A concerted rush bore him back across the feasting board, where Thorwald hacked through his mail and gashed the ribs beneath. Cormac struck back desperately, shattering Thorwald's sword and beating the sea king to his knees beneath the shock of the blow, but a club in the hands of a powerful carle crashed down on the Gael's unprotected head, laying the scalp open, and as he crumpled, Grimm Snorri's son struck the sword from his hand. Then, urged by Thorwald, the carles leaped upon him, smothering and crushing the half-senseless reaver by sheer weight of manpower. Even so, their task was not easy, but at last they had torn the steel fingers from the bull throat of one of their number, about which they had blindly locked, and bound the Gael hand and foot with cords not even his dynamic strength could break. The carle he had half-strangled gasped on the floor as they dragged Cormac upright to face the sea king who laughed in his face.

Cormac was a grim sight. He was red stained by the blood both of himself and his foes, and from the gash in his scalp a crimson trickle seeped down to dry on his scarred face. But his wild-beast vitality already asserted itself and there was no hint of a numbed brain in the cold eyes that returned Thorwald's domineering stare.

"Thor's blood!" swore the sea king. "I'm glad your comrade Wulfhere Hausakliufr—the Skull-splitter—was not with you. I have heard of your prowess as a killer, but to appreciate it, one must see for himself. In the last three minutes I have seen more weapon-play than I have seen in battles that lasted hours. By Thor, you ranged through my carles like a hunger-maddened wolf through a flock of sheep! Are all your race like you?"

The reaver deigned no reply.

"You are such a man as I would have for comrade," said Thorwald frankly. "I will forget all old feuds if you will join me." He spoke like a man who does not expect his wish to be granted.

Cormac's reply was merely a glimmer of cold scorn in his icy eyes.

"Well," said Thorwald, "I did not expect you to accede to my demand, and that spells your doom, because I cannot let such a foe to my race go free."

Then Thorwald laughed: "Your weapon-play has not been exaggerated, but your craft has. You fool—to match wits with a Viking! I knew you as soon as I laid eyes on you, though I had not seen you in years. Where on the North Seas is such a man as you, with your height, shoulder breadth—and scarred face? I had all prepared for you, before you had ceased telling me your first lie. Bah! A chief of Irish reavers. Aye—once, years ago. But now I know you for Cormac Mac Art an Cliuin, which is to say the Wolf, right-hand man of Wulfhere Hausakliufr, a Viking of the Danes. Aye, Wulfhere Hausakliufr, hated of my race.

"You desired my prisoner Hrut to trade for your cousin! Bah! I know you of old, by reputation at least. And I saw you once, years ago—

you came ashore with a lie on your lips to spy out my steading, to take report of my strength and weaknesses to Wulfhere, that you and he might steal upon me some night and burn the skalli over my head.

"Well, now you can tell me—how many ships has Wulfhere and where is he?"

Cormac merely laughed, a remarkably hard contemptuous laugh that enraged Thorwald. The sea king's beard bristled and his eyes grew cruel.

"You will not answer me, eh?" he swore. "Well, it does not matter. Whether Wulfhere went on to Makki Head or not, three of my dragon-ships will be waiting for him off the Point at dawn. Then mayhap when I carve the blood-eagle on Hrut I will have Wulfhere's back also for my sport—and you may look on and see it well done, ere I hang you from the highest tree on Golara. To the cell with him!"

As the carles dragged Cormac away, the Gael heard the querulous, uneasy voice of Grimm Snorri's son raised in petulant dispute with his chief. Outside the door he noted, no limp body lay in the red-stained dust. Brulla had either recovered consciousness and staggered away or been carried away by his tribesmen. These Picts were hard as cats to kill, Cormac knew, having fought their Caledonian cousins. A beating such as Brulla had received would have left the average man a crippled wreck, but the Pict would probably be fully recovered in a few hours, if no bones had been broken.

Thorwald Shield-hewer's steading fronted on a small bay, on the beach of which were drawn up six long, lean ships, shield railed and dragon beaked. As was usual, the steading consisted of a great hall—the skalli—about which were grouped smaller buildings—stables, storehouses and the huts of the carles. Around the whole stretched a high stockade, built, like the houses, of heavy logs. The logs of the stockade were some ten feet high, set deep in the earth and sharpened on the top. There were loopholes here and there for arrows and at regularly spaced intervals, shelves on the inner side on which the defenders might stand and strike down over the wall at the attackers. Beyond the stockade, the tall dark forest loomed menacingly.

The stockade was in the form of a horseshoe with the open side seaward. The horns ran out into the shallow bay, protecting the dragon-ships drawn up on the beach. An inner stockade ran straight across in front of the steading, from one horn to the other, separating the beach from the skalli. Men might swim out around the ends of the main stockade and gain the beach but they would still be blocked from the steading itself.

Thorwald's holdings seemed well protected, but vigilance was lax. Still, the Shetlands did not swarm with sea rovers then as they did at a later date. The few Norse holdings there were like Thorwald's—mere pirate camps from which the Vikings swooped down on the Hebrides, the Orkneys and Britain, where the Saxons were trampling a fading Roman-Celtic civilization—and on Gaul, Spain and the Mediterranean.

Thorwald did not ordinarily expect a raid from the sea and Cormac had seen with what contempt the Vikings looked on the natives of the Shetlands. Wulfhere and his Danes were different; outlawed even among their own people, they ranged even farther than Thorwald himself, and they were keen-beaked birds of prey, whose talons tore all alike.

Cormac was dragged to a small hut built against the stockade at a point some distance from the skalli and in this he was chained. The door slammed behind him and he was left to his meditations.

The Gael's shallow cuts had ceased to bleed, and inured to wounds—an iron man in an Age of iron—he gave them hardly a thought. Stung vanity bothered him; how easily he had slipped into Thorwald's trap, he whom kings had either cursed or blessed for his guile! Next time he would not be so overconfident, he mused; and a next time he was determined there should be. He did not worry overmuch about Wulfhere, even when he heard the shouts, scraping of slides and later the clack of oars that announced that three of Thorwald's longships were under way. Let them sneak to the Point and wait there till the dawn of Doom's Day! Neither he nor Wulfhere had been such utter fools as to trust themselves in the power of Thorwald's stronger force. Wulfhere had but one ship and some eighty men. They and the ship were even now hidden securely in a forest-screened cove on the other side of the island, which was less than a mile wide at this point. There was little chance of their being discovered by Thorwald's men and the risk of being spied out by some Pict was a chance that must be taken. If Wulfhere had followed their plan, he had run in after dark, feeling his way; there was no real reason why either Pict or Norseman should be lurking about. The shore about the cove was mainly wild, high cliffs, rugged and uninviting; moreover, Cormac had heard that the Picts ordinarily avoided that part of the island because of some superstitious reason. There were ancient stone columns on the cliffs and a grim altar that hinted of ghastly rites in bygone ages.

Wulfhere would lurk there until Cormac returned to him, or until a smoke drifting up from the Point assured him that Thorwald was on hand with the prisoner and meaning no treachery. Cormac had carefully said nothing about the signal that was to bring Wulfhere, though he had not expected to be recognized for what he was. Thorwald had been wrong when he assumed that the prisoner had been used only for a blind. The Gael had lied about himself and about his reason for wishing the custody of Hrut, but it was true when he had said that it was news of the Dane's captivity that brought him to Golara.

Cormac heard the cautious oars die away in silence. He heard the clash of arms and the shouts of the carles. Then these noises faded, all but the steady tramp of sentries, guarding against a night attack.

It must be nearly midnight, Cormac decided, glancing up at the stars gleaming through his small, heavily barred window. He was chained close to the dirt floor and could not even rise to a sitting posture. His back was against the rear wall of the hut, which was formed by the stockade, and as he reclined there, he thought he heard a sound that was not of the sighing of the night wind through the mighty trees without. Slowly he writhed about and found himself staring through a tiny aperture between two of the upright logs.

The moon had already set; in the dim starlight he could make out the vague outline of great, gently waving branches against the black wall of the forest. Was there a subtle whispering and rustling among those shadows that was not of the wind and the leaves? Faint and intangible as the suggestion of nameless evil, the almost imperceptible noises ran the full length of the stockade. The whole night seemed full of ghostly murmurings—as if the midnight forest were stirring and moving its darksome self, like a shadowy monster coming to uncanny life. "When the forest comes to life," the Pict had said—

Cormac heard, within the stockade, one carle call to another. His rough voice re-echoed in the whispering silence.

"Thor's blood, the trolls must be out tonight! How the wind whispers through the trees."

Even the dull-witted carle felt a hint of evil in the darkness and shadows. Gluing his eye to the crack, Cormac strove to pierce the darkness. The Gaelic pirate's faculties were as much keener than the average man's as a wolf 's are keener than a hog's; his eyes were like a cat's in the dark. But in that utter blackness he could see nothing but the vague forms of the first fringe of trees. Wait!

Something took shape in the shadows. A long line of figures moved like ghosts just under the shadows of the trees; a shiver passed along Cormac's spine. Surely these creatures were elves, evil demons of the forest. Short and mightily built, half stooping, one behind the other, they passed in almost utter silence. In the shadows their silence and their crouching positions made them monstrous travesties on men. Racial memories, half-lost in the misty gulfs of consciousness, came stealing back to claw with icy fingers at Cormac's heart. He did not fear them as a man fears a human foe; it was the horror of world-old, ancestral memories that gripped him—dim felt, chaotic dream-recollections of darker Ages and grimmer days when primitive men battled for supremacy in a new world.

For these Picts were a remnant of a lost tribe—the survivals of an elder epoch—last outposts of a dark Stone Age empire that crumbled before the bronze swords of the first Celts. Now these survivors, thrust out on the naked edges of the world they had once ruled, battled grimly for their existence.

There could be no accurate counting of them because of the darkness and the swiftness of their slinking gait, but Cormac reckoned that at least four hundred passed his line of vision. That band alone was equal to Thorwald's full strength and far outnumbered the men left in the steading now, since Thorwald had sent out three of his ships. The skulking figures passed as they had come, soundless, leaving no trace behind, like ghosts of the night.

Cormac waited in a silence that had become suddenly tense. Then without warning the night was shattered by one fearful death-yell! Pandemonium broke loose and a mad hell of sound burst on the air. And now the forest came to life! From all sides stocky figures broke cover and swarmed on the barricades. A lurid glare shed a ghastly light over all and Cormac tore savagely at his chains, wild with excitement. Monstrous events were occurring without, and here he was, chained like a sheep for the slaughter! He cursed incredibly.

The Norsemen were holding the wall; the clash of steel rose deafeningly in the night, the hum of arrows filled the air, and the deep fierce shouts of the Vikings vied with the hellish wolf-howling of the Picts. Cormac could not see, but he sensed the surging of human waves against the stockade, the plying of spears and axes, the reeling retreat and the renewed onset. The Picts, he knew, were without mail and indifferently armed. It was very possible that the limited force of Vikings could hold the stockade until Thorwald returned with the rest, as he would assuredly do when he saw the flame—but whence came the flame?

Someone was fumbling at the door. It swung open and Cormac saw the lean shambling frame and livid bearded face of Grimm Snorri's son limned against the red glare. In one hand he held a helmet and a sword Cormac recognized as his own, in the other a bunch of keys which jangled as his hand shook.

"We are all dead men!" squawked the old Viking. "I warned Thorwald! The woods are alive with Picts! There are thousands of them!

We can never hold the stockade until Thorwald returns! He is doomed, too, for the Picts will cut him off when he comes into the bay and feather his men with arrows before they can come to grips! They have swum around the outer horns of the stockade and set the three remaining galleys on fire! Osric would run like a fool with a dozen carles to save the ships and he had scarcely gotten outside the gates before he was down with a score of black shafts through him and his men were cut off and hemmed in by a hundred howling demons! Not a man of them escaped, and we barely had time to shut the gates when the whole screaming mob was battering at them!

"We have slain them by the scores, but for every one that drops, three spring to take his place. I have seen more Picts tonight than I knew were on Golara—or in the world. Cormac, you are a bold man; you have a ship somewhere off the isle—swear to save me and I will set you free! Mayhap the Picts will not harm you—that devil Brulla did not name you in his death rune.

"If any man can save me, it is you! I will show you where Hrut is hidden and we'll take him with us, and—" he threw a quick glance over his shoulder toward the roar of battle beachward, and went white. "Thor's blood!" he screamed. "The gates have given way and the Picts are inside the inner stockade!"

The howling rose to a crescendo of demoniac passion and fiendish exultation.

"Loose me, you gibbering fool!" raged Cormac, tearing at his chains. "You've time enough for babbling—"

Chattering with fear, Grimm Snorri's son stepped inside the hut, fumbling with the keys—even as his foot crossed the threshold a lean shape raced swift and silent as a wolf out of the flame-shot shadows. A dark arm hooked about the old Viking's withered neck, jerking his chin up. One fearful shriek burst from his writhing lips to break short in a ghastly gurgle as a keen edge whipped across his leathery throat.

Over the twitching corpse of his victim, the Pict eyed Cormac Mac Art, and the Gael stared back, expecting death but unafraid. Then in the glare of the burning ships, that made the cell hut as light as day, Cormac saw that the slayer was the chief, Brulla.

"You are he who slew Aslaf and Hordi. I watched through the door of the skalli before I dragged myself away to the forests," said the Pict, as calmly as though no inferno of combat was raging without. "I told my people of you and warned them not to harm you, if you still lived. You hate Thorwald as well as I. I will free you; glut your vengeance; soon will Thorwald return in his ships and we will cut his throat. There shall be no more Norse on Golara. All the free people of the isles hereabouts are gathering to aid us, and Thorwald is doomed!"

He bent over the Gael and released him. Cormac sprang erect, a fresh fire of confidence surging through his veins. He snatched his helmet with its flowing horsehair crest, and his long straight sword. He also took the keys from Brulla.

"Know you where was prisoned the Dane called Hrut?" he asked, as they stepped through the door. Brulla pointed across a seething whirlpool of flame and hacking swords.

"The smoke obscures the hut at present, but it lies next the storehouse on that side."

Cormac nodded and set off at a run. Where Brulla went he neither knew nor cared. The Picts had fired stable, storehouse and skalli, as well as the ships on the beach outside the inner stockade. About the skalli and here and there close to the stockade, which was also burning in a score of places, stubborn fighting went on, as the handful of survivors sold their lives with all the desperate ferocity of their breed. There were, indeed, thousands of the short, dark men, who swarmed about each tall blond warrior in a slashing, hammering mass. The heavy swords of the mailed Vikings took fearful toll, but the smaller men lashed in with a wild beast frenzy that made naught of wounds, and pulled down their giant foes by sheet weight of numbers. Once on the ground, the stabbing swords of the dark men did their work. Screams of death and yells of fury rent the flame-reddened skies, but as Cormac ran swiftly toward the storehouse, he heard no pleas for mercy. Driven to madness by countless outrages, the Picts were glutting their vengeance to the uttermost and the Norse people neither looked nor asked for mercy.

Blond-haired women, cursing and spitting in the faces of their killers, felt the knife jerked across their white throats, and Norse babes were butchered with no more compunction than their sires had shown in the slaughter—for sport—of Pictish infants.

Cormac took no part in this holocaust. None of these people was his friend—either race would cut his throat if the chance arose. As he ran he used his sword merely to parry chance cuts that fell on him from Pict and Norseman alike, and so swiftly he moved between staggering clumps of gasping, slashing men, that he ran his way across the open space without serious opposition. He reached the hut and a few seconds' work with the lock opened the heavy door. He had not come too soon; sparks from the burning storehouse nearby had caught on the hut thatch and already the interior was full of smoke. Through this Cormac groped his way toward a figure he could barely make out in the corner. There was a jangling of chains and a voice with a Danish accent spoke: "Slay me, in the name of Loki; better a sword thrust than this accursed smoke!"

Cormac knelt and fumbled at his chains. "I come to free you, oh Hrut," he gasped. A moment later he dragged the astonished warrior to his feet and together they staggered out of the hut, just as the roof fell in. Drawing in great draughts of air, Cormac turned and stared curiously at his companion—a splendid, red-maned giant of a man, with the bearing of a noble. He was half naked, ragged and unkempt from weeks of captivity, but his eyes gleamed with an unconquerable light.

"A sword!" he cried, those eyes blazing as they swept the scene. "A sword, good sir, in the name of Thor! Here is a goodly brawl and we stand idle!"

Cormac stooped and tore a reddened blade from the stiffening hand of an arrow-feathered Norseman.

"Here is a sword, Hrut," he growled, "but for whom will you strike—the Norse who have kept you cooped like a caged wolf and would have slain you—or the Picts who will cut your throat because of the color of your hair?"

"There can be but little choice," answered the Dane. "I heard the screams of women—"

"The women are all dead," grunted the Gael. "We cannot help them now; we must save ourselves. It is the night of the wolf—and the wolves are biting!"

"I would like to cross swords with Thorwald," the big Dane hesitated as Cormac drew him toward the flaming barrier.

"Not now, not now," the reaver rasped. "Bigger game is afoot, Thor—Hrut! Later we will come back and finish what the Picts leave—just now we have more than ourselves to think about, for if I know Wulfhere Skull-splitter he is already marching through the woods at double-quick time!"

The stockade was in places a smoldering mass of coals; Cormac and his companion battered a way through and, even as they stepped into the shadows of the trees outside, three figures rose about them and set upon them with bestial howls. Cormac shouted a warning, but it was useless. A whirling blade was at his throat and he had to strike to save himself. Turning from the corpse he had been loath to make, he saw Hrut, bestriding the mangled body of one Pict, take the barbed sword of the other in his left arm and split the wielder's skull with an overhand stroke.

Cursing, the Gael sprang forward. "Are you badly hurt?" Blood was gushing from a deep wound in Hrut's mighty arm.

"A scratch," the Dane's eyes blazed with the battle light. But despite his protests Cormac tore a strip from his own garments and bound the arm so as to staunch the flow of blood.

"Here, help me drag these bodies under the brush," growled the reaver. "I hated to strike—but when they saw your red beard it was our lives or theirs. I think Brulla would see our point of view, but if the rest find we killed their brothers neither Brulla nor the devil can keep their swords from our throats."

This done—"Listen!" commanded Hrut. The roar of battle had dwindled in the main to a crackle and roar of flames and the hideous and triumphant yelling of the Picts. Only in a single room in the flaming skalli, yet untouched by the fire, a handful of Vikings still kept up a stubborn defense. Through the noise of the fire there sounded a rhythmic clack-clack-clack!

"Thorwald is returning!" exclaimed Cormac, springing back to the edge of the forest to peer over the ruins of the stockade. Into the bay swept a single dragon-ship. The long ash oars drove her plunging through the water and from her rowers and from the men massed on poop and gunwale rose a roar of deep-toned ferocity as they saw the smoking ruins of the steading and the mangled bodies of their people. From the burning skalli came an echoing shout. In the smoldering glare that turned the bay to a gulf of blood, Cormac and Hrut saw the hawk face of Hakon Skel where he stood on the poop. But where were the other two ships? Cormac thought he knew and a smile of grim appreciation crossed his somber face.

Now the dragon-ship was sweeping in to the beach and hundreds of screaming Picts were wading out to meet it. Waist deep in water, holding their heavy black bows high to keep the cords dry, they loosed their arrows and a storm of shafts swept the dragon-ship from stem to stern. Full into the teeth of the deadliest gale it had ever faced the dragon-ship drove, while men went down in windrows along the gunwales, transfixed by the long black shafts that rent through linden-wood buckler and scale-mail armor to pierce the flesh beneath.

The rest crouched behind their shields and rowed and steered as best they could. Now the keel grated on the water-flooded sand and the swarming savages closed about her. By the hundreds they scrambled up the sides, the stern and the arching prow, while others maintained a steady fire from the water and the beach. Their marksmanship was almost uncanny. Flying between two slashing Picts a long shaft would strike down a Norseman. But when it came to handgrips, the advantage was immensely with the Vikings. Their giant stature, their armor and long swords, and their position on the gunwales above their foes made them for the moment invincible.

Swords and axes rose and fell, spattering blood and brains, and stocky shapes dropped writhing from the sides of the galley to sink like stones. The water about the ship grew thick with dead and Cormac caught his breath as he realized the lavishness with which the naked Picts were spending their lives. But soon he heard their chiefs shouting to them and he realized, as the attackers drew sullenly away, that their leaders were shouting for them to fall back and pick off the Vikings at long range.

The Vikings soon realized that also. Hakon Skel dropped with an arrow through his brain and with yells of fury the Norsemen began leaping from their ship into the water, in one desperate attempt to close with their foes and take toll in death.

The Picts accepted the challenge. About each Norseman closed a dozen Picts and the bay along the beach seethed and eddied with battle. The waves grew red as blood and corpses floated thick or littered the bottom, tripping the feet and clogging the arms of the living. The warriors penned in the skalli sallied forth to die with their tribesmen.

Then what Cormac had looked for occurred. A deep-chested roar thundered above the fury of the fight, and from the woods that fringed the bay burst Thorwald Shield-hewer, with the crews of two dragon-ships at his back. Cormac knew that, guessing what had occurred, he had sent the other ship on to draw the Picts out and give him time to land below the bay and march through the forest with the rest of his men.

Now in a solid formation, shield locking shield, they swept from the woods along the shore and bore down the beach toward their foes. With howls of unquenchable fury, the Picts turned on them with a rain of shafts and a headlong charge of stocky bodies and stabbing blades. But the arrows in the main glanced from the close-lapping shields and the mob-like rush met a solid wall of iron. But with the same desperation they had shown all during the fight, the Picts hurled charge after charge on the shield wall. It was a living sea that broke in red waves on that iron bulwark. The ground grew thick under foot with corpses, not all Pictish. But as often as a Norseman fell, his comrades locked their great shields close as ever, trampling the fallen under foot. No longer did the Vikings surge forward, but they stood like a solid rock and took not a single backward step. The wings of their wedge-shaped formation were forced inward as the Picts entirely surrounded them, until it was more like a square, facing all ways. And like a square of stone and iron it stood, and all the wild, blind charges of the Picts failed to shake it, though they hurled their bare breasts against the steel until their corpses formed a wall over which the living clambered.

Then suddenly, apparently without warning, they broke and fled in all directions, some across the flame-lit space of the steading, some into the forest. With yells of triumph the Vikings broke the formation and plunged after them, though Cormac saw Thorwald screaming frantic orders and beating at his men with the flat of his reddened sword. A trick! Cormac knew it as well as Thorwald, but the blind fighting frenzy of the carles betrayed them as their foes had guessed. The moment they streamed out loosely in pursuit, the Picts turned howling and a dozen Vikings went down before a hail of arrows. Before the rest could reform their position they were surrounded singly and in struggling clumps, and the work of death began. From a single massed battle, the combat became a score of single skirmishes on the beach—where the survivors of the dragon-ship had made their way—before the skalli's embers and in the fringe of the forest.

And suddenly as from a dream Cormac woke and cursed himself.

"By the blood of the gods, what a fool I am! Are we boys who have never seen a battle, to stand here gaping when we should be legging it through the forest?"

He was forced to fairly drag Hrut away and the two ran swiftly through the forest, hearing on all sides the clangor of arms and the shouts of death. The battle had spilled over into the forest and that grim and darksome wood was the scene of many a bloody deed. But Cormac and Hrut, warned by the sounds, managed to keep clear of such struggles, though once vague figures leaped at them from the shadows and, in the blind brief whirl of battle that followed, they never knew whether it was Picts or Norsemen who fell before their swords.

Then the sounds of conflict were behind them and in front sounded the tramp of many men. Hrut stopped short, gripping his red-stained sword, but Cormac pulled him on.

"Men marching in time; they can be none but Wulfhere's wolves!"

The next instant they burst into a glade, dimly lighted by the first whiteness of dawn, and from the opposite side strode a band of red-bearded giants, whose chief, looking like a very god of war, bellowed a welcome:

"Cormac! Thor's blood, it seems we've been marching through these accursed woods forever! When I saw the glow above the trees and heard the yelling I brought every carle on the ship, for I knew not but that you were burning and looting Thorwald's steading single-handed! What is forward—and who is this?"

"This is Hrut—whom we sought," answered Cormac. "Hell and the red whirlpools of war are what is forward—there's blood on your axe!"

"Aye—we had to hack our way through a swarm of small, dark fellows—Picts I believe you call 'em."

Cormac cursed. "We'll pile up a blood score that even Brulla can't answer for—"

"Well," grumbled the giant, "the woods are full of them, and we heard them howling like wolves behind us—"

"I had thought all would be at the steading," commented Hrut.

Cormac shook his head. "Brulla spoke of a gathering of clans; they have come from all the isles of the Hjaltlands and probably landed on all sides of the island—listen!"

The clamor of battle grew louder as the fighters penetrated deeper into the mazes of the forest, but from the way Wulfhere and his Vikings had come, there sounded a long-drawn yell like a pack of running wolves, swiftly rising higher and higher.

"Close ranks!" yelled Cormac, paling, and the Danes had barely time to lock their shields before the pack was upon them. Bursting from the thick trees a hundred Picts whose swords were yet unstained broke like a tidal wave on the shields of the Danes.

Cormac, thrusting and slashing like a fiend, shouted to Wulfhere: "Hold them hard—I must find Brulla. He will tell them we are foes of Thorwald and allow us to depart in peace!"

All but a handful of the original attackers were down, trodden under foot and snarling in their death throes. Cormac leaped from the shelter of the overlapping shields and darted into the forest. Searching for the Pictish chief in that battle-tortured forest was little short of madness, but it was their one lone chance. Seeing the fresh Picts coming up from behind them had told Cormac that he and his comrades would probably have to fight their way across the whole island to regain their galley. Doubtless these were warriors from some island lying to the east, who had just landed on Golara's eastern coast.

If he could find Brulla—he had not gone a score of paces past the glade when he stumbled over two corpses, locked in a death grapple. One was Thorwald Shield-hewer. The other was Brulla. Cormac stared at them and as the wolf yell of the Picts rose about him, his skin crawled. Then he sprang up and ran back to the glade where he had left the Danes.

Wulfhere leaned on his great axe and stared at the corpses at his feet. His men stolidly held their position.

"Brulla is dead," snapped the Gael. "We must aid ourselves. These Picts will cut our throats if they can, and the gods know they have no cause to love a Viking. Our only chance is to get back to our ship if we can. But that is a slim chance indeed, for I doubt not but that the woods are full of the savages. We can never keep the shield-wall position among the trees, but—"

"Think of another plan, Cormac," said Wulfhere grimly, pointing to the east with his great axe. There a lurid glow was visible among the trees and a hideous medley of howling came faintly to their ears. There was but one answer to that red glare.

"They've found and fired our ship," muttered Cormac. "By the blood of the gods, Fate's dice are loaded against us."

Suddenly a thought came to him.

"After me! Keep close together and hew your way through, if needs be, but follow me close!"

Without question they followed him through the corpse-strewn forest, hearing on each hand the sound of fighting men, until they stood at the forest fringe and gazed over the crumbled stockade at the ruins of the steading. By merest chance no body of Picts had opposed their swift march, but behind them rose a frightful and vengeful clamor as a band of them came upon the corpse-littered glade the Danes had just left.

No fighting was going on among the steading's ruins. The only Norsemen in sight were mangled corpses. The fighting had swept back into the forest whither the close-pressed Vikings had retreated or been driven. From the incessant clashing of steel within its depths, those who yet remained alive were giving a good account of themselves. Under the trees where bows were more or less useless, the survivors might defend themselves for hours, though, with the island swarming with Picts, their ultimate fate was certain.

Three or four hundred tribesmen, weary of battle at last, had left the fighting to their fresher tribesmen and were salvaging what loot they could from the embers of the storehouses.

"Look!" Cormac's sword pointed to the dragon-ship whose prow, driven in the sands, held her grounded, though her stern was afloat. "In a moment we will have a thousand yelling demons on our backs. There lies our one chance, wolves—Hakon Skel's *Raven*. We must hack through and gain it, shove it free and row off before the Picts can stop us. Some of us will die, and we may all die, but it's our only chance!"

The Vikings said nothing, but their fierce light eyes blazed and many grinned wolfishly. Touch and go! Life or death on the toss of the dice! That was a Viking's only excuse for living!

"Lock shields!" roared Wufihere. "Close ranks! The flying wedge formation—Hrut in the center."

"What—!" began Hrut angrily, but Cormac shoved him unceremoniously between the mailed ranks.

"You have no armor," he growled impatiently. "Ready old wolf? Then charge, and the gods choose the winners!"

Like an avalanche the steel-tipped wedge shot from the trees and raced toward the beach. The Picts looting the ruins turned with howls of amazement, and a straggling line barred the way to the water's edge. But without slacking gait the flying shield-wall struck the Pictish line, buckled it, crumpled it, hacked it down and trampled it under, and over its red ruins rushed upon the beach.

Here the formation was unavoidably broken. Waist deep in water, tripping among corpses, harried by the rain of arrows that now poured upon them from the beach, the Vikings gained the dragon-ship and swarmed up its sides, while a dozen giants set their shoulders against the prow to push it off the sands. Half of them died in the attempt, but the titanic efforts of the rest triumphed and the galley began to give way.

The Danes were the bowmen among the Viking races. Thirty of the eighty-odd warriors who followed Wulfhere wore heavy bows and quivers of long arrows strapped to their backs. As many of these as could be spared from oars and sweeps now unslung their weapons and directed their shafts on the Picts wading into the water to attack the men at the prow. In the first light of the rising sun the Danish shafts did fearful execution and the advance wavered and fell back. Arrows fell all about the craft and some found their marks, but crouching beneath their shields the warriors toiled mightily, and soon, though it seemed like hours, the dragon-ship rolled and wallowed free, the men in the water leaped and caught at chains and gunwale, and the long oars drove her out into the bay, just as a howling horde of wolfish figures swept out of the woods and down the beach. Their arrows fell in a rain, rattling harmlessly from shield rail and hull as the *Raven* shot toward the open sea.

"Touch and go!" roared Wulfhere with a great laugh, smiting Cormac terrifically between the shoulders. Hrut shook his head. To his humiliated anger, a big carle had been told off to keep a shield over him, during the fight.

"Many brave warriors are dying in yonder woods. It pains me to desert them thus, though they are our foes and would have put me to death."

Cormac shrugged his shoulders. "I, too, would have aided them had I seen a way. But we could have accomplished naught by remaining and dying with them. By the blood of the gods, what a night this has been! Golara is rid of her Vikings, but the Picts paid a red price! All of Thorwald's four hundred are dead now or soon will be, but not less than a thousand Picts have died outright in the steading and the gods only know how many more in the forest."

Wulfhere glanced at Hrut where he stood on the poop, outstretched hand on the sword whose reddened point rested on the deal planking. Unkempt, bloodstained, tattered, wounded, yet still his kingly carriage was unabated.

"And now that you have rescued me so boldly against incredible odds," said he, "what would you have of me besides my eternal gratitude, which you already have?"

Wulfhere did not reply; turning to the men who rested on their oars to gaze eagerly and expectantly up at the group on the poop, the Viking chief lifted his red axe and bellowed: "Skoal, wolves! Yell hail for Thorfinn Eagle-crest, king of Dane-mark!"

A thunderous roar went up to the blue of the morning skies that startled the wheeling seagulls. The tattered king gasped in amazement, glancing quickly from one to the other, not yet certain of his status.

"And now that you have recognized me," said he, "am I guest or prisoner?"

Cormac grinned. "We traced you from Skagen, whence you fled in a single ship to Helgoland, and learned there that Thorwald Shield-hewer had taken captive a Dane with the bearing of a king. Knowing you would conceal your identity, we did not expect him to know that he had a king of the Danes in his hands.

"Well, King Thorfinn, this ship and our swords are yours. We be outlaws, both from our own lands. You cannot alter my status in Erin, but you can inlaw Wulfhere and make Danish ports free to us."

"Gladly would I do this, my friends," said Thorfinn, deeply moved. "But how can I aid my friends, who cannot aid myself? I, too, am an outcast, and my cousin Eric rules the Danes."

"Only until we set foot on Danish soil!" exclaimed Cormac. "Oh, Thorfinn, you fled too soon, but who can foresee the future? Even as you put to sea like a hunted pirate, the throne was rocking under Eric's feet. While you lay captive on Thorwald's dragon-ship, Jarl Anlaf fell in battle with the Jutes and Eric lost his greatest supporter. Without Anlaf, his rule will crumble overnight and hosts will flock to your banner!"

Thorfinn's eyes lighted with a wondrous gleam. He threw his head back as a lion throws back his mane and flung up his reddened sword into the eye of the rising sun.

"Skoal!" he cried. "Head for Dane-mark, my friends, and may Thor fill our sail!"

"Aim her prow eastward, carles," roared Wulfhere to the men at the sweeps. "We go to set a new king on the throne of Dane-mark!"

Delenda Est

"It's no empire, I tell you! It's only a sham. Empire? Pah! Pirates, that's all we are!" It was Hunegais, of course, the ever moody and gloomy, with his braided black locks and drooping moustaches betraying his Slavonic blood. He sighed gustily, and the Falernian wine slopped over the rim of the jade goblet clenched in his brawny hand, to stain his purple, gilt-embroidered tunic. He drank noisily, after the manner of a horse, and returned with melancholy gusto to his original complaint.

"What have we done in Africa? Destroyed the big landholders and the priests; set ourselves up as landlords. Who works the land? Vandals? Not at all! The same men who worked it under the Romans. We've merely stepped into Roman shoes. We levy taxes and rents, and are forced to defend the land from the accursed Berbers. Our weakness is in our numbers. We can't amalgamate with the people; we'd be absorbed. We can't make allies and subjects out of them; all we can do is maintain a sort of military prestige—we are a small body of aliens sitting in castles and, for the present, enforcing our rule over a big native population, who, it's true, hates us no worse than they hated the Romans, but—"

"Some of that hate could be done away with," interrupted Athaulf. He was younger than Hunegais, clean shaven, and not unhandsome; and his manners were less primitive. He was a Suevi, whose youth had been spent as a hostage in the East Roman court. "They are orthodox; if we could bring ourselves to renounce Arian—"

"No!" Hunegais' heavy jaws came together with a snap that would have splintered lesser teeth than his. His dark eyes flamed with the fanaticism that was, among all the Teutons, the exclusive possession of his race. "Never! We are the masters! It is theirs to submit—not ours. We *know* the truth of Arian; if the miserable Africans cannot realize their mistake, they must be made to see it—by torch and sword and rack, if necessary!" Then his eyes dulled again, and with another gusty sigh from the depths of his belly, he groped for the wine jug.

"In a hundred years the Vandal kingdom will be a memory," he predicted. "All that holds it together now is the will of Genseric." He pronounced it Geiserich.

The individual so named laughed, leaned back in his carven ebony chair, and stretched out his muscular legs before him. Those were the legs of a horseman; but their owner had exchanged the saddle for the deck of a war galley. Within a generation, he had turned a race of horsemen into a race of sea rovers. He was the king of a race whose name had already become a term for destruction; and he was the possessor of the finest brain in the known world.

Born on the banks of the Danube and grown to manhood on that long trek westward, when the drifts of the nations crushed over the Roman palisades, he had brought to the crown forged for him in Spain all the wild wisdom the times could teach, in the feasting of swords and the surge and crush of races. His wild riders had swept the spears of the Roman rulers of Spain into oblivion. When the Visigoths and the Romans joined hands and began to look southward, it was the intrigues of Genseric which brought Attila's scarred Huns swarming westward, tusking the flaming horizons with their myriad lances. Attila was dead, now, and none knew where lay his bones and his treasures, guarded by the ghosts of five hundred slaughtered slaves; his name thundered around the world; but in his day he had been but one of the pawns moved resistlessly by the hand of the Vandal king.

And when, after Chalons, the Gothic hosts moved southward through the Pyrenees, Genseric had not waited to be crushed by superior numbers. Men still cursed the name of Boniface, who called on Genseric to aid him against his rival, Aetius, and opened the Vandal's road to Africa. His reconciliation with Rome had been too late; vain as the courage with which he had sought to undo what he had done. Boniface died on a Vandal spear, and a new kingdom rose in the south. And now Aetius, too, was dead, and the great war galleys of the Vandals were moving northward, the long oars dipping and flashing silver in the starlight, the great vessels heeling and rocking to the lift of the waves.

And in the cabin of the foremost galley, Genseric listened to the conversation of his captains, and smiled gently as he combed his unruly yellow beard with his muscular fingers. There was in his veins no trace of the Scythic blood which set his race somewhat aside from the other Teutons, from the long ago when scattered steppes riders, drifting westward before the conquering Sarmatians, had come among the people dwelling on the upper reaches of the Elbe. Genseric was pure German; of medium height, with a magnificent sweep of shoulders and chest, and a massive, corded neck, his frame promised as much of physical vitality as his wide blue eyes reflected mental vigor.

He was the strongest man in the known world, and he was a pirate—the first of the Teutonic sea raiders whom men later called Vikings; but his domain of conquest was not the Baltic nor the blue North Sea, but the sunlit shores of the Mediterranean.

"And the will of Genseric," he laughed, in reply to Hunegais' last remark, "is that we drink and feast and let tomorrow take care of itself."

"So you say!" snorted Hunegais, with the freedom that still existed among the barbarians. "When did you ever let a tomorrow take care of itself? You plot and plot, not for tomorrow alone, but for a thousand tomorrows to come! You need not masquerade with *us!* We are not Romans to be fooled into thinking *you* a fool—as Boniface was!"

"Aetius was no fool," muttered Thrasamund.

"But he's dead, and we are sailing on Rome," answered Hunegais, with the first sign of satisfaction he had yet evinced. "Alaric didn't get all the loot, thank God! And I'm glad Attila lost his nerve at the last minute—the more plunder for us."

"Attila remembered Chalons," drawled Athaulf. "There is something about Rome that lives—by the saints, it is strange. Even when the empire seems most ruined—torn, befouled, and tattered—some part of it springs into life again. Stilicho, Theodosius, Aetius—who can tell? Tonight in Rome there may be a man sleeping who will overthrow us all."

Hunegais snorted and hammered on the wine-stained board.

"Rome is as dead as the white mare I rode at the taking of Carthage! We have but to stretch our hands and grasp the plunder of her!"

"There was a great general once who thought as much," said Thrasamund drowsily. "A Carthaginian, too, by God! I have forgotten his name. But he beat the Romans at every turn. Cut, slash, that was his way!"

"Well," remarked Hunegais, "he must have lost at last, or he would have destroyed Rome."

"That's so!" ejaculated Thrasamund.

"We are not Carthaginians," laughed Genseric. "And who said aught of plundering Rome? Are we not merely sailing to the imperial city in answer to the appeal of the Empress who is beset by jealous foes? And now, get out of here, all of you. I want to sleep."

The cabin door slammed on the morose predictions of Hunegais, the witty retorts of Athaulf, the mumble of the others. Genseric rose and moved over to the table, to pour himself a last glass of wine. He walked with a limp; a Frankish spear had girded him in the leg long years ago.

He lifted the jeweled goblet to his lips—wheeled with a startled oath. He had not heard the cabin door open, but a man was standing across the table from him.

"By Odin!" Genseric's Arianism was scarcely skin-deep. "What do you in my cabin?"

The voice was calm, almost placid, after the first startled oath. The king was too shrewd often to evince his real emotions. His hand stealthily closed on the hilt of his sword. A sudden and unexpected stroke—

But the intruder made no hostile movement. He was a stranger to Genseric, and the Vandal knew he was neither Teuton nor Roman. He was tall, dark, with a stately head, his dark flowing locks confined by a dark crimson band. A curling black patriarchal beard swept his breast. A dim, misplaced familiarity twitched at the Vandal's mind as he looked.

"I have not come to harm you!" The voice was deep, strong and resonant. Genseric could tell little of his attire, since he was masked in a wide dark cloak. The Vandal wondered if he grasped a weapon under that cloak.

"Who are you, and how did you get into my cabin?" he demanded.

"Who I am, it matters not," returned the other. "I have been on this ship since you sailed from Carthage. You sailed at night; I came aboard then."

"I never saw you in Carthage," muttered Genseric. "And you are a man who would stand out in a crowd."

"I dwell in Carthage," the stranger replied. "I have dwelt there for many years. I was born there, and all my fathers before me. Carthage is my life!" The last sentence was uttered in a voice so passionate and fierce that Genseric involuntarily stepped back, his eyes narrowing.

"The folk of the city have some cause of complaint against us," said he; "but the looting and destruction was not by my orders; even then it was my intention to make Carthage my capital. If you suffered loss by the sack, why—"

"Not from your wolves," grimly answered the other. "Sack of the city? I have seen such a sack as not even you, barbarian, have dreamed of! They called you barbaric. I have seen what civilized Romans can do."

"Romans have not plundered Carthage in my memory," muttered Genseric, frowning in some perplexity.

"Poetic justice!" cried the stranger, his hand emerging from his cloak to strike down on the table. Genseric noted the hand was muscular yet white, the hand of an aristocrat. "Roman greed and treachery destroyed Carthage; trade rebuilt her, in another guise. Now you, barbarian, sail from her harbors to humble her conqueror! Is it any wonder that old dreams silver the cords of your ships and creep amidst the holds, and that forgotten ghosts burst their immemorial tombs to glide upon your decks?"

"Who said anything of humbling Rome?" uneasily demanded Genseric. "I merely sail to arbitrate a dispute as to succession—"

"Pah!" Again the hand slammed down on the table. "If you knew what I know, you would sweep that accursed city clean of life before you turn your prows southward again. Even now those you sail to aid plot your ruin—and a traitor is on board your ship!"

"What do you mean?" Still there was neither excitement nor passion in the Vandal's voice.

"Suppose I gave you proof that your most trusted companion and vassal plots your ruin with those to whose aid you lift your sails?"

"Give me that proof; then ask what you will," answered Genseric with a touch of grimness.

"Take this in token of faith!" The stranger rang a coin on the table, and caught up a silken girdle which Genseric himself had carelessly thrown down.

"Follow me to the cabin of your counsellor and scribe, the handsomest man among the barbarians—"

"Athaulf?" In spite of himself Genseric started. "I trust him beyond all others."

"Then you are not as wise as I deemed you," grimly answered the other. "The traitor within is to be feared more than the foe without. It was not the legions of Rome which conquered *me*—it was the traitors within my gates. Not alone in swords and ships does Rome deal, but with the souls of men. I have come from a far land to save your empire and your life. In return I ask but one thing: drench Rome in blood!"

For an instant the stranger stood transfigured, mighty arm lifted, fist clenched, dark eyes flashing fire. An aura of terrific power emanated from him, aweing even the wild Vandal. Then, sweeping his purple cloak about him with a kingly gesture, the man stalked to the door and through it, despite Genseric's exclamation and effort to detain him.

Swearing in bewilderment, the king limped to the door, opened it, and glared out on the deck. A lamp burned on the poop. A reek of unwashed bodies came up from the hold where the weary rowers toiled at their oars. The rhythmic clack vied with a dwindling chorus from the ships which followed in a long ghostly line. The moon struck silver from the waves, shone white on the deck. A single warrior stood on guard outside Genseric's door, the moonlight sparkling on his crested golden helmet and Roman corselet. He lifted his javelin in salute.

"Where did he go?" demanded the king.

"Who, my lord?" inquired the warrior stupidly.

"The tall man, dolt," exclaimed Genseric impatiently. "The man in the purple cloak who just left my cabin."

"None has left your cabin since the lord Hunegais and the others went forth, my lord," replied the Vandal in bewilderment.

"Liar!" Genseric's sword was a ripple of silver in his hand as it slid from its sheath. The warrior paled and shrank back.

"As God is my witness, king," he swore, "no such man have I seen this night."

Genseric glared at him; the Vandal king was a judge of men and he knew this one was not lying. He felt a peculiar twitching of his scalp, and turning without a word, limped hurriedly to Athaulf 's cabin. There he hesitated, then threw open the door.

Athaulf lay sprawled across a table in an attitude which needed no second glance to classify. His face was purple, his glassy eyes distended, and his tongue lolled out blackly. About his neck, knotted in such a knot as seamen make, was Genseric's silken girdle. Near one hand lay a quill, near the other ink and a piece of parchment. Catching it up, Genseric read laboriously.

"To her majesty the empress of Rome:

"I, thy faithful servant, have done thy bidding, and am prepared to persuade the barbarian I serve to delay his onset on the imperial city until the aid you expect from Byzantium has arrived. Then I will guide him into the bay I mentioned, where he can be caught as in a vise and destroyed with his whole fleet, and—"

The writing ceased with an erratic scrawl. Genseric glared down at him, and again the short hairs lifted on his scalp. There was no sign of the tall stranger, and the Vandal knew he would never be seen again.

"Rome shall pay for this," he muttered; the mask he wore in public had fallen away; the Vandal's face was that of a hungry wolf. In his glare, in the knotting of his mighty hand, it took no sage to read the doom of Rome. He suddenly remembered that he still clutched in his hand the coin the stranger had dropped on his table. He glanced at it, and his breath hissed between his teeth, as he recognized the characters of an old, forgotten language, the features of a man which he had often seen carved in ancient marble in old Carthage, preserved from Roman hate.

"Hannibal!" muttered Genseric.

The Ballad of King Geraint

This is the tale of a nameless fight,
In a land forgot to dream and sight,
And a people lost in the gloom and night.

King Geraint ruled the western land
From the Roman Wall to Channel's sand;
The Saxons held the eastern coast
By high-beaked galley and spear-tipped host.
They reached their hands from the eastern shore
And flooded the land with fire and gore.

King Geraint marched on the Watling Road,
Along the Ouse his banners showed.
Few his warriors but fierce his lords,
Dipped and reddened their worn swords.
He had scoured the land a-near and far,
He had sold his crown for the thews of war.
Knight and warrior and man-at-arms,
Yeoman drawn from the ravished farms,
Each was armed to suit his need,
Each one rode on a goodly steed.
The hoof-beat thunder sounded far—
So Geraint rode to his last red war.

Before them all King Geraint rode,
White was the great steed he bestrode,
A gift from the Ulster king, Leoghaire;
Gold in the sun was Geraint's hair.
His grey eyes flashed 'neath the helmet's crest
Like an eagle's that stoops from his craggy nest.
Tall and graceful and fair of face,
The warrior king of a fighting race.
Conal rode at King Geraint's right,
Closest friend feast or fight;
Mighty warrior and gallant knight.

Close there rode on the king's left side,
Donal, the chieftain of Strathclyde.
Dark was he, and hard of hand
As well befitted that desperate band
That held the hills of the Cumberland
Three hundred years from the Saxon horde.
There followed close with his great black sword
Cormac of Cornwall called the Hawk,
A savage branch on an ancient stalk.
More than half a pagan, he,
Ruling alone by the western sea;
Tall and lean with a dark hawk's face.
By his side rode, pace for pace,
Angus, a chief of the northern Scot,
With King Geraint he had cast his lot.
A giant he, and his fearful blows
Wrought destruction upon his foes.
Conmac rode in his armor bright,
Never was there more noble knight.
Like the British king, he too was fair,
With a golden beard and golden hair,
Blue were his eyes and pure his heart;
He ever took the weaker's part.
Learned was he and versed in art,
Read in all of the monkish books,
And yet though mild in air and looks
Never was knight more bold than he,
Flower of British chivalry.
With his banners floating like purple sails
Rode old Cadallon, the king of Wales.
White was his beard and his flowing hair,
But grey eyes gleamed like an eagle's stare.
Lord of the savage mountaineers,
Born and bred in the crash of spears.
A fierce and crafty old wolf was he;
Now he led his men from the western sea
With the single hope: to redden his shield
Ere he left his corpse on the battlefield.
There was one with a fearsome face,
A fighting man of a strange, lost race.
He was a Pict, Dulborn by name;

Under black brows, like cold black flame
His fierce eyes blazed at all the world;
His lips in a snarl were ever curled.
Short of stature but thick of limb,
Great was the shoulder breadth of him,
Hairy and apish and wild and grim.
Never a helmet would he wear
But the tangled shock of his own black hair.
A stunted giant, most strange to see—
A shape from the grisly past was he.
His people ruled, in the dark old days,
The western isles, and their altar blaze
Lighted the land, and they alone
Reigned in the grim old Age of Stone.
Now a scant remnant, hunted forth,
Lived like wolves in the misty north.
The Pict was banished, a lone exile;
God only knows what plot or guile,
What grisly crime or what fell deed
Barred Dulborn from his own dark breed.
When they exile, who are strange and fell,
Surely the deed was born in Hell!
But Dulborn rode to Geraint's court,
And followed him ever, life and morte.
His lips were locked and the heart inside,
And with him his secret lived and died.
Uther rode there, a broken king
Reft of his crown and everything
That makes life fair in the eyes of men.
His kingdom lay on the Humber when
Anlaf, king of the Angles, came
Riving the land with steel and flame.
In one wild night he was overthrown,
Lost his castle, his queen, his throne.
He saw his stricken vassals reel,
His queen's breast bared to the reddened steel,
His son crushed under the heathen heel,
His people enslaved, his warriors dead,
A crownless, landless king he fled.
Now he gazed at the vultures in the skies
And hollows of madness were under his eyes.

Few were the words that he had spent
Since he dropped at the gate of King Geraint,
Bloody and tattered and almost dead,
In the dawn that broke so deathly red.
Few were his words, but many his deeds,
From the Channel's shore to the banks of Tweed's,
And the ravens followed him over the meads.
There followed on King Geraint's trail
Two strong chiefs of the western Gael.
Friends abroad, though foes at home,
Seeking adventures beyond the foam,
They had come before and they came again
To strike a blow for their Brython kin.
One was Nial of whom men sing
That he was brother to Ulster's king.
Tall he was, and his shoulders broad;
In his hand his ivory-hilted sword
Flashed and leaped like a living flame,
Thus sing the bards who chant his fame.
His ringlets were curled and golden red,
Like a mist of flame about his head.
Red was his steed and his armor red,
A crimson flame from heel to head.
His comrade was Turlogh of Connacht;
In days of old the twain had fought
From dawn to dark till their shields were rent,
Swords shattered and strength and fury spent.
Now like old friends, they, side by side,
Ride with Geraint to the battle tide.
Not as tall as the Ulsterman
Was Turlogh, but broader in shoulder span.
If Nial was red, Turlogh was black
Like a phantom of Death in the battle wrack.
Eyes of a hot volcanic blue
Under black brows all Erin knew,
Burned with a passion that was not quenched
Till the shield was rent and the sword red-drenched.
Black was his armor, steed and shield;
So he rode to the battlefield.
With these ten knights and a thousand men
Geraint thundered through forest and fen.

* * * * *

Ceawlin, king of the Saxon hordes,
Marshalled his axes and his swords.
Gathered his ealdormen and thanes
From the smoking towns and the ravished plains.
Twelve thousand warriors owned his command
And he marshalled them on either hand.
Four thousand mounted on steeds he brought,
Eight thousand more on foot that fought.
His foremost lords were four in number:
Prince Osric who ruled from Ouse to Humber,
He was a lord of the Juttish strain;
Oswald, lord of the Sussex plain;
The Wessex ealdorman, Athelstane,
And Edric of Orkney Isles, a Dane.
King Ceawlin marshalled a thousand horse
To bar King Geraint's battle course.
He put Prince Osric in command,
With five strong chiefs at either hand:
Halfgar, Frisian sea-king he,
A name of fear in the narrow sea;
He knew not mercy, pity or ruth.
The thane Otho of the Black Boar's Tooth.
Athelred, cousin to the king,
And Rognor of the golden ring.
Oswick who ravaged London town
And slew three kings on The White Horse down.
The giant brothers, berserks they,
Tostig the Ogre and Athelney.
Fearsome were they, and huge and stark,
And unlike their race, most strangely dark.
Oswy the Jut, and the Norseman Rane,
And last and greatest, the viking Swane.
Half Saxon he, half northern Dane.
His torch had lighted a hundred shores,
Rome and Egypt had heard his oars.
Proud Massilia at his thrust
Had crumpled into the bloody dust.
Broad was he, with a cruel face,
Fiercest man of a savage race.

A thousand horse Ceawlin gave
To Oswald who ruled by the Sussex wave.
Ten chiefs likewise rode at his side:
Godric, fierce in his heathen pride.
Anlaf the Angle, Wutholwine,
Wulfhere, chieftain of Horsa's line,
Aella who ruled from Tweed to Tyne.
Gulla, and Gurth and Athelfrith,
Hakon the jarl, and Jan the Lith.
To all the foot he gave command
To Athelstane of the Iron Hand.
Ealdorman of Wessex, he,
Huge and fierce in his paganry.
Edric the Red, the Orkney Dane,
Shared the command with Athelstane.
Now twice a thousand horse remain.
Over them Ceawlin's Raven flew,
His spear arose and his trumpets blew.
Ceawlin rode in his heathen pride,
With mighty warriors on either side.
His brother Ulf on his right hand,
On his left, Leofwine of Helgoland.
Godwine of Mercia, Sweyn of Kent,
Eadelberht from the banks of Trent.
Eadwig, called by men The White,
Ealdred, jarl from the Isle of Wight.
Eadmund of York with his helmet bright,
Eadward of Northumbria whose sight
Might pierce the heavens or span a gulf;
Tostig the Raven and Rane the Wolf.
The bright steel flashed in the rising sun;
He gave his orders one by one.
King Geraint passed Corinium's walls.
The country shook to the trumpets' calls.
When sudden there charged across his course
Osric the prince, with a thousand horse.
They smote the spurs, they slacked the rein—
They crashed together on the plain.
King Geraint smote Prince Osric's shield,
At the shock both mighty chargers reeled.
But the Saxon spear to splinters flew,

And the king's lance rent the shield in two,
Shivered the hauberk's scales apart,
Rent the bosom and split the heart,
Stood a yard from the Saxon's back—
Prince Osric fell in his horse's track.
Geraint hath taken another spear,
Spurring his steed in mad career.
The heathen reel to his mighty thrust,
And white steed tramples them in the dust.
Conal at Halfgar drove amain,
Hurled him dead on the bloody plain;
But the Frisian spear his corselet tore,
Into his breast he felt it gore,
And out of the wound the life blood pour.
But he spoke no word of his deathly pain,
Following close by Geraint's rein,
And the heathen fell as he smote amain.
Otho of the Boar's Tooth ran
Full career at the Cornishman.
But the spear he wielded could not avail
'Gainst Cormac's coat of triple mail,
Or the great black sword, of a hundred fights
Which grisly Druids, in the deeps of nights
Had spelled with dark, unholy rites.
And it cleft the helmet and skull beneath,
Rending apart the monstrous teeth.
Donal, the chieftain of Strath-Clyde,
At Athelred bore through the battle tide.
The Saxon shattered his shield in twain,
But his own lance pierced the Saxon's brain—
Ceawlin's cousin lay on the plain.
Angus rushed like a bear at bay
At the giant berserk, Athelnay.
The horses reel, and the riders rock,
Both lances shiver at the shock!
They reel, they stagger, they charge, they close!
Front to front, with gigantic blows.
The Scotsman's shield is rent in twain,
He flings the fragments upon the plain;
His hauberk is pierced, his helmet rent—
Now the Saxon back in his saddle is bent!

The trumpets bray and the trumpets peal!
The Scot's sword shivers in sparks of steel!
The Saxon roared and spurred his horse,
But Angus met him in full mid-course,
With a mace he snatched from a dying hand—
He smote like a wave on a windy strand,
Shattered and shivered the whistling brand,
Battered the shield to a broken wreck,
Crushed the helmet down on the neck,
Shattered the skull like an empty shell,
Headlong the horse and rider fell!
Conmac hurled down Rognor slain,
Cadallon's lance rent Oswick's brain.
Uther at Oswy rode amain.
The Juttish spear gashed Uther's thigh
But he gave no heed and his flame-lit eye
Altered not in any part
As he broke his lance in the heathen's heart.
Rane's lance broke short on Nial's crest
And Nial pierced the Norseman's breast.
Tostig the Ogre slacked his rein
At the Pict Dulborn, he rode amain.
The Pict scorned sword or lance to bear,
As he scorned a helmet save his own hair.
A great black axe was all he bore;
But Tostig's lance in twain he shore,
And the next blow down through the shoulder tore
Rent the hauberk and cleft the bone,
The giant fell from his steed like stone;
Dulborn laughed at his dying groan.
Through the battle, Swane the viking sought
For the face of Turlogh of Connacht.
An ancient feud lay red between,
A long gone day and a traitor queen,
And a crashing of galleys black and lean.
Rending helmets and hauberk scales,
The viking crashed through the ranks of Wales.
His warriors died as they crowded in
'Neath the stabbing spears of Cadallon's men;
But Swane bore on and his sword dealt doom
Till a heap of corpses gave him room.

And in a voice that roared over all that fought,
He shouted for Turlogh of Connacht.
Like a wave that breaks on the sloping shale
Was the sudden charge of the fiery Gael.
He was stained with the blood of the viking's band,
His spear had shivered in his hand,
Now he held aloft his crimson brand.
His shield the viking's broadsword turned,
Along his arm the keen edge burned.
The red drops followed the slicing steel,
Turlogh cursed in the trumpet peal,
Rose in his stirrups, spurred and smote,
Breaking the shout in the viking's throat.
Hauberk and ribs gave at the blow
And Swane fell dead from his saddlebow.
Osric and all his lords lie slain,
Their bodies litter the broken plain.
Nor have the British men-at-arms
Proven weak in the loud alarms.
Geraint and his lords have rent the foes
And their warriors have followed swift and close,
Clearing the way with mighty blows.
A hundred Britons and Welsh lie dead,
But the shattered Saxons have turned and fled,
Those who are left alive to flee;
Most of them sleep with Eternity.

King Geraint spurred his great white steed,
His army followed him over the mead,
Till Oswald of Sussex barred his way—
Now trumpets roar and the chargers neigh
And the two hosts crash in the deadly fray.
The king was a thunderbolt of stone;
Steeds and riders were overthrown;
Ceorl and eorl went down before,
Seven thanes he overbore.
Conal was ever at his side,
Staining his sword in the crimson tide.
Chief Oswald was a man of war,
Fame of his deeds was blown afar.
Now he smote on the British line,

Cleft a Briton from chin to chine,
Severed another through the spine.
From another knight he dashed the brain,
Charged from the side at the king amain.
Conal's sight was growing dim,
He saw the fight in a red haze swim.
His sword arm hung like an arm of lead,
He scarce could lift his armored head,
His life was ebbing in spurts of red.
But even as waning sight was spent
He saw the peril of Geraint.
He reined about his weary horse
And barred the furious Saxon's course.
And the blow for the back of the king was stayed
By Conal's notched unsteady blade.
Rider and steed in one overthrow
Sank beneath that fearful blow.
King Geraint wheeled and he saw the end
Of his trusted comrade and boyhood friend.
His heart went cold and his lips went pale;
He smote the Saxon like a gale,
Rent his shield and his coat of mail.
Oswald lay by Conal's side
And over them washed the battle tide.
Godric, gleaming in silver scales,
Rode full tilt at the ranks of Wales.
At old Cadallon he aimed his spear,
Shouting an insult and a jeer.
The old king grinned as a wolf might grin
As the lances clashed with a ringing din.
The Saxon's broke on the Welshman's shield
And Godric dropped on the bloody field,
The shield fell from his nerveless hand
And his brains oozed out to clot the sand.
Hakon the jarl charged in to ride
At Donal, chieftain of Strath-Clyde.
Each at the other aimed his spear,
Crashed together in full career.
Fair and full and sudden the blow,
Each dropped dead from his saddlebow.
Uther crashed on the Saxon ranks,

Breaking the spears in lofty banks.
Sudden he saw, while the lances flew,
A form remembered, a face he knew.
A terrible scream tore from his throat,
That cut like a knife through the trumpet's note.
Anlaf turned at that deathly shriek,
A pallor sucked at his bearded cheek.
And a thought in his brain reeled to and fro—
That night on the Humber, long ago.
The face of his foe, at last, at last!
Uther came like a blinding blast.
Naught he made of the upflung guard,
Naught of the shield that sought to ward.
The first blow shattered the sword and shield,
The second hurled him to the field.
Uther leaped from his saddle red,
Hewed from his shoulders the Angle's head.
Into his saddle he leaped again,
Raged like a madman over the plain.
Took deep wounds that he did not feel,
His laughter howled through the trumpet's peal.
Ever he brandished the grinning head
While on his helmet drops of red
Fell like a sluggish fall of rain,
And he screamed with a terrible mirth insane.
Cormac crashed through the Saxon line,
Full on the chieftain Wutholwine.
And the Saxon rent his shield in twain,
As the Cornish sword crashed through his brain.
The Hawk was wild with the tang of war,
His way the Saxons could not bar
For the black sword hewed through plate and crest,
Cleaving the skull and the armored breast.
Lives are snuffed like candle flame
Beneath the sword no man may tame.
Conmac, knight sans stain or blame,
Rode where he saw the white shield shine
Of Wulfhere, chieftain of Horsa's line.
They spur, they meet with a thunder shake;
The horses rear and the lances break.
Now front to front they shower blows

While the squadrons reel and the tumult grows.
From the clashing steel the blue sparks fly—
And the fury dies in Wulfhere's eye;
Under his corselet the keen blade drinks,
The charger rears and the rider sinks.
Nial smote on the pagan horse
Quenching his ivory-hilted sword
In the first and best of the Saxon blood,
The red horse raged through the clashing flood.
Ceorl and eorl and chief went down
With rended breast or cloven crown.
Aella the chieftain of the Tyne,
He clove through the shoulder and the spine.
He hacked his way to Geraint's side
Where the heathen brake like a broken tide.
Nor faltered Turlogh of Connacht;
Red the destruction that he wrought.
His red sword shore through breast and brain,
His corpses littered the trampled plain
And the red blood fell in a grisly rain.
Gulla he slew, the Juttish thane.
Dulborn smote on the shield of Gurth,
Horse and rider crashed to the earth.
Gurth arose from that deadly fall
Where dead men lie and horses sprawl.
Leaped like a tiger on his foe,
Dented his shield with a savage blow,
Gashed the shoulder that lay below.
Dulborn laughed like the twang of a bow.
Rose in his stirrups, downward smote,
Cleaving the Saxon to the throat.
Angus the giant Northern chief
Ranged like a sickle through the sheaf.
His mace was clotted and dripping red
And still it crashed through plate and head,
Crumpling iron and steel and bone.
Horses and riders were overthrown.
In the very heart of the Saxon band
Two chiefs assailed him on either hand.
Athelfrith the Kentishman
With levelled spear upon him ran.

On the other side the chieftain Jan
Heaved his axe above his head
And a terrible blow at Angus sped.
At once they smote him, breast and head.
And the horses reeled to the triple shock
But Angus sat like a man of rock.
The spear broke short on his steel-clad breast,
The red axe shattered on his crest.
And the great mace crashed through the battle wrack
An iron thunderbolt, grim and black,
A double blow, forehand and back.
The first blow shattered Athelfrith,
And the second killed chief Jan the Lith.
And men cried out to see that deed
But the maddened Angus gave no heed.
He spurred his horse at the ringing spears
And his war-cry burst the Saxons' ears.
He smote to the left and to the right;
He was gripped with a fearful need to smite.
Helmets burst and the skulls gave way
Till the Saxons broke from the bloody fray.
And still the thundering Scot pursued
Till the plain with fallen men was strewed.
And still he had followed all that fled,
Till through the mists of dark and red
King Geraint's voice pierced his brain;
Reluctant he joined his fellows again.

Of all that rode across the plain
Six hundred men alone remain;
Donal and Conal both lie slain.
Uther's armor is hacked to a shred;
Crest to heel he is grim and red.
But he holds aloft dark Anlaf's head.
Seven deep wounds now sap his life
But he heeds them not as he seeks the strife.
And he laughs a laugh so wild and grim,
His comrades glance askance at him.
Dulborn, Cormac and Angus bleed
But of their wounds they take no heed.
Now front them on the open plain,

The heavy-armed ceorls of Athelstane
With his comrade Edric the Red, the Dane.
They have locked their shields in a solid wall
Their spears a-bristle above them all.
Grimmest arm of the Saxon war,
Geraint sees his setting star.
He bunches close his thinning ranks,
An iron bolt for the iron banks.
Shoulder to shoulder, flying fast
The Britons charge in a blinding blast.
And the spears give way and the shield-walls reel
To the blast of that avalanche of steel.
Geraint and Angus, knee to knee,
Crash like a black tide from the sea.
The black mace shatters the shields apart,
Breaking the spears—into the heart
Of the stabbing host the Scotsman tore
Steeping his iron mace in gore.
Now all the Britons thunder in
And the skies are rent by the battle din.
The howling Saxons ring them close,
They rock and sway in a waste of foes,
But cleave their way with terrible blows.
Uther rushed with a laugh and scream
Like a man who rides in a nightmare dream.
He slew a thane who had his stand
Between the chiefs of the Saxon band.
And Edric smote with a reddened brand
And Athelstane on the other hand.
Horse and rider they over-bore;
Uther fell and he rose no more.
Yet his hand was locked in the ghastly red
Hair of Anlaf's severed head,
In a grip that no man born could break,
And the hardiest warrior well might quake
At the smile which his bloody lips still froze;
So Uther lay in a ring of foes.
Geraint had seen King Uther slain;
Headlong he rushed on Athelstane,
Shattered the helmet on his head,
Dashed him earthward, broken and dead.

Then he turned on Edric; but at his side
Nial had ripped through the battle tide.
And the red horse hurled chief Edric down,
And the Gaelic sword edge cleft his crown.
The British knights are torn apart,
But still they cleave through the shield-wall's heart.
Singly or in struggling groups
The Saxons league the Celtic troops.
Many a rider is overthrown;
Cormac and Angus fight alone.
Conmac and Turlogh, knee to knee,
Blast their way through the iron sea.
Life blood dying his hauberk scales
Cadallon is ringed by the swords of Wales.
Still Geraint leads with his bloody brand,
With Dulborn and Nial on either hand,
Followed close by his dwindling band.
Cormac's black sword leaped and drank
Till his dying charger reeled and sank,
Pinning his rider to the ground,
And a hedge of spears bore in around.
Bleeding from many a grisly wound,
Cormac struggled and tore him clear,
Rose through the rain of sword and spear.
He braced his feet and he smote once more
Through iron and flesh the black sword tore.
Corpses rattled against his feet;
He scarcely felt the blades that beat
Hard on his helmet. Once again
The black sword crashed and men were slain.
Battle and sky were growing black;
Around him surged the battle wrack.
The warriors shouted and crowded back.
But the thick press held them hard and stayed
Within the sweep of the Cornish blade.
Cormac with both hands gripped his sword;
Little he felt the spears that gored.
The last red ounce of his life went out
In the swing that clove through the screaming rout.
He felt the keen edge cleave through flesh,
Iron and bone and brazen mesh.

He heard the clash of falling men,
They fell at his feet like trees and then
As the sword flashed round in that deathly arc
The world wavered and all went dark.
With a ghastly laugh the blood burst red
From his pallid lips and the chief fell dead.
The horse of Angus was overthrown,
He rose in a wave of foes alone.
He hurled his shield among the brand,
Gripped his mace in his mighty hands.
The Saxons rushed like a brainless wave,
Hewing and stabbing with spear and glaive.
He loomed above them like a tower,
A man of iron in that red hour.
His great voice roared through curse and yell;
The great black mallet rose and fell.
Shield nor helmet its blows withstood,
Brass or iron or steel-braced wood.
He struck as a bolt of thunder strikes.
They thrust with spears and heavy pikes;
They hewed at corselet and crested crown,
They gripped his legs to wrestle him down.
But the spears were splintered, the swords were bent,
And they staggered back when their strength was spent.
And Angus as he broke their brands,
Shook off the grasp of their nerveless hands.
He crushed their breasts and smashed their brains,
Ceorl and eorls and jarls and thanes
Fell like leaves on that fatal spot
To the berserk wrath of the giant Scot.
But still by hundreds they crowded in,
From all sides smote with a fearful din.
From every joint of his armor ran
The blood of the terrible Northern man.
His shattered helmet fell in twain,
The blood was starting from every vein.
His armor battered, torn and rent,
But he dealt his blows without stay or stint.
A terrible harvest Angus mowed;
High heaped the corpses he bestrode.
They lay about in a ghastly ring,

Leaving a space for his mace to swing.
He stood alone in an open space
Holding on high the great black mace.
The warriors pressed back from his blows;
So Angus glared at his ringing foes.
Silent they faltered, pressing back;
Under his thick brows, heavy and black,
The terrible eyes of the chieftain blazed,
The Saxons blanched and shrank as they gazed.
But their eorls lashed them with words of fire
And they charged once more with a desperate ire.
A whirlpool of iron, a storm of steel,
Through which the shrieks of the dying peal.
A whirl of swords and over all
The terrible mace's rise and fall!
And the Saxons broke—they turned and fled
And Angus stood on a heap of dead.
He swayed above those torn mounds,
With the ebb of a score of mortal wounds.
He sought to sound his battle-cry
As he saw his foes give way and fly;
He swung his iron mace on high,
And sank on a heap of dead, to die.

The Britons have cleft through the Saxon ranks;
Few there are left of that bold phalanx.
Geraint is wounded in the knee,
Not a knight from a gash is free.
Thrice was Dulborn's charger slain
But riderless horses race the plain.
Each time the black axe hewed a course
And gained the wielder another horse.
The ranks of the men-at-arms are reft;
Scarce two hundred now are left.
But behind them the shattered Saxon horde
Reels like a dragon broken and gored.
Their leaders and half their comrades slain
They break and eddy and swirl in vain,
And stream in flight across the plain.
And now to the bray of trumpet and drum
Full two thousand riders come.

Ceawlin rides in his armor bright
With mighty men at his left and right.
His brother Ulf, his banner rears,
The Raven banner above the spears.
Leofwine, Godwine, Sweyn of Kent,
Princes from Selsey to the Trent.
Warriors from Lindisfarne and York,
Jutes and Angles, fierce and stark,
Rode in the Saxon phalanx dark.
King Geraint turned to his faithful friends:
"Here the war and my kingdom ends.
"Many have died in this red fray,
"More shall die ere the death of day.
"Turn, I beg you, your steeds toward home;
"Seek your safety beyond the foam.
"Naught is left for a crownless king
"But a kingly death where the broadswords sing.
"But there is no need for you all to die;
"Turn, I beg you, to safety fly."
Cadallon's hauberk was seeping red;
But he laughed like a wolf as he shook his head:
"I turn my back when my foes are dead.
"I am a king in my own land
"Though my only crown is a bloody brand.
"I only wish to charge and close
"And gain to the thickest of my foes."
From his battered Welsh a fierce yell rose.
Said Conmac: "With my last-drawn breath
"I follow my king to life or death."
Nial's eyes blazed with a light
Mystic, more than mortal sight.
"Never in all the world," said he,
"Is one who touches in chivalry,
"Knighthood, honor without taint,
"And kingly courage, thou, Geraint!
"Come weal or evil, time or tide,
"Shoulder to shoulder with you I ride,
"And in death I will still be at your side."
Few were Turlogh's words and brief
As well befitted a Gaelic chief:
"While Geraint lives I follow the king."

Dulborn made his black axe sing
In a whistling arc through the parting air.
He shook back his tangled mane of hair.
Fiercely laughed in the battle joy
And the primal lust to rend and destroy.
"We waste good time in words," he said,
"Let us ride in and smite them dead."
So shoulder to shoulder the warriors rein
For the last red charge on that red plain.
Oh, who the minstrel that might sing
The last great fight of the British king!
"Surely," said Ulf, "these men are mad!"
Ceawlin's eyes were fierce and sad.
He laughed with wrath and little mirth.
"Mayhap—but madmen rule the earth.
"Osric and Oswald rode in vain,
"They and all their chiefs lie slain.
"And the Britons have broken Athelstane.
"Bitter the day for me, and black.
"When Geraint rides he turns not back."
Loud laughed the Viking Leofwine:
"See how they rush upon our line!
"Deep will I quench this sword of mine!
"Turn ye, Saxons, and leave their band
"To a single sword from Helgoland!
"From this keen edge no god can save
"The Wealish thrall and the British slave."
Eadmund of York from the king turned back,
His eyes with sudden wrath were black.
"Say ye so in your brainless pride?
"You will learn this day how the Britons ride!
"Not to the Saxons is the shame
"That they fall to a thunderstorm of flame!
"This is no war of churl and slave,
"But kings and warriors tried and brave.
"This is a war where ravens fly
"As desperate men go out to die.
"We shall see if you prove your arrogant boast
"If any one of the British host,
"Chieftain or warrior, smites your sword."
With brainless laughter the heathen roared.

Tostig the Raven was short in speech;
He had rushed his galleys on many a beach,
Fiercest of all the sea-kings, he,
Name of terror on land and sea.
Now he spoke: "We shall have our fill,
"These men are charging to die—and kill!"
Ceawlin made the battle sign
And his horde rushed hard on the charging line.

The standards reel and the riders rock,
The whole earth shudders at the shock.
And the charging Britons' desperate blows
Carry them into the heart of their foes.
On every side they are leagued amain
And the battle floods the trampled plain.
King Geraint charged as a hawk might fly
Where Ceawlin's standard broke the sky.
The Viking Leofwine barred his path,
First to taste of the Briton's wrath.
Leofwine's heart was fierce and stout
But now he felt his first black doubt
As the white steed crashed through the battle rout.
Ere he could draw a single breath
They loomed upon him, a bolt of death.
One mighty stroke snapped short his brand,
Shivered the shield in his iron hand,
Dashed him dead from his saddlebow
To lie on the beaten earth below.
Ceawlin spurred to meet his foe,
But Eadmund of York on his great bay horse
Barred the Saxon monarch's course.
Forced him back, despite his wrath,
And with forty spears across his path
Hedged the way to King Geraint
Who raged like a tiger, smote and rent,
Loomed o'er the fray like a drifting cloud
Heaping dead men in a grisly crowd.
On one side Nial of Ulster crashed,
On the other Dulborn smote and slashed.
And Turlogh and Conmac followed close,
Glutting their wrath with mighty blows;

With them there smote on the dark phalanx
The men-at-arms' swift falling ranks,
Who slashed and slaughtered and slew and died;
Silent, they neither moaned nor cried.
Cadallon swayed, but he still could grin,
To the Saxon center he shattered in;
Godwine the Mercian king he slew,
Eadelberht's skull he cleft in two.
Lodbrog rushed with a terrible blow;
Horse and steed in that overthrow,
Crashed—Cadallon the king lay dead
On his dying horse in a pool of red.
And his warriors who were left to die
Rushed with a yell that tore the sky.
Like a pack of grey wolves, gaunt and grim,
They tore chief Lodbrog limb from limb.
Leaped from their horses and made a wall
Where King Cadallon met his fall,
And around the corpse of their ancient king
Died in a red unbroken ring.
Conmac crashed through the battle tide
And the ranks gave back on either side.
No man his charge might halt or stay,
To the Raven banner he hewed his way.
His helmet was gone, his head was bare,
Like a flame of gold was his golden hair.
Ulf smote as hard as a warrior may,
But Conmac tossed his shield away,
Gripped the standard in his left hand,
And the other drove his crimson brand
Rending the hauberk scales apart,
Riving the bosom and the heart.
Ulf vanished in that sea of blood;
Up in his stirrups Conmac stood,
Brandished the Raven banner high,
Blackly limned in the cloudless sky—
From all the host came a mighty cry.
Then he broke and tore it and slashed in twain
And hurled the pieces on the plain.
The Saxons were mad with shame and rage,
Nothing but death could their hate assuage.

Ceawlin sees his brother dead
And his standard lost with the torn dead.
No shield or helmet Conmac bore
But bone and iron his sword edge shore,
And many a man went down before.
Warriors fell without name or number,
Till Eadward, chieftain of Northumber,
Spurred his steed with a deathly stroke;
Conmac's sword his helmet broke,
But Eadward clove that golden head
And the Briton fell from his saddle, dead.
Dulborn saw his comrade die;
He sounded a strange dark battle cry,
And charged, his great black axe to ply.
Seven chiefs in that charge he slew,
Smiting hauberk and helmet through,
Hewing bosoms and skulls in two.
Up in his stirrups Eadward stood,
Smote as only a chieftain could.
Full on the Pict's unhelmed head,
Dulborn laughed as the blow was sped.
For the tangled shock of his thick black mane
Stayed the sword edge and saved his brain.
Though the edge bit into the scalp beneath;
Dulborn laughed through his gnashing teeth.
His black axe crashed in a singing arc
And Eadward's eyes went strangely dark.
Under his armpit fell the stroke
As a woodsman's axe falls on the oak,
Cleaving hauberk and ribs and spine,
He died with never a groan or sign.
Dulborn was mad with the battle lust,
Horse and rider crashed to dust
Before the crash of his terrible axe
That rent through iron and bone like flax.
From Osgar of Kent he dashed the brain,
Fulk of Sussex he hewed in twain.
He smote and trampled them under horse;
Tostig the Raven barred his course.
The war cry roared from each warrior's throat,
Headlong they thundered, crashed and smote.

In full mid-air the swift strokes met,
The crimson axe and the broadsword wet;
And the sword to a thousand steel sparks flew,
And the axe with never a stay went through
The brazen shield that it split in two.
But notched and strained in many a test,
It broke on the Raven's iron crest.
And each at the other his charger drove,
Close clinched they struggled, tore and strove.
Both their daggers drank deep and well
Till from their plunging steeds they fell;
Down they crashed in the rolling thunder,
And the flying horses trampled them under.
All of the British men-at-arms
Sleep at rest from war's alarms.
All of his chivalry are reft,
None of his knights is to Geraint left.
Of all that followed his gleaming train
Only the Irish chiefs remain.
All of the three are wounded sore,
Head to heel they are steeped in gore.
Their shattered shields they have thrown away,
Splendor of God, what a fearful fray!
Snapped at the hilt was Turlogh's brand,
He snatched an axe from a dying hand.
"This is the end," King Geraint said,
"All our warriors and knights are dead.
"God grant us a knightly death this day!"
"Ever we ride at your side," said they.
And the white horse, red horse, and the black
Crashed once more through the battle wrack.
Their iron-shod hoofs in pools of red
Trampled the living with the dead.
With a blinding might that caught the breath,
Like a triple thunderbolt of death,
That bursts through clouds heaped dark blue,
The three great steeds came crashing through.
Under the hoofs that spurned the wold
Headlong, horses and riders rolled.
Men saw the great white charger loom
Like a flashing thundercloud of doom,

And the great red steed like a storm of hate,
And the huge black horse like a wind of Fate.
Whole ranks go down and the long lines reel
'Neath the frantic hoofs and the lashing steel.
King Geraint aimed his fearful rush
Where Ceawlin rode in the press and crush.
His path to the Saxon king was barred
By Eadwig and Ealdred and Athelgard,
Athelwald and the Kentish Sweyn,
Asgar and Dirck the Wessex thane,
Eadmund of York and the wolfish Rane.
Into their ranks King Geraint broke,
Smote with a headlong desperate stroke.
Eadwig the White went toppling down
With a shattered shield and a cloven crown.
Through Geraint's corselet Ealdred smote
Ere the King's sword ripped the life from his throat.
Nial smote hard of Athelgard,
Hurled him dead on the bloody sward.
Turlogh's axe dashed Athelwald dead
And the next stroke split Lord Asgar's head.
Geraint slew Dirck, the Wessex thane,
Nial shore through the breast of Rane.
Eadmund of York and his comrade Sweyn
Rein against the British king,
And the house carles close in a bristling ring
Ceawlin to guard from the red sword's swing.
King Geraint has taken his mortal wound,
The battle flows in a mist around.
The world is swaying and growing dim
But he sees Ceawlin's helmet swim
There in the mist, and he charges him.
'Tween Eadmund and Sweyn he made to ride
And they assail him from either side.
But Sweyn was dashed by his arm aside.
And ere he could turn, with a war cry grim
Nial of Ulster closed with him.
Eadmund, careless of his own life,
Spurred his steed in that deadly strife.
Parried the stroke that else had sheared
Ceawlin's head to his golden beard.

And Ceawlin struck, but his sword edge turned,
On Geraint's mail; the King's eyes burned
Into the eyes of his Saxon foe,
Again he smote and again the blow
At the very throat of his king was stayed
By the parry of Eadmund's faithful blade.
Then a great black shadow over him loomed,
On his shield the axe of Turlogh boomed.
But the chiefs had seized King Ceawlin's rein
And perforce raced across the plain,
Out of the reach of the British king
Who raged and smote in the closing ring.
Now while the fight had thundered on
A shadow over the plain had gone,
And a strange white mist fell over all,
Veiling the plain in a mystic pall.
Men could not see for half a pace
Through the strange white shroud before their face.
Turlogh and Eadmund dealt their blows
When sudden the mist swept down to close,
Hid friends from friends and foes from foes.
In the veiling mist Turlogh smote blind
Trusting to chance his foe to find.
He felt the axe on the helmet crash
And the chief go down with a sounding clash.
He heard in the mist the ring of steel,
The shout of men and the trumpet's peal.
He heard the clash of the flying swords
Where the King and Nial fought the lords,
But all was grisly and strange and white;
Forms rose and faded in his sight.
Unseen weapons dealt him blows,
He slew in the mist invisible foes.
And all the field was white and strange
Like a plain over which dead specters range.
Men groped like blind men through the tide
And no man knows how King Geraint died.
But sudden the mist was cleared away;
On a mighty heap of dead he lay,
Last great king of the British race
There on a kingly resting place,

On a mighty couch that was red and grim;
Nial of Ulster lay by him.
Round them lay in a silent ring
The greatest chiefs of the Saxon king,
Who fell where they his way had barred:
Eadwig, Ealdred and Athelgard,
Athelwald and the wolfish Rane,
Asgar and Dirck the Wessex thane,
Eadmund of York and the Kentish Sweyn.
Silent they lay and broken and dead
Save Eadmund of York alone, whose head
Was saved from Turlogh's blinded stroke,
Though the helmet into pieces broke.
Senseless he lay upon the plain
Till his people found him among the slain.
Turlogh reined the mighty black
And the weary, torn ranks gave back
Before the charger's thundering rush,
So Turlogh crashed through the serried crush.
They saw the black steed sweeping by,
The black knight etched against the sky,
Lifting a great black axe on high.
They shrank aside, they held their breath,
They thought him a thunderbolt of Death;
The ranks gave way, they made him room,
They thought him a harbinger of Doom.
A grim black phantom of Death and Fate,
Born in the worlds of Night and Hate.
So Turlogh rode, the single knight
Left alive from that terrible fight,
And vanished from the Saxons' sight.

The word went through the British land
From the Channel's shore to the Solway's strand;
Who is the minstrel fit to sing
Of the last great fight of Britain's king?—
The song of a race swift vanishing.

The Song of the Last Briton

The sea is grey in the death of day;
    Behind me lifts the night.
I'll flee no more from the ancient shore
    Where first I saw the light.

The Saxons come and the Saxons go
    With the ebb and surge of the tide;
Their galleys loom, grim shapes of doom,
    But here shall I abide.

My castles rust in crimson dust,
    Red ruin tossed in the drift—
But the sea is grey and the wolf's at bay
    And the ravens circle swift.

So come from your mists of Northern Sea
    Where the smoke-blue hazes melt.
Your dead shall lie where here I die,
    The last unconquered Celt.

Memories of Alfred

Here in old time King Alfred broke the Danes,
And all my dreams are of that ancient war
When red-haired jarls, close locked with shouting thanes
Bathed deep in slaughter till the evening star
Hung in the blue above the fading moon
And silence fell like sleep on Aethandune.

They live in me again, those dead, lost days,
And I am one with all that vanished host—
And memory of battles and forays
Stands at my elbow like a misty ghost.
For out of sleep that dead life is reborn
To rise and roar and follow Guthrum's horn.

At our first charge they wavered as to break,
But Alfred's war-cry fired their sluggish blood;
They stiffened—stood, their thirsty blades to slake,
And both hosts rolled together like a flood.
The spear-point kissed the heart, the sword, the throat,
And friend slew friend, not knowing whom he smote.

Dreaming on Downs

I marched with Alfred when he thundered forth
To break the crimson standards of the Dane;
I saw the galleys looming in the north
And heard the oar-locks and the sword's refrain.

And far across the pleasant Wessex downs
The chanting of the spearmen broke the lyre,
Till where the black thorn forest grimly frowns
We sang a song of doom and steel and fire.

Death rode his pale horse through the dreaming sky
All through that long red summer afternoon,
And night and silence fell, when silently
The dead men lay beneath a cold white moon.

Now Alfred sleeps with all the swords of yore,
(But o'er the downs a brooding shadow glides)
Untrampled flowers dream along the shore,
And Guthrum's galleys rust beneath the tides.

Now underneath this drowsy tree I lie
And turn old dreams upon my lazy knees,
Till ghostly giants fill the summer sky
And phantom oars awake the sleeping seas.

The Song of Horsa's Galley

From the Baltic Sea our galleys sweep
  To South and West and East,
We bring our bows from the Northern snows
  That the great grey wolves may feast.

To the outmost roads of the plunging sea
  Our dragon ships are hurled,
We have broken the chains of the Southern Danes
  And now we break the world.

Out of the dark of the misty north
  We come like shapes of the gloam
To harry again the Southland men
  And trample the arms of Rome.

The ravens circle above our prows
  And our chant is the song of the sea.
They hear our oars by a thousand shores
  And they know that the North is free.

Song Before Clontarf

Lean on your sword, red-bearded lord, and watch your victims crawl;
Under your feet they weakly beat the dust with their dying hands.
The red smokes roll from the serf's roof-pole and the chieftain's shattered hall—
But there are fires in the heather and a whetting of hungry brands.
The peaked prows loom like clouds of doom along each broken port;
The monks lie still on the heathered hill among the fallen stones.
Over the land like a god you stand, our maidens howl for your sport—
But kites await in the heather to tear the flesh from your bones.
Clouds and smoke for a broken folk, a lash for the bended back—
Thus you roared when your crimson sword blotted the moon on high,
But sea breaks and the world shakes to the battle's flying wrack,
And Death booms out of the heather to nail you in the sky.

The Grey God Passes

A voice echoed among the bleak reaches of the mountains that reared up gauntly on either hand. At the mouth of the defile that opened on a colossal crag, Conn the thrall wheeled, snarling like a wolf at bay. He was tall and massively, yet rangily, built, the fierceness of the wild dominant in his broad, sloping shoulders, his huge hairy chest and long, heavily muscled arms. His features were in keeping with his bodily aspect—a strong, stubborn jaw, low slanting forehead topped by a shock of tousled tawny hair which added to the wildness of his appearance no more than did his cold blue eyes. His only garment was a scanty loincloth. His own wolfish ruggedness was protection enough against the elements—for he was a slave in an age when even the masters lived lives as hard as the iron environments which bred them.

Now Conn half-crouched, sword ready, a bestial snarl of menace humming in his bull throat, and from the defile there came a tall man, wrapped in a cloak beneath which the thrall glimpsed a sheen of mail. The stranger wore a slouch hat pulled so low that from his shadowed features only one eye gleamed, cold and grim as the grey sea.

"Well, Conn, thrall of Wolfgar Snorri's son," said the stranger in a deep, powerful voice, "whither do you flee, with your master's blood on your hands?"

"I know you not," growled Conn, "nor how you know me. If you would take me, whistle up your dogs and make an end. Some of them will taste steel ere I die."

"Fool!" There was deep scorn in the reverberant tone. "I am no hunter of runaway serfs. There are wilder matters abroad. What do you smell in the sea wind?"

Conn turned toward the sea, lapping greyly at the cliffs far below. He expanded his mighty chest, his nostrils flaring as he breathed deeply.

"I smell the tang of the salt-spume," he answered.

The stranger's voice was like the rasp of swords. "The scent of blood is on the wind—the musk of slaughter and the shouts of the slaying."

Conn shook his head, bewildered. "It is only the wind among the crags."

"There is war in your homeland," said the stranger somberly. "The spears of the South have risen against the swords of the North and the death-fires are lighting the land like the midday sun."

"How can you know this?" asked the thrall uneasily. "No ship has put in to Torka for weeks. Who are you? Whence come you? How know you these things?"

"Can you not hear the skirl of the pipes, the clashing of the axes?" replied the tall stranger. "Can you not smell the war-reek the wind brings?"

"Not I," answered Conn. "It is many a long league from Torka to Erin, and I hear only the wind among the crags and the gulls screeching over the headlands. Yet if there is war, I should be among the weapon-men of my clan, though my life is forfeit to Melaghlin because I slew a man of his in a quarrel."

The stranger gave no heed, standing like a statue as he gazed far out across the reaches of hazy barren mountains and misty waves.

"It is the death-grip," he said, like one who speaks to himself. "Now comes the reaping of kings, the garnering of chiefs like a harvest. Gigantic shadows stalk red-handed across the world, and night is falling on Asgaard. I hear the cries of long-dead heroes whistling in the void, and the shouts of forgotten gods. To each being there is an appointed time, and even the gods must die . . ."

He stiffened suddenly with a great shout, flinging his arms seaward. Tall, rolling clouds, sailing gigantically before the gale, veiled the sea. Out of the mist came a great wind and out of the wind a whirling mass of clouds. And Conn cried out. From out the flying clouds, shadowy and horrific, swept twelve shapes. He saw, as in a nightmare, the twelve winged horses and their riders, women in flaming silver mail and winged helmets, whose golden hair floated out on the wind behind them, and whose cold eyes were fixed on some awesome goal beyond his ken.

"The Choosers of the Slain!" thundered the stranger, flinging his arms wide in a terrible gesture. "They ride in the twilight of the North! The winged hooves spurn the rolling clouds, the web of Fate is spun, the Loom and Spindle broken! Doom roars upon the gods and night falls on Asgaard! Night and the trumpets of Ragnarok!"

The cloak was blown wide in the wind, revealing the mighty, mail-clad figure; the slouch hat fell aside; the wild elf-locks blew free. And Conn shrank before the blaze of the stranger's eye. And he saw that where the other eye should have been, was but an empty socket. Thereat panic seized him, so that he turned and ran down the defile as a man flees demons. And a fearsome backward glance showed him the stranger etched against the cloud-torn sky, cloak blowing in the wind, arms flung high, and it seemed to the thrall that the man had grown monstrously in stature, that he loomed colossal among the clouds, dwarfing the mountains and the sea, and that he was suddenly grey, as with vast age.

II

Oh Masters of the North, we come with tally of remembered dead,
Of broken hearth and blazing home, and rafters crashing overhead.
A single cast of dice we throw to balance, by the leaden sea,
A hundred years of wrong and woe with one red hour of butchery.

The spring gale had blown itself out. The sky smiled blue overhead and the sea lay placid as a pool, with only a few scattered bits of driftwood along the beaches to give mute evidence of her treachery. Along the strand rode a lone horseman, his saffron cloak whipping out behind him, his yellow hair blowing about his face in the breeze.

Suddenly he reined up so short that his spirited steed reared and snorted. From among the sand dunes had risen a man, tall and powerful, of wild, shock-headed aspect, and naked but for a loincloth.

"Who are you," demanded the horseman, "who bear the sword of a chief, yet have the appearance of a masterless man, and wear the collar of a serf withal?"

"I am Conn, young master," answered the wanderer, "once an outlaw, once a thrall—always a man of King Brian's, whether he will or no. And I know you. You are Dunlang O'Hartigan, friend of Murrogh, son of Brian, prince of Dal Cais. Tell me, good sir, is there war in the land?"

"Sooth to say," answered the young chief, "even now King Brian and King Malachi lie encamped at Kilmainham, before Dublin. I have but ridden from the camp this morning. From all the lands of the Vikings King Sitric of Dublin has summoned the slayers, and Gaels and Danes are ready to join battle—and such a battle as Erin has never seen before."

Conn's eyes clouded. "By Crom!" he muttered, half to himself, "it is even as the Grey Man said—yet how could he have known? Surely it was all a dream."

"How come you here?" asked Dunlang.

"From Torka in the Orkneys in an open boat, flung down as a chip is thrown upon the tide. Of yore I slew a man of Meath, kern of Melaghlin, and King Brian's heart was hot against me because of the broken truce; so I fled. Well, the life of an outlaw is hard. Thorwald Raven, Jarl of the Hebrides, took me when I was weak from hunger and wounds, and put this collar on my neck." The kern touched the heavy copper ring encircling his bullneck. "Then he sold me to Wolfgar Snorri's son on Torka. He was a hard master. I did the work of three men, and stood at his back and mowed down carles like wheat when he brawled with his neighbors. In return he gave me crusts from his board, a bare earth floor to sleep on, and deep scars on my back. Finally I could bear it no more, and I leaped upon him in his own skalli and crushed his skull with a log of firewood. Then I took his sword and fled to the mountains, preferring to freeze or starve there rather than die under the lash.

"There in the mountains,"—again Conn's eyes clouded with doubt—"I think I dreamed," he said. "I saw a tall grey man who spoke of war in Erin, and in my dream I saw Valkyries riding southward on the clouds . . .

"Better to die at sea on a good venture than to starve in the Orkney mountains," he continued with more assurance, his feet on firm ground. "By chance I found a fisherman's boat, with a store of food and water, and I put to sea. By Crom! I wonder to find myself still alive! The gale took me in her fangs last night, and I know only that I fought the sea in the boat until the boat sank under my feet, and then fought her in her naked waves until my senses went from me. None could have been more surprised than I when I came to myself this dawn lying like a piece of driftwood on the beach. I have lain in the sun since, trying to warm the cold tang of the sea out of my bones."

"By the saints, Conn," said Dunlang, "I like your spirit."

"I hope King Brian likes it as well," grunted the kern.

"Attach yourself to my train," answered Dunlang. "I'll speak for you. King Brian has weightier matters on his mind than a single blood feud. This very day the opposing hosts lie drawn up for the death-grip."

"Will the spear-shattering fall on the morrow?" asked Conn.

"Not by King Brian's will," answered Dunlang. "He is loath to shed blood on Good Friday. But who knows when the heathen will come down upon us?"

Conn laid a hand on Dunlang's stirrup leather and strode beside him as the steed moved leisurely along.

"There is a notable gathering of weapon-men?"

"More than twenty thousand warriors on each side; the bay of Dublin is dark with the dragon-ships. From the Orkneys comes Jarl Sigurd with his raven banner. From Man comes the Viking Brodir with twenty longships. From the Danelagh in England comes Prince Amlaff, son of the King of Norway, with two thousand men. From all lands the hosts have gathered—from the Orkneys, the Shetlands, the Hebrides—from Scotland, England, Germany, and the lands of Scandinavia.

"Our spies say Sigurd and Brodir have a thousand men armed in steel mail from crown to heel, who fight in a solid wedge. The Dalcassians may be hard put to break that iron wall. Yet, God willing, we shall prevail. Then among the other chiefs and warriors there are Anrad the berserk, Hrafn the Red, Platt of Danemark, Thorstein and his comrade-in-arms Asmund, Thorleif Hordi, the Strong, Athelstane the Saxon, and Thorwald Raven, Jarl of the Hebrides."

At that name Conn grinned savagely and fingered his copper collar. "It is a great gathering if both Sigurd and Brodir come."

"That was the doing of Gormlaith," responded Dunlang.

"Word had come to the Orkneys that Brian had divorced Kormlada," said Conn, unconsciously giving the queen her Norse name.

"Aye—and her heart is black with hate against him. Strange it is that a woman so fair of form and countenance should have the soul of a demon."

"God's truth, my lord. And what of her brother, Prince Mailmora?"

"Who but he is the instigator of the whole war?" cried Dunlang angrily. "The hate between him and Murrogh, so long smoldering, has at last burst into flame, firing both kingdoms. Both were in the wrong—Murrogh perhaps more than Mailmora. Gormlaith goaded her brother on. I did not believe King Brian acted wisely when he gave honors to those against whom he had warred. It was not well he married Gormlaith and gave his daughter to Gormlaith's son, Sitric of Dublin. With Gormlaith he took the seeds of strife and hatred into his palace. She is a wanton; once she was the wife of Amlaff Cauran, the Dane; then she was wife to King Malachi of Meath, and he put her aside because of her wickedness."

"What of Melaghlin?" asked Conn.

"He seems to have forgotten the struggle in which Brian wrested Erin's crown from him. Together the two kings move against the Danes and Mailmora."

As they conversed, they passed along the bare shore until they came into a rough broken stretch of cliffs and boulders; and there they halted suddenly. On a boulder sat a girl, clad in a shimmering green garment whose pattern was so much like scales that for a bewildered instant Conn thought himself gazing on a mermaid come out of the deeps.

"Eevin!" Dunlang swung down from his horse, tossing the reins to Conn, and advanced to take her slender hands in his. "You sent for me and I have come—you've been weeping!"

Conn, holding the steed, felt an impulse to retire, prompted by superstitious qualms. Eevin, with her slender form, her wealth of shimmering golden hair, and her deep mysterious eyes, was not like any other girl he had ever seen. Her entire aspect was different from the women of the Norse-folk and of the Gaels alike, and Conn knew her to be a member of that fading mystic race which had occupied the land before the coming of his ancestors, some of whom still dwelt in caverns along the sea and deep in unfrequented forests—the De Danaans, sorcerers, the Irish said, and kin to the faeries.

"Dunlang!" The girl caught her lover in a convulsive embrace. "You must not go into battle—the weird of far-sight is on me, and I know if you go to the war, you will die! Come away with me—I'll hide you—I'll show you dim purple caverns like the castles of deep-sea kings, and shadowy forests where none save my people has set foot. Come with me and forget wars and hates and prides and ambitions, which are but shadows without reality or substance. Come and learn the dreamy splendors of far places, where fear and hate are naught, and the years seem as hours, drifting forever."

"Eevin, my love!" cried Dunlang, troubled. "You ask that which is beyond my power. When my clan moves into battle, I must be at Murrogh's side, though sure death be my portion. I love you beyond all life, but by the honor of my clan, this is an impossible thing."

"I feared as much," she answered, resigned. "You of the Tall Folk are but children—foolish, cruel, violent—slaying one another in childish quarrels. This is punishment visited on me who, alone of all my people, have loved a man of the Tall Folk. Your rough hands have bruised my soft flesh unwittingly, and your rough spirit as unwittingly bruises my heart."

"I would not hurt you, Eevin," began Dunlang, pained.

"I know," she replied, "the hands of men are not made to handle the delicate body and heart of a woman of the Dark People. It is my fate. I love and I have lost. My sight is a far sight which sees through the veil and the mists of life, behind the past and beyond the future. You will go into battle and the harps will keen for you; and Eevin of Craglea will weep until she melts in tears and the salt tears mingle with the cold salt sea."

Dunlang bowed his head, unspeaking, for her young voice vibrated with the ancient sorrow of womankind; and even the rough kern shuffled his feet uneasily.

"I have brought you a gift against the time of battle," she went on, bending lithely to lift something which caught the sun's sheen. "It may not save you, the ghosts in my soul whisper—but I hope without hope in my heart."

Dunlang stared uncertainly at what she spread before him.

Conn, edging closer and craning his neck, saw a hauberk of strange workmanship and a helmet such as he had never seen before—a heavy affair made to slip over the entire head and rest on the neckpieces of the hauberk. There was no movable vizor, merely a slit cut in the front through which to see, and the workmanship was of an earlier, more civilized age, which no man living could duplicate.

Dunlang looked at it askance, with the characteristic Celtic antipathy toward armor. The Britons who faced Caesar's legionaries fought naked, judging a man cowardly who cased himself in metal, and in later ages the Irish clans entertained the same conviction regarding Strongbow's mailclad knights.

"Eevin," said Dunlang, "my brothers will laugh at me if I enclose myself in iron, like a Dane. How can a man have full freedom of limb, weighted by such a garment? Of all the Gaels, only Turlogh Dubh wears full mail."

"And is any man of the Gael less brave than he?" she cried passionately. "Oh, you of the Tall People are foolish! For ages the ironclad Danes have trampled you, when you might have swept them out of the land long ago, but for your foolish pride."

"Not altogether pride, Eevin," argued Dunlang. "Of what avail is mail or plated armor against the Dalcassian ax which cuts through iron like cloth?"

"Mail would turn the swords of the Danes," she answered, "and not even an ax of the O'Briens would rend this armor. Long it has lain in the deep-sea caverns of my people, carefully protected from rust. He who wore it was a warrior of Rome in the long ago, before the legions were withdrawn from Britain. In an ancient war on the border of Wales, it fell into the hands of my people, and because its wearer was a great prince, my people treasured it. Now I beg you to wear it, if you love me."

Dunlang took it hesitantly, nor could he know that it was the armor worn by a gladiator in the days of the later Roman empire, nor wonder by what chance it had been worn by an officer in the British legion. Little of that knew Dunlang who, like most of his brother chiefs, could neither read nor write; knowledge and education were for monks and priests; a fighting man was kept too busy to cultivate the arts and sciences. He took the armor, and because he loved the strange girl, agreed to wear it—"If it will fit me."

"It will fit," she answered. "But I will see you no more alive."

She held out her white arms and he gathered her hungrily to him, while Conn looked away. Then Dunlang gently unlocked her clinging arms from about his neck, kissed her, and tore himself free.

Without a backward glance he mounted his steed and rode away, with Conn trotting easily alongside. Looking back in the gathering dusk, the kern saw Eevin standing there still, a poignant picture of despair.

III

The campfires sent up showers of sparks and illumined the land like day. In the distance loomed the grim walls of Dublin, dark and ominously silent; before the walls flickered other fires where the warriors of Leinster, under King Mailmora, whetted their axes for the coming battle. Out in the bay, the starlight glinted on myriad sails, shield rails and arching serpent-prows. Between the city and the fires of the Irish host stretched the plain of Clontarf, bordered by Tomar's Wood, dark and rustling in the night, and the Liffey's dark, star-flecked waters.

Before his tent, the firelight playing on his white beard and glinting from his undimmed eagle eyes, sat the great King Brian Boru, among his chiefs. The king was old—seventy-three winters had passed over his lion-like head—long years crammed with fierce wars and bloody intrigues. Yet his back was straight, his arm unwithered, his voice deep and resonant. His chiefs stood about him, tall warriors with war-hardened hands and eyes whetted by the sun and the winds and the high places; tigerish princes in their rich tunics, green girdles, leathern sandals and saffron mantles caught with great golden brooches.

They were an array of war-eagles—Murrogh, Brian's eldest son, the pride of all Erin, tall and mighty, with wide blue eyes that were never placid, but danced with mirth, dulled with sadness, or blazed with fury; Murrogh's young son, Turlogh, a supple lad of fifteen with golden locks and an eager face—tense with anticipation of trying his hand for the first time in the great game of war. And there was that other Turlogh, his cousin—Turlogh Dubh, who was only a few years older but who already had his full stature and was famed throughout all Erin for his berserk rages and the cunning of his deadly ax-play. And there were Meathla O'Faelan, prince of Desmond or South Munster, and his kin—the Great Stewards of Scotland—Lennox, and Donald of Mar, who had crossed the Irish Channel with their wild Highlanders—tall men, somber and gaunt and silent. And there were Dunlang O'Hartigan and O'Hyne, chief of Connacht. But O'Kelly, brother chief of the O'Hyne, and prince of Hy Many, was in the tent of his uncle, King Malachi O'Neill, which was pitched in the camp of the Meathmen, apart from the Dalcassians, and

King Brian was brooding on the matter. For since the setting of the sun, O'Kelly had been closeted with the King of Meath, and no man knew what passed between them.

Nor was Donagh, son of Brian, among the chiefs before the royal pavilion, for he was afield with a band ravaging the holdings of Mailmora of Leinster.

Now Dunlang approached the king, leading with him Conn the kern.

"My Lord," quoth Dunlang, "here is a man who was outlawed aforetime, who has spent vile durance among the Gall, and who risked his life by storm and sea to return and fight under your banner. From the Orkneys in an open boat he came, naked and alone, and the sea cast him all but lifeless on the sand."

Brian stiffened; even in small things his memory was sharp as a whetted stone. "Thou!" he cried. "Aye, I remember him. Well, Conn, you have come back—and with your red hands!"

"Aye, King Brian," answered Conn stolidly, "my hands are red, it is true, and so I look to washing off the stain in Danish blood."

"You dare stand before me, to whom your life is forfeit!"

"This alone I know, King Brian," said Conn boldly, "my father was with you at Sulcoit and the sack of Limerick, and before that followed you in your days of wandering and was one of the fifteen warriors who remained to you when King Mahon, your brother, came seeking you in the forest. And my grandsire followed Murkertagh of the Leather Cloaks, and my people have fought the Danes since the days of Thorgils. You need men who can strike strong blows, and it is my right to die in battle against my ancient enemies, rather than shamefully at the end of a rope."

King Brian nodded. "Well spoken. Take your life. Your days of outlawry are at an end. King Malachi would perhaps think otherwise, since it was a man of his you slew, but—" He paused; an old doubt ate at his soul at the thought of the King of Meath. "Let it be," he went on, "let it rest until after the battle—mayhap that will be world's end for us all."

Dunlang stepped toward Conn and laid hand on the copper collar. "Let us cut this away; you are a free man now."

But Conn shook his head. "Not until I have slain Thorwald Raven who put it there. I'll wear it into battle as a sign of no quarter."

"That is a noble sword you wear, kern," said Murrogh suddenly.

"Aye, my Lord. Murkertagh of the Leather Cloaks wielded this blade until Blacair the Dane slew him at Ardee, and it remained in the possession of the Gall until I took it from the body of Wolfgar Snorri's son."

"It is not fitting that a kern should wear the sword of a king," said Murrogh brusquely. "Let one of the chiefs take it and give him an ax instead."

Conn's fingers locked about the hilt. "He would take the sword from me had best give me the ax first," he said grimly, "and that suddenly."

Murrogh's hot temper blazed. With an oath, he strode toward Conn, who met him eye to eye and gave back not a step.

"Be at ease, my son," ordered King Brian. "Let the kern keep the blade."

Murrogh shrugged. His mood changed. "Aye, keep it and follow me into battle. We shall see if a king's sword in a kern's hands can hew as wide a path as a prince's blade."

"My lords," said Conn, "it may be God's will that I fall in the first onset—but the scars of slavery burn deep in my back this night, and I will not be backward when the spears are splintering."

IV

Therefore your doom is on you,
Is on you and your kings. . . .
—*Chesterton*

While King Brian communed with his chiefs on the plains above Clontarf, a grisly ritual was being enacted within the gloomy castle that was at once the fortress and palace of Dublin's king. With good reason did Christians fear and hate those grim walls; Dublin was a pagan city, ruled by savage heathen kings, and dark were the deeds committed therein.

In an inner chamber in the castle stood the Viking Brodir, somberly watching a ghastly sacrifice on a grim black altar. On that monstrous stone writhed a naked, frothing thing that had been a comely youth; brutally bound and gagged, he could only twist convulsively beneath the dripping, inexorable dagger in the hands of the white-bearded wild-eyed priest of Odin.

The blade hacked through flesh and thew and bone; blood gushed, to be caught in a broad, copper bowl, which the priest, with his red-dappled beard, held high, invoking Odin in a frenzied chant. His thin, bony fingers tore the yet pulsing heart from the butchered breast, and his wild half-mad eyes scanned it with avid intensity.

"What of your divinations?" demanded Brodir impatiently.

Shadows flickered in the priest's cold eyes, and his flesh crawled with a mysterious horror. "Fifty years I have served Odin," he said—

"Fifty years divined by the bleeding heart, but never such portents as these. Hark, Brodir!—If ye fight not on Good Friday, as the Christians call it, your host will be utterly routed and all your chiefs slain; if ye fight on Good Friday, King Brian will die—but he will win the day."

Brodir cursed with cold venom.

The priest shook his ancient head. "I cannot fathom the portent—and I am the last of the priests of the Flaming Circle, who learned mysteries at the feet of Thorgils. I see battle and slaughter—and yet more—shapes gigantic and terrible that stalk monstrously through the mists. . ."

"Enough of such mummery," snarled Brodir. "If I fall I would take Brian to Helheim with me. We go against the Gaels on the morrow, fall fair, fall foul!" He turned and strode from the room.

Brodir traversed a winding corridor and entered another, more spacious chamber, adorned, like all the Dublin king's palace, with the loot of all the world—gold-chased weapons, rare tapestries, rich rugs, divans from Byzantium and the East—plunder taken from all peoples by the roving Norsemen; for Dublin was the center of the Vikings' wide-flung world, the headquarters whence they fared forth to loot the kings of the earth.

A queenly form rose to greet him. Kormlada, whom the Gaels called Gormlaith, was indeed fair, but there was cruelty in her face and in her hard, scintillant eyes. She was of mixed Irish and Danish blood, and looked the part of a barbaric queen, with her pendant earrings, her golden armlets and anklets, and her silver breastplates set with jewels. But for these breastplates, her only garments were a short silken skirt which came halfway to her knees and was held in place by a wide girdle about her lithe waist, and sandals of soft red leather. Her hair was red-gold, her eyes light grey and glittering. Queen she had been, of Dublin, of Meath, and of Thomond. And queen she was still, for she held her son Sitric and her brother Mailmora in the palm of her slim white hand. Carried off in a raid in her childhood by Amlaff Cauran, King of Dublin, she had early discovered her power over men. As the child-wife of the rough Dane, she had swayed his kingdom at will, and her ambitions increased with her power.

Now she faced Brodir with her alluring, mysterious smile, but secret uneasiness ate at her. In all the world there was but one woman she feared, and but one man. And the man was Brodir. With him she was never entirely certain of her course; she duped him as she duped all men, but it was with many misgivings, for she sensed in him an elemental savagery which, once loosed, she might not be able to control.

"What of the priest's words, Brodir?" she asked.

"If we avoid battle on the morrow we lose," the Viking answered moodily. "If we fight, Brian wins, but falls. We fight—the more because my spies tell me Donagh is away from camp with a strong band, ravaging Mailmora's lands. We have sent spies to Malachi, who has an old grudge against Brian, urging him to desert the king—or at least to stand aside and aid neither of us. We have offered him rich rewards and Brian's lands to rule. Ha! Let him step into our trap! Not gold, but a bloody sword we will give him. With Brian crushed we will turn on Malachi and tread him into the dust! But first—Brian."

She clenched her white hands in savage exultation. "Bring me his head! I'll hang it above our bridal bed."

"I have heard strange tales," said Brodir soberly. "Sigurd has boasted in his cups."

Kormlada started and scanned the inscrutable countenance. Again she felt a quiver of fear as she gazed at the somber Viking with his tall, strong stature, his dark, menacing face, and his heavy black locks which he wore braided and caught in his sword-belt.

"What has Sigurd said?" she asked, striving to make her voice casual.

"When Sitric came to me in my skalli on the Isle of Man," said Brodir, red glints beginning to smolder in his dark eyes, "it was his oath that if I came to his aid, I should sit on the throne of Ireland with you as my queen. Now that fool of an Orkneyman, Sigurd, boasts in his ale that *he* was promised the same reward."

She forced a laugh. "He was drunk."

Brodir burst into wild cursing as the violence of the untamed Viking surged up in him. "You lie, you wanton!" he shouted, seizing her white wrist in an iron grip. "You were born to lure men to their doom! But you will not play fast and loose with Brodir of Man!"

"You are mad!" she cried, twisting vainly in his grasp. "Release me, or I'll call my guards!"

"Call them!" he snarled, "and I'll slash the heads from their bodies. Cross me now and blood will run ankle-deep in Dublin's streets. By Thor! There will be no city left for Brian to burn! Mailmora, Sitric, Sigurd, Amlaff—I'll cut all their throats and drag you naked to my ship by your yellow hair. Dare to call out!"

She dared not. He forced her to her knees, twisting her white arm so brutally that she bit her lip to keep from screaming.

"You promised Sigurd the same thing you promised me," he went on in ill-controlled fury, "knowing neither of us would throw away his life for less!"

"No! No!" she shrieked. "I swear by the ring of Thor!" Then, as the agony grew unbearable, she dropped pretense. "Yes—yes, I promised him—oh, let me go!"

"So!" The Viking tossed her contemptuously onto a pile of silken cushions, where she lay whimpering and disheveled. "You promised me and you promised Sigurd," he said, looming menacingly above her, "but your promise to me you'll keep—else you had better never been born. The throne of Ireland is a small thing beside my desire for you—if I cannot have you, no one shall."

"But what of Sigurd?"

"He'll fall in battle—or afterward," he answered grimly.

"Good enough!" Dire indeed was the extremity in which Kormlada had not her wits about her. "It's you I love, Brodir; I promised him only because he would not aid us otherwise."

"Love!" The Viking laughed savagely. "You love Kormlada—none other. But you'll keep your vow to me or you'll rue it." And, turning on his heel, he left her chamber.

Kormlada rose, rubbing her arm where the blue marks of his fingers marred her skin. "May he fall in the first charge!" she ground between her teeth. "If either survive, may it be that tall fool, Sigurd—methinks he would be a husband easier to manage than that black-haired savage. I will perforce marry him if he survives the battle, but by Thor! he shall not long press the throne of Ireland—I'll send him to join Brian."

"You speak as though King Brian were already dead." A tranquil voice behind Kormlada brought her about to face the other person in the world she feared besides Brodir. Her eyes widened as they fell upon a slender girl clad in shimmering green, a girl whose golden hair glimmered with unearthly light in the glow of the candles. The queen recoiled, hands outstretched as if to fend her away.

"Eevin! Stand back, witch! Cast no spell on me! How came you into my palace?"

"How came the breeze through the trees?" answered the Danaan girl. "What was Brodir saying to you before I entered?"

"If you are a sorceress, you know," sullenly answered the queen.

Eevin nodded. "Aye, I know. In your own mind I read it. He had consulted the oracle of the sea-people—the blood and the torn heart,"—her dainty lips curled with disgust—"and he told you he would attack tomorrow."

The queen blenched and made no reply, fearing to meet Eevin's magnetic eyes. She felt naked before the mysterious girl who could uncannily sift the contents of her mind and empty it of its secrets.

Eevin stood with bent head for a moment, then raised her head suddenly. Kormlada started, for something akin to fear shone in the were-girl's eyes.

"Who is in this castle?" she cried.

"You know as well as I," muttered Kormlada. "Sitric, Sigurd, Brodir."

"There is another!" exclaimed Eevin, paling and shuddering. "Ah, I know him of old—I feel him—he bears the cold of the North with him, the shivering tang of icy seas. . ."

She turned and slipped swiftly through the velvet hangings that masked a hidden doorway Kormlada had thought known only to herself and her women, leaving the queen bewildered and uneasy.

In the sacrificial chamber, the ancient priest still mumbled over the gory altar upon which lay the mutilated victim of his rite. "Fifty years I have served Odin," he maundered. "And never such portents have I read. Odin laid his mark upon me long ago in a night of horror. The years fall like withered leaves, and my age draws to a close. One by one I have seen the altars of Odin crumble. If the Christians win this battle, Odin's day is done. It comes upon me that I have offered up my last sacrifice. . ."

A deep, powerful voice spoke behind him. "And what more fitting than that you should accompany the soul of that last sacrifice to the realm of him you served?"

The priest wheeled, the sacrificial dagger falling from his hand. Before him stood a tall man, wrapped in a cloak beneath which shone the gleam of armor. A slouch hat was pulled low over his forehead, and when he pushed it back, a single eye, glittering and grim as the grey sea, met his horrified gaze.

Warriors who rushed into the chamber at the strangled scream that burst hideously forth, found the old priest dead beside his corpse-laden altar, unwounded, but with face and body shriveled as by some intolerable exposure, and a soul-shaking horror in his glassy eyes. Yet, save for the corpses, the chamber was empty, and none had been seen to enter it since Brodir had gone forth.

Alone in his tent with the heavily armed gallaglachs ranged outside, King Brian was dreaming a strange dream. In his dream a tall grey giant loomed terribly above him and cried in a voice that was like thunder among the clouds, "Beware, champion of the white Christ! Though you smite my children with the sword and drive me into the dark voids of Jotunheim, yet shall I work you rue! As you smite my children with the sword, so shall I smite the son of your body, and as I go into the dark, so shall you go, likewise, when the Choosers of the Slain ride the clouds above the battlefield!"

The thunder of the giant's voice and the awesome glitter of his single eye froze the blood of the king who had never known fear, and with a strangled cry, he woke, starting up. The thick torches which burned outside illumined the interior of his tent sufficiently well for him to make out a slender form.

"Eevin!" he cried. "By my soul! It is well for kings that your people take no part in the intrigues of mortals, when you can steal under the very noses of the guards into our tents. Do you seek Dunlang?"

The girl shook her head sadly. "I see him no more alive, great king. Were I to go to him now, my own black sorrow might unman him. I will come to him among the dead tomorrow."

King Brian shivered.

"But it is not of my woes that I came to speak, My Lord," she continued wearily. "It is not the way of the Dark People to take part in the quarrels of the Tall Folk—but I love one of them. This night I talked with Gormlaith."

Brian winced at the name of his divorced queen. "And your news?" he asked.

"Brodir strikes on the morrow."

The king shook his head heavily. "It vexes my soul to spill blood on the Holy Day. But if God wills it, we will not await their onslaught—we will march at dawn to meet them. I will send a swift runner to bring back Donagh. . ."

Eevin shook her head once more. "Nay, great king. Let Donagh live. After the battle the Dalcassians will need strong arms to brace the scepter."

Brian gazed fixedly at her. "I read my doom in those words. Have you cast my fate?"

Eevin spread her hands helplessly. "My Lord, not even the Dark People can rend the Veil at will. Not by the casting of fates, or the sorcery of divination, not in smoke or in blood have I read it, but a weird is upon me and I see through flame and the dim clash of battle."

"And I shall fall?"

She bowed her face in her hands.

"Well, let it fall as God wills," said King Brian tranquilly. "I have lived long and deeply. Weep not—through the darkest mists of gloom and night, dawn yet rises on the world. My clan will revere you in the long days to come. Now go, for the night wanes toward morn, and I would make my peace with God."

And Eevin of Craglea went like a shadow from the king's tent.

V

The war was like a dream; I cannot tell
How many heathen souls I sent to Hell.
I only know, above the fallen ones
I heard dark Odin shouting to his sons,
And felt amid the battle's roar and shock
The strife of gods that crashed in Ragnarok.
—*Conn's Saga*

Through the mist of the whitening dawn men moved like ghosts and weapons clanked eerily. Conn stretched his muscular arms, yawned cavernously, and loosened his great blade in its sheath. "This is the day the ravens drink blood, My Lord," he said, and Dunlang O'Hartigan nodded absently.

"Come hither and aid me to don this cursed cage," said the young chief. "For Eevin's sake I'll wear it; but by the saints! I had rather battle stark naked!"

The Gaels were on the move, marching from Kilmainham in the same formation in which they intended to enter battle. First came the Dalcassians, big rangy men in their saffron tunics, with a round buckler of steel-braced yew wood on the left arm, and the right hand gripping the dreaded Dalcassian ax. This ax differed greatly from the heavy weapon of the Danes; the Irish wielded it with one hand, the thumb stretched along the haft to guide the blow, and they had attained a skill at ax-fighting never before or since equaled. Hauberks they had none, neither the gallaglachs nor the kerns, though some of their chiefs, like Murrogh, wore light steel caps. But the tunics of warriors and chiefs alike had been woven with such skill and steeped in vinegar until their remarkable toughness afforded some protection against sword and arrow.

At the head of the Dalcassians strode Prince Murrogh, his fierce eyes alight, smiling as though he went to a feast instead of a slaughtering. On one side went Dunlang in his Roman corselet, closely followed by Conn, bearing the helmet, and on the other the two Turloghs—the son of Murrogh, and Turlogh Dubh, who alone of all the Dalcassians always went into battle fully armored. He looked grim enough, despite his youth, with his dark face and smoldering blue eyes, clad as he was in a full shirt of black mail, mail leggings and a steel helmet with a mail drop, and bearing a spiked buckler. Unlike the rest of the chiefs, who preferred their swords in battle, Black Turlogh fought with an ax of his own forging, and his skill with the weapon was almost uncanny.

Close behind the Dalcassians were the two companies of the Scottish, with their chiefs, the Great Stewards of Scotland, who, veterans of long wars with the Saxons, wore helmets with horsehair crests and coats of mail. With them came the men of South Munster commanded by Prince Meathla O'Faelan.

The third division consisted of the warriors of Connacht, wild men of the west, shock headed and naked but for their wolfskins, with their chiefs O'Kelly and O'Hyne. O'Kelly marched as a man whose soul is heavy, for the shadow of his meeting with Malachi the night before fell gauntly across him.

Somewhat apart from the three main divisions marched the tall gallaglachs and kerns of Meath, their king riding slowly before them.

And before all the host rode King Brian Boru on a white steed, his white locks blown about his ancient face and his eyes strange and fey, so that the wild kerns gazed on him with superstitious awe.

So the Gaels came before Dublin, where they saw the hosts of Leinster and Lochlann drawn up in battle array, stretching in a wide crescent from Dubhgall's Bridge to the narrow river Tolka which cuts the plain of Clontarf. Three main divisions there were—the foreign Northmen, the Vikings, with Sigurd and the grim Brodir; flanking them on the one side, the fierce Danes of Dublin, under their chief, a somber wanderer whose name no man knew, but who was called Dubhgall, the Dark Stranger; and on the other flank the Irish of Leinster, with their king, Mailmora. The Danish fortress on the hill beyond the Liffey River bristled with armed men where King Sitric guarded the city.

There was but one way into the city from the north, the direction from which the Gaels were advancing, for in those days Dublin lay wholly south of the Liffey; that was the bridge called Dubhgall's Bridge. The Danes stood with one horn of their line guarding this entrance, their ranks curving out toward the Tolka, their backs to the sea. The Gaels advanced along the level plain which stretched between Tomar's Wood and the shore.

With little more than a bowshot separating the hosts, the Gaels halted, and King Brian rode in front of them, holding aloft a crucifix. "Sons of Goidhel!" his voice rang like a trumpet call. "It is not given me to lead you into the fray, as I led you in days of old. But I have pitched my tent behind your lines, where you must trample me if you flee. You will not flee! Remember a hundred years of outrage and infamy! Remember your burned homes, your slaughtered kin, your ravaged women, your babes enslaved! Before you stand your oppressors! On this day our good Lord died for you! There stand the heathen hordes which revile His Name and slay His people! I have but one command to give you—conquer or die!"

The wild hordes yelled like wolves and a forest of axes brandished on high. King Brian bowed his head and his face was grey.

"Let them lead me back to my tent," he whispered to Murrogh. "Age has withered me from the play of the axes and my doom is hard upon me. Go forth, and may God stiffen your arms to the slaying!"

Now as the king rode slowly back to his tent among his guardsmen, there was a taking up of girdles, a drawing of blades, a dressing of shields. Conn placed the Roman helmet on Dunlang's head and grinned at the result, for the young chief looked like some mythical iron monster out of Norse legendry. The hosts moved inexorably toward each other.

The Vikings had assumed their favorite wedge-shaped formation with Sigurd and Brodir at the tip. The Northmen offered a strong contrast to the loose lines of the half-naked Gaels. They moved in compact ranks, armored with horned helmets, heavy scale-mail coats reaching to their knees, and leggings of seasoned wolf-hide braced with iron plates; and they bore great kite-shaped shields of linden wood with iron rims, and long spears. The thousand warriors in the forefront wore long leggings and gauntlets of mail as well, so that from crown to heel they were steelclad. These marched in a solid shield-wall, bucklers overlapping, and over their iron ranks floated the grim raven banner which had always brought victory to Jarl Sigurd—even if it brought death to the bearer. Now it was borne by old Rane Asgrimm's son, who felt that the hour of his death was at hand.

At the tip of the wedge, like the point of a spear, were the champions of Lochlann—Brodir in his dully glittering blue mail, which no blade had even dented; Jarl Sigurd, tall, blond bearded, gleaming in his golden-scaled hauberk; Hrafn the Red, in whose soul lurked a mocking devil that moved him to gargantuan laughter even in the madness of battle; the tall comrades, Thorstein and Asmund; Prince Amlaff, roving son of the King of Norway; Platt of Danemark; Athelstane the Saxon; Jarl Thorwald Raven of the Hebrides; Anrad the berserk.

Toward this formidable array the Irish advanced at quick pace in more or less open formation and with scant attempt at any orderly ranks. But Malachi and his warriors wheeled suddenly and drew off to the extreme left, taking up their position on the high ground by Cabra. And when Murrogh saw this, he cursed under his breath, and Black Turlogh growled, "Who said an O'Neill forgets an old grudge? By Crom! Murrogh, we may have to guard our backs as well as our breasts before this fight be won!"

Now suddenly from the Viking ranks strode Platt of Danemark, his red hair like a crimson veil about his bare head, his silver mail gleaming. The hosts watched eagerly, for in those days few battles began without preliminary single combats.

"Donald!" shouted Platt, flinging up his naked sword so that the rising sun caught it in a sheen of silver. "Where is Donald of Mar? Are you there, Donald, as you were at Rhu Stoir, or do you skulk from the fray?"

"I am here, rogue!" answered the Scottish chief as he strode, tall and gaunt, from among his men, flinging away his scabbard.

Highlander and Dane met in the middle space between the hosts, Donald cautious as a hunting wolf, Platt leaping in reckless and headlong, eyes alight and dancing with a laughing madness. Yet it was the wary Steward's foot which slipped suddenly on a rolling pebble, and before he could regain his balance, Platt's sword lunged into him so fiercely that the keen point tore through his corselet-scales and sank deep beneath his heart. Platt's mad yell of exultation broke in a gasp. Even as he crumpled, Donald of Mar lashed out a dying stroke that split the Dane's head, and the two fell together.

Thereat a deep-toned roar went up to the heavens, and the two great hosts rolled together like a tidal wave. Then were struck the first blows of the battle. There were no maneuvers of strategy, no cavalry charges, no flights of arrows. Forty thousand men fought on foot, hand to hand, man to man, slaying and dying in red chaos. The battle broke in howling waves about the spears and axes of the warriors. The first to shock were the Dalcassians and the Vikings, and as they met, both lines rocked at the impact. The deep roar of the Norsemen mingled with the yells of the Gaels and the Northern spears splintered among the Western axes. Foremost in the fray, Murrogh's great body heaved and strained as he roared and smote right and left with a heavy sword in either hand, mowing down men like corn. Neither shield nor helmet stood beneath his terrible blows, and behind him came his warriors slashing and howling like devils. Against the compact lines of the Dublin Danes thundered the wild tribesmen of Connacht, and the men of South Munster and their Scottish allies fell vengefully upon the Irish of Leinster.

The iron lines writhed and interwove across the plain. Conn, following Dunlang, grinned savagely as he smote home with dripping blade, and his fierce eyes sought for Thorwald Raven among the spears. But in that mad sea of battle where wild faces came and went like waves, it was difficult to pick out any one man.

At first both lines held without giving an inch; feet braced, straining breast to breast, they snarled and hacked, shield jammed hard against shield. All up and down the line of battle blades shimmered and flashed like sea spray in the sun, and the roar of battle shook the ravens that wheeled like Valkyries overhead. Then, when human flesh and blood could stand no more, the serried lines began to roll forward or back. The Leinstermen flinched before the fierce onslaught of the Munster clans and their Scottish allies, giving way slowly, foot by foot, cursed by their king, who fought on foot with a sword in the forefront of the fray.

But on the other flanks, the Danes of Dublin under the redoubtable Dubhgall had held against the first blasting charge of the Western tribes, though their ranks reeled at the shock, and now the wild men in their wolfskins were falling like garnered grain before the Danish axes.

In the center, the battle raged most fiercely; the wedge-shaped shield-wall of the Vikings held, and against its iron ranks the Dalcassians hurled their half-naked bodies in vain. A ghastly heap ringed that rim wall as Brodir and Sigurd began a slow, steady advance, the inexorable onstride of the Vikings, hacking deeper and deeper into the loose formation of the Gaels.

On the walls of Dublin Castle, King Sitric, watching the fight with Kormlada and his wife, exclaimed, "Well do the sea kings reap the field!"

Kormlada's beautiful eyes blazed with wild exultation. "Fall, Brian!" she cried fiercely. "Fall, Murrogh! And fall too, Brodir! Let the keen ravens feed!" Her voice faltered as her eyes fell upon a tall, cloaked figure standing on the battlements, apart from the people—a somber grey giant, brooding over the battle. A cold fear stole over her and froze the words on her lips. She plucked at Sitric's cloak. "Who is he?" she whispered, pointing.

Sitric looked and shuddered. "I know not. Pay him no heed. Go not near him. When I but approached him, he spoke not or looked at me, but a cold wind blew over me and my heart shriveled. Let us rather watch the battle. The Gaels give way."

But at the foremost point of the Gaelic advance, the line held. There, like the convex center of a curving ax-blade, fought Murrogh and his chiefs. The great prince was already streaming blood from gashes on his limbs, but his heavy swords flamed in double strokes that dealt death like a harvest, and the chiefs at his side mowed down the corn of battle. Fiercely Murrogh sought to reach Sigurd through the press. He saw the tall Jarl looming across the waves of spears and heads, striking blows like thunderstrokes, and the sight drove the Gaelic prince to madness. But he could not reach the Viking.

"The warriors are forced back," gasped Dunlang, seeking to shake the sweat from his eyes. The young chief was untouched; spears and axes alike splintered on the Roman helmet or glanced from the ancient cuirass, but, unused to armor, he felt like a chained wolf.

Murrogh spared a single swift glance; on either side of the clump of chiefs, the gallaglachs were falling back, slowly, savagely, selling each foot of ground with blood, unable to halt the irresistible advance of the mailed Northmen. These were falling, too, all along the battleline, but they closed ranks and forced their way forward, legs braced hard, bodies strained, spears driving without cease or pause; they plowed on through a red surf of dead and dying.

"Turlogh!" gasped Murrogh, dashing the blood from his eyes. "Haste from the fray for Malachi! Bid him charge, in God's name!"

But the frenzy of slaughter was on Black Turlogh; froth flecked his lips and his eyes were those of a madman. "The Devil take Malachi!" he shouted, splitting a Dane's skull with a stroke like the slash of a tiger's paw.

"Conn!" called Murrogh, and as he spoke he gripped the big kern's shoulder and dragged him back. "Haste to Malachi—we need his support."

Conn drew reluctantly away from the melee, clearing his path with thunderous strokes. Across the reeling sea of blades and rocking helmets he saw the towering form of Jarl Sigurd and his lords—the billowing folds of the raven banner floated above them as their whistling swords hewed down men like wheat before the reaper.

Free of the press, the kern ran swiftly along the battleline until he came to the higher ground of Cabra where the Meathmen thronged, tense and trembling like hunting hounds as they gripped their weapons and looked eagerly at their king. Malachi stood apart, watching the fray with moody eyes, his lion's head bowed, his fingers twined in his golden beard.

"King Melaghlin," said Conn bluntly, "Prince Murrogh urges you to charge home, for the press is great and the men of the Gael are hard beset."

The great O'Neill lifted his head and stared absently at the kern. Conn little guessed the chaotic struggle which was taking place in Malachi's soul—the red visions which thronged his brain—riches, power, the rule of all Erin, balanced against the black shame of treachery. He gazed out across the field where the banner of his nephew O'Kelly heaved among the spears. And Malachi shuddered, but shook his head.

"Nay," he said, "it is not time. I will charge—when the time comes."

For an instant king and kern looked into each others' eyes. Malachi's eyes dropped. Conn turned without a word and sped down the slope. As he went, he saw that the advance of Lennox and the men of Desmond had been checked. Mailmora, raging like a wild man, had cut down Prince Meathla O'Faelan with his own hand, a chance spear-thrust had wounded the Great Steward, and now the Leinstermen held fast against the onset of the Munster and Scottish clans. But where the Dalcassians fought, the battle was locked; the Prince of Thomond broke the onrush of the Norsemen like a jutting cliff that breaks the sea.

Conn reached Murrogh in the upheaval of slaughter. "Melaghlin says he will charge when the time comes."

"Hell to his soul!" cried Black Turlogh. "We are betrayed!"

Murrogh's blue eyes flamed. "Then in the name of God!" he roared, *"Let us charge and die!"*

The struggling men were stirred at his shout. The blind passion of the Gael surged up, bred of desperation; the lines stiffened, and a great shout shook the field that made King Sitric on his castle wall whiten and grip the parapet. He had heard such shouting before.

Now, as Murrogh leaped forward, the Gaels awoke to red fury as in men who have no hope. The nearness of doom woke frenzy in them, and, like inspired madmen, they hurled their last charge and smote the wall of shields, which reeled at the blow. No human power could stay the onslaught. Murrogh and his chiefs no longer hoped to win, or even to live, but only to glut their fury as they died, and in their despair they fought like wounded tigers—severing limbs, splitting skulls, cleaving breasts and shoulder bones. Close at Murrogh's heels, flamed the ax of Black Turlogh and the swords of Dunlang and the chiefs; under that torrent of steel the iron line crumpled and gave, and through the breach the frenzied Gaels poured. The shield formation melted away.

At the same moment the wild men of Connacht again hurled a desperate charge against the Dublin Danes. O'Hyne and Dubhgall fell together and the Dublin men were battered backward, disputing every foot. The whole field melted into a mingled mass of slashing battlers without rank or formation. Among a heap of torn Dalcassian dead, Murrogh came at last upon Jarl Sigurd. Behind the Jarl stood grim old Rane Asgrimm's son, holding the raven banner. Murrogh slew him with a single stroke. Sigurd turned, and his sword rent Murrogh's tunic and gashed his chest, but the Irish prince smote so fiercely on the Norseman's shield that Jarl Sigurd reeled backward.

Thorleif Hordi had picked up the banner, but scarce had he lifted it when Black Turlogh, his eyes glaring, broke through and split his skull to the teeth. Sigurd, seeing his banner fallen once more, struck Murrogh with such desperate fury that his sword bit through the prince's morion and gashed his scalp. Blood jetted down Murrogh's face, and he reeled, but before Sigurd could strike again, Black Turlogh's ax licked out like a flicker of lightning. The Jarl's warding shield fell shattered from his arm, and Sigurd gave back for an instant, daunted by the play of that deathly ax. Then a rush of warriors swept the raging chiefs apart.

"Thorstein!" shouted Sigurd. "Take up the banner!"

"Touch it not!" cried Asmund. "Who bears it, dies!" Even as he spoke, Dunlang's sword crushed his skull.

"Hrafn!" called Sigurd desperately. "Bear the banner!"

"Bear your own curse!" answered Hrafn. "This is the end of us all."

"Cowards!" roared the Jarl, snatching up the banner himself and striving to gather it under his cloak as Murrogh, face bloodied and eyes blazing, broke through to him. Sigurd flung up his sword—too late. The weapon in Murrogh's right hand splintered on his helmet, bursting the straps that held it and ripping it from his head, and Murrogh's left-hand sword, whistling in behind the first blow, shattered the Jarl's skull and felled him dead in the bloody folds of the great banner that wrapped about him as he went down.

Now a great roar went up, and the Gaels redoubled their strokes. With the formation of shields torn apart, the mail of the Vikings could not save them; for the Dalcassian axes, flashing in the sun, hewed through chainmesh and iron plates alike, rending linden shield and horned helmet. Yet the Danes did not break.

On the high ramparts, King Sitric had turned pale, his hands trembling where he gripped the parapet. He knew that these wild men could not be beaten now, for they spilled their lives like water, hurling their naked bodies again and again into the fangs of spear and ax. Kormlada was silent, but Sitric's wife, King Brian's daughter, cried out in joy, for her heart was with her own people.

Murrogh was striving now to reach Brodir, but the black Viking had seen Sigurd die. Brodir's world was crumbling; even his vaunted mail was failing him, for though it had thus far saved his skin, it was tattered now. Never before had the Manx Viking faced the dreaded Dalcassian ax. He drew back from Murrogh's onset. In the crush, an ax shattered on Murrogh's helmet, knocking him to his knees and blinding him momentarily with its impact. Dunlang's sword wove a wheel of death above the fallen prince, and Murrogh reeled up.

The press slackened as Black Turlogh, Conn and young Turlogh drove in, hacking and stabbing, and Dunlang, frenzied by the heat of battle, tore off his helmet and flung it aside, ripping off his cuirass.

"The Devil eat such cages!" he shouted, catching at the reeling prince to support him, and even at that instant Thorstein the Dane ran in and drove his spear into Dunlang's side. The young Dalcassian staggered and fell at Murrogh's feet, and Conn leaped forward to strike Thorstein's head from his shoulders so that it whirled grinning still through the air in a shower of crimson.

Murrogh shook the darkness from his eyes. "Dunlang!" he cried in a fearful voice, falling to his knees at his friend's side and raising his head.

But Dunlang's eyes were already glazing. "Murrogh! Eevin!" Then blood gushed from his lips and he went limp in Murrogh's arms.

Murrogh leaped up with a shout of demoniac fury. He rushed into the thick of the Vikings, and his men swept in behind him.

On the hill of Cabra, Malachi cried out, flinging doubts and plots to the wind. As Brodir had plotted, so had he. He had but to stand aside until both hosts were cut to pieces, then seize Erin, tricking the Danes as they had planned to betray him. But his blood cried out against him and would not be stilled. He gripped the golden collar of Tomar about his neck, the collar he had taken so many years before from the Danish king his sword had broken, and the old fire leaped up.

"Charge and die!" he shouted, drawing his sword, and at his back the men of Meath gave tongue like a hunting pack and swarmed down into the field.

Under the shock of the Meathmen's assault, the weakened Danes staggered and broke. They tore away singly and in desperate slashing groups, seeking to gain the bay where their ships were anchored. But the Meathmen had cut off their retreat, and the ships lay far out, for the tide was at flood. All day that terrific battle had ranged, yet to Conn, snatching a startled glance at the setting sun, it seemed that scarce an hour had passed since the first lines had crashed together.

The fleeing Northmen made for the river, and the Gaels plunged in after them to drag them down. Among the fugitives and the groups of Norsemen who here and there made determined stands, the Irish chiefs were divided. The boy Turlogh was separated from Murrogh's side and vanished in the Tolka, struggling with a Dane. The clans of Leinster did not break until Black Turlogh rushed like a maddened beast into the thick of them and struck Mailmora dead in the midst of his warriors.

Murrogh, still blood-mad, but staggering from fatigue and weakened by loss of blood, came upon a band of Vikings who, back-to-back, resisted the conquerors. Their leader was Anrad the Berserk, who, when he saw Murrogh, rushed furiously upon him. Murrogh, too weary to parry the Dane's stroke, dropped his own sword and closed with Anrad, bearing him to the ground. The sword was wrenched from the Dane's hand as they fell. Both snatched at it, but Murrogh caught the hilt and Anrad the blade. The Gaelic prince tore it away, dragging the keen edge through the Viking's hand, severing nerve and thew; and, setting a knee on Anrad's chest, Murrogh drove the sword thrice through his body. Anrad, dying, drew a dagger, but his strength ebbed so swiftly that his arm sank. And then a mighty hand gripped his wrist and drove home the stroke he had sought to strike, so that the keen blade sank beneath Murrogh's heart. Murrogh fell back dying, and his last glance showed him a tall grey giant looming above, his cloak billowing in the wind, his one glittering eye cold and terrible. But the mazed eyes of the surrounding warriors saw only death and the dealing of death.

The Danes were all in flight now, and on the high wall King Sitric sat watching his high ambitions fade away, while Kormlada gazed wild eyed into ruin, defeat and shame.

Conn ran among the dying and the fleeing, seeking Thorwald Raven. The kern's buckler was gone, shattered among the axes. His broad breast was gashed in half a dozen places; a sword edge had bitten into his scalp when only his shock of tangled hair had saved him. A spear had girded into his thigh. Yet now in his heat and fury he scarcely felt these wounds.

A weakening hand caught at Conn's knee as he stumbled among dead men in wolfskins and mailed corpses. He bent and saw O'Kelly, Malachi's nephew, and chief of the Hy Many. The chief 's eyes were glazing in death. Conn lifted his head, and a smile curled the blue lips.

"I hear the war cry of the O'Neill," he whispered. "Malachi could not betray us. He could not stand from the fray. The Red Hand—to—Victory!"

Conn rose as O'Kelly died, and caught sight of a familiar figure. Thorwald Raven had broken from the press and now fled alone and swiftly, not toward the sea or the river, where his comrades died beneath the Gaelic axes, but toward Tomar's Wood. Conn followed, spurred by his hate.

Thorwald saw him, and turned, snarling. So the thrall met his former master. As Conn rushed into close quarters, the Norseman gripped his spear shaft with both hands and lunged fiercely, but the point glanced from the great copper collar about the kern's neck. Conn, bending low, lunged upward with all his power, so that the great blade ripped through Jarl Thorwald's tattered mail and spilled his entrails on the ground.

Turning, Conn saw that the chase had brought him almost to the king's tent, pitched behind the battlelines. He saw King Brian Boru standing in front of the tent, his white locks flowing in the wind, and but one man attending him. Conn ran forward.

"Kern, what are your tidings?" asked the king.

"The foreigners flee," answered Conn, "but Murrogh has fallen."

"You bring evil tidings," said Brian. "Erin shall never again look on a champion like him." And age like a cold cloud closed upon him.

"Where are your guards, My Lord?" asked Conn.

"They have joined in the pursuit."

"Let me then take you to a safer place," said Conn. "The Gall fly all about us here."

King Brian shook his head. "Nay, I know I leave not this place alive, for Eevin of Craglea told me last night I should fall this day. And what avails me to survive Murrogh and the champions of the Gael? Let me lie at Armagh, in the peace of God."

Now the attendant cried out, "My king, we are undone! Men blue and naked are upon us."

"The armored Danes," cried Conn, wheeling.

King Brian drew his heavy sword.

A group of bloodstained Vikings were approaching, led by Brodir and Prince Amlaff. Their vaunted mail hung in shreds; their swords were notched and dripping. Brodir had marked the king's tent from afar, and was bent on murder, for his soul raged with shame and fury and he was beset by visions in which Brian, Sigurd, and Kormlada spun in a hellish dance. He had lost the battle, Ireland, Kormlada—now he was ready to give up his life in a dying stroke of vengeance.

Brodir rushed upon the king, Prince Amlaff at his heels. Conn sprang to bar their way. But Brodir swerved aside and left the kern to Amlaff, as he fell upon the king. Conn took Amlaff's blade in his left arm and smote a single terrible blow that rent the prince's hauberk like paper and shattered his spine. Then the kern sprang back to guard King Brian.

Then even as he turned, Conn saw Brodir parry Brian's stroke and drive his sword through the ancient king's breast. Brian went down, but even as he fell he caught himself on one knee and thrust his keen blade through flesh and bone, cutting both Brodir's legs from under him. The Viking's scream of triumph broke in a ghastly groan as he toppled in a widening pool of crimson. There he struggled convulsively and lay still.

Conn stood looking dazedly around him. Brodir's company of men had fled, and the Gaels were converging on Brian's tent. The sound of the keening for the heroes already rose to mingle with the screams and shouts that still came from the struggling hordes along the river. They were bringing Murrogh's body to the king's tent, walking slowly—weary, bloody men, with bowed heads. Behind the litter that bore the prince's body came others—laden with the bodies of Turlogh, Murrogh's son; of Donald, Steward of Mar; of O'Kelly and O'Hyne, the western chiefs; of Prince Meathla O'Faelan; of Dunlang O'Hartigan, beside whose litter walked Eevin of Craglea, her golden head sunk on her breast.

The warriors set down the litters and gathered silently and wearily about the corpse of King Brian Boru. They gazed unspeaking, their minds dulled from the agony of strife. Eevin lay motionless beside the body of her lover, as if she herself were dead; no tears stood in her eyes, no cry or moan escaped her pallid lips.

The clamor of battle was dying as the setting sun bathed the trampled field in its roseate light. The fugitives, tattered and slashed, were limping into the gates of Dublin, and the warriors of King Sitric were preparing to stand siege. But the Irish were in no condition to besiege the city. Four thousand warriors and chieftains had fallen, and nearly all the champions of the Gael were dead. But more than seven thousand Danes and Leinstermen lay stretched on the blood-soaked earth, and the power of the Vikings was broken. On Clontarf their iron reign was ended.

Conn walked toward the river, feeling now the ache of his stiffening wounds. He met Turlogh Dubh. The madness of battle was gone from Black Turlogh, and his dark face was inscrutable. From head to foot he was splattered with crimson.

"My Lord," said Conn, fingering the great copper ring about his neck, "I have slain the man who put this thrall-mark on me. I would be free of it."

Black Turlogh took his red-stained axhead in his hands and, pressing it against the ring, drove the keen edge through the softer metal. The ax gashed Conn's shoulder, but neither heeded.

"Now I am truly free," said Conn, flexing his mighty arms. "My heart is heavy for the chiefs who have fallen, but my mind is mazed with wonder and glory. When will ever such a battle be fought again? Truly, it was a feast of the ravens, a sea of slaughter. . ."

His voice trailed off, and he stood like a statue, head flung back, eyes staring into the clouded heavens. The sun was sinking in a dark ocean of scarlet. Great clouds rolled and tumbled, piled mountainously against the smoldering red of the sunset. A wind blew out of them, biting, cold, and, borne on the wind, etched shadowy against the clouds, a vague, gigantic form went flying, beard and wild locks streaming in the gale, cloak billowing out like great wings—speeding into the mysterious blue mists that pulsed and shimmered in the brooding North.

"Look up there—in the sky!" cried Conn. "The grey man! It is he! The grey man with the single terrible eye. I saw him in the mountains of Torka. I glimpsed him brooding on the walls of Dublin while the battle raged. I saw him looming above Prince Murrogh as he died. Look! He rides the wind and races among the tall clouds. He dwindles. He fades into the void! He vanishes!"

"It is Odin, god of the sea-people," said Turlogh somberly. "His children are broken, his altars crumble, and his worshippers fallen before the swords of the South. He flees the new gods and their children, and returns to the blue gulfs of the North which gave him birth. No more will helpless victims howl beneath the daggers of his priests—no more will he stalk the black clouds." He shook his head darkly. "The Grey God passes, and we too are passing, though we have conquered. The days of the twilight come on amain, and a strange feeling is upon me as of a waning age. What are we all, too, but ghosts waning into the night?"

And he went on into the dusk, leaving Conn to his freedom—from thralldom and cruelty, as both he and all the Gaels were now free of the shadow of the Grey God and his ruthless worshippers.

The Dark Man

For this is the night of the drawing of swords,
And the painted tower of the heathen hordes
Leans to our hammers, fires and cords,
Leans a little and falls.

—*Chesterton*

A biting wind drifted the snow as it fell. The surf snarled along the rugged shore and farther out the long leaden combers moaned ceaselessly. Through the gray dawn that was stealing over the coast of Connacht a fisherman came trudging, a man rugged as the land that bore him. His feet were wrapped in rough cured leather; a single garment of deerskin scantily sheltered his body. He wore no other clothing. As he strode stolidly along the shore, as heedless of the bitter cold as if he were the shaggy beast he appeared at first glance, he halted. Another man loomed up out of the veil of falling snow and drifting sea-mist. Turlogh Dubh stood before him.

This man was nearly a head taller than the stocky fisherman, and he had the bearing of a fighting man. No single glance would suffice, but any man or woman whose eyes fell on Turlogh Dubh would look long. Six feet and one inch he stood, and the first impression of slimness faded on closer inspection. He was big but trimly molded; a magnificent sweep of shoulder and depth of chest. Rangy he was, but compact, combining the strength of a bull with the lithe quickness of a panther. The slightest movement he made showed that steel trap coordination that makes the super-fighter. Turlogh Dubh—Black Turlogh, once of the Clan na O'Brien. And black he was as to hair, and dark of complexion. From under heavy black brows gleamed eyes of a hot volcanic blue. And in his clean-shaven face there was something of the somberness of dark mountains, of the ocean at midnight. Like the fisherman, he was a part of this fierce western land.

On his head he wore a plain vizorless helmet without crest or symbol. From neck to mid-thigh he was protected by a close-fitting shirt of black chain mail. The kilt he wore below his armor and which reached to his knees, was of plain drab material. His legs were wrapped with hard leather that might turn a sword edge, and the shoes on his feet were worn with much traveling.

A broad belt encircled his lean waist, holding a long dirk in a leather sheath. On his left arm he carried a small round shield of hide-covered wood, hard as iron, braced and reinforced with steel, and having a short, heavy spike in the center. An ax hung from his right wrist, and it was to this feature that the fisherman's eyes wandered. The weapon with its three-foot handle and graceful lines looked slim and light when the fisherman mentally compared it to the great axes carried by the Norsemen. Yet scarcely three years had passed, as the fisherman knew, since such axes as these had shattered the northern hosts into red defeat and broken the pagan power forever.

There was individuality about the ax as about its owner. It was not like any other the fisherman had ever seen. Single-edged it was, with a short three-edged spike on the back and another on the top of the head. Like the wielder, it was heavier than it looked. With its slightly curved shaft and the graceful artistry of the blade, it looked the weapon of an expert—swift, lethal, deadly, cobra-like. The head was of finest Irish workmanship, which meant, at that day, the finest in the world. The handle, cut from the heart of a century-old oak, specially fire-hardened and braced with steel, was as unbreakable as an iron bar.

"Who are you?" asked the fisherman with the bluntness of the west.

"Who are you to ask?" answered the other.

The fisherman's eyes roved to the single ornament the warrior wore—a heavy golden armlet on his left arm.

"Clean-shaven and close-cropped in the Norman fashion," he muttered. "And dark—you'd be Black Turlogh, the outlaw of Clan na O'Brien. You range far; I heard of you last in the Wicklow hills preying off the O'Reillys and the Oastmen alike."

"A man must eat, outcast or not," growled the Dalcassian.

The fisherman shrugged his shoulders. A masterless man—it was a hard road. In those days of clans, when a man's own kin cast him out he became a son of Ishmael with a vengeance. All men's hands were against him. The fisherman had heard of Turlogh Dubh—a strange, bitter man, a terrible warrior and a crafty strategist, but one whom sudden bursts of strange madness made a marked man even in that land and age of madmen.

"It's a bitter day," said the fisherman apropos of nothing.

Turlogh stared somberly at his tangled beard and wild matted hair. "Have you a boat?"

The other nodded toward a small sheltered cove where lay snugly anchored a trim craft built with the skill of a hundred generations of men who had torn their livelihood from the stubborn sea.

"It scarce looks seaworthy," said Turlogh.

"Seaworthy? You who were born and bred on the western coast should know better. I've sailed her alone to Drumcliff Bay and back, and all the devils in the wind ripping at her."

"You can't take fish in such a sea."

"Do ye think it's only you chiefs that take sport in risking their hides? By the saints, I've sailed to Ballinskellings in a storm—and back too—just for the fun of the thing."

"Good enough," said Turlogh. "I'll take your boat."

"Ye'll take the devil! What kind of talk is this? If you want to leave Erin, go to Dublin and take ship with your Dane friends."

A black scowl made Turlogh's face a mask of menace. "Men have died for less than that."

"Did you not intrigue with the Danes?—and is that not why your clan drove you out to starve in the heather?"

"The jealousy of a cousin and the spite of a woman," growled Turlogh. "Lies—all lies. But enough. Have you seen a long serpent beating up from the south in the last few days?"

"Aye—three days ago we sighted a dragon-beaked galley before the scud. But she didn't put in—faith, the pirates get naught from the western fishers but hard blows."

"That would be Thorfel the Fair," muttered Turlogh, swaying his ax by its wrist-strap. "I knew it."

"There has been a ship-harrying in the south?"

"A band of reavers fell by night on the castle on Kilbaha. There was a sword-quenching—and the pirates took Moira, daughter of Murtagh, a chief of the Dalcassians."

"I've heard of her," muttered the fisherman. "There'll be a whetting of swords in the south—a red sea-plowing, eh, my black jewel?"

"Her brother Dermod lies helpless from a sword-cut in the foot. The lands of her clan are harried by the MacMurroughs in the east and the O'Connors from the north. Not many men can be spared from the defense of the tribe, even to seek for Moira—the clan is fighting for its life. All Erin is rocking under the Dalcassian throne since great Brian fell. Even so, Cormac O'Brien has taken ship to hunt down her ravishers—but he follows the trail of a wild goose, for it is thought the raiders were Danes from Coningbeg. Well—we outcasts have ways of knowledge—it was Thorfel the Fair who holds the isle of Slyne, that the Norse call Helni, in the Hebrides. There he has taken her—there I follow him. Lend me your boat."

"You are mad!" cried the fisherman sharply. "What are you saying? From Connacht to the Hebrides in an open boat? In this weather? I say you are mad."

"I will essay it," answered Turlogh absently. "Will you lend me your boat?"

"No."

"I might slay you and take it," said Turlogh.

"You might," returned the fisherman stolidly.

"You crawling swine," snarled the outlaw in swift passion, "a princess of Erin languishes in the grip of a red-bearded reaver of the north and you haggle like a Saxon."

"Man, I must live!" cried the fisherman as passionately. "Take my boat and I shall starve! Where can I get another like it? It is the cream of its kind!"

Turlogh reached for the armlet on his left arm. "I will pay you. Here is a torc that Brian Boru put on my arm with his own hand before Clontarf. Take it; it would buy a hundred boats. I have starved with it on my arm, but now the need is desperate."

But the fisherman shook his head, the strange illogic of the Gael burning in his eyes. "No! My hut is no place for a torc that King Brian's hands have touched. Keep it—and take the boat, in the name of the saints, if it means that much to you."

"You shall have it back when I return," promised Turlogh, "and mayhap a golden chain that now decks the bull neck of some northern rover."

The day was sad and leaden. The wind moaned and the everlasting monotone of the sea was like the sorrow that is born in the heart of man. The fisherman stood on the rocks and watched the frail craft glide and twist serpent-like among the rocks until the blast of the open sea smote it and tossed it like a feather. The wind caught the sail and the slim boat leaped and staggered, then righted herself and raced before the gale, dwindling until it was but a dancing speck in the eyes of the watcher. And then a flurry of snow hid it from his sight.

Turlogh realized something of the madness of his pilgrimage. But he was bred to hardships and peril. Cold and ice and driving sleet that would have frozen a weaker man, only spurred him to greater efforts. He was as hard and supple as a wolf. Among a race of men whose hardiness astounded even the toughest Norseman, Turlogh Dubh stood out alone. At birth he had been tossed into a snowdrift to test his right to survive. His childhood and boyhood had been spent on the mountains, coast and moors of the west. Until manhood he had never worn woven cloth upon his body; a wolfskin had formed the apparel of this son of a Dalcassian chief. Before his outlawry he could out-tire a horse, running all day long beside it. He had never wearied at swimming. Now, since the intrigues of jealous clansmen had driven him into the wastelands and the life of the wolf, his ruggedness was such as cannot be conceived by a civilized man.

The snow ceased, the weather cleared, the wind held. Turlogh necessarily hugged the coastline, avoiding the reefs against which it seemed again and again that his craft would be dashed. With tiller, sail and oar he worked tirelessly. Not one man out of a thousand of seafarers could have accomplished it, but Turlogh did. He needed no sleep; as he steered he ate from the rude provisions the fisherman had provided him. By the time he sighted Malin Head the weather had calmed wonderfully. There was still a heavy sea, but the gale had slackened to a sharp breeze that sent the little boat skipping along. Days and nights merged into each other; Turlogh drove eastward. Once he put into shore for fresh water and to snatch a few hours' sleep.

As he steered he thought of the fisherman's last words: "Why should you risk your life for a clan that's put a price on your head?"

Turlogh shrugged his shoulders. Blood was thicker than water. The mere fact that his people had booted him out to die like a hunted wolf on the moors did not alter the fact that they *were* his people. Little Moira, daughter of Murtagh na Kilbaha, had nothing to do with it. He remembered her—he had played with her when he was a boy and she a babe—he remembered the deep grayness of her eyes and the burnished sheen of her black hair, the fairness of her skin. Even as a child she had been remarkably beautiful—why, she was only a child now, for he, Turlogh, was young and he was many years her senior. Now she was speeding north to become the unwilling bride of a Norse reaver. Thorfel the Fair—the Handsome—Turlogh swore by gods that knew not the Cross. A red mist waved across his eyes so that the rolling sea swam crimson all about him. An Irish girl a captive in the skalli of a Norse pirate—with a vicious wrench Turlogh turned his bows straight for the open sea. There was a tinge of madness in his eyes.

It is a long slant from Malin Head to Helni straight out across the foaming billows, as Turlogh took it. He was aiming for a small island that lay, with many other small islands, between Mull and the Hebrides. A modern seaman with charts and compass might have difficulty in finding it. Turlogh had neither. He sailed by instinct and through knowledge. He knew these seas as a man knows his house. He had sailed them as a raider and an avenger, and once he had sailed them as a captive lashed to the deck of a Danish dragon-ship. And he followed a red trail. Smoke drifting from headlands, floating pieces of wreckage, charred timbers showed that Thorfel was ravaging as he went. Turlogh growled in savage satisfaction; he was close behind the Viking, in spite of the long lead. For Thorfel was burning and pillaging the shores as he went, and Turlogh's course was like an arrow's.

He was still a long way from Helni when he sighted a small island slightly off his course. He knew it of old as one uninhabited, but there he could get fresh water. So he steered for it. The Isle of Swords it was called, no man knew why. And as he neared the beach he saw a sight which he rightly interpreted. Two boats were drawn up on the shelving shore. One was a crude affair, something like the one Turlogh had, but considerably larger. The other was a long low craft—undeniably Viking. Both were deserted. Turlogh listened for the clash of arms, the cry of battle, but silence reigned. Fishers, he thought, from the Scotch isles; they had been sighted by some band of rovers on ship or on some other island, and had been pursued in the long rowboat. But it had been a longer chase than they had anticipated, he was sure; else they would not have started out in an open boat. But inflamed with the murder lust, the reavers would have followed their prey across a hundred miles of rough water, in an open boat, if necessary.

Turlogh drew inshore, tossed over the stone that served for anchor and leaped upon the beach, ax ready. Then up the shore a short distance he saw a strange red huddle of forms. A few swift strides brought him face to face with mystery. Fifteen red-bearded Danes lay in their own gore in a rough circle. Not one breathed. Within this circle, mingling with the bodies of their slayers, lay other men, such as Turlogh had never seen. Short of stature they were, and very dark; their staring dead eyes were the blackest Turlogh had ever seen. They were scantily armored, and their stiff hands still gripped broken swords and daggers. Here and there lay arrows that had shattered on the corselets of the Danes, and Turlogh observed with surprize that many of them were tipped with flint.

"This was a grim fight," he muttered. "Aye, this was a rare sword-quenching. Who are these people? In all the isles I have never seen their like before. Seven—is that all? Where are their comrades who helped them slay these Danes?"

No tracks led away from the bloody spot. Turlogh's brow darkened.

"These were all—seven against fifteen—yet the slayers died with the slain. What manner of men are these who slay twice their number of Vikings? They are small men—their armor is mean. Yet—"

Another thought struck him. Why did not the strangers scatter and flee, hide themselves in the woods? He believed he knew the answer.

There, at the very center of the silent circle, lay a strange thing. A statue it was of some dark substance and it was in the form of a man. Some five feet long—or high—it was, carved in a semblance of life that made Turlogh start. Half over it lay the corpse of an ancient man, hacked almost beyond human semblance. One lean arm was locked about the figure; the other was outstretched, the hand gripping a flint dagger which was sheathed to the hilt in the breast of a Dane. Turlogh noted the fearful wounds that disfigured all the dark men. They had been hard to kill—they had fought until literally hacked to pieces, and dying, they had dealt death to their slayers. So much Turlogh's eyes showed him. In the dead faces of the dark strangers was a terrible desperation. He noted how their dead hands were still locked in the beards of their foes. One lay beneath the body of a huge Dane, and on this Dane Turlogh could see no wound; until he looked closer and saw the dark man's teeth were sunk, beastlike, into the bull throat of the other.

He bent and dragged the figure from among the bodies. The ancient's arm was locked about it, and he was forced to tear it away with all his strength. It was as if, even in death, the old one clung to his treasure; for Turlogh felt that it was for this image that the small dark men had died. They might have scattered and eluded their foes, but that would have meant giving up their image. They chose to die beside it. Turlogh shook his head; his hatred of the Norse, a heritage of wrongs and outrages, was a burning, living thing, almost an obsession, that at times drove him to the point of insanity. There was, in his fierce heart, no room for mercy; the sight of these Danes, lying dead at his feet, filled him with savage satisfaction. Yet he sensed here, in these silent dead men, a passion stronger than his. Here was some driving impulse deeper than his hate. Aye—and older. These little men seemed very ancient to him, not old as individuals are old, but old as a race is old. Even their corpses exuded an intangible aura of the primeval. And the image—

The Gael bent and grasped it, to lift it. He expected to encounter great weight and was astonished. It was no heavier than if it had been made of light wood. He tapped it, and the sound was solid. At first he thought it was of iron; then he decided it was of stone, but such stone as he had never seen; and he felt that no such stone was to be found in the British Isles or anywhere in the world he knew. For like the little dead men it looked *old*. It was as smooth and free from corrosion as if carved yesterday, but for all that, it was a symbol of antiquity, Turlogh knew. It was the figure of a man who much resembled the small dark men who lay about it. But it differed subtly. Turlogh felt somehow that this was the image of a man who had lived long ago, for surely the unknown sculptor had had a living model. And he had contrived to breathe a touch of life into his work. There was the sweep of the shoulders, the depth of the chest, the powerfully molded arms; the strength of the features was evident. The firm jaw, the regular nose, the high forehead, all indicated a powerful intellect, a high courage, an inflexible will. Surely, thought Turlogh, this man was a king—or a god. Yet he wore no crown; his only garment was a sort of loincloth, wrought so cunningly that every wrinkle and fold was carved as in reality.

"This was their god," mused Turlogh, looking about him. "They fled before the Danes—but died for their god at last. Who are these people? Whence come they? Whither were they bound?"

He stood, leaning on his ax, and a strange tide rose in his soul. A sense of mighty abysses of time and space opened before; of the strange, endless tides of mankind that drift forever; of the waves of humanity that wax and wane with the waxing and waning of the sea tides. Life was a door opening upon two black, unknown worlds—and how many races of men with their hopes and fears, their loves and their hates, had passed through that door—on their pilgrimage from the dark to the dark? Turlogh sighed. Deep in his soul stirred the mystic sadness of the Gael.

"You were a king, once, Dark Man," he said to the silent image. "Mayhap you were a god and reigned over all the world. Your people passed—as mine are passing. Surely you were a king of the Flint People, the race whom my Celtic ancestors destroyed. Well—we have had our day and we, too, are passing. These Danes who lie at your feet—they are the conquerors now. They must have their day—but they too will pass. But you shall go with me, Dark Man, king, god or devil though you be. Aye, for it is in my mind that you will bring me luck, and luck is what I shall need when I sight Helni, Dark Man."

Turlogh bound the image securely in the bows. Again he set out for his sea-plowing. Now the skies grew gray and the snow fell in driving lances that stung and cut. The waves were gray grained with ice and the winds bellowed and beat on the open boat. But Turlogh feared not. And his boat rode as it had never ridden before. Through the roaring gale and the driving snow it sped, and to the mind of the Dalcassian it seemed that the Dark Man lent him aid. Surely he had been lost a hundred times without supernatural assistance. With all his skill at boat handling he wrought, and it seemed to him that there was an unseen hand on the tiller, and at the oar; that more than human skill aided him when he trimmed his sail.

And when all the world was a driving white veil in which even the Gael's sense of direction was lost, it seemed to him that he was steering in compliance with a silent voice that spoke in the dim reaches of his consciousness. Nor was he surprized when at last, when the snow had ceased and the clouds had rolled away beneath a cold silvery moon, he saw land loom up ahead and recognized it as the isle of Helni. More, he knew that just around a point of land was the bay where Thorfel's dragon-ship was moored when not ranging the seas, and a hundred yards back from the bay lay Thorfel's skalli. He grinned fiercely. All the skill in the world could not have brought him to this exact spot—it was pure luck—no, it was more than luck. Here was the best place possible for him to make an approach—within half a mile of his foe's hold, yet hidden from sight of any watchers by this jutting promontory. He glanced at the Dark Man in the bows—brooding, inscrutable as the sphinx. A strange feeling stole over the Gael—that all this was his work; that he, Turlogh, was only a pawn in the game. What was this fetish? What grim secret did those carven eyes hold? Why did the dark little men fight so terribly for him?

Turlogh ran his boat inshore, into a small creek. A few yards up this he anchored and stepped out on shore. A last glance at the brooding Dark Man in the bows, and he turned and went hurriedly up the slope of the promontory, keeping to cover as much as possible. At the top of the slope he gazed down on the other side. Less than half a mile away Thorfel's dragon-ship lay at anchor. And there lay Thorfel's skalli, also the long low building of rough-hewn log emitting the gleams that betokened the roaring fires within. Shouts of wassail came clearly to the listener through the sharp still air. He ground his teeth. Wassail! Aye, they were celebrating the ruin and destruction they had committed—the homes left in smoking embers—the slain men—the ravished girls. They were lords of the world, these Vikings—all the southland lay helpless beneath their swords. The southland folk lived only to furnish them sport—and slaves—Turlogh shuddered violently and shook as if in a chill. The blood-sickness was on him like a physical pain, but he fought back the mists of passion that clouded his brain. He was here, not to fight but to steal away the girl they had stolen.

He took careful note of the ground, like a general going over the plan of his campaign. He noted that the trees grew thick close behind the skalli; that the smaller houses, the storehouses and servants' huts were between the main building and the bay. A huge fire was blazing down by the shore and a few carles were roaring and drinking about it, but the fierce cold had driven most of them into the drinking hall of the main building.

Turlogh crept down the thickly wooded slope, entering the forest which swept about in a wide curve away from the shore. He kept to the fringe of its shadows, approaching the skalli in a rather indirect route, but afraid to strike out boldly in the open lest he be seen by the watchers that Thorfel surely had out. Gods, if he only had the warriors of Clare at his back as he had of old! Then there would be no skulking like a wolf among the trees! His hand locked like iron on his ax-haft as he visualized the scene—the charge, the shouting, the bloodletting, the play of the Dalcassian axes—he sighed. He was a lone outcast; never again would he lead the swordsmen of his clan to battle.

He dropped suddenly in the snow behind a low shrub and lay still. Men were approaching from the same direction in which he had come—men who grumbled loudly and walked heavily. They came into sight—two of them, huge Norse warriors, their silver-scaled armor flashing in the moonlight. They were carrying something between them with difficulty and to Turlogh's amazement he saw it was the Dark Man. His consternation at the realization that they had found his boat was gulfed in a greater astonishment. These men were giants; their arms bulged with iron muscles. Yet they were staggering under what seemed a stupendous weight. In their hands the Dark Man seemed to weigh hundreds of pounds; yet Turlogh had lifted it lightly as a feather! He almost swore in his amazement. Surely these men were drunk. One of them spoke, and Turlogh's short neck hairs bristled at the sound of the guttural accents, as a dog will bristle at the sight of a foe.

"Let it down; Thor's death, the thing weighs a ton. Let's rest."

The other grunted a reply and they began to ease the image to the earth. Then one of them lost his hold on it; his hand slipped and the Dark Man crashed heavily into the snow. The first speaker howled.

"You clumsy fool, you dropped it on my foot! Curse you, my ankle's broken!"

"It twisted out of my hand!" cried the other. "The thing's alive, I tell you!"

"Then I'll slay it," snarled the lamed Viking, and drawing his sword, he struck savagely at the prostrate figure. Fire flashed as the blade shivered into a hundred pieces, and the other Norseman howled as a flying sliver of steel gashed his cheek.

"The devil's in it!" shouted the other, throwing his hilt away. "I've not even scratched it! Here, take hold—let's get it into the ale hall and let Thorfel deal with it."

"Let it lie," growled the second man, wiping the blood from his face. "I'm bleeding like a butchered hog. Let's go back and tell Thorfel that there's no ship stealing on the island. That's what he sent us to the point to see."

"What of the boat where we found this?" snapped the other. "Some Scotch fisher driven out of his course by the storm and hiding like a rat in the woods now, I guess. Here, bear a hand; idol or devil, we'll carry this to Thorfel."

Grunting with the effort, they lifted the image once more and went on slowly, one groaning and cursing as he limped along, the other shaking his head from time to time as the blood got into his eyes.

Turlogh rose stealthily and watched them. A touch of chilliness traveled up and down his spine. Either of these men was as strong as he, yet it was taxing their powers to the utmost to carry what he had handled easily. He shook his head and took up his way again.

At last he reached a point in the woods nearest the skalli. Now was the crucial test. Somehow he must reach that building and hide himself, unperceived. Clouds were gathering. He waited until one obscured the moon, and in the gloom that followed, ran swiftly and silently across the snow, crouching. A shadow out of the shadows he seemed. The shouts and songs from within the long building were deafening. Now he was close to its side, flattening himself against the rough-hewn logs. Vigilance was most certainly relaxed now—yet what foe should Thorfel expect, when he was friends with all northern reavers, and none else could be expected to fare forth on a night such as this had been?

A shadow among the shadows, Turlogh stole about the house. He noted a side door and slid cautiously to it. Then he drew back close against the wall. Someone within was fumbling at the latch. Then the door was flung open and a big warrior lurched out, slamming the door to behind him. Then he saw Turlogh. His bearded lips parted, but in that instant the Gael's hands shot to his throat and locked there like a wolf trap. The threatened yell died in a gasp. One hand flew to Turlogh's wrist, the other drew a dagger and stabbed upward. But already the man was senseless; the dagger rattled feebly against the outlaw's corselet and dropped into the snow. The Norseman sagged in his slayer's grasp, his throat literally crushed by that iron grip. Turlogh flung him contemptuously into the snow and spat in his dead face before he turned again to the door.

The latch had not fastened within. The door sagged a trifle. Turlogh peered in and saw an empty room, piled with ale barrels. He entered noiselessly, shutting the door but not latching it. He thought of hiding his victim's body, but he did not know how he could do it. He must trust to luck that no one saw it in the deep snow where it lay. He crossed the room and found it let into another parallel with the outer wall. This was also a storeroom, and was empty. From this a doorway, without a door but furnished with a curtain of skins, let into the main hall, as Turlogh could tell from the sounds on the other side. He peered out cautiously.

He was looking into the drinking hall—the great hall which served as banquet, council and living hall of the master of the skalli. This hall, with its smoke-blackened rafters, great roaring fireplaces, and heavily laden boards, was a scene of terrific revelry tonight. Huge warriors with golden beards and savage eyes sat or lounged on the rude benches, strode about the hall or sprawled full length on the floor. They drank mightily from foaming horns and leathern jacks, and gorged themselves on great pieces of rye bread, and huge chunks of meat they cut with their daggers from whole roasted joints. It was a scene of strange incongruity, for in contrast with these barbaric men and their rough songs and shouts, the walls were hung with rare spoils that betokened civilized workmanship. Fine tapestries that Norman women had worked; richly chased weapons that princes of France and Spain had wielded; armor and silken garments from Byzantium and the Orient—for the dragon-ships ranged far. With these were placed the spoils of the hunt, to show the Viking's mastery of beasts as well as men.

The modern man can scarcely conceive of Turlogh O'Brien's feeling toward these men. To him they were devils—ogres who dwelt in the north only to descend on the peaceful people of the south. All the world was their prey to pick and choose, to take and spare as it pleased their barbaric whims. His brain throbbed and burned as he gazed. As only the Gael can hate, he hated them—their magnificent arrogance, their pride and their power, their contempt for all other races, their stern, forbidding eyes—above all else he hated the eyes that looked scorn and menace on the world. The Gaels were cruel but they had strange moments of sentiment and kindness. There was no sentiment in the Norse makeup.

The sight of this revelry was like a slap in Black Turlogh's face, and only one thing was needed to make his madness complete. This was furnished. At the head of the board sat Thorfel the Fair, young, handsome, arrogant, flushed with wine and pride. He *was* handsome, was young Thorfel. In build he much resembled Turlogh himself, except that he was larger in every way, but there the resemblance ceased. As Turlogh was exceptionally dark among a dark people, Thorfel was exceptionally blond among a people essentially fair. His hair and mustache were like finespun gold and his light gray eyes flashed scintillant lights. By his side—Turlogh's nails bit into his palms. Moira of the O'Briens seemed greatly out of place among these huge blond men and strapping yellow-haired women. She was small, almost frail, and her hair was black with glossy bronze tints. But her skin was fair as theirs, with a delicate rose tint their most beautiful women could not boast. Her full lips were white now with fear and she shrank from the clamor and uproar. Turlogh saw her tremble as Thorfel insolently put his arm about her. The hall waved redly before Turlogh's eyes and he fought doggedly for control.

"Thorfel's brother, Osric, to his right," he muttered to himself; "on the other side Tostig, the Dane, who can cleave an ox in half with that great sword of his—they say. And there is Halfgar, and Sweyn, and Oswick, and Athelstane, the Saxon—the one *man* of a pack of sea-wolves. And name of the devil—what is this? A priest?"

A priest it was, sitting white and still in the rout, silently counting his beads, while his eyes wandered pityingly toward the slender Irish girl at the head of the board. Then Turlogh saw something else. On a smaller table to one side, a table of mahogany whose rich scrollwork showed that it was loot from the southland, stood the Dark Man. The two crippled Norsemen had brought it to the hall, after all. The sight of it brought a strange shock to Turlogh and cooled his seething brain. Only five feet tall? It seemed much larger now, somehow. It loomed above the revelry, as a god that broods on deep dark matters beyond the ken of the human insects who howl at his feet. As always when looking at the Dark Man, Turlogh felt as if a door had suddenly opened on outer space and the wind that blows among the stars. Waiting—waiting—for whom? Perhaps the carven eyes of the Dark Man looked through the skalli walls, across the snowy waste, and over the promontory. Perhaps those sightless eyes saw the five boats that even now slid silently with muffled oars, through the calm dark waters. But of this Turlogh Dubh knew nothing; nothing of the boats or their silent rowers; small, dark men with inscrutable eyes.

Thorfel's voice cut through the din: "Ho, friends!" They fell silent and turned as the young sea king rose to his feet. "Tonight," he thundered, "I am taking a bride!"

A thunder of applause shook the smoky rafters. Turlogh cursed with sick fury.

Thorfel caught up the girl with rough gentleness and set her on the board.

"Is she not a fit bride for a Viking?" he shouted. "True, she's a bit shy, but that's only natural."

"All Irish are cowards!" shouted Oswick.

"As proved by Clontarf and the scar on your jaw!" rumbled Athelstane, which gentle thrust made Oswick wince and brought a roar of rough mirth from the throng.

"'Ware her temper, Thorfel," called a bold-eyed young Juno who sat with the warriors; "Irish girls have claws like cats."

Thorfel laughed with the confidence of a man used to mastery. "I'll teach her her lessons with a stout birch switch. But enough. It grows late. Priest, marry us."

"Daughter," said the priest, unsteadily, rising, "these pagan men have brought me here by violence to perform Christian nuptials in an ungodly house. Do you marry this man willingly?"

"No! No! Oh God, no!" Moira screamed with a wild despair that brought the sweat to Turlogh's forehead. "Oh most holy master, save me from this fate! They tore me from my home—struck down the brother that would have saved me! This man bore me off as if I were a chattel—a soulless beast!"

"Be silent!" thundered Thorfel, slapping her across the mouth, lightly but with enough force to bring a trickle of blood from her delicate lips. "By Thor, you grow independent. I am determined to have a wife, and all the squeals of a puling little wench will not stop me. Why, you graceless hussy, am I not wedding you in the Christian manner, simply because of your foolish superstitions? Take care that I do not dispense with the nuptials, and take you as slave, not wife!"

"Daughter," quavered the priest, afraid, not for himself, but for her, "bethink you! This man offers you more than many a man would offer. It is at least an honorable married state."

"Aye," rumbled Athelstane, "marry him like a good wench and make the best of it. There's more than one southland woman on the cross benches of the north."

What can I do? The question tore through Turlogh's brain. There was but one thing to do—wait until the ceremony was over and Thorfel had retired with his bride. Then steal her away as best he could. After that—but he dared not look ahead. He had done and would do his best. What he did, he of necessity did alone; a masterless man had no friends, even among masterless men. There was no way to reach Moira to tell her of his presence. She must go through with the wedding without even the slim hope of deliverance that knowledge of his presence might have lent. Instinctively his eyes flashed to the Dark Man standing somber and aloof from the rout. At his feet the old quarreled with the new—the pagan with the Christian—and Turlogh even in that moment felt that the old and new were alike young to the Dark Man.

Did the carven ears of the Dark Man hear strange prows grating on the beach, the stroke of a stealthy knife in the night, the gurgle that marks the severed throat? Those in the skalli heard only their own noise and those who reveled by the fires outside sang on, unaware of the silent coils of death closing about them.

"Enough!" shouted Thorfel. "Count your beads and mutter your mummery, priest! Come here, wench, and marry!" He jerked the girl off the board and plumped her down on her feet before him. She tore loose from him with flaming eyes. All the hot Gaelic blood was roused in her.

"You yellow-haired swine!" she cried. "Do you think that a princess of Clare, with Brian Boru's blood in her veins, would sit at the cross bench of a barbarian and bear the tow-headed cubs of a northern thief? No—I'll never marry you!"

"Then I'll take you as a slave!" he roared, snatching at her wrist.

"Nor that way, either, swine!" she exclaimed, her fear forgotten in fierce triumph. With the speed of light she snatched a dagger from his girdle, and before he could seize her she drove the keen blade under her heart. The priest cried out as though he had received the wound, and springing forward, caught her in his arms as she fell.

"The curse of Almighty God on you, Thorfel!" he cried, with a voice that rang like a clarion, as he bore her to a couch nearby.

Thorfel stood nonplussed. Silence reigned for an instant, and in that instant Turlogh O'Brien went mad.

"Lamh Laidir Abu!" the war-cry of the O'Briens ripped through the stillness like the scream of a wounded panther, and as men whirled toward the shriek, the frenzied Gael came through the doorway like the blast of a wind from hell. He was in the grip of the Celtic black fury beside which the berserk rage of the Viking pales. Eyes glaring and a tinge of froth on his writhing lips, he crashed among the men who sprawled, off guard, in his path. Those terrible eyes were fixed on Thorfel at the other end of the hall, but as Turlogh rushed he smote to the right and left. His charge was the rush of a whirlwind that left a litter of dead and dying men in his wake.

Benches crashed to the floor, men yelled, ale flooded from upset casks. Swift as was the Celt's attack, two men blocked his way with drawn swords before he could reach Thorfel—Halfgar and Oswick. The scarred-faced Viking went down with a cleft skull before he could lift his weapon, and Turlogh, catching Halfgar's blade on his shield, struck again like lightning and the keen ax sheared through hauberk, ribs and spine.

The hall was in a terrific uproar. Men were seizing weapons and pressing forward from all sides, and in the midst the lone Gael raged silently and terribly. Like a wounded tiger was Turlogh Dubh in his madness. His eery movement was a blur of speed, an explosion of dynamic force. Scarce had Halfgar fallen before the Gael leaped across his crumpling form at Thorfel, who had drawn his sword and stood as if bewildered. But a rush of carles swept between them. Swords rose and fell and the Dalcassian ax flashed among them like the play of summer lightning. On either hand and from before and behind a warrior drove at him. From one side Osric rushed, swinging a two-handed sword; from the other a house carle drove in with a spear. Turlogh stooped beneath the swing of the sword and struck a double blow, forehand and back. Thorfel's brother dropped, hewed through the knee, and the carle died on his feet as the backlash return drove the ax's back spike through his skull. Turlogh straightened, dashing his shield into the face of the swordsman who rushed him from the front. The spike in the center of the shield made a ghastly ruin of his features; then even as the Gael wheeled cat-like to guard his rear, he felt the shadow of Death loom over him. From the corner of his eye he saw the Dane Tostig swinging his great two-handed sword, and jammed against the table, off balance, he knew that even his superhuman quickness could not save him. Then the whistling sword struck the Dark Man on the table and with a clash like thunder, shivered to a thousand blue sparks. Tostig staggered, dazedly, still holding the useless hilt, and Turlogh thrust as with a sword; the upper spike of his ax struck the Dane over the eye and crashed through to the brain.

And even at that instant, the air was filled with a strange singing and men howled. A huge carle, ax still lifted, pitched forward clumsily against the Gael, who split his skull before he saw that a flint-pointed arrow transfixed his throat. The hall seemed full of glancing beams of light that hummed like bees and carried quick death in their humming. Turlogh risked his life for a glance toward the great doorway at the other end of the hall. Through it was pouring a strange horde. Small, dark men they were, with beady black eyes and immobile faces. They were scantily armored, but they bore swords, spears and bows. Now at close range they drove their long black arrows pointblank and the carles went down in windrows.

Now a red wave of combat swept the skalli hall, a storm of strife that shattered tables, smashed the benches, tore the hangings and the trophies from the walls, and stained the floors with a red lake. There had been less of the dark strangers than Vikings, but in the surprize of the attack, the first flight of arrows had evened the odds, and now at handgrips the strange warriors showed themselves in no way inferior to their huge foes. Dazed by surprize and the ale they had drunk, with no time to arm themselves fully, the Norsemen yet fought back with all the reckless ferocity of their race. But the primitive fury of their attackers matched their own valor, and at the head of the hall, where a white-faced priest shielded a dying girl, Black Turlogh tore and ripped with a frenzy that made valor and fury alike futile.

And over all towered the Dark Man. To Turlogh's shifting glances, caught between the flash of sword and ax, it seemed that the image had grown—expanded—heightened; that it loomed giant-like over the battle; that its head rose into the smoke-filled rafters of the great hall; that it brooded like a dark cloud of death over these insects who cut each other's throats at its feet. Turlogh sensed in the lightning swordplay and the slaughter that this was the proper element of the Dark Man. Violence and fury were exuded by him. The raw scent of fresh-spilled blood was good to his nostrils and these yellow-haired corpses that rattled at his feet were as sacrifices to him.

The storm of battle rocked the mighty hall. The skalli became a shambles where men slipped in pools of blood, and slipping, died. Heads spun grinning from slumping shoulders. Barbed spears tore the heart, still beating, from the gory breast. Brains splashed and clotted the madly driving axes. Daggers lunged upward, ripping bellies and spilling entrails upon the floor. The clash and clangor of steel rose deafeningly. No quarter was asked or given. A wounded Norseman had dragged down one of the dark men, and doggedly strangled him regardless of the dagger his victim plunged again and again into his body.

One of the dark men seized a child who ran howling from an inner room, and dashed its brains out against the wall. Another gripped a Norse woman by her golden hair and hurling her to her knees, cut her throat, while she spat in his face. One listening for cries of fear or pleas for mercy would have heard none; men, women or children, they died slashing and clawing, their last gasp a sob of fury, or a snarl of quenchless hatred.

And about the table where stood the Dark Man, immovable as a mountain, washed the red waves of slaughter. Norseman and tribesman died at his feet. How many red infernos of slaughter and madness have your strange carved eyes gazed upon, Dark Man?

Shoulder to shoulder Sweyn and Thorfel fought. The Saxon Athelstane, his golden beard a-bristle with the battle-joy, had placed his back against the wall and a man fell at each sweep of his two-handed ax. Now Turlogh came in like a wave, avoiding, with a lithe twist of his upper body, the first ponderous stroke. Now the superiority of the light Irish ax was proved, for before the Saxon could shift his heavy weapon, the Dalcassian ax licked out like a striking cobra and Athelstane reeled as the edge bit through the corselet into the ribs beneath. Another stroke and he crumpled, blood gushing from his temple.

Now none barred Turlogh's way to Thorfel except Sweyn, and even as the Gael leaped like a panther toward the slashing pair, one was ahead of him. The chief of the dark men glided like a shadow under the slash of Sweyn's sword, and his own short blade thrust upward under the shirt of mail. Thorfel faced Turlogh alone. Thorfel was no coward; he even laughed with pure battle-joy as he thrust, but there was no mirth in Black Turlogh's face, only a frantic rage that writhed his lips and made his eyes coals of blue fire.

In the first whirl of steel Thorfel's sword broke. The young sea king leaped like a tiger at his foe, thrusting with the shards of the blade. Turlogh laughed fiercely as the jagged remnant gashed his cheek, and at the same instant he cut Thorfel's left foot from under him. The Norseman fell with a heavy crash, then struggled to his knees, clawing for his dagger. His eyes were clouded.

"Make an end, curse you!" he snarled.

Turlogh laughed. "Where is your power and your glory, now?" he taunted. "You who would have for unwilling wife an Irish princess—you—"

Suddenly his hate strangled him, and with a howl like a maddened panther he swung his ax in a whistling arc that cleft the Norseman from shoulder to breast-bone. Another stroke severed the head, and with the grisly trophy in his hand he approached the couch where lay Moira O'Brien. The priest had lifted her head and held a goblet of wine to her pale lips. Her cloudy gray eyes rested with slight recognition on Turlogh—but it seemed at last she knew him and she tried to smile.

"Moira, blood of my heart," said the outlaw heavily, "you die in a strange land. But the birds in the Cullane hills will weep for you, and the heather will sigh in vain for the tread of your little feet. But you shall not be forgotten; axes shall drip for you and for you shall galleys crash and walled cities go up in flames. And that your ghost go not unassuaged into the realms of Tirna-n-Oge, behold this token of vengeance!"

And he held forth the dripping head of Thorfel.

"In God's name, my son," said the priest, his voice husky with horror, "have done—have done. Will you do your ghastly deeds in the very presence of—see, she is dead. May God in His infinite justice have mercy on her soul, for though she took her own life, yet she died as she lived, in innocence and purity."

Turlogh dropped his ax head to the floor and his head was bowed. All the fire of his madness had left him and there remained only a dark sadness, a deep sense of futility and weariness. Over all the hall there was no sound. No groans of the wounded were raised, for the knives of the little dark men had been at work, and save their own, there were no wounded. Turlogh sensed that the survivors had gathered about the statue on the table and now stood looking at him with inscrutable eyes. The priest mumbled over the corpse of the girl, telling his beads. Flame ate at the farther wall of the building, but none heeded it. Then from among the dead on the floor a huge form heaved up unsteadily. Athelstane the Saxon, overlooked by the killers, leaned against the wall and stared about dazedly. Blood flowed from a wound in his ribs and another in his scalp where Turlogh's ax had struck glancingly.

The Gael walked over to him. "I have no hatred for you, Saxon," said he, heavily, "but blood calls for blood and you must die."

Athelstane looked at him without an answer. His large gray eyes were serious but without fear. He too was a barbarian—more pagan than Christian; he too realized the rights of the blood-feud. But as Turlogh raised his ax, the priest sprang between, his thin hands outstretched, his eyes haggard.

"Have done! In God's name I command you! Almighty Powers, has not enough blood been shed this fearful night? In the name of the Most High, I claim this man."

Turlogh dropped his ax. "He is yours; not for your oath or your curse, not for your creed but for that you too are a man and did your best for Moira."

A touch on his arm made Turlogh turn. The chief of the strangers stood regarding him with inscrutable eyes.

"Who are you?" asked the Gael idly. He did not care; he felt only weariness.

"I am Brogar, chief of the Picts, Friend of the Dark Man."

"Why do you call me that?" asked Turlogh.

"He rode in the bows of your boat and guided you to Helni through wind and snow. He saved your life when he broke the great sword of the Dane."

Turlogh glanced at the brooding Dark One. It seemed there must be a human or superhuman intelligence behind those strange stone eyes. Was it chance alone that caused Tostig's sword to strike the image as he swung it in a death blow?

"What is this thing?" asked the Gael.

"It is the only god we have left," answered the other somberly. "It is the image of our greatest king, Bran Mak Morn, he who gathered the broken lines of the Pictish tribes into a single mighty nation, he who drove forth the Norseman and Briton and shattered the legions of Rome, centuries ago. A wizard made this statue while the great Morni yet lived and reigned, and when he died in the last great battle, his spirit entered into it. It is our god.

"Ages ago we ruled. Before the Dane, before the Gael, before the Briton, before the Roman, we reigned in the western isles. Our stone circles rose to the sun. We worked in flint and hides and were happy. Then came the Celts and drove us into the wildernesses. They held the southland. But we throve in the north and were strong. Rome broke the Britons and came against us. But there rose among us Bran Mak Morn, of the blood of Brule the Spear-slayer, the friend of King Kull of Valusia who reigned thousands of years ago before Atlantis sank. Bran became king of all Caledon. He broke the iron ranks of Rome and sent the legions cowering south behind their Wall.

"Bran Mak Morn fell in battle; the nation fell apart. Civil wars rocked it. The Gaels came and reared the kingdom of Dalriadia above the ruins of the Cruithni. When the Scot Kenneth MacAlpine broke the kingdom of Galloway, the last remnant of the Pictish empire faded like snow on the mountains. Like wolves we live now among the scattered islands, among the crags of the highlands and the dim hills of Galloway. We are a fading people. We pass. But the Dark Man remains—the Dark One, the great king, Bran Mak Morn, whose ghost dwells forever in the stone likeness of his living self."

As in a dream Turlogh saw an ancient Pict who looked much like the one in whose dead arms he had found the Dark Man, lift the image from the table. The old man's arms were thin as withered branches and his skin clung to his skull like a mummy's, but he handled with ease the image that two strong Vikings had had trouble in carrying.

As if reading his thoughts Brogar spoke softly: "Only a friend may with safety touch the Dark One. We knew you to be a friend, for he rode in your boat and did you no harm."

"How know you this?"

"The Old One," pointing to the white-bearded ancient. "Gonar, high priest of the Dark One—the ghost of Bran comes to him in dreams. It was Grok, the lesser priest and his people who stole the image and took to sea in a long boat. In dreams Gonar followed; aye, as he slept he sent his spirit with the ghost of the Morni, and he saw the pursuit by the Danes, the battle and slaughter on the Isle of Swords. He saw you come and find the Dark One, and he saw that the ghost of the great king was pleased with you. Wo to the foes of the Mak Morn! But good luck shall fare the friends of him."

Turlogh came to himself as from a trance. The heat of the burning hall was in his face and the flickering flames lit and shadowed the carven face of the Dark Man as his worshippers bore him from the building, lending it a strange life. Was it, in truth, that the spirit of a long-dead king lived in that cold stone? Bran Mak Morn loved his people with a savage love; he hated their foes with a terrible hate. Was it possible to breathe into inanimate blind stone a pulsating love and hate that should outlast the centuries?

Turlogh lifted the still, slight form of the dead girl and bore her out of the flaming hall. Five long open boats lay at anchor, and scattered about the embers of the fires the carles had lit, lay the reddened corpses of the revelers who had died silently.

"How stole ye upon these undiscovered?" asked Turlogh. "And whence came you in those open boats?"

"The stealth of the panther is theirs who live by stealth," answered the Pict. "And these were drunken. We followed the path of the Dark One and we came hither from the Isle of the Altar, near the Scottish mainland, from whence Grok stole the Dark Man."

Turlogh knew no island of that name but he did realize the courage of these men in daring the seas in boats such as these. He thought of his own boat and requested Brogar to send some of his men for it. The Pict did so. While he waited for them to bring it around the point, he watched the priest bandaging the wounds of the survivors. Silent, immobile, they spoke no word either of complaint or thanks.

The fisherman's boat came scudding around the point just as the first hint of sunrise reddened the waters. The Picts were getting into their boats, lifting in the dead and wounded. Turlogh stepped into his boat and gently eased his pitiful burden down.

"She shall sleep in her own land," he said somberly. "She shall not lie in this cold foreign isle. Brogar, whither go you?"

"We take the Dark One back to his isle and his altar," said the Pict. "Through the mouth of his people he thanks you. The tie of blood is between us, Gael, and mayhap we shall come to you again in your need, as Bran Mak Morn, great king of Pictdom, shall come again to his people some day in the days to come."

"And you, good Jerome? You will come with me?"

The priest shook his head and pointed to Athelstane. The wounded Saxon reposed on a rude couch made of skins piled in the snow.

"I stay here to attend to this man. He is sorely wounded."

Turlogh looked about. The walls of the skalli had crashed into a mass of glowing embers. Brogar's men had set fire to the storehouses and the long galley, and the smoke and flame vied luridly with the growing morning light.

"You will freeze or starve. Come with me."

"I will find sustenance for us both. Persuade me not, my son."

"He is a pagan and a reaver."

"No matter. He is a human—a living creature. I will not leave him to die."

"So be it."

Turlogh prepared to cast off. The boats of the Picts were already rounding the point. The rhythmic clack of their oarlocks came clearly to him. They looked not back, bending stolidly to their work.

He glanced at the stiff corpses about the beach, at the charred embers of the skalli and the glowing timbers of the galley. In the glare the priest seemed unearthly in his thinness and whiteness, like a saint from some old illuminated manuscript. In his worn pallid face was a more than human sadness, a greater than human weariness.

"Look!" he cried suddenly, pointing seaward. "The ocean is of blood! See how it swims red in the rising sun! Oh, my people, my people, the blood you have spilt in anger turns the very seas to scarlet! How can you win through?"

"I came in the snow and sleet," said Turlogh, not understanding at first. "I go as I came."

The priest shook his head. "It is more than a mortal sea. Your hands are red with blood and you follow a red sea-path, yet the fault is not wholly with you. Almighty God, when will the reign of blood cease?"

Turlogh shook his head. "Not so long as the race lasts."

The morning wind caught and filled his sail. Into the west he raced like a shadow fleeing the dawn. And so passed Turlogh Dubh O'Brien from the sight of the priest Jerome, who stood watching, shading his weary brow with his thin hand, until the boat was but a tiny speck far out on the tossing wastes of the blue ocean.

The Gods of Bal-Sagoth

1. Steel in the Storm

Lightning dazzled the eyes of Turlogh O'Brien and his foot slipped in a smear of blood as he staggered on the reeling deck. The clashing of steel rivaled the bellowing of the thunder, and screams of death cut through the roar of waves and wind. The incessant lightning flicker gleamed on the corpses sprawling redly, the gigantic horned figures that roared and smote like huge demons of the midnight storm, the great beaked prow looming above.

The play was quick and desperate; in the momentary illumination a ferocious bearded face shone before Turlogh, and his swift ax licked out, splitting it to the chin. In the brief, utter blackness that followed the flash, an unseen stroke swept Turlogh's helmet from his head and he struck back blindly, feeling his ax sink into flesh, and hearing a man howl. Again the fires of the raging skies sprang, showing the Gael the ring of savage faces, the hedge of gleaming steel that hemmed him in. Back against the mainmast Turlogh parried and smote; then through the madness of the fray a great voice thundered, and in a flashing instant the Gael caught a glimpse of a giant form—a strangely familiar face. Then the world crashed into fire-shot blackness.

Consciousness returned slowly. Turlogh was first aware of a swaying, rocking motion of his whole body which he could not check. Then a dull throbbing in his head racked him and he sought to raise his hands to it. Then it was he realized he was bound hand and foot—not an altogether new experience. Clearing sight showed him that he was tied to the mast of the dragon-ship whose warriors had struck him down. Why they had spared him, he could not understand, because if they knew him at all, they knew him to be an outlaw—an outcast from his clan, who would pay no ransom to save him from the very pits of Hell.

The wind had fallen greatly but a heavy sea was flowing, which tossed the long ship like a chip from gulf-like trough to foaming crest. A round silver moon, peering through broken clouds, lighted the tossing billows. The Gael, raised on the wild west coast of Ireland, knew that the serpent ship was crippled. He could tell it by the way she labored, plowing deep into the spume, heeling to the lift of the surge. Well, the tempest which had been raging on these southern waters had been enough to damage even such staunch craft as these Vikings built.

The same gale had caught the French vessel on which Turlogh had been a passenger, driving her off her course and far southward. Days and nights had been a blind, howling chaos in which the ship had been hurled, flying like a wounded bird before the storm. And in the very rack of the tempest a beaked prow had loomed in the scud above the lower, broader craft, and the grappling irons had sunk in. Surely these Norsemen were wolves and the bloodlust that burned in their hearts was not human. In the terror and roar of the storm they leaped howling to the onslaught, and while the raging heavens hurled their full wrath upon them, and each shock of the frenzied waves threatened to engulf both vessels, these sea wolves glutted their fury to the utmost—true sons of the sea, whose wildest rages found echo in their own bosoms. It had been a slaughter rather than a fight—the Celt had been the only fighting man aboard the doomed ship—and now he remembered the strange familiarity of the face he had glimpsed just before he was struck down. Who—?

"Good hail, my bold Dalcassian, it's long since we met!"

Turlogh stared at the man who stood before him, feet braced to the lifting of the deck. He was of huge stature, a good half head taller than Turlogh who stood well above six feet. His legs were like columns, his arms like oak and iron. His beard was of crisp gold, matching the massive armlets he wore. A shirt of scale-mail added to his warlike appearance as the horned helmet seemed to increase his height. But there was no wrath in the calm gray eyes which gazed tranquilly into the smoldering blue eyes of the Gael.

"Athelstane, the Saxon!"

"Aye—it's been a long day since you gave me this," the giant indicated a thin white scar on his temple. "We seem fated to meet on nights of fury—we first crossed steel the night you burned Thorfel's skalli. Then I fell before your ax and you saved me from Brogar's Picts—alone of all the folk who followed Thorfel. Tonight it was I who struck you down." He touched the great two-handed sword strapped to his shoulders and Turlogh cursed.

"Nay, revile me not," said Athelstane with a pained expression. "I could have slain you in the press—I struck with the flat, but knowing you Irish have cursed hard skulls, I struck with both hands. You have been senseless for hours. Lodbrog would have slain you with the rest of the merchant ship's crew but I claimed your life. But the Vikings would only agree to spare you on condition that you be bound to the mast. They know you of old."

"Where are we?"

"Ask me not. The storm blew us far out of our course. We were sailing to harry the coasts of Spain. When chance threw us in with your vessel, of course we seized the opportunity, but there was scant spoil. Now we are racing with the sea-flow, unknowing. The steer sweep is crippled and the whole ship lamed. We may be riding the very rim of the world for aught I know. Swear to join us and I will loose you."

"Swear to join the hosts of Hell!" snarled Turlogh. "Rather will I go down with the ship and sleep forever under the green waters, bound to this mast. My only regret is that I cannot send more sea wolves to join the hundred-odd I have already sent to Purgatory!"

"Well, well," said Athelstane tolerantly, "a man must eat—here—I will loose your hands at least—now, set your teeth into this joint of meat."

Turlogh bent his head to the great joint and tore at it ravenously. The Saxon watched him a moment, then turned away. A strange man, reflected Turlogh, this renegade Saxon who hunted with the wolf pack of the North—a savage warrior in battle, but with fibers of kindliness in his makeup which set him apart from the men with whom he consorted.

The ship reeled on blindly in the night, and Athelstane, returning with a great horn of foaming ale, remarked on the fact that the clouds were gathering again, obscuring the seething face of the sea. He left the Gael's hands unbound but Turlogh was held fast to the mast by cords about legs and body. The rovers paid no heed to their prisoner; they were too much occupied in keeping their crippled ship from going down under their feet.

At last Turlogh believed he could catch at times a deep roaring above the wash of the waves. This grew in volume, and even as the duller-eared Norsemen heard it, the ship leaped like a spurred horse, straining in every timber. As by magic the clouds, lightening for dawn, rolled away on each side, showing a wild waste of tossing gray waters, and a long line of breakers dead ahead. Beyond the frothing madness of the reefs loomed land, apparently an island. The roaring increased to deafening proportions, as the longship, caught in the tide rip, raced headlong to her doom. Turlogh saw Lodbrog rushing about, his long beard flowing in the wind as he brandished his fists and bellowed futile commands. Athelstane came running across the deck.

"Little chance for any of us," he growled as he cut the Gael's bonds, "but you shall have as much as the rest—"

Turlogh sprang free. "Where is my ax?"

"There in that weapon-rack. But Thor's blood, man," marveled the big Saxon, "you won't burden yourself now—"

Turlogh had snatched the ax and confidence flowed like wine through his veins at the familiar feel of the slim, graceful shaft. His ax was as much a part of him as his right hand; if he must die he wished to die with it in his grip. He hastily slung it to his girdle. All armor had been stripped from him when he had been captured.

"There are sharks in these waters," said Athelstane, preparing to doff his scale mail. "If we have to swim—"

The ship struck with a crash that snapped her masts and shivered her prow like glass. Her dragon beak shot high in the air and men tumbled like tenpins from her slanted deck. A moment she poised, shuddering like a live thing, then slid from the hidden reef and went down in a blinding smother of spray.

Turlogh had left the deck in a long dive that carried him clear. Now he rose in the turmoil, fought the waves for a mad moment, then caught a piece of wreckage that the breakers flung up. As he clambered across this, a shape bumped against him and went down again. Turlogh plunged his arm deep, caught a sword-belt and heaved the man up and on his makeshift raft. For in that instant he had recognized the Saxon, Athelstane, still burdened with the armor he had not had time to remove. The man seemed dazed. He lay limp, limbs trailing.

Turlogh remembered that ride through the breaker as a chaotic nightmare. The tide tore them through, plunging their frail craft into the depths, then flinging them into the skies. There was naught to do but hold on and trust to luck. And Turlogh held on, gripping the Saxon with one hand and their raft with the other, while it seemed his fingers would crack with the strain. Again and again they were almost swamped; then by some miracle they were through, riding in water comparatively calm and Turlogh saw a lean fin cutting the surface a yard away. It swirled in and Turlogh unslung his ax and struck. Red dyed the waters instantly and a rush of sinuous shapes made the craft rock. While the sharks tore their brother, Turlogh, paddling with his hands, urged the rude raft ashore until he could feel the bottom. He waded to the beach, half carrying the Saxon; then, iron though he was, Turlogh O'Brien sank down, exhausted and soon slept soundly.

2. Gods from the Abyss

Turlogh did not sleep long. When he awoke the sun was just risen above the sea rim. The Gael rose, feeling as refreshed as if he had slept the whole night through, and looked about him. The broad white beach sloped gently from the water to a waving expanse of gigantic trees. There seemed no underbrush, but so close together were the huge boles, his sight could not pierce into the jungle. Athelstane was standing some distance away on a spit of sand that ran out into the sea. The huge Saxon leaned on his great sword and gazed out toward the reefs.

Here and there on the beach lay the stiff figures that had been washed ashore. A sudden snarl of satisfaction broke from Turlogh's lips. Here at his very feet was a gift from the gods; a dead Viking lay there, fully armed in the helmet and mail shirt he had not had time to doff when the ship foundered, and Turlogh saw they were his own. Even the round light buckler strapped to the Norseman's back was his. Turlogh did pause to wonder how all his accouterments had come into the possession of one man, but stripped the dead and donned the plain round helmet and the shirt of black chain mail. Thus armed he went up the beach toward Athelstane, his eyes gleaming unpleasantly.

The Saxon turned as he approached. "Hail to you, Gael," he greeted. "We be all of Lodbrog's ship-people left alive. The hungry green sea drank them all. By Thor, I owe my life to you! What with the weight of my mail, and the crack my skull got on the rail, I had most certainly been food for the sharks but for you. It all seems like a dream now."

"You saved my life," snarled Turlogh, "I saved yours. Now the debt is paid, the accounts are squared, so up with your sword and let us make an end."

Athelstane stared. "You wish to fight me? Why—what—?"

"I hate your breed as I hate Satan!" roared the Gael, a tinge of madness in his blazing eyes. "Your wolves have ravaged my people for five hundred years! The smoking ruins of the Southland, the seas of spilled blood call for vengeance! The screams of a thousand ravished girls are ringing in my ears, night and day! Would that the North had but a single breast for my ax to cleave!"

"But I am no Norseman," rumbled the giant in worriment.

"The more shame to you, renegade," raved the maddened Gael. "Defend yourself lest I cut you down in cold blood!"

"This is not to my liking," protested Athelstane, lifting his mighty blade, his gray eyes serious but unafraid. "Men speak truly who say there is madness in you."

Words ceased as the men prepared to go into deadly action. The Gael approached his foe, crouching panther-like, eyes ablaze. The Saxon waited the onslaught, feet braced wide apart, sword held high in both hands. It was Turlogh's ax and shield against Athelstane's two-handed sword; in a contest one stroke might end either way. Like two great jungle beasts they played their deadly, wary game, then—

Even as Turlogh's muscles tensed for the death-leap, a fearful sound split the silence! Both men started and recoiled. From the depths of the forest behind them rose a ghastly and inhuman scream. Shrill, yet of great volume, it rose higher and higher until it ceased at the highest pitch, like the triumph of a demon, like the cry of some grisly ogre gloating over its human prey.

"Thor's blood!" gasped the Saxon, letting his sword-point fall. "What was that?"

Turlogh shook his head. Even his iron nerve was slightly shaken. "Some fiend of the forest. This is a strange land in a strange sea. Mayhap Satan himself reigns here and it is the gate to Hell."

Athelstane looked uncertain. He was more pagan than Christian and his devils were heathen devils. But they were none the less grim for that.

"Well," said he, "let us drop our quarrel until we see what it may be. Two blades are better than one, whether for man or devil—"

A wild shriek cut him short. This time it was a human voice, blood-chilling in its horror and despair. Simultaneously came the swift patter of feet and the lumbering rush of some heavy body among the trees. The warriors wheeled toward the sound, and out of the deep shadows a half-naked woman came flying like a white leaf blown on the wind. Her loose hair streamed like a flame of gold behind her, her white limbs flashed in the morning sun, her eyes blazed with frenzied terror. And behind her—

Even Turlogh's hair stood up. The thing that pursued the fleeing girl was neither man nor beast. In form it was like a bird, but such a bird as the rest of the world had not seen for many an age. Some twelve feet high it towered, and its evil head with the wicked red eyes and cruel curved beak was as big as a horse's head. The long, arched neck was thicker than a man's thigh and the huge taloned feet could have gripped the fleeing woman as an eagle grips a sparrow.

This much Turlogh saw in one glance as he sprang between the monster and its prey who sank down with a cry on the beach. It loomed above him like a mountain of death and the evil beak darted down, denting the shield he raised and staggering him with the impact. At the same instant he struck, but the keen ax sank harmlessly into a cushioning mass of spiky feathers. Again the beak flashed at him and his sidelong leap saved his life by a hair's breadth. And then Athelstane ran in, and bracing his feet wide, swung his great sword with both hands and all his strength. The mighty blade sheared through one of the tree-like legs below the knee, and with an abhorrent screech, the monster sank on its side, flapping its short heavy wings wildly. Turlogh drove the back-spike of his ax between the glaring red eyes and the gigantic bird kicked convulsively and lay still.

"Thor's blood!" Athelstane's gray eyes were blazing with battle lust. "Truly we've come to the rim of the world—"

"Watch the forest lest another come forth," snapped Turlogh, turning to the woman who had scrambled to her feet and stood panting, eyes wide with wonder. She was a splendid young animal, tall, clean limbed, slim and shapely. Her only garment was a sheer bit of silk hung carelessly about her hips. But though the scantiness of her dress suggested the savage, her skin was snowy white, her loose hair of purest gold and her eyes gray. Now she spoke hastily, stammeringly, in the tongue of the Norse, as if she had not so spoken in years.

"You—who are you men? Whence come you? What do you on the Isle of the Gods?"

"Thor's blood!" rumbled the Saxon; "she's of our own kind!"

"Not mine!" snapped Turlogh, unable even in that moment to forget his hate for the people of the North.

The girl looked curiously at the two. "The world must have changed greatly since I left it," she said, evidently in full control of herself once more, "else how is it that wolf and wild bull hunt together? By your black hair, you are a Gael, and you, big man, have a slur in your speech that can be naught but Saxon."

"We are two outcasts," answered Turlogh. "You see these dead men lining the strand? They were the crew of the dragon-ship which bore us here, storm driven. This man, Athelstane, once of Wessex, was a swordsman on that ship and I was a captive. I am Turlogh Dubh, once a chief of Clan na O'Brien. Who are you and what land is this?"

"This is the oldest land in the world," answered the girl. "Rome, Egypt, Cathay are as but infants beside it. I am Brunhild, daughter of Rane Thorfin's son, of the Orkneys, and until a few days ago, queen of this ancient kingdom."

Turlogh looked uncertainly at Athelstane. This sounded like sorcery.

"After what we have just seen," rumbled the giant, "I am ready to believe anything. But are you in truth Rane Thorfin's son's stolen child?"

"Aye!" cried the girl, "I am that one! I was stolen when Tostig the Mad raided the Orkneys and burned Rane's steading in the absence of its master—"

"And then Tostig vanished from the face of the earth—or the sea!" interrupted Athelstane. "He was in truth a madman. I sailed with him for a ship-harrying many years ago when I was but a youth."

"And his madness cast me on this island," answered Brunhild; "for after he had harried the shores of England, the fire in his brain drove him out into unknown seas—south and south and ever south until even the fierce wolves he led murmured. Then a storm drove us on yonder reef, though at another part, rending the dragon-ship even as yours was rended last night. Tostig and all his strong men perished in the waves, but I clung to pieces of wreckage and a whim of the gods cast me ashore, half-dead. I was fifteen years old. That was ten years ago.

"I found a strange terrible people dwelling here, a brown-skinned folk who knew many dark secrets of magic. They found me lying senseless on the beach and because I was the first white human they had ever seen, their priests divined that I was a goddess given them by the sea, whom they worship. So they put me in the temple with the rest of their curious gods and did reverence to me. And their high priest, old Gothan—cursed be his name!—taught me many strange and fearful things. Soon I learned their language and much of their priests' inner mysteries. And as I grew into womanhood the desire for power stirred in me; for the people of the North are made to rule the folk of the world, and it is not for the daughter of a sea king to sit meekly in a temple and accept the offerings of fruit and flowers and human sacrifices!"

She stopped for a moment, eyes blazing. Truly, she looked a worthy daughter of the fierce race she claimed.

"Well," she continued, "there was one who loved me—Kotar, a young chief. With him I plotted and at last I rose and flung off the yoke of old Gothan. That was a wild season of plot and counterplot, intrigue, rebellion and red carnage! Men and women died like flies and the streets of Bal-Sagoth ran red—but in the end we triumphed, Kotar and I! The dynasty of Angar came to an end on a night of blood and fury and I reigned supreme on the Isle of the Gods, queen and goddess!"

She had drawn herself up to her full height, her beautiful face alight with fierce pride, her bosom heaving. Turlogh was at once fascinated and repelled. He had seen rulers rise and fall, and between the lines of her brief narrative he read the bloodshed and carnage, the cruelty and the treachery—sensing the basic ruthlessness of this girl-woman.

"But if you were queen," he asked, "how is it that we find you hunted through the forests of your domain by this monster, like a runaway serving wench?"

Brunhild bit her lip and an angry flush mounted to her cheeks. "What is it that brings down every woman, whatever her station? I trusted a man—Kotar, my lover, with whom I shared my rule. He betrayed me; after I had raised him to the highest power in the kingdom, next to my own, I found he secretly made love to another girl. I killed them both!"

Turlogh smiled coldly: "You are a true Brunhild! And then what?"

"Kotar was loved by the people. Old Gothan stirred them up. I made my greatest mistake when I let that old one live. Yet I dared not slay him. Well, Gothan rose against me, as I had risen against him, and the warriors rebelled, slaying those who stood faithful to me. Me they took captive but dared not kill; for after all, I was a goddess, they believed. So before dawn, fearing the people would change their minds again and restore me to power, Gothan had me taken to the lagoon which separates this part of the island from the other. The priests rowed me across the lagoon and left me, naked and helpless, to my fate."

"And that fate was—this?" Athelstane touched the huge carcass with his foot.

Brunhild shuddered. "Many ages ago there were many of these monsters on the isle, the legends say. They warred on the people of Bal-Sagoth and devoured them by the hundreds. But at last all were exterminated on the main part of the isle and on this side of the lagoon all died but this one, who had abided here for centuries. In the old times hosts of men came against him, but he was greatest of all the devil-birds and he slew all who fought him. So the priests made a god of him and left this part of the island to him. None comes here except those brought as sacrifices—as I was. He could not cross to the main island, because the lagoon swarms with great sharks which would rend even him to pieces.

"For a while I eluded him, stealing among the trees, but at last he spied me out—and you know the rest. I owe my life to you. Now what will you do with me?"

Athelstane looked at Turlogh and Turlogh shrugged. "What can we do, save starve in this forest?"

"I will tell you!" the girl cried in a ringing voice, her eyes blazing anew to the swift working of her keen brain. "There is an old legend among this people—that men of iron will come out of the sea and the city of Bal-Sagoth will fall! You, with your mail and helmets, will seem as iron men to these folk who know nothing of armor! You have slain Groth-golka the bird-god—you have come out of the sea as did I—the people will look on you as gods. Come with me and aid me to win back my kingdom! You shall be my right-hand men and I will heap honors on you! Fine garments, gorgeous palaces, fairest girls shall be yours!"

Her promises slid from Turlogh's mind without leaving an imprint, but the mad splendor of the proposal intrigued him. Strongly he desired to look on this strange city of which Brunhild spoke, and the thought of two warriors and one girl pitted against a whole nation for a crown stirred the utmost depths of his knight-errant Celtic soul.

"It is well," said he. "And what of you, Athelstane?"

"My belly is empty," growled the giant. "Lead me to where there is food and I'll hew my way to it, through a horde of priests and warriors."

"Lead us to this city!" said Turlogh to Brunhild.

"Hail!" she cried flinging her white arms high in wild exultation. "Now let Gothan and Ska and Gelka tremble! With ye at my side I'll win back the crown they tore from me, and this time I'll not spare my enemy! I'll hurl old Gothan from the highest battlement, though the bellowing of his demons shake the very bowels of the earth! And we shall see if the god Golgoroth shall stand against the sword that cut Groth-golka's leg from under him. Now hew the head from this carcass that the people may know you have overcome the bird-god. Now follow me, for the sun mounts the sky and I would sleep in my own palace tonight!"

The three passed into the shadows of the mighty forest. The interlocking branches, hundreds of feet above their heads, made dim and strange such sunlight as filtered through. No life was seen except for an occasional gaily hued bird or a huge ape. These beasts, Brunhild said, were survivors of another age, harmless except when attacked. Presently the growth changed somewhat, the trees thinned and became smaller and fruit of many kinds was seen among the branches. Brunhild told the warriors which to pluck and eat as they walked along. Turlogh was quite satisfied with the fruit, but Athelstane, though he ate enormously, did so with scant relish. Fruit was light sustenance to a man used to such solid stuff as formed his regular diet. Even among the gluttonous Danes the Saxon's capacity for beef and ale was admired.

"Look!" cried Brunhild sharply, halting and pointing. "The spires of Bal-Sagoth!"

Through the trees the warriors caught a glimmer, white and shimmery, and apparently far away. There was an illusory impression of towering battlements, high in the air, with fleecy clouds hovering about them. The sight woke strange dreams in the mystic deeps of the Gael's soul, and even Athelstane was silent as if he too were struck by the pagan beauty and mystery of the scene.

So they progressed through the forest, now losing sight of the distant city as treetops obstructed the view, now seeing it again. And at last they came out on the low shelving banks of a broad blue lagoon and the full beauty of the landscape burst upon their eyes. From the opposite shores the country sloped upward in long gentle undulations which broke like great slow waves at the foot of a range of blue hills a few miles away. These wide swells were covered with deep grass and many groves of trees, while miles away on either hand there was seen curving away into the distance the strip of thick forest which Brunhild said belted the whole island. And among those blue dreaming hills brooded the age-old city of Bal-Sagoth, its white walls and sapphire towers clean-cut against the morning sky. The suggestion of great distance had been an illusion.

"Is that not a kingdom worth fighting for?" cried Brunhild, her voice vibrant. "Swift now—let us bind this dry wood together for a raft. We could not live an instant swimming in that shark haunted water."

At that instant a figure leaped up from the tall grass on the other shore—a naked, brown-skinned man who stared for a moment, agape. Then as Athelstane shouted and held up the grim head of Groth-golka, the fellow gave a startled cry and raced away like an antelope.

"A slave Gothan left to see if I tried to swim the lagoon," said Brunhild with angry satisfaction. "Let him run to the city and tell them—but let us make haste and cross the lagoon before Gothan can arrive and dispute our passage."

Turlogh and Athelstane were already busy. A number of dead trees lay about and these they stripped of their branches and bound together with long vines. In a short time they had built a raft, crude and clumsy, but capable of bearing them across the lagoon. Brunhild gave a frank sigh of relief when they stepped on the other shore.

"Let us go straight to the city," said she. "The slave has reached it ere now and they will be watching us from the walls. A bold course is our only one. Thor's hammer, but I'd like to see Gothan's face when the slave tells him Brunhild is returning with two strange warriors and the head of him to whom she was given as sacrifice!"

"Why did you not kill Gothan when you had the power?" asked Athelstane.

She shook her head, her eyes clouding with something akin to fear: "Easier said than done. Half the people hate Gothan, half love him, and all fear him. The most ancient men of the city say that he was old when they were babes. The people believe him to be more god than priest, and I myself have seen him do terrible and mysterious things, beyond the power of a common man.

"Nay, when I was but a puppet in his hands, I came only to the outer fringe of his mysteries, yet I have looked on sights that froze my blood. I have seen strange shadows flit along the midnight walls, and groping along black subterranean corridors in the dead of night I have heard unhallowed sounds and have felt the presence of hideous beings. And once I heard the grisly slavering bellowings of the nameless Thing Gothan has chained deep in the bowels of the hills on which rests the city of Bal- Sagoth."

Brunhild shuddered.

"There are many gods in Bal-Sagoth, but the greatest of all is Gol-goroth, the god of darkness who sits forever in the Temple of Shadows. When I overthrew the power of Gothan, I forbade men to worship Gol-goroth, and made the priest hail, as the one true deity, A-ala, the daughter of the sea—myself. I had strong men take heavy hammers and smite the image of Golgoroth, but their blows only shattered the hammers and gave strange hurts to the men who wielded them. Gol-goroth was indestructible and showed no mar. So I desisted and shut the doors of the Temple of Shadows which were opened only when I was overthrown and Gothan, who had been skulking in the secret places of the city, came again into his own. Then Golgoroth reigned again in his full terror and the idols of A-ala were overthrown in the Temple of the Sea, and the priests of A-ala died howling on the red-stained altar before the black god. But now we shall see!"

"Surely you are a very Valkyrie," muttered Athelstane. "But three against a nation is great odds—especially such a people as this, who must assuredly be all witches and sorcerers."

"Bah!" cried Brunhild contemptuously. "There are many sorcerers, it is true, but though the people are strange to us, they are mere fools in their own way, as are all nations. When Gothan led me captive down the streets they spat on me. Now watch them turn on Ska, the new king Gothan has given them, when it seems my star rises again! But now we approach the city gates—be bold but wary!"

They had ascended the long swelling slopes and were not far from the walls which rose immensely upward. Surely, thought Turlogh, heathen gods built this city. The walls seemed of marble and with their fretted battlements and slim watchtowers, dwarfed the memory of such cities as Rome, Damascus and Byzantium. A broad white winding road led up from the lower levels to the plateau before the gates and as they came up this road, the three adventurers felt hundreds of hidden eyes fixed on them with fierce intensity. The walls seemed deserted; it might have been a dead city. But the impact of those staring eyes was felt.

Now they stood before the massive gates, which to the amazed eyes of the warriors seemed to be of chased silver.

"Here is an emperor's ransom!" muttered Athelstane, eyes ablaze. "Thor's blood, if we had but a stout band of reavers and a ship to carry away the plunder!"

"Smite on the gate and then step back, lest something fall upon you," said Brunhild, and the thunder of Turlogh's ax on the portals woke the echoes in the sleeping hills.

The three then fell back a few paces and suddenly the mighty gates swung inward and a strange concourse of people stood revealed. The two white warriors looked on a pageant of barbaric grandeur. A throng of tall, slim, brown-skinned men stood in the gates. Their only garments were loincloths of silk, the fine work of which contrasted strangely with the near nudity of the wearers. Tall waving plumes of many colors decked their heads, and armlets and leglets of gold and silver, crusted with gleaming gems, completed their ornamentation. Armor they wore none, but each carried a light shield on his left arm, made of hard wood, highly polished, and braced with silver. Their weapons were slim-bladed spears, light hatchets and slender daggers, all bladed with fine steel. Evidently these warriors depended more on speed and skill than on brute force.

At the front of this band stood three men who instantly commanded attention. One was a lean hawk-faced warrior, almost as tall as Athelstane, who wore about his neck a great golden chain from which was suspended a curious symbol in jade. One of the other men was young, evil eyed; an impressive riot of colors in the mantle of parrot feathers which swung from his shoulders. The third man had nothing to set him apart from the rest save his own strange personality. He wore no mantle, bore no weapons. His only garment was a plain loincloth. He was very old; he alone of all the throng was bearded, and his beard was as white as the long hair which fell about his shoulders. He was very tall and very lean, and his great dark eyes blazed as from a hidden fire. Turlogh knew without being told that this man was Gothan, priest of the Black God. The ancient exuded a very aura of age and mystery. His great eyes were like windows of some forgotten temple, behind which passed like ghosts his dark and terrible thoughts. Turlogh sensed that Gothan had delved too deep in forbidden secrets to remain altogether human. He had passed through doors that had cut him off from the dreams, desires and emotions of ordinary mortals. Looking into those unwinking orbs Turlogh felt his skin crawl, as if he had looked into the eyes of a great serpent.

Now a glance upward showed that the walls were thronged with silent dark-eyed folk. The stage was set; all was in readiness for the swift, red drama. Turlogh felt his pulse quicken with fierce exhilaration and Athelstane's eyes began to glow with ferocious light.

Brunhild stepped forward boldly, head high, her splendid figure vibrant. The white warriors naturally could not understand what passed between her and the others, except as they read from gestures and expressions, but later Brunhild narrated the conversation almost word for word.

"Well, people of Bal-Sagoth," said she, spacing her words slowly, "what words have you for your goddess whom you mocked and reviled?"

"What will you have, false one?" exclaimed the tall man, Ska, the king set up by Gothan; "you who mocked at the customs of our ancestors, defied the laws of Bal-Sagoth, which are older than the world, murdered your lover and defiled the shrine of Gol-goroth? You were doomed by law, king and god and placed in the grim forest beyond the lagoon—"

"And I, who am likewise a goddess and greater than any god," answered Brunhild mockingly, "am returned from the realm of horror with the head of Groth-golka!"

At a word from her, Athelstane held up the great beaked head, and a low whispering ran about the battlements, tense with fear and bewilderment.

"Who are these men?" Ska bent a worried frown on the two warriors.

"They are iron men who have come out of the sea!" answered Brunhild in a clear voice that carried far; "the beings who have come in response to the old prophesy, to overthrow the city of Bal-Sagoth, whose people are traitors and whose priests are false!"

At these words the fearful murmur broke out afresh all up and down the line of the walls, till Gothan lifted his vulture head and the people fell silent and shrank before the icy stare of his terrible eyes.

Ska glared bewilderedly, his ambition struggling with his superstitious fears.

Turlogh, looking closely at Gothan, believed that he read beneath the inscrutable mask of the old priest's face. For all his inhuman wisdom, Gothan had his limitations. This sudden return of one he thought well disposed of, and the appearance of the white-skinned giants accompanying her, had caught Gothan off his guard, Turlogh believed, rightly. There had been no time to properly prepare for their reception. The people had already begun to murmur in the streets against the severity of Ska's brief rule. They had always believed in Brunhild's divinity; now that she returned with two tall men of her own hue, bearing the grim trophy that marked the conquest of another of their gods, the people were wavering. Any small thing might turn the tide either way.

"People of Bal-Sagoth!" shouted Brunhild suddenly, springing back and flinging her arms high, gazing full into the faces that looked down at her, "I bid you avert your doom before it is too late! You cast me out and spat on me; you turned to darker gods than I! Yet all this will I forgive if you return and do obeisance to me! Once you reviled me—you called me bloody and cruel! True, I was a hard mistress—but has Ska been an easy master? You said I lashed the people with whips of rawhide—has Ska stroked you with parrot feathers?

"A virgin died on my altar at the full tide of each moon—but youths and maidens die at the waxing and the waning, the rising and the setting of each moon, before Gol-goroth, on whose altar a fresh human heart forever throbs! Ska is but a shadow! Your real lord is Gothan, who sits above the city like a vulture! Once you were a mighty people; your galleys filled the seas. Now you are a remnant and that is dwindling fast! Fools! You will all die on the altar of Gol-goroth ere Gothan is done and he will stalk alone among the silent ruins of Bal-Sagoth!

"Look at him!" her voice rose to a scream as she lashed herself to an inspired frenzy, and even Turlogh, to whom the words were meaningless, shivered. "Look at him where he stands there like an evil spirit out of the past! He is not even human! I tell you, he is a foul ghost, whose beard is dabbled with the blood of a million butcheries—an incarnate fiend out of the mist of the ages come to destroy the people of Bal-Sagoth!

"Choose now! Rise up against the ancient devil and his blasphemous gods, receive your rightful queen and deity again and you shall regain some of your former greatness. Refuse, and the ancient prophesy shall be fulfilled and the sun will set on the silent and crumbled ruins of Bal-Sagoth!"

Fired by her dynamic words, a young warrior with the insignia of a chief sprang to the parapet and shouted: "Hail to A-ala! Down with the bloody gods!"

Among the multitude many took up the shout and steel clashed as a score of fights started. The crowd on the battlements and in the streets surged and eddied, while Ska glared, bewildered. Brunhild, forcing back her companions who quivered with eagerness for action of some kind, shouted: "Hold! Let no man strike a blow yet! People of Bal-Sagoth, it has been a tradition since the beginning of time that a king must fight for his crown! Let Ska cross steel with one of these warriors! If Ska wins, I will kneel before him and let him strike off my head! If Ska loses, then you shall accept me as your rightful queen and goddess!"

A great roar of approval went up from the walls as the people ceased their brawls, glad enough to shift the responsibility to their rulers.

"Will you fight, Ska?" asked Brunhild, turning to the king mockingly. "Or will you give me your head without further argument?"

"Slut!" howled Ska, driven to madness. "I will take the skulls of these fools for drinking cups, and then I will rend you between two bent trees!"

Gothan laid a hand on his arm and whispered in his ear, but Ska had reached the point where he was deaf to all but his fury. His achieved ambition, he had found, had faded to the mere part of a puppet dancing on Gothan's string; now even the hollow bauble of his kingship was slipping from him and this wench mocked him to his face before his people. Ska went, to all practical effects, stark mad.

Brunhild turned to her two allies. "One of you must fight Ska."

"Let me be the one!" urged Turlogh, eyes dancing with eager battle-lust. "He has the look of a man quick as a wildcat, and Athelstane, while a very bull for strength, is a thought slow for such work—"

"Slow!" broke in Athelstane reproachfully. "Why, Turlogh, for a man my weight—"

"Enough," Brunhild interrupted. "He must choose for himself."

She spoke to Ska, who glared red eyed for an instant, then indicated Athelstane, who grinned joyfully, cast aside the bird's head and unslung his sword. Turlogh swore and stepped back. The king had decided that he would have a better chance against this huge buffalo of a man who looked slow, than against the black-haired tigerish warrior, whose catlike quickness was evident.

"This Ska is without armor," rumbled the Saxon. "Let me likewise doff my mail and helmet so that we fight on equal terms—"

"No!" cried Brunhild. "Your armor is your only chance! I tell you, this false king fights like the play of summer lightning! You will be hard put to hold your own as it is. Keep on your armor, I say!"

"Well, well," grumbled Athelstane, "I will—I will. Though I say it is scarcely fair. But let him come on and make an end of it."

The huge Saxon strode ponderously toward his foe, who warily crouched and circled away. Athelstane held his great sword in both hands before him, pointed upward, the hilt somewhat below the level of his chin, in position to strike a blow to right or left, or to parry a sudden attack.

Ska had flung away his light shield, his fighting sense telling him that it would be useless before the stroke of that heavy blade. In his right hand he held his slim spear as a man holds a throwing dart, in his left a light, keen-edged hatchet. He meant to make a fast, shifty fight of it, and his tactics were good. But Ska, having never encountered armor before, made his fatal mistake in supposing it to be apparel or ornament through which his weapons would pierce.

Now he sprang in, thrusting at Athelstane's face with his spear. The Saxon parried with ease and instantly cut tremendously at Ska's legs. The king bounded high, clearing the whistling blade, and in midair he hacked down at Athelstane's bent head. The light hatchet shivered to bits on the Viking's helmet and Ska sprang back out of reach with a bloodlusting howl.

And now it was Athelstane who rushed with unexpected quickness, like a charging bull, and before that terrible onslaught Ska, bewildered by the breaking of his hatchet, was caught off his guard—flat-footed. He caught a fleeting glimpse of the giant looming over him like an overwhelming wave and he sprang in, instead of out, stabbing ferociously. That mistake was his last. The thrusting spear glanced harmlessly from the Saxon's mail, and in that instant the great sword sang down in a stroke the king could not evade. The force of that stroke tossed him as a man is tossed by a plunging bull. A dozen feet away fell Ska, king of Bal-Sagoth, to lie shattered and dead in a ghastly welter of blood and entrails. The throng gaped, struck silent by the prowess of that deed.

"Hew off his head!" cried Brunhild, her eyes flaming as she clenched her hands so that the nails bit into the palms. "Impale that carrion's head on your sword-point so that we may carry it through the city gates with us as token of victory!"

But Athelstane shook his head, cleansing his blade: "Nay, he was a brave man and I will not mutilate his corpse. It is no great feat I have done, for he was naked and I full-armed. Else it is in my mind, the brawl had gone differently."

Turlogh glanced at the people on the walls. They had recovered from their astonishment and now a vast roar went up: "A-ala! Hail to the true goddess!" And the warriors in the gateway dropped to their knees and bowed their foreheads in the dust before Brunhild, who stood proudly erect, bosom heaving with fierce triumph. Truly, thought Turlogh, she is more than a queen—she is a shield woman, a Valkyrie, as Athelstane said.

Now she stepped aside and tearing the golden chain with its jade symbol from the dead neck of Ska, held it on high and shouted: "People of Bal-Sagoth, you have seen how your false king died before this golden-bearded giant, who being of iron, shows no single cut! Choose now—do you receive me of your own free will?"

"Aye, we do!" the multitude answered in a great shout. "Return to your people, oh mighty and all-powerful queen!"

Brunhild smiled sardonically. "Come," said she to the warriors; "they are lashing themselves into a very frenzy of love and loyalty, having already forgotten their treachery. The memory of the mob is short!"

Aye, thought Turlogh, as at Brunhild's side he and the Saxon passed through the mighty gates between files of prostrate chieftains; aye, the memory of the mob is very short. But a few days have passed since they were yelling as wildly for Ska the liberator—scant hours had passed since Ska sat enthroned, master of life and death, and the people bowed before his feet. Now—Turlogh glanced at the mangled corpse which lay deserted and forgotten before the silver gates. The shadow of a circling vulture fell across it. The clamor of the multitude filled Turlogh's ears and he smiled a bitter smile.

The great gates closed behind the three adventurers and Turlogh saw a broad white street stretching away in front of him. Other lesser streets radiated from this one. The two warriors caught a jumbled and chaotic impression of great white stone buildings shouldering each other; of sky-lifting towers and broad stair-fronted palaces. Turlogh knew there must be an ordered system by which the city was laid out, but to him all seemed a waste of stone and metal and polished wood, without rhyme or reason. His baffled eyes sought the street again.

Far up the street extended a mass of humanity, from which rose a rhythmic thunder of sound. Thousands of naked, gaily plumed men and women knelt there, bending forward to touch the marble flags with their foreheads, then swaying back with an upward flinging of their arms, all moving in perfect unison like the bending and rising of tall grass before the wind. And in time to their bowing they lifted a monotoned chant that sank and swelled in a frenzy of ecstasy. So her wayward people welcomed back the goddess A-ala.

Just within the gates Brunhild stopped and there came to her the young chief who had first raised the shout of revolt upon the walls. He knelt and kissed her bare feet, saying: "Oh great queen and goddess, thou knowest Zomar was ever faithful to thee! Thou knowest how I fought for thee and barely escaped the altar of Gol-goroth for thy sake!"

"Thou hast indeed been faithful, Zomar," answered Brunhild in the stilted language required for such occasions, "nor shall thy fidelity go unrewarded. Henceforth thou art commander of my own bodyguard." Then in a lower voice she added: "Gather a band from your own retainers and from those who have espoused my cause all along, and bring them to the palace. I do not trust the people any more than I have to!"

Suddenly Athelstane, not understanding the conversation, broke in: "Where is the old one with the beard?"

Turlogh started and glanced around. He had almost forgotten the wizard. He had not seen him go—yet he was gone! Brunhild laughed ruefully.

"He's stolen away to breed more trouble in the shadows. He and Gelka vanished when Ska fell. He has secret ways of coming and going and none may stay him. Forget him for the time being; heed ye well—we shall have plenty of him anon!"

Now the chiefs brought a finely carved and highly ornamented palanquin carried by two strong slaves, and Brunhild stepped into this, saying to her companions: "They are fearful of touching you, but ask if you would be carried. I think it better that you walk, one on each side of me."

"Thor's blood!" rumbled Athelstane, shouldering the huge sword he had never sheathed. "I'm no infant! I'll split the skull of the man who seeks to carry me!"

And so up the long white street went Brunhild, daughter of Rane Thorfin's son in the Orkneys, goddess of the sea, queen of age-old Bal-Sagoth. Borne by two great slaves she went, with a white giant striding on each side with bared steel, and a concourse of chiefs following, while the multitude gave way to right and left, leaving a wide lane down which she passed. Golden trumpets sounded a fanfare of triumph, drums thundered, chants of worship echoed to the ringing skies. Surely in this riot of glory, this barbaric pageant of splendor, the proud soul of the North-born girl drank deep and grew drunken with imperial pride.

Athelstane's eyes glowed with simple delight at this flame of pagan magnificence, but to the black-haired fighting-man of the West, it seemed that even in the loudest clamor of triumph, the trumpet, the drum and the shouting faded away into the forgotten dust and silence of eternity. Kingdoms and empires pass away like mist from the sea, thought Turlogh; the people shout and triumph and even in the revelry of Belshazzar's feast, the Medes break the gates of Babylon. Even now the shadow of doom is over this city and the slow tides of oblivion lap the feet of this unheeding race. So in a strange mood Turlogh O'Brien strode beside the palanquin, and it seemed to him that he and Athelstane walked in a dead city, through throngs of dim ghosts, cheering a ghost queen.

3. The Fall of the Gods

Night had fallen on the ancient city of Bal-Sagoth. Turlogh, Athelstane and Brunhild sat alone in a room of the inner palace. The queen half-reclined on a silken couch, while the men sat on mahogany chairs, engaged in the viands that slave girls had served them on golden dishes. The walls of this room, as of all the palace, were of marble, with golden scrollwork. The ceiling was of lapis lazuli and the floor of silver-inlaid marble tiles. Heavy velvet hangings decorated the walls and silken cushions; richly made divans and mahogany chairs and tables littered the room in careless profusion.

"I would give much for a horn of ale, but this wine is not sour to the palate," said Athelstane, emptying a golden flagon with relish. "Brunhild, you have deceived us. You let us understand it would take hard fighting to win back your crown—yet I have struck but one blow and my sword is thirsty as Turlogh's ax which has not drunk at all. We hammered on the gates and the people fell down and worshipped with no more ado. And until a little while ago, we but stood by your throne in the great palace room, while you spoke to the throngs that came and knocked their heads on the floor before you—by Thor, never have I heard such clattering and jabbering! My ears ring till now—what were they saying? And where is that old conjurer Gothan?"

"Your steel will drink deep yet, Saxon," answered the girl grimly, resting her chin on her hands and eyeing the warriors with deep moody eyes. "Had you gambled with cities and crowns as I have done, you would know that seizing a throne may be easier than keeping it. Our sudden appearance with the bird-god's head, your killing of Ska, swept the people off their feet. As for the rest—I held audience in the palace as you saw, even if you did not understand, and the people who came in bowing droves were assuring me of their unswerving loyalty—ha! I graciously pardoned them all, but I am no fool. When they have time to think, they will begin to grumble again. Gothan is lurking in the shadows somewhere, plotting evil to us all, you may be sure. This city is honeycombed with secret corridors and subterranean passages of which only the priests know. Even I, who have traversed some of them when I was Gothan's puppet, know not where to look for the secret doors, since Gothan always led me through them blindfolded.

"Just now, I think I hold the upper hand. The people look on you with more awe than they regard me. They think your armor and helmets are part of your bodies and that you are invulnerable. Did you not note them timidly touching your mail as we passed through the crowd, and the amazement on their faces as they felt the iron of it?"

"For a people so wise in some ways they are very foolish in others," said Turlogh. "Who are they and whence came they?"

"They are so old," answered Brunhild, "that their most ancient legends give no hint of their origin. Ages ago they were a part of a great empire which spread out over the many isles of this sea. But some of the islands sank and vanished with their cities and people. Then the red-skinned savages assailed them and isle after isle fell before them. At last only this island was left unconquered, and the people have become weaker and forgotten many ancient arts. For lack of ports to sail to, the galleys rotted by the wharves which themselves crumbled into decay. Not in the memory of man has any son of Bal-Sagoth sailed the seas. At irregular intervals the red people descend upon the Isle of the Gods, traversing the seas in their long war canoes which bear grinning skulls on the prows. Not far away as a Viking would reckon a sea voyage, but out of sight over the sea rim lie the islands inhabited by these red men who centuries ago slaughtered the folk who dwelt there. We have always beaten them off; they cannot scale the walls, but still they come and the fear of their raid is always hovering over the isle.

"But it is not them I fear; it is Gothan, who is at this moment either slipping like a loathly serpent through his black tunnels or else brewing abominations in one of his hidden chambers. In the caves deep in the hills to which his tunnels lead, he works fearful and unholy magic. His subjects are beasts—serpents, spiders, and great apes; and men—red captives and wretches of his own race.

Deep in his grisly caverns he makes beasts of men and half-men of beasts, mingling bestial with human in ghastly creation. No man dares guess at the horrors that have spawned in the darkness, or what shapes of terror and blasphemy have come into being during the ages Gothan has wrought his abominations; for he is not as other men, and has discovered the secret of life everlasting. He has at least brought into foul life one creature that even he fears, the gibbering, mowing, nameless Thing he keeps chained in the furtherest cavern that no human foot save his has trod. He would loose it against me if he dared. . . .

"But it grows late and I would sleep. I will sleep in the room next to this, which has no other opening than this door. Not even a slave girl will I keep with me, for I trust none of these people fully. You shall keep this room, and though the outer door is bolted, one had better watch while the other sleeps. Zomar and his guardsmen patrol the corridors outside, but I shall feel safer with two men of my own blood between me and the rest of the city."

She rose, and with a strangely lingering glance at Turlogh, entered her chamber and closed the door behind her.

Athelstane stretched and yawned. "Well, Turlogh," said he lazily, "men's fortunes are unstable as the sea. Last night I was the picked swordsman of a band of reavers and you a captive. This dawn we were lost outcasts springing at each other's throats. Now we are sword brothers and right-hand men to a queen. And you, I think, are destined to become a king."

"How so?"

"Why, have you not noticed the Orkney girl's eyes on you? Faith there's more than friendship in her glances that rest on those black locks and that brown face of yours. I tell you—"

"Enough," Turlogh's voice was harsh as an old wound stung him. "Women in power are white-fanged wolves. It was the spite of a woman that—" He stopped.

"Well, well," returned Athelstane tolerantly, "there are more good women than bad ones. I know—it was the intrigues of a woman that made you an outcast. Well, we should be good comrades. I am an outlaw, too. If I should show my face in Wessex I would soon be looking down on the countryside from a stout oak limb."

"What drove you out on the Viking path? So far have the Saxons forgotten the ocean-ways that King Alfred was obliged to hire Frisian rovers to build and man his fleet when he fought the Danes."

Athelstane shrugged his mighty shoulders and began whetting his dirk.

"I had a yearning for the sea even when I was a shock-headed child in Wessex. I was still a youth when I killed a young earl and fled the vengeance of his people. I found refuge in the Orkneys and the ways of the Vikings were more to my liking than the ways of my own blood. But I came back to fight against Canute, and when England submitted to his rule, he gave me command of his house-carles. That made the Danes jealous because of the honor given a Saxon who had fought against them, and the Saxons remembered I had left Wessex under a cloud once, and murmured that I was overly well favored by the conquerors. Well, there was a Saxon thane and a Danish jarl who one night at feast assailed me with fiery words and I forgot myself and slew them both.

"So England—was—again—barred—to—me. I—took—the—Viking—path—again—"

Athelstane's words trailed off. His hands slid limply from his lap and the whetstone and dirk dropped to the floor. His head fell forward on his broad chest and his eyes closed.

"Too much wine," muttered Turlogh. "But let him slumber; I'll keep watch."

Yet even as he spoke, the Gael was aware of a strange lassitude stealing over him. He lay back in the broad chair. His eyes felt heavy and sleep veiled his brain despite himself. And as he lay there, a strange nightmare vision came to him. One of the heavy hangings on the wall opposite the door swayed violently and from behind it slunk a fearful shape that crept slavering across the room. Turlogh watched it apathetically, aware that he was dreaming and at the same time wondering at the strangeness of the dream. The thing was grotesquely like a crooked gnarled man in shape, but its face was bestial. It bared yellow fangs as it lurched silently toward him, and from under penthouse brows small, reddened eyes gleamed demoniacally. Yet there was something of the human in its countenance; it was neither ape nor man, but an unnatural creature horribly compounded of both.

Now the foul apparition halted before him, and as the gnarled fingers clutched his throat, Turlogh was suddenly and fearfully aware that this was no dream but a fiendish reality. With a burst of desperate effort he broke the unseen chains that held him and hurled himself from the chair. The grasping fingers missed his throat, but quick as he was, he could not elude the swift lunge of those hairy arms, and the next moment he was tumbling about the floor in a death grip with the monster, whose sinews felt like pliant steel.

That fearful battle was fought in silence save for the hissing of hard-drawn breath. Turlogh's left forearm was thrust under the apish chin, holding back the grisly fangs from his throat, about which the monster's fingers had locked. Athelstane still slept in his chair, head fallen forward. Turlogh tried to call to him, but those throttling hands had shut off his voice—were fast choking out his life. The room swam in a red haze before his distended eyes. His right hand, clenched into an iron mallet, battered desperately at the fearful face bent toward his; the beast-like teeth shattered under his blows and blood splattered, but still the red eyes gloated and the taloned fingers sank deeper and deeper until a ringing in Turlogh's ears knelled his soul's departure.

Even as he sank into semi-unconsciousness, his falling hand struck something his numbed fighting-brain recognized as the dirk Athelstane had dropped on the floor. Blindly, with a dying gesture, Turlogh struck and felt the fingers loosen suddenly. Feeling the return of life and power, he heaved up and over, with his assailant beneath him. Through red mists that slowly lightened, Turlogh Dubh saw the ape-man, now encrimsoned, writhing beneath him, and he drove the dirk home until the dumb horror lay still with wide staring eyes.

The Gael staggered to his feet, dizzy and panting, trembling in every limb. He drew in great gulps of air and his giddiness slowly cleared. Blood trickled plentifully from the wounds in his throat. He noted with amazement that the Saxon still slumbered. And suddenly he began to feel again the tides of unnatural weariness and lassitude that had rendered him helpless before. Picking up his ax, he shook off the feeling with difficulty and stepped toward the curtain from behind which the ape-man had come. Like an invisible wave a subtle power emanating from those hangings struck him, and with weighted limbs he forced his way across the room. Now he stood before the curtain and felt the power of a terrific evil will beating upon his own, menacing his very soul, threatening to enslave him, brain and body. Twice he raised his hand and twice it dropped limply to his side. Now for the third time he made a mighty effort and tore the hangings bodily from the wall. For a flashing instant he caught a glimpse of a bizarre, half-naked figure in a mantle of parrot feathers and a headgear of waving plumes. Then as he felt the full hypnotic blast of those blazing eyes, he closed his own eyes and struck blind. He felt his ax sink deep; then he opened his eyes and gazed at the silent figure which lay at his feet, cleft head in a widening crimson pool.

And now Athelstane suddenly heaved erect, eyes flaring bewilderedly, sword out. "What—?" he stammered, glaring wildly. "Turlogh, what in Thor's name's happened? Thor's blood! That is a priest there, but what is this dead thing?"

"One of the devils of this foul city," answered Turlogh, wrenching his ax free. "I think Gothan has failed again. This one stood behind the hangings and bewitched us unawares. He put the spell of sleep on us—"

"Aye, I slept," the Saxon nodded dazedly. "But how came they here—"

"There must be a secret door behind these hangings, though I cannot find it—"

"Hark!" From the room where the queen slept there came a vague scuffling sound, that in its very faintness seemed fraught with grisly potentialities.

"Brunhild!" Turlogh shouted. A strangled gurgle answered him. He thrust against the door. It was locked. As he heaved up his ax to hew it open, Athelstane brushed him aside and hurled his full weight against it. The panels crashed and through their ruins Athelstane plunged into the room. A roar burst from his lips. Over the Saxon's shoulder Turlogh saw a vision of delirium. Brunhild, queen of Bal-Sagoth, writhed helpless in midair, gripped by the black shadow of a nightmare. Then as the great black shape turned cold flaming eyes on them Turlogh saw it was a living creature. It stood, man-like, upon two tree-like legs, but its outline and face were not of a man, beast or devil. This, Turlogh felt, was the horror that even Gothan had hesitated to loose upon his foes; the archfiend that the demoniac priest had brought into life in his hidden caves of horror. What ghastly knowledge had been necessary, what hideous blending of human and bestial things with nameless shapes from outer voids of darkness?

Held like a babe in arms Brunhild writhed, eyes flaring with horror, and as the Thing took a misshapen hand from her white throat to defend itself, a scream of heart-shaking fright burst from her pale lips. Athelstane, first in the room, was ahead of the Gael. The black shape loomed over the giant Saxon, dwarfing and overshadowing him, but Athelstane, gripping the hilt with both hands, lunged upward. The great sword sank over half its length into the black body and came out crimson as the monster reeled back. A hellish pandemonium of sound burst forth, and the echoes of that hideous yell thundered through the palace and deafened the hearers. Turlogh was springing in, ax high, when the fiend dropped the girl and fled reeling across the room, vanishing in a dark opening that now gaped in the wall. Athelstane, clean berserk, plunged after it.

Turlogh made to follow, but Brunhild, reeling up, threw her white arms around him in a grip even he could hardly break. "No!" she screamed, eyes ablaze with terror. "Do not follow them into that fearful corridor! It must lead to Hell itself! The Saxon will never return! Let you not share his fate!"

"Loose me, woman!" roared Turlogh in a frenzy, striving to disengage himself without hurting her. "My comrade may be fighting for his life!"

"Wait till I summon the guard!" she cried, but Turlogh flung her from him, and as he sprang through the secret doorway, Brunhild smote on the jade gong until the palace re-echoed. A loud pounding began in the corridor and Zomar's voice shouted: "Oh queen, are you in peril? Shall we burst the door?"

"Hasten!" she screamed, as she rushed to the outer door and flung it open.

Turlogh, leaping recklessly into the corridor, raced along in darkness for a few moments, hearing ahead of him the agonized bellowing of the wounded monster and the deep fierce shouts of the Viking. Then these noises faded away in the distance as he came into a narrow passageway faintly lighted with torches stuck into niches. Face down on the floor lay a brown man, clad in gay feathers, his skull crushed like an eggshell.

How long Turlogh O'Brien followed the dizzy windings of the shadowy corridor he never knew. Other smaller passages led off to each side but he kept to the main corridor. At last he passed under an arched doorway and came out into a strange vasty room.

Somber massive columns upheld a shadowy ceiling so high it seemed like a brooding cloud arched against a midnight sky. Turlogh saw that he was in a temple. Behind a black, red-stained stone altar loomed a mighty form, sinister and abhorrent. The god Gol-goroth! Surely it must be he. But Turlogh spared only a single glance for the colossal figure that brooded there in the shadows. Before him was a strange tableau. Athelstane leaned on his great sword and gazed at the two shapes which sprawled in a red welter at his feet. Whatever foul magic had brought the Black Thing into life, it had taken but a thrust of English steel to hurl it back into the limbo from whence it came. The monster lay half-across its last victim—a gaunt, white-bearded man whose eyes were starkly evil, even in death.

"Gothan!" ejaculated the startled Gael.

"Aye, the priest—I was close behind this troll or whatever it is, all the way along the corridor, but for all its size it fled like a deer. Once one in a feather mantle tried to halt it, and it smashed his skull and paused not an instant. At last we burst into this temple, I close upon the monster's heels with my sword raised for the death-cut. But Thor's blood! When it saw the old one standing by that altar, it gave one fearful howl and tore him to pieces and died itself, all in an instant, before I could reach it and strike."

Turlogh gazed at the huge formless thing. Looking directly at it, he could form no estimate of its nature. He got only a chaotic impression of great size and inhuman evil. Now it lay like a vast shadow blotched out on the marble floor. Surely black wings beating from moonless gulfs had hovered over its birth, and the grisly souls of nameless demons had gone into its being.

And now Brunhild rushed from the dark corridor with Zomar and the guardsmen. And from outer doors and secret nooks came others silently—warriors, and priests in feathered mantles, until a great throng stood in the Temple of Darkness.

A fierce cry broke from the queen as she saw what had happened. Her eyes blazed terribly and she was gripped by a strange madness.

"At last!" she screamed, spurning the corpse of her archfoe with her heel. "At last I am true mistress of Bal-Sagoth! The secrets of the hidden ways are mine now, and old Gothan's beard is dabbled in his own blood!"

She flung her arms high in fearful triumph, and ran toward the grim idol, screaming exultant insults like a mad woman. And at that instant the temple rocked! The colossal image swayed outward, and then pitched suddenly forward as a tall tower falls. Turlogh shouted and leaped forward, but even as he did, with a thunder like the bursting of a world, the god Gol-goroth crashed down upon the doomed woman, who stood frozen. The mighty image splintered into a thousand great fragments, blotting from the sight of men forever Brunhild, daughter of Rane Thorfin's son, queen of Bal-Sagoth. From under the ruins there oozed a wide crimson stream.

Warriors and priests stood frozen, deafened by the crash of that fall, stunned by the weird catastrophe. An icy hand touched Turlogh's spine. Had that vast bulk been thrust over by the hand of a dead man? As it had rushed downward it had seemed to the Gael that the inhuman features had for an instant taken on the likeness of the dead Gothan!

Now as all stood speechless, the acolyte Gelka saw and seized his opportunity.

"Gol-goroth has spoken!" he screamed. "He has crushed the false goddess! She was but a wicked mortal! And these strangers, too, are mortal! See—he bleeds!"

The priest's finger stabbed at the dried blood on Turlogh's throat and a wild roar went up from the throng. Dazed and bewildered by the swiftness and magnitude of the late events, they were like crazed wolves, ready to wipe out doubts and fear in a burst of bloodshed. Gelka bounded at Turlogh, hatchet flashing, and a knife in the hand of a satellite licked into Zomar's back. Turlogh had not understood the shout, but he realized the air was tense with danger for Athelstane and himself. He met the leaping Gelka with a stroke that sheared through the waving plumes and the skull beneath, then half a dozen lances broke on his buckler and a rush of bodies swept him back against a great pillar. Then Athelstane, slow of thought, who had stood gaping for the flashing second it had taken this to transpire, awoke in a blast of awesome fury. With a deafening roar he swung his heavy sword in a mighty arc. The whistling blade whipped off a head, sheared through a torso and sank deep into a spinal column. The three corpses fell across each other and even in the madness of the strife, men cried out at the marvel of that single stroke.

But like a brown, blind tide of fury the maddened people of Bal-Sagoth rolled on their foes. The guardsmen of the dead queen, trapped in the press, died to a man without a chance to strike a blow. But the overthrow of the two white warriors was no such easy task. Back-to-back they smashed and smote; Athelstane's sword was a thunderbolt of death; Turlogh's ax was lightning. Hedged close by a sea of snarling brown faces and flashing steel they hacked their way slowly toward a doorway. The very mass of the attackers hindered the warriors of Bal-Sagoth, for they had no space to guide their strokes, while the weapons of the seafarers kept a bloody ring clear in front of them.

Heaping a ghastly row of corpses as they went, the comrades slowly cut their way through the snarling press. The Temple of Shadows, witness of many a bloody deed, was flooded with gore spilled like a red sacrifice to her broken gods. The heavy weapons of the white fighters wrought fearful havoc among their naked, lighter-limbed foes, while their armor guarded their own lives. But their arms, legs and faces were cut and gashed by the frantically flying steel and it seemed the sheer number of their foes would overwhelm them ere they could reach the door.

Then they had reached it, and made desperate play until the brown warriors, no longer able to come upon them from all sides, drew back for a breathing space, leaving a torn red heap before the threshold. And in that instant the two sprang back into the corridor and seizing the great brazen door, slammed it in the very faces of the warriors who leaped howling to prevent it. Athelstane, bracing his mighty legs, held it against their combined efforts until Turlogh had time to find and slip the bolt.

"Thor!" gasped the Saxon, shaking the blood in a red shower from his face. "This is close play! What now, Turlogh?"

"Down the corridor, quick!" snapped the Gael, "before they come on us from this way and trap us like rats against this door. By Satan, the whole city must be roused! Hark to that roaring!"

In truth, as they raced down the shadowed corridor, it seemed to them that all Bal-Sagoth had burst into rebellion and civil war. From all sides came the clashing of steel, the shouts of men, and the screams of women, overshadowed by a hideous howling. A lurid glow became apparent down the corridor and then even as Turlogh, in the lead, rounded a corner and came out into an open courtyard, a vague figure leaped at him and a heavy weapon fell with unexpected force on his shield, almost felling him. But even as he staggered he struck back and the upper spike on his ax sank under the heart of his attacker, who fell at his feet. In the glare that illumined all, Turlogh saw his victim differed from the brown warriors he had been fighting. This man was naked, powerfully muscled and of a copperish red rather than brown. The heavy animal-like jaw, the slanting low forehead showed none of the intelligence and refinement of the brown people, but only a brute ferocity. A heavy war-club, rudely carved, lay beside him.

"By Thor!" exclaimed Athelstane. "The city burns!"

Turlogh looked up. They were standing on a sort of raised courtyard from which broad steps led down into the streets and from this vantage point they had a plain view of the terrific end of Bal-Sagoth. Flames leaped madly higher and higher, paling the moon, and in the red glare pigmy figures ran to and fro, falling and dying like puppets dancing to the tune of the Black Gods. Through the roar of the flames and the crashing of falling walls cut screams of death and shrieks of ghastly triumph. The city was swarming with naked, copper-skinned devils who burned and ravished and butchered in one red carnival of madness.

The red men of the isles! By the thousands they had descended on the Isle of the Gods in the night, and whether stealth or treachery let them through the walls, the comrades never knew, but now they ravened through the corpse-strewn streets, glutting their bloodlust in holocaust and massacre wholesale. Not all the gashed forms that lay in the crimson running streets were brown; the people of the doomed city fought with desperate courage, but outnumbered and caught off guard, their courage was futile. The red men were like bloodhungry tigers.

"What ho, Turlogh!" shouted Athelstane, beard a-bristle, eyes ablaze as the madness of the scene fired a like passion in his own fierce soul. "The world ends! Let us into the thick of it and glut our steel before we die! Who shall we strike for—the red or the brown?"

"Steady!" snapped the Gael. "Either people would cut our throats. We must hack our way through to the gates, and the Devil take them all. We have no friends here. This way—down these stairs. Across the roofs in yonder direction I see the arch of a gate."

The comrades sprang down the stairs, gained the narrow street below and ran swiftly in the way Turlogh indicated. About them washed a red inundation of slaughter. A thick smoke veiled all now, and in the murk chaotic groups merged, writhed and scattered, littering the shattered flags with gory shapes. It was like a nightmare in which demoniac figures leaped and capered, looming suddenly in the fire-shot mist, vanishing as suddenly. The flames from each side of the streets shouldered each other, singeing the hair of the warriors as they ran. Roofs fell in with an awesome thunder and walls crashing into ruin filled the air with flying death. Men struck blindly from the smoke and the seafarers cut them down and never knew whether their skins were brown or red.

Now a new note rose in the cataclysmic horror. Blinded by the smoke, confused by the winding streets, the red men were trapped in the snare of their own making. Fire is impartial; it can burn the lighter as well as the intended victim; and a falling wall is blind.

The red men abandoned their prey and ran howling to and fro like beasts, seeking escape; many, finding this futile, turned back in a last unreasoning storm of madness as a blinded tiger turns, and made their last moments of life a crimson burst of slaughter.

Turlogh, with the unerring sense of direction that comes to men who live the life of the wolf, ran toward the point where he knew an outer gate to be; yet in the windings of the streets and the screen of smoke, doubt assailed him. From the flame-shot murk in front of him a fearful scream rang out. A naked girl reeled blindly into view and fell at Turlogh's feet, blood gushing from her mutilated breast. A howling, red-stained devil, close on her heels, jerked back her head and cut her throat a fraction of a second before Turlogh's ax ripped the head from its shoulders and spun it grinning into the street. And at that second a sudden wind shifted the writhing smoke and the comrades saw the open gateway ahead of them, aswarm with red warriors. A fierce shout, a blasting rush, a mad instant of volcanic ferocity that littered the gateway with corpses, and they were through and racing down the slopes toward the distant forest and the beach beyond. Before them the sky was reddening for dawn; behind them rose the soul-shaking tumult of the doomed city.

Like hunted things they fled, seeking brief shelter among the many groves from time to time, to avoid groups of savages who ran toward the city. The whole island seemed to be swarming with them; the chiefs must have drawn on all the isles within hundreds of miles for a raid of such magnitude. And at last the comrades reached the strip of forest, and breathed deeply as they came to the beach and found it abandoned save for a number of long skull-decorated war canoes.

Athelstane sat down and gasped for breath. "Thor's blood! What now? What may we do but hide in these woods until those red devils hunt us out?"

"Help me launch this boat," snapped Turlogh. We'll take our chance on the open main—"

"Ho!" Athelstane leaped erect, pointing. "Thor's blood, a ship!"

The sun was just up, gleaming like a great golden coin on the sea rim. And limned in the sun swam a tall, high-pooped craft. The comrades leaped into the nearest canoe, shoved off and rowed like mad, shouting and waving their oars to attract the attention of the crew. Powerful muscles drove the long slim craft along at an incredible clip, and it was not long before the ship stood about and allowed them to come alongside. Dark-faced men, clad in mail, looked over the rail.

"Spaniards," muttered Athelstane. "If they recognize me, I had better stayed on the island!"

But he clambered up the chain without hesitation, and the two wanderers fronted the lean somber-faced man whose armor was that of a knight of Asturias. He spoke to them in Spanish and Turlogh answered him, for the Gael, like many of his race, was a natural linguist and had wandered far and spoken many tongues. In a few words the Dalcassian told their story and explained the great pillar of smoke which now rolled upward in the morning air from the isle.

"Tell him there is a king's ransom for the taking," put in Athelstane. "Tell him of the silver gates, Turlogh."

But when the Gael spoke of the vast loot in the doomed city, the commander shook his head.

"Good sir, we have no time to secure it, nor men to waste in the taking. Those red fiends you describe would hardly give up anything—though useless to them—without a fierce battle and neither my time nor my force is mine. I am Don Roderigo del Cortez of Castile and this ship, the *Gray Friar,* is one of a fleet that sailed to harry the Moorish Corsairs. Some days agone we were separated from the rest of the fleet in a sea skirmish and the tempest blew us far off our course. We are even now beating back to rejoin the fleet if we can find it; if not, to harry the infidel as well as we may. We serve God and the king and we cannot halt for mere dross as you suggest. But you are welcome aboard this ship and we have need of such fighting men as you appear to be. You will not regret it, should you wish to join us and strike a blow for Christendom against the Moslems."

In the narrow-bridged nose and deep dark eyes, as in the lead ascetic face, Turlogh read the fanatic, the stainless cavalier, the knight errant. He spoke to Athelstane: "This man is mad, but there are good blows to be struck and strange lands to see; anyway, we have no other choice."

"One place is as good as another to masterless men and wanderers," quoth the huge Saxon. "Tell him we will follow him to Hell and singe the tail of the Devil if there be any chance of loot."

4. Empire

Turlogh and Athelstane leaned on the rail, gazing back at the swiftly receding Island of the Gods, from which rose a pillar of smoke, laden with the ghosts of a thousand centuries and the shadows and mysteries of forgotten empire, and Athelstane cursed as only a Saxon can.

"A king's ransom—and after all that bloodletting—no loot!"

Turlogh shook his head. "We have seen an ancient kingdom fall—we have seen the last remnant of the world's oldest empire sink into flames and the abyss of oblivion, and barbarism rear its brute head above the ruins. So pass the glory and the splendor and the imperial purple—in red flames and yellow smoke."

"But not one bit of plunder—" persisted the Viking.

Again Turlogh shook his head. "I brought away with me the rarest gem upon the island—something for which men and women have died and the gutters run with blood."

He drew from his girdle a small object—a curiously carved symbol of jade.

"The emblem of kingship!" exclaimed Athelstane.

"Aye—as Brunhild struggled with me to keep me from following you into the corridor, this thing caught in my mail and was torn from the golden chain that held it."

"He who bears it is king of Bal-Sagoth," ruminated the mighty Saxon. "As I predicted, Turlogh, you are a king!"

Turlogh laughed with bitter mirth and pointed to the great billowing column of smoke which floated in the sky away on the sea rim.

"Aye—a kingdom of the dead—an empire of ghosts and smoke. I am Ard-Righ of a phantom city—I am King Turlogh of Bal-Sagoth and my kingdom is fading in the morning sky. And therein it is like all other empires in the world—dreams and ghosts and smoke."

The Outgoing of Sigurd the Jerusalem-Farer

The fires roared in the skalli-hall,
And a woman begged me stay—
But the bitter night was falling
And the cold wind calling
Across the moaning spray.

How could I stay in the feasting-hall
When the wild wind walked the sea?
The feet of the winds drew out my soul
To the grey waves and the cloud's scroll
Where the gulls wheel and the whales roll,
And the abyss roars to me.

Man the sweeps and bend the sail—
We need no oars tonight,
For the sharp sleet drives before the gale
That dashes the spray across the rail
To freeze on helmet and corselet scale,
And the waves are running white.
I could not hide in the feasting-hall
Where the great fires light the rooms—
For the winds are walking the night for me
And I must follow where gaunt lands be,
Seeking, beyond some nameless sea,
The dooms beyond the dooms.

Marching Song of Connacht

The men of the East are decked in steel,
They march with a trumpets' din,
They glitter with silks and golden scales,
And high kings boast their kin—
We of the West wear the hides of wolves,
But our hearts are steel within.

They of the East ride gallant steeds,
Their spears are long and brown;
Their shields are set with sparkling stones,
And each knight wears a crown—
We fight on foot as our forebears fought,
And we drag the rider down.

We race the steed of the Saxon knight
Across the naked fen—
They of the East are full of pride,
Cubs of the Lion's den.
They boast they breed a race of kings—
But we of the West breed Men.

Reuben's Birthright

The Black Prince scowled above his lance and wrath in his hot eyes lay,
"I would that you rode with the spears of France and not at my side today.
"A man may parry an open blow, but I know not where to fend;
"I would that you were an open foe instead of a sworn friend.

"You came to me in an hour of need, and your heart I thought I saw;
"But you are one of a rebel breed that knows not king or law.
"You—with your ever-smiling face and a black heart under your mail,
"With the haughty strain of the Norman race and the wild, black blood of the Gael.

"Thrice in a night fight's close-locked gloom my shield by merest chance
"Has turned a sword that thrust like doom—I wot 'twas not of France!
"And in a dust cloud, blind and red, as we charged the Provence line
"An unseen axe struck Fitzjames dead, who gave his life for mine.

"Had I proofs, your head should fall this day or ever I rode to strife—
"Are you but a wolf to rend and slay, with naught to guide your life?
"No gleam of love in a lady's eyes? No honor or faith or fame?"
I raised my face to the brooding skies and laughed at my own black shame.

"I followed the skene of the Geraldine from Meath to the western sea,
"Till a careless word that I scarcely heard bred hate in the heart of me.
"Then I lent my sword to the Western chiefs, for half of my blood is Gael,
"And we cut like a sickle through the sheafs as we harried the lines of the Pale.

"But Dermod O'Connor wild with wine, called me a dog at heel,
"And I cleft his bosom to the spine and fled to the black O'Neill.
"We harried the chieftains of the south, we shattered the Norman bows,
"We wasted the world from Cork to Louth, we trampled our fallen foes.

"But Conn Ruadh put on me a slight before the Gaelic lords,
"And I betrayed him in the night to the red O'Donnell swords.

"I am no thrall to any man, no vassal to any king;
"I owe no vow to any clan, nor faith to anything.

"Traitor—but not for fear or gold, but the fire in my own black brain,
"For the coins I loot from the broken hold I throw to the winds again.
"And I am true to myself alone, through pride and the traitor's part—
"I would give my life to shield your throne, or rip from your breast the heart

"For a look or a word, scarce thought or heard. I follow a fading fire,
"Past bead and bell and the hangman's cell, like a harp-call of desire.
"I may not see the road I ride for the witch-fire lamps that gleam,
"But phantoms glide at my bridle-side, and I follow a nameless dream."

The Black Prince shuddered and shook his head and crossed himself amain:
"Go, in God's name, and never," he said, "ride in my sight again."
The starlight silvered my bridle-rein, the moonlight burned my lance
As I rode back from the wars again through the pleasant hills of France.

As I rode from a task undone—not for the lord's command,
Nor life nor limb, but the shifting whim that stayed my wayward hand.
As I rode to tell Lord Amory of the dark Fitzgerald line
If the Black Prince died it needs must be by another hand than mine.

The Ghost in the Doorway

The supernatural has always played a great part, not alone in the folklore, but in the actual history of Ireland. Aside from the Duine Sidh, the spirits of the earth; the Leprechaun, or Leithphrogan; the Geancanach; the Clobher-ceann; and such like spirits or fairies common to the whole isle and race, there are local sprites, and scarcely a single great Irish family but has their own particular apparition or ghost.

The following is a translation from the memoirs, in Gaelic, of Captain Turlogh Kirowan, who held his commission in the armies of France during the reign of Louis ___, in 16__. Captain Kirowan's life was a turbulent one. He was born in the city of Galway, but his mother was an O'Sullivan of County Kerry. He was foremost in all the plots and revolts against English rule, and it was in 16__, during the incredible severities of Cromwell's bloody rule in Ireland, that the following event transpired. Kirowan was well known to Cromwell, both for his valor and his craft, and the red-handed hypocrite, croaking blasphemies about the divine will of God while he slaughtered right and left, had placed a high price on the Galwayman's head. Be assured that Cromwell was looking for Kirowan, but only by proxy. That psychopathic Puritan was in his element when it came to massacring women and children, but he had no desire to meet Turlogh Kirowan man to man.

After the collapse of Irish resistance in Munster, Turlogh, who had come down from the North to aid in the war, found himself alone and hunted in the county of Clare. The rest is taken from his unpublished memoirs, being a free translation, and leaving out the quaint chronology of the time:

"Now as night fell I set out across the moors and presently came to the ruins of a castle. This was now a great desolate heap of masonry rising up alone in wild and lonely surroundings, far from any human habitation. I determined to conceal myself there until after the moon had set, before taking up my journey again, for I was sorely in need of rest and sleep.

"I entered the ruins and my heart was heavy within me, for, thought I, this heap of broken stone may well typify the woes of Ireland. For I knew that in past years it had been a stronghold of the great O'Brien clan, and these crumbling walls had re-echoed to the sound of mirth and song and laughter. But the Normans under Fitzmaurice had taken the castle and slaughtered the defendants some three hundred years ago, and the ruined castle had been left to the bats and owls.

"I wrapped my cloak about me and, still a prey to melancholy conjectures, lay down in the shadows of the great hall and fell asleep. I must have slept some two hours when I was awakened. I started up, wondering if I had been discovered. The moon shone through the rent and torn roof and illumined the jagged gap of the doorway. And while I looked, suddenly a man came into this doorway and halted on the threshold.

"To my amazement, I saw he was clad in the kilts and accoutrement of an Irish chieftain of five hundred years ago. He was clearly etched in the moonlight and I saw he was a tall, broad-shouldered man, splendidly built, and in his right hand he gripped a broken sword. His left hand clutched his breast, and I saw blood trickling through the fingers. I started forward, but he pointed back toward where he had evidently come with the broken sword and said distinctly in Gaelic: 'Take care! The red beard is coming!—'

"As I halted in amazement, he slumped to the floor, his sword falling from his hand and his left hand falling away from his breast, wherein I observed a ghastly wound. Now this struck me as strange and eery—for though the broken sword fell on the stone flags of the floor, it made no clash or clang of any sort. I ran to the fallen warrior, but even as I stooped to raise him—he was no more! He did not fade or grow dim—he simply was not there when I bent toward him, though for a moment it seemed as though I could see the faint outline of a body on the stone flags.

"My mind in a turmoil, I began to cogitate on this mysterious happening and by and by came to the conclusion that I had been dreaming and had seen all this in my sleep. But so perturbed was I that, remembering the phantom's curious words, I rose and, taking my rapier and cloak, I made my way out of the castle by another doorway and concealed myself outside among some bushes. I scarce had done so when I was aware of the approach of a large number of men.

"These very warily surrounded the castle while others stole inside, all going cautiously and holding their swords so they would not clank. It was a part of a company of Roundheads, and I recognized their officer, a Captain Balston, a large man with a huge red beard. Seeing this and remembering the apparition's words concerning a man with a red beard, I was almost struck speechless.

"While they were concerned with the castle, I stole away and, making good haste on foot across the moors, I presently came upon a number of tethered horses under the charge of a soldier who was either asleep or drunk. Taking one of these, I made good my escape and presently came to Galway, whence I took ship for France, arriving at Bordeaux safely, to greet my family who had already fled.

"I told them my tale, and on the telling of it, an old friend of the family, Lady Nuala O'Brien, who had gone into exile with them, cried out: 'Lad, you have seen your ancestor, Conmac O'Sullivan, a chief of your mother's blood!'

"She then said: 'As you know, that castle in olden days played an important part in the history of my clan. Some five hundred years ago, before the great Brian Boru broke the Danes at Clontarf, these reavers made a raid into Clare and were stealing upon that castle to surprize the merrymakers therein, when they were surprized by a small party of the O'Sullivans, just out of earshot of the castle. The Danes slaughtered these Irish, but Conmac O'Sullivan, a mighty fighter, slew until his sword broke, and then, bursting away, outran the Danes to the castle. Reeling into the doorway of the hall, while all within halted their amusements and stared at him, he spoke those very words: "Take care! The Red Beard is coming!—" Then he fell and died of his wounds.

"'Thus warned, the O'Briens had time to man the walls and close the gates before the Danes were upon them, and after a stubborn siege, the pirates were beaten away, and their leader, Lamh Derg, or Red Beard, was killed. So it is certain that your ancestor came to warn you, otherwise you had assuredly been taken.'

"Which is very true."

Black Michael's Story

The moon above the Kerry hills
Had risen half a span
When we went out from Knocknaree
To card a Saxon man.

We laid him naked on the ditch—
God save this soul of mine!—
The howls of him as hard we dragged
The cats along his spine!

A great, full-blooded man he was,
That beat poor Tom O'Rourke—
The hardest English landlord, now,
From Donegal to Cork.

'Twas: "Damn your eyes, pay rent or starve!
Get out, with all your brats!"
But faith, the howling of him now
Was louder than the cats'!

Och, maybe he remembered then,
The swelling Saxon toad,
How he evicted Biddy Flynn
To die beside the road.

I hope that he remembered too—
The while the tomcats clung—
My cousin Mike O'Flaherty
That his conviction hung.

He cursed the king in agony,
He damned the Penal Laws—
Och, quite a different man he was
Beneath those ripping claws!

His squealing dwindled to a moan,
His back was bloody beef;
We threw him in the thorny ditch
Like any common thief.

The wind was stealing from the sea,
The night was strange and still;
We heard him weeping like a child
As we went down the hill.

And then above our oaths and jests
There sounded from the wood
A cry so wild and sweet and sad
It chained us where we stood.

Some night bird rended by an owl—
I felt black sorrow rise;
I turned to speak to Dermod Shea,
And tears were in his eyes.

Dermod's Bane

If your heart is sick in your breast and a blind, black curtain of sorrow is between your brain and your eyes so that the very sunlight is pale and leprous—go to the city of Galway, in the county of the same name, in the province of Connaught, in the country of Ireland.

In the grey old City of Tribes as they call it, there is a dreamy soothing spell that is like enchantment, and if you are of Galway blood, no matter how far away, your grief will pass slowly from you like a dream, leaving only a sad sweet memory, like the scent of a dying rose. There is a mist of antiquity hovering over the old city which mingles with sorrow and makes one forget. Or you can go out into the blue Connaught hills and feel the salt sharp tang of the wind off the Atlantic, and life seems faint and far away, with all its sharp joys and bitter sorrows, and no more real than the shadows of the clouds which pass.

I came to Galway as a wounded beast crawls back to his lair in the hills. The city of my people broke upon my gaze for the first time, but it did not seem strange or foreign. It seemed like a homecoming to me, and with each day passing the land of my birth seemed farther and farther away and the land of my ancestor closer.

I came to Galway with an aching heart. My twin sister, whom I loved as I never loved anyone else, had died. Her going was swift and unexpected. It seemed to my mazed agony that one moment she was laughing beside me with her cheery smile and bright grey Irish eyes, and the next, the cold bitter grass was growing above her. Oh, my soul to God, not your Son alone endured crucifixion.

A black cloud like a shroud locked about me and in the dim borderland of madness I sat alone, tearless and speechless. My grandmother came to me at last, a great grim old woman, with hard haunted eyes that held all the woes of the Irish race.

"Let you go to Galway, lad. Let you go to the old land. Maybe the sorrow of you will be drowned in the cold salt sea. Maybe the folk of Connaught can heal the wound that is on you—" . . . . I went to Galway.

Well, the people were kind there—all those great old families, the Martins, the Lynches, the Deanes, the Dorseys, the Blakes, the Kirowans—families of the fourteen great families who rule Galway.

Out on the hills and in the valleys I roved and talked with the kindly, quaint country folk, many of whom still spoke the good old Erse language which I could speak haltingly.

There, on a hill one night before a shepherd's fire I heard again the old legend of Dermod O'Connor. As the shepherd unfolded the terrible tale in his rich brogue, interlaced with many Gaelic phrases, I remembered that my grandmother had told me the tale when I was a child, but I had forgotten most of it.

Briefly the story is this: there was a chief of the Clan na O'Connor and his name was Dermod, but people called him the Wolf. The O'Connors were kings in the old days, ruling Connaught with a hand of steel. They divided the rule of Ireland with the O'Briens in the South—Munster—and the O'Neills in the North—Ulster. With the O'Rourkes they fought the MacMurraughs of Leinster and it was Dermot MacMurraugh, driven out of Ireland by the O'Connors, who brought in Strongbow and his Norman adventurers. When Earl Pembroke, whom men called Strongbow, landed in Ireland, Roderick O'Connor was king of Ireland in name and claim at least. And the clan O'Connor, fierce Celtic warriors that they were, kept up their struggle for freedom until at last their power was broken by a terrible Norman invasion. All honor to the O'Connors. In the old times my people fought under their banners—but each tree has a rotten root. Each great house has its black sheep. Dermod O'Connor was the black sheep of his clan and a blacker one never lived.

His hand was against all men, even his own house. He was no chieftain, fighting to regain the crown of Erin or to free his people; he was a red-handed reaver and he preyed alike on Norman and Celt; he raided into The Pale and he carried torch and steel into Munster and Leinster. The O'Briens and the O'Carrolls had cause to curse him, and the O'Neills hunted him like a wolf.

He left a trail of blood and devastation wherever he rode, and at last of his band, dwindling from desertions and constant fighting, he alone remained, hiding in caves and hills, butchering lone travelers for the sheer lust of blood that was on him, and descending on lonely farmer's houses or shepherd's huts to commit atrocities on their womenfolk. He was a giant of a man and the legends make of him something inhuman and monstrous. It must be truth that he was strange and terrible in appearance.

But his end came at last. He murdered a youth of the Kirowan clan and the Kirowans rode out of the city of Galway with vengeance in their hearts. Sir Michael Kirowan met the marauder alone in the hills—Sir Michael, a direct ancestor of mine, whose very name I bear. Alone they fought with only the shuddering hills to witness that terrible battle, till the clash of steel reached the ears of the rest of the clan who were riding hard and scouring the countryside.

They found Sir Michael badly wounded and Dermod O'Connor dying with a cleft shoulder bone and a ghastly wound in his breast. But such was their fury and hatred, that they flung a noose about the dying robber's neck and hanged him to a great tree on the edge of a cliff overlooking the sea.

"And," said my friend the shepherd, stirring the fire, "the peasant folk still point out the tree and call it Dermod's Bane, after the Danish manner, and men have seen the great outlaw o' nights, and him gnashing his great tushes and spouting blood from shoulder and breast and swearin' all manner o' ill on the Kirowans and their blood for all time to come.

"And so, sir, let you not walk in the cliffs over the sea by night for you are of the blood he hates and the same name of the man who felled him is on you. For let you laugh if so be your will, but the ghost of Dermod O'Connor the Wolf is abroad o' dark night and the moon out of the sky, and him with his great black beard and ghastly eyes and boar tushes."

They pointed me out the tree, Dermod's Bane, and strangely like a gallows it looked, standing there as it had stood for how many hundred years I do not know, for men live long in Ireland and trees live longer. There were no other trees near and the cliff rose sheer from the sea for four hundred feet. Below was only the deep sinister blue of the waves, deep and dark, breaking on the cruel rocks.

I walked much in the hills at night for when the silence of the darkness was on the world and no speech or noises of men to hold my thoughts, my sorrow was dark on my heart again and I walked on the hills where the stars seemed close and warm. And often my mazed brain wondered which star *she* was on, or if she had turned to a star.

One night the old, sharp agony returned unbearably. I rose from my bed—for I was staying at the time in a little mountain inn—and dressed and went into the hills. My temples throbbed and there was an unbearable weight about my heart. My dumb frozen soul shrieked up to God, but I could not weep. I felt I must weep or go mad. For never a tear had passed my eyelids since—

Well, I walked on and on, how long or how far I do not know. The stars were hot and red and angry and gave me no comfort that night. At first I wanted to scream and howl and throw myself on the ground and tear the grass with my teeth. Then that passed and I wandered as in a trance. There was no moon and in the dim starlight the hills and their trees loomed dark and strange. Over the summits I could see the great Atlantic lying like a dusky silver monster and I heard her faint roaring.

Something flitted in front of me and I thought that it was a wolf. But there have been no wolves in Ireland for many and many a year. Again I saw the thing, a long low shadowy shape. I followed it mechanically. Now in front of me I saw a cliff overlooking the sea. On the cliff's edge was a single great tree that loomed up like a gibbet. I approached this.

Then in front of me, as I neared the tree, a vague mist hovered. A strange fear spread over me as I watched stupidly. A form became evident. Dim and silkily, like a shred of moon-mist, but with an undoubted human shape. A face—I cried out!

A vague, sweet face floated before me, indistinct, mist-like—yet I made out the shimmery mass of dark hair, the high pure forehead, the red curving lips—the serious soft grey eyes.

"Moira!" I cried in agony and rushed forward, my aching arms spread wide, my heart bursting in my bosom.

She floated away from me like a mist blown by a breeze; now she seemed to waver in space—I felt myself staggering wildly on the very edge of the cliff, whither my blind rush had led me. As a man wakes from a dream I saw in one flashing instant the cruel rocks four hundred feet below. I heard the hungry lapping of the waves—as I felt myself falling forward I saw the vision, but now it was changed hideously. Great tusklike teeth gleamed ghoulishly through a matted black beard. Terrible eyes blazed under penthouse brows; blood flowed from a wound in the shoulder and a ghastly gash in the broad breast—

"Dermod O'Connor!" I screamed, my hair bristling. "Avaunt, fiend out of Hell—"

I swayed out for the fall I could not check, with death waiting four hundred feet below. Then a soft small hand closed on my wrist and I was drawn irresistibly back. I fell, but back on the soft green grass at the lip of the cliff, not to the keen-edged rocks and waiting sea below. Oh, I knew—I could not be wrong. The small hand was gone from my wrist, the hideous face gone from the cliff edge—but that grasp on my wrist that drew me back from my doom—how could I fail to recognize it? A thousand times had I felt the dear touch of that soft hand on my arm or in my own hand. Oh, Moira, Moira, pulse of my heart, in life and in death you were ever at my side.

And now for the first time I wept and lying on my stomach with my face in my hands, I poured my racked heart out in scalding, blinding and soul-easing tears, until the sun came up over the blue Galway hills and limned the branches of Dermod's Bane with a strange new radiance.

Now, did I dream or was I mad? Did in truth, the ghost of that long dead outlaw lead me across the hills to the cliff under the death-tree, and there assume the shape of my dead sister to lure me to my doom? And did in truth the real hand of that dead sister, brought suddenly to my side by my peril, hold me back from death?

Believe or disbelieve as you will. To me it is a fact. I saw Dermod O'Connor that night and he led me over the cliff; and the soft hand of Moira Kirowan dragged me back and its touch loosened the frozen channels of my heart and brought me peace. For the wall that bars the living from the dead is but a thin veil, I know now, and so sure as a dead woman's love conquered a dead man's hate, so sure shall I some day in the world beyond, hold my sister in my arms again.

The Cairn on the Headland

"And the next instant this great red loon was shaking me like a dog shaking a rat. 'Where is Meve MacDonnal?' he was screaming. By the saints, it's a grisly thing to hear a madman in a lonely place at midnight screaming the name of a woman dead three hundred years."

—*The Longshoreman's Tale.*

"This is the cairn you seek," I said, laying my hand gingerly on one of the rough stones which composed the strangely symmetrical heap.

An avid interest burned in Ortali's dark eyes. His gaze swept the landscape and came back to rest on the great pile of massive weatherworn boulders.

"What a wild, weird, desolate place!" he said. "Who would have thought to find such a spot in this vicinity? Except for the smoke rising yonder, one would scarcely dream that beyond that headland lies a great city! Here there is scarcely even a fisherman's hut within sight."

"The people shun the cairn as they have shunned it for centuries," I replied.

"Why?"

"You've asked me that before," I replied impatiently. "I can only answer that they now avoid by habit what their ancestors avoided through knowledge."

"Knowledge!" he laughed derisively. "Superstition!"

I looked at him somberly with unveiled hate. Two men could scarcely have been of more opposite types. He was slender, self-possessed, unmistakably Latin with his dark eyes and sophisticated air. I am massive, clumsy and bear-like, with cold blue eyes and tousled red hair. We were countrymen in that we were born in the same land; but the homelands of our ancestors were as far apart as South from North.

"Nordic superstition," he repeated. "I cannot imagine a Latin people allowing such a mystery as this to go unexplored all these years. The Latins are too practical—too prosaic, if you will. Are you sure of the date of this pile?"

"I find no mention of it in any manuscript prior to 1014 A. D.," I growled, "and I've read all such manuscripts extant, in the original. MacLiag, King Brian Boru's poet, speaks of the rearing of the cairn immediately after the battle, and there can be little doubt but that this is the pile referred to. It is mentioned briefly in the later chronicles of the Four Masters, also in the Book of Leinster, compiled in the late 1150s, and again in the Book of Lecan, compiled by the MacFirbis about 1416. All connect it with the battle of Clontarf, without mentioning why it was built."

"Well, what is the mystery about it?" he queried. "What more natural than that the defeated Norsemen should rear a cairn above the body of some great chief who had fallen in the battle?"

"In the first place," I answered, "there is a mystery concerning the existence of it. The building of cairns above the dead was a Norse, not an Irish, custom. Yet according to the chroniclers, it was not Norsemen who reared this heap. How could they have built it immediately after the battle, in which they had been cut to pieces and driven in headlong flight through the gates of Dublin? Their chieftains lay where they had fallen and the ravens picked their bones. It was Irish hands that heaped these stones."

"Well, was that so strange?" persisted Ortali. "In old times the Irish heaped up stones before they went into battle, each man putting a stone in place; after the battle the living removed their stones, leaving in that manner a simple tally of the slain for any who wished to count the remaining stones."

I shook my head.

"That was in more ancient times; not in the battle of Clontarf. In the first place, there were more than twenty thousand warriors, and four thousand fell here; this cairn is not large enough to have served as a tally of the men killed in battle. And it is too symmetrically built. Hardly a stone has fallen away in all these centuries. No, it was reared to cover something."

"Nordic superstitions!" the man sneered again.

"Aye, superstitions if you will!" fired by his scorn, I exclaimed so savagely that he involuntarily stepped back, his hand slipping inside his coat. "We of North Europe had gods and demons before which the pallid mythologies of the South fade to childishness. At a time when your ancestors were lolling on silken cushions among the crumbling marble pillars of a decaying civilization, my ancestors were building their own civilization in hardships and gigantic battles against foes human and inhuman.

"Here on this very plain the Dark Ages came to an end and the light of a new era dawned faintly on a world of hate and anarchy. Here, as even you know, in the year 1014, Brian Boru and his Dalcassian ax-wielders broke the power of the heathen Norsemen forever—those grim anarchistic plunderers who had held back the progress of civilization for centuries.

"It was more than a struggle between Gael and Dane for the crown of Ireland. It was a war between the White Christ and Odin, between Christian and pagan. It was the last stand of the heathen—of the people of the old, grim ways. For three hundred years the world had writhed beneath the heel of the Viking, and here on Clontarf that scourge was lifted forever.

"Then, as now, the importance of that battle was underestimated by polite Latin and Latinized writers and historians. The polished sophisticates of the civilized cities of the South were not interested in the battles of barbarians in the remote northwestern corner of the world—a place and peoples of whose very names they were only vaguely aware. They only knew that suddenly the terrible raids of the sea kings ceased to sweep along their coasts, and in another century the wild age of plunder and slaughter had almost been forgotten—all because a rude, half-civilized people who scantily covered their nakedness with wolf hides rose up against the conquerors.

"Here was Ragnarok, the fall of the gods! Here in very truth Odin fell, for his religion was given its death blow. He was last of all the heathen gods to stand before Christianity, and it looked for a time as if his children might prevail and plunge the world back into darkness and savagery. Before Clontarf, legends say, he often appeared on earth to his worshipers, dimly seen in the smoke of the sacrifices where naked human victims died screaming, or riding the wind-torn clouds, his wild locks flying in the gale, or, appareled like a Norse warrior, dealing thunderous blows in the forefront of nameless battles. But after Clontarf he was seen no more; his worshipers called on him in vain with wild chants and grim sacrifices. They lost faith in him, who had failed them in their wildest hour; his altars crumbled, his priests turned gray and died, and men turned to his conqueror, the White Christ. The reign of blood and iron was forgotten; the age of the red-handed sea kings passed. The rising sun slowly, dimly, lighted the night of the Dark Ages, and men forgot Odin, who came no more on earth.

"Aye, laugh if you will! But who knows what shapes of horror have had birth in the darkness, the cold gloom, and the whistling black gulfs of the North? In the southern lands the sun shines and flowers blow; under the soft skies men laugh at demons. But in the North who can say what elemental spirits of evil dwell in the fierce storms and the darkness? Well may it be that from such fiends of the night men evolved the worship of the grim ones, Odin and Thor, and their terrible kin."

Ortali was silent for an instant, as if taken aback by my vehemence; then he laughed. "Well said, my Northern philosopher! We will argue these questions another time. I could hardly expect a descendant of Nordic barbarians to escape some trace of the dreams and mysticism of his race. But you cannot expect me to be moved by your imaginings, either. I still believe that this cairn covers no grimmer secret than a Norse chief who fell in the battle—and really your ravings concerning Nordic devils have no bearing on the matter. Will you help me tear into this cairn?"

"No," I answered shortly.

"A few hours' work will suffice to lay bare whatever it may hide," he continued as if he had not heard. "By the way, speaking of superstitions, is there not some wild tale concerning holly connected with this heap?"

"An old legend says that all trees bearing holly were cut down for a league in all directions, for some mysterious reason," I answered sullenly. "That's another mystery. Holly was an important part of Norse magic-making. The Four Masters tell of a Norseman—a white-bearded ancient of wild aspect, and apparently a priest of Odin—who was slain by the natives while attempting to lay a branch of holly on the cairn, a year after the battle."

"Well," he laughed, "I have procured a sprig of holly—see?—and shall wear it in my lapel; perhaps it will protect me against your Nordic devils. I feel more certain than ever that the cairn covers a sea king—and they were always laid to rest with all their riches: golden cups and jewel-set sword hilts and silver corselets. I feel that this cairn holds wealth, wealth over which clumsy-footed Irish peasants have been stumbling for centuries, living in want and dying in hunger. Bah! We shall return here at about midnight, when we may be fairly certain that we will not be interrupted—and you will aid me at the excavations."

The last sentence was rapped out in a tone that sent a red surge of bloodlust through my brain. Ortali turned and began examining the cairn as he spoke, and almost involuntarily my hand reached out stealthily and closed on a wicked bit of jagged stone that had become detached from one of the boulders. In that instant I was a potential murderer if ever one walked the earth. One blow, quick, silent and savage, and I would be free forever from a slavery bitter as my Celtic ancestors knew beneath the heels of the Vikings.

As if sensing my thoughts, Ortali wheeled to face me. I quickly slipped the stone into my pocket, not knowing whether he noted the action. But he must have seen the red killing instinct burning in my eyes, for again he recoiled and again his hand sought the hidden revolver.

But he only said: "I've changed my mind. We will not uncover the cairn tonight. Tomorrow night perhaps. We may be spied upon. Just now I am going back to the hotel."

I made no reply, but turned my back upon him and stalked moodily away in the direction of the shore. He started up the slope of the headland beyond which lay the city, and when I turned to look at him, he was just crossing the ridge, etched clearly against the hazy sky. If hate could kill, he would have dropped dead. I saw him in a red-tinged haze, and the pulses in my temples throbbed like hammers.

I turned back toward the shore, and stopped suddenly. Engrossed with my own dark thoughts, I had approached within a few feet of a woman before seeing her. She was tall and strongly made, with a strong stern face, deeply lined and weatherworn as the hills. She was dressed in a manner strange to me, but I thought little of it, knowing the curious styles of clothing worn by certain backward types of our people.

"What would you be doing at the cairn?" she asked in a deep, powerful voice. I looked at her in surprise; she spoke in Gaelic, which was not strange of itself, but the Gaelic she used I had supposed was extinct as a spoken language: it was the Gaelic of scholars, pure, and with a distinctly archaic flavor. A woman from some secluded hill country, I thought, where the people still spoke the unadulterated tongue of their ancestors.

"We were speculating on its mystery," I answered in the same tongue, hesitantly, however, for though skilled in the more modern form taught in the schools, to match her use of the language was a strain on my knowledge of it.

She shook her head slowly. "I like not the dark man who was with you," she said somberly. "Who are you?"

"I am an American, though born and raised here," I answered. "My name is James O'Brien."

A strange light gleamed in her cold eyes.

"O'Brien? You are of my clan. I was born an O'Brien. I married a man of the MacDonnals, but my heart was ever with the folk of my blood."

"You live hereabouts?" I queried, my mind on her unusual accent.

"Aye, I lived here upon a time," she answered, "but I have been far away for a long time. All is changed—changed. I would not have returned, but I was drawn back by a call you would not understand. Tell me, would you open the cairn?"

I started and gazed at her closely, deciding that she had somehow overheard our conversation.

"It is not mine to say," I answered bitterly. "Ortali—my companion—he will doubtless open it and I am constrained to aid him. Of my own will I would not molest it."

Her cold eyes bored into my soul.

"Fools rush blind to their doom," she said somberly. "What does this man know of the mysteries of this ancient land? Deeds have been done here whereof the world reechoed. Yonder, in the long ago, when Tomar's Wood rose dark and rustling against the plain of Clontarf, and the Danish walls of Dublin loomed south of the river Liffey, the ravens fed on the slain and the setting sun lighted lakes of crimson. There King Brian, your ancestor and mine, broke the spears of the North. From all lands they came, and from the isles of the sea; they came in gleaming mail and their horned helmets cast long shadows across the land. Their dragon-prows thronged the waves and the sound of their oars was as the beat of a storm.

"On yonder plain the heroes fell like ripe wheat before the reaper. There fell Jarl Sigurd of the Orkneys, and Brodir of Man, last of the sea kings, and all their chiefs. There fell, too, Prince Murrogh and his son Turlogh, and many chieftains of the Gael, and King Brian Boru himself, Erin's mightiest monarch."

"True!" My imagination was always fired by the epic tales of the land of my birth. "Blood of mine was spilled here, and, though I have passed the best part of my life in a far land, there are ties of blood to bind my soul to this shore."

She nodded slowly, and from beneath her robes drew forth something that sparkled dully in the setting sun.

"Take this," she said. "As a token of blood tie, I give it to you. I feel the weird of strange and monstrous happenings—but this will keep you safe from evil and the people of the night. Beyond reckoning of man, it is holy."

I took it, wonderingly. It was a crucifix of curiously worked gold, set with tiny jewels. The workmanship was extremely archaic and unmistakably Celtic. And vaguely within me stirred a memory of a long-lost relic described by forgotten monks in dim manuscripts.

"Great heavens!" I exclaimed. "This is—this must be—this *can* be nothing less than the lost crucifix of Saint Brandon the Blessed!"

"Aye." She inclined her grim head. "Saint Brandon's cross, fashioned by the hands of the holy man in the long ago, before the Norse barbarians made Erin a red hell—in the days when a golden peace and holiness ruled the land."

"But, woman!" I exclaimed wildly, "I cannot accept this as a gift from you! You cannot know its value! Its intrinsic worth alone is equal to a fortune; as a relic it is priceless—"

"Enough!" Her deep voice struck me suddenly silent. "Have done with such talk, which is sacrilege. The cross of Saint Brandon is beyond price. It was never stained with gold; only as a free gift has it ever changed hands. I give it to you to shield you against the powers of evil. Say no more."

"But it has been lost for three hundred years!" I exclaimed. "How—where . . . ?"

"A holy man gave it to me long ago," she answered. "I hid it in my bosom—long it lay in my bosom. But now I give it to you; I have come from a far country to give it to you, for there are monstrous happenings in the wind, and it is sword and shield against the people of the night. An ancient evil stirs in its prison, which blind hands of folly may break open; but stronger than any evil is the cross of Saint Brandon which has gathered power and strength through the long, long ages since that forgotten evil fell to the earth."

"But who are you?" I exclaimed.

"I am Meve MacDonnal," she answered.

Then, turning without a word, she strode away in the deepening twilight while I stood bewildered and watched her cross the headland and pass from sight, turning inland as she topped the ridge. Then I, too, shaking myself like a man waking from a dream, went slowly up the slope and across the headland. When I crossed the ridge it was as if I had passed out of one world into another: behind me lay the wilderness and desolation of a weird medieval age; before me pulsed the lights and the roar of modern Dublin. Only one archaic touch was lent to the scene before me: some distance inland loomed the straggling and broken lines of an ancient graveyard, long deserted and grown up in weeds, barely discernible in the dusk. As I looked I saw a tall figure moving ghostily among the crumbling tombs, and I shook my head bewilderedly. Surely Meve MacDonnal was touched with madness, living in the past, like one seeking to stir to flame the ashes of dead yesterdays. I set out toward where, in the near distance, began the straggling window-gleams that grew into the swarming ocean of lights that was Dublin.

Back at the suburban hotel where Ortali and I had our rooms, I did not speak to him of the cross the woman had given me. In that at least he should not share. I intended keeping it until she requested its return, which I felt sure she would do. Now as I remembered her appearance, the strangeness of her costume returned to me, with one item which had impressed itself on my subconscious mind at the time, but which I had not consciously realized. Meve MacDonnal had been wearing sandals of a type not worn in Ireland for centuries. Well, it was perhaps natural that with her retrospective nature she should imitate the apparel of the past ages which seemed to claim all her thoughts.

I turned the cross reverently in my hands. There was no doubt that it was the very cross for which antiquarians had searched so long in vain, and at last in despair had denied the existence of. The priestly scholar, Michael O'Rourke, in a treatise written about 1690, described the relic at length, chronicled its history exhaustively and maintained that it was last heard of in the possession of Bishop Liam O'Brien, who, dying in 1595, gave it into the keeping of a kinswoman; but who this woman was, it was never known, and O'Rourke maintained that she kept her possession of the cross a secret, and that it was laid away with her in her tomb.

At another time my elation at discovering this relic would have been extreme, but, at the time, my mind was too filled with hate and smoldering fury. Replacing the cross in my pocket, I fell moodily to reviewing my connections with Ortali, connections which puzzled my friends, but which were simple enough.

Some years before I had been connected with a certain large university in a humble way. One of the professors with whom I worked—a man named Reynolds—was of intolerably overbearing disposition toward those whom he considered his inferiors. I was a poverty-ridden student striving for life in a system which makes the very existence of a scholar precarious. I bore Professor Reynolds' abuse as long as I could, but one day we clashed. The reason does not matter; it was trivial enough in itself. Because I dared reply to his insults, Reynolds struck me and I knocked him senseless.

That very day he caused my dismissal from the university. Facing not only an abrupt termination of my work and studies, but actual starvation, I was reduced to desperation, and I went to Reynolds' study late that night intending to thrash him within an inch of his life. I found him alone in his study, but the moment I entered, he sprang up and rushed at me like a wild beast, with a dagger he used for a paperweight. I did not strike him; I did not even touch him. As I stepped aside to avoid his rush, a small rug slipped beneath his charging feet. He fell headlong and, to my horror, in his fall the dagger in his hand was driven into his heart. He died instantly. I was at once aware of my position. I was known to have quarreled, and even exchanged blows with the man. I had every reason to hate him. If I were found in the study with the dead man, no jury in the world would not believe that I had murdered him. I hurriedly left by the way I had come, thinking that I had been unobserved. But

Ortali, the dead man's secretary, had seen me. Returning from a dance, he had observed me entering the premises, and, following me, had seen the whole affair through the window. But this I did not know until later.

The body was found by the professor's housekeeper, and naturally there was a great stir. Suspicion pointed to me, but lack of evidence kept me from being indicted, and this same lack of evidence brought about a verdict of suicide. All this time Ortali had kept quiet. Now he came to me and disclosed what he knew. He knew, of course, that I had not killed Reynolds, but he could prove that I was in the study when the professor met his death, and I knew Ortali was capable of carrying out his threat of swearing that he had seen me murder Reynolds in cold blood. And thus began a systematic blackmail.

I venture to say that a stranger blackmail was never levied. I had no money then; Ortali was gambling on my future, for he was assured of my abilities. He advanced me money, and, by clever wire-pulling, got me an appointment in a large college. Then he sat back to reap the benefits of his scheming, and he reaped full fold of the seed he sowed. In my line I became eminently successful. I soon commanded an enormous salary in my regular work, and I received rich prizes and awards for researches of various difficult nature, and of these Ortali took the lion's share—in money at least. I seemed to have the Midas touch. Yet of the wine of my success I tasted only the dregs.

I scarcely had a cent to my name. The money that had flowed through my hands had gone to enrich my slaver, unknown to the world. A man of remarkable gifts, he could have gone to the heights in any line, but for a queer streak in him, which, coupled with an inordinately avaricious nature, made him a parasite, a bloodsucking leech.

This trip to Dublin had been in the nature of a vacation for me. I was worn out with study and labor. But he had somehow heard of Grimmin's Cairn, as it was called, and, like a vulture that scents dead flesh, he conceived himself on the track of hidden gold. A golden wine cup would have been, to him, sufficient reward for the labor of tearing into the pile, and reason enough for desecrating or even destroying the ancient landmark. He was a swine whose only god was gold.

Well, I thought grimly, as I disrobed for bed, all things end, both good and bad. Such a life as I had lived was unbearable. Ortali had dangled the gallows before my eyes until it had lost its terrors. I had staggered beneath the load I carried because of my love for my work. But all human endurance has its limits. My hands turned to iron as I thought of Ortali, working beside me at midnight at the lonely cairn. One stroke, with such a stone as I had caught up that day, and my agony would be ended. That life and hopes and career and ambitions would be ended as well, could not be helped. Ah, what a sorry, sorry end to all my high dreams! When a rope and the long drop through the black trap would cut short an honorable career and a useful life! And all because of a human vampire who feasted his rotten lust on my soul, and drove me to murder and ruin.

But I knew my fate was written in the iron books of doom. Sooner or later I would turn on Ortali and kill him, be the consequences what they might. And I had reached the end of my road. Continual torture had rendered me, I believe, partly insane. I knew that at Grimmin's Cairn, when we toiled at midnight, Ortali's life would end beneath my hands, and my own life be cast away.

Something fell out of my pocket and I picked it up. It was the piece of sharp stone I had caught up off the cairn. Looking at it moodily, I wondered what strange hands had touched it in old times, and what grim secret it helped to hide on the bare headland of Grimmin. I switched out the light and lay in the darkness, the stone still in my hand, forgotten, occupied with my own dark broodings. And I glided gradually into deep slumber.

At first I was aware that I was dreaming, as people often are. All was dim and vague, and connected in some strange way, I realized, with the bit of stone still grasped in my sleeping hand. Gigantic, chaotic scenes and landscapes and events shifted before me, like clouds that rolled and tumbled before a gale. Slowly these settled and crystallized into one distinct landscape, familiar and yet wildly strange. I saw a broad bare plain, fringed by the gray sea on one side, and a dark, rustling forest on the other; this plain was cut by a winding river, and beyond this river I saw a city—such a city as my waking eyes had never seen: bare, stark, massive, with the grim architecture of an earlier, wilder age. On the plain I saw, as in a mist, a mighty battle. Serried ranks rolled backward and forward, steel flashed like a sunlit sea, and men fell like ripe wheat beneath the blades. I saw men in wolfskins, wild and shock headed, wielding dripping axes, and tall men in horned helmets and glittering mail, whose eyes were cold and blue as the sea. And I saw myself.

Yes, in my dream I saw and recognized, in a semi-detached way, myself. I was tall and rangily powerful; I was shock headed and naked but for a wolf hide girt about my loins. I ran among the ranks yelling and smiting with a red ax, and blood ran down my flanks from wounds I scarcely felt. My eyes were cold blue and my shaggy hair and beard were red.

Now for an instant I was cognizant of my dual personality, aware that I was at once the wild man who ran and smote with the gory ax, and the man who slumbered and dreamed across the centuries. But this sensation quickly faded. I was no longer aware of any personality other than that of the barbarian who ran and smote. James O'Brien had no existence; I was Red Cumal, kern of Brian Boru, and my ax was dripping with the blood of my foes.

The roar of conflict was dying away, though here and there struggling clumps of warriors still dotted the plain. Down along the river half-naked tribesmen, waist-deep in reddening water, tore and slashed with helmeted warriors whose mail could not save them from the stroke of the Dalcassian ax. Across the river a bloody, disorderly horde was staggering through the gates of Dublin.

The sun was sinking low toward the horizon. All day I had fought beside the chiefs. I had seen Jarl Sigurd fall beneath Prince Murrogh's sword. I had seen Murrogh himself die in the moment of victory, by the hand of a grim mailed giant whose name none knew. I had seen, in the flight of the enemy, Brodir and King Brian fall together at the door of the great king's tent.

Aye, it had been a feasting of ravens, a red flood of slaughter, and I knew that no more would the dragon-prowed fleets sweep from the blue North with torch and destruction. Far and wide the Vikings lay in their glittering mail, as the ripe wheat lies after the reaping. Among them lay thousands of bodies clad in the wolf hides of the tribes, but the dead of the Northern people far outnumbered the dead of Erin. I was weary and sick of the stench of raw blood. I had glutted my soul with slaughter; now I sought plunder. And I found it—on the corpse of a richly-clad Norse chief which lay close to the seashore. I tore off the silver-scaled corselet, the horned helmet. They fitted as if made for me, and I swaggered among the dead, calling on my wild comrades to admire my appearance, though the harness felt strange to me, for the Gauls scorned armor and fought half-naked.

In my search for loot I had wandered far out on the plain, away from the river, but still the mail-clad bodies lay thickly strewn, for the bursting of the ranks had scattered fugitives and pursuers all over the countryside, from the dark waving Wood of Tomar, to the river and the seashore. And on the seaward slope of Drumna's headland, out of sight of the city and the plain of Clontarf, I came suddenly upon a dying warrior. He was tall and massive, clad in gray mail. He lay partly in the folds of a great dark cloak, and his sword lay broken near his mighty right hand. His horned helmet had fallen from his head and his elf-locks blew in the wind that swept out of the west.

Where one eye should have been was an empty socket and the other eye glittered cold and grim as the North Sea, though it was glazing with the approach of death. Blood oozed from a rent in his corselet. I approached him warily, a strange cold fear, that I could not understand, gripping me. Ax ready to dash out his brains, I bent over him, and recognized him as the chief who had slain Prince Murrogh, and who had mown down the warriors of the Gael like a harvest. Wherever he had fought, the Norsemen had prevailed, but in all other parts of the field, the Gaels had been irresistible.

And now he spoke to me in Norse and I understood, for had I not toiled as slave among the sea people for long bitter years?

"The Christians have overcome," he gasped in a voice whose timbre, though low-pitched, sent a curious shiver of fear through me; there was in it an undertone of icy waves sweeping along a Northern shore, as of freezing winds whispering among the pine trees. "Doom and shadows stalk on Asgaard and here has fallen Ragnarok. I could not be in all parts of the field at once, and now I am wounded unto death. A spear—a spear with a cross carved in the blade; no other weapon could wound me."

I realized that the chief, seeing mistily my red beard and the Norse armor I wore, supposed me to be one of his own race. But a crawling horror surged darkly in the depths of my soul.

"White Christ, thou hast not yet conquered," he muttered deliriously. "Lift me up, man, and let me speak to you."

Now, for some reason I complied, and as I lifted him to a sitting posture, I shuddered and my flesh crawled at the feel of him, for his flesh was like ivory—smoother and harder than is natural for human flesh, and colder than even a dying man should be.

"I die as men die," he muttered. "Fool, to assume the attributes of mankind, even though it was to aid the people who deify me. The gods are immortal, but flesh can perish, even when it clothes a god. Haste and bring a sprig of the magic plant—even holly—and lay it on my bosom. Aye, though it be no larger than a dagger point, it will free me from this fleshly prison I put on when I came to war with men with their own weapons. And I will shake off this flesh and stalk once more among the thundering clouds. Woe, then, to all men who bend not the knee to me! Haste; I will await your coming."

His lion-like head fell back, and feeling shudderingly under his corselet, I could distinguish no heartbeat. He was dead, as men die, but I knew that locked in that semblance of a human body, there but slumbered the spirit of a fiend of the frost and darkness.

Aye, I knew him: Odin, the Gray Man, the One-eyed, the god of the North who had taken the form of a warrior to fight for his people. Assuming the form of a human he was subject to many of the limitations of humanity. All men knew this of the gods, who often walked the earth in the guise of men. Odin, clothed in human semblance, could be wounded by certain weapons, and even slain, but a touch of the mysterious holly would rouse him in grisly resurrection. This task he had set me, not knowing me for an enemy; in human form he could only use human faculties, and these had been impaired by onstriding death.

My hair stood up and my flesh crawled. I tore from my body the Norse armor, and fought a wild panic that prompted me to run blind and screaming with terror across the plain. Nauseated with fear, I gathered boulders and heaped them for a rude couch, and on it, shaking with horror, I lifted the body of the Norse god. And as the sun set and the stars came silently out, I was working with fierce energy, piling huge rocks above the corpse. Other tribesmen came up and I told them of what I was sealing up—I hoped forever. And they, shivering with horror, fell to aiding me. No sprig of magic holly should be laid on Odin's terrible bosom. Beneath these rude stones the Northern demon should slumber until the thunder of Judgment Day, forgotten by the world which had once cried out beneath his iron heel. Yet not wholly forgot, for, as we labored, one of my comrades said: "This shall be no longer Drumna's Headland, but the Headland of the Gray Man."

That phrase established a connection between my dreamself and my sleeping self. I started up from sleep exclaiming: "Gray Man's Headland!"

I looked about dazedly, the furnishings of the room, faintly lighted by the starlight in the windows, seeming strange and unfamiliar until I slowly oriented myself with time and space.

"Gray Man's Headland," I repeated, "Gray Man—Graymin—Grimmin—*Grimmin's Headland!* Great God, the thing under the cairn!"

Shaken, I sprang up, and realized that I still gripped the piece of stone from the cairn. It is well known that inanimate objects retain psychic associations. A round stone from the plain of Jericho has been placed in the hand of a hypnotized medium, and she has at once reconstructed in her mind the battle and siege of the city, and the shattering fall of the walls. I did not doubt that this bit of stone had acted as a magnet to drag my modern mind through the mists of the centuries into a life I had known before.

I was more shaken than I can describe, for the whole fantastic affair fitted in too well with certain formless vague sensations concerning the cairn which had already lingered at the back of my mind, to be dismissed as an unusually vivid dream. I felt the need of a glass of wine, and remembered that Ortali always had wine in his room. I hurriedly donned my clothes, opened my door, crossed the corridor and was about to knock at Ortali's door, when I noticed that it was partly open, as if someone had neglected to close it carefully. I entered, switching on a light. The room was empty.

I realized what had occurred. Ortali mistrusted me; he feared to risk himself alone with me in a lonely spot at midnight. He had postponed the visit to the cairn, merely to trick me, to give him a chance to slip away alone.

My hatred for Ortali was for the moment completely submerged by a wild panic of horror at the thought of what the opening of the cairn might result in. For I did not doubt the authenticity of my dream. It was no dream; it was a fragmentary bit of memory, in which I had relived that other life of mine. Gray Man's Headland—Grimmin's Headland, and under those rough stones that grisly corpse in its semblance of humanity—I could not hope that, imbued with the imperishable essence of an elemental spirit, that corpse had crumbled to dust in the ages.

Of my race out of the city and across those semi-desolate reaches, I remember little. The night was a cloak of horror through which peered red stars like the gloating eyes of uncanny beasts, and my footfalls echoed hollowly so that repeatedly I thought some monster loped at my heels.

The straggling lights fell away behind me and I entered the region of mystery and horror. No wonder that progress had passed to the right and to the left of this spot, leaving it untouched, a blind back-eddy given over to goblin-dreams and nightmare memories. Well that so few suspected its very existence.

Dimly I saw the headland, but fear gripped me and held me aloof. I had a vague, incoherent idea of finding the ancient woman, Meve MacDonnal. She was grown old in the mysteries and traditions of the mysterious land. She could aid me, if indeed the blind fool Ortali loosed on the world the forgotten demon men once worshiped in the North.

A figure loomed suddenly in the starlight and I caromed against him, almost upsetting him. A stammering voice in a thick brogue protested with the petulancy of intoxication. It was a burly longshoreman returning to his cottage, no doubt, from some late revel in a tavern. I seized him and shook him, my eyes glaring wildly in the starlight.

"I am looking for Meve MacDonnal! Do you know her? Tell me, you fool! Do you know old Meve MacDonnal?"

It was as if my words sobered him as suddenly as a dash of icy water in his face. In the starlight I saw his face glimmer whitely and a catch of fear was at his throat. He sought to cross himself with an uncertain hand.

"Meve MacDonnal? Are ye mad? What would ye be doin' with *her?*"

"Tell me!" I shrieked, shaking him savagely. "Where is Meve MacDonnal?"

"There!" he gasped, pointing with a shaking hand where dimly in the night something loomed against the shadows. "In the name of the holy saints, begone, be ye madman or devil, and l'ave an honest man alone! There—there ye'll find Meve MacDonnal—where they laid her, full three hundred years ago!"

Half-heeding his words I flung him aside with a fierce exclamation, and, as I raced across the weed-grown plain, I heard the sounds of his lumbering flight. Half blind with panic, I came to the low structures the man had pointed out. And floundering deep in weeds, my feet sinking into musty mold, I realized with a shock that I was in the ancient graveyard on the inland side of Grimmin's Headland, into which I had seen Meve MacDonnal disappear the evening before. I was close by the door of the largest tomb, and with an eery premonition I leaned close, seeking to make out the deeply carven inscription. And partly by the dim light of the stars and partly by the touch of my tracing fingers, I made out the words and figures, in the half-forgotten Gaelic of three centuries ago: "Meve MacDonnal—1565-1640."

With a cry of horror I recoiled and, snatching out the crucifix she had given me, made to hurl it into the darkness—but it was as if an invisible hand caught my wrist. Madness and insanity—but I could not doubt: Meve MacDonnal had come to me from the tomb wherein she had rested for three hundred years to give me the ancient, ancient relic entrusted to her so long ago by her priestly kin. The memory of her words came to me, and the memory of Ortali and the Gray Man. From a lesser horror I turned squarely to a greater, and ran swiftly toward the headland which loomed dimly against the stars toward the sea.

As I crossed the ridge I saw, in the starlight, the cairn, and the figure that toiled gnome-like above it. Ortali, with his accustomed, almost superhuman energy, had dislodged many of the boulders; and as I approached, shaking with horrified anticipation, I saw him tear aside the last layer, and I heard his savage cry of triumph, that froze me in my tracks some yards behind him, looking down from the slope. An unholy radiance rose from the cairn, and I saw, in the north, the aurora flame up suddenly with terrible beauty, paling the starlight. All about the cairn pulsed a weird light, turning the rough stones to a cold shimmering silver, and in this glow I saw Ortali, all heedless, cast aside his pick and lean gloatingly over the aperture he had made—and I saw there the helmeted head, reposing on the couch of stones where I, Red Cumal, placed it so long ago. I saw the inhuman terror and beauty of that awesome carven face, in which was neither human weakness, pity nor mercy. I saw the soul-freezing glitter of the one eye, which stared wide open in a fearful semblance of life. All up and down the tall, mailed figure shimmered and sparkled cold darts and gleams of icy light, like the northern lights that blazed in the shuddering skies. Aye, the Gray Man lay as I had left him more than nine hundred years before, without a trace of rust or rot or decay.

And now as Ortali leaned forward to examine his find, a gasping cry broke from my lips—for the sprig of holly worn in his lapel in defiance of "Nordic superstition," slipped from its place, and in the weird glow I plainly saw it fall upon the mighty mailed breast of the figure, where it blazed suddenly with a brightness too dazzling for human eyes. My cry was echoed by Ortali. The figure moved; the mighty limbs flexed, tumbling the shining stones aside. A new gleam lighted the terrible eye and a tide of life flooded and animated the carven features.

Out of the cairn he rose, and the northern lights played terribly about him. And the Gray Man changed and altered in horrific transmutation. The human features faded like a fading mask; the armor fell from his body and crumbled to dust as it fell; and the fiendish spirit of ice and frost and darkness that the sons of the North deified as Odin, stood up nakedly and terribly in the stars. About his grisly head played lightnings and the shuddering gleams of the aurora. His towering anthropomorphic form was dark as shadow and gleaming as ice; his horrible crest reared colossally against the vaulting arch of the sky.

Ortali cowered, screaming wordlessly, as the taloned malformed hands reached for him. In the shadowy indescribable features of the Thing there was no tinge of gratitude toward the man who had released it—only a demoniac gloating and a demoniac hate for all the sons of men. I saw the shadowy arms shoot out and strike. I heard Ortali scream once—a single unbearable screech that broke short at the shrillest pitch. A single instant a blinding blue glare burst about him, lighting his convulsed features and his upward-rolling eyes; then his body was dashed earthward as by an electric shock, so savagely that I distinctly heard the splintering of his bones. But Ortali was dead before he touched the ground—dead, shriveled and blackened, exactly like a man blasted by a thunderbolt, to which cause, indeed, men later ascribed his death.

The slavering monster that had slain him lumbered now toward me, shadowy tentacle-like arms outspread, the pale starlight making a luminous pool of his great inhuman eye, his frightful talons dripping with I know not what elemental forces to blast the bodies and souls of men.

But I flinched not, and in that instant I feared him not, neither the horror of his countenance nor the threat of his thunderbolt dooms.

For in a blinding white flame had come to me the realization of why Meve MacDonnal had come from her tomb to bring me the ancient cross which had lain in her bosom for three hundred years, gathering unto itself unseen forces of good and light, which war forever against the shapes of lunacy and shadow.

As I plucked from my garments the ancient cross, I felt the play of gigantic unseen forces in the air about me. I was but a pawn in the game—merely the hand that held the relic of holiness, that was the symbol of the powers opposed forever against the fiends of darkness. As I held it high, from it shot a single shaft of white light, unbearably pure, unbearably white, as if all the awesome forces of Light were combined in the symbol and loosed in one concentrated arrow of wrath against the monster of darkness. And with a hideous shriek the demon reeled back, shriveling before my eyes. Then with a great rush of vulture-like wings, he soared into the stars, dwindling, dwindling among the play of the flaming fires and the lights of the haunted skies, fleeing back into the dark limbo which gave him birth, God only knows how many grisly eons ago.

Black Harps in the Hills

Let Saxons sing of Saxon kings,
Red faced swine with a greasy beard—
Through my songs the Gaelic broadsword sings,
The pibrock skirls and the sporran swings,
For mine is the blood of the Irish kings
That Saxon monarchs feared.

The heather bends to a marching tread,
The echoes shake to a marching tune—
For the Gael has supped on bitter bread,
And follows the ghosts of the mighty dead,
And the blue blades gleam and the pikes burn red
In the rising of the moon.

Norseman reaver or red haired Dane,
Norman baron or English lord—
Each of them reeled to a reddened rain,
Drunken with fury and blind with pain,
Till the black fire spilled from the Gaelic brain
And the steel from the broken sword.

But never the chiefs in death lay still,
Never the clans lay scattered and few—
But a new face rose and a new voice roared,
And a new hand gripped the broken sword,
And the fleeing clans were a charging horde,
And the old hate burned anew!

Brian Boruma, Shane O'Neill,
Art McMurrough and Edward Bruce,
Thomas Fitzgerald—ringing steel
Shakes the hills and the trumpets peal,
Skulls crunch under the iron heel!
Death is the only truce!

Clontarf, Benburg, and Yellow Ford—
The Gael with red Death rides alone!
Lamh derg abu! And the riders reel
To Hugh O'Donnell's girding steel
And the lances of Tyrone!

Edward Fitzgerald, Charles Parnell,
Robert Emmet—I smite the harp!
Wolfe Tone and Napper Tandy—hail!
The song that you sang shall never fail
While one brain burns with the fire of the Gael
And one last sword is sharp—

Lamh laidir abu! Lamh derg abu!
Munster and Ulster, north and south,
The old hate flickers and burns anew,
The heather shakes and the pikes gleam blue.
And the old clans charge as they charged with you
Into Death's red grinning mouth!

We have not won and we have not lost—
Fire in Kerry and Fermanagh—
We have broken the teeth in the Saxon's boast
Though our dead have littered each heath and coast,
And by God, we will raise another host!
Slainte—Erin go bragh.

Appendix 1

James Allison

Unfinished Tales

Brachen the Kelt

Once I was Brachan the Kelt. . . . . .

If you ask me how I know, I can only retort by asking you in turn how you know that you were you yesterday or last month or last year. And if you cannot tell me how you know, why you remember, the fact remains unchanged; and because I cannot tell you how I remember the myriad shapes that have borne my spirit down the long chain of reincarnations, that memory is none the less vital and existent. I am James Allison, and I was Brachan. Let that suffice.

It was long ago. That statement is indefinite, but it cannot be improved upon. How many millenniums have passed since Brachan walked the world I do not know, because there are no landmarks in my memory of Brachan's life to fix his century. I can only say that it was long ago, in the youth of the world as we know it.

I was Brachan, tall, yellow haired, blue eyed, magnificently thewed, member of one of the great basic races, now extinct. I say extinct, because there lives in the world today no single pureblooded Aryan. But in Brachan's day the race was as yet unmixed. It was Brachan, perhaps, who began that mixing and mingling of races; Brachan, the mate of Taramis, from whose loins sprang tribes and nations.

I was born far to the east of the land in which I grew to manhood, on the open steppes by the shores of that great inland sea which in those dim times stretched from the Arctic Ocean to the Indian Sea, separating the primitive Aryans from the primitive Mongolians. There on the western shores of that great sea my people dwelt in great numbers, already, following the grass north by summer and south by winter. But we had no herds then; it was the great droves of grass-eaters we followed—the wild cattle, the bison and the horses which as yet no man had ridden. We were hunters, fishers, and plunderers. And already we were splitting off in tribes that wandered west and south in century-long hegiras.

So the steppes with their rolling expanses of waving grass and the horsehide tents along the shores of the inland sea remain but as dim memories in my mind. For as a child I was carried in the long trek westward that brought the culture of bronze to the shores of the distant Atlantic . . . . I can hear the rising clamor of the historians who would rise to refute me.

I am well aware of the curious mistake they make in dating the invasion of the first Aryans into western Europe, and the advent of the Bronze Age. We came, they said, in clumsy wagons drawn by oxen. We had already tamed and domesticated dogs, and were horsemen. By that time, say the historians, the beginnings of civilization were evident along the shores of the Mediterranean and the valleys of the great southern rivers.

I can only state facts. I was a child in the first Aryan clan to come into western Europe, then a great empty land of forests and rivers inhabited only by scattered tribes of dark-skinned aborigines. We were called Kelts, which was merely the designation of our clan. Neither in appearance nor in language did we at that time differ from our kinsmen of the far east. We had not learned to domesticate dogs, nor ride horses, nor shape a wagon wheel. We marched on foot, and we were ten years on the road. Yet we bore weapons and implements of bronze, and understood the art of weaving rushes into baskets, and of manufacturing flax into cloth.

If these facts tend to upset established conceptions and scientific theories, I am sorry, but I do not see what I can do about it. The historians undoubtedly confuse the first Aryan invasion with the migration of the Gauls, which occurred centuries later. They were our Aryan kin, and they found the formerly not too extensive Keltic clan grown into many tribes, and spread over many lands. Our language differed only as Saxon differs from modern English, and we intermarried and intermingled until we became as one race, and the terms Kelt and Gaul were synonymous.

But the Keltic clan was the first of all Aryans to set foot in Europe. My clearest memories are of rolling hills covered with oaks and firs, with rich grassy valleys between, stretching to cliffs where the blue sea broke in incessant surges—there I grew from childhood to early manhood, and it was as a young man that I finally drifted away from the range of my clan and wandered southward to where, far beyond the dreaming blue hills that rimmed the hazy horizon there awaited the love of Taramis and the horror of the Shaggy One.

Why I left the homelands of my clan I do not know; perhaps stronger in me than in my tribesmen burned the restless urge of wandering. Southward I went . . . . . . It was a strange, fierce world in those dim days. On a nameless island in the Mediterranean a group of swart skin-clad fishermen dwelt in a cluster of rude mud huts that was to grow centuries later into lion-gated Knossos. But where the Mediterranean rolls now, there were only great lakes and rivers. There were an eastern and a western lake, and a high rim of land kept the distant ocean from bursting over into the vast valley that was the Mediterranean basin in those days. Already the sea was gnawing at that rim, and when it burst—but it did not burst in Brachan's lifetime, though in another, later life I witnessed that cataclysm that wiped out a thriving civilization and gave rise to a cycle of tales wherein the world is destroyed by flood . . . . . .

But forgive my meanderings. My memories throng so thick upon me, of so many lives, that I am prone to digress, to wander into irrelevant channels. It is hard to follow the course of one life among the multitudes that I remember as you remember the days that throng thick on your heels.

Oh, it was a long wandering that led me at last to the village of the Amelians. I travelled on foot and alone, hunting and being hunted, slaying and battling the slayers. It was no easy road I trod, nor one unopposed. Lions roamed through what is now Europe, gigantic brutes, huger and fiercer than any today existent. There were cave bears, saber-toothed tigers, giant buffalo and elks, panthers . . . . but as always, the grimmest hunter, the fiercest beast of prey, was man.

Yet in the village of Amelia, with its wooden huts and their thatches rising above the points of the stockade, I found a welcome. I do not know what possessed King Jogah of Amelia to welcome me, a stranger, or why he did not order his warriors to feather me with arrows from the loopholes as I strode from the forest, across the fields of barley, toward the heavy gate. Perhaps it was curiosity. No man of Amelia had ever seen a man like me, nor had they dreamed that such men dwelt in the world, for the Keltic drift had not yet reached those southern valleys.

The men of Amelia were hard, sinewy, wiry, else they could not have lived in that age, for all their bows and their tall stockade. But they lacked my height and the might of my muscles. They were white men, but black of hair and dark of eye, and their skins were of a faint olive hue. Their old men had scanty beards, which were greatly esteemed.

But how shall I speak of Taramis? I can tell you her body was a poem in supple rhythm, that her skin was a rich luscious olive, that her thick, burnished black locks fell over shoulders exquisitely molded; that her dark eyes gleamed and smoldered with the vital life of the primitive; that her limbs were lissome and ripe with young womanhood—but I have not painted even a dim likeness to the vibrant figure that was Taramis, the daughter of King Jogah.

From the moment I first saw her, bearing water from the spring, the gourd on her glossy head, her slim body swaying in a poem of rhythm, I loved her—I desired her—with all the fierce passion of my race. To her own people Taramis was beautiful; to me, this dark-haired woman of the strangers was the ultimate fulfillment of all desire. When I looked at her, merely looked at her, my brain swam with dizziness and the blood beat like war drums in my ears. Love? Desire? What does James Allison know of the terms? What do you, what does any weak modern know? Ashes of passion burnt out when the earth was young—pale, dim reflections of a flame that once shook the worlds—passion that topples kingdoms, slaughters tribes, breaks down cities and uproots mountains—this we knew in the youth of the earth. Oh, I have loved as well as slain and wandered in my time, when I was Man in the youth of the world. I have renounced crowns to win the woman of my choice, and I have destroyed empires for the same reason; I have mated on reeking battlefields, with the crimson of the slaying still clotted on my fingers, and the screams of the dying resounding in my ears. But enough. It is of an earlier, simpler age I would tell—of the love of Taramis and the horror of the Shaggy One.

When I came to speak the language of Amelia—and that was not long, for it was simple and Kelts were always linguists, even in those dim days—I asked for her—asked? A Kelt did not *ask* for anything, save from his own chief. I demanded her, and had her father laughed at me for a giftless wanderer, I was ready to make a red slaughter in his palace-hut before numbers overcame me. For the desire of Taramis was a white-hot brand in my bosom.

But old King Jogah did not laugh. He tugged his long beard, and he stared at me, and he stared at his warriors. And then he set me a task. And therein he could not lose, for if I failed he was rid of a restless and turbulent guest, and if I won, he was rid of a horror that had haunted the land since time immemorial.

I have often wondered, as James Allison, in what distant land the men of Amelia had their beginning. They had dim legends of a far trek from the southeast, and in years to come, in my far wanderings, I came upon people of their blood again. Yet there were differences—and in all the modern world today there is no race who shows their characteristics, even mongrel as we have become.

But it is certain that their ancestors came to the valleys of Amelia centuries before, and there they found a race already in possession—a grim, hairy race which were like men, yet hideously unlike. Long and horrible had been the war, but at last the true men conquered, the beast-men fled into the barren hills, there to wage a desultory warfare for another century.

In the ending of a race sometimes its survivals take strange and terrible forms. So this subrace culminated in the Shaggy One. That is what they called him. Last of all his race, he lurked high in the grim hills, a horror too grisly to dream of, a retrogression of a race originally horribly low in the scale of human development—yet horribly advanced in certain shuddersome branches.

He brooded high in the hills, descending from time to time to make raids in the valleys, with the cunning and ferocity of a fiend. Parties which went out to slay him never came back, or their survivors straggled back, mad with fear at what they had seen. The head of this prehistoric demon was the price I should pay for Taramis.

At dawn, at the first dim light of dawn, I fared forth from the village of Amelia, and the young men played on reed pipes the wailing dirge for the dead. But I was Brachan, a Kelt and a sword-slayer, and I laughed as the gates of the village closed behind me.

Only one weapon I bore, the sword men called Skull-biter. Oh, I could sing a whole saga of that shimmering blade! It has glittered down through history like a star of war and slaughter. There is no blade like it, nor has there ever been. It was the sword of Goliath and with it David smote off the giant's head on that bloody field. It was the two-edged sword of Islam, and gleamed in the unsteady hands of Muhammad the Prophet; aye, and by devious ways it preceded the Moslems into Europe, and with it in his hands Roland died in the Pass of Roncesvalles. Richard the Lion Hearted bore it, not dreaming that he wielded the very brand of Durandal of which Blondin sang. Akbar hewed with it a road to empire; it was the sword of Attila; and today it hangs in the palace of some Afghan prince, awaiting the day when fate shall bring it forth again, to drink deep of the red wine of blood.

I forged it myself, I, Brachan the Kelt, mixing in the bronze the blood of men and of tigers, and by a curious process, never to be duplicated, the bronze took on the hardness and toughness of Damascus steel, unbreakable, unperishable. A hand's breadth wide below the guard it was, tapering to a sharp point, with a curious curving slant that lent the double edges almost a concave edge. The pommel was a heavy ball of bronze . . . . . . but Skull-biter was a sword among swords. I can no more describe the beauty of her, the balance and the springy swiftness, than I can describe the beauty of my other mistress, Taramis.

I went into the hills with Skull-biter slung to my shoulders. Through a maze of ravines and crags I made my way, until I came to a high cliff and far up upon it I saw a cave. And up the cliff to that cave led steps, niched in the rock—laboriously, perhaps, with a flint hand axe, gripped in a hairy, brutish hand.

I, James Allison, wonder at the incredible recklessness of Brachan, which was unbelievable, even in a Kelt. Up that dizzy ladder I went, not knowing what awaited me above, and whether it slept or was awake. But I had trailed the thing's bloody misshapen footprints from a countryside where it had torn a man limb from limb and sucked his blood, and I believed it was sluggish and heavy with slaughter and satiation.

Into the cave I came on tiptoe, lightly, Skull-biter in my hand, and I saw the monster sleeping, horribly like a man, on a great slab of rock, resting his head on his arm. I stood staring in wonder for a moment. The Shaggy One was much like an ape, yet he was no more an ape than I was. He was taller than I—upright on his gnarled, bowed legs I am sure he would have towered seven feet in height. He was covered with shaggy black hair, shot with silver. He had a strange grotesque head, but it was not the head of an ape. The forehead was very low and slanting, but the back of the head was large and well developed. The nose was flattish, the nostrils flaring; the ears were close set, and twitched in his slumber; the mouth was wide, the lips loose.

Then, as he awoke with a start, before he could rise, I swung my sword and hewed the head from the giant sloping shoulders. The head fell to the rock floor of the cavern, the headless body reared upright, spouting blood, then staggered and toppled down, grasping horribly at the empty air. I did not delay. A nameless horror brooded over that cavern. The Shaggy One dead was more terrible to me than the Shaggy One alive. Yet part of that terror I was forced to carry with me. I took up the severed head and dropped it into the leathern bag I carried, and I returned to the village of Amelia.

It was a great wedding feast they gave us, old Jogah and his people of Amelia. Let me describe to you Jogah's palace hut. In the first place it was a house of no mean proportions, built of planks sawed with incredible effort out of huge tree trunks, and a thatched roof. It was crudely and mightily built; it might have withstood the onrush of a hurricane. It was a long building, and for the first half a corridor ran through it, with rooms on each side, each room having one outer window and one door, opening into the corridor. In these rooms slept the warriors attached to Jogah's personal court. In one of these Taramis and I were to sleep. Passing from between these rooms, the corridor opened out into one huge hall-like chamber. A great table occupied the central part of this hall, with benches ranged about it, and benches also ranged the walls where the lesser folk could sit and feast. At the head of the table, facing the entrance, was Jogah's carven throne. Behind that throne were other rooms, three side by side; he occupied the central room with his eldest wife, while his other two wives had each a room on the side. Behind these rooms were other chambers where slept the children of the king and his various wives. The floor was of wood, carpeted only with rushes.

[. . .]

Genseric's Son

Long, long ago an infant son was born to Gudrun of the Shining Locks, the wife of Genseric the Sworder, in their horsehide lodge on the frozen snows of Vanaheim. When the man-child's first wail of life broke upon the icy waste, Genseric lifted him in his mighty hand and searched him for any blemish, as was the custom of the Vanir and their brothers the Æsir. And he frowned, for the infant's left leg was crooked.

Immemorial custom had decreed that only the perfect should live; but Genseric turned to Gudrun questioningly, for hers was the last word in the matter. But Gudrun, with the rack of her throes still upon her, threw back fiercely and proudly her thick shining tresses, and said harshly: "I have four sons of fair, straight limbs; shall I give them a crippled frog for a brother?"

So Genseric went from the tent into the chill grey dawn, carrying the man-child naked. The smoke of his breath clotted his beard, and his shod feet crunched in the frozen crust. There was frost upon his sword hilt, and the icy air bit through his furs and the mail beneath.

Far out on the misty waste he laid the infant, its body turning blue in the wind that wailed out of the murky depths that veiled the horizons. He laid his hand on his sword, then blown to his ears from afar came the long howling of the great grey wolves. So he turned and strode back across the waste, like a dark phantom of the indefinite dawn, and behind him the cry of the pack rose to a crescendo of exultation and died away.

But even before the sun had thrust its way through the icy mists and low-lying clouds to turn the snow fields to a floating plain of blinding fire, old Bragi came to Genseric's tent, with his grey beard and his haunted eyes and the strangeness in his soul that an ancient sword cut upon his head had made his.

"I saw you lay the child upon the snow," quoth old Bragi. "I saw as I returned across the chill wastes in the grey birth of dawn. I heard the howling of the wolves as you turned away, and soon the swift patter of their feet over the crust. Their eyes were green in the murk, and their tongues lolled red as hunger between their white fangs. They came about the infant where it lay upon the snow, and stirred its limbs with their muzzles, yet harmed it not. By the icy blood of Ymir, they howled like the fiends of the wastes about it, and a great grey she-wolf lay down beside it and gave it her teats. Its fingers clutched at her stiff grey ice-clotted hair, and it sucked at her dugs as a wolf cub suckles. Then fear fell upon me, and I fled swiftly. Yet it is the truth I speak."

So Genseric and his brothers went forth into the waste, until they came to the spot where the babe was left. But the infant was gone, and all about the spot where it had lain were the tracks of wolves. There was no blood on the snow, but the tracks of many wolves led westward into the plains of eternal ice and snow. And afterwards, in the horsehide tents of Vanaheim and of Asgard, over the flickering fires was told the tale of Genseric's fifth born, the man-child who was taken by the wolves.

I was that man-child. I, whom men now call James Allison, in another, weaker, softer age and clime. I cannot tell you how I possess this knowledge, any more than you can tell me how it is that the events of yesterday, and the days before, and the years before remain indelibly impressed upon that part of your consciousness we call memory, so that you can call them into life again by speech and writing. You know, that is all; aye, and I *know*. As you remember your days, I remember my lives. Your memory of your days is unbroken by the nights of sleep which separate them, nor is the memory of my lives broken by the alternating nights of deeper sleep we call death. In that night I have gone ten thousand times, and out of that night ten thousand times have I awakened, as I shall awake again and again throughout the long ages until the destruction of the planet that spawned it shall at last and ultimately break the chain of flesh and blood and bone figments which have successively cloaked the undying spirit that is *I*.

Even the destruction of the planet cannot kill that spirit, whether its end be blackening frost under a dead, icy sun, or the melting wrath of cosmic fires. Let the earth burst like an iridescent bubble floating in the gulf of infinity, yet *life* is not destroyed. I have seen visions, vast and terrible and wonderful, of the cataclysm that shall not destroy the spirit that is me, but hurl it into unguessed infinities, into undreamed oceans of suns and stars beyond the ken of man, to take up the endless succession anew in gorgeous, weird worlds beyond the echoing voids.

But I have no lust to plumb those dreaming deeps. I am of the earth, earthly. Out of the dust I have sprung, and into the dust I have returned, not once, but a million times, to rise in eternal resurrection, clothed in a new flesh and burning youth, like fresh and shining raiment. I look not beyond the horizons of the planet that gave me birth. My feet are deep in the mysteries of her grasses and her pools; her dew is in my hair, and her sun is hot gold on my naked shoulders;

under my hands the warm earth pulses with life that gave the races of man being, and my arms embrace the living trunks of her trees; they are no less her children than am I; the speech of their leaves no less articulate than mine.

Oh, I have been many men in many lands! As I lay here waiting for death to free me from this broken, unsound body, I do not see the dingy walls, the cobwebbed ceiling, the cheap prints that pass for pictures; they do not limit my vision, nor the houses and the oak groves and the hills beyond; not the horizons themselves are my boundaries. I see the flaming dawns I have known of old, the far lands, the broad, foaming seas—white cliffs against the clear cold blue, with a smother of sparkling froth about their foot, and the cry of gulls. I see pageantry, and pride, and glory, the shine of the sun on golden corselets, the breaking of spears, the spreading of purple sails, and the dark eyes of women who have loved me.

Oh, I see all the men that have been I! The brave, the fearful, the strong, the weak, the kind, the cruel, the living, loving, hating, lusting, swilling, gorging, fighting, betraying, swaggering figures that have borne equally with one another the transient, restless spirit that now animates the frail and sickly frame that men call James Allison.

What have I not been? King, warrior, slave. I died at Marathon, at Arbela, at Cannae, at Chalons, at Clontarf, at Hastings, at Agincourt, at Austerlitz, at San Jacinto, and at Gettysburg. I was a nameless, yellow-haired chieftain riding a half-wild stallion when we brought bronze into western Europe; I bore spear and shield in the Macedonian phalanx when the plains of India shook to the tread of Alexander; I pulled a strong bow at Poitiers, when our whistling clouds of arrows broke the chivalry of France; and I heard the creak of leather, the tinkling of spurs and the singing of the night riders when we drove the lowing herds of longhorns up the dim trail men call the Chisholm to build a new young empire of leather and beef and steel.

What could I not tell you of this my planet, and the life that teems upon it; how could I not refute the chroniclers and the sages, and laugh to scorn the historians and the philosophers!

But I will rather go back beyond their ken, into an age of which they have no cognizance. I will tell you of the man-child of Genseric and of Gudrun of the Shining Locks, who was suckled by wolves.

Oh, the tale is no new one. Every race has its legends of a babe who tugged at the breasts of a she-wolf. It is the heritage of all Aryan peoples, and from them other races have borrowed.

But it was from the actuality of the son of Genseric and Gudrun that all these tales sprang. Romulus was suckled by a harlot, and his sons called her a wolf through courtesy and evasion. But the milk of the grey she-wolf was the only sustenance the son of Genseric knew.

I never had a name, as men are named, though in the years of my life I was called many things by many tribes. I was the Strong One. That was what my many names signified, in whatever tongue they were framed. I remember that a tribe of the Æsir called me Ghor, and since that is as good a name as another I will call the son of Genseric and of Gudrun by that name.

[. . .]

The Guardian of the Idol

Synopsis

The story begins with Gorm, the Cro-Magnon, lying bound beside the altar of the Neolithic people, having been branded with the symbol of sacrifice. The Neolithic people lived in a village of mud and wattle huts, surrounded by a palisade. The hut stood on the low bluffs of a neck of land which ran out into a broad river. Part way between the village and the land there was another barrier of palisades spanning the neck and running out into the water, which was haunted by a flesh-eating fish in great numbers. None of the Neolithic men could swim, they having wandered up from the south with their domesticated dogs—all of which they had eaten in a year of famine—their oxen and their stone polishers and pieces of pottery and woven flax garments.

Amidst the horrors of primitive worship, Gorm's companion, a young hunter, was sacrificed, and in the confusion a flaming brand was knocked out of the fire and fell close to Gorm's limbs. The fire burned part way through, searing his flesh, and nerved to desperation, he snapped his bonds, burst through the crowd and leaped into the river where he was attacked by the savage fishes. They slashed and tore him, but he managed to get across the river before the Neolithic people could follow him in canoes, dug out of tree trunks.

For weeks he lay in the deep forest, recovering from his wounds, and during that time he made his comments on his own people and the Neolithic people. Recovering, and burning with the shame of his branding, he set out to steal and destroy the god of the Neolithic people—a wooden idol set up in a dark grove in the midst of a canyon inhabited by a still older survival—one of the grisly Neandertal men, almost destroyed by the Cro-Magnon people.

This canyon was surrounded on all sides except one by comparatively high cliffs. Gorm, to draw the Neandertal to the upper end of the canyon, went along the cliffs and showed himself to the monster, then fell back out of sight and built a green wood fire, thinking that the monster would remain watching it, expecting the Cro-Magnon to try to invade the canyon from that direction. Meanwhile Gorm hurried back along the cliffs and entered the canyon from the lower end. But the Neandertal had peculiarities beyond the range of real humans. When Gorm entered the sacred grove he saw the Neandertal standing before him, or rather the image of the beast. A sound behind him made him wheel to meet the real monster. After a savage battle he overcame it and found the idol. The Neolithic people believed all their souls were contained in their idol and had gone all together and placed the idol in the grove, knowing the Neandertal would act as an involuntary guard of it. He could not climb and they placed it high up in a great oak.

Gorm broke off the head and burned the body, and taking the head with him, returned to the Neolithic village. Presenting himself at the palisade across the neck, he displayed the head to the guard and struck him down while he stood paralyzed with fear and amazement. Then he went on to the village, and in the first fire of dawn, showed the head of the god to the villagers who immediately all went mad, burst through the palisade and tumbled into the river.

Draft

Once I was Gorm, of the Bison People. I cannot explain to you how I remember this, any more than I can explain the phenomenon that causes me, and you, to remember the events of yesterday and yesteryear. I am James Allison, dying of a malady that baffles all modern science, and I was Gorm, of the Bison People, who lived in a far clime and a far age. More I cannot say. I *was;* I *am;* I cannot dispute the evidences of ten thousand years that teach me I *shall be again*. Enough; I am James Allison; I was Gorm; and in the voices of Gorm and of James Allison I shall tell my tale, the tale of Gorm, who lived when the world was young and mankind was weak, and few. And I will begin at the point where I, Gorm of the Bison People, lay bound hand and foot beside the altar stone of the River People, with the howling of maddened worshippers in my ears, and the hideous mask of their priest bending over me, its plumes rippling in the breeze that drove the smoke of the fires in billowing whorls that dimmed the ring of savage faces.

Closer and closer bent that bestial visage, through the eye slits of which gleamed the beady black eyes of the priest who wore it. And closer and closer to my naked breast sank the hand gripping a white-hot flint held in a cleft stick—I did not close my eyes as that hell-hot shard touched my bosom and ploughed the flesh. A wisp of smoke curled up from my breast but I made no sound, nor showed my keen agony by the flicker of an eyelash or the twitch of a muscle. From the River People rose a maddened howl; the priest straightened, waving the branding stone and screaming. And on my breast, burned indelibly, showed the symbol of the sacrifice.

Soon a knife of flint, plunging into my heart as I lay on the blackly stained stone, would flood that smoking symbol with red blood, that the gods of the River People might be appeased and send rice fat in the marshes and barley thick in the fields.

One victim lay already on the altar—a youth of my own people, though of a different tribe, captured about the same time as myself. Now the people began circling the altar stone and the ring of fires, chanting and leaping in their grotesque dance—I wish that I might reconstruct that primeval scene.

The village of the River People stood on the extremity of a neck of land which ran into the great river. This neck, at the end, broadened and was roughly circular, and their mud and wattle huts occupied almost the entire space. Their palisade, made of upright, pointed logs sunk in the earth, stood at the very rim of the low bluffs which surrounded the end of the peninsula. The altar stone, merely a flat rock topping a heap of stones, stood in the center of the village where a space was left clear. Fires, built to form a triangle, enclosed the stone and the priest who stood beside the stone, and the victims who lay upon it and beside it.

Around this triangle the River People danced and mouthed—short, but thickly-muscled folk, with shocks of bushy hair and black glittering eyes, clad in garments of skins and crudely woven flax. They were dark-skinned folk. I, Gorm, was typical of my people, being tall and broad shouldered, with grey eyes and tawny hair.

The priest chanted; he lifted a flint knife, and when it fell it was quenched in the heart of the Bison man who lay on the altar. At the spurt of crimson the people howled like wolves and some rent their garments and leaped into the fires, scattering sparks. One brand, struck by a heedless foot, flew through the air and fell beside me, searing my flesh, but falling so the flame touched the thongs that bound my legs. I lay still, setting my teeth against the bite of the flame. Then, when the priest had torn out the heart of his victim, and cast it into the flame, I exerted my agony-steeled thews and snapped the thongs.

In an instant I was up and racing toward the palisade. Men and women howled and scattered before me as I smote right and left with a flaming brand snatched from a fire. Arrows whistled about me as I climbed the [. . .]

Akram the Mysterious

Once I was Hengibar the Wanderer. I cannot explain my knowledge of this fact by any occult or esoteric maunderings, nor shall I try. A man remembers his past life; I remember my past *lives*. Just as a normal man recalls the shapes that were he in childhood, boyhood and youth, so I recall the shapes that have been I in forgotten ages. Why this memory is mine I cannot say, any more than I can explain the myriad phenomena of nature which confront me and every other mortal daily. But as I lie waiting for death to free me from my lifelong disease, I see with a clear, sure sight the grand vistas of lives that trail out behind me. I see the men who have been I, and I see the beasts that have been I. For my memory does not end at the becoming of Man. How could it, when the Beast so shades into Man that there is no clearly defined line to mark the boundaries of bestiality? At this instant I see a dim twilight vista, among the gigantic trees of a primordial forest that never knew the sound of a leather-shod foot. I see a vast, shaggy, shambling bulk that lumbers clumsily yet swiftly, sometimes upright, sometimes on all fours. He delves under rotten logs for grubs and insects, and his small ears twitch continually. He lifts his head and bares yellow fangs. He is primordial, bestial, anthropoid; yet he is James Allison, and I recognize the kinship. Kinship? Say rather oneness. There is no question of kin. I am he; he is I. My flesh is soft and white and hairless; his is dark and tough and shaggy with black hair. Yet we are one, and already in his feeble, shadowed brain are beginning to stir and sting and tingle the man-thoughts and the man-dreams—crude, chaotic, fleeting, yet the basis for all the high and lofty visions that men have dreamed in all the long following ages.

Nor does my knowledge cease there. It goes back, back, down vistas I dare not follow—to abysses too dark and awful for the human mind to plumb. Yet even there I am aware of my identity, my individuality. I tell you, the individual is never lost, either in the pit from which we once emerged, blind, squalling and noisome, or in that eventual Nirvana into which we shall one day sink—which I have glimpsed afar off, shining as a blue twilight lake among the mountains of the stars.

But enough. I would tell you of Hengibar. Oh, it was long, long ago! How long I dare not say. Why should I seek for paltry human comparisons to describe a realm indescribably, incomprehensibly distant?

I was Hengibar. And when I, the weakling, the cripple, think of Hengibar, I could shout for joy. Aye, for the sheer blind tingling joy of physical might. Oh, the clean blood singing through the strong veins, pumped by a heart stronger than a dynamo! Oh, the great thews rippling under bronzed skin! Who said the mind is the only measurement of man? I say to you that the blood, the muscles, the bones, the hard fibre of the flesh are as much Man as the grey mush of the brain and the dreams it grinds out. Because modern man is soft and white and weak he scorns the physical magnificence of the primitive. What does he know of physical power? What does a blind man know of sight? I tell you, there is no man on earth today who understands the surging glory of muscular power as do I, who lie here with limbs drawn and flabby, and thews weak as rotten cordage. Already much of me is dead; for that matter every civilized man carries about with him masses of dead, atrophied or withered tissue.

But when I was Hengibar every cell, tissue and fibre of my great frame was quick and vibrant and electric with stinging life. My senses were like whetted knives. My eyes made out microscopic details unknown to the dull eyes of moderns. I heard sounds men have not heard for a thousand centuries, since civilization blunted their sensations.

My eyes were blue, my hair yellow—not the colorless, straw-like hue of so many modern blonds, but a living gold with the flame of the sun caught in it. Where I was not burnt bronze by the sun, my skin was white as milk. My loins were girt with a bit of leopard skin. With either hand I could wield my heavy flint-headed axe.

I was akin to the folk with whom I wandered, but not one with them. Like me they were tall and blue eyed, but their hair was flaming crimson. They were of Vanaheim and I was of Asgard, the natural divisions of Nordheim, that shadowy, semi-mythical homeland of all proto-Aryans. In Hengibar's day the bulk of the Nordheimr still dwelt there, in their horsehide tents among the snows: golden-haired Æsir and red-haired Vanir, warring among themselves, from time to time sending forth drifts of tribes that wandered around the world and left their traces in strange far places.

I must have been born on one of those century-long drifts. Who my people were I never knew. The Vanir of Wolfang the One-eyed found me as a baby in a dark primordial forest of a far western land, alone and naked, my lips smeared with the blood of a wolf cub I had strangled with my infant fingers and was devouring raw and yet warm. I snarled at them like a tiger whelp, they said. Wolfang, seeing my yellow hair, had been about to dash out my brains with his axe, but when he grasped the nape of my neck, I writhed my head about, uttering no whimper, and sank my milk-teeth into the hairy skin of his forearm.

"By Ymir," he rumbled, "the young one has wolf-blood in him. We will keep him, and he will become a mighty man—a manslayer and an eater of raw meat. He will repay the clan for his rearing in days to come."

Aye, and I did, by the ice-sheathed beard of Ymir! In war and hunt none surpassed me in my growing up, and it was as a full grown warrior that I came to the devil-haunted valley of Akram.

We were a large tribe, for those days and time. Our fighting men alone numbered more than a hundred and seventy. Living mainly by the hunt, and by plunder, it followed that no section would support our clan long at a time. So our life was a continuous search for meat, and in that long trek men were born, grew old and died.

I was one of the scouts ranging many miles ahead of the main column when we came to the foothills of the mountains beyond which lay Akram the mysterious. I saw them first when the dark forest thinned—blue ramparts mounting swiftly to the sky, slope piled upon slope.

I knew the only scout ahead of me was Wulfgar, and I wondered if he had gone up into the hills or was ranging along the forest for meat. I wondered no longer when I found him—or what was left of him—among the thinning trees. The corpse sprawled in the damp forest mold, the perfection of its limbs mocked and belied by its horrible mutilation.

From the arrow-mark in the breast, and the footprints in the loam, I quickly reconstructed the scene. Wulfgar had come carelessly from the deeper forest. A man had crouched behind a clump of bushes, evidently watching him. I could imagine the rest—the sudden twang of the bowstring, the thud of the shaft into Wulfgar's heart, then the quick stroke of axe or blade that completed the task. The slayer's footprints differed from any I had ever seen. They were not like the tracks made by the narrow high-arched feet of the Nordheimr; they were the marks of wide, flat, splayfeet. And they led toward the blue-masked hills.

The language is too weak to describe the fury that seethed in my soul as I looked down on the headless carrion that had been Wulfgar of the Vanir. Death was our constant companion in those grim days. Slaying and dying was our main occupation. But in this case it was more than my personal friendship for Wulfgar that prompted my rage. He had been shot down from ambush without a chance to strike a blow; that had been largely due to his carelessness, and I cursed him for a fool, even while I lusted for his slayer's blood. But killing him in that manner, and taking his head, was a slap in the face of the whole tribe. I cannot explain to you Hengibar's feelings on the matter; but the taking of a man's head was a shameful thing, the crowning insult to his clan, and only wholesale slaughter could wipe it out.

It was a part of the clan-feeling, and since that emotion is unknown to modern man, it is useful for me to try to explain why, as Hengibar stood over his mutilated tribesman, his blood hammered in his ears, his veins swelled, and the sky swam yellow and red-streaked to his maddened gaze.

I left the corpse where it lay. The tribe would find and dispose of it, or the jungle creatures would pick its bones bare. It did not matter; the ultimate indignity had been offered to it, and my first duty was to find the man who took Wulfgar's head and kill him in as bloody and horrible a manner as I could.

I started on the unknown hunter's trail, and I did not go leisurely. The long patience of the wild was not mine. I burned with impatience to wash out my clan's dishonor in blood. I begrudged every instant the killer lived, every breath he drew, every step he took on the green earth.

It was not hard to follow his tracks through the thinning forest. Even when the loam gave way to rocky hill-soil I had no difficulty in tracing the spoor. Mine were not the atrophied senses of modern men. I was alive and alert and awake to all that spread before my eyes and ears. The cry of an insect, the rasp of a wing against a branch, the brushing of grass blades together, all held clear meanings for me, that I could read and understand as you understand the expositions of your teachers and lecturers. A displaced grass tuft, a crushed particle of moss, a bent twig—these served me as well as signposts and highway guides serve the modern traveler. I have trailed a man across a stretch of naked rocks, and not gone astray. But the fellow I followed up into the hills of Akram left a trail a child of the Vanir could have followed. He was a clumsy, blundering fellow, who could never have trapped a Vanir save by pure chance. I realized this as I followed his plain spoor, and my fury was further fanned by the thought of such a stupid dolt taking the head of a brother warrior.

Wulfgar's body had been cold, and the spoor was not fresh. I knew that the slayer had hours start on me. I knew also that my swift pace was cutting down his lead. I wished to come up with him before he reached his village—for it was pretty obvious that he had a village within reach, or he would not have burdened himself with the head. So swiftly and vengefully I followed the trail into the mountains.

As I climbed higher and higher, I began to hear a weird whistling ahead of me and above me, and at moonrise I came to the highest point of the pass through which ran the trail and found the source of the noise. On poles, driven upright into the earth, scores of human skulls were fastened. Holes had been knocked in them with fiendish cunning, and the wind blowing through them sang eerily. My flesh crawled at that sorcery, but I did not falter.

After several hours' swift traveling, I came out onto the slopes overlooking a broad valley, and wondered at what I saw. For in the red glow of the sinking moon, I saw the outlines of a walled town—I who had never seen any habitation except the horsehide tents of my people, and the thatched huts of the barley people. For some time I stood struck dumb and speechless. Such a sight was beyond my wildest imagination. My mind refused to comprehend it. Think, my civilized brothers, try to think just what the sight of a walled city would be to a primitive whose most magnificent idea of architecture was embraced by a mud hut with a thatch roof. Nothing in all my past experience or the experience of my people prepared me for such a sight. None of them had ever dreamed of the existence of stone walls and ordered streets.

What could they mean but habitations of gods? And by my reactions, or rather by my actions, I realize that Hengibar was a remarkable person. For I neither fell on my face and worshipped, nor fled howling with fear. Confronted by that incredible phenomenon, I reasoned that, men or gods, the slayers of Wulfgar were within those walls; and grasping my axe more firmly, I went down the grassy slopes toward that citadel of mystery.

The valley was crisscrossed with ditches—irrigation ditches, watering once fertile fields, though of course I could not know their meaning. But I saw and recognized the marks of rapine. The ditches were dry or filled with scummy water; they were broken; the fields had been laid waste.

Between the fields and the walls lay a strip of grassy ground, dotted with clusters of palms; many of these had been broken down, as if in wanton destruction. But they gave me cover, and I glided through the shadowy starlight until I crouched in a clump of palms near the great gate and glared murderously at the man who squatted there.

The scent of him was in my nostrils, causing the short hair of my neck to bristle with hatred. His scent was not like the scent of any man I had ever encountered. I could see him well enough in the starlight—for my eyes were like whetted swords—to make out his characteristics. He was tall and powerfully made, though smooth where I was knotty with muscles. His head was round, and his hair fell over his shoulders in lanky strands. His eyes were oblique and they glimmered like a beast's in the starlight. He wore a loincloth and he held a spear in his hands.

His senses, compared to mine, were dull. He neither heard, smelled nor saw me. At last, wearied of his posture, he rose, stretched himself, and began to walk leisurely up and down before the gate. And like a shadow I crawled from the palms and glided upon him. He was yawning and stretching his arms again when I came up to his back and smote him in the middle of the back, somewhat above the waist. The keen flint blade sheared through his spine and he fell without a sound and died.

Then I turned to the gate, and pushed cautiously upon it. It swung open and I stole through. As I realized that I was within the walls, the panic of the wild swept upon me, and I fought it down. The town lay before me.

Let me describe that town, which seemed vaster, more inexplicable and more incredible to Hengibar than London would seem to a Zulu savage. For the black man knows Kaffir villages containing hundreds of huts, and Hengibar did not. Yet that city was only a small one, after all, and laid out on plain, simple lines. It was in the form of an oblong. There were three streets, running parallel. The main street ran from the gate to the great structure that took up the entire further end of the town. On each side of the street stood small, trim stone houses, square, flat roofed, one storied, with only a few yards separating each house from its neighbor. Behind these houses, on either side, ran a narrower street, lined by houses built squarely against the outer wall. The further end of the town was occupied by a comparatively large building, surrounded by a half-circle of palm trees.

I saw no lights; no one moved. The streets lay empty. Yet as I slunk down the main street, keeping in the shadows of the houses, I knew that men lay about me—many men. Their scent cloyed the air, and my hair prickled with hate.

As I slid shadowlike past a doorway, someone muttered within, as a man grunts in his sleep, harried by evil dreams. And at the sound all fear and caution were swept out of my brain by a red wave of berserk fury, and bloodlust.

With a bloodthirsty snarl I launched myself against the door and through its splintering remnants burst into the darkness beyond it. I could see nothing, but men were in the room with me, and my axe, flailing in the dark, crushed a human skull. Someone heaved up, yelling in alarm, and my axe found him glancingly, changing his yells to screams of pain and fear. He rushed wildly for the door and plunged through, still shrieking, and I was at his heels, slashing and hacking in silent fury. He burst into the street, and ran staggeringly down it, splattering blood at every step and screaming like a stuck pig. On all sides men were rousing in the houses, were casting open doors and shouting to each other in their alien tongue, but I gave no heed. There was room in my brain only for the bloodlust, and I bounded after the fleeing man, felled him with a terrific blow from behind, and pouncing on his writhing body, struck him again and again until he lay still beneath my dripping axe.

Then I looked up, as a panther glares up from its prey, and saw men swarming out of the houses all along the street. Torches tossed wildly, and glinted on spearheads. With a snarl I wheeled away and sprang for the cover of the shadows between the houses. A man barred my way, torch held on high. I went straight for him, and as the torchlight fell on my blazing eyes, snarling blood-spattered features and dripping axe, he cried out and recoiled as a man recoils from a tiger. The next instant my axe rose and fell, cutting his shriek short, and over his torn form I sprang to the shadows between the houses.

Then began a grim game of hide-and-seek. All up and down the main street torches wavered, spears gleamed, and men ran and shouted. Apparently the houses built against the wall were uninhabited. The furnishings in them were broken, and the scent of stale blood, long dried, was heavy in the air.

Their arrangement was so simple even I fathomed it quickly. And I took refuge in them, gliding out on the other side when the hunters approached too closely. And truth to tell, there seemed to be no great zest in their search, and they were loath to leave the main street. I glided among the houses along the wall, vengeful, skulking like an old panther, and soon I came upon one bolder than his brothers, who peered among the shadows, torch in one hand and spear in the other. He was alone. And he was remarkably dull of senses. I was almost at his shoulder when he turned and saw me, and he shrieked and tried to avoid the axe that swept down in a glittering arc. His skull cracked like an eggshell, but his scream brought his fellows on the run.

I slunk back into the shadows, and there was a great jabbering when they found the body. As they crowded about, in the glare of the torches, I saw that their skins were yellow instead of white. They waved their spears and gibbered, and finally, bunched into a compact group, they back away toward the main street, their spears menacing all points of the compass. Whatever their courage by daylight, it was feeble by night, and a fierce contempt rose in me to supplement the hatred I felt for them. For their feet were flat and broad and splay, and I knew one of them was the man I sought.

They showed no signs of leaving the torch-lit street.

[…]

Appendix 2
Cormac Mac Art

Unfinished Tales

Tigers of the Sea

Chapter 1

"Tigers of the sea! Men with the hearts of wolves and thews of fire and steel! Feeders of ravens whose only joy lies in slaying and dying! Giants to whom the death song of the sword is sweeter than the love song of a girl!"

The tired eyes of King Gerinth were shadowed.

"This is no new tale to me; for a score of years such men have assailed my people like hunger-maddened wolves."

"Take a page from Caesar's book," answered Conal the minstrel, as he lifted a wine goblet and drank deep. "Have we not read in the Roman books how he pitted wolf against wolf? Aye—that way he conquered our ancestors, who in their day were wolves also."

"And now they are more like sheep," murmured the king, a quiet bitterness in his voice, "In the years of the peace of Rome, our people forgot the arts of war. Now Rome has fallen and we fight for our lives. And cannot even protect our women."

Conal set down the goblet and leaned across the finely carved oak table.

"Wolf against wolf!" he cried, "You have told me—as well I knew!—that no warriors could be spared from the borders to search for your sister, the princess Helen—even if you knew where she is to be found. Therefore, you must enlist the aid of other men. And these men I have just described to you are as superior in ferocity and barbarity to the savage Angles that assail us, as the Angles themselves are superior to our softened peasantry."

"But would they serve under a Briton against their own blood," demurred the king, "And would they keep faith with me?"

"They hate each other as much as we hate them both," answered the minstrel. "Moreover, you can promise them the reward—only when they return with the princess Helen."

"Tell me more of them," requested King Gerinth.

"Wulfhere the Skull-splitter, the chieftain, is a red-bearded giant like all his race. He is crafty in his way, but leads his Vikings mainly because of his fury in battle. He handles his heavy, long shafted axe as lightly as if it were a toy, and with it he shatters the swords, shields, helmets and skulls of all who oppose him. When Wulfhere crashes through the ranks, stained with blood, his crimson beard bristling and his terrible eyes blazing, and his great axe, clotted with brains and blood, few there are who dare face him.

"But it is on his right-hand man that Wulfhere depends for advice and council. That one is crafty as a serpent and is known to we Britons of old—for he is no Viking at all by birth, but a Gael of Erin, by name Cormac Mac Art, called *an Cliuin*, or the Wolf. Of old he led a band of Irish reavers and harried the coasts of the British Isles and Gaul and Spain—aye, and he preyed also on the Vikings themselves. But civil war broke up his band and he joined the forces of Wulfhere—they are Danes and dwell in a land south of the people who are called Norsemen.

"Cormac Mac Art has all the guile and reckless valor of his race. He is tall and rangy, a tiger where Wulfhere is a wild bull. His weapon is the sword, and his skill is incredible. The Viking rely little on the art of fencing. Their manner of fighting is to deliver mighty blows with the full sweep of their arms. Well, the Gael can deal a full arm blow with the best of them, but he favors the point. In a world where the old time skill of the Roman swordsman is almost forgotten, Cormac Mac Art is well-nigh invincible. He is cool and deadly as the wolf for which he is named, yet at times, in the fury of battle, a madness comes upon him that transcends the frenzy of the Berserk. At such times he is more terrible than Wulfhere and men who would face the Dane, flee before the blood-lust of the Gael."

King Gerinth nodded. "And you could find these men for me?"

"Lord king, even now they are within reach. In a lonely bay on the western coast, in a little frequented region, they have beached their dragon-ship and are making sure that it is fully seaworthy before moving against the Angles. Wulfhere is no sea king. He has but one ship. But so swiftly he moves and so fierce is his crew that the Angles, Jutes and Saxons fear him more than any of their other foes. He revels in battle. He will do as you wish him, if the reward is great enough."

"Promise him anything you will," answered Gerinth. "It is more than a princess of the realm that has been stolen—it is my little sister."

His fine, deeply lined face was strangely tender as he spoke.

"Let me attend to it," said Donal, refilling his goblet. "I know where these Vikings are to be found. I can pass among them; but I tell you before I start that it will take your majesty's word, from your own lips, to convince Cormac Mac Art of—anything! Those Western Celts are more wary than the Vikings themselves."

Again King Gerinth nodded. He knew that the minstrel had walked strange paths and that though he was loquacious on most subjects he was tight-lipped on others. Donal was blest or cursed with a strange and roving mind and his skill with the harp opened many doors to him that axes could not open. Where a warrior had died, Donal of the Harp walked unscathed. He knew well many fierce sea kings who were but grim legends and myths to most of the people of Britain, but Gerinth had never had cause to doubt the minstrel's loyalty.

Chapter 2

Wulfhere of the Danes fingered his crimson beard and scowled abstractedly. He was a giant, his breast muscles bulged like twin shields under his scale-mail corselet. The horned helmet on his head added to his great height and with his huge hand knotted about the long shaft of a great axe, he made a picture of rampant barbarism not easily forgotten. But for all his evident savagery, the chief of the Danes seemed slightly bewildered and undecided. He turned and growled a question to a man who sat near.

This man was tall and rangy. He was big and powerful, and though he lacked the massive bulk of the Dane, he more than made up for it by the tigerish litheness that was apparent in his every move. He was dark, with a smooth-shaven face and square-cut black hair. He wore none of the golden armlets or ornaments of which the Vikings were so fond. His mail was of chain mesh and his helmet, which lay beside him, was crested with flowing horsehair.

"Well, Cormac," growled the pirate chief, "what think you?"

Cormac Mac Art did not reply directly to his friend. His cold, narrow, grey eyes gazed full into the blue eyes of Donal the minstrel. Donal was a thin man of more than medium height. His wayward unruly hair was yellow. Now he bore neither harp nor sword and his dress was whimsically reminiscent of a court jester. His thin patrician face was as inscrutable at the moment as the sinister scarred features of the Gael.

"I trust you as much as I trust any man," said Cormac. "But I must have more than your mere word on the matter. How do I know that this is not some trick to send us on a wild goose chase, or mayhap into a nest of our enemies? We have business on the east coast of Britain—"

"The matter of which I speak will pay you better than the looting of some pirate's den," answered the minstrel, "If you will come with me, I will bring you to a man who may be able to convince you. But you must come alone, you and Wulfhere."

"A trap," grumbled the Dane. "Donal, I am disappointed in you—"

Cormac, looking deep into the minstrel's strange eyes, shook his head slowly.

"No, Wulfhere; if it be a trap, Donal too is duped and that I cannot believe."

"If you believe that," said Donal, "why can you not believe my mere word in regard to the other matter."

"That is different," answered the reaver. "Here only my life and Wulfhere's is involved. The other concerns every member of our crew. It is my duty to them to require every proof. I do not think you lie; but you may have been lied to."

"Come, then, and I will bring you to one whom you will believe in spite of yourself."

Cormac rose from the great rock whereon he had been sitting, and donned his helmet. Wulfhere, still grumbling and shaking his head, shouted an order to the Vikings who sat grouped about a small fire a short distance away, cooking a haunch of venison. Others were tossing dice in the sand and others still working on the dragon-ship which was drawn up on the beach. Thick forest grew close about this cove and that fact, coupled with the wild nature of the region, made it an ideal place for a pirate's rendezvous.

"All seaworthy and shipshape," grumbled Wulfhere, referring to the galley, "On the morrow we could have sailed forth on the Viking path again—"

"Be at ease, Wulfhere," advised the Gael. "If Donal's man does not make matters sufficiently clear for our satisfaction, we have but to return and take the path."

"Aye—if we return."

"Why, Donal knew of our presence. Had he wished to betray us, he could have led a troop of Gerinth's horsemen upon us, or surrounded us with British bowmen. Donal, at least, I think, means to deal squarely with us as he has done in the past. It is the man behind Donal I mistrust."

The three had left the small bay behind them and now walked along in the shadow of the forest. The land tilted upward rapidly and soon the forest thinned out to straggling clumps and single gnarled oaks that grew between and among huge boulders, broken as if in a Titan's play. The landscape was rugged and wild in the extreme. And at last they rounded a cliff and saw a tall man, wrapped in a purple cloak, standing beneath a mountain oak. He was alone and Donal walked quickly toward him, beckoning his companions to follow. Cormac showed no sign of what he thought, but Wulfhere growled in his beard, as he gripped the shaft of his axe and glanced suspiciously on all sides, as if expecting a horde of swordsmen to burst out of ambush. The three stopped before the silent man and Donal doffed his feathered cap. The man dropped his cloak and Cormac gave a low exclamation.

"By the blood of the gods! King Gerinth himself!"

He made no movement to kneel or to uncover his head, nor did Wulfhere. These wild rovers of the sea acknowledged the rule of no king. Their attitude was the respect accorded a fellow warrior; that was all. There was neither insolence nor deference in their manner, though Wulfhere's eyes did widen slightly as he gazed at the man whose keen brain and matchless valor had for years and against terrific odds stemmed the triumphant march of the Saxons to the Western sea.

The Dane saw a tall, slender man with a weary aristocratic face and kindly grey eyes. Only in his black hair was the Latin strain in his veins evident. Behind him lay the ages of a civilization now crumbled to dust before the onstriding barbarians. He represented the last far-flung remnant of Rome's once mighty empire, struggling on the waves of barbarism which had engulfed the rest of that empire in one red inundation. Cormac, while possessing the true Gaelic antipathy for his Cymric kin in general, sensed the pathos and valor of this brave, vain struggle, and even Wulfhere, looking into the far-seeing eyes of the British king, felt a trifle awed. Here was a people, with their back to the wall, fighting grimly for their lives, and at the same time vainly endeavoring to uphold the culture and ideals of an age already gone forever. The gods of Rome had faded under the ruthless heel of Goth and Vandal. Flaxen-haired savages reigned in the purple halls of the vanished Caesars. Only in this far-flung isle a little band of Romanized Celts clung to the traditions of yesterday.

"These are the warriors, your majesty," said Donal and Gerinth nodded and thanked with the quiet courtesy of a born nobleman.

"They wish to hear again from your lips, what I have told them," said the bard.

"My friends," said the king quietly, "I come to ask your aid. My sister, the princess Helen, a girl of twenty years of age, has been stolen—how, or by whom, I do not know. She rode into the forest one morning attended only by her maid and a page and she did not return. It was on one of those rare occasions when our coasts were peaceful, but when search parties were sent out, they found the page dead and horribly mangled in a small glade deep in the forest. The horses were found later, wandering loose, but of the princess Helen and her maid there was no trace. Nor was there ever a trace found of her, though we combed the kingdom from border to sea. Spies sent among the Angles and Saxons found no sign of her and we at last decided that she had been taken captive and borne away by some wandering band of seafarers, who roaming inland, had seized her and then taken to sea again.

"We are helpless to carry on such a search as must be necessary if she is to be found. We have no ships—the last remnant of the British fleet was destroyed in the sea-fight off Cornwall by the Saxons. And if we had ships, we could not spare the men to man them, not even for the princess Helen. The Angles press hard on our eastern borders and Cerdic's brood raven upon us from the south. In my extremity I appeal to you. I cannot tell you where to look for my sister. I cannot tell you how to recover her if found. I can only say: in the name of God, search the ends of the world for her, and if you find her, return with her and name your price."

Wulfhere glanced at Cormac as he always did in matters that required thought.

"Better that we set a price before we go," grunted the Gael.

"Then you agree?" cried the king, his fine face lighting.

"Not so fast," returned the wary Gael. "Let us first bargain. It is no easy task you set us—to comb the seas for a girl of whom nothing is known save that she was stolen. How if we search the oceans and return empty-handed?"

"Still I will reward you," answered the king, "I have gold in plenty—would I could trade it for warriors—but I have Vortigern's example before me."

"If we go and bring back the princess, alive or dead," said Cormac, "you shall give us a hundred pounds of virgin gold, and ten pounds of gold for each man we lose on the voyage. If we do our best and cannot find the princess, you shall still give us ten pounds for every man slain in the search, but we will waive further reward. We are not Saxons, to haggle over money. Moreover, in either event you will allow us to overhaul our longship in one of your bays, and furnish us with material enough to replace such equipment as may be damaged during the voyage. Is it agreed?"

"You have my word and my hand on it," answered the king, stretching out his arm and as their hands met, Cormac felt the nervous strength in the Briton's fingers.

"You sail at once?"

"As soon as we can return to the cove."

"I will accompany you," said Donal suddenly. "And there is another."

He whistled suddenly and came nearer to sudden decapitation than he guessed; the sound was too much like a signal of attack to leave the wolf-like nerves of the seafarers untouched. Cormac and Wulfhere, however, relaxed as a single man came from the bushes.

"This is Marcus, of a noble British house," said Donal. "The betrothed of the princess Helen. He too will accompany us if he may."

The young man was above medium height and well built. He was in full chain-mail armor and the crested helmet of a legionary, and was girt with a straight thrusting sword. His eyes were grey, but in his black hair and the faint olive-brown tint of his complexion, he showed that the warm blood of the South ran far more strongly in his veins than in those of his king. He was undeniably handsome though now his face was shadowed with worry.

"You will allow me to accompany you, will you not?" he addressed himself to Wulfhere. "The game of war is not unknown to me and even if I were a weakling, this waiting in ignorance of the fate of my promised bride is worse than death."

"Come if you will," growled Wulfhere. "It's like we'll need all the swords we can muster before the cruise is over. King Gerinth, have you no hint whatever of who took the princess?"

"None. We found only a single trace of anything out of the ordinary in the forests. Here it is."

The king drew from his garments a tiny object and passed it to the chieftain. Wulfhere stared unenlightened at the small polished flint arrow head which lay in his huge palm. Cormac took it and looked closely at it. His face was inscrutable but his cold eyes flickered momentarily. Then the Gael said a strange thing:

"I will not shave today, after all."

Chapter 3

The fresh wind filled the sails of the dragon-ship and the rhythmic clack of many oars answered the deep-chested chant of the rowers. Cormac Mac Art, in full armor, the horsehair of his helmet floating in the breeze, leaned on the rail of the poop deck. Wulfhere banged his axe on the deck planking and roared an unnecessary order at the steersman.

"Cormac," said the huge Viking, "who is king of Britain?"

"Who is king of Hades when Pluto is away?" asked the Gael.

"Read me no runes from your knowledge of Roman myths," growled Wulfhere.

"Rome ruled Britain as Pluto rules Hades," answered Cormac. "Now Rome has fallen and the lesser demons are battling among themselves for mastery. Some eighty years ago the legions were withdrawn from Britain when Alaric and his Goths sacked the imperial city. Vortigern was king of Britain then—or rather, made himself so when the Britons had to look for themselves for aid. He let the wolves in, himself, when he hired Hengist and Horsa and their Jutes to fight off the Picts, as you know. The Saxons and Angles poured in after them like a red wave and Vortigern fell. Britain is split into three Celtic kingdoms now, with the pirates holding all the eastern coast and slowly but surely forcing their way westward. The southern kingdom, Damnonia and the country extending to Caer Odun is ruled over by Uther Pendragon. The middle kingdom, from Uther's lines to the foot of the Cumbrian mountains is held by Gerinth. North of his kingdom is the realm known by the Britons as Strath-Clyde—King Garth's domain. His people are the wildest of all the Britons, for many of them are tribes which were never fully conquered by Rome. Also, in the most westwardly tip of Damnonia and among the western mountains of Gerinth's land, are barbaric tribes who never acknowledged Rome and do not now acknowledge either of the three kings. The whole land is a prey to robbers and bandits and the three kings are not always at peace among themselves, owing to Uther's waywardness, which is tinged with madness, and Garth's innate savagery. Were it not that Gerinth acts as a buffer between them, they would have been at each others' throats long ago.

"As it is they seldom act in concert, for long. The Jutes, Angles and Saxons who assail them are forever at war among themselves also, as you know, but a never-ending supply streams across the Narrow Seas in their long, low galleys."

"As well I know," growled the Dane, "having sent some score of those galleys to Midgaard. Some day my own people will come and take Britain from them."

"It is a land worth fighting for," responded the Gael. "What think you of the men we have shipped aboard?"

"Donal we know of old. He can tear the heart from my breast with his harp when he is so minded, or make me a boy again. And in a pinch we know he can wield a sword. As for the Roman—" so Wulfhere termed Marcus, "he has the look of a seasoned warrior."

"His ancestors were commanders of British legions for three centuries and before that they trod the battlefields of Gaul and Italy with Caesar. It is but the remnant of Roman strategy lingering in the British knights that have enabled them to beat back the Saxons thus far. But Wulfhere, what think you of my beard?" The Gael rubbed the bristly stubble that covered his face.

"I never saw you so unkempt before," grunted the Dane, "save when we had fled or fought for days so you could not be hacking at your face with a razor."

"It will hide my scars in a few days," grinned Cormac. "When I told you to head for Ara in Dalriadia did naught occur to you?"

"Why, I assumed you would ask for news of the princess among the wild Scots there."

"And why did you suppose I would expect them to know?"

Wulfhere shrugged his shoulders. "I am done seeking to reason out your actions."

Cormac drew from his pouch the flint arrowhead. "In all the British Isles there is but one race who makes such points for their arrows. They are the Picts of Caledonia, who ruled these isles before the Celts came, in the age of stone. Even now they tip their arrows often with flint, as I learned when I fought under King Gol of Dalriadia. There was a time, soon after the legions left Britain, when the Picts ranged like wolves clear to the southern coast. But the Jutes and Angles and Saxons drove them back into the heather country, and for so long has King Garth served as a buffer between them and Gerinth that he and his people have forgotten their ways."

"Then you think Picts stole the princess? But how did they—"

"That is for me to learn; that's why we are heading for Ara. The Dalriadians and the Picts have been alternately fighting with each other and against each other for over a hundred years. Just now there is peace between them and the Scots are likely to know much of what goes on in the Dark Empire as the Pictish kingdom is called—and dark it is, and strange. For these Picts come of an old, old race and their ways are beyond our ken."

"And we will capture a Scot and question him?"

Cormac shook his head. "I will go ashore and mingle with them; they are of my race and language."

"And when they recognize you," grunted Wulfhere, "they will hang you to the highest tree. They have no cause to love you. True, you fought under King Gol in your early youth, but since then you have raided Dalriadia's coasts more than once—not only with your Irish reavers, but with me, likewise."

"And that is why I am growing a beard, old sea-dragon," laughed the Gael.

Chapter 4

Night had fallen over the rugged western coast of Caledon. Eastward loomed against the stars the distant mountains; westward the dark seas stretched away to uncharted gulfs and unknown shores. The *Raven* rode at anchor on the northern side of a wild and rugged promontory that ran out into the sea, hugging close those beetling cliffs. Under cover of darkness Cormac had steered her inshore, threading the treacherous reefs of that grim shore with a knowledge born of long experience. Cormac Mac Art was Erin born, but all the isles of the Western Sea had been his stamping ground since the day he had been able to lift his first sword.

"And now," said Cormac, "I go ashore—alone."

"Let me go with you!" cried Marcus, eagerly, but the Gael shook his head.

"Your appearance and accent would betray us both. Nor can you either, Donal, for though I know the kings of the Scots have listened to your harp, you are the only one besides myself who knows this coast and if I fail to return you must take her out."

The Gael's appearance was vastly altered. A thick short beard masked his features, concealing his scars. He had laid aside his horsehair-crested helmet and his finely worked mail shirt, and had donned the round helmet and crude scale-mail corselet of the Dalriadians. The arms of many nations were part of the *Raven's* cargo.

"Well, old sea-wolf," said he with a wicked grin, as he prepared to lower himself over the rail, "you have said nothing but I see a gleam in your eyes; do you also wish to accompany me? Surely the Dalriadians could have nothing but welcome for so kind a friend who has burnt their villages and sunk their hide-bottomed boats."

Wulfhere cursed him heartedly. "We seafarers are so well loved by the Scots that my red beard alone would be enough to hang me. But even so, were I not captain of this ship, and my duty to it, I'd chance it rather than see you go into danger alone, and you such an empty-headed fool!"

Cormac laughed deeply. "Wait for me until dawn," he instructed, "and no longer."

Then dropping from the after rail he struck out for the shore, swimming strongly in spite of his mail and weapons. He swam along the base of the cliffs and presently found a shelving ledge from which a steep incline led upward. It might have taxed the agility of a mountain goat to have made the ascent there, but Cormac was not inclined to make the long circuit about the promontory. He climbed straight upward and after a considerable strain of energy and skill, he gained the top of the cliffs and made his way along them to the point where they joined a steep ridge on the mainland. Down the southern slope of this he made his way toward the distant twinkle of fires that marked the Dalriadian town of Ara.

He had not taken half a dozen steps when a sound behind him brought him about, blade at the ready. A huge figure bulked dimly in the starlight.

"Hrut! What in the name of seven devils—"

"Wulfhere sent me after you," rumbled the big carle. "He feared harm might come to you."

Cormac was a man of irascible temper. He cursed Hrut and Wulfhere impartially. Hrut listened stolidly and Cormac knew the futility of arguing with him. The big Dane was a silent, moody creature whose mind had been slightly affected by a sword cut on the head. But he was brave and loyal and his skill at woodcraft was second only to Cormac's.

"Come along," Cormac concluded his tirade. "But you cannot come into the village with me. You understand that you must hide outside the walls?"

The carle nodded, and motioning him to follow, Cormac took up his way at a steady trot. Hrut followed swiftly and silently as a ghost for all his bulk. Cormac went swiftly, for he would be crowded indeed to accomplish what he had set out to do, and return to the dragon-ship by midday. But he went warily for he expected momentarily to meet a party of warriors, leaving or returning from the town. But luck was with him, and soon he crouched among the trees within arrow shot of the village.

"Hide here," he whispered to Hrut. "On no account come any nearer the town. If you hear a brawl, wait until an hour to dawn, and if you have heard naught from me, go back to Wulfhere. Do you understand?"

The usual nod was the answer and as Hrut faded back among the trees, Cormac went boldly toward the village. Ara was built close to the shore of a small, landlocked bay and Cormac saw the crude hide coracles of the Dalriadians drawn up on the beach. In these they swept south in fierce raids on the Britons and Saxons, or crossed to Ulster for supplies and reinforcements. Ara was more of an army camp than a town, the real seat of Dalriadia lying some distance inland. The village was not a particularly imposing-looking place, with its few hundred wattle and mud huts surrounded by a low wall of rough stones, but Cormac knew the temper of its inhabitants. What the Caledonian Gaels lack in wealth and armament they made up in unquenchable ferocity. A hundred years of ceaseless conflict with Pict, Roman, Briton and Saxon had left them little opportunity to cultivate the natural seeds of civilization that was their heritage from their native land. The Gaels of Caledonia had gone backward a step; they were behind their Irish cousins in culture and artisanship, but they had not lost an iota of the Gaelic fighting fury.

Their ancestors had come into Caledonia from Ulahd into which they had been driven by a stronger tribe of the southern Irish. Cormac, born in what was later known as Connacht, was a son of these conquerors, and felt himself not only distinct from these transplanted Gaels, but from their cousins in northern Erin. Still, he had spent enough time among these people to deceive them, he felt.

He strode up to the crude gate and shouted for entrance before he was perceived by the guard, who were prone to be lax in their vigilance in the face of apparent quietude—a universal Celtic trait. A harsh voice ordered him to stand still, while a torch thrust above the gate shone its flickering light full on him. In its illumination Cormac could see, framed above the gate, fierce faces with unkempt beards and cold grey or blue eyes.

"Who are you?" one of the guards demanded.

"Partha Mac Othna, of Ulahd. I have come to take service under your chief, Eochaidh Mac Ailbe."

"Your garments are dripping wet."

"An they were not it would be a marvel," answered Cormac. "There was a boat load of us set sail from Ulahd this morning. On the way a Saxon sea rover ran us down and all but I perished in the waves and the arrows the pirates rained upon us. I caught a piece of the broken mast and essayed to float."

"And what of the Saxon?"

"I saw the sails disappear southward. Mayhap they raid the Britons."

"How is it that the guard along the beach did not see you when you finally came ashore?"

"I made shore more than a mile to the south and glimpsing the lights through the trees, came here. I have been here aforetime and knew it to be Ara, whither I was bound."

"Let him in," growled one of the Dalriadians, "His tale rings true."

The clumsy gate swung open and Cormac entered the fortified camp of his hereditary foes. Fires blazed between the huts and gathered close about the gate was the curious throng who had heard the guard challenge Cormac. Men, women and children partook of the wildness and savagery of their hard country. The women, splendidly built amazons, with loose-flowing hair, stared at him curiously, and dirty-faced, half-naked children peered at him from under shocks of tangled hair. And Cormac noted that each held a weapon of sorts. Brats scarcely able to toddle held a stone or a piece of wood. This symbolized the fierce life they led, when even the very babes had learned to snatch up a weapon at the first hint of alarm—aye, and to fight like wounded wildcats if need be. Cormac noted the fierceness of the people, their lean, hard savagery. No wonder Rome had never broken these people!

Some fifteen years had passed since Cormac had fought in the ranks of these ferocious warriors. He had no fear of being recognized by any of his former comrades. Nor, with his thick beard as a disguise, did he expect recognition as Wulfhere's comrade.

Cormac followed the warrior who led him toward the largest hut in the village. This, the pirate was sure, housed the chieftain and his folk. There was no elegance in Caledonia. King Gol's palace was a wattled hut. Cormac smiled to himself as he compared this village with the cities he had seen in his wanderings. But it was not walls and towers that made a city, he reflected, but the people within.

He was escorted into the great hut where a score of warriors were drinking from leather jacks about a crudely carved table. At the head sat the chief, known to Cormac of old, and at his elbow the inevitable minstrel—a characteristic of Celtic court life, however crude the court. Cormac involuntarily compared this skin-clad shock-headed kern to the cultured and chivalrous Donal.

"Son of Ailbe," said Cormac's escort, "here is a weapon-man from Erin who wishes to take service under you."

"Who is your chief?" hiccupped Eochaidh and Cormac saw that the Dalriadian was drunk.

"I am a free wanderer," answered the Wolf. "Aforetime I followed the bows of Donn Ruadh Mac Finn, flaith na Ulahd."

"Sit ye down and drink," ordered Eochaidh with an uncertain wave of his hairy hand. "Later I will talk with you."

No more attention was paid to Cormac, except the Scots made a place for him and a shock-headed gilly filled his cup with the fiery potheen so relished by the Gaels. The wolf's ranging eye took in all the details of the scene, passed casually over the Dalriadian fighting men and rested long on two men who sat almost opposite him. One of these Cormac knew—he was a renegade Norseman, Sigrel by name, who had found sanctuary among the foes of his race. Cormac's pulse quickened as he caught the evil eyes of the man fixed narrowly on him, but the sight of the man beside the Norseman made him forget Sigrel for the moment.

The man was short and strongly made. He was dark, much darker than Cormac himself, and from a face as immobile as an idol's. Two black eyes glittered reptile-like. His square-cut black hair was caught back and confined by a narrow silver band about his temples and he wore only a loincloth and a broad leather girdle from which hung a short barbed sword. A Pict! Cormac's heart leaped. He had intended drawing Eochaidh into conversation at once, and by the means of a tale he had already fabricated, to draw from him any information he might have of the whereabouts of the princess Helen. But the Dalriadian chief was too drunk for that now. He roared barbaric songs, pounded the board with his sword hilt in accompaniment to the wild strains of his minstrel's harp, and between times guzzled potheen at an astounding rate. All were drunk—all save Cormac and Sigrel, who furtively eyed the Gael over the rim of his goblet.

While Cormac racked his brain for a convincing way of drawing the Pict into conversation, the minstrel concluded one of his wild chants with a burst of sound and a rhyme that named Eochaidh Mac Ailbe, "Wolf of Alba, greatest of raven-saters!"

The Pict reeled drunkenly to his feet, dashing his drinking jack down on the board. The Picts habitually drank a smooth ale made from the heather blossom. The fiery barley malt brewed by the Gaels maddened them. This particular Pict's brain was on fire. His face, no longer immobile, writhed demoniacally and his eyes glowed like coals of black fire.

"True, Eochaidh Mac Ailbe is a great warrior," he cried in his barbaric Gaelic, "But even he is not the greatest warrior in Caledonia! Who is greater than King Brogar, the Dark One, who rules the ancient throne of Pictdom? And next to him is Grulk! I am Grulk the Skull-cleaver! In my house in Grothga there is a mat woven of the scalps of Britons, Angles, Saxons—aye, and Scots!"

Cormac shrugged his shoulders in impatience. The drunken boastings of this savage would be likely to bring him a sword-thrust from the drink-fired Scots, that would cut off all chance of learning anything from him. But the Pict's next words electrified the Gael.

"Who of all Caledonia has taken a more beautiful woman from the southern Britons than Grulk?" he shouted, reeling and glaring. "There were five of us in the hide-bottomed boat the gale blew southward. We went ashore in Gerinth's realm for fresh water. And there we came upon three Britons deep in the forest—one lad and two beautiful maidens. The boy showed fight, but I, Grulk, leaping upon his shoulders, bore him to earth and disemboweled him with my sword. The women we took into our boat and fled northward and gained the coast of Caledonia and took the women to Grothga!"

"Words and empty words," sneered Cormac, leaning across the table. "There are no such women in Grothga now!" Taking a long chance.

The Pict howled like a wolf and fumbled drunkenly for his sword.

"When old Gonar, the high priest, looked on the face of the most finely dressed one—she who called herself Atalanta—he cried out that she was sacred to the moon god—that the symbol was upon her breast, though none but he could see. So he sent her, with the other, Marcia, to the Isle of Altars, in the Shetlands, in a long boat the Scots lent him, with fifteen warriors. The girl Atalanta is the daughter of a British nobleman and she will be acceptable in the eyes of Golka of the moon."

"How long since they departed for the Shetlands?" asked Cormac, as the Pict showed signs of making a quarrel of it.

"Three weeks; the night of The Nuptuals of the Moon is not yet. But you said I lied—"

"Drink and forget it," growled a warrior, thrusting a brimming goblet at him. The Pict seized it with both hands and thrust his face into the liquor, guzzling ravenously, while the liquid slopped down on his bare chest. Cormac rose from his bench. He had learned all he wished to know, and he believed the Scots were too drunk to notice his casual departure from the hut. Outside it might be a different matter to get past the wall. But no sooner had he risen than another was on his feet. Sigrel the renegade Viking came around the table toward him.

"What, Partha," he said maliciously, "is your thirst so soon satisfied?"

Suddenly he thrust out a hand and pushed back the Gael's helmet from his brows. Cormac angrily struck his hand away, and Sigrel leaped back with a yell of ferocious triumph.

"Eochaidh! Men of Caledonia! A thief and a liar is among you!"

The drunken warriors gaped stupidly.

"This is Cormac *an Cliuin,*" shouted Sigrel, reaching for his sword, "Cormac Mac Art, the reaver, comrade of Wulfhere the Viking!"

Cormac moved with the volcanic quickness of a wounded tiger. Steel flashed in the flickering torchlight and Sigrel's head rolled grinning beneath the feet of the astounded revelers. A single bound carried the reaver to the door and he vanished while the Scots were struggling to their feet, roaring bewilderedly and tugging at their swords.

In an instant the whole village was in an uproar. Men had seen Cormac leap from the chief's hut with his red-stained sword in his hand and they gave chase without asking the reason for his flight. The partially sobered feasters came tumbling out of the hut yelling and cursing and when they shouted the real identity of their erstwhile guest, a thunderous roar of rage went up and the whole village joined vengefully in the chase.

Cormac, weaving in and out among the huts like a flying shadow, came to an unguarded point of the wall, and without slackening his headlong gait, cleared the low barrier with a bound and raced toward the forest. A quick glance over his shoulder showed him that his escape had been seen. Warriors were swarming over the wall, weapons in their hands.

It was some distance to the first thick tangle of trees. Cormac took it full speed, running low and momentarily expecting an arrow between his shoulders. But the Dalriadians had no skill at archery and he reached the fringe of the forest unscathed.

He had outfooted the fleet Caledonians, all save one who had distanced his fellows by a hundred yards and was now close upon the reaver's heels. Cormac wheeled to dispose of this single foe, and even as he turned a stone rolled under his foot and flung him to his knee. He flung up his blade to block the sword that hovered over him like the shadow of Doom, but before it could fall, a giant shape catapulted from the trees, a heavy sword crashed down, and the Scot fell limply across Cormac, his skull shattered.

The Gael flung off the corpse and leaped to his feet. The yelling pursuers were close now, and Hrut, snarling like a wild beast, faced them, but Cormac seized his wrist and dragged him back among the trees. The next instant they were fleeing in the direction from which they had first come to Ara, ducking and dodging among the trees.

Behind them, and presently on either side they heard the crashing of men through the underbrush and savage yells. Hundreds of warriors had joined in the hunt of their archenemy. Cormac and Hrut slackened their speed and went warily, keeping in the deep shadows, flitting from tree to tree, now lying prone in the bushes to let a band of searchers go by. They had progressed some little distance when Cormac was galvanized by the deep baying of hounds far behind them.

"We are ahead of our pursuers now, I think," muttered the Gael. "We might make a dash of it and gain the ridge and from thence the promontory and the ship. But they have loosed the wolf hounds on our trail and if we take that way, we will lead them and the warriors straight to Wulfhere's ship. There are enough of them to swim out and board her and take her by storm. We must swim for it."

Cormac turned westward, almost at right angles to the course they had been following and they quickened their pace recklessly. And emerging into a small glade ran full into three Dalriadians who assailed them with yells. Evidently they had not been ahead of their hunters as far as Cormac had thought, and the Gael hurling himself fiercely into the fray, knew that the fight must be short or else the sound would bring scores of warriors hastening to the spot.

One of the Scots engaged Cormac while the other two fell upon the giant Hrut. A buckler turned Cormac's first vicious thrust and the Dalriadian's sword beat down on his helmet, biting through the metal and into the scalp beneath. But before the warrior could strike again, Cormac's sword cut his left leg from under him, through the knee, and as he crumpled another stroke shore through his neck cords.

In the meantime Hrut had killed one of his opponents with a bear-like stroke that rended the upflung shield as though it had been paper and crushed the skull it sought to guard, and as Cormac turned to aid him, the remaining foe leaped in with the desperate recklessness of a dying wolf, and it seemed to the Gael that his stabbing sword sank halfway to the hilt in the Dane's mighty bosom. But Hrut gripped the Scot's throat in his huge left hand, thrust him away and struck a blow that shore through corselet and ribs and left the broken blade wedged in the dead man's spinal column.

"Are you hurt badly, Hrut?" Cormac was at his side, striving to undo the Dane's rent corselet so that he might staunch the flow of blood. But the carle pushed him away.

"A scratch," he said thickly. "I've broken my sword—let us haste."

Cormac cast a doubtful look at his companion, then turned and hurried on in the direction they had been following. Seeing that Hrut followed with apparent ease, and hearing the baying of the hounds grow nearer, Cormac increased his gait until the two were running fleetly through the midnight forest. At length they heard the lapping of the sea, and even as Hrut's breathing grew heavy and labored they emerged upon a steep rocky shore, where the trees overhung the water. To the north, jutting out into the sea could be seen the vague bulk of the promontory behind which lay the *Raven*. Three miles of rugged coast lay between the promontory and the bay of Ara. Cormac and Hrut were at a point a little over halfway between, and slightly nearer the promontory than the bay.

"We swim from here," growled Cormac, "and it's a long swim to Wulfhere's ship, around the end of the promontory—for the cliffs are too steep to climb on this side—but we can make it and the hounds can't follow our tracks in the water—what in the name of the gods—"

Hrut had reeled and pitched headlong the steep bank, his hands trailing in the water. Cormac reached him instantly and turned him on his back; but the Dane's fierce face was already set. Cormac tore open his corselet and felt beneath it for an instant, then withdrew his hand and swore in amazement at the vitality that had enabled the carle to run for nearly half a mile with that terrible wound beneath his heart. The Gael hesitated, then to his ears came the deep baying of the hounds.

With a bitter curse he tore off his helmet and corselet and threw them aside, kicking off his sandals. Drawing his sword belt up another notch he waded out into the water and then struck out strongly.

In the darkness before dawn Wulfhere, pacing the deck of his dragon-ship, heard a faint sound that was not the lapping of the waves against the hull or the cliffs. With a quick word to his comrades, the Dane stepped to the rail and peered over. Marcus and Donal pressed close behind him, and presently saw a ghostly figure clamber out of the water and up the side. Cormac Mac Art, bloodstained and half naked, clambered over the rail and snarled:

"Out oars, wolves, and pull for the open sea, before we have half a thousand Dalriadians on our backs! And head her prow for the Shetlands—the Picts have taken Gerinth's sister there."

"Where's Hrut?" rumbled Wulfhere, as Cormac started toward the sweep-head.

"Drive a brass nail into the main mast," snarled the Gael. "Gerinth owes us ten pounds already."

The bitterness in his eyes belied the harsh callousness of his words.

Chapter 5

Marcus paced the deck of the dragon-ship. The wind filled the sails and the long ash oars of the rowers sent the long lean craft hurtling through the water but to the impatient Briton it seemed that they moved at a snail's pace.

"But why did the Pict call her Atalanta?" he cried, turning to Cormac, "True, her maid was named Marcia—but we have no real proof that the woman with her is the princess Helen."

"We have all the proof in the world," answered the Gael. "Do you think the princess would admit her true identity to her abductors? If they knew they held Gerinth's sister, they would have half his kingdom as ransom."

"But what did the Pict mean by the Nuptials of the Moon?"

Wulfhere looked at Cormac and Cormac started to speak, shot a quick glance at Marcus and hesitated.

"Tell him," nodded Donal. "He must know eventually."

"The Picts worship strange and abhorrent gods," said the Gael. "As is well known to we who roam the sea, eh Wulfhere?"

"Right," growled the giant. "Many a Viking has died on their altar stones."

"One of their gods is Golka of the Moon. Every so often they present a captured virgin of high rank to him. On a strange, lonely isle in the Shetlands stands a grim black altar, surrounded by columns of stone, such as you have seen at Stonehenge. On that altar when the moon is full, the girl is sacrificed to Golka."

Marcus shuddered; his nails bit into his palms.

"Gods of Rome, can such things be?"

"Rome has fallen," grunted the Skull-splitter, "Her gods are dead. They will not aid us. But fear not." He lifted his gleaming, keen edged axe. "Here is that which will aid us! Let me lead my wolves into the stone circle and we will give Golka such a blood-sacrifice as he has never dreamed of!"

"Sail on the port bow!" came the sudden shout of the lookout in the cross-trees. Wulfhere wheeled suddenly, beard bristling. A few moments later all on board could make out the long low lines of the strange craft.

"A dragon-ship," swore Cormac, "and making full speed with oar and sail—she means to cut across our bows, Wulfhere."

The chieftain swore, his cold blue eyes beginning to blaze. His whole body quivered with eagerness and a new roaring note came into the voice that bellowed commands to his crew.

"By the bones of Thor, he must be a fool! But we'll give him his fill!"

Marcus caught the Dane's mighty arm and swung him about.

"Our mission is not to fight every sea-thief we meet," the Briton cried angrily. "You were engaged to search for the princess Helen; we must not jeopardize this expedition. Now we have at last a clue; will you throw away our chances merely to glut your foolish lust for battle?"

Wulfhere's eyes flamed.

"This to me on my own deck?" he roared. "I'll not show my stern to any rover for Gerinth and all his gold! If its fight he wants, its fight he'll get."

"The lad's right, Wulfhere," said Cormac quietly. "But by the blood of the gods we'll have to run for it, for yon ship is aimed straight for us and I see a running about on the deck that can mean naught but preparation for a sea-fight."

"And run we cannot," said Wulfhere in deep satisfaction. "For I know her—that ship is Rudd Thorwald's *Fire-Woman,* and he is my life-long enemy. She is as fleet as the *Raven* and if we flee we will have her hanging on our stern all the way to the Shetlands. We must fight!"

"Then let us make it short and desperate," snapped Cormac,

scowling. "There's scant use in trying to ram her; run alongside and we'll take her by storm."

"I was born in a sea-fight, and I sank dragon-ships before I ever saw you," roared Wulfhere, "Take the sweep-head." He turned to Marcus. "Hast ever been in a sea-brawl, youngster?"

"No, but if I fail to go further than you can lead, hang me to your dragon-beak!" snapped the angered Briton.

Wulfhere's cold eyes glinted in amused appreciation, as he turned away.

There was little maneuvering of ships in that primitive age. The Vikings attained the seacraft they had in a later day. The long, low serpents of the sea drove straight for each other, while warriors lined the sides of each, yelling and clashing sword on shield.

Marcus, leaning on the rail, glanced at the wolfish warriors beside and below him, and glanced across the intervening waves at the fierce, light-eyed, yellow-bearded Vikings who lined the sides of the opposing galley—Jutes they were, and hereditary enemies of the red-maned Danes. The young Briton shuddered involuntarily, not from fear but because of the innate, ruthless savagery of the scene, as a man might shudder at a pack of ravening wolves, without fearing them.

And now there came a giant twanging of bowstrings and a rain of death leaped through the air. Here the Danes had the advantage; they were the bowmen of the North Sea. The Jutes, like their Saxon cousins, knew little of archery. Arrows came whistling back but their flight lacked the deadly accuracy of the Danish shafts. Marcus saw men go down in windrows aboard the Jutish craft, while the rest crouched behind the shields that lined the sides. The three men at the sweep-head fell and the long sweep swung in a wide erratic arc; the galley lost way and Marcus saw a blond giant he instinctively knew to be Rudd Thorwald himself, leap to the sweep-head. Arrows rattled off his mail like hailstornes, and then the two crafts ran alongside with a rending and crashing of oars and a grinding of timbers.

The wolf-yell of the Vikings split the skies and in an instant all was a red chaos. The grappling hooks bit in, gripping keel to keel. Shields locked, the double line writhed and rocked as each crew sought to beat the other back from its bulwarks and gain the opposing deck. Marcus, thrusting and parrying with a wild-eyed giant across the rails, saw in a quick glance over his foe's shoulder, Rudd Thorwald rushing from the sweep-head to the rail. Then his straight sword was through the Jute's throat and he flung one leg over the rail. But before he could leap into the other ship, another howling devil was hacking and hewing at him, and only a shield suddenly flung above his head saved his life. It was Donal the minstrel who had come to his aid.

Toward the waist of the ship, Wulfhere surged on through the fray and one mighty sweep of his great axe cleared a space for him for an instant. In that instant he was over the rail on the deck of the *Fire-Woman* and Cormac, Thorfinn, Edric and Snorri were close behind him. Snorri died the moment his feet touched the *Fire-Woman's* deck and a second later a Juttish axe split Edric's skull, but already the Danes were pouring through the breach made in the lines of the defenders and in a moment the Jutes were fighting with their backs to the wall.

On the blood-slippery deck the two Viking chieftains met. Wulfhere's axe hewed the shaft of Rudd Thorwald's spear in twain, but before the Dane could strike again, the Jute snatched a sword from a dying hand and the edge bit through Wulfhere's corselet over his ribs. In an instant the Skull-splitter's mail was dyed red, but with a mad roar he swung his axe in a two-handed stroke that rent Rudd Thorwald's armor like paper and cleft through shoulder bone and spine. The Juttish chief fell dead in a red welter of blood and the Juttish warriors, disheartened, fell back, fighting desperately.

The Dane yelled with fierce delight. But the battle was not over. The Jutes knowing there was no mercy for the losers of a sea-fight, battled stubornly. Marcus was in the thick of it, with Donal close at his side. A strange madness had gripped the young Briton. To his mind, distorted momentarily by the fury of the fray, it seemed that these Jutes were holding him back from Helen. They stood in his way and while he and his comrades wasted time with them, Helen might be in desperate need of rescue. A red haze burned before Marcus' eyes and his sword wove a web of death in front of him. A huge Jute dented his shield with a sweeping axe-head and Marcus flung his shield away, ripping the warrior open with the other hand.

"By the blood of the gods," Cormac rasped, "I never heard before that Romans went berserk, but—"

Marcus had forced his way over the corpse littered benches to the poop. A sword battered down on his helm as he leaped upward but he paid no heed; even as he thrust mechanically, his eyes fell on a strangely incongruous ornament suspended from the Jute's bull neck from a slender golden chain. On the end of that chain glittering against his broad mailed chest hung a tiny jewel—a single ruby carved in the symbol of the acanthus. Marcus cried out like a man with a death under his heart and like a madman plunged in blindly, scarcely knowing what he did. He felt his blade sink deep and the force of his charge hurled him to the poop deck on top of his victim.

Struggling to his knees, oblivious to the Hell of battle about him, Marcus tore the jewel from the pirate's neck and pressed it to his lips. Then he gripped the Jute's shoulders fiercely.

"Quick!" he cried in the tongue of the Angles, which the Jutes understood. "Tell me, before I rend the heart from your breast, tell me whence you got this gem!"

The Jute's eyes were already glazing. He was past acting on his own initiative. He heard an insistent voice questioning him, and answered dully, scarcely knowing that he did so: "From one of the girls we took—from the—Pictish boat."

Marcus shook him in agony: "What of them? Where are they?"

Cormac, seeing something was forward, had broken from the fight and now bent, with Donal, over the dying pirate.

"We—sold—them—" muttered the Jute in a fading whisper. "To—Thorleif Hordi's son—at—"

His head fell back; the voice ceased.

Marcus looked up at Donal with pain-haunted eyes.

"Look, Donal," he cried, holding up the chain with the ruby pendant. "See? It is Helen's! I myself gave it to her—she and Marcia were on this very ship—but now—who is this Thorleif Hordi's son?"

"Easy to say," broke in Cormac. "He is a Norse reaver who has established himself in the Hebrides. Be of good cheer, young sir; Helen is better off in the hands of the Vikings than in those of the Pictish savages of the Hjaltlands."

"But surely we must waste no time now!" cried Marcus. "The gods have cast this knowledge into out hands; if we tarry we may again be put upon a false scent!"

Wulfhere and his Danes had cleared the poop and waste, but on the after deck the survivors still stubbornly contended with their conquerors. There was scant mercy shown in a sea-fight of that age. Had the Jutes been victorious they would have spared none; nor did they expect or ask for mercy.

Cormac made his way through the waist of the ship where dead and dying lay heaped, and struggled his way through the yelling Danes to where Wulfhere stood plying his dripping axe. By main force he tore the Skull-splitter from his prey and jerked him about.

"Have done, old wolf," he growled. "The fight is won; Rudd Thorwald is dead. Would you waste steel on these miserable carles?"

"I leave this ship when no Jute remains alive!" thundered the battle-maddened Dane. Cormac laughed grimly.

"Have done! Bigger game is afoot! These Jutes will drink blood before you slaughter them all and we will need every man before the faring is over. From the lips of a dying Jute we have heard it—the princess is in the steading of Thorleif Hordi's son, in the Hebrides."

Wulfhere's beard bristled with ferocious joy. So many were his foes that it was hard to name a Viking farer with whom he had no feud.

"Is it so? Then, ho, wolves, leave the rest of these sea-rats to drown or swim as they will! We go to burn Thorleif Hordi's son's skalli over his head!"

Slowly, by words and blows, he beat his raging Danes off and marshalling them together, drove them over the gunwales into their own ship. The bleeding, battle weary Jutes watched them go, leaning on their reddened weapons in sullen silence. The toll taken had been terrific, but by far the greater loss had been aboard the *Fire-Woman.* From stem to stern dead men wallowed among the broken benches in a welter of crimson.

"Ho, rats!" Wulfhere shouted, as his Vikings cast off and the oars of the *Raven* began to ply. "I leave you your blood-gutted craft and the carrion that was Rudd Thorwald. Make the best you can of them and thank the gods that I spared your lives!"

The losers harkened in sullen silence, answering only with black scowls, all save one, a lean, wolfish figure of a warrior, who brandished a notched and bloody axe and shouted: "Mayhap you will curse the gods, someday, Skull-splitter, because you spared Halfgar Wolf's-tooth!"

It was a name, in sooth, that Wulfhere had cause to remember well in later days. But now the chief merely roared in laughter though Cormac frowned.

"It is a foolish thing to taunt beaten men, Wulfhere," said he. "But you have a nasty cut across your ribs. Let me see to it."

Marcus turned away with the gem that Helen had worn. The flood of savagery during the last few hours left him dazed and weary. But he had discovered strange, dark deeps in his own soul. A few minutes of fierce swordplay on the gunwales of a sea rover had sufficed to bridge the gap of three centuries. Coolness in action, a characteristic drilled into his forebears by countless Roman officers, and inherited by him, had been swept away in an instant before the wild, old Celtic fury before which Caesar had staggered on the Ceanntish beaches. For a few mad moments he had been one with the wild men about him. The shadows of Rome were fading; was he too, like all the world, reverting to the nature of his British ancestors, blood-brothers in savagery to Wulfhere Skull-splitter?

Chapter 6

"It is not far from here to Kaldjorn where Thorleif Hordi's son has built his steading," said Cormac glancing abstractedly at the mast where now sixteen brass nails gleamed dully.

The Norse were already establishing themselves in the Hebrides, the Orkneys and the Shetlands. Later these movements became permanent colonizations. At this time, however, their steadings were merely pirate camps.

"The Sudeyar lie to the east, just out of sight over the sea rim. We must resort to craft again. Thorleif Hordi's son has four longships and three hundred carles. We have one ship and less than eighty men. We cannot do as Wulfhere wishes—go ashore and burn Thorleif's skalli. And he will not be likely to give up such a prize as the princess Helen without a battle.

"This is what I suggest. Thorleif's steading is on the east side of the isle of Kaldjorn, which luckily is a small one. We will draw in under cover of night, on the west side. There are high cliffs there and the ship should be safe from detection for a time, since none of Thorleif's folk have any reason to wander about on the western part of the island. Then I will go ashore and seek to steal the princess."

Wulfhere laughed: "You will find it a more difficult matter to hoax the Norse than you did the Scots. Your looks will brand you as a Gael and they will cut the blood-eagle in your back."

"I will creep among them like a serpent and they will know naught of my coming," answered the Gael. "Your Norseman is a very dullard when it comes to stealth, and easy to deceive."

"I will go with you," broke in Marcus. "This time I will not be denied."

"While I must gnaw my thumb on the west side of the isle," grumbled Wulfhere enviously.

"Wait," said Donal. "I have a better plan, Cormac."

[...]

The Temple of Abomination
Early Draft

"Easy all," grunted Wulfhere Hausakliufr, "I see the glimmer of a stone building through the trees—Thor's blood, Cormac, are you leading us into a trap?"

The tall Gael shook his head, a frown darkening his sinister, scarred face.

"I never heard of a castle in these parts—the British tribes hereabouts don't build in stone—it may be an old Roman ruin—"

Wulfhere hesitated, glancing back at the compact lines of red-bearded, horn-helmed warriors. "Maybe we'd best send out a scout—"

Cormac Mac Art laughed jeeringly. "You barbarians still start at the name of Rome, and Alaric led his Goths through the Forum fifty years ago. Fear not, there are no legions in Britain—I think that is a Druidic temple. We have nothing to fear from them—we are moving against their hereditary enemies."

"And Cerdic's brood will howl like wolves when we strike them from the west instead of the south or east," grinned the huge Dane. "It was a crafty idea of yours, Cormac, to hide our dragon-ship on the west coast of Britain and march straight through British country to fall on the Saxons. But it's mad, too."

"There's method in my madness," responded the Gael. "I know that there are few warriors hereabouts; most of the chiefs are gathering about Arthur Pendragon for a great concerted drive. Pendragon! He's no more Uther Pendragon's son than you are. Uther was a black-bearded madman—more Roman than Briton and more Gaul than Roman. Arthur's as fair as Thorfinn there, but there's no hint of red in his hair and beard. And he's pure Celt—a waif from one of the wild western tribes that never bowed to Rome. It was Lancelot who put it into his head to make himself king."

"Is he smooth and polished like the Romans were?"

"Arthur? Ha! One of your Danes would look like a gentlewoman beside him. He's a shock-headed savage with a love for battle." Cormac grinned ferociously and touched his scars, "By the blood of the gods, he has a hungry sword! It's little gain we reavers from Erin have gotten on his coasts!"

"Would I could cross steel with him," grunted Wulfhere, thumbing the edge of his great axe. "What of Lancelot?"

"A renegade Gallo-Roman who has made an art of throat-cutting. He varies reading Petronius with plotting and intriguing. Gawaine is a pure-blooded Briton like Arthur, but he has Romanesque leanings. It's absurd to see him aping Lancelot—but he fights like a blood-hungry devil. Without these two Arthur would have been no more than a petty chieftain. He can neither read nor write."

"What has that to do with it?" rumbled the Dane. "Neither can I—there's the temple."

They had entered the tall grove in whose shadows crouched the small squat building, that seemed to leer out at them from behind a screening row of columns.

"I thought these Britons were mostly of a new sect called Christians," growled Wulfhere.

"The Romano-British mongrels are," assented Cormac. "The pure Celts hold to the old gods, as we of Erin. By the blood of the gods, we Gaels will never turn Christian while one Druid lives."

"What do these Christians?" asked Wulfhere curiously.

"They eat babies. What else, I do not know."

"But the Druids burn men in cages of green wood."

"A lie spread by Caesar and believed by fools," rasped Cormac impatiently. "Wait here—I'm of the same belief as these Britons, if I am of a different race. These druids will bless our expedition against the Saxons. I have little faith in their mummery, but it might help—"

The Gael strode between the columns and vanished. Wulfhere leaned on his axe; it seemed to him that from within came a faint rattle—like the hoofs of a goat on a marble floor.

"This is an evil place," muttered Thorfinn. "I thought I saw a strange face peering about the top of a column a moment agone."

"It was a funguous vine grown and twisted about," contradicted Hrothgar. "See how the fungus plants spring up all about the temple, how they twist and writhe like souls in torment—how human-like their appearance—"

"You are both mad," broke in Hakon Snorri's son. "It was a goat you saw—I saw the horns that grew upon its head—"

"Thor's blood!" snarled Wulfhere. "Be silent! Listen—"

Within the temple had sounded the echo of a sharp incredulous cry; me rasp of a sword from its scabbard, a strange slithering sound. Wulfhere glanced uncertainly about, then gripped his axe and started for the portals. From between the columns came Cormac Mac Art. The color was gone from his face and his eyes stared like a man who has looked into dark, nameless gulfs. Wulfhere's eyes fixed themselves on his sword and widened in slow horror. That blade was stained to the hilt with a green, leprous slime.

The Gael gestured toward the interior of the temple.

"Take your wolves in, Wulfhere," he said, "and let them loose—"

The Skull-splitter nodded stolidly and nodded to his warriors. With a clank of mail and a shimmer of axes the Danes strode into the temple. Cormac stepped out away from the columns and drew in a deep breath of pure air. He glanced at the writhing, snaky vines that clustered close and a strong shudder shook him. From within came an incessant clangor of steel, muffled blows—blows that sank deep in strange flesh. There was a frantic drumming as of many goats racing back and forth across the tiles. Once there sounded a strange cry that was partly like the death howl of a human, partly like the dying bleat of a goat, partly like the rending creak of a vine torn away.

Cormac wiped his forehead where the sweat beaded. "Not a Druidic temple—" No—not a temple where men deified the cleaner forms of Nature—creeping, crawling shapes of red chaos and howling insanity—slithering essences of blasphemy lurking like loathsome reptilian things in the ships of Rome—ghastly growths that spawned in the ooze of the Orient transplanted to cleaner lands—rooting themselves deep in good British soil—grisly pre-Druidic oaks that fed unnameable monstrosities beneath a gibbous moon. And the legends were true—slime of a decadent Greece writhing among ancient abominations—the goatlike satyrs, the mandrake—and a culminating horror—a ghastly cult older than Atlantis—vines and human things and goatish monstrosities that interwove and twined together—that set aside natural laws and mingled plant, beast and human in nameless creation.

Anthropoid, leprous shadows loping down colossal black basaltic corridors of pulsing, inhuman night. Mowing slavering abominations of an Elder World squatting on a lone bare hill in a grisly ring, howling brain-shattering incantations to a hag-moon. Titanic shapes of blasphemy and gibbering madness growing out of the night and silence of a midnight oak forest. Age-forgotten gods that ground writhing howling naked humans between their brutish jaws.

Wulfhere came from the temple with his Vikings behind him. To Cormac's questioning glance he shrugged his gigantic shoulders.

Cormac sheathed his sword with a clang; again he breathed deeply.

"On to Wessex," he growled, "We'll clean our steel in good Saxon blood."

[. . .]

The Temple of Abomination
Later Draft

"Easy all," grunted Wulfhere Hausakliufr. "I see the glimmer of a stone building through the trees—Thor's blood, Cormac, are you leading us into a trap?"

The tall Gael shook his head, a frown darkening his sinister, scarred face.

"I never heard of a castle in these parts—the British tribes hereabouts don't build in stone—it may be an old Roman ruin—"

Wulfhere hesitated, glancing back at the compact lines of bearded, horn-helmeted warriors: "Maybe we'd best send out a scout—"

Cormac Mac Art laughed jeeringly: "Alaric led his Goths through the Forum fifty years ago, yet you barbarians still start at the name of Rome. Fear not; there are no legions in Britain—I think this is a Druidic temple. We have nothing to fear from them—more especially as we are moving against their hereditary enemies."

"And Cerdic's brood will howl like wolves when we strike them from the west instead of the south or east," grinned the Skull-splitter. "It was a crafty idea of yours, Cormac, to hide our dragon-ship on the west coast and march straight through British country to fall on the Saxons. But it's mad, too."

"There's method in my madness," responded the Gael. "I know that there are few warriors hereabouts; most of the chiefs are gathering about Arthur Pendragon for a great concerted drive. Pendragon! He's no more Uther Pendragon's son than you are. Uther was a black-bearded madman—more Roman than Briton and more Gaul than Roman. Arthur is as fair as Eric there. And he's pure Celt—a waif from one of the wild western tribes that never bowed to Rome. It was Lancelot who put it into his head to make himself king—else he had still been no more than a wild chief raiding the borders."

"Is he smooth and polished like the Romans were?"

"Arthur? Ha! One of your Danes would look like a gentlewoman beside him. He's a shock-headed savage with a love for battle." Cormac grinned ferociously and touched his scars. "By the blood of the gods, he has a hungry sword! It's little gain we reavers from Erin have gotten on his coasts!"

"Would I could cross steel with him," grunted Wulfhere, thumbing the flaring edge of his great axe. "What of Lancelot?"

"A renegade Gallo-Roman who has made an art of throat-cutting. He varies reading Petronius with plotting and intriguing. Gawaine is a pure-blooded Briton like Arthur, but he has Romanesque leanings. It's amusing to see him aping Lancelot—but he fights like a blood-hungry devil. Without these two Arthur would have been no more than a bandit chief. He can neither read nor write."

"What has that to do with it?" rumbled the Dane. "Neither can I—there's the temple."

They had entered the tall grove in whose shadows crouched the broad, squat building that seemed to leer out at them from behind a screening row of columns.

"I thought these Britons were mostly of a new sect called Christians," growled Wulfhere.

"The Romano-British mongrels are," assented Cormac. "The pure Celts hold to the old gods, as we of Erin. By the blood of the gods, we Gaels will never turn Christian while one Druid lives."

"What do these Christians?" asked Wulfhere curiously.

"They eat babies, it is said."

"But the Druids burn men in cages of green wood."

"A lie spread by Caesar and believed by fools," rasped Cormac impatiently. "I am not upholding the Druids, especially, but wisdom of the elements and ages is not denied to them. These Christians teach meekness and the bowing of the neck to the blow."

"What?" The great Viking was sincerely amazed. "Is it their creed to take blows like a slave?"

"Aye—to return good for evil and to forgive their oppressors."

The giant meditated on this statement for a moment. "That is not a creed, but cowardice," he decided. "These Christians be all madmen. Cormac, if you recognize one of that breed point him out and I will try his faith." He lifted his axe meaningly. "For look you," he said, "that is an insidious and dangerous teaching which may spread like rust on the wheat and undermine the manhood of men, if it be not stamped out like a young serpent under heel."

"Let me but see one of these madmen," said Cormac grimly, "and I will begin the stamping. But let me see to this temple. Wait here—I'm of the same belief as these Britons, if I am of a different race. These Druids will bless our raid against the Saxons. Much is mummery but their friendship at least is desirable."

The Gael strode between the columns and vanished. The Hausakliufr leaned on his axe; it seemed to him that from within came a faint rattle—like the hoofs of a goat on a marble floor.

"This is an evil place," muttered Thorfinn Jarl's bane. "I thought I saw a strange face peering about the top of the column a moment agone."

"It was a fungus vine grown and twisted about," contradicted Black Hrothgar. "See how the fungoid plants spring up all about the temple, how they twist and writhe like souls in torment—how human-like their appearance—"

"You are both mad," broke in Hakon Snorri's son. "It was a goat you saw—I saw the horns that grew upon its head—"

"Thor's blood!" snarled Wulfhere. "Be silent! Listen!—"

Within the temple had sounded the echo of a sharp, incredulous cry; a sudden demonic rapping as of fantastic hoofs on marble flags; the rasp of a sword from its scabbard and a heavy blow. Wulfhere gripped his axe and took the first step of a headlong charge for the portals. Then between the columns came Cormac Mac Art. Wulfhere's eyes widened in slow horror, for never yet had he seen the steel nerves of the lean Gael shaken, yet now the color was gone from Cormac's face and his eyes stared like those of a man who has looked into dark, nameless gulfs. His blade dripped red.

"What in the name of Thor—?" growled Wulfhere, peering fearsomely into the shadow-haunted shrine.

Cormac wiped away beads of cold sweat and moistened his lips.

"By the blood of the gods," he said, "we have stumbled upon an abomination—or else I am mad. From the inner gloom it came bounding and capering suddenly and it almost had me in its grasp before I had sense enough to draw and strike."

"What?" queried the Dane nervously.

"The Thing! It leaped and capered like a goat but ran upright, and in the dim light it was not unlike a man."

"You are mad," said Wulfhere uneasily; his mythology did not include satyrs.

"Well," snapped Cormac, "the Thing lies upon the flags within; follow me and I will prove to you whether I am mad."

He turned and strode through the columns, and Wulfhere followed, axe ready, his Vikings trailing in behind him in close formation, and going warily. They passed between the columns which were plain and without ornamentation of any kind and entered the temple. Here they found themselves to be in a broad hall, flanked with squat pillars of black stone, and these indeed were carved. As upon a pedestal a squat figure squatted on the top of each, but in the dim light they could not make out what sort of beings they represented, though there was a vague abhorrent hint of abnormality about each shape.

"Well," said Wulfhere impatiently, "where is your monster?"

"There he fell," said Cormac, pointing with his sword, "and—by the black gods!"

The flags lay bare.

"Moon-mist and madness," said Wulfhere, shaking his head. "Celtic superstition—you see ghosts, Cormac!"

"Yes?" snapped the badgered Gael. "Who saw a troll on the beach of Helgoland and roused the whole camp with shouts and bellowings? Who kept the band under arms all night and kept men feeding the fires till they nearly dropped, to scare away the things of darkness?"

Wulfhere growled uncomfortably and glared at his warriors as if to challenge anyone to laugh.

"Look," said Cormac, bending closer. On the tiling was a wide smear of blood, fresh spilt. Wulfhere took a single glance and then straightened quickly, glaring into the shadows. His men bunched closer, facing outward, beards a-bristle. A tense silence reigned.

"Follow me," said Cormac in a low tone, and they pressed close at his heels as he walked warily down the broad corridor. Apparently no entrances opened between the brooding, evil pillars. Ahead of them the shadows paled and they came forth into a broad circular chamber with a domed ceiling. Around this chamber were more pillars, regularly spaced, and in the light that flowed somehow through the dome, the warriors saw the nature of these things and the shapes that crowned them. Cormac swore between his teeth and Wulfhere spat. The figures were human, and not even the most perverse and degenerate geniuses of decadent Greece and later Rome could have conceived such obscenities or breathed into the tortured stone such foul life. Cormac scowled. Here and there in the sculpturing the unknown artists had struck a chord of unrealness—a hint of abnormality beyond any human deformity. These touches roused in him a vague uneasiness, a crawling, shuddersome half-fear that lurked white maned and grisly at the back of his mind.

The thought that had been growing in his mind, that he had seen and slain an hallucination, vanished.

Besides the doorway through which they had entered the chamber, four other portals showed—narrow, arched doorways, apparently without doors. There was apparently no altar. Cormac strode to the center of the dome and looked up. The dome arched above him, sullen and broodingly. His gaze sought the floor on which he stood and he noted the pattern of the floor. It was of tiling rather than flags and laid in a design the lines of which converged to the center of the floor which was formed by a single broad octagonal slab. Even as he realized that he was standing on that slab, it fell away silently from under his feet and he felt himself plunging into an abyss beneath.

Only the Gael's superhuman quickness saved him. Thorfinn Jarl's bane was standing nearest him and, as the Gael dropped, he shot out a long arm and clutched at the Dane's swordbelt. The desperate fingers missed but closed on the scabbard and, as Thorfinn instinctively braced his legs, Cormac's fall was checked and he swung suspended, life hanging on the grip of his single hand and the strength of the scabbard loops. In an instant Thorfinn had seized his wrist, and Wulfhere, leaping forward with a roar of alarm, added the grasp of his huge hand. Between them they heaved the Gael up out of the gaping blackness, Cormac aiding them with a twist and a lift of his rangy form that swung his legs up over the brink.

"Thor's blood!" ejaculated Wulfhere, more shaken by the experience than was Cormac. "It was touch and go then! By Thor, you still hold your sword!"

"When I drop it, life will be no longer in me," answered Cormac. "I mean to carry it into Hell with me. But let me look into this gulf that opened so suddenly beneath me."

"More traps may fall," said Wulfhere nervously.

"I see the sides of the well," said Cormac, leaning and peering, "but my gaze is swiftly swallowed in darkness—what a foul stench drifts up from below."

"Come away," said Wulfhere hurriedly. "That stench was never born of earth—this well must lead into some Roman purgatory. Mayhap into the place—the cavern where the serpent drips venom on Loki."

Cormac paid no heed. "I see the trap now," said he. "That slab was balanced on a sort of pivot, and here is the catch that supported it. How it was worked I can't say, but this catch was released and the slab fell, held on one side by the pivot—" his voice trailed away.

"Blood!" he said. "Blood on the edge of the pit!"

"The thing you slashed," grunted Wulfhere, "it has crawled into the pit."

"Not unless dead things crawl," growled Cormac. "I killed it, I tell you. It was carried here and thrown in. Listen!"

The warriors bent close; from somewhere far down—an incredible distance it seemed—there came a sound—a nasty, squashy, wallowing sound, mingled with noises indescribable and unrecognizable.

With one accord the warriors drew away from the well and

exchanging silent glances backed away.

"This stone won't burn," growled Wulfhere, voicing a common thought. "There's no loot here and nothing human. Let's be gone."

"Wait!" the keen-eared Gael threw up his head like a hunting hound. He frowned and drew nearer to one of the arched openings.

"A human groan," he whispered. "Did you not hear it?"

Wulfhere bent his head, cupping palm to ear. "Aye—down that corridor."

"Follow me," snapped the Gael. "Stay close together. Wulfhere, grip my belt; Hrothgar, hold Wulfhere's, and Hakon, Hrothgar's. There may be more pits. The rest of you dress your shields and each man keep close touch with the next."

So in a compact mass they squeezed through the narrow portal and found the corridor much wider than they had thought. There it was darker, but further down the corridor they saw what appeared to be a patch of light.

They hastened to it and halted. Here indeed it was lighter, so that the unspeakable carven obscenities thronging the wall were cast into plain sight. This light came in from above, where the ceiling had been pierced with several openings. And chained to the wall among the foul carvings hung a naked human form. It was a man who sagged on the chains that held him half erect and Cormac thought him dead—and staring at the grisly mutilations that had been wrought upon him, decided it was better so. Then the head lifted slightly and a low groan sighed through the pulped lips.

"He lives, by Thor!" swore Wulfhere in amazement.

"Water, in God's name," whispered the man on the wall and Cormac, taking a well-filled flask from Hakon Snorri's son, held it to the creature's lips. The man drank in great gasping gulps, then lifted his head with a mighty effort. The Gael looked into deep eyes, strangely calm.

"God's benison on you, my lords," came the voice, faint and rattling, yet somehow suggesting that it had once been strong and resonant. "Has the long torment ended and am I in paradise at last?"

Wulfhere and Cormac glanced at each other curiously. Paradise! Strange indeed, thought Cormac, would such red-handed reavers as we look in the heaven of the humble ones.

"Nay, it is not Paradise," muttered the man deliriously, "for I am still galled by these heavy chains—"

Wulfhere bent and examined the chains that held him. Then with a grunt he raised his axe and, shortening his hold upon the haft, smote a short powerful blow. The links parted beneath the keen edge and the man slumped forward into Cormac's arms, free of the wall but with the heavy bands still upon wrists and ankles; these, Cormac saw, sank deeply into the flesh which the rough and rusty metal envenomed.

"I think you have not long to live, good sir," said Cormac. "Tell us how you are named and where is your village, so it may be we might tell your people of your passing."

"My name is Fabricus, my lord," said the victim, speaking with difficulty. "My town is that city which still holds the Saxon at bay."

"You are a Christian, by your words," said Cormac, and Wulfhere gazed curiously.

"I am but a humble priest of God, noble sir," whispered the other. "But you must not linger. Leave me here and go quickly lest evil befall you."

"By the blood of Thor," snorted Wulfhere, "I quit not this place until I see who it is that treats living beings so foully."

"Evil blacker than the dark side of the moon," muttered Fabricus. "Before it, the differences of man fade so that you seem to me like a brother of the blood and of the milk, Saxon."

"I am no Saxon, friend," rumbled the Dane.

"No matter," whispered the other. "All men in the rightful form of man are brothers—such is the word of the Lord; which I had not fully comprehended until I came to this place of abominations."

"Thor," muttered Wulfhere, "this is no Druidic temple?"

"Nay," it was the dying man who answered, "not a temple where men, even in heathenness, deify the cleaner forms of Nature—ah God, they hem me close—avaunt foul demons of the Outer Dark—creeping, creeping—crawling shapes of red chaos and howling insanity—slithering essences of blasphemy lurking like loathsome reptilian things in the ships of Rome—ghastly beings that spawned in the ooze of the Orient, transplanted to cleaner lands—rooting themselves deep in good British soil—grisly pre-Druidic oaks that feed unnamable monstrosities beneath a gibbous moon—"

The mutter of delirium faltered and faded, and Cormac shook the priest lightly. He aroused as a man waking slowly from deep sleep.

"Go, I beg of you," he whispered. "They have done their worst to me—but you—they will lap you round with evil spells—they will break your body as they have shattered mine—they will seek to break your souls as they had broken mine but for my everlasting faith in our good Lord God. He will come, the monster, the high priest of infamy, with his legions of the damned—listen!" The dying head lifted. "Even now he comes! Now may God protect us all!"

Cormac snarled like a wolf and the great Viking wheeled about, rumbling defiance like a lion at bay. Aye, something was coming down one of the smaller corridors which opened into that wider one. There was a myriad rattling of hoofs on the tiling—"Close the ranks!" snarled Wulfhere. "Make the shield wall, wolves, and die with your axes red!"

The Vikings quickly formed into a half-moon of steel, surrounding the dying priest and facing outward, just as a hideous horde burst from the dark opening into the comparative light. In a flood of black madness and red horror their assailants swept upon them. Most of them were goat-like creatures, that ran upright and had human hands and faces frightfully partaking of both goat and human. But among their ranks were shapes even more fearful. And behind them all, luminous with an evil light in the darkness of the winding corridor from which the horde emerged, Cormac saw an unholy countenance, human, yet more and less than human. Then on that solid iron wall the noisome horde broke.

The creatures were unarmed, but they were horned, fanged and taloned.

They fought as beasts fight, but with less of the beast's cunning and skill. And the Vikings, eyes blazing and beards abristle with the battle-lust, swung their axes in mighty strokes of death. Girding horn, slashing talon and gnashing fang found flesh and drew blood in streams, but protected by their helmets, mail, and overlapping shields, the Danes suffered comparatively little while their whistling axes and stabbing spears took ghastly toll among their unprotected assailants.

"Thor and the blood of Thor," cursed Wulfhere, cleaving a goat-thing clear through the body with a single stroke of his red axe, "mayhap ye find it a harder thing to slay armed men than to torture a naked priest, spawn of Helheim!"

Before that rain of hacking steel the hell-horde broke, but behind them the half-seen man among the shadows drove them back to the onslaught with strange chanting words, unintelligible to the humans who strove against his vassals. So his creatures turned again to the fray with desperate fury, until the dead things lay piled high about the feet of their slayers, and the few survivors broke and fled up and down the corridor. The Vikings would have scattered in pursuit but Wulfhere's bellow halted them. But as the horde broke, Cormac bounded across the sprawling corpses and raced down the winding corridor in pursuit of One who fled before him. His victim turned up another corridor and finally raced out into the domed main chamber, and there he turned at bay—a tall man with inhuman eyes and a strange dark face, naked but for fantastic ornaments.

With his strange, short, curved sword he sought to parry the Gael's headlong attack but Cormac drove his foe before him like straw before the wind. Whatever else this high priest might be, he was human, for he winced and cursed in a weird tongue as Cormac's long lean blade broke through his guard again and again and brought blood from head, chest and arm. Back Cormac drove him inexorably until he wavered on the very brink of the pit. And there, as the Gael's point girded into his breast, he reeled and fell backward with a wild cry that came up from untold depths. And far below rose sounds as of a grisly feast. And Cormac fiercely smiled.

[…]

Untitled

Between berserk battle rages, the black despair of melancholy fell like a pall on the soul of Wulfhere Skull-crusher. At such times he contemplated the emptiness of existence with an unerring perception that was not deceived by the mists and veils and cloaks that mask the naked core of life—which is Nothing. He saw the lies and myths and shams with which men pad reality as smoke fading into nothing, and freed of their false luster and tinsel glitter, he stared bleakly into the Abyss which is Existence—wherein, at the last, the voices and dreams and vanities of men tinkle hollowly and without reality. He saw the beginning and the end of Life—which is Nothing. Only to men like Wulfhere Skull-crusher is such vision allowed. And because not even such as he can long endure such vision, his baffled mind at last sought human feelings and emotions; he came to consider Hate, which comes nearer to being a reality in an unreal universe than any other dream or conception of man.

In hate, as in ale and battle, is a taste of oblivion, and oblivion is the best thing a man can seek. A man cannot wholly forget himself in love, for love is merely a self-seeking, motivated by a desire to increase one's pleasure; but hate seeks the destruction of another with such singleness of purpose that the hater loses himself in his pursuit, and the loss of self, if only temporarily, is the best reward for which a man may ask.

Hate grew in the mind of Wulfhere Skull-splitter as if to fill the gulf of Existence.

[. . .]

Appendix 3

Turlogh Dubh O'Brien

Unfinished Tales

Untitled

The Dane came in with a rush, hurling his huge body forward with surprizing speed, his red beard bristling. His axe sang as he struck. Turlogh O'Brien, avoiding death by a hair's breadth, smiled thinly. They made a strange contrast, those two men, as they played a grim game of life and death on that barren Wicklow moor. There was little difference in their heights, each being some six feet tall, but there the resemblance ceased. O'Brien was a big man but the Dane was a giant; the Gael was rangy-limbed, broad-shouldered, lean-waisted; he was all steel springs and whalebone. The Dane was paunchy, huge of legs and arms, with a great deal of fat. He looked slow but he moved like chain lightning. Moreover, Sigrel the Dane was red, with flaming hair and beard, and a red face. The outcast of the great O'Brien clan was dark. His hair was so black that no hair could be blacker, his complexion was dark, and from under heavy black brows gleamed a pair of volcanic blue eyes.

In those days there need be no personal quarrel to send Dane and Celt at each others' throats. The Vikings held Dublin and Drogheda and claimed lordship over all Leinster and Munster, but like later conquerors, they found the making good of this claim an everlasting, bloody task. Yet these men were known to each other and a personal element entered.

"Renegade!" grunted Sigrel, gritting his teeth as he drove his axe at Turlogh's head. "Outlaw! Brodir will laugh when—I—bring him—your skull!"

Turlogh swayed under the swishing death and the Dane leaped back from the Gael's underhand stroke.

"Then you'll have to put some speed into those great legs, red beard," O'Brien taunted. "Come—come—this draws out too long—here's my head—let you strike at it!"

He dropped his axe and thrust out his bare head tauntingly—and though Sigrel was a veteran fighter, and though he knew the craft and shiftiness of the O'Briens, he saw red and lunged savagely at that mocking face—too late he knew that he had been tricked, but with the realization came oblivion as the deadly O'Brien axe crashed through his skull.

"The Dalcassian stroke, eh?" a voice broke the sudden silence which followed the clash of steel.

Turlogh whirled. A tall finely-formed man stood close by. This man was taller than O'Brien but not as broad; his features were clean-cut and rather thin, more like a poet's than a fighting man's, but his garb was that of a warrior. He carried no axe, but a long straight sword hung at his side.

"I see from your colors that you are an O'Donnell," said Turlogh warily. "Might I be asking what you are doing so far from Tir-conal and you all alone?"

"You might be asking," agreed the O'Donnell, "but I might not be answering—not now at least."

Turlogh shrugged his shoulders. "Well enough; there's no love lost between our clans, but mine has cast me off, so I see no reason for renewing old warfare unless you are being set on it."

"Who is this man?" asked O'Donnell abruptly, indicating the dead Dane.

"And should I be knowing the name and degree of every row-footed sea-robber in Leinster?"

"He knew you."

"So you saw the whole fight, eh?"

"And heard it—from the first stroke to the last."

"Well, my stealthy bog-creeper from Ulster, this Dane's name was Sigrel and he was a small chief of sorts in the Danish holdings about Dublin. He knew me of old in a little matter of intrigue into which I was mixed without my knowledge, do you see, and which cost me my reputation both among the Danes and the Irish and which led to my ostracism by my clan—bad cess to them.

"It was his bad luck and my good luck which led us to meet here today—"

And so saying, but keeping a wary eye on O'Donnell all the while, Turlogh bent and went through the Dane's garments, frankly bent on loot. Seeing a shadow cross the fine face of the O'Donnell, Turlogh said impatiently:

"Do you not be vexing your Ulster soul on my account. An outcast must fend for himself as well as he may. The coins in this dead Dane's pouch will not be doing him any good, but will save me from the necessity of taking food and drink by force from some poor peasant—"

He stopped abruptly and straightened with a small rolled parchment in his hand. This he unrolled and scanned, then tossed to O'Donnell.

"Mayhap you can make sense of it. I cannot."

O'Donnell bent his brows above it, then, refolding it, placed the scrip among his garments. His face was immobile, but his eyes gleamed.

"Let us be talking together," he said. "It may be we can be of aid to each other."

Turlogh dropped his axe head to the earth and, leaning on the shaft, stared at the Ulsterman questioningly.

"My name," said the latter, "is Murtagh O'Donnell and of my rank it is neither here nor there, but why I come into Leinster alone like a foraging wolf, I will tell you.

"There is a chief of Tyrone and his name is Maelmora O'Neill."

Turlogh nodded; he knew the name, as who of the fighting men of Ireland, Dane or Gael, did not?

"Now give close heed. This O'Neill, coming from Rome on a merchant ship, fell into the hands of Swane Lodbrog who holds the isle of Mac Kir and recognizes no overlord. His galleys took the merchant ship and slew all except O'Neill, whom he took as slave. Now I have learned in devious ways that O'Neill is known to the Viking only as Maelmora More, or Big Myles, for O'Neill did not wish his true identity to be known, lest Swane demand a huge ransom from his clan.

"Swane is a madman in his way, who believes he can build an island kingdom on the small bit of earth which is the isle of Mac Kir. He is fortifying the whole island whereon there is much rock, and he has hundreds of slaves working in his quarries. Therein is toiling, like a common kern today, Maelmora O'Neill, second chief of the Hui Neill of Ulster."

"Well," said Turlogh, shouldering his axe, "doubtless there is a stupidity on me, and so I cannot see what connection there is between an O'Neill working in a stone quarry in an island between Leinster and France, and one of his hereditary enemies skulking about the moors of Wicklow alone."

Murtagh smiled. "You will see. The O'Neills hold prisoner Conmac O'Donnell, my sister's son. They ask for more than we can pay for ransom. So I come to Leinster alone, and alone I will go to Mac Kir and enter the service of Swane Lodbrog if necessary. Or I will parley with him for his strongest slave, as a man buys an ordinary serf. I will buy Maelmora O'Neill—"

Turlogh grinned with true Celtic appreciation of a trick.

"By the beard of Mananan McLir! I see your wisdom—but why tell me this?"

"Because I may need the aid of a strong ruthless outlaw. Aid me and you will never again need to loot the bodies of dead Danes. I will not be so exorbitant as Swane might be in the matter of ransom—the price the O'Neills shall pay for their chief will be the delivery of Conmac O'Donnell safe and sound."

[...]

The Shadow of the Hun

Prologue

A calm held the great warship in a level ring of the landless sea. The brass and gold work glittered in the sun, the idle sails flapped against the mast. On the high-flung poop three men sipped wine and conversed idly. Save for one feature, they were types as far apart as might be imagined; but in one way they were alike—each had the appearance of the born warrior.

Athelstane the Saxon was a giant; six and a half feet he towered from his sandals of bull's hide to his shock of flaxen hair. His crisp beard was as golden as the massive armlets he wore, his eyes large, calm and grey. He wore a corselet of scale mail and even as he drank and talked, he held across his knees his two-handed broadsword in its worn sheath.

Don Roderigo del Cortez was tall, dark and spare, clad in plain, unornamented armor. His dark eyes were deep and somber, his manner stately and courteous. He wore no beard but a thin mustache, and his only arm was a long narrow sword—forerunner of the rapier.

Turlogh Dubh O'Brien was not as tall as either of his companions, though he was well over six feet. His dark face was clean shaven, his black hair cropped short. From under heavy black brows gleamed his volcanic eyes—blue, and full of shifting gleams like clouds passing across some deep blue lake. Long limbed, deep chested, broad shouldered, his every motion betokened his iron strength and catlike litheness. He was, in some ways, more the complete fighting man than his friends, for he possessed a dynamic quickness the Saxon lacked, and sheer strength beyond the power of the slender Spaniard.

He was armed in black, closely worked chain mail, and a green girdle held a long dirk at his hip. Close by in a weapon rack rested more of his arms—a plain vizorless helmet with a mail drop, a round buckler with a keen spike in the center, and a single-handed axe. This axe partook of the lethal quality of its owner; with its keen single edge, perfectly made handle of oak that would notch a sword, it was the weapon of a master. It was lighter than most of the axes of the age, and built on different lines. A short keen spike on the back and one on the top of the head added to its deadly appearance.

"Don Roderigo," rumbled Athelstane, refilling his goblet, "what of these Easterners we are sailing against? Thor's blood, I have crossed steel with all the war-men of the Western world, but these I have not seen. Many of my comrades have fared to Mikligaard, but not I."

"The Saracens are brave and cruel warriors, good sir," answered the Don. "They fight with javelins and curved sabers. And they hate our fair Lord Christ, for they hold to Muhammad."

"As I gather it," pursued Athelstane, "east, whither we are sailing, lies the neck of water which divides Europe from Africa. The infidel Saracens hold both Africa and the greater part of Spain. And beyond lies, on one side of the Middle Sea, Italy and Greece, and on the other the eastern part of Africa and Holy Land which the Arab jackals defile. And thereabouts is Constantinople, or Mikligaard as the Vikings name it—and beyond, what?"

Don Roderigo shook his head. "Beyond lies Iran—Persia—and the wilderness wherein swarm pagan Turks and Tatars. Beyond—they tell wild tales of Hind and Cathay—but who knows? Between lies deserts and mountains full of pagans and evil spirits, dragons and—"

Turlogh suddenly interrupted with a shake of his head: "There are no dragons, Don Roderigo, though truth to tell there are many perils for the wanderer, both from beast and men."

The others glanced curiously at him. It was not often the Gaelic outcast opened his lips to speak of his long wanderings. But now it was his mood.

"I was some seven years younger," said he, "when I sailed one day from Erin on a raid—by my axe, it was a lengthy raid, for it was more than three years ere I set foot again on Irish land. Mind you, Athelstane, in those days of my outlawry I had a ship of my own—aye, and a crew."

"I remember," muttered the Saxon. "My Viking comrades had scathe thereby and villages smoked on England's western coast. But what of the unknown lands to the east whereof I spoke?"

"If you land on the south-easternmost coast of the Baltic Sea," answered Turlogh O'Brien, "and wander southward and eastward, you will come to a great inland sea—the Caspian Sea. Between them lie a vast land of forest and rivers, and wide, rolling plains, with few trees but grown with tall grass—a vast, grey, desolate land—"

Chapter 1

Across the leaden, grey steppes, beneath the grey, leaden sky flew a few herons. As far as eye could reach stretched the drab, waving grass, ruffled by a chill wind. A few scanty clusters of stunted trees broke the monotony and in the distance there was discernible the outline of a great river that wound, serpent-like, through the wilderness. Reeds grew tall and thick there and waterfowl circled above.

Turlogh O'Brien gazed out across the wastes and the gloomy desolation entered into his soul. Then he started. Out of the growth about the river broke four figures, which his keen eyes made out as horsemen, racing toward him—one in advance of the others. Turlogh held in his hand the reins of a great roan stallion. Now he mounted swiftly, unslung axe and buckler and rode into a sparse clump of trees which stood nearby. He did not believe the oncoming riders were coming to attack him; their attitude was such as to make him believe that the three behind pursued the fourth. And the Gael was curious to know what manner of men inhabited this wilderness.

They approached swiftly and soon Turlogh saw that his surmise was correct. The man in front swayed in his saddle, and one arm dangled limply. He guided his steed with the other hand and held a broken sword between his teeth. He was tall and young and he rode like the wind, his shock of yellow hair flying in the breeze. But the pursuers were swiftly closing the gap. They were shorter in stature than he they hunted, and mounted on smaller, nimbler steeds. As they approached the Celt's refuge, Turlogh saw they were very dark, were clad in light, silvered-mail shirts and wore turbans. They bore light round shields and curved scimitars.

Turlogh's mind was made up in an instant. This was none of his quarrel—but yonder three armed men hunted a wounded warrior, who was certainly of a tribe more akin to Turlogh's own people than the pursuers. These were Turks, the Gael decided, though he had supposed their ranges to lie considerably more to the south. An instinctive hatred burned up in his breast. It was the old, old feud between Aryan and Turanian, so strong that it sends the distant descendants of primitive warriors at each other's throats.

Now the yellow-haired youth thundered past the scanty grove, and now the foremost of the pursuers was almost abreast it. A lifted scimitar gleamed in a dark hand and a fierce yell of triumph rose to the skies—to be changed to a gasp of surprize as an unexpected shape shot from the trees.

Like a bolt from a catapult the great roan crashed full against the steed of the Turk. There was no time to rein about and avoid the impact. Striking from the side, the heavier horse hurled the lighter off its feet and headlong, flinging the rider underfoot where a lashing hoof dashed out his brains.

Turlogh reined about to meet the onset of the remaining Turks who howled like wolves in amazement and rage, but assailed him from either side. The Gael spurred to meet the nearest, ere the other could come at him from the other side. The curved scimitar lashed at Turlogh's head, but the Gael, guiding his horse with his knees, caught the blade on his shield and struck almost simultaneously. The keen edge bit through the turban and split the shaven skull beneath. As the Turk slumped from his saddle, Turlogh wheeled back to parry the scimitar that already hovered over him. The yellow-haired youth had seen the fray and was charging back to his rescuer's aid, but the fight was over before he could reach it.

The remaining Turk charged in from Turlogh's left, howling and hacking like a madman, believing the Gael could not reach him with his red axe without turning his steed or shifting the weapon to his left hand. But as he plunged in, slashing, the yellow-haired youth saw a trick of battle of which he had never heard. Turlogh rose in his stirrups, twisted in his saddle and reversed the usual procedure. He parried the whistling blade with his axe and struck with his buckler as a boxer strikes with a heavy cestus. The Turk's howl of triumph broke in a ghastly gurgle as the spike in the center of the shield tore his jugular vein. Blood flooded Turlogh's buckler and the Turk lurched to the earth where he died, clawing at his red-dabbled beard.

Turlogh turned to see the wounded youth reining his steed near. He spoke in a tongue the Gael could understand:

"I thank you, brother, whoever you are. These dog-brothers had carried my head back to Khogar Khan, had it not been for you. Four of them started me among the reeds of the river. One I slew—by Saint Piotr, he'll never eat sunflower seeds again. But they shattered my sword and broke my arm and I fled perforce. Tell me your name, that we may be brothers."

"My name is Turlogh Dubh, that is to say, Black Turlogh," answered the Gael. "My clan is the O'Brien, my land Erin. But now I am an outcast from my people and have wandered for many moons."

"I am Somakeld," said the youth, "and my people are the Turgaslavs, the steppes dwellers. My clan is camped just beyond yonder skyline. Come with me and let my people welcome you."

"Let me first see to that arm," said Turlogh, though the youth laughed at the scratch, as he called it. Turlogh, skilled in the dressing of wounds, set the broken bone and bandaged the deep saber slash as well as he could with mud and spider-webs taken from the stunted trees. Somakeld uttered no murmur of complaint and when the task was done, thanked the Celt with quiet courtesy. Then they rode toward the Slavic camp.

"How is it you speak my tongue?" asked the lad.

"I have wandered for months among the great forests," answered Turlogh. "The forest tribes are akin to the steppes dwellers and their tongue is much the same. But tell me this, Somakeld, whence come those Turks we slew? I have seen Tatars, who ride even into the great forests sometimes, but I had thought that the empire of the Turks lies far to the south."

"Aye, so it does," agreed Somakeld, "but these dogs were driven out by their kin."

Somakeld spoke at some length, and Turlogh found him to be far more frank and keen witted than the sullen forest people his late wanderings had led him among. Though a youth, the young Slav had journeyed far "—to the yellow sands of the south, where the caravans ply behind Rhoum and Bokhara, east beyond the Blue Sea (the Aral Sea), beyond the northern reaches of the Volga, and West to the great river called the Dneiper." His was a wandering, nomadic tribe and he himself had more than his share of the wanderlust.

These Turks were wilder, fiercer cousins to the Seljuks before whose onslaught the Arab caliphates of Islam were crumbling. This particular tribe had been overthrown in the incessant border warfare, either by the Persians or by some kindred Turkish clan, Somakeld was not sure. But they had fled the pasturelands of their ancestors and had wandered far beyond the loose boundaries of their race.

They had come into the steppes where the nomadic outposts of two rival races bickered and mingled—where the easternmost drift of the last Aryan wanderers snarled and snapped at the westernmost drift of the Tatar herders.

The usual desultory warfare had ensued—skirmishes and raids for women and horses on both sides. The roving bands of Tatars took first one side and then the other as their whims led them. But of late the war had taken on a new aspect. A new khan had arisen among the Turks who held the grazing lands beyond the river. This one was Khogar Khan, who gained his leadership by murdering the former khan. His ambition was great. He dreamed of power—of the sovereignty, not of a waste of grazing land and wandering tribes, but of a great empire, reaching from the heart of the steppes to the Caspian Sea. It was no mad vision, commented Somakeld, who had heard the old men talk of mushroom empires that sprang up almost overnight in the teeming mazes of the East, to sweep across the curve of the world like a prairie fire, and as quickly to burn itself out.

But Khogar Khan had one obstacle to overcome first—the Turgaslavs, hereditary lords of the steppes. His first, main step must be to crush them.

Already the Turks, fired by their warlike leader, had routed the Tatar clans in the vicinity, slaying many, forcing some into a sullen subjection and driving the rest away. Now the Moslems were gathering their forces for a powerful drive on their Aryan foes to the west. Riders were scouring the steppes, gathering the Turgaslavic clans. His people had no villages, Somakeld explained, but followed the grass. The various clans of the tribes were scattered wherever fancy might lead them, over a radius of a hundred miles.

Spies had reported the movements of the Turks, and it was while returning from a distant clan that Somakeld had encountered his hereditary foes. His tribe was not a large one, said the young Turgaslav, but for centuries they had overcome their foes. Once they numbered many thousands, but tribal wars had thinned them and branches of the tribe had split off and wandered westward, there to forget their pastoral life and become tillers of the soil. Somakeld sniffed in disdain.

"But you, my brother," he exclaimed suddenly, "you have not told me how you have come to wander alone so far from your own pastureland. Surely you were a chief among your own people."

Turlogh grinned bleakly. "Once I was a chief in an island far to the west, called Erin. My king was an ancient man and very wise, and his name was Brian Boru. But the great king fell in a mighty battle with red-bearded sea rovers called Danes, though his people won the battle. Then followed a time of feud and intrigue and the spite of a woman and the jealousy of a kinsman cast me forth from my clan, an outlaw to starve on the heath.

"But though I was no longer one of the Dal Cais, my heart was still bitter against the Danes who had ravaged my land for centuries and I drew to me certain masterless men and outlaws like myself, and by devious ways we took a galley from the Danes."

And with swift words Turlogh sought to picture for the young Slav that red phase in his restless and battle-haunted life.

His ship was *The Raven* which he re-named *Crom's Hate* after an old heathen Celtic god. Trickery and savage fighting won her, and the scum of the seas manned her. Not one of her crew but had a price on his head. To Turlogh flocked rogues and thieves and murderers, whose only virtue was the reckless abandon of desperate men who have nothing to live for.

Irish outlaws, Scottish criminals, runaway Saxon thralls, Welsh freebooters, gallows birds from Brittany—these steered and rowed *Crom's Hate* and fought and looted at their savage lord's command. There were men with cropped ears and slit noses, men with brands on face and shoulder, men whose limbs bore the marks of rack and shackle. They were without love and without hope and they fought like blood-hungry devils.

Their only law was the word of Turlogh O'Brien, and that law was adamantine. There was no sentiment between them; they snarled about him like wolves and he cursed them for the vermin they were. But they feared and respected his ferocity and fighting prowess and he recognized their desperate savagery. He made no attempt to impose his will upon them in ways of other leaders whose hand is not against the world. He demanded of them only that they follow him and fight like demons when he gave the word. Nor did he give an order twice. In the hellish environments in which he found himself, all the slumbering tiger awoke in the Gaelic chief and of all the red-handed crew he himself was the most terrible.

When he gave an order, a man obeyed instantly or drew his weapon as swiftly. For the penalty of disobedience or hesitancy was an instant dashing out of the mutineer's brains beneath the savage chieftain's axe. Men who had followed Turlogh O'Brien in the days before his outlawry would have gaped at him now as he stood on the bloodstained poop of *Crom's Hate*, eyes blaring and axe dripping, yelling commands to his motley horde in a voice that was like the maddened yell of a panther.

He was a pirate who preyed on pirates. Only when his supplies were at ebb would he swoop down and harry the fertile coasts of England, Wales or France. The almost insane hatred for the Vikings that burned in his heart sent him ravaging the strongholds of the raiders in the Hebrides, the Orkneys and even on the coasts of the Scandinavian mainlands. When driving sleet and winter gales lashed the western seas, Turlogh and his tatterdemalions rode the bitter wind, freezing, starving, suffering, to fall on their foes with torch and sword.

It was a hard service the Gael offered the men who came to him from chains or the shadow of the gallows. He promised them only a hard, bitter life, ceaseless toil and warfare and a bloody death. But he gave them a chance to strike back at the world and to glut themselves in slaughter—and men followed him.

When even the stout Norsemen had their longships in the ship-houses and were pent in sturdy skallis, drinking ale and listening to the skalds, Turlogh and his thieves roamed the foaming wastes, to smite their enemies in their security and leave smoldering embers of strong steadings.

It was a day in deep winter. A bitter gale lashed the Baltic, driving before it a stinging sleet that froze on mast and rower's bench. Waves burst clear across the low waist of the dragon-ship, drenching the rowers and clotting their beards with ice. Even these men, inured to all hardships, who lived like wolves, were on the point of collapse. On the foredeck, with one hand on the arching prow that terminated in a dragon's head, Turlogh O'Brien strained his eyes, striving to pierce the veil of sleet and freezing spray.

There was ice on Turlogh's mail, and blood that caked his shoes was frozen stiff. But he gave no heed; at birth he had been flung into a snowdrift to decide his right to live. He was harder than a wolf. And now his heart burned in him so fiercely that no outer cold could harm him.

He had ventured far, this voyage, and he had left smoldering ruins, slaked in crimson, on the coasts of Jutland and the shores that hem the Skaggerack. Not content, he had swept on up into the Baltic and now believed he was in what was called by some the Gulf of Finland.

Suddenly he sighted a flying shape in the mist and yelled fiercely. A longship! Some Viking farer who had put out to meet him, doubtless, having gotten wind of his ravaging and not wishing to be caught napping in his skalli, as had those sea kings whose skulls now adorned the shield-rail.

Turlogh, eyes fixed on that racing shadow, shouted a command to alter the course and lay her alongside. His lieutenant, a grim, one-eyed Scotsman, dared an objection.

"We've got to hold her in the wind; if we veer half a point, a broadside sea will break her in two. It's mad enough to venture among such seas in a ship with never a deck to her—"

"The devil takes care of his own!" yelled Turlogh. "Do as I say, you spawn of hell—there! She's faded into the sleet—I can't see her—"

The huge ice-crested waves tossed the long low craft like a chip. The Scotsman was right; only a madman would have ventured into those winter seas. But Turlogh had a tinge of madness in his soul that broke its rein at times.

Suddenly and without warning a beaked prow loomed out of the driving mist on their port bow. The men of *Crom's Hate* saw the horned helmets and the fierce blond faces of the Norsemen who lined the rail, yelling and brandishing their weapons.

"Run alongside and board her!" yelled Turlogh, as a cloud of arrows whistled through the howling wind. *Crom's Hate* leaped forward like a spurred horse, but an instant later the strongest man at the sweep, a giant Saxon with the brand of a runaway thrall on his face, dropped with an arrow in his heart, and the kicking sweep head resisted the efforts of his fellows. Turlogh yelled fiercely, and others sprang forward, but the galley, out of control, veered away, tossed and trembled to the impact of a broadside sea that swept half a score men overboard, and the Viking galley rammed her.

The iron beak of the Norsemen did not strike squarely, else it had sheared straight through the waist, but it ripped a great rent near her prow and scraped down the sides, with a deafening splintering of oars. The longships locked almost rail to rail, and the bulwarks were instantly thronged with howling, hacking figures that slew and died in a red holocaust of hate.

Men died like flies along the rails where axes shattered helm and skull, and swords broke in mailed bosoms. But the Scotch mate sought Turlogh where he slashed and hacked like a blood-hungry demon, and yelled: "The seas will tear us apart at any instant and *Crom's Hate* is sinking under our feet!"

"Lash them together!" yelled Turlogh, eyes ablaze and foam flecking his lips; his latent madness burst all bounds. "Lash them rail to rail and we'll drag these swine into Hell with us! We'll sink together and slay while we drown!"

And with his own hands he flung the first grappling hooks. The Vikings realized his intentions and sought to draw away, but too late. Locked together, there was no steering either ship. They were at the mercy of the winds and waves that tossed them and raced them dizzily along, while the crews closed in a last desperate grapple. Hacking and slashing in a red cataclysm of howling hell, Turlogh was vaguely aware that a great roaring ripped the din, like waves dashing on a rock-bound coast. But the berserk madness of slaying was on him and on all the rest, and they ceased not to howl and ply their red axes as the two tortured ships, mastless, prowless and with splintered oars and timbers, hurled headlong through the surf to shatter on the foaming coast.

Chapter 2

"And you alone lived?" asked Somakeld, breathlessly.

"I alone," answered Turlogh somberly. "Why, I know not. In the midst of the tumult, darkness fell upon me and I awaked in the hut of a strange people. Some whim of the waves cast me ashore when all the rest died. But not alone was I washed ashore. Many others the sea cast up, but only I had a spark of life in me. The rest were slain of wounds, water or cold. Many froze. I too, the people said, was almost frozen. And my buckler and axe were gripped in my hands so tightly they could not loosen them, and I still gripped them so when I came to myself.

"Well, these folks were Finns—kindly people who treated me well. With them I abode a space, but their land was a barren one of ice and snow and when the time came when I knew it was early spring in southern lands, I left them. I had a horse of theirs, and I wandered south through the great forests full of wolves and bears, and evil beasts whose shadows and footprints only I saw.

"I came upon fierce pagan tribes in these forests, some of which I fled from and some of which I tarried with. Some of these folk defied the grandsons of Rurik and I was well pleased to strike a blow against the Norsemen again. So I wandered for many months, first on the horse the Finns gave me, then on steeds I stole or bought, lastly on this great stallion that a pagan chief gave me. When I left the huts of the Finns it was late winter there. Now it is nearly winter again and I am still far from the southern lands my heart craves."

"Come with me and dwell in the tents of my people, oh, my brother," urged Somakeld. "We are a brave people and we love warlike deeds. You shall be a chief. The girls of the Turgaslavs are fair. Dwell with my people."

Turlogh shrugged his shoulders. "I will ride with you, Somakeld, for my steed is weary and I am hungry. I will abide with you awhile because there is the smell of war in the land—aye, the ravens are gathering and I would not be put aside when the swords come to their quenching."

Night had fallen when the companions rode up to the encampment of the Turgaslavs. Turlogh had seen Tatar camps and this Slavic camp did not differ materially from them. The same high lumbering wagons, the same peaked saddles heaped carefully about, the same rings about the fires, where women cooked meat and passed about drinking horns of milk and mead. The Aryan and the Turanian nomad had progressed and evolved on much the same lines. Turlogh realized that he was gazing on a phase of Aryan life which was swift passing. The Aryan nomad was gradually quitting the pastoral life in favor of the agricultural life, or was being absorbed by the Tatar nomads.

Turlogh saw plenty of evidence that amalgamation was already taking place among these ancient Aryan steppes-lords and the Mongolian peoples. Many of the Turgaslavs had the broad faces and black hair that betokened a Tatar strain, and there was a fair sprinkling of pure blood Tatars, though the bulk of the tribesmen were tall and big boned, with the light eyes and flaxen hair of the primitive Aryan. The admixture had already begun such as in later centuries was to produce the Cossacks.

The horses of these Aryan wanderers were tall and heavier than those ridden by the smaller Turks and Tatars, and their swords were long, straight and heavy, with both cutting edge and point. They were also armed with heavy axes, long spears and daggers, and bows, lighter and less effective than the bows of their Turanian rivals.

Their armor was crude and scanty, consisting largely of iron helmets, rude corselets of iron plates laced to heavy hide jackets, and round, wooden, leather-covered and iron-braced bucklers. They wore as clothing garments of sheepskin. The men were tall, upright in carriage and frank and open of countenance, while the women were pleasing in appearance.

Sentries on horseback roamed the steppe and these challenged the companions, but gave back at the word from Somakeld. A moon was rising as Turlogh and the youth trotted up the slope of the slight eminence whereon was pitched the Slavic camp, and sweeping the plains with his keen glance, Turlogh saw dark shadowy figures and lurching bulks cross the distant horizons, converging toward the camp on the rise.

"My people answer the call of war," said Somakeld, and the Gael nodded, his eyes glittering in the gloom as dim ancestral memories stirred vaguely in the sleeping deeps of his soul. Aye, the clans were gathering to feed the ravens as the Aryan clans had gathered in the dim lost ages—as the Gael's own ancestors had gathered on these very steppes, lurching along in clumsy wagons, or swinging on half-wild horses.

As they rode up to the fires a shout of welcome greeted them. Turlogh instantly picked out the chief—his name, as Somakeld had said, Hroghar Skel. He was old, but his long beard was still flaxen and when he rose to greet the stranger with simple stateliness, the Gael saw that he was mighty in stature and that age had not dimmed his eagle eye nor withered his iron muscles.

"Your face is new to me," said the chieftain in a deep calm voice. "You are neither Slav, Turk nor Tatar. But whoever you be, dismount and rest your steed. Eat and drink at our fires tonight."

"This is a noted warrior, oh ataman," exclaimed Somakeld. "A bogatyr, a hero! He has come to aid us against the Turks! By the honor of my clan, three Turks he sent to howl at the gates of Hell this day!"

The ancient inclined his lion-like head: "Our lives are yours, bogatyr."

As Turlogh swung from his saddle he noted another man squatted by the fire, a man in early-middle life it seemed, with the broad, short build of the Tatar. This man had the bearing of a chief and beneath his sheepskins was the sheen of silks and the glimmer of silvered mail. His broad dark face was immobile, but his small beady eyes flickered as they rested on the splendid roan stallion. Behind the chief squatted a slim handsome youth, evidently his son. The Tatar's eyes rested long on the roan stallion.

Turlogh saw to his horse before he attended to his own needs, and assured that the roan was well cared for, he took a seat at the chieftain's fire. Somakeld, proud of his new acquaintance and of his own admission to the fire of the leaders, told the tale of his meeting with the Gael, and repeated the story of Turlogh's wanderings. All listened interestedly and the newcomers, who were arriving in a steady stream, pressed close to gaze curiously at the Celt and to hear whispered versions of his exploits from folk of the outer rings.

"You have the look of an eagle, bogatyr," said Hroghar Skel. "Little matter to tell me you were a chief in your own land—well I know that you are a ruler of men. Well, the men of the Turgaslav need keen swords and strong wills. Khogar Khan moves against us and who knows how the war may go? The Turks are mighty fighters, and they have scattered like birds before the winds, the warriors of Chaga Khan." And he nodded at the Tatar who sat drinking mare's milk.

"Aye," the Tatar's voice was like the rasp of a sword from its scabbard, "they were like wolves among sheep—by Erlik, they are madmen!"

"There is madness in them so that they fight as a steppes fire burns the grass," nodded Hroghar Skel. "There is magic in them that upholds them in the teeth of the spears. Khogar Khan claims descent from that red-handed scourge of old times—Attila the Hun. And more—he wears in his girdle the very sword which the Hun quenched in the blood of kings."

Turlogh gave a surprized exclamation.

The beady eyes of Chaga Khan turned on him.

"I saw it," the Tatar grunted, poising his drinking jack. "It was a red flame in his hand and with it he fed the kites. By Erlik, old Death ran before his steed and a black wind howled behind. When he smote, it was as if a horde smote and no man could stand before him. He heaped my warriors in crimson ranks behind him to mark his course."

Silence reigned for a space. The night wind sighed through the high grass and the lurching rumble of distant wagons was heard, and the challenge of the outposts. Hroghar Skel shook his head and his iron hand was twisted in his beard.

"They gather fast—by dawn all the clans of the Turgaslav will be encamped and clamoring to be led against their enemies. But a cold doubt lies at the base of my brain. It is more than mortal men we fight."

All eyes turned toward Turlogh. Primitive people are swift to snatch at portents and supernatural conclusions. It seemed to them that Turlogh's coming was no chance thing, but that strange forces that work behind the veil had sent him to their aid. But the Gael merely said: "I will sleep."

As he stretched out on the sheepskins in Hroghar's tent, again deep ancestral feelings stirred in the Gael as he listened to the night sounds of the nomadic camp. All seemed friendly and familiar to him, the crackle of the fires, the scents of the cooking pots, the smell of sweaty leather and horseflesh, the jingle of bridles and the creak of saddles, the singing of the tribesmen and their laughter. These Slavs were of the very foundations of the Aryan race—the root and the stock. They clung close to that pristine existence that Turlogh's ancestors had abandoned so many centuries ago. Somakeld's people were fundamental—strong and clean with primal life and principle. They were knit close to the tie-ribs of existence, to the raw, red realities of life.

As he drifted into slumber, Turlogh's last vague waking thoughts were that though half a world lay between them and his people, the blood of these nomads was his own, and after centuries of wandering in alien lands, he had come home at last. Then he sank into sleep haunted by dreams wherein he, light eyed, wild, skin clad, traversed endless leagues of forest and plain in lurching, oxen-pulled wagons, or on the backs of half wild horses, and in company of his wild, light-eyed, skin-clad kind, roared and slashed in nameless battles in dim, lost lands, fought man and beast and foaming torrents, and trampled tottering civilizations that were old when the world was young—so in his dreams he wandered and fought again down dim, lost ages.

Chapter 3

Hroghar swept his hand around in a gesture that took in all the camp, where women cooked food and mended harness and men whetted swords.

"These are all my people. I can muster but seven hundred warriors, strong able men, neither too young nor too old to fight. Some three hundred Tatars hunt with us; they will fight for us as long as the arrows fly, but we cannot depend upon them to stand when it comes to sword strokes. Khogar Khan has a good thousand riders, and five hundred Tatar allies."

"What of Chaga Khan?" demanded Turlogh.

Hroghar shook his head.

"The Tatars are like wolves that make a ring about two warring bulls, to devour the loser. Chaga Khan sent to us to ask for aid but joined battle before we could come to his help. He feels he owes us nothing. His people have withdrawn far to the east. He waits to see how we will stand up against the Turks. These Tatars who cleave to us, and they whom Khogar Khan has impressed into his service, are of small roving clans. Chaga Khan's tribe is the most powerful one in this part of the steppes. Despite his defeat by the Turks, he can still muster a thousand riders."

"Then in the name of the Devil," snapped Turlogh, "can you not make him understand that if he joined forces with you, you would defeat the Turks?"

The old Slav shrugged his shoulders. "Little use to argue with a Tatar. Khogar Khan struck fear into him and he is afraid to go up against the Turk. And I am not so sure that he wishes to aid me, anyway. He will watch which way the feather falls. If we win, he will come back to his old pasture lands. If the Turk wins, he may retire further into the East, even into the deserts of his people, or he may join forces with Khogar Khan. He believes that the Turk will be a great conqueror, like Attila his ancestor, and it is good to follow the banners of a conqueror."

"Then why not ally yourself to Khogar Khan?" Turlogh watched the old chief's face narrowly. The mighty hand on the spear shaft shook with anger; Hroghar's eyes blazed.

"We white-skins have been lords of the steppes for untold ages. Hence went conquering hordes to people the world. When we were many, we lashed the dark-faced people back into the Eastern deserts. Now that we are weak and few, we make them the same reply our ancestors made: 'Death to you, dog-brothers!' Our fair Lord God made us the masters of all other races. If I treat with these Moslem jackals for peace, may the heart rot in my bosom!"

Turlogh grinned hardly and bleakly. "There is iron in you, old man! But you have overlooked one thing—even if we win, the tribe will be greatly weakened, and Chaga Khan and his jackals may swoop down and wipe out what is left of us."

Hroghar plucked his beard: "True; but what can we do?"

The Gael shrugged his shoulders: "How will you fight these Turks?"

"Why, lord sir, in the same manner we always fight; we will mount our steeds and gallop across the steppes until we meet their horde and then we will shout our war cry and charge in and cut them down like grain."

"And will they not bend their bows and shoot you out of your saddles before you can come to grips?" Turlogh growled.

"There will be a flight of arrows," agreed the Turgaslav, "but these Turks are not like the Tatars; they like sword strokes. They will loose a cloud of shafts as they charge and then rush in with naked steel. Chaga Khan's warriors had the better of it as long as the battle was an exchange of arrows, but when the Turks rode in among them, they could not stand before them. The Moslems are bigger men and better armed."

"Good," grunted Turlogh. "You are bigger men than the Turks and will have the same advantage with them that they had with the Tatars. But the Turgaslavs must come swiftly to an exchange of sword strokes if they are to win."

[. . .]

Miscellanea

Poems and Unfinished Tales

The King's Service

Prologue

The slow rise and headlong fall of Rome shook the Western world. In the mushroom growth of the East, the downfall of imperial cities caused only a momentary ripple in the swarming tides of restless humanity, and their very memory faded from the minds of men even as the crawling jungle, the drifting desert, effaced the crumbling walls and shattered towers.

Such a kingdom was Nagdragore, whose eagle-crested rajahs levied tribute from the Deccan when yellow-haired barbarians were stalking red-handed through the gates of Rome.

The glories of Nagdragore have been forgotten for a thousand years. Not even in the misty gulf of the Hindu legend where a hundred lost dynasties sleep unheeded, does any hint of that vanished realm linger. Nagdragore is one with a thousand nameless ruins—a crumbling mass of shattered stone and broken marble, lost in the waving green deeps of the blind crawling jungle.

This tale is of the times of Nagdragore's lost splendor, before she decayed and fell before the ravages of the White Hun, Tatar and Mogul; a tale of the Age that saw her gleam like a scintillant jewel on the dusky breast of India, when her imperial towers rose golden, white and purple in the blue, gazing with the pride of assured destiny across the green-girdling, white-foaming Gulf of Cambay.

Chapter 1

"The mists are clearing."

Hairy calloused hands rested on long ash oars and frosty eyes peered through the thinning veil. The ship was a strange one for Eastern waters; it was long, lean, low in the waist, high of stern and bows, the prow curving up into a carved dragon's head. The open build, the shield-rail, the prow marked her as a raider as clearly as did her crew—huge, flaxen-bearded warriors with cold, light eyes.

On the poop stood a small group of men and one of these, a brooding-eyed, lowering-browed giant, cursed in his beard.

"The hordes of Helheim know where we be, or in which direction be land; yet water and food grow scant—Hrothgar, you say you sense land to the eastward, but by Thor—"

A sudden shout went up from the crew, as the rowers set their oars aback and stared with dropped jaws. Before them the fog was thinning swiftly and now hanging in the dim sky a sudden blaze of gems and marble burst upon their eyes. They glimpsed, awedly, the turrets and spires and battlements of a mighty city in the sky.

"By the blood of Loki!" swore the Viking chief. "It's Midgaard!"

Another on the poop laughed. The Viking turned to him irritably. This man was unlike his companions; he alone bore no weapons and wore no mail, yet the rest eyed him with a sort of sullen respect. There was in his bearing a natural, lion-like dignity, a nobility of manner and a realization of power without arrogance. He was tall, as broad-shouldered and powerful as any man there, and there was about him a certain cat-like litheness that most of the massive-limbed warriors lacked. His hair was as golden as theirs, his eyes as blue, but no one would have mistaken him for one of them. His strong face, browned by the sun, was quick and mobile with the whimsical half-mockery of the Celt.

"Donn Othna," said the pirate chieftain angrily, "what is your jest now?"

The other shook his head. "I only laughed to think that in yon blaze of beauty a Saxon could see the city of his cold, savage gods who build with swords and skulls rather than marble and gold."

The breeze lifted the mists and the city shone more clearly. Port, harbor and walls grew out of the fading grey with astonishing swiftness.

"Like a city of a dream," muttered Hrothgar, his cold eyes strange with wonder. "The fog was thicker than we thought, that we should have so nearly approached such a port unknowing. Look at the craft which throng her wharves. What now, Athelred?"

The giant scowled. "They have already spied us; if we flee now we will have a score of galleys swooping after us, I think. And we must have fresh water—what think you, Donn Othna?"

The Celt shrugged his mighty shoulders.

"Who am I to think anything? I am no chief among you—but if we cannot flee—and to turn now would in sooth arouse suspicion—we must put on a bold front. I see yonder many trading crafts which have the look of far-farers and it may be that these people trade with many nations and will not fall on us at sight. Not all folk are Saxons!"

Athelred snarled churlishly and shouted at the steersman who had been resting on the long sweep, staring agape. The long ash oars began to churn the waves again and the galley boldly swept toward the dreaming harbor. Already other craft were putting out to meet them. Strangely built, richly carved galleys manned by dark-skinned men swept upon alongside and the Saxons perforce lay to, while Athelred hailed their leaders.

The Vikings gazed in amazement at the costly ornamented ships, and at the hawk-faced, turbaned warriors whose apparel shone in silver and silk, and whose weapons shimmered with gold chasings and sparkling gems; they gaped at the heavy steel bows, the round silver-spiked, gold-braced bucklers, the long slim spears, and curved sabers. And meanwhile the Orientals stared back in equal wonder at these white-skinned, flaxen-haired giants, with their horned helmets, scale-mail shirts and flaring-edged axes.

A tall, black-bearded chief stood on the ornate deck of the nearer craft and shouted to Athelred who answered him in his own tongue. Neither could understand the other and the Saxon chief began to fume with the dangerous impatience of the barbarian. There was tension in the air. The Vikings stealthily laid down their oars and felt for their axes, and aboard the other crafts bowstrings slid into the nocks of barbed arrows. Then Donn Othna, on a long chance, shouted a greeting in the Latin tongue. A change was instantly seen in the opposing chief.

He waved his arm and answered with a single word in the same tongue, which Donn Othna took to mean a friendly reply. The Celt spoke further, but the chief repeated the single Latin word and with a wave of his arm, indicated that the strangers should precede him into the port. The carles, at a growl from their chief, again took up their oars and the dragon-ship swept into the harbor and alongside the wharf with an escort of wallowing galleys on either side.

There the Eastern chief came alongside and by gestures indicated that they were to stay aboard their own craft for a while. Athelred's beard bristled at this, but there was nothing else to do. The chief strode away with a clatter of weapons and a number of tall, bearded warriors unobtrusively took up their position on the wharves. They appeared not to notice the strangers, but Donn Othna noted that they outnumbered the dragon-ship's crew and that they bore wicked bows.

A great concourse of people came upon the wharves, gesticulating and shouting in wonder, gazing wide-eyed at the grim white giants who stared back equally fascinated. The archers thrust back the crowd roughly, forcing them to leave a wide space clear. Donn Othna smiled; more than his more stolid companions did he appreciate the gaudy panorama of color before him.

"Donn Othna," it was Athelred growling beside him, "on which side stand you?"

"What do you mean?"

The giant waved a huge hand toward the warriors on the wharves.

"If it comes to a pitched battle will you fight for us, or will you stab me in the back?"

The big Celt laughed cynically. "Strange words to a prisoner. What avail would be a single sword against yon hosts?" Then his manner changed. "Bring me the sword your men took from me; if I am to aid you I would not seem a thrall in the eyes of these people."

Athelred growled in his beard at the abrupt command, but his eyes fell before the cold gaze of the other and he shouted a command. A huge warrior presently mounted the poop, bringing with him a long heavy sword in a leather sheath, attached to a broad silver-buckled belt. Donn Othna's eyes sparkled as he took the weapon and fastened it about his waist. He laid hand on the jeweled ivory hilt with its heavy silver cross-guard and drew it half from the scabbard. The double-edged blade, of a sinister blue, hummed faintly.

"By Thor!" muttered Hrothgar. "Your sword sings, Donn Othna!"

"It sings for its homecoming, Hrothgar," answered the Celt. "Now I know that yon shore is the land of Hind, for it was here that my sword was born from furnace and forge and wizard's hammer, dim ages ago. It was once a great saber, belonging to a mighty Eastern emperor, whom Alexander conquered. And Alexander took it with him into Egypt where it abode until the Romans came and a consul took it for his own. Not liking the curved shape, he had a sword-maker of Damascus reshape the blade—for the Romans used straight thrusting swords. It came into Britain with Caesar and was lost to the Gaels in a great battle in the west. I myself took it from Eochaidh Mac Ailbe, king of Erin, whom I slew in a sea-fight off the western coast."

"A sword for a prince," said Hrothgar in open admiration. "Look—one comes!"

With a great shouting and clanking of arms, a mighty concourse swept down to the wharves. A thousand warriors in shining armor, on Arab barbs, camels and grunting elephants escorted one who sat in a throne-like chair high on the back of a great elephant. Donn Othna saw a lean, haughty face, black-bearded and hawk-nosed; deep dark eyes, liquid and yet keen, surveyed the westerners. The Celt realized that this king, lord or whoever he was, was not of the same race as his subjects.

The cavalcade halted before the dragon-ship, trumpets split the skies in a ripping fanfare, cymbals clashed deafeningly and then a gaudily dressed chieftain spurred forward, salaamed deeply from his saddle and burst into a grandiloquent flight of words which meant exactly nothing to the gaping Occidentals. The personage on the throne-chair checked his vassal with a languid wave of a white, jewel-decked hand and spoke in clear, liquid Latin:

"He is saying, my friends, that the exalted son of the gods, the beloved of Brahma, the great rajah Constantius, does you the stupendous, unheard of and entirely astounding honor of coming to greet you in person."

All eyes turned toward Donn Othna, the only man aboard the long-serpent who could understand the words. The huge Saxons eyed him eagerly like great, puzzled children and it was on him that the eyes of the Orientals focused. The tall Celt stood, arms folded, head thrown back, meeting the gaze of the rajah squarely, and for all the splendor and trappings of the Oriental, his kingship was no less apparent than the royalty of the westerner. There two natural born leaders of men faced each other, recognizing each other's regal birthright.

"I am Donn Orthna, a prince of Britain," said the Celt. "This chief is Athelred of the Saxons. We have sailed for many a weary moon and desire only peace and a chance to trade for food and water. What city is this?"

"This is Nagdragore, one of the chief principalities of India," answered the rajah. "Come ashore—ye are my guests. It's many a day since I turned my face eastward and I am hungry to speak with one in the old tongue of Rome and hear the news of the west."

"What says he? Is it peace or war? Where be we?" the questions rained on the Briton.

"We are indeed in the land of Hind," answered Donn Othna. "But yonder king is no Indian. If he be not a Greek, then I am a Saxon! He bids us be his guests ashore—that may well mean prisoners, but we have no choice. Mayhap he means to deal fairly with us."

Chapter 2

Donn Othna lifted a cup carved of a single jewel and drank deeply. He set it down and gazed across the richly carved teakwood table at the rajah who lounged sensuously on the silken divan. They were alone in the room except for the huge black mute who, naked except for a silk loincloth, stood just behind Constantius, holding a wide-bladed scimitar nearly as long as himself.

"Well, prince," said the rajah, toying idly with a great sapphire on his finger, "have I not played squarely with you and your men? Even now they gorge and guzzle on such meat and drink as they never dreamed existed, and rest themselves on silken couches, while musicians play stringed music for their pleasure and girls lithe as panthers dance for them. I have not even taken their axes from them—as for you, here you feast with me alone—yet I see suspicion in your eyes."

Donn Othna indicated the sword which he had unbuckled and laid on a polished bench.

"I had not unslung Alexander's sword did I not trust you. As for the Saxons—Crom's jest! They are like bears in a palace. Had you sought to disarm them their wonder had turned to desperate rage and those same axes had drunk deep in the red tides. It is not suspicion you see in my eyes but wonder. By the gods! When I was a shock-headed boy on the western marches I wondered at Tara in Erin, and gaped at Caer Odun. Then when I was a youth and raided into Roman territory, I thought Corinium, Aquae Sulis, Ebbracum and Lundinium were the mightiest cities of all the earth. When I came into manhood the memory of those was paled by my first sight of Rome, though it was crumbling under the defiling feet of Goth and Vandal. And Rome seems but a village when I gaze at the jewel-crowned spires and golden-chased towers of Nagdragore!"

Constantius nodded, a tinge of bitterness in his eyes. "It is an empire worth fighting for, and once I had dreams of spanning the land of India from sea to sea—but tell me of Rome and Byzantium—it has been a long time since I turned my face eastward. Then the German barbarians were overrunning the Roman borders, Genseric was pillaging the imperial city herself, and rumors of a strange and terrible people came even to Byzantium which writhed under the heel of the Ostrogoth."

"The Huns!" exclaimed Donn Othna, his face lighting fiercely. "Aye, they came out of the East like a wind of death—like a swarm of locusts. They drove the Goths, the Franks and the Vandals before them and the Teutons trampled Rome in their flight. Then with the sea before them, they could fly no further. They turned at bay—the two hosts met at Chalons—by the gods, there was a sword-quenching! There the ravens fed and the axes were glutted redly! They rolled on us like a black wave, and as a wave breaks on the rocks, they broke on the German shield-wall and the ranks of Aetius' legions."

"You were there?" exclaimed Constantius.

"Aye! With five hundred of my tribesmen!" Donn Othna's fierce eyes blazed and he smote his fist resoundingly upon the table. "We sailed with those British legions who went to the succor of Rome—and came no more to their native soil. On the plains of Gaul and Italy their bones rot—and those of many a western clansman who never bowed to Rome, but who followed his civilized kin to the wars.

"All day we fought and, at the end, the Huns broke—by Crom, my sword was red and clotted from pommel to point, and I could scarcely lift my arm. Of my five hundred warriors, fifty lived!

"Well—Votigern had called in the Jutes to aid him against the Picts, and the Angles and Saxons followed them like hungry wolves. I returned to Britain and in the whirlwind of war that swept the southern coasts, I fell captive to this Athelred, who knowing my name and rank, wished to hold me for ransom. But a strange thing came to pass—"

Donn Othna paused and laughed shortly.

"We of the west hate long and well, and our Gaelic cousins make a cult of revenge, but by Crom, I never knew what the lust for vengeance could be until we sighted the ships of Asgrimm the Angle. This sea-king has an old feud with Athelred and he gave chase with his ten long-serpents. By Crom, he chased us half around the world! He hung to our stern like a hunting dog and we could not elude him.

"We raced him around the coast of Gaul and down past Spain, and when we would have turned into the Mediterranean he crowded us close and drove us past the Gates of Hercules. South and forever south we fled, past sullen, steaming coasts, dank with swamp or dark with jungle, where black people wild and naked shouted and shot arrows at us.

"At last we rounded a cape and headed east, and somewhere there we shook off our pursuers. Since then we have sailed and rowed at random. So you see, King Constantius, my news is nearly a year old."

The rajah's deep dark eyes were pensive with inner thought. He sighed and drank deep of the goblet the black slave filled and tasted first.

"Nearly twenty years ago I sailed from Byzantium with Cyprian traders bound for Alexandria. I was but a youth, ignorant and full of wonder at the world, but with royal blood in my veins. From Alexandria I wandered by devious ways to Damascus and there I joined a caravan returning to Shiraz in Persia. Later I sought pearls on the Gulf of Oman and it was there that I was taken captive by a Maldive pirate who sold me on the slave block at Nagdragore. I need not repeat to you the devious route by which I reached the throne.

"The old dynasty was crumbling, ready to fall; Nagdragore was harried by incessant wars with neighboring kingdoms. It was a red trail, black with plot and treachery that I followed, but today I am rajah of Nagdragore—though the throne rocks beneath my feet."

Constantius rested his elbows on the table and his chin in his hands; his great brooding eyes fixed themselves on the blond giant opposite him.

"You are a prince likewise, though your palace be a wattle hut," he said. "We be of the same world, though I had my birth at one end, and you at the other end of that world. I need men I can trust. My kingdom is divided against itself and I play one chief against the other to the hurt of Nagdragore, but to mine own gain. My chief foes are Anand Mulhar and Nimbaydur Singh. The one is rich, cowardly and avaricious—too cautious and too suspicious to oppose me openly. The other is young, passionate, romantic and brave—but a victim of moneylenders who watch the way the fish leaps.

"The common people hate me because they love Nimbaydur Singh who has a trace of royal blood in his veins. The nobles—the Rajputs—dislike me because I am an outlander. But I rule the moneylenders and, through them, Nagdragore.

"The war is a more or less secret one in which I am ground between Anand Mulhar on the one side and Nimbaydur Singh on the other, yet still hold in my hands the reins of power. They hate each other too much to combine against me.

"But it is the silent assassin's dagger I have to fear. I half trust my guard, but half trust is little better than full suspicion and far more dangerous. That is why I came down to the wharves to greet you myself. Will you and these barbarians remain here in the palace and do battle for me if the occasion arise?

"I could not make you officially my bodyguard. It would offend the nobles and all would rise instantly. But I will ostensibly make you part of the army; you will remain here in the palace and you, prince, shall be my cup companion."

Donn Othna grinned a slow, lazy grin, and reached for the wine pitcher.

"I will talk to Athelred," said he. "I think he will agree."

Chapter 3

The Briton found Athelred sitting cross-legged on a silken couch, tearing at a huge quarter of roast lamb, between enormous gulps of Indian wine. The Saxon growled a greeting and continued to gorge and guzzle, while Donn Othna seated himself and glanced quizzically about him. The pirate crew sprawled at ease among the cushions on the marble floor or wandered about the great room, gazing curiously up at the jeweled dome high overhead or staring out the golden-barred windows into courts with flowering trees and exotic blossoms scenting the air, or into colonnaded chambers where fountains flung a silvery sheen high into the air. They were curious and delighted as children and suspicious as wolves. Each kept his curved-handled, wicked-headed axe close to his hand.

"What now, Donn Othna?" mumbled Athelred, munching away without a pause.

"What would you?" parried the Briton.

"Why," the pirate waved a half-gnawed bone about him, "here's loot that would make Hengist's eyes open and Cerdic's mouth water. Let us do this—in the night we will rise stealthily and set fire to the palace; then in the confusion we will snatch such plunder as we can easily bear away and hack our way to our ship which lies unguarded along the docks. Then, ho, for the western seas! When my people see what we bring, there will be a hundred dragon-ships following us! We will plunder Nagdragore as Genseric plundered Rome and carve us out a kingdom with our axes."

"Would it draw your sea-wolves from Britain," said Donn Othna grimly, "I might agree. But it's a plan too mad for even a Saxon to try. Even if I could overlook the treachery to our host, we could never cover half the distance to the ship. A hundred and fifty men cut their way through fifty thousand? Think no more of it."

"What then?" growled Athelred. "By Thor, it seems our positions have changed! Aboard ship you were our prisoner. Now it seems we are yours! We are hereditary foes—how do I know you mean to deal squarely with us? How do I know what you and the king have been jabbering to each other? Maybe you plan to cut our throats."

"And not knowing, you must take my word for it," answered the prince calmly. "I have no love for you or your race, though I know you as brave men. But here it is to our advantage to act in concert. Without me you have no interpreter; without you I have no armed force to strengthen my claim to respect. Constantius has offered us service in his palace guards. I trust him no more than you trust me; he will deal us false the moment it is to his advantage. But until such time, it is to our advantage to comply with his request. If I know men, niggardliness is not one of his faults. We will live well on his bounty. Just now he needs our swords. Later that need may pass and we may take ship again—but understand, Athelred, this service I do you now is my ransom. I am no longer your prisoner and if I go aboard your ship again, I am a free man, whom you will set on British soil without price."

"I swear it by my sword," grunted Athelred, and Donn Othna nodded, satisfied, knowing the blunt Saxon was a man of his word.

"The East is fraught with unlimited possibilities," said the Briton. "Here a bold heart and a keen sword can accomplish as much as they can in the West and the reward is greater, if more fleeting. Just now, I doubt if Constantius trusts me fully. I must prove that we can be of value to him."

The chance came sooner than he had hoped. In the days following, Donn Othna and his comrades abode in the mazes of the Eastern city, wondering at the strange contrasts—the splendor and riches of the nobles, the poverty and squalor of the poor. Nor was the least paradox he who sat upon the throne.

Donn Othna sat in the golden-leaf chamber and drank wine with the rajah Constantius, while the great silent black man served them. The British prince gazed in wonder at the rajah. Constantius drank deep and unwisely. He was drunk, his strange eyes darker and more liquid than ever.

"You are a relief as well as a protection to me, Donn Othna," said he, with a slight hiccup. "I can be my true self with you—at least I assume it to be my true self. I trust you because you bring the clean, straightforward power of the western winds and the clean salt tang of the western seas with you. I need not be forever on my guard—I tell you, Donn Othna, this business of empire is not one that makes for ease or happiness. Had I to live my life over again, I would rather be what once I was—a clean-limbed, brown-skinned youth, diving for pearls in the Oman Gulf and flinging them away to dark-eyed Arab girls.

"But the purple is my curse and my birthright, just as it's yours. I am rajah not because I was wise or foolish but because I have the blood of emperors in my veins and I followed a destiny I could not avoid. You, too, will live to press a throne and curse the crown that wearies your tired neck. Drink!"

Donn Othna waved away the proffered goblet.

"I have drunk enough and you far too much," he said bluntly. "By Crom, I have found ou to be much of a hashish eater and more of a drunkard. You are incredibly wise and incredibly foolish. How can a man like you be a king?"

Constantius laughed. "A question that had cost another man his head. I will tell you why I am king: because I can flatter men and see through their flattery; because I know the weaknesses of strong men; because I know how to use money; because I have no scruples whatever, and resort to any method, fair or foul, to gain my ends. Because, being born to the West and raised in the East, the guile of both worlds is in me. Because, though I am in the main a fool, I have flashes of real genius, beyond the power of a consistently wise man. And because—and all my other gifts were useless without it—I have the power of molding women as wax in my hands. Let me look in any woman's eyes and hold her close to me, and she is my slave forever."

Donn Othna shrugged his mighty shoulders and set down his goblet.

"The East draws me with a strange fascination," said he, "though I had rather rule a tribe of shock-headed Cymry. But, by Crom, your ways are devious and strange."

Constantius laughed and rose, unsteadily. The retiring of the rajah was attended to only by the great black mute. Donn Othna slept in a chamber adjoining the golden-leaf room.

And now Donn Othna, dismissing his own slave, stepped to the heavily barred window that looked out on an inner court, and breathed deep the spice scents of the Orient. The dreaming antiquity of India touched his eyelids with slumberous fingers and in the deeps of his soul dim racial memories stirred. After all, he felt a certain kinship with these hawk-faced, keen-eyed Rajputs. They were of his blood, if the ancient legends were true, that told of the days when the sons of Aryan were one great tribe, in the mist-dim ages before Nimbaydur Singh's ancestors broke from the nation in that great southern drift, and before Donn Othna's ancestors took up the long trek westward.

A faint sound brought him back to the present. A quick stride took him across the room where he gazed into the golden-leaf chamber through a cloth-of-gold curtain. A dancing girl had entered the chamber and Donn Othna wondered how she had gotten past the swordsmen stationed outside the door. She was a slim young thing, lithe and beautiful, her scanty silken girdle and golden breastplates accentuating her sinuous loveliness. She approached the huge black who stared at her in sullen wonder and menace. She approached him, her red lips pleading, her deep eyes luring, her little hands outstretched and upturned beseechingly. Donn Othna could not understand her low tones—though he had learned much of the Rajput language—but he saw the black shake his bullet head and lift his huge scimitar threateningly.

She was close to the mute now—and she moved like a striking cobra. From somewhere about her scanty garments she flashed a dagger and with the same motion she flicked it under the mute's heart. He swayed like a great black idol, the sword fell from his nerveless hands and he fell across it, his face writhing in the agony of effort as his withered tongue sought to sound a warning to his master. Then blood burst from that silently gaping mouth and the great slave lay still.

The girl sprang quickly and silently toward the door, but Donn Othna was ahead of her in a single bound. She checked herself for a fleeting second, then sprang at his throat like a fury. The dances of the East make their devotees lithe and steel-like in every thew. Ages later when westerners again invaded the East, they found that a slim nautch girl could prove more than a match for a man. But those men had never tugged at a galley oar, wielded a twenty pound battle-axe or reined four wild chariot horses back on their haunches. Donn Othna caught the feline fury that was thrusting so earnestly for his life, disarmed her with little effort and tucked her under his arm like a child.

He was rather uncertain as to his next step when out of the royal bedchamber came the rajah, his eyes still clouded somewhat with wine. A single glance showed him what had occurred.

"Another woman assassin?" he asked casually. "My throne against your sword, Donn Othna, Anand Mulhar sent her. Nimbaydur Singh is too upright for such tricks—the poor fool." He casually touched the body of his faithful slave with his toe, but made no comment.

"What shall I do with the spitfire?" asked Donn Othna. "She's too young to hang and if you let her go—"

Constantius shook his head. "Neither one nor the other; let me have her."

Donn Othna handed her to the rajah as if she were an infant, glad to be rid of the scratching, biting little devil. But at the first touch of Constantius' hands she fell quiet, trembling like a high-strung steed. The rajah sat down on a divan and forced the girl to her knees before him, without harshness and without mercy. She whimpered a little, far more afraid of the Greek's calmness than she had been of Donn Othna's anger. One white jeweled hand held her slim wrists, the other rested on her head forcing her to look up into the rajah's face with eyes that sought desperately to escape his steady stare.

"You are very young and very foolish," said Constantius in a deliberate tone. "You came here to murder me because some evil master sent you—" his hand slowly caressed her as a man pets a dog. "Look into my eyes—I am your rightful master. I will not harm you; you will remain with me and you will love me."

"Yes, master," the girl answered in a small voice like a girl in a trance; her eyes did not try to evade Constantius now; they were very wide and filled with a strange new light; she leaned to the rajah's caress. He smiled and the quality of that smile made him strangely handsome.

"Tell me who you are and who sent you," he commanded, and to Donn Othna's utter amazement, the girl bowed her head obediently.

"I am Yatala; my master Anand Mulhar sent me to kill you, master. For more than a moon now, I have danced in the palace. For my master put me on the block and so contrived that your wizar bought me among other dancing girls. It was well planned, master. I came tonight and made eyes at the guards without; then when they let me approach, seeing that I was little and unarmed, I blew a secret dust into their eyes, so that deep sleep came upon them. Then taking a dagger from one, I entered—and you know the rest, master."

She hid her face on Constantius' knees and the rajah looked up at Donn Othna with a lazy smile.

"What think you of my power over women now, Donn Othna?"

"You are a devil," answered the prince frankly. "I would have taken oath no torture could have wrung from that girl what she has just told you freely—hark!"

A stealthy footstep sounded without. The girl's eyes flared with sudden terror.

"Beware, my lord!" she cried. "That is Tamur, Anand Mulhar's strangler—he followed me to make sure—"

Donn Othna whirled toward the door—it opened to reveal a terrible shape. Tamur was taller and heavier than the powerful Briton. Naked except for a loincloth, his dusky bronze skin rippled over knots and coils of iron muscles. His limbs were like oak and iron, yet lithe and springy as a tiger's, his shoulders incredibly wide. A short tree-like neck upheld a bestial head. The low, slanting forehead, the flaring nostrils, the cruel gash of a mouth, the close-set ears, the ape-like shaven skull, all betrayed the human beast, the born blood-letter. In his girdle was twisted the implement of his trade—a sinister silken cord. In his right hand he bore a curved saber.

Donn Othna took in this formidable figure in one glance, then he was springing to the attack with the headlong savagery of his race. His sword flashed through the air in a blazing blue arc just as the other struck. Here was no hesitant caution on either side. Both sprang and struck simultaneously, quick to fling all on a single blow. And in midair the curved blade and the straight blade met with a resounding clash. The scimitar shivered to a thousand ringing sparks and, before the Briton could strike again, the strangler dropped his hilt and, like a striking snake, caught his white-skinned foe in a fierce grip.

The British prince let go his sword, useless at such close quarters, and returned the grapple. In an instant he knew that he was pitted against a skilled and cruel wrestler. The smooth, naked body of the Indian was like a great snake and as hard to hold. But not for naught had Donn Othna held his own with trained Roman wrestlers of old. Now he blocked and fended shrewd thrust of knee and elbow, and the clutch of iron fingers that sought cruel, maiming holds, while he launched an attack of his own. The thin veneer of civilization, acquired from contact with his Romanized neighbors, had vanished in the heat of battle, and it was a whiteskinned barbarian, wild as any Goth or Saxon, who tore and snarled in the golden-leaf room of Nagdragore's rajahs.

Donn Othna saw, over Tamur's heaving shoulder, Constantius approaching with the sword he had dropped and, blue eyes blazing with battle-lust, he snarled for the rajah to keep back and let him finish his own fight.

Chest to chest, the giants strove, reeling back and forth, close clinched, but still upright, each foiling every effort of the other. Tamur's thumb gouged at Donn Othna's eye, but the prince sank his head against the other's massive chest, shifted his hold, and the strangler was forced to cease gouging and break the Briton's hold, to save his own spine.

Again Tamur caught Donn Othna's arm in a sudden bonebreaking crossbar grip that had snapped the elbow like a twig had not the British prince suddenly driven his head hard and desperately into the Indian's face. Blood spattered as Tamur's head snapped back and Donn Othna, following his advantage, back-heeled him and threw him. Both crashed heavily on the floor, but the strangler writhed from under the Briton, and the latter found his neck menaced by a grip that bent his head back at a sickening angle.

With a gasp he tore free, just as Tamur drove his knee agonizingly into the Briton's groin. Then as the white man's iron grip involuntarily relaxed, the brown man leaped free, whipping the deadly cord from his girdle. Donn Othna rose more slowly, nauseated with the pain of that foul thrust, and Tamur, with an inhuman croak of triumph, sprang and cast his cord. The Briton heard the girl scream, as he felt the thin length whip like a serpent about his throat, instantly cutting off his breath. But at the same instant he struck out blindly and terrifically, his clenched iron fist meeting Tamur's jaw like a mallet meeting a ship's side. The strangler dropped like a log and Donn Othna, gasping, tore the cord from his tortured throat and flung it aside, just as Tamur scrambled to his feet, eyes glaring like a madman's.

The Briton fell on him raging, battering him with sledgehammer blows, gained from long hours of practice with the cestus. Such an attack was beyond Tamur's skill to cope with; the East has not the instinct of striking with the clenched fist. A swing that smashed full in his mouth splattered blood and splintered teeth and he retaliated with the only sort of blow he knew—an open-handed, full-armed slap to the side of the head that staggered Donn Othna and filled his eyes with momentary spark-shot darkness. But instantly he returned the blow with a smash that sank deep in Tamur's midriff and dropped him to his knees, gasping and writhing.

The strangler grappled Donn Othna's legs and dragged him down, and once more they battled and tore close-clinched. But the ravening Briton felt his foe grow weaker; and redoubling the fury of his attack, like a tiger maddened by the blood scent, he bore the Indian backward and down, sought and found a deadly hold at last, and strangled the strangler, sinking his iron fingers deeper and deeper until he felt the life flow out from under them, and the writhing body stiffened.

Then Donn Othna rose and shook the blood and sweat from his eyes and smiled grimly at the spellbound rajah who stood like one frozen, still dangling Alexander's sword.

"Well, Constantius," said Donn Othna, "you see I am worthy of your trust."

[. . .]

Where Are Your Knights, Donn Othna?

Now that the kings have fallen,
Now that the gods have fled,
Now that the cities smolder
In a riot of ghastly red—

Where are your knights, Donn Othna?
Where the sword that was bright?
The skies are choked with ravens—
Where will you ride tonight?

"I left my knights in a valley
"Far and dim in the west;
"They were weary with endless battle,
"And I left them to their rest.

"We fed the hungry vultures
"When we rent the ranks apart,
"And I left my good sword broken
"In a sea-king's cruel heart.

"On a crimson couch and royal
"Each good knight lies asleep;
"They heed not the trumpet's clamor,
"Nor the night-wind's restless sweep.

"The hounds of Death ran howling,
"And red the rune they bayed—
"I cannot wake my warriors,
"I cannot mend my blade.

"But there are shields unbroken
"And ravens yet to feed,
"And though deep-notched and crimson
"This axe will serve my need.

“East where the ravens gather,
“Where the death fires glimmer bright,
“Where the sea-kings roar and triumph,
“I ride alone tonight.”

No More the Serpent Prow

The House of Asgard passes with the night;
The House of Vanaheim in clouds and mist;
The House of Gael is fading like the sight
Of eyes that cold Nylyara's lips have kissed.
The dragon-ships are rotting on the shore;
Forgot the shouts that shook the foaming deep;
And like a slow, foul tide wave, ever more,
Out of the East the drooling mist waves creep.

Untitled

"I," said Chuchulain, "was a man, at least. If you will pardon my seeming vanity, I believe I might say that of all the Red Branch kings—"

"Well," said I, "I know your reputation well enough to grant you that, and you will pardon my seeming lack of enthusiasm. I realize it was not your fault that you were born in Ulster—"

"From your tone," he remarked, "I infer that it was *your* ancestors with whom I—ah—well, to put it plainly yet modestly—"

"You need not conclude your remarks," I broke in. "Your set had the advantage of transmitting *your* side of that little affair through the ever busy mouths of Ulster bards—whereas we of Connacht—well, somewhere in the shuffle the records must have gotten lost or burned—"

"Let old ghosts lie," said he. "Surely you have the Connacht gift of gab—I remember how Queen Medhbh—with all due respect to her—bamboozled me into throwing away my victory right when—well, it was not to rake up old legends that I came here tonight. I wish to talk about the present."

[. . .]

The Harp of Alfred

I heard the harp of Alfred
    As I went o'er the downs,
When thorn-trees stood at even
    Like monks in dusky gowns;
I heard the music Guthrum heard
    Beside the wasted towns;

When Alfred, like a peasant,
    Came harping down the hill,
And the drunken Danes made merry
    With the man they sought to kill,
And the Saxon king laughed in their beards
    And bent them to his will.

I heard the harp of Alfred
    As twilight waned to night;
I heard ghost armies tramping
    As the dim stars flamed white;
And Guthrum walked at my left hand,
    And Alfred at my right.

Viking's Vision

A white sea was flowing, a bitter wind was blowing;
Our chanting shook the cormorants that wheeled about our bows.
South—Deathward we were sailing, and Aslaf gripped the railing,
A hungry dagger at his hip, a hate upon his brows.

We sang for red tomorrows to bring the Southland sorrows
In sunken ship and plundered town and wives and daughters raped.
We sang of castles falling, gold lost beyond recalling,
Till Aslaf wheeled and cursed at us till every mouth there gaped.

"Go tell your lusts to devils, you ape-faced swines of evils!
"Or save the breath you waste today for shout and battle shock!"
And as he ceased to thunder, I caught my breath in wonder
To see a tremor in that hand which might have crushed a rock.

Fire smote the Southland beaches 'mid women's wails and screeches.
We drove the bees to cover and we broke them from their hives.
Where blades their blue sparks showered and maidens shrank and cowered,
We plunged our souls in glory and we plunged our swords in lives.

In armor rent and battered lay dead men still and scattered.
The light that lit the burning towns shone red on gems and gold.
And for each man's desire were girls as fair as fire—
But Aslaf's frown was on his brow as if his heart were cold.

We came all drunk and roaring, gold coins and gems a-pouring
Into his lap—the fairest girls, and praises and acclaim.
With wolfish snarl of anger, he cursed our drunken clangor,
And tossed the loot upon the earth—his eyes were icy flame.

"Swine of the tavern benches! What boot these naked wenches?
These twinkling stones and yellow gauds, what mean them all to me?
A weird is come upon me; the hand of Fate is on me,
And over all the clamor sounds the calling of the sea.

"I have no rest in sleeping; I hear strange waters sweeping
Long beaches where no Viking's foot has ever trod before.
I take in this ale no pleasure, for still I hear the measure
Of long and even waves that break upon an unknown shore.

"West where lost winds are sighing, a new strange world is lying!
Its vales and mountains fill my dreams, its calling breaks my sleep.
And dust is battle glory, the while a mystic story
Each west wind brings to haunt my heart across the roaring deep.

"My prow has plowed the Baltic, and passed these rocks basaltic
From high above the narrow gates that lock the Middle Sea;
And that dark Afric river that feeds the sea forever,
And I have seen the waters break on Byzantium's lea.

"But there are seas unparted, and there are coasts uncharted,
And o'er the waves a whisper comes that I am first to go,
The hour of doom is striking the twilight of the Viking!
To ship! We seek the Fate that waits beyond the sunset's glow."

Thor's Son

Serpent prow on the Afric coast,
Doom on the Moorish town;
And this is the song the steersman sang
As the dragon-ship swept down:

I followed Asgrim Snorri's son around the world and half-way back,
And 'scaped the hate of Galdjerhrun who sank our ship off Skagerack.
I lent my sword to Hrothgar then; his eyes were ice, his heart was hard;
He fell with half his weapon-men to our own kin at Mikligard.

And then for many a weary moon I labored at the galley's oar
Where men grow maddened by the rune of row-locks clacking evermore.
But I survived the reeking rack, the toil, the whips that burned and gashed,
The spiteful Greeks that scarred my back and trembled even while they lashed.

They sold me on an Eastern block; in silver coins their price was paid,
They girt me with a chain and lock, I laughed and they were sore afraid.
I toiled among the olive trees until a night of hot desire
Brought me a breath of outer seas and filled my veins with curious fire.

Then I arose and broke my chain and laughed to know that I was free,
And battered out my master's brain and fled and gained the open sea.
Beneath a copper sun adrift, I shunned the proa and the dhow,
Until I saw a sail uplift, and saw and knew the dragon prow.

Oh, East of sands and sunlit gulf, your blood is thin, your gods are few;
You could not break the Northern wolf and now the wolf has turned on you.
The fires that light the coast of Spain fling shadows on the Eastern strand.
Masters, your slave has come again with torch and axe in his red hand!

To Harry the Oliad Men

When the first winds of summer the roses brought,
    And the fields were a-blossom again,
The warriors went riding from green Connacht
    To harry the Oliad men.

Cail of the Sword, we called our lord,
    He harried the East and the North—
Oh, the blades dripped red and the ravens fed
    When Cail and his wolves went forth.

The war-cloud rolled like the wind before—
    And the gods of the North were old—
The sea-folk fled from the purple shore
    As the white birds flee the cold.

Hy-Brasil

There's a far, lone island in the dim red West
Where the sea-waves are crimson with the red of burnished gold,
(Sapphire in the billows, gold upon the crest)
An island that is older than the continents are old.

For when in dim Atlantis a thousand jeweled spires
Burned through the twilight in the ocean's dusky smile,
And when mystic Lemuria glowed with myriad gemming fires
Strange ships went sailing to seek the wondrous isle.

And when the land of Britain was a forest for the deer
And the mammoth roamed the mountains and the plains were veiled in snow,
When the dawn had swept the ocean and the air was crystal clear
The ape-man looking sea-ward caught the distant topaz glow.

When Drake went down to Darien and Cortez sailed the Main
And the wide blue Pacific lay like a summer dream,
From the gold-decked bridges of the galleons of Spain
Far upon the skyline they saw the island gleam.

It flashes in the Baltic, dimly glimpsed through driving snow,
And it lights the Indian Ocean when the waves are lying still,
It dreams along the sea-rim in the twilight's golden glow,
And mariners have named it The Isle of Hy-Brasil.

For sailing ships are anchored close, about that ancient isle,
Ships that roamed the oceans in the dim dawn days,
Coracles from Britain, triremes from the Nile,
Anchored round the harbors, mile on countless mile,
Ships and ships and shades of ships, fading in the haze.

And there's a Roman galley with its seven banks of oars,
And there's a golden barge-boat that knew the Caesar's hand,
And there's a sombre pirate craft with shattered cabin doors,
And there's a sturdy bireme that sailed to the Holy Land.

Main masts lifting like a forest of the south,
Beaked prows looming and the scarlet courses furled,
Dim decks heel-marked, warped by rain and drouth,
Rift in the cross-trees, drift of the southern seas;
Dim ships, strong ships, from all about the world.

High ships, proud ships, towering at their poops,
Galleons flaunting their pinnacles of pride,
Battleships and merchantmen and long, lean sloops,
Flagships floating with the schooners on the tide.

And there's a Viking Serpent that sailed the northern seas,
That knew the stride of giants, ferocious gods of brawn,
And there's a lateened rover that billowed to the breeze,
There a ship that sailed from Tyre when the waves were tinged with fire
And the first skies of history were rosying to dawn.

The Good St. Brandon knew it when he turned him to the West
When he left the world behind him as he ventured far away,
And his fearless keel went plowing the ocean's sapphire crest
Till he won unto Hy-Brasil which no other mortal may.

For the island is Hy-Brasil, the paradise of ships,
Where the dim ghost crafts lie anchored and at rest,
Where the sea wind never rages and the sea rain never drips,
There they dream away the days in the mystic, sapphire haze
About the isle of Hy-Brasil, far off amid the West.

Heritage

My people came from Munster and rugged Nevis-side;
Their hearts were black with ancient wrongs and hate and bitter pride.
Their souls were wild and restless, with swift and changing moods;
They knew red Border forays and dark unholy feuds.
And first within my cradle, on the day that I was born,
I heard the songs the rebels sang to give the gallows scorn.

But when the Springtime standards march in a great green waving host,
I never dream of Inverness or the rugged Kerry coast.
I never dream of a barren land where the keening sea-wind shrills;
My dreams are all of Devon downs and the good green southern hills.

I never see the surging Lorne or the sullen Kenmare's flow,
But I have walked through Dartmoor nights with all the winds that blow.
I know the quaint ale-houses beneath the oaks whose shade
Was flung when lost Lundinium fell before the Roman raid.
I know the croon of sleepy streams, and the brown, time-carven towns,
But best of all the fall of night across the dreaming downs.

I never walked there waking, in dream alone I trod,
But Devon is my heritage by tree and hill and sod.
Beyond the years of yearning, and lust and blood and flame,
My people rode in Devon before the Saxon came.

Oh, wattle hut and barley, oh, feast and song and tale!
Oh, land of dreamy legend, and the good brown British ale!
My heritage is barren, my feet are doomed to roam;
I may not drink from Devon springs nor break the Devon loam.

But when the kings are fallen and when the empires pass,
And when the gleaming cities are wasted stone and grass,
When the younger peoples topple and break their gods in vain,
They that were lords of all the earth may get them home again.
Gods, hurl the haughty deathwards and shake the iron thrones
That my kin shall ride in Devon above the Saxon's bones.

Singing Hemp

Aslaf sat in the dragon bows
And smote on his soulless harp,
And he sang of the winds and the cold sea-path
And the sword-edge bitter and sharp.

"Ravens whetting their iron beaks,
"Black in the blood-red dawn,
"And the quenchless fire of the mad desire
"That drives the Viking on.

'The wind that blows to the night-black gulfs
"It bears the Southland's groans;
"We turn not back on the red sea-track
"Till the white sea has our bones.

"Sons of the frost—the cold blue souls
"Of the cloud-rack, torn and whirled,
"Are the fires that rise in the Viking's eyes,
"Oh, blind black wolf of the world!"

The Return of the Sea-Farer

Thorfinn, Thorfinn, where have you been?
And whence do you come, in the rain and the night?
The grey ocean surges have swallowed your men
And your dragon-ship sleeps where the wolf-waves roll white.

On your corselet is crusted the salt of the sea,
And the blown spray is frozen to ice in your hair,
Your keen sword is broken, and still hauntingly
Your eyes like a fey-woman's distantly stare.

Were there figures unnamed in the seas of the West,
Were there scale-crusted dragons that shattered your ships?
Were there ocean-fiends riding the dark billows' crest,
Or icy sea-women with death on their lips?

"Bare stretch the seas to the set of the sun;
"No mermaid or kraken opposes the keel—
"Of the lies of the women and priests are they spun,
"To naked winds only the blue billows reel.

"West, ever west, like a sea-gull we fled,
"The wind in our sails and the spray in our teeth,
"And the moon or the sun a cold radiance shed
"Through the fathomless fathoms that thundered beneath.

"Then at last rose in wrath the monster we dared,
"The wind's maddened stallions neighed death all around,
"The white fangs of the hounds of the ocean were bared—
"And we tossed like a rat in the teeth of the hound.

"Lashed into blindness, we staggered in flight,
"We reeled to the rush of the howling white host—
"And then like a phantom born out of the night,
"Through the fury and madness, I glimpsed a strange coast.

"Eastward and eastward the gale hurled us on,
"And the dragon-ship staggered at each stroke and strain,
"Till she sank like a stone in a frenzy of dawn
"And the sea cast me forth from her bosom again.

"I am haunted by dreams that are stronger than ghosts.
"They lift me and thrill me with weird second-sight—
"Who can rest or be still who has seen nameless coasts?—
"Has glimpsed a new world in the storm and the night?"

Heritage

Saxon blood in the veins of me,
Gaelic wine in my brain—
But deep in the dreaming soul of me
The restless fire of the Dane.
The fire that smolders half asleep,
Desire that burns and frets,
That makes me dream of cold blue seas
And the fishers' shining nets.

That makes me dream of flying foam
And cracking sails unfurled,
And tall sea-clouds and the wet sea-track
That leads around the world.

Viking's Trail

From the sullen cliffs and the grim fiords
    Where the naked shorelines frown
We turned our prows toward the sun-spun south
    Where a weak king held the crown;
Past the scarlet sand of Helgoland
    The dragon-ships swept down.

In the restless seas of the Hebrides
    The sun in the cold clear blue
Shone on the decks of red-stained deal,
    Raven-banner and plunging keel,
Bronze boar-helmet and grey sword-steel
    And the beards of each berserk crew.

The warning fires leaped up at dawn
    As the Southland coast we raised
From looming headland and barren dune
    The beacon signals blazed.

But it was no beacon smoke that hung
    A-sway in the evening breeze
For the smoldering towns on the fertile downs
    And the wrecks along the leas
Marked red the trail of the Serpent sail
    And told that we swept the seas.

To a Friend

I toiled beside you in the galley's chains
　Through long, long days of deathly toil the same.
　North born, from some far Viking land you came;
The dark Milesian fury coursed my veins.
　Then came a night of battle, blood and flame,
And we rose up and shook our tangled manes
　And wiped out days and nights of fear and shame
With rage that laved the decks in gore and brains.

The years have stretched to eons—vanished quite
　That day we burst the grim forecastle door.
Yet let them have a care who mock our might—
　The hour may come as in those days before
When we shall rise and bellow to the night
　And plunge our hands in hot red blood once more.

Twilight on Stonehenge

Great columns loom against the brooding sky;
  Like giants of another world they stand,
  Flinging their shadows far across the land—
Across the sunset's path their shadows lie;
Above, between, the lone, gray sea-gulls fly.
  And now the moon rides like a smoldering brand
  And mid those shadows, hewn by Titan's hand
Glides shades of eld, ghost shapes, dim-seen and sly.

The crimson moon rides higher o'er the brake,
  The darkness fades, the shadows merge and melt;
    Across the fen the sea-wind's whisper comes
    Bearing the discord of forgotten drums—
That speak to ghosts alone where bird and snake
  Drowse in the last, lone stronghold of the Celt.

The House of Gael

The ancient boast, the ancient song;
The ghostly dream that clings and stays,
A guest unbidden, overlong,
A stranger in unfriendly days.
The yester-ages men know not,
The dust consumes the broken spears—
The spectre of a harp forgot
Comes chanting down the dying years.
Why should I bid a phantom stay?
Retain the out-worn lay and tale?
My day was done with yesterday,
And eons claim the House of Gael.

www.ingramcontent.com/pod-product-compliance
Lightning Source LLC
Chambersburg PA
CBHW051425190726
48289CB00001B/52